OSSI
Odyssey

Olim in Tempus

MARK L. WILLIAMS

INK START MEDIA
5710 W Gate City Blvd Ste K #284
Greensboro, NC 27407

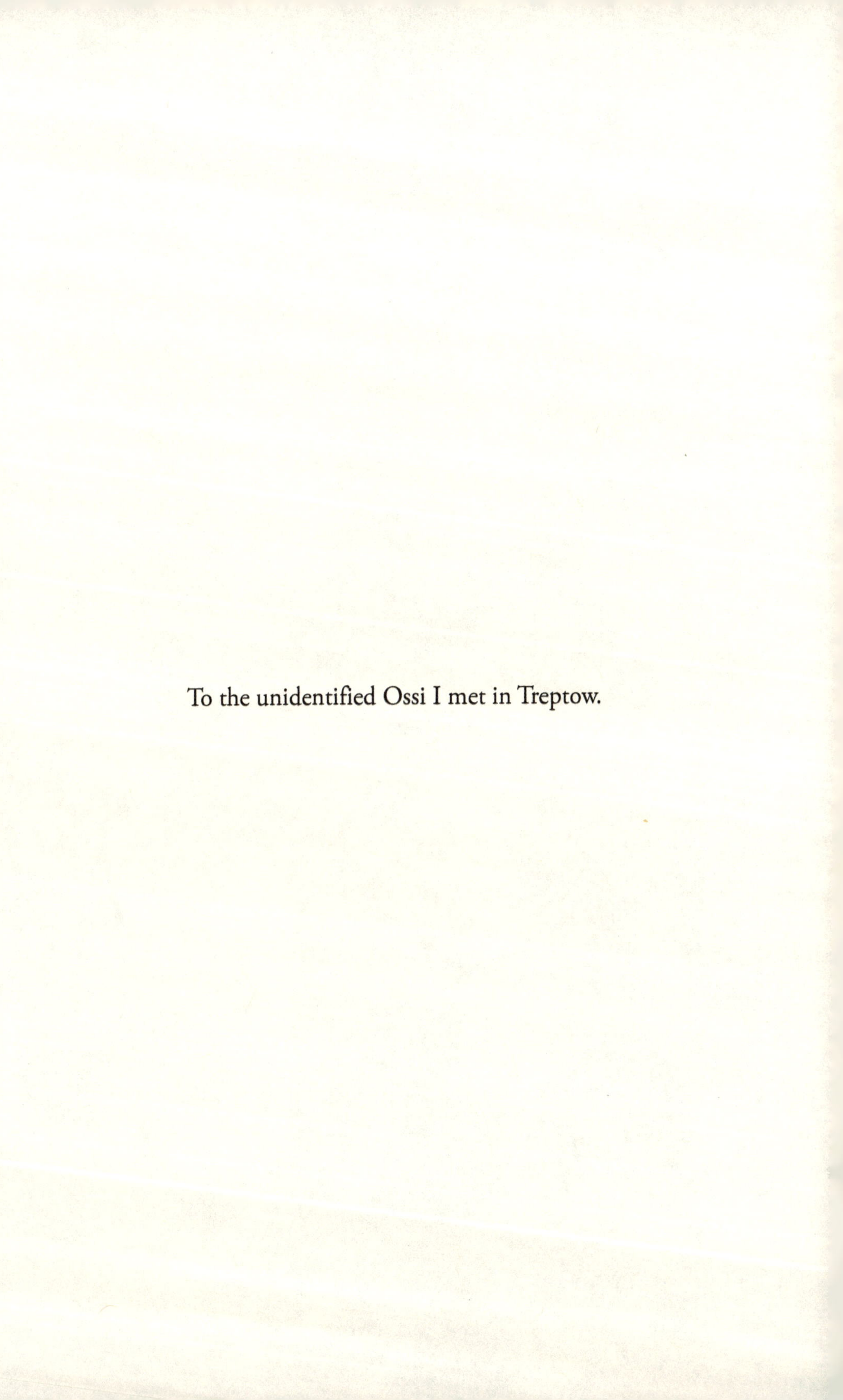

To the unidentified Ossi I met in Treptow.

Prologue

Ute Kaufmann took her first breath in a modest German city perched, precariously, on the shoulder of the larger, more cosmopolitan Nürnberg. Even before she became acquainted with the narrow, bustling streets of her birthplace, she was immersed in the peculiar sub-culture of the Swabs. In one semblance or another, the Kaufmann family was Swabish for at least three hundred years – possibly longer. Predictably, there were a few marriages outside the Swabish culture, but these *unworthies* were absorbed into the fabric so completely that none of their descendants claimed conflicting pedigree. Nevertheless, certain anomalies existed.

Within the Kaufman family, for example, in the mists of the early eighteenth century, the religion of Rome slipped quietly away to be replaced by the fervor of the stubborn Meister Luther. As if to allay this embarrassment, the twentieth-century branch of the family set aside public practice of their faith save for major holy days when members of the clan sat quietly, almost apologetically, in the pews furthest from the pulpit and nearest the door. Ute readily testified that her parents were ardent believers, but – atypical for Swabes – they kept religion near the hearth and out of public view.

Ute's earliest memories were the not-so-subtle Swabish dictums. First among these was the difference between Bavarians and the Swabish. Second was the "*tradition,*" if not outright insistence that Swabes and Bavarians do not – *should not* – mix. As a wholesaler (Kaufmann by name; Kaufmann by trade), the family patriarch enjoyed a thriving business among Bavarian merchants. Beyond the ledger sheet and the obligatory schmoozing, Heinrich Kaufmann und Sohn was seldom represented at swank Bavarian soirées – a practice promoted and maintained by both ethnic contingents. At school, Ute mixed with Bavarian children and most of her teachers were Bavarian. There, existed no appreciable friction beyond what one finds in any school. However, Ute's closest friends were all Swabes.

Aside from the cultural lore of Swabia, Ute was privy to certain family "adjuncts." These were propounded, primarily on family experiences rather than anything endemically Swabish. As one would expect, Ute learned that Swabes married Swabes. Time introduced an additional maxim in the wake of many, many wars: *never marry a soldier*.

The fruit of such indoctrination was predictable. Ute's brother, Dieter, married a deliciously lovely Bavarian girl and set aside the Swabish boisterousness to take on the reserved – almost aloof – Bavarian manner. He started a nice, quiet, Bavarian family. Under ordinary circumstances, this breech of etiquette would have stirred up a hornet's nest in the Swabish circle. Dieter's faux pas, however, merely cocked eyebrows. After Ute's abominations, Dieter's transgressions were, comparatively, innocuous.

Upon completion of her schooling, Ute obtained a job with a local department store. Her Swabish attributes, a tenacious work ethic and tooth-aching honesty, were tremendous advantages. When she made a mistake, as she frequently did in her early days, she not only admitted it, she announced it to all and sundry with the addendum that she'd not repeat the error. In an amazingly short period, she made nearly all possible blunders and became the person her employer most relied upon. Even Bavarians admire probity. That, coupled with efficiency and alacrity, made Ute popular with the management. She lived at home, but that is not an unusual circumstance, even in modern-day Europe.

One afternoon, an Ami soldier in mufti ambled into the store. Ute identified him by the close-cropped hair and clothes that screamed Western hemisphere. He was purposeful in his search and quickly found that which he sought. Ute was behind the register. The soldier made some remark in German so mangled Ute couldn't decipher a single word.

Swabish politeness brushed aside her natural reticence; she responded in English. The soldier's face lit with appreciation. He grinned, accepted his purchase and blushed slightly while enunciating a recognizable "*auf wiedersehn.*" The entire incident brought the girl a moment of mirth, but the memory of the encounter hardly survived the soldier's disappearance.

More than a month went by before Ute found herself enjoying a day at the zoo. It was her favorite haunt. The admission price was more than a lowly department store employee cared to pay, but the amusement she found was magnified by the nature of the place. She'd visited other zoos, but they were built for people. The Nürnberg Zoo, she maintained, was designed for animals.

Avoiding low tree branches, Ute reveled in the spring afternoon. Sunlight spilled around. The lush foliage provided amusing shadows. As a Swabish girl, she didn't require friends or relatives to escort her. It was a place she wished to share only with the animals.

She was in no hurry to leave. On the contrary, she was determined to lounge about on benches and enjoy the day. Swabish thrift demands that paying a large sum for entry, one must enjoy every nook and cranny. All the amenities were, after all, provided.

She emerged from the public ladies' room with freshly scrubbed hands, ready to purchase one of the ubiquitous wursts. The aroma had teased her nose and appetite for some while. Focused as was she on the appealing sausages, Ute paid no heed to the man preceding her in line. As he turned to leave, Ute was unexpectedly accosted.

"I know you!"

With no one nearby, other than the man at the Imbiss, she must be the addressee. It was unsettling, being publicly hailed in English and by a man! She examined a recognized face.

"You're the girl who speaks English."

It was bad form to point out that most girls of her generation spoke English. Still, she was flattered the Ami soldier recognized her, though she dared not postulate why.

They shared a bench and conversed in English and tried, with moderate success, not to appear unattractive while masticating and preventing *senf* from dripping onto their clothes. The soldier attempted to speak German, but it was futile. They relied on English. Ute caught herself before correcting the man's grammar. It was rude and supercilious – both strictly forbidden under her Swabish code. Then, of course, she mightn't be as proficient in conversational English as her school marks indicated.

It remains beyond the scope of the present narrative to detail the ensuing courtship, nor is there need to recount the upset, both for Ute's family and the Swabish community in general. One is invited to imagine the heart-numbing, breath-ceasing shock when Ute announced her acceptance of an Ami marriage proposal. Many times, in subsequent years, Ute recalled the admonition of marrying soldiers. Even though the European theatre was, relatively, calm, there were moments when the Cold War threatened to become blazing hot.

How Ute's heart froze when the phone rang in the late or early hours. Then, there were those unending days – Ute counted them – when her husband disappeared into the landscape of Southeast Asia leaving her to contemplate life as a widow. Their posting to Fort Campbell was, also, a trial. So fearful was she when her husband announced he was slated for a live-fire range, that he ceased making mention. No explanations could placate her until a junior officer advised him to invite Ute to an exercise.

There were regulations, of course, but none a good top sergeant couldn't navigate. It came to pass that Ute Foster *nee* Kaufmann, found herself perched atop a tracked vehicle wearing a steel helmet and a flak jacket while witnessing the sight of her husband and his crew sending ordinance clanking into rusted hulks far down range. She was no longer apprehensive. It would take a deranged genius months of planning to thwart all the safety precautions and visit injury on someone.

Still, she couldn't be with her husband every time he went to a range; thus, she'd sit quietly at home, trying not to think about it and wringing her hands in worry whenever she did. When Sergeant First Class Aaron Foster was ordered back to Germany, Ute was thrilled.

"You'd better start being nice to me," she teased. "I'll go home to Mother."

She did, as it turned out, but not from tempestuousness. As a member of the cavalry, SFC Foster was engaged in frequent exercises. If, Ute figured, her husband would be away from home for three or more days, there was no reason for her to be alone. Rather than reflect on her husband's life expectancy should the Soviet forces spill across the border (thirty seconds was a generous estimate), the Swabish woman enjoyed time with her family.

It was an arduous process to overcome Ute's transgressions, but Swabish people seldom nurture grudges. Ute's marriage to an Ami soldier made Dieter's misdemeanors little more than annoyances. Ultimately, she was no less welcome in the Kaufmann abode than when she lived there. Similarly, Aaron's infrequent visits were the excuse for proper Swabish – a.k.a., loud – celebrations. Too many sins, however, defy even the most studied attempts at amends.

Ute promised she would raise her children in the best Swabish tradition. As the months turned into years and children tarried, the prospective grandparents grew increasingly restless. Then, the word arrived with one of Ute's welcome visits. She'd seen service doctors and civilian doctors, but she waited until examined, tested, and poked by a Swabish specialist.

Ute Foster was barren.

It was ruinous news for the Kaufmanns and their army-wife daughter. They spent a weekend in grief. Still, there were plenty of celebrations over the blessings remaining. Then, several months later, Ute created an egregious wound that revived the family tumult.

She brought into her home a foundling.

War and Revelation

Oregon, 1986-1987

The Pride of Fair Seas Charter Company was the *Mary R.*, a forty-eight-foot, twin-inboard, sport cruiser laid down in Portland in 1912. Over the years, the craft changed hands several times before Ed Barker bought it and carried out the latest in a series of overhauls. She was well-tended and prudently used, but served, almost exclusively, to ferry sport fisherman on day trips. Indeed, it was for this that Barker bought the craft. Gemini circumstances, however, delivered "Captain" Foster to her helm.

The expected overhaul was delayed by cash-flow problems. Too much of the company's assets were tied up in maintenance and equipment. Though Barker's company had ample collateral, the process of securing a loan proved cumbersome. When *Mary*'s overhaul began, the man, to whom command was promised, was diagnosed with cancer and faced lengthy and problematic treatments. Though Aaron Foster secured the proper documents to skipper the craft, Barker was unwilling to trust a fishing vessel to a novice pilot.

Coastal fishermen are a jealous lot. It required years of experience to learn the ins and outs of the trade. Competent as Aaron Foster was, he was new to the fishing community and hardly worthy to ferry a group of well-heeled but highly demanding sportsmen.

The second felicitous event began just as the *Mary R.* came out of the yard. A single pod of whales was caught off the tiny entrance to the local harbor. The migration period was over; whale law dictated that all transients remain in limbo until the next migration. The pod became a magnet for tourists.

Few people paused at the wide-spot on U.S. highway 101 long enough for a cup of coffee. Suddenly, transients invested in whale watching. One of Barker's competitors began sending day fishermen to Fair Seas to facilitate lucrative whale cruises. Barker was grateful for the referrals – until he realized how much more money he could make. Suddenly, the formula made sense. Three of Barker's boats would continue catering to sports fishermen.

The *Mary R.*, however, was diverted to the whale industry. Aaron Foster's lack of fishing experience ceased being an issue. Indeed, when the whales vacated their feeding place, Barker could keep one of the boats home and rotate Foster around on the remaining three until he learned enough to take out live-bait customers on his own.

Ed Barker, however, squeezed nickels until the buffalo bellowed. So long as there were whales, there were people plunking down folding money for a close look. The pod must have had great connections, because the little town on the edge of the big ocean was seldom left without these living tourist attractions. Aaron Foster remained on permanent "whale watch."

Barker ran four to six tours a day with the whales, depending upon the weather and time of year. Further, whale watching required no fishing gear, no bait, and none of the added expenses incurred in the fishing business. All Barker had to pay for was the skipper, the Coast Guard approved "mate" (re: safety regulations) and fuel. During the summer months, Kathy Foster lived on the *Mary R.* and, with a little conniving, she served as first mate. She knew CPR; she knew first aid; she knew quite a bit about everything – and, as a minor, Barker paid her pennies.

He did part with a few dollars every week, under the table. Kathy's dad made it possible for Barker to afford it. Kathy Foster loved going out on the *Mary R.*, and she loved communing with the whales. Nevertheless, there were times – no matter how infrequent – when she wished to remain ashore. Without a mate, the *Mary R.* couldn't sail, and Barker balked at paying anyone a proper wage.

Kathy, fluent in German, matched Ed Barker swear word for swear word. In the end, Barker won because he held Aaron's job hostage. Kathy might do or say anything, but if her father's wages were on the line, she'd surrender. Still, Barker relented just often enough to ensure the continuation of their verbal battles. The cranky, aging Barker enjoyed these bi-lingual duels.

The Fisherman's Inn is a local greasy spoon perched on the edge of the bay – "the smallest navigable harbor in the world," if local propaganda holds true. Waiting table for tourists, truckers and the less imaginative locals, Ute Foster had a half-dozen picture windows through which to check the comings and goings of the *Mary R.*, and the status of her crew. When the weather worsened, she'd turn terse until she viewed the craft puttering safely into sheltered water.

The only uniform in the Fisherman's Inn was a white apron and a name tag. Ute's pseudonym was Judy. She started out playing the game willingly enough, but there came a time when one customer too many asked what U-T-E stood for. Kathy would be quick enough to say something witty and, probably, off color. Ute's repartee was not so skilled; she assumed the alias (and the name badge) of a former employee.

Kathy often rode her bike up the hill to Mr. James's market. She spent part of Ed Barker's *Schwartzgeld* on cookies, ice cream, or an occasional book. She was never tempted to buy ham openly, but she burned with guilt over her, thus far, undetected thefts. It was a guilt she couldn't dismiss.

The Pig War raged without truce.

One morning, Kathy sat at the counter of the Fisherman's Inn nursing a cup of cocoa and an attitude. The previous evening marked the greatest engagement of the war. As it proved inconclusive, both sides retired from the field licking wounds. Resentment festered.

Ute brought out a plate of bacon and eggs for a trucker seated just three stools further down the counter. She cast a glance at Kathy who replied by making a face. The bacon smelled so good! Kathy's resentment revived. She'd have said something brusque were she not in a public place. She composed and revised an acid comment to serve up at the first opportunity.

The girl kept a careful watch over her shoulder. She was irked to find the *Mary R.* in motion. How her father got aboard without her notice stoked her temper. There were ninety wooden steps from the sidewalk to the dock and it was time she went to work for Scrooge MacBarker. She slid off the stool and started for the door.

She did not know what toxic comment she'd hurl at her father while boarding – she had ninety steps to compose an aria – but she knew either bacon or ham would be a subject or, at least, a direct object. As she neared the inner door of the café's unique entrance, a hand gripped her shoulder and whirled her around. Before Kathy regained equilibrium, her mother's arms held her tight long enough to generate acute embarrassment. Then, as suddenly as the attack came, it was over. Ute cantered back behind the counter and into the kitchen.

Kathy wasn't sure, but she thought Ute's face was contorted. The hair at the back of Kathy's neck prickled. She was certain her mother was fighting back tears. It wasn't until she threw her leg over the railing that she remembered her initial intention. Aaron Foster stood on the bridge expectantly.

With no venom to hurl, Kathy looked away. She lifted the hinged portion of the railing she deigned to use. A half dozen passengers moved forward, clutching their tickets. Behind them, thumping down the long stairway as if afraid of being left behind, other passengers rushed toward the boat while producing frivolous banter.

"After we cast off, get up here."

Aaron Foster's voice took an abrupt tone. Kathy hated to be on the defensive and silently derided herself for not launching the first volley. Even in a fight, Swabish civility must be observed. Her father had given an order. Until she knew it was personal, rather than nautical, Kathy was obligated to obey.

Once everyone was aboard, she advised the passengers of the location of the life vests, reminded them to remain on deck, and use the railing whenever standing or moving about. She cast off the stern line then sprinted adroitly to the bow to do the same there, hauling fenders aboard and stowing them as she went. She was in no hurry to get to the bridge, however. She waited until a few adventurers slid up to the foredeck. As Kathy made her way back onto the poop, *Mary R.* passed under the highway bridge.

The conversations of the passengers echoed off the rock walls and the steel and concrete span. She climbed the ladder quickly enough and plopped down beside her father looking back at the frothing wake. Even at her devilish worst, she knew better than to speak. The *Mary R.* was slithering out of the bay between two natural rock sentries far enough apart to allow the passage of small craft. Any miscalculation or sudden swell could turn the boat into splinters and any survivors into casualties.

Kathy saw the harbor entrance behind, and knew they were in the channel. Still, Aaron said nothing. She watched as the scene became a vista – the bridge, the traffic gliding across it, the businesses fronting the highway, and the people receding into mere splashes of color. Still, Aaron remained silent.

It was Gary Swofford! That little snot! He snitched. He told his mom who called Aaron and gave him an ear full. That's why her father's order was so gruff. Her blood boiling, Kathy prepared her defense. Athena Swofford was a great woman. It would not do for Kathy to attack her – as if she could. Who could smear someone with the name of a Greek goddess?

Athena, like Ute, was a waitress at the Fisherman's Inn. She was ever perky, witty and gave as good as she got from customers. Once upon a time, she was a woman in love. Her family did not approve. She married anyway and was ushered out of the clan.

It was all fun and games for three years. When she discovered herself in the family way, the fun ended. Her husband did not want children. Athena did. The argument ended the morning she woke to discover herself abandoned.

"*Well, Mr. Swofford,*" Kathy thought, "*whoever and wherever you are, I'm with you. The world would be a much better place if Gary were not in it.*"

He knew Kathy couldn't abide the German mangling of her name, Ka-TEE. It drove her up the wall. Stupidly, she told him about this peeve when she mistook him for human. Mindlessly, she detailed the frustrations of the Pig War. Then, one afternoon, they fell into an argument.

It was unfair; Kathy was winning the verbal brawl without breaking a sweat. That was when Gary goaded her,

"Shove a schnitzel up your dress, Ka-TEE!"

Her fist was in his face that instant. Somehow, he hadn't expected that reaction; he stumbled backwards with his hands over his mouth. He tried to say something, but when he saw blood on his hands, he slunk away. Instead of staying and fighting like a man, he ran home to Mommy. Aaron Foster intended to scold her.

Kathy organized her defense.

Exhibit A: she never wore dresses – despised them, in fact. Exhibit B: Gary had no right to taunt her with pig meat. Exhibit C: Ka-TEE. As with exhibit B, the jury would consider his pronunciation an open invitation to reprisal. If Aaron Foster had a triple digit IQ, he'd praise Kathy for self-restraint. She only split Gary's lip; she had grounds to kill him.

"Kathy, there's no time or place to tell you this," the skipper said at long last. "We should have told you years ago, but – I guess neither your mother –"

When he stopped, the hairs on the back of Kathy's neck stood again. That sudden, mysterious hug became ominous. She was off guard; she continued to stare at the shore, bobbing on the horizon. It took five minutes to clear the channel. She'd not stand watch until then.

"Kathy, Ute and I weren't married for very long before we learned –"

Another incomplete sentence hung in the air like a storm cloud. Kathy broke out in goose flesh. Her father did not stutter or stammer. Had Gary died? Did he drown in his own blood? Would the police meet them at the dock? Athena was not at work that morning. Previously, Kathy gave it no thought. Suddenly, Athena's absence was ominous.

"Kathy!" she jumped at the sharp tone.

She turned her head to find her father diverting attention from the channel buoys.

"Are you listening to me?"

She should have phrased a reply. Instead, she nodded emphatically.

Captain Foster appeared relieved and returned to his duties.

"We found out that we couldn't have children."

Kathy focused on the arch of the highway bridge. Her father's words caused unease, but she was too stunned to figure out why.

"I was on border patrol one morning," he went on quickly. "We saw a Soviet officer through our glasses at a rail crossing. He looked to be reading the riot act to some guys in civilian clothes and some officers – they looked like officers – in East German uniforms. We decided to look around. There was snow on the ground, so when we found tracks –"

Kathy sensed rather than saw him wipe a sweaty palm on his pants.

"The tracks went into the woods. I left the vehicle and driver behind. Me and another guy followed the tracks. The Germans were there. Some farmer called, I guess. He was poaching, probably. Tracks in snow – makes it easier."

There was an uncomfortable silence. Kathy waited, still unaware of the implications of the story, but very aware that it was difficult for her father to relate it.

"They'd taken you to hospital – had pulled you from under some woman's coat. All blue, they said, more dead than alive, they said. Didn't expect you to live, they said. The guy with me understood German pretty good. They'd covered a body, but they hadn't moved her – yet."

The second person pronoun rang through her head like the thunder of a thousand bronze bells. Kathy was stunned. She heard her father, but reality evaded her. She knew he had problems speaking. His story disturbed her, but she couldn't grasp it.

"I told your – I told Ute. She was on the phone for hours, calling everybody she could think of. I think – I think she wanted to make sure you were okay. She – well, I think we know where you get your stubbornness. The more they put her off, the more determined she was. Ute got it into her head that she was going to take care of you – didn't trust you in the care of people who didn't give a rat's ass. The German paper-pushers didn't like her interfering because I'm American. Ute had a fit. She spent months and months getting the run-around, but she kept on. I hardly ever saw her. She was never at home. She and her brother were – well, I gave up. They didn't. The day she brought you home –"

His voice broke and he wiped away his tears.

Kathy stood up, bounded back down onto the deck, worked her way forward and began searching for tell-tale spouts. They managed to get within twenty yards of a blue. There were expressions of wonder, gratitude and awe. Many camera shutters clicked. Kathy remained her normal animated self until the *Mary R.* turned for home.

She answered questions and even exchanged banter with the passengers. When she returned to the bridge, she resumed her place with the same sober expression she wore previously.

"Maybe you wondered why we celebrate your birthday and Thanksgiving together. That was Ute's idea. As near as anyone can figure, you were born about that time. The Germans don't have Thanksgiving, but Americans do, and Ute figured we had something to – be – thankful for. The birth document was issued by the West Germans. The stuffed shirt at the registry didn't care for the name Ute picked. You know, in Germany, the government decides what parents are permitted to name a child. He wanted to put Katherine or, at least, Katarina, but Ute is like a Moray eel – when she gets her teeth in something, she lets go only when she's ready. She wanted Kathy – just Kathy. It isn't completely unknown in Germany. In America it isn't as popular as it used to be, but it's always short for something. Ute wanted Kathy – just plain Kathy – the one – the only."

Kathy counted the buoys as they slid aft. She knew they were near the harbor entrance.

"I'm not half-Swabish?"

"Highly doubtful."

"Am I even German?"

"Probably, but there is no way to be certain."

She crossed her arms over her jacketed chest and continued to study the wake of the boat.

"Why don't we go to church much? Why didn't we make you go to Sunday school? Why the big deal about pork? Ute felt a responsibility. If, one day, you found out that you were Jewish, maybe, or something else, you'd hate us for stuffing you full of pork and making you go to church –"

Kathy snorted. The very idea of hating her parents was absurd.

"We should have told you long ago, I know. We wanted to, but – Ute was afraid. I guess that fight last night pushed her over the edge. She wanted to tell you this morning, but she couldn't – well – she just couldn't. So – this was hard. Thanks for not being difficult."

Kathy swallowed hard.

"Why was Mom afraid?"

She forced herself to speak loudly enough to be heard above the engines.

"She was afraid that you wouldn't want her to be your mother anymore."

Kathy thought back to the mysterious, tearful hug.

This was too much!

She launched herself into action. Vacating the bridge, she rushed down into the hold. There, away from prying eyes, she threw herself onto a bunk and cried.

Flirting with Treason

German Democratic Republic
1987

Two beds filled a cramped room with no space for a third. Jürgen had the larger; polished cherry it was. Likely crafted in the nineteenth century, its history was obscure; it was war salvage. The previous owners had no need of it. An alternate story insisted the bed belonged to a prominent Jewish family until their pelf was seized. Regardless, Herr Jacobs, the elder, purchased it through services rendered.

It was high off the floor in the style of by-gone days. Heike Jacobs required aid to mount it. Her brother, the brawny athlete, jumped up onto it. The second bed was Nadine's. Though, also, pre-war vintage, it was more modern.

In former times, the sisters shared it in perfect tranquility. Later, however, they outgrew it and Heike, the youngest, was placed on a pallet on the floor nearest the window. Over the years, the child transformed it into a comfortable little nest. It was drafty under the window. In the winter months, Heike wore a woolen cap to bed. In the heat of the summer, air movement was welcome.

It was only right and proper for Heike to be banished. She was the youngest. She was not Jacobs by blood. Heike's real parents were traitors. Shortly after her birth, they attempted to smuggle her out of the DDR. She hated them. She hoped never to meet them – hoped she'd never know anything about them.

Heike was a Jacobs, by law and by choice. She'd fight like a tigress should anyone question her filial loyalty.

She lay on her stomach squinting at a tattered Russian textbook. She was not "quick of study," but she was highly motivated.

Heike Jacobs was on a mission to erase the shame of her traitorous past by becoming a productive member of the State. She entertained ambitions of party membership, an honor many desired but few achieved. Heike was determined to produce a record of accomplishments no one dare overlook. A prestigious record, however, is predicated on impressive school marks. Herr Jacobs the elder, Rolf, was unquestioningly deserving of party membership. So, also, were Jürgen and Nadine, both respected members of the *Freie Deutsche Jungend* (FDJ).

None of them were ever nominated. Of course, her siblings were still young. Should one, or both, achieve party membership, Heike's chances would increase. She, however, rejected nepotism. Heike valued nothing unearned.

Russian was her enemy. She refused to accept anything less than complete mastery. Thus, on a warm summer's day which lured others outdoors, she locked in battle with a tenacious foe.

The letters contorted under her burning eyes. Thankfully, the Slavic tongue is phonetic. Heike could, and often did, read entire passages aloud with only vague notions of meaning. Her difficulties resided in syntax and her rudimentary knowledge of the Russian lexicon. She required a higher-level vocabulary.

"Words, words, words," quoth the Prince of Denmark.

As an admirer of the Bard, Heike recalled quotes and allusions, but these seldom brought succor – certainly not under the present circumstance. Pushkin's diction taunted. Wrinkles of anger mingled with those of hate. She refused to seek refuge in either glossary or footnotes. If she could – through cerebral labor and stubbornness – decipher a word through context, she'd carry its meaning to the grave.

So focused was she on her self-imposed torture that Heike remained unaware of Nadine's presence until she announced herself. Heike was not startled; she was annoyed. All her assigned chores were dispatched. She expected privacy – had, in fact, demanded it. Nadine had no jurisdiction.

Nature was not kind to Nadine. True, Heike was but one of many who envied the silky texture of the shimmering, blond hair Nadine kept short and neatly trimmed. It was, unfortunately, thin and Nadine's pink scalp resembled a scar where she parted her tresses above the left ear. Her face was an oval and her features so unremarkable that Nadine seldom drew attention. The physical fortunes of the family were visited upon Jürgen; Nadine – poor, poor Nadine – was forced to navigate the world on wit and charm.

Alas, she possessed little of either,

"Jürgen sent me," Nadine advanced, fearful of stirring Heike's temper.

"I'm busy."

Nadine took a breath. She didn't want a scene.

"This is important."

Jürgen was not one to disturb Heike without cause. Moreover, it was unlike him to dispatch Nadine as a summoner. In the circumstances, it was curiosity above mental fatigue that forced her into a truce.

The Jacobs's abode was tiny enough, even by European standards. There was one large room downstairs with a cramped kitchen in the back accessed by a low, narrow arch. The bathroom, a contortionist's nightmare, was tucked under the stairs when – weeks prior to the war – indoor plumbing was introduced. Seated on the miniature couch, quiet and serine was Frau Jacobs, her light brown hair liberally streaked with gray and pulled back into a bun.

"We will be in the park, Mutti," Nadine announced.

Frau Jacobs's eyes flashed momentarily, then, she receded into the seclusion of whatever remained of her mind. When Heike first knew her, Mutti was the cheery personification of unlimited and unreserved love. Her arms were always open, and her heart full. Then, slowly, she metamorphosed into a state of quiet reserve as some malevolent thief robbed her of her senses. Though she appeared to understand when her children and her husband addressed her, she seldom spoke.

She handled household tasks unaided, but her former alacrity deserted her. When not engaged, she sat quietly and stared at things only she could see. Heike forced a smile; it didn't come naturally. She owed so very much to the shadow of a woman who once welcomed her into the tiny house. Frau Jacobs treated Heike exactly as if she were her own.

Once on the sun-drenched street, the sisters set out briskly for the public expanse wrapped around the modest Ilm River like a cloak of green sable.

"Did you hear the story about the Polish dog and the German dog passing each other on a bridge between the two countries?"

Heike admitted that she hadn't. She didn't care for jokes.

"The dog from the DDR asked the Polish dog why he wanted to go to Germany. 'I have to eat,' said the Polish dog. 'Why do you want to go into Poland?' The German dog said, 'I have to bark.'"

Instinctively, Heike looked about – careful not to be obvious. She satisfied herself they were beyond earshot.

In the DDR, one learns to be anxious without looking anxious.

"Where did you hear that?" she hissed.

"Be patient," Nadine whispered in reply.

Some minutes later, they were at the bank of the river. They skirted that meandering stream before turning back toward the city. Climbing a lazy incline, they walked through a gap in a hedge and ducked under the low-lying branches of an ancient oak. Once clear, they discovered Jürgen sitting, Indian style, in the grass. Heike bulked momentarily. He was in the company of eight others.

They formed a circle in an unprotected space. The nearest tree was a good ten meters distant.

"*Why don't you just post a sign?*" Heike thought to herself.

Approaching, Heike recognized Günther Neubert.

Her heart raced.

Günther and Jürgen were best friends and classmates. Günther was the most handsome youth in Weimar, by Heike's reckoning. She was glad Nadine pried her from the Slavs. To be in the company of Günther Neubert was an honor she "dreamed not of."

Her legs, suddenly rubber, caused her to lag. Was it the sight of Günther or the realization that she approached something subversive?

The moment she settled onto the grass with these people, her chances of party membership were at risk. Still, to be near Günther, it was worth the gamble.

Once settled into the space provide by relative strangers, Heike noticed Liselotte 'Lilo' Kruger. The slim, leggy blond, seemed two meters tall. Heike would have recognized her before had she stood. Seated with her long legs folded, Lilo wasn't so conspicuous. To the rest of the world – the male portion – Lilo was a beauty.

Her long blond hair splashed off broad shoulders and – *zu weiter*. Had Heike the skills of the Bard, she'd paint a brilliant poetic portrait devoid of hyperbole. However, and for good reason, Heike was immune to Lilo's allure. She was stung by the Folly twins, Inattention and Envy. Were she not focused on the image making her blood race, she'd have noticed Lilo curled up against Günther like a fawning kitten.

Young Heike dare not entertain hope. It was enough to admire her "Romeo" from a distance. She was determined to enjoy the sweet and abide the bitter.

"I still say she's too young," an unidentified boy said.

Heike cast a glance at the speaker. She knew him by sight but not by name. She looked at Jürgen, then at Nadine, kneeling across the circle from her, then back at Günther (as furtively possible without appearing furtive).

"Give the girl a chance," Jürgen replied.

There was a subdued surge of mirth. Heike resented inside jokes. Those created at her expense, she resented more so. Only the presence of Jürgen and Günther kept her from launching a rude remark.

"Heike," Jürgen began, "have you heard the story about the German dog and the Polish dog?"

She cast a glance at Nadine and found her visage impassive.

"Yes," she admitted.

Despite the distance from potential eavesdroppers, she avoided the risk of a repetition. She, habitually, limited herself to monosyllabic responses. In the DDR, elaboration was often needless and always dangerous.

"Well," he continued, "this is where we bark. This is a larger group than most, but we are all on track for party membership, so we're innocuous enough, I suppose. Still, even we need a place where we can speak. One cannot formulate constructive ideas if denied open discussion, *na*? One of our number left for an apprenticeship; we desire fresh blood, so to speak – bright, ambitious and as dedicated to the socialist cause as we are. Naturally, I thought of you, but I could hardly suggest it, could I?"

"So, Günther suggested it," a girl next to Lilo volunteered.

Heike looked Günther in the eye. Her vision was momentarily blurred by the world's undulation. Instantly, she was propelled into a fantasy world where a thirteen-year-old girl and a seventeen-year-old boy could – but, when Lilo rested her head on Günther's shoulder, the fantasy galloped through images of severed limbs and a mutilated face. She felt herself blush and hoped no one realized it was the product of shame and envy rather than embarrassment.

"We do insist on one rule that must never, never be broken," Jürgen advanced with a tone both ominous and profoundly serious, "nothing we talk about within this group, nothing that is said from one person to another in this group, must ever be repeated beyond this group. Do you understand?"

Her attention momentarily diverted from Günther; Heike was about to nod her head. At the last moment, she caught herself. She was well-schooled on the proper means of sealing a vow.

"I will never repeat anything said in this group to anyone beyond it."

Jürgen nodded approval and rocked back.

"I've known Heike for twelve years," he announced. "I've never known her to violate a confidence."

"Nor I," Nadine added without prompting.

"Well," Günther nodded, "that is a glowing recommendation."

Heike maintained her poise with great difficulty. Günther, first in her youthful heart, endorsed her as a person of honor.

"There is one thing," Nadine began, solemnity.

All eyes turned upon the speaker. Heike, experiencing breathing problems, narrowed her eyes. Was her sister turning petty? She and Nadine seldom saw eye-to-eye. Indeed, their differences often graduated to violence.

Despite her tinder years, the rage in Heike's heart magnified her ferocity. Nadine suffered physically during these encounters. If Nadine introduced grievances, she would pay.

"We all know how Heike came to us. She's teased at school. Sometimes, it's nasty. If anybody holds her family's history against her, speak up."

Günther nodded his approval, but it was Lilo, letting go of Günther's arm for the occasion, who elaborated.

"Nadine is right. If anybody feels resentment, let's discuss it."

Another group member, known to Heike only by sight, seconded the sentiment.

"A person can carry that kind of thing around for a long time," he philosophized. "Then, at exactly the worst moment, it explodes. Better to hurt feelings now than risk disaster later."

There was a quick burst of mumblings and a tacit cross-examination by those assembled.

"You two live with her," someone previously unknown asked. "Do you know of any reason why we should doubt your sister's loyalty?"

Jürgen, true to his character, did not respond at once. As with all important matters, he thought it over carefully and objectively. Nadine watched him closely. Her answer was formulated long before the question was asked, but Jürgen was her elder. It was her place to defer.

"I cannot think of a single reason," he announced.

Automatically, all eyes settled onto Nadine who shook her head slowly.

"Not a single one," she echoed.

And that, in the parlance of popular literature, was that. Heike Jacobs was a member of young barkers. She was too wise to insert herself into the conversational flow that day. In the DDR, particularly, people avoided appearing presumptuous or precocious. Heike realized the organization had, hitherto, existed quite well without her. If asked a direct question, she'd reply in a direct and terse manner. Since no one did, she kept silent.

Despite remaining out of earshot, the group discussed innocuous topics. The most enterprising Stasi agent would have naught to report.

The group, after all, was based on the faithful and party hopefuls. Everyone, save Heike, was a leader in the FDJ. All but two held awards. Because their FDJ affiliation, they concluded the session by standing and exchanging the organizational salute.

"*Freundschaft*," Günter announced with the accepted gesture.

"*Freundschaft*," the others, including Heike, responded.

Again, the girl felt her legs wobble and her heart race. She was too young to become a member of the FDJ. Still, giving the salute and the proper salutation, she imagined herself in the blue shirt that bore the proud emblem on her sleeve of the glowing, golden rays of the rising sun. True, only those who courted social disaster refused membership. One could not expect a good job or university placement without FDJ endorsement. If conscripted into the army, one might never experience promotion.

There was nothing special about wearing the blue shirt. People such as Günther, Jürgen, Lilo, Nadine and, soon, Heike were certain to thrive and excel in the organization. That would provide the first important step on the path to party membership.

Heike swathed herself in the dream of a noteworthy FDJ career. Of course, she imagined herself stepping into the ranks of the party, but another part of her dream was equally exciting. As a respected leader of the party, she'd not only be worthy of her country, she'd be worthy of Günther. They would be equals.

Pain shot up her body and burrowed into her head. Heike let go a rude word.

"What's wrong?" Jürgen asked.

He was a step ahead of his sisters, leading the way homeward. He paused to investigate.

Heike bent down to rub her ankle. Only when pain subsided, did she examine the cobblestones.

"I twisted my ankle," she protested.

Nadine had no problem locating the offending stone. She stomped on the guilty protrusion without result.

"You'd think they could keep the streets in proper repair," Nadine muttered.

"Ja," Heike agreed, thoughtlessly.

A moment later, as she limped along, Heike shivered. For the first time in her life, she had criticized the party. If any outsider heard, the trio might face reprisals.

* * *

Influences

He sat, unforgettable, with one arm akimbo and clutching a scroll, one foot dangling over a skull. He leaned forward slightly as if watching a drama playing out in the city park. She was accustomed to his presence. His confident, smug expression demanded attention. Shakespeare, alone of the city's statuary, was seated – and not on a horse. More to the point, he appeared casual. He looked real. He was the friendliest effigy in the city, and Heike never passed without studying him.

At school, Heike learned statues represented people of accomplishment. They symbolized, not only the person, but the profound ideas the person promoted for the benefit of *das Volk*. Goethe and Schiller shook hands in front of the theatre; Liszt and Herder appeared cold and arrogant, Ernst Thälmann was angry – so much so that Heike avoided him whenever possible. Neptune, a personal favorite, looked rather jolly, holding a trident in his hand and with a fountain at his feet.

Shakespeare, however, struck her as affable.

She was, perhaps, five when she asked after this curious image. Nadine was along. As the elder sister, by a hundred days, Nadine felt responsible for educating her adopted sister. Shakespeare, however, was an unknown. Therefore, she pouted until Mutti waxed eloquently in a narration swallowing them both.

As a young girl, Mutti related cheerily, her class was ushered into the National Theater. It was an assault on the senses: the language was bold if archaic, the costumes strange but magical, and the action was mesmerizing. After the performance, the students were allowed a few minutes with the cast. Only then did Mutti understand that the entire program was authored by a long-dead Englishman.

"It was," Mutti confessed, "the happiest, most satisfying day of my school life."

Nadine was moved only momentarily. Heike, however, was enraptured. The statue in the park graduated from life-like figure to the most important person beyond her family. If this man's words made Frau Jacobs happy, he deserved veneration.

Over the years, he became Heike's spiritual guru.

"Oh, what beautiful poetry, *Liebchen*!"

The passage of time and her mother's descent into inarticulation did not blunt the memory of Anne Jacobs's gushing praise.

Heike's knowledge of the theatre was predicated on her teachers' praise of Goethe and Schiller; they were Germans. They'd lived and worked in the city. Mutti's exaltation remained a beacon. Until she experienced Shakespeare, Heike's adulation of the local heroes remained conditional.

Jürgen inherited his mother's personality. It mattered not that Heike was not his real sister. He treated her as if she was his mother's youngest child. He adopted his mother's pet name for her, '*little mouse.*' Unable to mount Jürgen's high bed, she sat at the foot of the neighboring one she and Nadine once shared and asked about the famous Englishman.

Jürgen had yet to see a Shakespeare play. However, he'd sampled his work. He explained, in direct and respectful language, how the local Shakespearian society so worshipped the bard that it attempted to "adopt" him and "make him German." It was during the Romantic Movement when, otherwise, intelligent people entertained fantastic notions. Still, the statue in the park was tangible evidence that once, in Weimar, there existed dedicated admirers.

"I'd like to see some of his things," Heike announced.

Jürgen could easily have echoed the words of others when confronted by Heike's youthful exuberance. He could, for example, remind her of her youth. That, however, never crossed his mind. Jürgen was not, thankfully, like other people; he took after his mother.

Jürgen knew so much. Moreover, he was the family repository of "unauthorized" history.

"Let me see what I can do," he nodded.

Three years later, for her birthday, Heike was presented with the worm-eaten remains of the complete-works of Shakespeare. The front cover and several of the introductory pages were missing; the binding was in shreds and the print so small that Heike's young eyes could read it only under strong light. Nevertheless, with Jürgen's aid, she began.

She started with *The Winter's Tale* for reasons she couldn't explain. It was slow going at first. The German was decidedly old and caked with formality, but she wanted to share the thrill Anne Ecke once experienced. It came gradually, but her mind began to resonate with the meter. She understood how people can fall in love with poetry and words.

When the play's statue came to life, however, Heike became Shakespeare's slave. She shared her experience in the dark with Nadine. It was frustrating. Her summation of the plot was uninteresting and devoid of craftmanship. Heike grasped for the Bard's words but recalled few. She created her own words – bold, gripping words – verbal painting.

Eventually, Jürgen said something inaudible though complementary. Nadine said nothing, but Heike heard her sniff, proof that she was as moved by Heike's words just as Heike was moved by the master. Encouraged by this experience, Heike flew to the park to sit in the shadow of her most appreciated teacher. She read to him the words from her mangled text. Frequently, she would look up to see if her love for him could bring *his* statue to life.

She never managed. However, she imagined that, occasionally, the corners of Shakespeare's mouth curled up into a faint smile. She launched into *Much Ado*, suppling her with laughs while teaching her how people can be tragically gullible. From this, she followed the master into *Julius Caesar*, which proved tedious, but not without its moments. She discovered a soulmate in Portia. She read and reread the scene between Brutus and Portia.

How she loved him!

Heike admired this quality. She was in love herself. She'd never admit it. She, certainly, wouldn't declare it. Merely thirteen, no logic or reason could shake her one fundamental conclusion: she loved Günther Neubert. All the signs were evident and undeniable – shortness of breath at the sight of him, a gnawing in the stomach, a tingling in her body, loss of appetite, the inability to concentrate, and the futility of banishing him from her thoughts.

Portia's speeches mirrored Heike's feelings for Günther. Could she love a man as completely as Cato's daughter loved hers? She knew the Romeo and Juliet story. Even in the DDR, one must be extremely isolated to avoid the hundreds of allusions to that romance. However, she was unprepared to discover that Juliet was thirteen.

The Russian language seized her anew. It was three months before she could make alternate use of her spare time. In the interim, she exchanged important ideas and observations with Günther. Lilo clung to him like wet clothes. Nevertheless, the object of her affections never referenced her age and never dismissed her as a mere child; Günther treated her as Jürgen did – with patience and respect.

Heike Jacobs perched on the ground near the Bard, her ragged, riddled text in hand. Looking up from the tiny letters of *Midsummer Night's Dream*, she found the placid face of a genius.

"Are you teasing me?" she demanded.

She need not keep her voice down. Though summer abounded, most found it too hot to venture out. Even had they, Heike was hardly worthy of note. In work pants, sitting on the ground, clutching a disintegrating volume, Heike was an immature eccentric and unworthy of attention.

Poor Helena!

Heike fought back tears. Helena's love was "*as constant as the North Star.*" Driven to insanity by torment and magic, her love for Demetrius never wavers. She offers to be his spaniel, just to be near him.

Days later, Heike and Nadine set out for school. Unexpectedly, the sisters saw Günther spilling onto the street amid a quartet of younger children. Heike's pulse rocketed; her breathing became labored. Nadine was no fool, she knew from that day in the park, that Heike was infatuated. Twice, she teased her with unveiled references to her malady. Heike bristled; Nadine relented. Suddenly, Nadine opted to prod.

"Run on ahead and talk to Günther," she urged.

"Why don't you?"

Nadine had an answer for that but kept silent.

"Go on. You know he likes you more than he likes me."

Heike scowled. Her elder sister assumed Heike was a victim of puppy love. Nadine had suffered through that delightful affliction and couldn't blame *Maus*. However, there is a cure: reality. Nadine intended Heike to get a full dose.

"Go on, Heike. Run up and say hello. Günther will take it from there."

Maus shook her head emphatically. Nadine continued to prod, and Heike continued to resist. Suddenly, the exasperated Nadine exploded.

"*Blöte Kuh!*"

The second she threw the insult, Nadine sprinted ahead. Heike was not above violence. Discretion urged the elder to seek the safety of distance. She pulled even with Günther. After a moment, he looked for Maus. He waved but didn't wait. He and Nadine conversed, and Heike was thankful to be beyond earshot. She wallowed in the torture of her own making.

Heike folded the pages closed. She would have slammed the book shut in frustration, but she'd condemn herself to chasing and sorting hundreds of pages until Shakespeare's words returned to order.

She walked to the base of the statue,

"Is this my destiny?" she asked with a quivering voice. "Do I have to satisfy myself following Günther and Lilo around?"

The statue had no answer.

She ambulated with slow, aimless steps.

If she could not have the man she wanted, she must endure a life alone. Once a member of the Party, she'd make the required sacrifices. She'd work hard and harder. She'd divert all her energy to obtaining a place in the government. Heike Jacobs would face long odds and, somehow, lead her country toward utopia.

The expression of her love for Günther and – to her regret, Lilo – would be providing a nation where they and their children would thrive and prosper. Her blood rushed with the image of her emerging, battle-scared but unbowed, atop a vista from which she could look out upon a great and prosperous nation. That would be the manifestation of her love for Günther.

Shakespeare would show the way. He found humor and a brighter world in the depths of tragedy. If Heike were denied the man she loved, she'd be Helena who lived on behalf of him. It was proper. Had Romeo and Juliet lived, they'd be happy and together, but what could they contribute to the world? Through death, they ended a foolish, needless feud. Helena would sacrifice everything for Demetrius. If I cannot be in love, Heike concluded, I will do great things through love.

She clutched her tattered folio to her breast and sighed. An endless path stretched out before her, filled with obstacles, pitfalls, and detours. It would take more than bravery to get her from where she was to the realization of her dream. It required tools and skills she'd yet to discover. If waging war with Russian was any gauge, Heike's chances were not good.

She exchanged her sigh for a deep breath of determination. She must leave her source of inspiration and begin her struggle.

She followed the footpath to the crest of the slope. The road she must travel did not exist. Heike must blaze her own trail. Symbolically, she left that path and headed into the trees and vegetation that filled the city park. She ducked under a tree branch and dodged between two shoulder-high bushes and discovered her first disastrous obstacle.

Lilo!

She was striding with a purpose along the major pathway leading through the park. Heike could not identify her visage; she was too far away. However, her flowing hair, stature, and long strides made it impossible to mistake her for a stranger.

Heike stepped back between the bushes. She wasn't properly concealed, but she would avoid observation unless Lilo initiated a search.

The Amazon was on a mission. Her long strides ate up distance with amazing alacrity. She tugged at the open collar of her shirt momentarily, making her appear like a huge, menacing praying mantis.

Lilo trooped past Heike. She was headed south. When Heike felt safe, she angled for the path in a northerly direction. Twice, she looked over her shoulder. Lilo was no longer in sight. She slowed her space and transferred her energy to battling her shame and cowardice.

Government scouts blundered. They should have discovered Lilo years before. During a competition among regional sports clubs, Lilo easily defeated all commers in the three distance races. Her long legs gobbled up huge expanses of track. Unlike most girls her size, Lilo's legs were little more than a blur once she hit her stride.

She was selected for training camp on the spot. There must have been many red faces and a barrage of invectives from on high. How had the government missed discovering Lilo's talent? She was nearly good enough to have a spot on the national team without government training. Imagine what she could do with years of proper handling!

The Olympic hopeful was due to leave for camp the following week. Heike would be relieved over the departure, but she scolded herself for avoiding her nemesis. To congratulate her and wish her well wouldn't have hurt Heike a bit. To begin her quest for a meaningful future by acting like a frightened dog was a very bad start.

Heike neared the *Tempelherrenhaus*. In olden times, it was a music conservatory and, later, a social hall. Famous men and women gathered there for evenings of intellectual and cultural stimulation. Johann Sebastian Bach and Franz Liszt performed and conducted recitals within its walls. Goethe and Schiller gave readings, lectures, and led discussions. Then, in 1945, a bomb destroyed it.

Weimar was not a target. There were no war factories, troop concentrations, or transportation hubs in or near the city. However, a single bomb was jettisoned, and an important monument evaporated.

Heike passed through the archway as an act of respect. Once "inside," there was nothing but scrub growth. There was no surviving evidence of the floor and only portions of the foundations. Once, this temple was a pulsating center of culture.

Heike turned to her right and carefully negotiated her way through a tangle of nettles. She was within sight of the pedestrian path when she was arrested.

"*Hallo*, Heike!"

The familiar voice made the blood rush through her body. She discovered Günther laying a few meters away. His head rested on a bookbag. One ankle was propped on his opposite knee. It was through the triangle formed by his folded leg that he'd spied her. He waved to her with the book was reading.

Her heart raced anew. She faced chores at home, but she couldn't leave Günther alone in the park. Her quaking knees might fail her. Cautiously, she approached the reclining figure.

"What are you reading?" she asked.

She couldn't *not* speak. Her voice was little more than a squeak. She felt her face turn scarlet. Günther, ever the gentleman, pretended not to notice either her voice or her countenance.

"*Huckleberry Finn*," he reported with a broad grin.

She could make out the cover as she came near, but her eyes were blurred.

"In English?"

He nodded.

"It's torture," he announced. "It's in dialect and it takes me forever to decipher the code."

She stood like a statue. Her conversational well was dry. She resisted the urge to run, but her trembling could hardly escape his notice. The longer she stood, the more pronounced her terror. She feared that she might pass out – as if her current predicament was not humiliating enough.

He sat up and folded his legs Indian style.

Günther pounded the ground beside him with an open hand.

"Sit down," he invited, "let's chat."

"…*my little body is weary of this great world.*"

She wished she hadn't underlined that.

Frustrated and eager for something cogent, he'd asked to examine Heike's tattered volume. Predictably, he found the passage from *Merchant* almost immediately.

He studied it for, seemingly, eons before his eyes left the text.

"What language did you choose for school?"

During a group meeting, Heike announced she'd not continue Russian. As with everything, Günther remembered.

"English," she announced, sheepishly.

Jürgen and Nadine had pursued French. Nadine shone in French. She'd make an excellent tutor for Heike. Nevertheless, Heike opted to leap into uncharted waters. If she struggled with English, as she had with Russian, there'd be no one to rescue her.

"Why English?"

It was a fair question. She pointed to her abused volume.

"It's that important?"

She nodded but averted her eyes. When the silence became oppressive, she broke it.

"He speaks to me. I want to read him. Translations are unreliable."

"That's four years of English – at least."

She knew. She'd continue English at university if mastery was her goal. To fully appreciate Shakespeare, she must think in English. That was problematical. No matter how hard she tried with Russian, she relied on mental translations to keep from losing her way.

"I saw Lilo just a moment ago."

She gestured stupidly with her arm in the direction from whence she'd come. Heike examined the nettles and the arched entrance of a building long gone. Günther must be diverted. It was foolish to tarry. It was foolish to kneel at his invitation. It was foolish to act childishly.

"What do you wish?"

Lilo's whereabouts, apparently, were of no concern. Heike refused to look at him further. She was distant and furtive. He'd known her most of her life but only as his best friend's sister. Suddenly, he wanted to plumb her depths. Heike sensed this. It made her very nervous.

She took a deep breath and rubbed her hands on the thighs of her pants while looking, nervously – hopefully – for any sign of Lilo. Moments before, she had eschewed the sinewy athlete. Suddenly, she needed a deliverer.

"I don't wish," she declared. "Wishing is for dreamers. Dreams are for the idle. Hard work produces, not wishing."

She made her speech to her surroundings. Any look at or toward Günther would compound her mortification.

"Bravo! Very adroit and ideologically sound. But this is me, Heike; not a meeting of the FDJ or SED. If wishing were a power, what would you ask?"

Heike blundered. She didn't pause to study.

"I want Mutti back."

There followed a prolonged and stunned silence. She didn't dare look his way; Günther could not pry his eyes from her.

"You've obviously thought about this," he concluded.

"Every day."

"It's so like you."

"What is?"

"That you place other people first."

She shrugged.

"Mutti was a good teacher. I've never heard her *wish* for anything. I never appreciated that until – I remember the many things she did. Things we never noticed –"

He failed to mock her. Tentatively, she looked in his direction and relaxed slightly.

"Let me tell you something bizarre."

She couldn't gauge his expression properly. He was merely in her peripheral view.

"Whenever we made Mutti proud, or whenever we were upset, Mutti made us a nice, hot cup of cocoa. Did Jürgen's tell you?"

Günther nodded his head. That much she could see.

"She still does."

He blinked hard.

"Where does she get cocoa?"

"Where does she keep it?" Heike challenged.

She forgot her fear and shame. Heike looked directly at him as if pleading.

"We've turned the kitchen inside out. We searched constantly when we were younger. We still look. We'd never steal, but – where is it?"

Günther rubbed his chin.

"She was born in that house," he mused. "Her father was a known socialist. He probably made secret places to hide things from the Gestapo."

"Mutti was so young when they took Opa," Heike reminded.

Günther had no further ideas.

"I'm no longer curious," Heike confessed. "If I find that hiding place, it will rob Mutti of something she has left."

This produced a stunned expression on her listener's face. The child was at a loss to know what she'd done, or what he thought. She averted her eyes again.

"Where in Shakespeare did you find that?" he asked.

"Nowhere."

Only the tree leaves rustling in the breeze dared speak. Children squealed with delight in the distance, Günther and Heike remained mute.

"Do you ever cry?" he asked at last.

"What is that to you?" she prickled, turning her head.

"Jürgen says you never cry. He's never seen you."

She wanted to read his expression. The topic was exceedingly odd. An indefinable fear gripped her; she felt herself trembling. Heike pursed her lips and shook her head. She didn't want him to sense her fear.

"People who cry are out of control and weak. I cannot be weak."

"That is a pity," he remarked, sotto voce.

This eerie exchange begged a question. Heike let his comment linger in the air. It refused to go away.

"Why a pity?" she asked to break the agonizing silence.

"If you cry, I'd have an excuse to hold you."

She drew a quick breath and looked up. She couldn't help herself. She wanted to see a mocking smile. At the same moment, she feared she wasn't being mocked.

Heike panicked. What must she look like? Eyes popping out of their sockets and mouth half open, Heike must appear exactly as she was, a child. She remained stunned as Günther came to her and folded her in his arms.

She didn't speak. Her tongue abandoned her. Her trembling ceased. Her head rested, blissfully, against his chest.

"You're a treasure," he whispered.

Modesty availed itself. She pictured Lilo stumbling onto this farcical scene. Perhaps, Nadine, or a classmate, might find her in Günther's arms. She pushed against his chest with her hands. Her protest was symbolic. Heike did not want to free herself.

"Günther," she hissed for fear she'd be overheard. "I'm only thirteen!"

What she could have said – would have said, if she could think, was that Lilo...

"Juliet was thirteen," he reminded.

Her feeble attempts terminated. She dedicated herself to the joy of the sensation. She suspected she'd never nestle with him again.

"Well," he said, freeing her, "my self-indulgence is over. Forgive me."

He remained so near – only a few centimeters. He was so close, she felt his body heat. She looked into his eyes. For several seconds, there was nothing in her life but his eyes.

"Maybe, you're young," he concluded, "but you're very adult."

She swallowed hard and tried to speak, but words evaded her. Desperately, she threw her arms around his neck and felt the reassurance of his arms gathering her anew. A moment later, he kissed her. It was timid – almost apologetic, but his lips briefly pressed against hers. Heike's head swirled.

* * *

Once Kathy knew the cause, the Pig War ended.

Kathy Foster was not the gregarious imp she'd been portrayed by the adults in her family's social circle. She was, in fact, taciturn and made friends slowly, if at all. She admired her parents but resented their admonition of pork in any form. She took little pride in being "half-Swabish." It was, for her, a souvenir of sorts, rather like attaching decals to one's luggage. Before the *Mary R.* disgorged her passengers, Kathy's attitude changed.

Ute was Swabish and proud of it.

The first order of business was to scold the woman royally for daring to think that Kathy would cease wanting her as a mother. To prove it, Kathy would whole-heartedly embrace her Swabish inheritance. Swabish people are gregarious and honest.

Kathy confessed to Aaron of shoplifting two small "canlets" of ham from the local market. She insisted upon making restitution on the condition that Ute, her mother, would never learn of her crime.

"She should know," Aaron advised.

"She's Swabish," Kathy reminded, "if she knows I'm a thief, it will hurt her as much as if I stabbed her with a carving knife."

Aaron thought Kathy's comparison was hyperbolic, but there was no doubt about her genuine feelings. He agreed to accompany her to the grocery manager. She confessed. She'd pay for her crimes on the proviso that her mother not be informed. Similarly, Kathy's penance included apologizing to Gary for striking him. She'd, additionally, throw herself on Athena's mercy; she fully expected punishment.

"This won't make you Swabish, you know," Aaron warned.

"It will help me live up to Mom's expectations," she replied.

She must strive to be the "new, improved" Kathy – for her adoptive mother's sake.

Apologizing to Athena was easy. She was the bouncy, flirtatious woman who teased local customers who cheerfully teased back. She was marginally attractive and very wary. Falling, foolishly, heels over teakettle made her distrustful of herself.

Athena gave Kathy a champion frown. The girl wasn't the least concerned. Athena liked her very much and was not about to throw her overboard for a thoughtless lapse of decorum. Gary, though –

Kathy and Gary were classmates. However, had their mother's not worked together at the Fisherman's Inn, they mightn't have established a relationship. He was an unassuming little imp, but his visage was described (by Kathy's mother), as "angelic." They dispatched three grades together (beginning when Kathy skipped over the fifth grade). Kathy held a height advantage until Gary's summer growth spirt amazed her and horrified Athena. It was a financial hardship to keep the boy in clothes.

When Kathy scraped her knuckles on his teeth, she hated him. Learning she was a foundling prompted her to dedicate herself to honoring Ute's heritage. Being Swabish, even by fraud, meant being honorable. Carrying a grudge would not serve. As the aggressor, it was incumbent upon her to make amends.

She mounted Harry, her bike, and initiated a search.

Harry, as with many of the Foster family "luxuries," was a yard-sale purchase. It was a boy's bike, *Junge Fahrrad* (*auf Deutsch*). Kathy preferred *Herrad*. She anglicized it to *Harry*. They'd been together for years. Sadly, however, she was growing up, and Harry's utility was nearing its end. As with Kathy's wardrobe, she'd remain faithful until Harry became untenable.

Gary was practicing with his sling shot. He braced when he caught sight of her. To his credit, he never considered using a weapon against her – even in self-defense. If, however, she intended to strike him again, he'd be ready.

"I'm sorry I lost my temper," she began while dismounting. "I'm sorry, Gary. Sorry and ashamed. If there's anything I can do to make up for – hitting you –"

Here was a golden opportunity.

He played his hand with great skill – both figuratively and literally.

The opportunity came two days later. They knelt on opposite sides of the Foster yard-sale coffee table, playing cards. Nearby, a garage-sale portable hi-fi belched a Brenda Lee selection. The Foster record library was made up of used and discarded albums found or bought. It was an eclectic collection, but Kathy treasured it. She sang along with Brenda, Perry Como, Jo Stafford, and others unknown to most people her age. Not, however, Gary.

He enjoyed playing cards with Kathy. Her singing voice was pleasing. She didn't need to sing duets with Brenda Lee; Kathy could sing an acapella solo and capture the attention of any passerby. Gary knew better than complement the tempestuous girl on her singing prowess. Kathy was convinced she lacked both talent and aptitude. She considered any complement disingenuous and mocking. So, Gary played his hand and never allowed Kathy to know how much he enjoyed her voice.

"Looking forward to high school?" He asked.

Kathy made a noise. School was not on her list of favorites.

"You could try out for the freshman cheerleading team," he suggested, sounding both casual and indifferent.

She studied her hand.

"If you try out for football," she replied.

Gary remained deadpan. Inside, he bubbled. She'd sucker punched him. Despite her apology, and his feelings for her, he lusted to get even. Kathy's attitude toward cheerleaders, especially their attire, was widely known. Cheering would mortify her; wearing those short, short skirts would shame her; pretending interest in football or basketball would drive her insane.

It was *sooooooooooooo* easy!

Kathy threw herself into singing along with bossa nova hits her father – um, Aaron – was given. It took only a week before mastering Portuguese. She didn't have a clue what the words meant, or how accurately she pronounced them, but the rhythm and freshness of the Brazilian music made her giddy.

"Do you have to be Lutheran to go to church?" she asked quietly while drying the dinner dishes.

"Not hardly," was the reply of a woman misled by American colloquialisms.

The dishes were stacked in their assigned places before the morose daughter spoke again.

"Would you mind if I went to church with you?"

"Not hardly."

Kathy didn't see the look Ute cast Aaron. Had she noted, it wouldn't have mattered. There was more to her sudden interest in church than a desire to regain her mother's regard, though, admittedly, that was an essential part. The Reverend Mr. Rademacher was an Americanized German.

Rademacher conferenced with Kathy in her first language. Ute Foster was as adroit, but there was a pronounced difference: Rev. Rademacher represented detachment. Kathy could speak with him on subjects she'd never introduce at home.

"Do you know anything about the Jewish religion?" she asked.

Rev. Rademacher wasn't only knowledgeable, he shared. He knew Kathy's history. He suspected the source of her curiosity. The elder Fosters were not privy to these colloquies; Kathy and Rev. Rademacher's jealously protected confidentiality. Regardless, the home tensions eased, and the Foster family returned to near normal.

After four consecutive days on whale-watch, Kathy earned shore leave. Barker knew Kathy's long-hour days were generating unwelcome interest from local troublemakers. Child labor laws, lawyers, publicity – Scrooge opted for discretion. Ignorant of Barker's motives, Kathy woke early to enjoy every minute of her leisure time. She and Harry were on the move early.

Minutes shy of eight, she slid onto the stool at the end of the counter in the Fisherman's Inn. She spun about to see if the *Mary R.* was quayside. This took three seconds Spinning back to rest her elbows on the counter, she found a steaming mug of coffee.

Athena!

Gary's mother knew Kathy drank herself into caffeine stupors on the briny. She knew Ute disapproved while Aaron remained ambivalent. Whenever possible, Athena served Kathy. Ute would comment; Athena would joke. Provided Kathy limit herself to a single half-filled mug, it went no further.

A hotcake platter with a side of patty sausage flew past with Athena in tow. The waitress took her time returning to the kitchen. Business was slow, the summer tourists were only beginning to stir. Crowds seldom gathered before nine.

"Ya get fired?"

Athena enjoyed her Southern drawl despite never being further south than Modesto.

Kathy's flippant response was stayed by Ute's return from a table of three.

"Kathy!" she scolded.

Athena intervened quickly.

"Aw, that ain't straight coffee, gal. I diluted it."

Ute knew her leg was being pulled, but she stifled protest. The chef rang the bell for an order up, and Ute was off.

"With whiskey," Athena added, *almost*, under her breath.

This was articulated as Kathy took a sip. It was a near thing. Had her control not held, Athena would have gotten sprayed. Kathy reached for a napkin to check the coffee rivulet on her chin.

"I was just at your place. Gary's not home."

"Nah! The damned fool started football practice yesterday mornin'. He's gonna have ta hitch a ride back, 'cause I ain't takin' off work."

Kathy's surprise was complete.

"Bastard!" she hissed.

"Whoa, Nelly!" Athena whispered – or as near a whisper as Athena would ever produce.

"Yer momma will warm your britches if she hears ya say that."

Kathy locked on Athena's concerned eyes.

"He got me," she reported, "that conniving little brat got me. I'll kill him!"

Athena planted her elbows on the counter and leaned forward, her forehead nearly touching Kathy's.

"Take a number, hon!"

DDR

Fall 1988

Anne Ecke remained a national celebrity in the DDR. Her father was a hell-raising socialist of the Spartacus League. His revolutionary fervor moderated with age. However, he once met Karl Liebknecht. He attended two of Rosa Luxemburg's addresses; her eloquence reverberated through his soul for the remainder of his days.

When the League's grab for power failed, Liebknecht and Luxemburg were murdered, Werner Ecke maintained a low profile. He held positions as a civil servant and newspaper publisher while, under his convivial personality, his socialist views matured. Werner Ecke came to Weimar as a part of the contingent meeting in the city theatre to draft a republican constitution. He believed a weak republic was the best avenue for the incubation of the socialist movement which, in turn, would lead to a strong socialist state. Though too young to engage in the proceedings, he was a delegate's trusted secretary.

Werner was too likeable to enflame the masses. He was, in the words of an admirer, "a remarkable ordinary". During the birth of the short-lived Republic, he met a local girl. Though young, she was as infatuated with the genial socialist as he was captivated by her simple charms. They corresponded voluminously for eight years until he returned to edit a socialist newspaper.

The couple wed soon after. Anne Ecke was the only war-surviving child of their union. When Hitler seized power, Ecke's newspaper closed, and he remained unemployed and unemployable – a shadowy figure in a small house on a small street. Together with other socialists, Ecke established an underground network, cooperating with anyone opposed to the dictatorship. Ecke wasn't particular.

If a person or group opposed Hitler, Ecke was a willing partner. Hitler must be deposed. Without this, true socialism had no chance. Eventually, his underground activities were exposed. In 1944, he was escorted from his home never to be seen again. His exact fate remains a mystery.

Many stories linger; most conflicting and none confirmed. Despite the Nazi's best efforts, Ecke became a cult figure. At war's end, stories about Ecke's underground activities reached a fever pitch and were entrenched in legend. Anne Ecke was nine years old when she was first subjected to veneration. As the only surviving Ecke, she was awarded the best educational opportunities.

To mark what would have been Werner Ecke's sixtieth birthday, the city government organized a celebration. Anne Ecke, then a university student, was guest of honor. After copious amounts of alcohol, the local party leader brought Anne to the podium. She was awarded party membership. Subsequently, the party boss urged her to make a request; if possible, he'd grant it.

The girl enjoyed libation enough to take the weaving party leader at his word. She became maudlin and cried. She worshiped the father she barely knew. Her one wish was to live in her birth house, where she'd last seen Papa. Eighteen months later, the house was hers, complements of a grateful party and country.

Rolf Jacobs is a bull of a man, all muscle and bellow. Few people dared thwart him. His industry is legend. He excelled in trade school. A genius with machines, he went to the Weimar bus barn for his school practicum and stayed.

Because of his honesty and work ethic, he was soon a supervisor. His leadership skills were effective; underlings knew slackness wasn't tolerated. How a boisterous, uncouth bully attracted a demure, petite Anne was impossible. Yet, they met, and within a year, they wed.

Rolf feared no one, to include the ubiquitous party martinets. However, he was contrite and respectful in the presence of his wife. He never raised his voice to her and, despite all bets to the contrary, he never mistreated her by word or deed. When an infrequent dispute arose, Rolf surrendered unconditionally.

When Anne's mind began abandoning her, Rolf became more contrite and gentler. He was a tyrant with the children: they must serve their mother in all things. They did, as much from respect and love as fear of Rolf's wrath. Their chores were constant and demanding.

Anne once swept and washed the steps every day; the children, each in turn, inherited the chore. As she once washed, cleaned dishes, changed the beds and mended, so did the children, each in turn. As Anne went shopping daily, so did the children, each in turn.

Jacobs family life was remarkably pedestrian. Rolf bellowed and bullied and kept the children in abject fear. Though he seldom showed them the back of his hand, it was enough to check any rebellion. If Anne mediated, her ever-open arms became a sanctuary. If Anne didn't intervene, Rolf's punishment was quick and memorable.

After castigation, the offender rushed to Anne's embrace, reassured that he or she was loved and appreciated. Because of Rolf, Heike's first genuine romance proved frustrating in the extreme. Günther was, rightfully, afraid of Rolf. If he came to the house asking for her or, worse, if he came home with her, he might find himself, literally, tossed onto the cobblestones. Similarly, the children were seldom allowed outside once Rolf returned from work.

There were exceptions. However, if one "invented" an exception, Rolf taught them that the price of prevarication ran high. Thus, Heike and Günther romanced within the barking clique or after-school venues. Heike existed from stolen kiss to stolen kiss and floated on the wonder that such an accomplished young man would grace her with his attentions.

Though Jürgen might know from Günther, and Nadine strongly suspected, Heike's *"siblings"* never pressed. Should Rolf ask, neither dared lie. Ignorance was safer. Should Rolf ask Heike a direct question, she was on her own.

Heike fanned the fledgling flame of hope. Somehow, she and Günther would find a life together. Rolf was formidable, and Heike's lineage invited the sword of vengeance. The slightest misstep would bring the blade down upon the spawn of treason. Her greatest fear, however, was too big to ignore: *Lilo.*

Lilo's ran distances in eye-popping time. The government seized her. She bid farewell at a group meeting.

She sensed Günther's feelings were fading. It didn't show in their parting hug, however. Heike turned green. Lilo embraced them all that afternoon – including young Heike; there were no tears. She was aiming for Olympic medals.

To her credit, Lilo was skeptical. She was starting very late. Typically, she'd give her all in national service – as would any citizen. One group member, Nicole Hase, was Lilo's close friend. Despite an admirable visage, Nicole was too short, stocky, and imposing to turn heads.

Her timorousness during exchanges kept her on the fringe. When she spoke, it was to offer tepid support for or timid objection to the proposals of others. On that last day, during hugs, Nicole responded with fervor. They exchanged hushed words, after which Nicole brushed away her tears, turned on her heel and chugged off prior to dismissal.

Subsequently, Nicole eschewed the group. Heike thought nothing of it until she noticed Nicole waiting for a bus at *Goetherplatz.* Waiting for a bus herself, Heike caught Nicole examining her from across the street. They nodded hello.

Heike had no reason to speak; there was nothing to say. To cross over and ask a question – any question – was considered forward. In the DDR, prying was dangerous. At any rate, Nicole's reasons for abandoning the group were hers alone. Heike dug for her fare as she boarded her bus. Her head down, she didn't recognize the driver until after the coins were in the tray.

"*Tag*, Heike," the driver nodded.

The woman's strawberry-blond hair was her only aesthetic attribute.

"*Tag*, Frau Willing."

Heike was handed a ticket. She took the first available seat and kept her eyes on that part of Frau Willing's face reflected in the overhead mirror. She looked ancient. Frau Willing's presence in the Jacobs' home was frequent before – well, *before.*

Heike wanted to question the driver but dared not. For Frau Willing, the professional, driving came first. Getting off, Heike was tempted to invite her to visit some evening. She squelched it. They had only imitation coffee (it was foul), some wine (dishwater) for refreshments.

There was cocoa, of course, but only Anne dispensed that. Though Anne would beam upon seeing a familiar face, it would prove a quiet evening. Heike lifted a hand of farewell and *Frau* Willing nodded an *auf Wiedersehn.*

Abendsbrot was exactly that. Bread, lightly buttered – when butter was obtainable – with wurst or, when available, cheese. If the designated shopper found fresh vegetables – radishes, carrots, lettuce – Nadine would slice them up for open-faced sandwiches. These light morsels were washed down with tea or coffee. Frau Jacobs took her food in the kitchen, but she sat near the table with an expression of approval while watching her family eat.

If someone did not meet the matriarch's expectation, a frown appeared. No one liked grotesqueness presiding over the evening table, so everyone strove to ensure the serving plate was empty. After the meal, Herr Jacobs sat with his wife on the couch. They relaxed together while the children tended the chores. Sometimes, the radio served up light-music.

Newspapers made Rolf prickly. He read selected portions directly and saved the irritating bits for later in the evening. He quietly recounted the events of his day or discussed inconsequential matters. His wife smiled or nodded. No one knew if she understood, but the after-meal monologues appeared to please her.

"I saw Frau Willing today," Heike announced, drying the mug Nadine handed her.

Nadine replied by making a noise in her throat. The memory of Willing's frequent visits struck a nostalgic chord. Heike wanted to advance the idea of inviting her, but it died in her sister's silence.

The dishes were done, and the sink properly washed and rinsed. Heike shook out the towel and hung it in the proper place while Nadine stowed the soap and checked to ensure all items were in their assigned positions.

"Do you want Jürgen's bed?"

Heike was stunned. Since the kitchen was little more than a walk-in closet, there was no way Nadine could escape until Heike passed though the curtained arch.

"No!" she whispered emphatically.

Nadine had little patience. The fact that she didn't push Heike through the arch with a sardonic remark spoke volumes. Everyone knew that Jürgen and Günther were leaving for national service. Everyone knew there would be more space in the children's room. Previously, no one made overt comments. There was no predicting how Frau Jacobs would react to her son's disappearance. Nadine's breaking silence was a serious breach.

"I can't get into the damned thing."

"And I can? You're the athletic one."

"No."

"We will find something for you to step up on. Now, shut it!"

As Heike turned, Nadine grabbed her arm. This was not done. Only Rolf could grab – or Mutti when still in possession of her mind. Not even Jürgen would be so bold. Heike's fist clinched. Only the presence of Frau Jacobs on the other side of the veiled entrance kept her from launching.

"You deserve it."

"Deserve? I'm not even family."

The hand dropped, and Heike marched. She respectfully nodded to Rolf and Anne in passing. Nadine followed. They ascended the stairs to find the bedroom door open. The splash of light confirmed that Jürgen had properly swept and mopped the landing and dusted the shrunk which housed the family's clothes – few though they were. Heike swept and mopped that morning, but family ritual required "evening patrol." Frau Jacobs was sure to express unease if anything was amiss.

Jürgen perched on his bed in t-shirt and shorts. It was common for people, especially children, to share unisex accommodations in the DDR; biological mysteries seldom lingered for long. He was reading; Jürgen always read or studied. The shallow tin of wash water lay under his bed, together with a cleaning cloth. It was Nadine's turn to swab the bathroom, she'd empty the water and clean both tin and rag upon completion of her mission.

"What are you reading?" Heike asked.

She didn't care. Faced with translating a passage from Goethe into English, any excuse to delay mind-numbing work for a few precious seconds was welcome.

"It's a book of verse Lilo left," he reported.

"As if we have room to store books," Nadine mumbled.

The Jacobs children's bookcase was a tidy pile on the floor next to the entrance. There were proper shelves downstairs; the bedroom floor was for schoolbooks.

"Any good?"

Nadine growled audibly. She knew Heike was stalling. There was a math test on the morrow. Nadine was petulant.

"Ponderous," he sighed. "I thought it esoteric. I'm beginning to think it's just bad."

"May I have a go?"

Heike measured all poetry against the Bard. She was curious but in no hurry. Jürgen shut the book and tossed it in a lazy arc across the room. Heike caught it but rendered no thanks. Nadine was boiling.

She opened the book to read the first page that fell open. Thirty seconds were all she managed before becoming restless. It was a difficult text, to be sure. She flipped through the pages and examined titles, pausing now and then to survey Lilo's margin notes and highlights. She found a curious message inside the front cover.

Propertius
Vergangen

The entry was in pencil, but Lilo placed large, black marks around the verb. In pen and, with colored ink, she'd underscored it. This might be the idle doodling of a frustrated Amazon. Who could trudge through the heavy verbiage before being reduced to childish entertainments? Heike interpreted the marks as pique, not boredom.

Heike flipped through the pages more. Twice, she encountered a check followed by p.v. Propertius, *Vergangen* abbreviated – *oder*? She examined the poetry closest to the margin notes. One had featured a soul in anguish, the other rated a hand-printed addendum: *the tyranny of doubt.*

Enough was enough. Heike Jacobs had problems of her own.

* * *

School officials initiated an on-going gag. Assigned seating in Gymnasium was random. From her first day, Heike shared a worktable with Heiko Müller. Other students rotated from year to year and term to term, Heike and Heiko, however, were always assigned together. The first day of new levels, Heike entered her assigned class to find Heiko leaning back in a chair and looking bored.

"*'Morgan*, Heiko."

"*'Morgan*, Heike."

She pulled out the companion chair and settled in,

"We aren't assigned," he reminded.

"Patience," she responded.

The first subject was algebra, as if they hadn't had their fill the previous year. The teacher strode into class with a briefcase firmly in one hand and a seating chart in another. He called out names and assigned desks. Heike and Heiko moved forward one row, but, as always, they shared the same table. When the literature teacher strode in, she looked quickly at the chart and then squarely at Heike and Heiko.

"She's in on it," Heiko whispered.

Heike nodded.

During the morning break, Heike bought a "coffee" and sipped while milling around the common area. It was a pleasant day, and the fresh air was invigorating. She found a patch of sunlight filtering through the surrounding trees and settled down beside the cool stones of the building. Her thoughts (curses) were reserved for the upcoming English class. She was adrift and knew it.

With Günther gone for the army, she was stung by double remorse. Jürgen, her trusted tutor, was, also, a soldier. Why, she wondered, couldn't people leave well enough alone? When the German language migrated to that soggy island, it was orderly. Then the French and the Norse and the Church and an entire gang of malevolent brigands raped it to produce a bastard.

Though Heike remained determined to read Shakespeare as written, she despaired. There were traps galore. The spelling was arbitrary, the grammar a product of folly, many verbs unforgivably weak, and the nouns, all of them, were homeless. Heike was in a fine temper when Heiko crept up unnoticed.

"Have you seen what's coming to *Kino*?" he asked, innocently.

Heike snorted.

"*Heißer Sommer*. It was a *Scheiß* movie when they made it, and it's a *Scheiß* movie still."

She was obligated to express this opinion on two grounds: first, she was in a snit because of the English course hanging ominously in her immediate future; second, she adored the movie, but was old enough – and sophisticated enough – to be above such silliness.

In the late 1960s, Frank Schöbel and Chris Doerk were DDR hit-parade idols. The government enlisted them to appear in a teen musical aimed to placate the masses. Everybody knew of the Elvis films. Indeed, Elvis was very popular in the DDR. The *Volk* lusted after forbidden *Wessi*, Elvis-like musicals.

The answer was, *Heißer Sommer*, a paper-thin plot garnished with two pop icons and music as near rock-and-roll as authorities allowed. It was unrealistic and carried no party message, but it proved addictive. A younger Heike saw it three times and was eager to see it again. Later, on her knees and scrubbing the stairs, she understood. She'd been a brainless fool!

Heiko intended to ask her to the movies. She, thoughtlessly, vetoed the offer before he had the chance to ask.

Would she have accepted? Of course! Since Günther's departure, she hadn't so much as a post card. She was angry at first, then hurt. If Günther provided reason to believe he liked her beyond anemic little kisses and clever conversation, she'd remain his Helena. She hadn't looked for a boyfriend.

Heiko was a friend and nothing more. He wasn't particularly handsome, and she didn't care for his blond hair spilling down his back like a girl's. Moreover, his interest was music; Heike couldn't read a note. His attitude towards the FDJ was tepid. Nevertheless, they could have enjoyed the film together.

On the appointed Saturday, Heike and Nadine met on a triangular traffic island fronting the school. They often pondered its existence amid a dearth of motor traffic. Indeed, the students used the school's front street as a promenade.

Heißer Sommer was, basically, fun and music. Nowhere, from opening credits to final fade, did it touch reality. It was a decadent imitation of the toxic American cinema. While neither Heike nor Nadine admitted it, they looked forward to viewing, again, a movie that the Party never should have allowed.

They walked a good distance to find a long line at the cinema kiosk. Others were just as anxious to see the film – again. Amid them was Heiko, next to him, roughly two-thirds his height, stood a rosy-cheeked girl with short, mismanaged hair. *Girl* was the proper word. She owned a round, youthful face. However, the buttons of her blouse were called upon to resist dangerous stress. It was obvious what Heiko saw in the little imp.

Heike turned green. Were she not such a fool, she'd be standing next to Heiko rather than *Fräulein* Wonderchest. She grabbed Nadine and guided her out of Heiko's line of sight. They got inside the cinema undetected, but it was a hollow victory. Heiko sat a few rows ahead – next to HER.

Robbed of any chance to enjoy the movie, Heike turned sour. Nadine fell victim to the contagion. She spent more time casting glances at the toxic figure at her side than watching the screen. Something was very wrong. Nadine realized it might prove injurious to inquire. Thus, Nadine squirmed in her seat in a vain effort to ignore a ticking time bomb.

The silence between sisters continued during their exit. They sprinted across the busy street whereupon Heike paused at the curb to look back. Nadine stood, unquestioningly, nearby. Heiko and his full-figured companion exited the movie-house together. They, obviously, enjoyed it and chatted gaily about it.

Then, the girl's smile radiated warmth enough to melt the ice in Heike's heart. She recognized the same smile she'd seen nearly every school day of her life. Her shoulders slumped and air fled her body. Heiko, as had Heike, escorted his sister to the cinema!

Oregon

Fall 1988

Athena Swofford's car mocked the word. It was roughly a twenty-five-mile round trip from her *house* – another euphemism – to the high school. Gary's morning practice began at nine o'clock and the afternoon practice at three. It was a considerable risk to drive Gary to morning practice. Chances were excellent that the car would break down between the signs proclaiming U.S. 101 and Resume Speed.

Gary would leave morning practice, bruised and beaten, sleep for an hour or so in the shade under the stadium bleachers. Once awake, he'd hobble to a convenience store for a sandwich and juice. After the second practice, he rode home with two older boys and slept until Athena returned to fix dinner.

Gary hardly cast a shadow. Though he ran like blazes with the others, he was too small and frail for serious work. He spent most of his time holding tackling dummies. Little good these heavy monsters proved when hulk after hulk, each carrying twenty to fifty more pounds than Gary, slammed into them. With each vicious hit, dummy and dummy-holder went sprawling.

No one expected "Gold Dust" to return for the second day of practice, but he did – as well as the third, the fourth, the fifth and the

Saturday practices. Kathy spent no time in reflection. A deal was a deal. She was obligated to audition for yell squad.

Sitting in the pew beside Ute, waiting for the service to begin, Kathy was increasingly annoyed. Even Aaron showed signs of irritation each time his wife's head snapped about to monitor the entry doors. Finally, as the organist took her place and adjusted her music, Ute waved.

Kathy looked toward the double doors and found Athena in a hat, dress, and heels. She recalled Ute's intention to invite Athena to church but thought nothing of it until the woman hustled up the aisle. In her wake, bent and hobbling, was Gary the Sneak.

Athena waltzed into the narrow space between pews and settled down. It took Gary much longer. Slowly, tentatively, he lowered himself into a sitting position; his face was contorted. Kathy squeezed past Athena to sit beside her son. All her thoughts of homicide evaporated.

"What's wrong?" she asked.

The organ music was, appropriately, dirge-like.

"A little stiff," he replied.

Athena snorted.

"A little? He couldn't pull on his pants this morning."

"I'll be okay," he assured, "after stretching and running a lap, I'm fine."

"Run a – Gary Swofford, you aren't going to practice tomorrow!"

He did not reply. Athena pretended not to hear. Kathy wanted to grab Gary's arm and shake him, but she feared breaking his brittle bones.

"You tricked me," she confessed, "not fair and square, but you got me. There's no point on going back. You won."

Gary nodded. Kathy alternated between hating and pitying Gary.

To prove himself as pig-headed as Kathy, Gary returned to practice on Monday morning and – to the amazement of all – survived. Even the older boys, the juniors and seniors who were merciless in their taunting, teasing and hitting, began to soften. No one ever saw a person take so much punishment without complaint. By the end of the second week, upper classmen were competing for the honor of providing Gary rides to and from practice. This relieved Athena of hazardous morning excursions.

At the end of daily doubles, Gary "made" the freshman squad. This was no other place for him. Players and coaches admired Gary's tenacity. The varsity captains met with the coaches. They agreed to allow Gary to suit up for varsity games as a team amulet.

Kathy was enraged. Convinced that Gary Swofford was one breath away from death's door, she cursed his thick-headedness. Similarly, she cursed her humiliation over a forced audition for a group she abhorred.

She was on the bus when Gary boarded. He saw her sitting alone in a fifth-row seat. He correctly judged, by her visage, that Kathy was in no mood for conversation. He didn't say hello. He aimed for an empty seat further back. Unexpectedly, she seized his arm and, with mortifying ease, yanked him into the seat beside her.

"The least you can do is keep some creep from sitting next to me," she snapped.

That was the whole of their conversation.

When Kathy stepped off the bus, she looked for trouble. As if on cue, a target, literally, stepped in front of her.

The girl's smile was perfect; her blond hair was perfect; her skirt and her blouse and her shoes were perfect. Everyone deferred to her. Teachers and students greeted her as if she were royalty. Her royal highness responded in a perfectly confident, cheerful, and well-modulated voice.

Kathy hated her!

She followed the blond debutant to the main doors. Blondie allowed a willing flunky to open the portal for her. At that precise moment, Kathy, made an impatient charge for the adjoining door and stepped on the heel of a "princess slipper."

She lusted for a jungle shriek, a flood of tears and a public lament for the perfect yellow flats – no longer perfect. Kathy was amazed and disappointed; the girl cast a look at Kathy with the most amazing smile. It beamed. The brain-dead glamour girl mistook a deliberate assault for an accident. Pretty Polly, apparently, could not read Kathy's belligerent expression.

"Thank-you, Jessie," she addressed the door slave as she passed through. "Ever the gentleman."

Kathy Foster wanted to slap the girl's perfect face before wrapping her hands around her perfect neck and squeezing a perfect tongue out of her perfect head. The only deterrent was the realization that such a sequence of events would be difficult to pass off as accidental.

Kathy went blandly from class to inane class. English, algebra, science for rocks, and physical education were the core requirements. For electives, the frosh were – to quote the only repeatable Barker expletive – "bupkis."

Chorus appeared the most innocuous, but Kathy's interest in the discipline was blunted when the entire class, one at a time, "registered" their voices. When Kathy's turn came, she performed, like a trained seal – twice!

The dreaded announcement came just prior to lunch break.

"All interested freshman girls need to sign up in Ms. Killen's room for rally tryouts." Kathy knew the announcement was aimed at one *dis*interested girl.

Informed of the location of Ms. Killen's room, Kathy took a deep breath and marched bravely down the hall. There were two girls in front of her and one behind. This allowed her to sign the paper on the teacher's desk and march out without making eye contact. She made a deal and she'd stick to it, but resentment burned. She took some comfort in her "audition." She'd make a laughingstock of herself Thursday and be summarily dismissed. Her insidious obligation would end.

Eating lunch in silence, Swabish scruples struck with a vengeance. Gary could have walked away after that first murderous morning practice. Several boys, older and much bigger than Gary, quit after the third or fourth practice. Yet, there stood Gary, bent, bruised, a collection of lacerations from scalp to toe, but indefatigable. He made the frosh team – if that counted as an accomplishment.

Should Kathy give anything other than her best, it would constitute a breach of promise. By locally accepted standards, there'd be not a single recrimination. By Swabish standards, however –

Damn!

It was bad enough to adhere to Swabish values despite recent revelations. It was unthinkable for Gary Swofford, who hadn't a drop of Swabish blood in his ancestry, to outshine her. As the day wound down,

Kathy entertained visions of getting Gary on the *Mary R.* and pushing him into the Pacific. If he could swim back to shore, she'd shake his hand and buy him coffee. If he didn't – oh, well!

The last class was German I. She wanted to take Spanish, but the class was packed by the time she registered. Her next pick was German III or even German IV, but upper classmen got priority. Thus, Kathy would languish for an entire year with "*Was ist los,*" and "*Auf Wiedersehn.*" Nearing the end of her first day in high school, Kathy's year was, already, a disaster.

Complete? Hardly. Her disaster was a work-in-progress.

She sat sullen and silent studying the desk-top graffiti of the scholars preceding her. Kathy sensed an unexplained movement. The male teacher, looking as dejected as Kathy, sat on the front edge of his desk, swinging one foot absent-mindedly. Suddenly, he was on his feet. When Kathy investigated, her blood boiled anew.

"Welcome, Molly," the obsequious twit saluted, "I saw your name on the roster."

"Yep," replied the perfect smile of the perfect blond in perfect clothes (except for one shoe). "I'm taking the plunge."

The prima-damned-donna turned to survey the classroom. Kathy suspected her royal highness was selecting a throne. When she discovered it, she'd order the occupant to vacate. Doubtless, the slave would obey. Everyone, of course, save Kathy, who would respond to the royal whim with a four-letter aria.

Unexpectedly, the well-togged queen made no demands of the peasantry. Instead, she made an announcement.

"When two vowels go walking, the second does the talking."

With this slice of doggerel, she made an exaggerated curtsey and moved towards the nearest empty desk – the one next to Kathy. She watched the royal personage smooth out her skirt and settle into the desk with finishing-school ease. Once seated, she placed the palms of her hands flat on the desk in a manner suggesting she expected no further attention.

"*Sind Sie Deutsch?*"

The question was spontaneous. Kathy asked without realizing. The queen turned to speak.

"Meine Mutti," she replied, *"und du?"*

The queen spoke in a northern dialect, but Kathy bristled at *du*. Kathy hadn't used it; what made this supercilious society girl think she could get away with it? Kathy forced herself to retain her calm while reflecting. Miss Oregon admitted she wasn't German. The reasonable assumption, then: she's American.

Americans neither knew nor used *Sie*. Americans used only *du*, from the mightiest to the lowest. If Kathy were going to hate this girl – and she entertained doubts – *du* was not a black mark.

"I – ah, it's a long story," she replied with more reserve than was her wont.

The queen's expression changed. Kathy expected mockery or sarcasm. Instead, Kathy found herself exploring the face of a curious young girl. The bell rang, and the curious face turned into one of strict attention. Whatever else this perfectly attired person was, she didn't socialize during class.

The moment the bell clamored; Kathy felt a gentle hand on her forearm. The blond, who remained mute throughout class, was a sudden torrent of German verbiage.

"I have tennis practice now. Must you catch a bus?"

"Genau."

"Let me walk with you. What did you mean 'it's a long story?' Are you German? *Ja, oder nein?"*

The queen's tone was unexpectantly disarming.

Kathy explained her family history, so far as she knew it. Confined to English, she'd have resented the crush of the crowd, but she was confident that only the Queen knew enough German to understand. There were, leaving the school, as many salutations as were directed toward the fashion plate that morning. Though the blonde returned each one, it was clear that she attended Kathy closely.

"Gott im Himmel!" she exclaimed at last, "I'd be out of my head. Are you okay? What are you going to do?"

"There's not much I can do. My *Onkle* Dieter worked on this since my – adoption. I'm just a border incident."

"Hang in there, kid," Molly said with an unexpected switch of languages, "if there is anything I can do, I will."

Somehow, through a mystery Kathy couldn't fathom, she believed her. "*Danke.*"

"We'll talk tomorrow," Molly promised.

* * *

It was small consolation to be the last girl selected to frosh rally. True to Gary's example, she gave her best, but Kathy couldn't enjoy it. She was a year younger than the other girls which made her feel doubly oafish. There was, however, one benefit: Kathy and Molly had time in the locker room before and after their respective practices. It was a comfort to speak German with a peer. Moreover, Molly Waldron was perceptive and mature.

Kathy's-age Jayme Waldron was as fluent in German as her sister, but she was more "real." One look at Jayme's slovenly clothes and blowsy hair was enough. Kathy knew she'd discovered a kindred spirit. Though the junior-high girl was graced with excellent features, so much so that she might surpass Molly's attributes, she scorned make-up and preferred jeans and shirts.

"Mom came from a poor family," Jayme explained one afternoon while she and Kathy watched Molly practice.

"She always wanted to look good, but her folks couldn't afford nice things. When Molly came, she got only neat stuff."

"What happened to you?"

Jayme wasn't offended.

"I don't put up with mom's crap. I mean, I used to wear clothes Molly outgrew, but I always got in trouble when I ripped them or got them dirty. When we went shopping, I'd throw fits. I don't want to look like Lady Di, damn it!"

"But Molly does," Kathy presumed.

"She's Miss Goody Two-shoes – always happy, always caring, always the peace-maker. If mom wants her to look like the prom queen, she'll put up with it because she knows it hurts Mom if she won't. Me, I don't care how Mom feels, I stand up for myself. So long as Molly is perfect, I can live my own life."

"You and Molly must fight a lot."

Jayme snorted.

"Mol will walk barefoot over hot coals and broken glass before she'd fight. It's so neat, though. I can talk to Molly anytime about anything, and she's too polite to tell me to go to hell. When Mom or Dad get on my case, I just run to Mol, and she makes with the fairy-godmother routine."

Kathy felt horrible. She'd be happy to fight with a sibling if only to confirm her own existence.

The school colors, scarlet on white, demanded attention. Ute was mesmerized by the sharp pleats and the bold high school initials. There was nothing like it in her culture. Having lived in America or in base housing for half her life, she grew familiar with traditions.

She begged Kathy to release the uniform from the cleaner's plastic cocoon and put it on. She searched for a camera. She couldn't wait to dispatch glossy prints of Kathy to her parents in Germany and Aaron's parents in Milton-Freewater. Kathy refused. She wanted to crawl under a rock.

She was a jeans and shirt person. She didn't *do* makeup or manage her hair, a vain habit in coastal winds. Kathy was on the yell squad. Membership, despite despicable circumstances, brought obligations. Swabs honored obligations.

Sitting on her bed, in near tears, Kathy examined that skirt. Not only would her legs be on display, but she'd attend school with her butt, practically, hanging out. Princess Molly could not fathom the problem. Jayme, however, suffered for her.

"Damned Swabish!" Jayme spat.

Kathy and Gary were friends again, but not without strain. Athena scrambled down the ninety-some steps to jump onto the *Mary R.* one brisk fall Saturday during a "break." She paid no heed to the assembly anxious to board, but she captured the crew's attention.

"I need Kathy's car a sec," she bellowed to Aaron.

"I can't leave here with the engines running," he bellowed back.

Athena made hand gestures to the waiting ticket holders and hustled Kathy down the cabin steps, ignoring the *NO PASSENGERS ALLOWED* sign.

"What planet are you from?" she demanded.

The girl replied with empty, Orphan-Annie eyes.

"That boy, Gary Foster; know him?"

Kathy nodded.

"Well, he's got a crush on you, gal."

At last Kathy found a handle. She smiled. Athena was teasing.

"Too bad," she began, thinking in high gear. "I'm dating the Pope."

"You think I'm joking? You dare!"

Kathy attempted to waft the subject away with the back of a hand.

"When Gary came home talkin' 'bout you, I didn't give it a thought, but he don't shut up. 'Kathy did this…', 'Kathy did that…', 'Kathy smeared ink on her English paper.' Absolute crapula, and no end. I'm damned tired of it."

"Are you kidding?" Kathy demanded.

"What do I have to do? Tattoo it on your butt? Don't tell me – oh, please don't tell me you haven't noticed how he looks at you."

"How he looks at me?"

This conversation was bizarre.

"Oh, God! When he ain't lookin' goof eyes at ya, he's tracking your every move like a hound on the scent."

Kathy turned and leaned back against the compartment containing the crew's rain slicks. She stared at nothing and reviewed the previous several days.

"He drools over Molly," she informed the irate mother.

"Oh, I bet he's getting an eye-full of babes," Athena nodded, "but the drool is for you."

Kathy shot her a glance and found Athena's face frozen with earnestness.

"Kathy, I know I ain't much when it comes to bein' a wife or mother, but when it comes to guys, I'm aces high. I can tell when a guy is smitten. I ain't tryin' to play cupid, because – no offense, girl – you're a pain in the ass! I don't welcome the day you start hangin' around the house, but you best wake up and smell the jet fuel or you'll end up a little ol' lady sittin' alone in the park talkin' to pidgins."

Kathy didn't believe a word. Still, if Athena went to all that trouble, and exercise to kid around –

She began paying attention. At the end of a week's observations, Kathy wasn't wholly convinced, but she was no longer dismissive. Gary was meek and mild, to be certain, but he had depth. He proved much to many with unexpected and inexplicable resources during combat with boys both older and bigger. He wasn't very sneaky, however. Twice, Kathy surprised him while casting "goof-eyes" at her.

* * *

Costal society is fluid, but the bond between the Fosters and the Waldrons constituted an oddity. The Waldron family was upper income; the patriarch was career Air Force and, upon separation, started a small but lucrative electronics business. Mrs. Waldron, the quintessential farmer's daughter, utilized her status as a military spouse to pursue educational opportunities otherwise beyond reach. She obtained citizenship and a degree in accounting. She was the secretary for a local bank manager.

The twin income kept the family well off, and Molly well attired. Jayme, meanwhile, never lacked sporting equipment. The Fosters remained only a step above hand-to-mouth. Regardless, there was a common, unshakable, bond: both matriarchs shared German roots. Ute Foster and Hilde Waldron became instant friends.

Soon enough, there was an exchange of evening dinners during which Aaron Foster and Michael Waldron discovered a mutual interest in the sea. Though strictly an amateur sailor, Michael entertained notions of designing and building a craft of his own. Aaron had some expertise in craft design. As the wives chatted in German, the men spoke the language of the sea. The girls babbled away however they pleased. Often, they switched languages in mid-sentence.

The Waldron girls drew Kathy into tennis. She made no secret of her displeasure of the freshman cheer squad; she counted the days until her sentence expired. Still, by learning tennis, the trio shared after-school hours together. Molly was an accomplished player, but she lacked Jayme's "killer instinct." College scouts were attracted by Molly's win-loss record, but when they watched her practicing with Jayme, they discovered the real prospect.

While Kathy languished in the hell of "butt shaking and enthusiasm faking," she watched Gary struggle through frosh games as wide receiver – a useless position for a team lacking a passing game. He was persistent, however, and blocked by throwing his body in front of much larger players and made himself as annoying as chiggers at a picnic. Once in a great while, he allowed a ball carrier to cut behind his block and gain additional yards. At the end of the game, of course, his body was mostly purple and blue.

Neither her fellow cheerleaders nor their coach expressed dismay over Kathy's frequently announced retirement. Her heart, clearly, wasn't in it. Upon discovering the reason behind her try out, they teased her. The fact that Kathy and Molly were thick precluded serious resentment. Molly was Miss Popularity, and students balked over taunting her shadow.

The Waldron sisters knew they had a college future. Jayme would be a tennis star while Molly's scholastic standing was certain to attract scholarships. Regardless, the Waldron economy could support both girls. Kathy's options resided entirely with her mother; Ute remained a German citizen. Her adopted daughter qualified for a government subsidized university billet, *if* she qualified. It was a plan formulated years prior, and the reason Ute eschewed American citizenship.

"It's a huge responsibility," Kathy announced in partial jest. "I have to get a university degree before mom can be American."

Ute was less facetious. She loved Aaron and lived where he lived. However, she loved her German heritage. She married a soldier, she married a foreigner, adopted a foundling, and lived in America. Each of these trespasses placed a strain on the Kaufmanns. The wounds needed time to heal, and Ute would not tempt further.

The choir teacher, Mr. Davidson, gently leaned on Kathy. He managed to get her to the point – but not beyond – of recognizing her vocal quality. Until he was on firmer ground, however, he'd not push. Nevertheless, he invented ways to showcase her. When Kathy expressed a desire to read music, he exploited it as a means of breaking down her resistance.

For her Thanksgiving birthday, Kathy invited the Waldron sisters. It was too bold to suggest they sacrifice their own Thanksgiving, so she avoided the subject. Mrs. Foster proved far more resourceful. When Kathy woke up on her birthday, after an extra hour of sleep, she found her father lounging at the table with the local paper and a mug of coffee.

Kathy, still in pajamas and a tattered robe, shuffled to the pot and poured a mug. She yawned audibly and sat across from Aaron. She pondered what to have for breakfast, but her half-closed lids made thinking a chore.

"Happy birthday," her father bid through his paper.

Kathy yawned once more and took a sip of the coffee.

"Where's mom?"

"At the café."

Kathy was not amused. The Fisherman's Inn was closed on Thanksgiving. She didn't fathom her father's joke, but she was too groggy to care. She quietly sipped her coffee. When the mug was empty, she prepared toast. Aaron put the paper aside and watched her. It was disquieting.

"Where's mom?"

"I told you."

She grew annoyed. She fished for something sardonic, but Aaron spoke first.

"Your mother has permission to use the kitchen for your birthday dinner."

"Are you serious? Are we feeding an army?"

"Pretty near. The Swoffords, the Rademachers, and the Waldrons."

"You're kidding!"

He shrugged. If Kathy didn't believe, he wasn't going to fuss.

"It must be in health-department order when we leave," he warned. "We have to swab and wash up. That includes birthday girls."

Kathy didn't care. For a memorable Birthgiving, Kathy would scrape barnacles.

Kathy Foster knew about too many cooks. The quartet in the kitchen that day, however, were heedless. While Athena devoted her attention to the turkey, Ute Foster conjured three Swabish dishes and

Hilde Waldron contributed genuine farm delights she learned as a child. Mrs. Rademacher, an American of German birth, contributed two major-league sauces. Moreover, there were birthday cakes and pies previously prepared severally by six bakers. When Aaron and Kathy arrived, the place was as alive as if it were a business day.

There was too much; Aaron was dispatched to deliver a plate to Ed Barker, the curmudgeon by nature, who, likely, feasted on cold beans from a can. On his return, he invited a hungry Japanese couple ambushed by an unexpected holiday. Tables were pushed together in the shape of a capital I so the assembly could dine together.

As the guest of honor, Kathy was pressed into delivering a few remarks. After Rev. Rademacher's blessing, she stood. At her right was Molly, and on her left, Gary. Jayme perched at the end of the table next to her sister.

"I won't be but a moment," she promised. "Opa Kaufmann, in Germany, often tells me if there are twenty Bavarians in a restaurant, there must be twenty tables. If you have twenty Swabs, you need only one table! Let's eat."

The food was eroded as people enjoyed a boisterous Swabish gathering. The poor Japanese couple were shell-shocked at first, but the festive good cheer was contagious; they grew as loud and merry as everyone else. The adults tempered their appetite with wine or, perhaps, tempered their drinking with food.

Before birthday cakes and pies were sliced, Athena – who consumed more wine than was prudent – started singing Brenda Lee songs. Kathy joined in. This rafter-rattling duet, in normal circumstances, would have moderated their enthusiasm. However, the audience egged them on. In the end, the singers decided that Brenda Lee deserved more respect.

There were no gifts. This family tradition began with Kathy in diapers. It was, after all, the elder Fosters who made their thankfulness manifest by toasting Kathy who considered a birthday feast ample enough. Christmas was fast approaching, and, on the Foster's income, two gift-giving ceremonies so near were needlessly extravagant.

When everyone finished, the table contained enough food to feed a village. Stuffed with guilt, the group initiated a meals-on-wheels project. The local Coast Guard contingent was on duty as were local police. If they secured paper or plastic plates and something to cover them, the men could cruise around and distribute Thanksgiving cheer.

By this time, Kathy was comfortable enough with the market manager to call him at home. Quickly, she explained their predicament. Plastic wrap was plentiful, but the need for disposable plates was acute. He agreed to meet her at the store so she could purchase what was needed. Aaron offered to drive her up the hill, but Kathy's coat was buried under a mountain of wraps.

"Take mine," Molly offered, lifting it from the hall tree.

Predictably, it was pricy with a fur-trimmed hood and worthy enough to be featured in Vogue. It mightn't be real fur, but Kathy didn't care. She pulled it on and promised to be extra careful.

Two doors lead into the café; the first fronted the street, and the second was set at right angles. The object was to prevent ocean winds from sweeping and gusting into the establishment. The owners mounted a mirror inside the first door. Women, especially, paused for emergency hair care before entering.

As the establishment was closed, the entry light remained off. All artificial light was behind Kathy and created a ghostly atmosphere. With Aaron two steps behind, Kathy opened the inner door. As she pivoted and reached for the front door, she caught a reflection of herself in the glass. Over her shoulder, she saw the mirror's reflection as well; she wore Molly's coat; the hood was up.

Kathy kept moving into the November chill. The hair on her neck prickled, but not from the cold. Kathy quaked from the memory of her momentary reflection. She sensed that, had she turned around and faced the mirror, a stranger's face would glare back at her.

She sat pensively as Aaron drove; she tried to convince herself that her imagination was irrational and fatuous. She considered the event the invention of a giddy schoolgirl, but the image remained vivid.

Kathy could not dismiss the feeling that she'd caught a glimpse of her sister.

Weimar

January 1989

The icy wind blew strong. Shakespeare was covered in hoarfrost. The bitterness of winter was not confined to weather. The barkers no longer lounged on carpets of grass. They met indoors, inviting danger.

The walls might not have ears, but there were windows, doors, and adjoining rooms. Any undetected person might catch a careless word or phrase and race to the authorities. During Heike's tenure, discussions skirted contentious topics. At the first sign of discomfort, a member would terminate debate with platitudes of how party leaders knew what they were doing. Everyone abided by this tacit by-law and avoided treason.

The one notable exception was a meeting in a youth center. A member had a key and was armed with assurances it would be vacant. The group gathered in a small room where administrative files were kept. They left the door slightly ajar and assigned a "guard." He kept a vigilant eye on the adjoining common area.

Should anyone appear, he'd swing the door wide, because a closing door was certain to arouse suspicion. Should the door open, the conversation would switch to a critique of *Heißer Sommer*; Heike was tasked with leading this "emergency" discussion.

Matters became heated. Nadine questioned economic policy. She insisted that judicious use of paint would reduce required maintenance, particularly with city structures. Most buildings and houses, including that of Anne Ecke, were disintegrating.

"The economic planners have better uses for lead," an older boy explained.

This hint went unheeded.

"So, a building rots and falls down. Calculate the resources and man hours to rebuild. For a fraction of that cost, we lengthen the building's life."

"The government knows what it's doing," someone announced, emphatically.

"We don't have the information the planners have," another reminded.

Nadine ignored them.

"The economic planners ignore us," she hissed.

"Shut up, Nadine," someone snarled.

"Forty years and no paint," Nadine snapped. "That's negligence!"

Two people responded simultaneously, making their responses unintelligible. One of the boys moved to silence Nadine physically, but Heike interceded. The door flew open and exploded against the stop; everyone froze. Heike was frightened and forgot her duty. Everyone stared at the door guard and, silently, awaited fate.

The door sentry shrugged.

"I had to shut her up," he explained softly.

Nadine's face was beet red. She realized the danger she'd subjected the group. The subject was closed, but Nadine fumed.

"It's cold in here," she announced. "I'm going for coffee."

Heike was tempted to follow but didn't. If Nadine carried her temper onto the street and renewed her passionate argument, they'd risk arrest. It was safer to let her cool off, alone.

That weekend, Nadine invited Heike to a play, Shakespeare's *Richard II*. They applied to Rolf for post-*abendsbrot*-curfew dispensation. It was granted, brusquely.

Nadine led the way through icy, slushy streets to an ill-designed, post-war building, cheaply built and shoddily maintained. Nadine rang an apartment buzzer, taking care that Heike didn't see which.

Once admitted, they climbed five flights to pass through an open door and into a gabled garret. There was no heat and few chairs. Twenty other people sat bundled and silent. The play began. The actors, like the audience, were heavily attired. The intimacy of the room allowed them to speak in conversational tones. Each line passed through a billowy cloud of breath.

Richard II came on stage from behind a hanging sheet.

Heike gasped. The actor, though youngish, had lines on his forehead and under his eyes. He wore glasses with thick, black rims. His hair was white and slicked back, he was the image of Erich Honecker. The man forced to abandon his throne was not Shakespeare's Richard; it was the East German head of state.

Heike closed her eyes and waited for the horror to end – or the police to arrive. She wanted to leave, but that would ignite fears of betrayal. Heike and Nadine might be assaulted. The parody was shaved to fifty minutes. The temperature, alone, demanded brevity.

No applause greeted the conclusion, for obvious reasons. Rather than depart as a stampeding heard, the cast released the audience in groups of two or three and cautioned them to exit quietly. Heike and Nadine were the fourth group. They trod slowly and softly. They heard television audio filtering through apartment doors at every landing.

They opened the door quietly and let it catch behind them. They marched through the frozen night air for three blocks in silence.

"I can't believe you did this!" Heike attacked, keeping her voice low.

Nadine didn't reply. Perhaps, she hadn't realized the subversive nature of the play.

"*Pabst* will kill us!"

"Who will tell?" Nadine demanded.

"What if he asks around? What if he finds out about this? *Scheiße!* He'd beat us both."

In all actuality, Heike hoped for a beating. If anyone other than Rolf Jacobs discovered how they spent the evening, they'd get much worse.

The girls remained mute while completing their chores.

"You're a reformer!" Heike accused as they made ready for bed. Nadine let her silence respond.

* * *

It wasn't enough for Nadine to compromise the group. It wasn't enough to lure Heike into treasonous attics. She'd, also, spoke her mind at the optics company where she served her practicum. The management shifted her from tracking production figures and inventory to cleaning floors and toilets. Doubtless, the authorities were notified.

Heike spent one day a week at the bus barn. She aided the office staff with the more tedious duties. She didn't serve because she wanted a career in public transportation; she had no career path. Once in the Party, she'd be assigned one. Public transport was as good an option as any. Besides, an essential part of her practicum was for others to gauge her abilities and attitude.

A prison stint would destroy a career path.

Nadine's big mouth threatened her leadership position in the FDJ. She'd lost the trust of the optics firm. Her Stasi file, doubtless, expanded. Heike would be tainted. Her university prospects were compromised along with her chances for party membership. Rolf, also, would become a suspect.

Heike longed to talk with Jürgen or Günther. They'd know how to meet the crisis. She could run to the grotto and consult with the Bard, but the weather was horrid. When not freezing, or pouring rain, it snowed and gusted.

"*Guten Tag, Fräulein* Jacobs."

With her hood thrown up over her head and eyes on the slippery sidewalk, Heike didn't see Frau Willing until directly in front of her. She wore a thick coat, but her strawberry blond hair, pulled tightly back into a ponytail, was uncovered. Her face, never much to look upon, was spotted with cold. There were heavy lines under her eyes.

"*Fräulein?*" Heike queried.

"You're grown woman," the driver replied with her country dialect.

"I'm fourteen."

"Maybe, but you too big to call familiar. If you like not, I can call you Big Girl."

Frau Willing was on her way into the office but paused to share this exchange. Heike was appreciative. It was a welcome diversion from black thoughts.

"You're the first person to call me *Fräulein*."

"'Nice fit."

"I – like it."

"Don't like so much," the driver warned. "You get married next month and become *Frau*."

Heike thought of Günther. She hadn't heard from him since the army swallowed him. Similarly, after her abrupt rebuff, Heiko was attentive toward another girl.

"I doubt I shall marry soon."

"Poor *Knaben*. Bad luck for them. How is Frau Jacobs?"

"*Wie immer*."

The driver's visage reflected pain. She harbored fond memories of a dear friend.

"I must go. We see again, okay?"

Heike nodded and resumed the journey home. Unexpectedly, she heard Frau Willing calling.

"Hey, Fräulein, you learn drive yet?"

Heike stopped and turned.

"I'm fourteen," she reminded.

"Papa teach me when I am twelve. You much behind. I teach to drive."

Heike waved and moved on. She saw little practicality in learning to drive a tractor or a horse-drawn cart.

Oregon

January 1989

After the Thanksgiving vision, Kathy turned moody. She never communicated her vision lest people think her insane. The more she told herself it was an optical illusion, the less she believed it. Perhaps, her biological parents were insane, and she'd inherited the gene.

Since the day Athena 'assaulted' her, Kathy's feelings towards Gary altered. She was aware but ambivalent. Though flattered by the attention, she felt unworthy.

Molly and Kathy were best friends, but they lived miles apart and seldom met outside school. Gary was closer, but there was a barrier between; his feelings went beyond camaraderie. She didn't want to enter the world of dating and fawning. He was short, light and not very handsome. Primarily, however, she felt freakish; she had no real family, and the birthday visitation rattled her.

Eventually, she succumbed.

They stood at the sea wall. The tide was ushered in by a persistent gale. They leaned into the wind. To overcome the noise of wind and waves, they yelled. It was not the proper time, and Gary was not the proper person.

Yet...

"Don't tell anybody! Please! Not anybody. Promise, Gary. Don't send me to the Looney bin. Promise!"

Gary, shocked and distraught, would promise to stick his face in a fan to satiate her.

"Pie in the sky!" she concluded, "I probably don't have a living relation."

His heart broke.

"What about your trip this summer?"

She glared at him. Whatever the joke, she wasn't receptive – even if she understood it. Gary was no Rhodes Scholar, but he could read and interpret her expression.

"Aren't your folks sending you to Germany?"

Kathy scoffed.

Kathy and her "foster" mother had visited twice in past years, but, since Aaron's retirement, they hadn't the money.

"We can't afford it," she pronounced, leaving a choice epithet unspoken.

"Mom says your mom told her about a charter flight. It's cheaper."

"We don't have the money," Kathy repeated.

There was, she realized, a reason why Ute and Aaron didn't discuss this with her. She loved Oma and Opa so much. However, she didn't want to go. They'd been so loving and gracious to her in the past; now that they knew that Kathy knew… Had it all been a sham? Even if it weren't, there was *Onkle* Dieter and *Tante* "Nose-in-the-air," the Bavarian side of the family.

They hated Kathy. Pretending to tolerate her only served to make their hatred more obvious. A German visit must include the obligatory visit with her Bavarian relations – an event sure to produce sparks on both sides. Kathy's existence made them resentful, and feigned politeness exacerbated hard feelings.

Kathy Foster understood why these people resented and, perhaps, hated her. Now, the "border incident" was cognizant of the root cause, she feared attitudes would worsen. No longer would anyone be forced to pretend that Kathy was family. Before, they may have wished that Kathy would step out into traffic; now, they'd be tempted to push her onto the Autobahn.

She dreaded the possibility of seeing her non-family family.

Not until much later did she realize why she told Gary her secret.

Weimar

February 1989

Heike wasn't curious about Frau Willing's office appearance that frigid day. In the DDR curiosity was discouraged. Regardless, people learned things. A few days following their encounter, Rolf reported during Abendsbrot.

Frau Willing was summoned before an administrative board to explain how her bus was an impediment to navigation for more than an hour – this in a country where one is paid regardless of performance. The Polizei filed a report. This promoted "impediment to traffic" to "counter-revolutionary behavior." Upon receipt of the police report, transport authorities ordered Frau Willing to appear. Herr Jacobs, working near the administrator's office, was privy to unsanctioned information.

Heike and Nadine, despite their war of silence, exchanged surprised expressions.

Heike was ashamed for assuming simple peasants were unworthy of praise. Frau Willing responded to Heike's informal summons. She asked for Fräulein Jacobs, a form of address Heike considered alien. She was caught punching mileage figures into a pre-war calculator to verify previously tabulated data. She'd no wish to shirk her duty, but she refused to keep the driver waiting.

Heike nodded; the driver settled into a much-abused wooden chair and waited. When Heike finished, she folded several meters of paper and clipped it to the inside of a file folder. She placed the document package upon the desk from whence it came. The material was two years old. It waited for a supervisor to decide its fate.

"You want learn drive?" Frau Willing asked.

Willing the Reliable! The peasant woman, as with Herr Jacobs, adhered to an old-fashioned work ethic. The bus she drove must cough and rumble in strict accordance with a printed schedule. She never dawdled when on the clock. Similarly, if she made a promise, she followed through. In a nation of shoddy labor practices, Herr Jacobs and Frau Willing were two giants of productivity.

"You have an auto?"

The woman looked askance at her inquisitor. Frau Willing was single; she lived on the bus route. For her a car was bourgeois decadence.

"Your Papa has auto," she reminded.

Heike froze. The Jacobs family waited five years for the Trabi. By all rights, they dare not expect a car for an additional two years. Herr Jacobs, as with every DDR citizen, was familiar with the "underground" economy. He traded his way up the waiting list.

The cream-colored automobile was hardly six weeks old. Both Heike and Nadine got considerable exercise keeping it polished to Rolf's satisfaction. Had Frau Willing proposed driving a Panzer through the town square, Heike's amazement would have been no less.

"Pabst won't let me near the car," Heike objected.

The bus driver held up a hand to allow a single key to dangle from a knotted chord.

"Herr Jacobs say lessons do good to you."

The girl cast an instinctive glance towards the shop floor. There was a substantial wall between her and the maintenance crew. It was not so substantial, however, to blunt Rolf's booming voice. It wasn't that Heike doubted Willing's word, but Rolf's surrendering the vehicle for Heike's benefit was "eccentric."

"Come," the woman prompted, "I have not so much time."

Heike grabbed her coat and followed her mentor out the door. She feared Rolf's reaction should she damage the Trabi. Hopefully, Frau

Willing would provide a buffer. Before squeezing into the tiny package, Frau Willing lifted the hood and kept the shivering girl occupied until she became familiar with engine nomenclature. A small, simple engine required a brief introduction.

"So, when I tell, you know what I mean, no?"

Heike nodded without understanding.

Heike put on the Trabi, but the driver's seat was adjusted to accommodate Rolf's mass. She adjusted for her shorter legs. During the procedure, Heike seized her opportunity.

"Did you really deliver a baby?"

Frau Willing's mood changed.

"Stupid!" she spat. "Woman say baby come; hospital say baby come not; send woman home. Well, baby come, and bus people act like murder happen. Much noise – no help. It left to me to help poor woman. Somebody must to do."

Only Shakespeare could rival Willing's eloquence.

"I couldn't have done it," Heike admitted.

Frau Willing wasn't buying.

"Fräulein Jacobs, you hear woman screaming for help and only stupid geese honking until your head split, you do. Either must to kill stupid geese or help woman. Helping woman cause fewer trouble."

The bus driver took no pride in her actions. Instead, she nurtured an attitude. Reliving the incident lit a fuse.

"Husband get to bus before ambulance. If police not make fuss, I could drive to hospital and not to need ambulance. Poor woman get better care on bus!"

She was treading on the edge of disaster with her narrative. If Heike were low enough to report Frau Willing to the authorities, it would provide an opportunity to vent her anger anew – and for the record! Maybe, sedition was the only available means to bring about change. Heike hoped not. It would mean Nadine was right.

The first lesson consisted of fundamentals. Heike was introduced to the clutch and brake pedals. She was encouraged to test their resistance as the teacher lectured her in both theory and application in her coarse dialect. The function of the foot throttle was explained. Finally, she was talked through the choreography: clutch, gear engagement and throttle.

Heike was a slave to this regimen until her mentor was satisfied.

"Now, start motor."

A moment later a billowing, noxious cloud swirled lazily around the machine. Heike held her breath and followed her instructor's orders. Clutch in, shift to reverse, ease up on the clutch. Backing out of the parking space was noisy and slow, but Willing did not criticize. Once free, they lurched across and around the parking area. Willing remained stoic, her terse instructions were mixed with words of encouragement.

That first lesson consisted of several short-distance "drives" followed by a complete stop, a shift into neutral, and a continuation of their tiny parking-area circuit. In their quarter hour's journey, Heike brought both the auto and the motor to an instant stop when she detected another vehicle in motion. Even though their speed hardly surpassed a baby's crawl, both Heike and Frau Willing braced to avoid injury. Heike expected an explosion of invective from her tutor. Instead, Patience calmly suggested a more gradual application of the brake.

"We should quit," Heike suggested. "I'm going to break something."

Patience was not concerned.

"I show you how to fix. Drive now."

Assured that Patience was accomplished in Trabi repair, Heike continued with her adventure. Moisture gathered on her palms and brow in defiance of the temperature. Finally, she was allowed into a parking space. She switched off the motor, let out the clutch and a loud sigh.

"How your family?" Patience asked.

"Mutti and Pabst are as ever."

Patience owed Heike a platitude. Instead, the stoic expression changed to one of disapproval.

"Nadine?" she prompted.

"We haven't spoken for days."

"Fight over Knaben?"

The speculation was playful, but the tone subdued. Heike let go another sigh. She'd carried her load too long. Patience had imprudently vented earlier; it was only fair that Heike take advantage of a sympathetic ear.

"Do you know Shakespeare?"

"Nice enough street."

"Not the street – the writer."

It was Frau Willing's turn to exhale audibly.

"Read schedules; read maintenance books; read construction notices. I, a simple spoon carver only."

Heike bristled at the ethnic slur. Many people referred, derogatorily, to the peasant, forest dwellers as spoon carvers. They were the object of jokes and unflattering stories. Heike objected to them. She was well versed in "proper" socialist values. The spoon-carver epithet did not mesh with "all men are brothers."

She realized Frau Willing was pained by barbs aimed at her uncultured, under-educated background. Avoiding condescension, Heike narrated the gist of her *Richard II* experience. She avoided geographical references. She omitted the mention of an attic stage. Despite wanting to trust others, Heike dared not.

Most people resented knowing too much. If asked by the authorities to speak, one was forced to disclose matters injurious to others or risk injury by pleading ignorance. What, for example, would Heike do if a Vopo insisted she repeat Frau Willing's criticisms of the local hospital? If such a question were raised, it meant they knew the answer. Far better ignorance. Still, a person could never not know the pain and concerns of a friend – that would preclude ever having friends.

"I haven't spoken to her since."

"Tough do," Patience nodded. "So, what now you want?"

The answer was so immediate that Heike wondered how it had evaded her.

"I want my sister back."

Patience nodded knowingly.

"Tell her."

Heike could think of a dozen reasons why this was impossible. Strangely, she hadn't the courage to articulate any. The price of her cowardice was self-reproach and shame.

"Next week? Same time?" Patience asked.

Heike looked as disturbed as she felt.

"It isn't fair, Frau Willing. I have nothing to give you in return."

"Not so, Fräulein. I teach you drive; you teach me Shakespeare."

Instantly, Heike felt excitement multiplied by gratitude.

She scurried to the nearest bus line and shivered. Heike, eventually, disembarked at the stop nearest the city library. There she found a welcome opportunity to warm up, and a chance to examine one of the few English language volumes housed there. It was a history of the United States, though, in truth, it was a history of the American socialist movement. The volume, intended as a language tool, was elementary enough for her to digest.

English and Heike had a tenuous relationship. She abandoned Huck Finn after three pages. She tried again with a German translation at her elbow but fared little better. The German language made the narration tedious; English slang made it unintelligible.

The volume she sought was in place, few would read it. It was too thin for the title to appear on the spine. She snapped it up and retired to the nearest vacant table. She flipped through the pages. She recognized it, not by page number, but by a crude pencil sketch of Samuel Gompers in a straw hat.

The text was innocuous, and its theme familiar and obvious. The terse caption under the drawing caused her stomach to churn.

"Show me a country in which there are no strikes, and I'll show you a country in which there is no freedom."

Heike read Gompers words without trembling. The language was clear enough, and she was certain that there was neither ambiguity nor a translation error. Still, Heike found it difficult to understand how such a quote appeared in a book available to the masses. Reading it caused people to think.

It, certainly, got Heike thinking.

Heike learned lessons well and thoroughly. Previously, there existed the State and the Party. There was never any doubt what was politically correct and proper. She adhered to socialist cause and dedicated herself to its advancement. Then, unexpectedly, the recorded words of an English-Jewish immigrant to America, slapped her in the face and bought restless nights.

Doubt is reasonable but deadly. One did not stray from the Party path; one did not question Party decisions. How, she had wondered, could Nadine become obsessed with the production of lead-based paint?

It was so trivial! How, exactly, was Nadine's foolishness different from Heike's? For Nadine, the question was one of production priorities; for Heike, it was the condition of the worker.

How easy it is to dismiss. One never heard of work stoppages in the DDR. It was a socialist state administered by a socialist government. Heike was not *yet* a worker. How could she know what conditions existed in the workplace?

Still, after reading Gompers, Heike began noticing bus-office grumblings. Those muttered complaints were nearly inaudible save to a young girl with a restless mind. Then, there was Frau Willing's tirade in the car –

Had these sentiments hovered about her, unnoticed, for the whole of her life? Were they a recent phenomenon? Either way, awareness of dissatisfaction created avenues of urgent speculation. Heike needed to talk with someone – someone she trusted.

She closed the book and returned it carefully lest some suspicious eye fall upon it. Satisfied she hadn't been observed, she hurried home. For the first time in many days, she must speak to Nadine.

Oregon Coast

March 1989

"Barbie?"

The force of this articulated moniker caused Kathy to blink in shock and amazement.

"That's terrible," Molly protested with unusual animation. "Kathy Foster, I hate you!"

Molly's ubiquitous smile blunted the effectiveness.

"I'm sorry," Kathy muttered.

"The whole school probably says it now. Kathy, you're horrible!"

Confession, Kathy concluded, may be good for the soul, but it was hard on the nerves. The moment she disclosed her trespass, she knew it was a mistake. Now, she must live with it. Still, Molly's gestures and attitude made clear that their friendship remained unshaken.

Kathy felt unworthy and ashamed.

She was not deceived by Molly's practiced *sang-froid* (trafficking with the Waldrons exposes one to patrician words and phrases). It would take time to win back Molly's polished graces. This called for a conference with Jayme who, despite her youth and rebellious ways, was the unquestioned expert on Molly's foibles and vulnerabilities.

It was Kathy who engineered the sleepover. She hardly expected a positive response. After seeing Molly's spacious and immaculately manicured bedroom, Barbie could never be comfortable in Kathy's small, slovenly space. Molly, however, was enthusiastic and lobbied for permission. Mrs. Waldron suggested Kathy spend the weekend in roomier accommodations, but Molly longed to spend two days on the *Mary R.* as a guest of the first mate.

It was a twenty-minute hike from school to the Waldron home where Jayme waited in the driveway. Molly had great hopes for autumn. Kathy, free of yell obligations and determined to avoid future blackmail snares, promised to join Molly on the tennis court. It guaranteed time together and, for away matches, they'd partner on the bus. Jayme, an in-coming freshman, was sure to make the team.

Jayme was the athlete. Molly possessed a fluid, almost ballet-like style. Jayme was an epileptic blur. Jayme attacked the net with such ferocity that she sometimes flew into and over it. As a middle schooler, she stepped onto the high-school courts for practice matches.

She beat Molly regularly and notched up victories against two other varsity players. Then she built a similar record against the boys. Whenever weather and wind cooperated, Molly coached Kathy in the rudiments. It was Jayme, however, who helped polish the clumsy neophyte.

No one, Kathy least of all, expected she'd amount to much, but she participated for the society. Still, on a particularly brisk, drizzly, March afternoon, the girls practiced volleys against each other and the garage door. Kathy hated chasing errant balls. She quickly developed a talent for getting a borrowed racket on the pesky yellow spheres. Her satisfaction was magnified by the absence of a net which would nullify many of her returns.

Wet and panting, Kathy enjoyed a hot shower and a change of clothes. Molly attempted to outfit her, but Kathy feared soiling or tearing Barbie's things. Jayme's cut-off and patched jeans were more her speed. The similarly proffered sweatshirt was bulky enough, so no one noticed the jeans weren't snapped.

As Molly took her turn in the shower, Jayme draped her legs over the arms of an easy chair and reached for the television remote. Kathy, hoping for a game of Ping-Pong or, at least, a video, hovered expectantly behind the rec-room sofa. After flipping through the afternoon tripe, Jayme settled on a sports channel. Kathy sighed and sat down on the sofa to await the return of Guardian Barbie.

"Molly's never been away from home before."

Kathy stared blankly at the TV. Not for several seconds did the announcement register. She turned to look at Jayme who returned the look.

"You're kidding!"

Jayme shook her head and watched a highlight reel of double plays.

"Aren't you?"

Again, the shake of the head.

Kathy was dumbfounded. She invited her friend as if it were a pedestrian matter. Unexpectedly, it was a milestone. At the age of six, Kathy spent several days with Oma and Opa while Aaron and Ute took a bus tour of Italy. The following summer, Kathy spent a long weekend with Granny and Grampy in sheep country near Milton-Freewater.

In a few more months, she'd board a plane for Germany. The realization that Barbie had never traveled beyond her parental shadows never occurred. An innocuous sleepover turned ominous.

"I'll pack a few things," Molly called from upstairs.

Jayme never batted an eye.

"How'd your mom and dad meet?" Kathy asked.

She expected Jayme to shrug or put her off. Instead, the budding athlete warmed to the question.

"Dad was on leave and was making a tour of World War II battle fields," Jayme reported with amusement. "Mom was helping Opa deliver milk when Dad asked directions. I've seen pictures of Mom in her dairy-maid suit. Yuk! After a day or two, Dad asked directions to the farm. He wanted to see Mom. They started writing letters."

Jayme tore her eyes from the television and grinned at Kathy.

"I don't believe a word of it," the tennis prodigy appended.

Kathy nodded. Battle fields on the Lüneberger Heide? Kathy, no historical scholar, was dubious.

"Good tank country," Aaron might say.

She made a note to ask. After years in the cavalry and two tours in Germany, he'd know about the fighting up north. Her gambit accepted; Kathy related how Ute met Aaron. She did so with practiced ease. It kept her mind occupied and Jayme, amazingly, appeared interested.

Thankfully, Molly materialized before additional diversions were required. Kathy tried not to laugh. Molly wore a blue jump suit with a red and white, broad-stripped pullover. Looking like some perky model posing for *Seventeen*, Molly's attire was too flashy for the sea-side environment. The coast, save for Molly, was not a venue for modish togs, and Barbie's outfit looked more outrageous than her cover-girl school attire.

When Mrs. Waldron returned from work, she helped herself to a glass of fruit juice before carrying Molly's bag to the car. Kathy half expected Jayme to stand in the door and wave a big white hanky as her sister left the nest for the first time. It was a relief when Jayme remained downstairs and, presumably, draped over the chair facing the TV. Similarly, Mrs. Waldron radiated calm while chauffeuring the girls to the tiny bay next to the big ocean. Still, Kathy waited for someone to blubber hysterically. It was, alas, very straight forward; a little hug and a peck on the cheek, and Mrs. Waldron drove away.

"Let's walk along the sea wall," Kathy suggested, pulling on a pair of her own jeans.

Molly was enthusiastic. While Kathy tied her shoes, Molly got out of her clown suit and produced a pair of jeans and one of Jayme's sweatshirts. She changed without fanfare, but, as they stepped into the afternoon wind, Kathy realized she'd witnessed a quiet rebellion.

* * *

The sea was brusque. Several squalls lashed up against the shore pushing moderate waves before them. The whales broached merrily; Kathy and Molly kept a sharp lookout. The wind flattened spouts and hid them amid rising swells. The marine mammals hugged the shore, and Aaron wouldn't risk getting too near the rocks.

Kathy spotted a pair of plumes to port, Captain Foster turned into the wind and the bow of the *Mary R.* slapped against the sea. Three of the passengers leaned over the rail and screamed at the ocean. Kathy left Molly, turning green, leaning against the cabin. Refusing to display their lunches on the quarter deck, the queasy gathered at the rail. With the boat charging into troughs, it was too easy to let go the railing and lurch into the angry water.

Kathy's job was averting "*man overboard!*" Failing this, her task was rescue. Though untried, she was prepared. As Aaron neared a mommy and her calf, he reduced power. Despite Barker's insistence that his skippers "climb right up the dorsal," Aaron, habitually, surrendered the right-of-way to the marine mammals.

A whale could damage, if not sink, his craft. However, his greatest concern was drawing blood with the twin props. The pitching and rolling of the *Mary R.* increased in inverse proportion to reduction of steerageway. Molly raced for the rail and Kathy tensed. Responsible for both ends of the boat, she cursed her inability to be everywhere at once. She knew Molly and trusted her to keep her head; she'd focus on strangers and ignored the whales.

"You want to sit this one out?" Kathy asked after tying up.

Molly, white as a sheet, abandoned her ever-ready smile in favor of a scowl. Not trusting her voice, she shook her head.

"Mol, you've got guts!"

Molly cringed over Kathy's choice of words. Kathy's pang of regret was displaced by admiration. After her own bouts with sea sickness, Kathy swore never to sail again. The lure of the Pacific, however, proved too powerful. Similarly, Barbie rejected a legitimate reason to abandon ship.

"Why?" she asked, later, over coffee in the Fisherman's Inn.

"I didn't come here to be alone."

Her color returned, and smile mended, Molly conquered motion sickness, but it took nearly four round trips.

She could have enjoyed the warmth of the café or joined Gary in his Saturday patrol of the sea wall. Despite her pathetic clothes, Molly was easily the "toast of the coast," or would be had she occupied one of the sidewalk benches. She'd not be companionless for long.

"I want to be with you."

A lump came to Kathy's throat. Molly's casual sentiment struck deep. It reminded Kathy of someone she sensed rather than saw on Thanksgiving Day. Why, should she lust after an unknown?

"I don't want to be alone," Kathy murmured without realizing it.

"Huh?"

Molly stared. Ugly wrinkles marched across her forehead. She was used to Kathy's eccentricities, but cryptic remarks were, hitherto, unknown.

* * *

Molly refused to sleep in Kathy's bed. Kathy refused to sleep comfortably with a guest consigned to the floor. They agreed to "go camping" with two sleeping bags in cramped quarters.

The lights switched out, they conversed in low, relaxed tones.

"What was your dad doing on the Lüneberger Heide?"

"Chasing Mom."

"Before that."

"Why?"

Kathy didn't answer.

Earlier, Kathy opened Ute's road atlas. She scanned the area around Lüneberg in search of Mrs. Waldron's village. It was too tiny for listing. However, she searched for inconsequential specks not represented in the index. She got as far as Bergen and slammed the volume shut. Thus, ended a specious tale of romance.

She kept her discovery close. Perhaps, Molly suspected; perhaps, not.

"I admire you going to Germany by yourself. I doubt I could do it."

"You speak fluent German," Kathy noted. "You'd have no trouble."

"I still don't think I could do it," she admitted.

Kathy recalled Jayme's revelation.

"It's so wasteful," she sighed. "Mom and Dad shell out a fortune and for what? It's not like I can look in a phone book and find my other family."

"But you get to know this family better."

She considered for a moment.

"I'm not sure I want to."

"Oh, poo!" Molly exclaimed in language harsh by Waldron standards.

"You're not on that Bavarian thing again? What if your people are Bavarian? Will you hate yourself?"

It was a slap in the face. Molly's conjecture was unlikely. She might have Bavarian roots. Just as likely, she might share the Austrian birthplace of Hitler. She could be Romanian or Polish or Albanian; it was *not* knowing that weighed her down.

Her longing kept her awake. This condition purchased a jaw-dropping revelation: Barbie, of all people, snored!

Weimar, DDR

March 1989

The days crept by like snails trapped in amber. With each hesitant step forward, Heike arrived at a critical decision that might cost her life. Nadine welcomed Heike's overture with tears and a rib-snapping hug. Heike was equally emotional, but the chasm remained. Nadine was a reformer, if not a counter-revolutionary, and she didn't bother hiding it.

People were whispering. Nadine's furtive glances and facial expressions betrayed her. The "sisters" avoided talking politics. Should the Stasi pounce, the family's only protection was the desperate resort: *"I didn't know! We never discussed it."*

The explosion over economic priorities and the subversive *Richard II* were volatile. Coupled with her *demotion* at the optic works, and rumors at school, an arrest could be imminent. No matter how adamant the denials, the entire family would be implicated. Rolf could lose his job, Anne could lose the house, Jürgen could be expelled from university and Heike denied entrance.

Not a hearth in Weimar would welcome them. The honored memory of Anne's father would not protect them from ostracism – or lengthy prison terms. Heike's duty was to tell the authorities. By presenting evidence against Nadine, she'd save herself, and, just maybe, her adoptive parents – and Jürgen. It was the right thing to do.

Günther!

Her decision was predicated in the park the day she caught him reading Huck Finn. Heike, unable to fathom the babble of the American dialect, had, over several weeks, navigated a German translation. Huck, realizing his duty, vowed to turn Jim over to the authorities. He balked; *Freundschaft* was more important than duty.

In *Richard III*, Clarence, a man guilty of trusting his brother, learns, at death's door, that his brother arranged his murder. Could treason against one's country be worse than betraying one's family? Troilus asks of Cressida what she finds offensive.

"*Mine own company,*" she replies.

If the reward for betraying Nadine was promotion to General Secretary and, thereby, the power to set all national issues aright, Heike must refuse. The worst punishment possible was to experience Cressida's heart-wrenching sentiment. The more Heike wrestled with her dilemma, the clearer her course. She could, if forced, live in a prison. Regardless, she'd die before condemning Nadine to one.

She roamed the library, calmly browsing the stacks. No one suspected from her casual attitude the monumental decision she'd reached. Indeed, there was no visible sign to mark the moment her fate was determined. She examined the spines with feigned casualness.

Her mind turned to Günther. Save for a pair of post cards, she'd no word since his departure. Her lips burned from his kisses, but she no longer believed there was any substance behind them. Günther's silence ended childish hopes. Still, he wasn't treasonous.

He helped Heike invest in a new concept of herself; he had confidence in her when others, including Heike, were ambivalent. Günther found her a *Kind* and left her a *Fräulein*.

She found herself amid classical literature. Seeking diversion, she found *The Aeneid*. That was Vergil, she knew.

Suddenly, she paused and looked at the titles preceding. *Plautus*. Not right. No other Ps. She made a quick scan and found an anthology of Roman verse. She snapped it up and examined the table of contents.

Propertius!

Quietly, she retired to the nearest table and opened the volume. In cold blood she flipped pages, reading titles until,

Vergangen

The one I love has left. Has left.

Comrade, you tell me my distress is baseless?
Those we love are our enemies.
Killing me would be a little thing.

The monarch of yesterday's love becomes tomorrow's
fool.
Thus, is love.

Troy had proud towers.
I think of gifts given and songs sung.
But in all our time together, never once were said the
words
"I love you."

Heike sobbed. She wasn't worthy to live near other people. She spied on them and read their thoughts like a British spy. True enough, the poem stabbed her heart, but her grief was for Lilo. Heike invaded another's soul.

It mattered not that she loathed the concept of Lilo and Günther together. What mattered most to Heike was Lilo's pain. She appreciated the pain – indeed, she shared it. Next to Günther and Lilo as a couple, the most despised concept was a union of Lilo and Heike. Yet, they were united by the same devastating remorse; they were sisters!

She closed the book.

Sisters

The word lulled calmly atop the tempestuous waves of rage and hurt. It went almost unnoticed until the tumult subsided. Then, it drifted, wind-blown. Finally, it bobbed placidly in the renewed calm of her brain.

Sisters? Brothers?

Was Heike an only child? She hated those who tried to steal her away from her country. For those, she had nothing but contempt. But – others?

Heike Jacobs was alone. She needed someone. Günther was *Vergangen* as was Jürgen. Nadine, spiritually, was slipping away. Mutti – dear, dear Mutti – was far away. Could there be – dared she hope?

* * *

Winter left a last, spiteful snow flurry. Heike hadn't seen it coming, but she knew enough to protect herself. Typically, however, she neglected her gloves. Jürgen's coat was missing the top button. To protect her body, she clasped the coat closed.

Her hands were frozen when she arrived in August Baudert Platz. She quickened her pace toward the *Bahnhof.* She rushed through the heavy door, her lungs aching, and heart nearly bursting. Nearly as cold inside as out, Heike was sheltered from the merciless wind. She let go the coat and cupped her hands over her mouth; she puffed into them urgently until feeling returned.

She shuffled to the Mitropa Café and paused. She feared her trek wasted. Heike had asked Nadine. Nadine, little more than a baby herself when Heike arrived, shrugged. They opted not to ask Herr Jacobs. Were Frau Jacobs of sound mind…Well?

Jürgen would know something. Jürgen, mysteriously, collected hordes of forbidden information. He reveled stories about local history during the NS time. Nadine and Heike were incredulous. Over time, however, his stories were confirmed, and the girls regarded him a sage.

Alas, Jürgen was gone. It wouldn't do to write or call. This was delicate. The Stasi might intercept fragments of Heike's curiosity.

"Jürgen and Nicole were thick for years," Nadine reminded.

It was a slender hope, but Heike had naught else to quench her thirst. Nicole worked at the Bahnhof café.

The swirl of air swathed her. Predictably, transients huddled over coffee and cake while waiting. Trains seldom ran on time; passengers expected long waits. When the weather was good, it was a trivial ordeal. When the weather was foul, sheltered places filled quickly.

There was no mistaking Nicole despite substantial weight loss. The way she flitted between the counter and patrons demonstrated high energy. There should be two service people out front. The work ethic of the DDR presupposed that worker absenteeism was a given. Rolf Jacobs delivered orations on how subordinates wandered in and out without explanation.

There was always a queue somewhere for goods; the café staff, save for Nicole, waited patiently for a chance at scarce goods. Heike's hope surged. She perched at the first empty table. It might require several minutes for service. This was a given in the DDR, Heike seized the opportunity to wiggle out of Jürgen's coat and allow warm air to caress her.

Finally, the full-bodied woman navigated her way around and through tables and chairs. Watching the large, white apron, Heike recalled a scene in Shakespeare where an ample woman, similarly adorned, was compared to a ship under sail. Though Nicole had shed weight, she remained formidable.

"*Genossin.*"

The socialist salutation, appropriate for people of their generation, lacked sincerity. There was a sardonic edge that grated. What, she wondered, had she done to Nicole?

"You have real coffee?"

Nicole eyed her coldly.

"Ja."

Nicole dragged out the reply, rich in subtext. Undoubtedly, there was real coffee on the premises. Whether Heike would experience it remained moot.

"*Eine Tasse, bitte.*"

"*Sofort.*"

The patron entertained herself with a myriad of conjectures concerning Nicole's abrasive attitude. Rather than waste time pondering the cause, she steeled herself against it. Jürgen's clearly stated rule: When you want something, you mustn't display hostility.

It was a prolonged wait. In her defense, the waitress couldn't ignore the multitude to please Heike. Still, when she arrived with a tray, silver-plated (once upon a long-time ago), Heike examined the black sludge and wondered when it was brewed.

"I need to talk," she said boldly but softly.

"I get off at four."

"I'll wait on the square."

"Four, then."

She was gone.

Heike stared at the coffee. She considered adding something. However, the sugar in the bowl was caked and broke off in chunks. Who knew what liquids had splashed into that bowl? The milk on the tiny server looked suspicious.

She pulled coins from her pocket. She made certain to leave Nicole something, ever mindful that too much is as offensive as too little. She wanted to talk, not get pushed in the face.

* * *

By four o'clock, the weather entered its third season. Heike wore the coat only because it was a trial to carry it. She left it unbuttoned and welcomed a gentle breeze. She selected a bench with a clear view of the station's main entrance. The café had a separate, employee entrance; Heike kept the west end under observation.

It was nearly four thirty when Nicole emerged. She found Heike and crossed the street. She sat next to her. Heike explained her predicament and asked if Jürgen ever shared information.

"You're asking me to remember after a long time," Nicole replied. "I wasn't interested."

Heike pretended to be understanding and gently prodded with carefully formulated questions. She didn't want to put ideas into Nicole's head; she was interested only in Nadine's memory.

"There was an arrest on New Year's morning," Nicole advanced. "Your parents tried for the West."

New Year's Day! That must be 1974. The Jacobs family records showed Heike's date of birth was November 12, 1973.

"One child?"

She couldn't help herself.

After several moments, Nicole shook her head.

"I don't know. Jürgen spoke of it, but, like I said, I wasn't interested. I can't remember. You must ask him."

Heike nodded and expressed thanks.

Nicole re-crossed the street. Heike watched her enter a cab. She watched as it exited the square. Heike remained with her thoughts. The interview proved unsatisfactory, yet she experienced amazing tension. It was, however, unlike the dread of Nadine's possible arrest.

This anxiety was different. It fed upon itself and promoted hope; Heike drew strength from it. Somewhere, she imagined, there were others who shared her blood and genes. *He, she* or *they* might be in the West. Unexpectedly, it didn't matter. A bond exists, a bond stronger than geography and politics.

It was a hope. Only a hope. Until hope was dashed to pieces by a brutal, capricious reality, Heike would carry it. Perhaps, one day, someone would read her mind as Heike read Lilo's.

Cogito, ergo sum.

Who penned that? French? Pre-Hegelian for certain. However, another philosopher emerged on that fickle spring day. Heike Jacobs synthesized Shakespeare, Twain, and her own felicity to arrive at an unshakable aphorism: *I am not alone.*

The Oregon Coast

May 1989

The migrating whales abounded. The ocean settled into a placid pool under a week of azure skies. For Kathy, however, the afternoon fog was suffocating, and the geysers produced by transient sea mammals lost appeal. She was outgrowing Harry and their afternoon outings became less frequent. Practicing volleys with Jayme was a chore, and conversations with Gary were labored.

Molly's boldness surprised one and all with her sudden proclivity for the word *no*. This was partnered by her ability to strike up animated conversations with a certain soon-to-be graduate. The opportunities for Kathy to be alone with Molly were few.

Ute assumed Kathy's personality deficiency was the result of adolescence. In a superhuman effort to avoid nagging, she suffered through Kathy's taciturn behavior. Whenever she or Aaron sounded her out, Kathy retreated into a shell.

In April, the cacophony raised by Polish Solidarity forced the Communists to agree into a power-sharing scheme and – forty years delayed – free elections. Kathy hunched over the kitchen table with Ute, listening to short-wave broadcasts from Germany. They heard reporters blabbing excitedly. Something was happening in the East – and it wasn't confined to Poland. Stories seeped out of Romania and East Germany.

Kathy remained silently attentive. After signoff, she padded softly to her room and closed the door. Aaron and Ute exchanged glances.

The Fisherman's Inn experienced lulls between breakfast and lunch. During one such, Ute discovered Kathy at a window seat looking into the harbor. Athena waited table, a coffee ewer in hand. Ute took up a mug from under the counter.

"Have Ramon make an oyster sandwich. Can you watch the counter for a bit?"

"I can handle it," Athena assured.

Ute filled a mug, sat across from Kathy, and made her offering.

"Thanks," the girl said softly, accepting the mug.

Ute said nothing. She waited.

"Taking a break?" Kathy asked, abrasively.

"I'm on strike."

For the first time in many, many days, Kathy peered out of her cave. "What?"

"I'm staying here until you tell me about the monkey on your back."

Kathy looked at Athena and back at her mother.

"Gary and I had words."

Ute didn't move. She stared. The atmosphere grew tense.

"He thinks it's great I'm flying to Germany, but it's all dash."

"Dash?" Ute repeated. "I'm only glad Molly doesn't swear like a sailor. There's no telling what'll come out of your mouth. Why *dash*?"

"You're spending a fortune on this."

"Don't you want to see Omie and Opie?"

"Of course, but – but – Uncle Dieter. I mean, you haven't spoken in years."

"That's nothing to do with you."

"*Doch, doch*! I *am* the reason."

Ute shook her head vigorously.

"No, Kathy. *I'm* the reason. Dieter insisted we tell you about the adoption years ago – and he was right. He avoided us because he and his family don't abide lying. Sooner or later, someone would say something in front of you. He's angry with me."

Kathy wasn't convinced. She assumed a childish pout.

"No one knows more about you than Dieter. He's has a huge file. He's always collecting information."

"And what good is it? He can't tell me if I have a family."

"Kathy!"

The teen bit her lip in repentance.

"You know what I mean."

"Of course," Ute nodded. "But you've two cousins crazy about their American relative."

"Oh, jolly."

"Will you stop with this Bavarian crap!"

Momentarily, Kathy expected Ute to reach across the table and grab her. She straightened her posture and scooted back in her chair, just in case.

"He's my brother and they're his children."

"Molly and I had this conversation," she announced, flatly.

It was Ute's turn to lean back. She put one hand in her lap; one remained flat on the table.

"I want this for you and for my brother. I want to go. I must make up for all those stupid, empty years, but your – father –"

She stopped and examined Kathy. The girl betrayed no sign of prickliness.

"Your father suggested that, if only one person can go, it must be you."

"Why?"

It was a question devoid of emotion.

"I have a family; you're looking for one."

Kathy sighed.

"What did your grandfather do during the war?"

Kathy expected to see a sharp reaction. She was disappointed. Ute's brows narrowed, but they betrayed no umbrage.

"I won't tell you."

"Why not?"

"For two reasons. One night, after dinner, *Vati* and Mutti sat us down and told Dieter and me all about it. They wouldn't risk our hearing it from someone else. Kathy, there are certain things I don't want to know. Ask your uncle. He may not say either. If you insist, I'll tell you where to look, but I won't tell you something I never wanted to know myself."

Kathy weighed that.

"What's the second reason?"

Ute's reply was instantaneous.

"He – *my* Opa – is part of my family, not yours."

"But Opie was in the Hitler Youth –"

"So was my mother," Ute nodded. "That's how they met."

"They met in the Hitler Youth?"

Ute remained patience personified.

"It wasn't like Girl Scouts. You didn't join. It was blackmail. Refusing to join got entire families in trouble."

Athena arrived with fried oysters snuggled in a bun along with lettuce and tomatoes. The monument was surrounded by French fries. Athena warmed up the coffee, said a few cheery words, and deduced the patrons didn't welcome interruption. She left quickly.

"On the house," Ute announced.

"Dash! You're paying for it yourself."

Ute shrugged.

"Enjoy."

Kathy hesitated. She didn't want to appear eager. After a respectful while, she reached for the red squeeze bottle and smothered the fries. Ute didn't make a face.

"My mother sang in the choir," Ute began. "When the bombing started, they sang to boost morale. That was her job in the girls' version of the Hitler Youth. When things got really bad, she was sent to a farm in the country and away from bombs. There were other kids. They helped with the farm work – there was no one else except old men and a few women."

Kathy listened as she munched fries – she, habitually, saved the oysters for "dessert."

"That winter, one of the younger boys got very sick. It was twelve miles to the nearest doctor and no gas for the car, so they put him on a sled. Your Oma and another girl volunteered to pull it. They couldn't go in daylight. American and British planes owned the sky, and they couldn't tell the difference between kids pulling a sled and troops hauling supplies, so, they went at night. They dragged that boy without a map or a compass, but they saved his life. That's why Oma has that red nose and red cheeks. Skin damage."

Kathy nodded. She wondered if she'd ever teased Omie about her Rudolph-the-Red-Nose. It glowed after she drank coffee. How brutal to make fun?

"She told that story to Vati," Ute added. "He told me. Mutti never talks about the war. I caught her once after dinner. She was licking sauce off the plate. She was embarrassed, of course. She giggled and said, '*Just like in the war.*' That, Kathy, is the only mention she ever made to me."

Kathy nearly gagged. She pushed the plate away.

"Sorry. I didn't want to upset you. Let me tell you about the happiest day of my life. Was it when I met your father – or when I knew I was in love? My wedding day was very happy. And – oh God! – the day we got you…! That was a great, great, great day! But – sorry, Kathy – the happiest day of my life was very ordinary.

"It was a beautiful spring day. A Sunday, I'm sure, because there was no school. I woke up wanting to sing. I threw open the window and let the world in. I was listening to the BBC; I don't know why. I didn't listen, except when they played Lilly Bolero before the news. I raced downstairs, hopped on my bike, and sped around the block. I'd rush back upstairs and listen to a military band play Lilly Bolero – I pictured them in red uniforms and bear-skin hats marching past Buckingham Palace. Then, back onto the bike and another race around the block.

"I don't remember Dieter. He may have been with friends. Vati and Mutti worked in the garden. My heart was beating so fast, and the air was so fresh and tingly with spring and the sun was so warm! I don't recall a time when I was so excited for so long and so happy to be alive!"

Kathy eyed the sandwich. She felt Ute's enthusiasm but couldn't share it.

"A few weeks ago, I remembered it again and realized something. I was riding my bike and no bombs fell, no planes strafed; there were no piles of rubble, no police spying on me, no tanks roaring down the streets. I realize, now, that millions of people died so I could have that one, perfect, spring day. If the war never happened and Hitler still ran the country – It's – sobering."

Kathy slammed her elbow on the table and rested her head on a fist.

"And my family – my other family, might be in a concentration camp."

"Maybe. I doubt it."

"Molly's dad was visiting concentration camps when he met her mom," Kathy announced.

"She told you?"

"I figured it out. Omie and Opie met in the Hitler Youth; Mr. and Mrs. Waldron met in a KZ; I'm a stinking border incident! Not exactly the formula for a romance novel, huh?"

Ute pushed the plate back under Kathy's nose and rested her arms on the table. She picked up a fry and swathed it with ketchup. She made delicate little circles in the air with the dripping red end.

"Open up the hanger, the plane's coming in for a landing."

"Stop it!" Kathy demanded. "I'm too old for that."

Ute smiled and made noises.

"Not until you open the hanger," she warned.

Kathy lunged if only to silence Ute before embarrassing her further. Ute managed to get her fingers out of the way just in time. Kathy hoped to teach her a lesson. There was a moment of pensive munching under Ute's wide smile. Kathy battled with herself, only to relent. When she reached for the sandwich, Ute pushed herself back from the table.

"In case you don't know it, Kathy. It doesn't matter where you came from."

Kathy rolled her eyes.

"I know, I know," Ute muttered. "It sounds silly, but think about it."

Kathy watched Ute saunter back to the counter. The talk didn't make her feel better, but it made her feel differently.

Weimar

June 1989

Heike left the house. She and Nadine discussed Poland. For the first time, a Communist Party faced election-day opponents. *Solidarity*, the previously "illegal" trade union, ran a slate of candidates. They swept into office by a large margin.

Such news was, of course, highly edited before DDR citizens were informed. However, word-of-mouth, was faster and more accurate than "official" news. In the past, in Hungary, in Czechoslovakia, and in the DDR, Soviet tanks quelled opposition. Through tact and patience, Heike expressed reservations. Nadine's face turned beet-red; veins bulged in her neck.

She argued loudly. Heike considered cracking Nadine's skull to terminate her dangerous arguments. However, Heike vowed never again to raise a hand against her sister. Instead, she fled the house.

It was rainy and chilly. Should she return for a jacket and umbrella, Nadine would expand her arguments. Dodging through the streets, she reached a café. Her clothes dripped and her hair was plastered to her face. She adjourned to the restroom and repaired what damage she could.

Following a serving of steamy, rich soljanka, she was moderately warmed and her clothes moderately dry. She ordered coffee for dessert. She intended to return home but nurtured misgivings. The drizzle dissipated. As was her wont, she directed her feet towards Shakespeare. She was careful, however, to monitor the weather.

There were few people about. Those who were carried umbrellas. They weren't strolling; they marched with expeditious steps. Only Heike paused. Expecting no one, she walked through a gap in the hedge and discovered a sinister vision.

She squealed.

He was a bull of a man – broad shoulders and a barrel chest. He was as amazed as she. Clearly, he hadn't expected anyone to stray from the path. Otherwise, he'd have hidden before she swerved, very nearly, into him.

He wore a Soviet uniform, greenish-brown woolen pants, and tunic with splashes of red on and around the insignia. The uniform was sodden, particularly around the shoulders and thighs. His was a young face, and it radiated fear.

Soviets and Germans, both military and civilian, mingled only within clearly defined parameters. To meet in a public place devoid of supervision was forbidden. Despite the ubiquitous symbol of Soviet and German hands clasped in friendship, animosity remained. The Soviets never forgot over twenty million people murdered by the Germans. Similarly, Germans cultivated hatred over Soviet brutal rape fests and murdering civilians and prisoners.

With sixty years of resentment and hatred towards each other, a blood bath remained one thoughtless word away. Heike considered it wasteful to learn the language of her "Soviet allies" when they were forbidden to mingle. Discovered together, unsupervised, they faced serious consequences. She wanted to flee, but she held her ground. The burly figure looked as if he could break Heike's spine with minimal effort. However, his babyish, frightened expression marked him as harmless. After several awkward moments, the boy held two fingers near his face. She recognized the sign and shook her head.

"*Sigareta?*" he squeaked in Russian.

"I smoke not," she replied, as well as her unpracticed tongue allowed.

"*Sigareta?*" he asked, gesturing again.

Heike took a breath.

"I have a cigarette not," she said, slowly and distinctly.

He dropped his hand. He'd suffered defeat. For a moment, she thought he'd burst into tears.

"Where are your comrades?"

He didn't look up. He spoke to his feet.

"Comrades! When the rain come, they went into shelter. Not me. I want to be not with soldiers."

Heike looked about furtively. This was dangerous.

"You shouldn't be here," she scolded.

He wasn't moved by her Russian. Did he think her an informant? If he became frightened enough, and desperate enough, he might use his huge hands for something other than begging cigarettes.

"Where are you from?"

She hoped her question would allay suspicion. His fear melted into a morose, unseeing glare.

"Georgia," he replied, almost hopefully. "You know it?"

"*Da.*"

She wasn't truthful. Georgia was in the south – somewhere. It wasn't, she recalled, very large. Stalin was born there. Jürgen told her that – school texts provided little information about him.

"My father grows tobacco. Good tobacco. Good for cigarettes."

Heike wanted to avoid that subject.

"What is your name?"

It was the first Russian sentence she learned. It was the one she was least likely to exercise.

"Vasile."

The pause was short and uncomfortable. Once the rain subsided, people were sure to come out. The more eyes in the park, the greater their chance of discovery.

"Is Vasile a Georgian name?"

He shrugged.

Georgia, tobacco – he's a peasant! He didn't know his own heritage. Remarkable! She'd stumbled onto the Soviet equivalent of a spoon-carver. That changed everything. Frau Willing, her friend and ally, was a peasant.

"It is not safe for you to be alone."

Another shrug.

"It could be trouble," she prompted.

This earned a snort, but it wasn't aimed at her. It was, unmistakably, a reflection of attitude. She intruded no further but took advantage of the silence to scan the most likely avenues of approach. It wasn't her place to state the obvious. Her concerns outran her Russian vocabulary, beyond sentences memorized by rote, her Russian grammar was stretched to the limit.

"My brother was killed in Afghanistan," the soldier announced bitterly. "Mother nearly died from that. I am called to the army and sent to here. How can they make trouble more?"

He spoke slowly allowing her to digest some words and deduce the meanings of others.

"My comrade is a soldier," she began. "He could go to university, but he stays in army."

The boy was interested.

"Why?"

"Duty."

He didn't understand.

"He felt it is his duty," she elaborated, wondering why she defended Günther.

Was he really a friend? It was clear Heike Jacobs cast no shadow in Günther's eyes.

"Duty?"

Had she used the right word? She looked around while searching for a substitute.

"He knows he must do."

He nodded.

"Ah, duty."

She'd used the wrong word. She recognized the correct one when he uttered it. Likely, the error marked her a fool.

"My duty is my family," he expanded. "I need to help my father with work and look after my sisters. Sisters do not know duty."

"You are not running away?"

"I think about running all the time, but where is to home? I can ask not, true?"

Heike looked around once again, realizing that time, their mutual enemy, was sprinting away.

"You can help your sisters by example, Vasile," she said quickly.

She hoped her Russian communicated her intentions.

She reached out and touched his arm. He started. If he did not appreciate the danger before, he was fully aware of it at that moment.

"You must be best soldier. When you return, you bring best example. You do what is needed; do it well. You do duty. Your sisters see. Your sisters learn duty from you."

He shook his arm free. He stepped back.

"Duty, Vasile."

"So easy to say," he whispered.

"Duty to your family means above everything."

"The army is not good," he muttered.

"You don't do for army. You do for family. Lead with example."

"And you? You not in army."

"I live for family."

He nervously looked about.

"You think?"

"I know. Think not of Vasile. That makes hard. Think of family. Be example. They will listen, Vasile. They will follow good example."

He smirked.

"Sergeant Vasile. That sound good."

She nodded.

"The better example you be, the fewer orders you must do."

Somehow, the notion appealed to him.

"A sergeant with no yell," he mused. "That is funny. I be that sergeant."

"Start now," Heike encouraged, "before someone sees."

He nodded and set off.

She hoped her advice was sound.

* * *

She didn't speak of her chance meeting. No one – especially Nadine – must know. As a candidate for questioning by the authorities, the less Nadine knew, the safer Heike and the family were.

Should she be questioned about talking with a Soviet soldier, she knew him only as Vasile. There must be thousands, but how many stationed near Weimar were Georgian? Heike knew enough to get him in grave trouble. Unease made her nervous, and nervousness was compounded by additional shouting matches. With Frau Jacobs in the next room, their kitchen "shouting" was muted, but exchanges were white hot.

Finally, Heike drained the dish water and left Nadine to finish drying and putting away the dishes. She paused briefly to exchange smiles with the saintly woman who happily watched her husband read the less provocative portions of the paper. It was a forced smile. Heike was angry. She was so angry; she came near striking Nadine.

She was kept in check through the vow she made. Above this, she wished to save Frau Jacobs distress. Certain borders are not crossed. Seething, she escorted a book to the far end of the room, an empty space where her sleeping pallet once lay. Sitting on the floor, behind her bed, provided a buffer.

The girls smoldered; neither spoke. Neither intended to speak. Nadine didn't climb onto her bed. She'd see Heike from the summit. Thus, she settled on the floor with her back against the door. Suppose, Heike thought, this was the moment the Stasi comes. Wasn't her duty to stand with Nadine rather than oppose her?

How far Heike had journeyed. Formerly, she was dedicated to the State; all sacrifices and labors were predicated on her country only. Now, Heike Jacobs resolved to sacrifice everything – her life, if need be – for the family. If she were a simple peasant like Vasile, she'd have no qualms. Soon to join the FDJ, Heike was conflicted; regardless, she must put Nadine first.

Heike and Nadine debated. Heike knew her arguments were sound. Nadine rebutted with emotion and provocative phrases proving, in Heike's estimation, she was wrong. The younger girl became enraged over Nadine's refusal to bow to evidence and logic.

Without further reflection, Heike slammed her book shut and crabbed her way around the beds. Nadine sat tensed and ready to defend herself. Her scowl was hateful and horrid. Suddenly, she found herself warding off a hug.

"I'm sorry," Heike gushed.

That was all she dared say, but it was enough. After her initial shock, Nadine got her arms out from between them and returned the hug.

"I'm sorry, too" she whispered.

The next moment, they were braced against the door. If the Stasi came for Nadine, they'd have a chore entering. The officers would be confronted by a united front.

* * *

Heiko was insistent. He hadn't sought Heike, but when they met in a bookstore, he made it imperative that she see him home. She was suspicious, naturally, but she was hardly alarmed. Yes, he expressed interest once, but she frightened him off.

"Is your sister home?" Heike asked, ashamed of hating her without realizing her identity.

"No, it's safe."

He was unaware of how ominous this sounded.

"Safe for what?" she asked, reasonably.

"You'll see."

She was on her guard. He ushered her up the street.

"I should say, you'll hear."

She was instantly curious. Heiko's enthusiasm was contagious. Moreover, he sensed Heike's reticence and deduced the reason for it. By stressing the word *hear*, his invitation became acceptable.

Heiko fumbled excitedly with his keys at the door of the apartment building. Together, they climbed two flights of stairs where, once more, Heiko's excited fingers trembled. Once inside, he called out, but no one replied.

"Sit right there," he instructed, pressing her gently onto a worn sofa.

Heike shrugged off the sling and let her shoulder bag drop onto the threadbare carpet. She watched the giddy Heiko disappear; she heard rustling. He reappeared with a brown paper sleeve which he set delicately next to a turntable. Carefully, he extracted a disc, placed it on the machine, lifted the arm, and rested it, delicately, onto the record.

Moments later, Heike's eyes grew large. She made an emergency survey. There were two cracked windows. She rushed to close them – quickly! She looked through them and was, momentarily, relieved to discover no one. She turned and leaned against the wall.

"Are you crazy?" she whispered.

Heiko's thousand-watt smile radiated through the room.

"I want to play that kind of music," he announced.

"Where? It isn't permitted!"

His smile remained undamaged.

"Maybe, someday. It's the kind of jazz the Wessies play in special clubs."

"We have Ossi clubs," she reminded. "They have bars on the windows."

He remained dauntless.

"Do you like it?"

She listened briefly but couldn't, honestly, say she did. Rash judgments, she realized, are very tricky. Once, she hated Hanna. That evaporated the moment Heike realized her identity.

"I'm in a band," he announced.

She knew. He played trombone. Sitting next to a comrade every day at school, one learns things. Heike heard the group at a recent festival. They did *not* play the music she was hearing.

"We play this," he announced. "Well, we try."

"Where do you practice? No, don't answer! AND, I don't want to know where you got this record. Heiko, the Stasi may be watching me!"

He nodded knowingly.

"Nadine?" he asked.

Heike scurried back to the sofa and sat down on the forward edge. She leaned forward expectantly.

"You know?"

He shrugged.

"It stands to reason, doesn't it? Her practicum went badly. FDJ leaders spoke with her."

"Then, you know this is dangerous. If the Stasi talks to Nadine, they'll talk to me. What if they ask me about this?"

He pondered the question. Heike felt he'd arrive at a profound conclusion or, at least, some clever subterfuge. Instead, he frightened her even more.

"I like blue-grass music. It's an American jazz form. I hope, someday, to get a banjo. Maybe, I'll make one. It might be difficult learning to play. Still, it will be fun."

"Heiko, please! Don't you understand? You're making me a spy! The Stasi will force me to cooperate to make things easier for Nadine. Then we're all in trouble. I won't get into the Party or uni – that's assuming we don't all go to prison."

Heiko became serious. He looked hard into Heike's pleading eyes and sighed. He got up and paced about the room before lifting the needle from the record and putting it away.

"You still want to be in the Party?"

"Yes; I want to make a difference."

Heiko digested this and settled back into a chair.

"We all say that. You will be in the FDJ soon. I'll bet potatoes you'll become a leader. Good luck, Heike. It's what you want. I want to play music I like, even if no one hears. Is that unreasonable?"

Heike averted her eyes. It was difficult to comprehend when smart people make mistakes. If the Party declared certain music "unacceptable," there must be good reasons.

"Let me ask you, Heike. Suppose you, one day, become General Secretary. Do you feel your judgment will be seriously flawed because Nadine asks questions, or a classmate plays forbidden music?"

She didn't answer.

She couldn't answer.

She sank onto the floor, propped her head against her hand and dove deep into confused thought. Heiko let her wrestle for several moments before hiding his contraband. When he returned, he brought a mug of steaming coffee.

The aroma prickled. Heike perked up. She nodded thanks, accepted it, and took an experimental sip. Heiko returned to his seat and waited,

"It's so difficult for me to know what is right."

She looked up to find his serious expression.

"Funny, isn't it?" he began quietly. "We've been twins ever since we were assigned the same station. You were so close, I never appreciated how remarkable you are. No wonder Hanna admires you."

"Stop that!" Heike warned irascibly. "She doesn't know me."

"You know Rosa Luxemburg?" he countered.

"Well," Heike responded, examining her coffee. "I'm not Rosa Luxemburg."

"But you set an example, Heike – the way you act and talk and present yourself. Hanna notices and takes it to heart. She confessed she's envious of me because I'm with you every day."

"Please, don't do this, Heiko. There's no way I can live up to people's expectations. I can't even live up to my own."

Heiko slapped his thighs and produced a resounding pop. Startled, Heike looked up to find him smiling anew.

"That's the beauty of it!" he gleamed. "That's why you're an inspiration – and not just for Hanna. There are many who feel this way. You don't try to be something; you're real."

"But I'm confused. Rosa knew what to do. She knew where she was going –"

"And she knew she would die," Heiko injected.

"I'm not that brave. I don't want to be murdered or go to prison. And," she added with special emphasis, "I don't know what I want. I don't know where I'm going."

Heiko laughed.

"Come on," he said, standing, "I'll walk you to town where you can get my decedent, subversive, counter-revolutionary music out of your ears."

He offered his hand, and she accepted it. He placed the mug on an end table, grabbed her bag and offered it to her. He held the door for her. Heike, temporarily stunned, accepted his courtesies.

"Why did you laugh back there?" she asked. "Do you think it's funny that a person doesn't want to be killed or sent to prison."

"I think it's human."

"Then, why laugh?"

"Because you're the only intelligent person I know who admits confusion."

She began to pout.

"I don't find that encouraging," she admitted. "I know my family means more to me than anything. At least, I've figured that out."

Heiko nodded.

"Still dissatisfied?"

Heike nodded.

"Just a thought," he prompted. "You have two families, oder?"

They walked silently on. She frowned, as she often did, and kept her thoughts close. Heiko's question struck her with the emotional force of a military invasion.

Fürth and the Hinterland

June 1989

Despite long association, the relationship between Gary and Kathy blurred. They were best friends and worst enemies, but when they slammed into blunt-force puberty, neither knew what they expected of themselves or each other. They retired to neutral corners to plot. Plotting gave way to procrastination.

The two spoke awkwardly at church while sitting next to each other. Their daily bus rides were, frequently, marked by prolonged silence. Kathy opted to spend her free time with Molly; Gary accompanied a quartet of footballers who, once, attempted to murder him on the practice field. Though Kathy was pleased he'd earned their respect, she was jealous for reasons she could not define.

When school ended, she and Gary rode the bus in silence. It was impossible to speak with a boisterous end-of-year celebration surrounding them, but neither joined in. Gary de-bussed first. Kathy gave him a half-hearted slap on the elbow with the back of her hand. He didn't notice or, if he did, failed to acknowledge it.

Three days later, Ute took the day off and drive Kathy to the airport. Aaron would take a day off to meet her on her return.

Molly said her good-byes by phone. Kathy saw nothing of Gary.

It was early. Before her shift, Athena came up the hill to wish *bon voyage*. With her, was Gary, as contrite and shy as a child on the first day at school. After the obligatory chit-chat, it was time for good-byes. Athena stepped forward and wrapped her arms around Kathy, wished her a good flight, and a happy summer.

The moment Athena released her; Gary took over. He not only got his arms around her, he kissed her, unabashedly, on the lips. The female trio was stunned.

"I guess, that's a good-bye," Kathy announced, her face reddening.

"Don't forget to come back," Gary reminded, emphatically.

If there was ever a companionable silence, what followed was decidedly *not*. Kathy, flustered and embarrassed beyond words, was strangely excited. For weeks, she wished she had the presence of mind to kiss him back. Athena and Ute were half shocked, and half pleased.

"Well…" Ute began, unpoised.

"Yes, well…" Athena echoed, equally challenged.

It remained for Kathy to break the spell by getting into the passenger seat.

Most of the journey to the airport was lost as Kathy remained in a daze. It persisted through much of the flight and ceased only when sleep descended. She dreamed of Gary's kiss and the tricks she devised to encourage him to do it again.

* * *

Since departing with her Ami husband for the New World, Ute's first several letters home contained a common theme. She missed real German bread and butter. On her first return visit, Ute was met by her parents, fresh bread and a pot of butter. They found a secluded spot, sliced the bread, buttered it, and feasted merrily.

This became a family tradition.

Kathy hardly expected the custom to extend to her; she hadn't a drop of Kaufmann blood. However, she delighted in sharing the traditional reunion meal with her grandparents. The message was unmistakable.

It was wonderful to be back in Germany. The sights and sounds overwhelmed her. She felt at home; she felt she could live the rest of her life there and never want for more. Despite her delight, Kathy realized that, all-too-soon, she'd lust after an ocean breeze and saltwater spray.

On all previous visits, Kathy slept in Uncle Dieter's room. Ute, predictably, preferred the comfort of her own room. Keeping with tradition, Kathy's luggage was deposited in Dieter's chamber. Oma encouraged her to rest.

Kathy examined the well-maintained museum. There was a nautical chart of the Bodensee tacked to the sloping ceiling. Dieter had taken sailing lessons there. Though he never had a boat of his own, the chart remained.

She lay on the bed and tried to sleep. Instead, she sat blurry-eyed, groggy, and half dazed by Gary's kiss. Several minutes passed. Twice she dozed only to snap to attention when her head dropped.

Finally, Kathy studied the chart she knew well. She'd memorized many soundings and navigation aids. Kathy could pilot the *Mary R.* safely over and around the Bodensee with adroitness, should the opportunity ever come. Suddenly, however, sound sleep under that chart was impossible.

Quietly, she gathered her things and carried them across the landing to Ute's room. There, as ever, were displayed Ute's dolls, books, drawings, and several items she left behind before decamping with the man she loved. How she enjoyed sitting with Ute in this room and having her many questions answered about the objects on display. When Kathy was very young, Ute read to her from the books that shaped both their young years.

The old radio sat on the nightstand. She recalled the part it played in the happiest day of Ute Kaufmann's life. She promised herself to fiddle with it. Could she tune in the BBC?

Kathy quietly closed the door and sat on her mother's – Ute's – bed. She fell onto her back, kicked off her shoes, and swung her feet up. With her hands resting on her stomach, she was asleep in seconds.

* * *

Oma gently prodded her awake. The woman chuckled and confessed her momentary fright upon discovering Dieter's room vacant. If there were objections to Kathy's relocation, they remained unexpressed.

It was a sumptuous dinner. There were meat and potatoes, and rich, creamy gravy smothering all save the delectable red cabbage. There was sliced, German bread and butter. It was the best of Swabish food served by an accomplished Swabish cook.

After her gluttony, Kathy helped store the residuals before tackling the dishes. The Kaufmann's had a dishwasher, but Frau Kaufmann used it only once a week to sterilize. As a traditional Swabish housewife, Oma was ever mindful: slothfulness is a sin.

Uncomfortable from overeating, Kathy feigned nonchalance. Adjourning to the living room, she sat on the couch and loosed her jeans to relieve the suffering. Oma, as was her wont, watched the news. Opa, as was his wont, absorbed the financial pages of the paper. It was Oma's duty to alert her husband to any pressing news, but she seldom did.

Since the Luftwaffe no longer flew F-104s, the country wasn't littered with crash sites. Though political matters were furiously debated, the average person remained, largely, untouched. Swabish abodes serve independent people who find satisfaction and happiness with and through themselves.

Few words were exchanged. After the news, Oma switched to a regional channel featuring a comic stage play. The Bavarians actors spoke a thick dialect, but Kathy's ears were attuned. Obviously, the play wasn't written by a Bavarian; the humor was based upon stereotypes even Kathy recognized as inaccurate. Still, it generated laughter; even Opa set aside his paper and joined the mirth.

Suddenly, Opa exploded. Kathy, not comprehending, looked quizzically in his direction.

"They don't feed you in America, *Schatz*?"

He was pointing at the open snap of her jeans. Kathy colored.

"If I lived here," she reported, "I'd weigh a thousand kilo."

Opa laughed again.

"If we feed you Bavarian food, you'd disappear!"

Kathy and Oma smiled. Bavarian food might appeal to some, but only those unfortunates who'd yet to experience Swabish cooking. As the actors took their bows before a live audience, the atmosphere turned too serious for Kathy's taste.

"Tomorrow afternoon, Marion and the kinder will take you to lunch," Oma stated.

"I doubt I will be hungry by then," Kathy responded.

"No matter," her grandmother continued. "It is a getting-to-know you occasion. You need not eat anything if you don't wish."

Kathy's expansive stomach knotted. She knew there was no way to avoid the Bavarian side of the family.

* * *

Kathy came down for her favorite German meal of the day and Frau Kaufmann didn't disappoint. The table was as picturesque as a photo in *Good Housekeeping*. There was a basket of fresh brötchen, croissants and freshly sliced, dark, multi-grain bread – all accompanied by a pitcher of orange juice, fresh butter, an array of jams and a platter of thinly sliced meat and cheese. She presupposed that pork was not represented among the cold cuts, but that no longer hurt. Kathy was sufficiently tempted by Swiss cheese slices.

Additionally, brown eggs nested in a wicker basket near freshly brewed coffee. She sat at the place reserved. She transferred one of the eggs to her egg cup, rubbed her hands, and reached for the breadbasket.

"I'm glad you're hungry," Opa commented, watching her over his coffee.

"Oh, I'm not hungry," Kathy admitted. "But I always have appetite for *Frühstück*."

Opa laughed his deep, resonant, trademark laugh. So long as Opa laughed, all was well with the world.

After breakfast, Kathy went upstairs to fiddle with the radio. She managed to find the BBC, but she didn't wait to hear if they still played Lilly Bolero at the top of the hour. She was restless and worried about the pending outing. To calm herself, she walked slowly around the block and settled down in the living room to leaf through a few of Opa's books.

"Don't make it hard on them," Oma pleaded, joining her.

"For you, Oma, I promise."

The answer pleased Frau Kaufmann, but it left Kathy anxious. She hated pretend.

Marion Kaufmann drove a sparkling white BMW from which emerged Kathy's two pretend cousins. She'd seen them before, but they seldom exchanged words.

Michael was barely nine. It was he who bounded out of the car first. For him, any visit to Oma's was an occasion of great importance. He didn't ignore Kathy, exactly, but he couldn't wait to be swallowed by Oma's special hug.

Bernard was nearly twelve. He, too, was excited about a visit to Oma, but felt that showing excitement was beneath him. Marion, the "Bavarian Ice Princess," stepped out of the car like royalty. She was slim and attractive – perhaps, more so than Ute.

"*Wo ist Opa?*" Misha asked.

He hopped at Oma's feet as if propelled by a mighty spring.

"He's running errands, *Schatz*. He won't be long."

Bernard collected his hug with stoic silence; this didn't rest well with Kathy. Marion exchanged pleasantries with her mother-in-law, but quickly turned to Kathy with hand extended. The girl hesitated before accepting it.

"How was your trip?"

"Long," Kathy replied, "and tiring."

"I'm sure. You brought your appetite, of course."

Oma's chuckle communicated volumes.

"Care to come in for a minute?" Oma offered.

Mischa was hopping again. He wanted to eat first and visit later. As discretion is, etc., Marion relented. Kathy turned toward the shiny BMW.

"Let your cousin sit in front," Marion spoke firmly to her elder son.

Bernard looked at Kathy. She expected hostility but discovered none. Rather, Bernard appeared pleased. Kathy felt unexpectedly magnanimous.

"I prefer riding in back," she announced.

"It's your party," Marion replied.

Bernard flashed a friendly grin. Before she realized, she found his grin at the back door. She'd never had a door opened for her before.

"*Bitte*," Bernd beamed.

"*Danke*," she replied.

"I put it to the boys where to eat," Marion reported, backing out of the drive.

"We know you don't like Bavarian," Mischa announced, making her feel guilty.

"And I don't like Swabish," Bernard muttered.

"I thought Greek might be nice," Marion advanced, completing the circuit, "Let Kathy decide."

"Greek is fine. I like Greek."

"Who doesn't?" Mischa asked, appending a slurping sound.

The restaurant was not far. The Greeks were boisterous and accommodating. The Bavarian patrons were, predictably, reserved and spoke in low, guarded tones. Even the effusive Mischa turned down his volume. Still, with the Greek staff cracking wise, Kathy was mollified.

She hated eating in a tomb, which is probably what it would be at a Bavarian place where frosty napkins sprouted out of expensive crystal wine glasses and waiters dressed like undertakers. Much to Kathy's relief and surprise, the conversation flowed easily. There was not a single awkward pause. Mischa was exceedingly conversant. Bernard, precocious and cultured, came across as a likable fraud.

Marion presided over the table by supplying welcome bits of exposition to the boys' shorthand narrations. Though they did ask the odd question about life in America, it was more important to inform Kathy about Bavarian life. They spoke of school and sports and cultural events. Unexpectedly, it was a pleasant get-acquainted affair.

Later, everyone gathered in the Kaufmann living room presided over by the booming voice and commanding figure of Opa Kaufmann. Oma served up cake and coffee. Bernard wanted tea and Mischa chocolate milk. At last, the trio left, and Kathy trundled upstairs for a little nap. She felt satisfied but prayed her meeting with Onkle Dieter would prove as pleasant.

It wasn't.

She sat in the living room as Dieter and his father talked business. Though Opa retired from the wholesale firm his grandfather founded, he took an active interest. He made sure his former employees were well treated. Further, he wasn't above reproving his son if he suspected the employees were growing restless.

They spoke of orders, money and market trends – all very, very boring for Kathy. However, she knew the routine from visits past: business first then, and only then, social concerns. Left to her own devices, she'd be in the kitchen with Oma. The evening meal of the previous night was a welcome-home dinner. It was a special event.

The Kaufmann household returned to its normal routine – the big meal was at midday with the evening meal the traditional Abendsbrot. Still, Oma was creative in concocting cute little tomato sandwiches or egg and cheese or myriads of delightful snacks. Kathy enjoyed laboring at Oma's side – and learning useful skills. Finally, business ended and Opa made a lame excuse to exit the room. It was, now, Kathy and Darth Vader.

"Well," Dieter began pretentiously, "welcome to Germany, Kathy. I trust my sister is well."

Kathy assured him she was.

"I've made copies of items you may find interesting. I say *may* because you might not be interested with some things. I can't decide for you; I copied everything."

He snatched up his brief case and produced a document binder two-inches thick. It contained documents and notes Dieter made over the years, to include the addresses and phone numbers of both the officials with whom he dealt and the private interviews he conducted. There were notes of his interview with Aaron Foster and the two crewmates with him that day. There was a copy of Kathy's document, a government issued item used in lieu of an official birth certificate. There was a copy of the adoption papers.

"This map –" Kathy noted.

Dieter left his chair and came around behind her. There were three maps in the file.

"You were found there," he reported, "here's the farmhouse. The man died four years ago. His widow moved in with family in Bamberg."

"Where is this place?" she asked, drawing a finger over the page.

"On the border, about two hour's drive, perhaps."

She turned and looked at him.

"Can we go there?"

He never batted an eye.

"Saturday?"

She nodded.

He moved across the room like a man of action. He took up his brief case and headed for the front door.

"I shall come by about nine o'clock," he announced. "Meanwhile, look through the file. If you have questions, I'll attempt to answer them on our way."

"Danke," she said automatically.

He was nearly to the door when thoughts arrested him. He turned around.

"I imagined you'd want to do this, so I've made arrangements. Normally, I work Saturdays to noon."

"I don't want to take you away from work," she sputtered, suddenly defensive.

"As I said, I made arrangements. I wish I could be more help. There must be a thousand things you want to know. Be patient with me; everything I know is in your hands."

She looked down at the folder.

"You've been busy," she observed.

"I did it for Ute."

"You haven't spoken in years," Kathy reminded.

Dieter retraced his steps.

"I never quit, Kathy. Believe me. I never stopped asking questions; I never stopped looking for answers. Now, I work for you. I won't stop until you tell me."

She never heard her uncle speak so.

"I have no right to tell you what you have to do," she announced.

"You're the only one with the right," he corrected. "It is your life, Kathy. When Ute didn't let you make your own choices – Well, we have different ideas. When you think this has gone far enough, I can walk away."

She blinked before looking again at the map. Eventually, she found her voice.

"I'll let you know," she muttered.

"See you Saturday morning," he assured.

* * *

There were few majestic trees in the wooded area, so designated by the map. The majority were scrawny, pathetic examples of Central European fauna. Had the landowner the will, he'd have cleared the area ages ago and put it under the plow. Save for the birds, no animals were in evidence. A few deer left transient signs, but they, apparently, didn't linger in the anemic copse.

Kathy and Dieter stepped into a tiny clearing. A mat of leaves made crisp by dry weather lay undisturbed. The sun rippled through the sparse greenery which, come fall, would become the next layer of carpet. A few hardy plants grew through the leaves, but they were poor representatives.

There was one feature distinguishing this clearing from the others. Nailed to a tree was a small, wooden cross. Once upon a time, there was legible lettering across the horizontal portion, but years of weathering robbed it of all but a few samples of peeling paint.

Kathy surveyed the area. From where she stood, there was no sign of human habitation. She imagined what it looked like in the middle of winter, in the dark of night, and with three or four inches of snow on the ground. It was a bleak, dismal spot. It gave her a chill.

There was no call to speak. She knew the narrative. The cross marked the tree up against which Kathy's mother was found. Judging by her trail in the snow, it was the last of many times the exhausted, half-frozen woman fell. She crawled to the tree, propped herself against it, and died.

The farmer found her in the early hours of New Year's Day, 1974. Was she still alive? Was there some flickering sign of life the farmer failed to notice? He didn't examine. Instead, he hurried to his house and phoned the authorities.

The police discovered the woman wasn't alone. From under her flimsy coat, they extracted a child, nearly dead. Had an ambulance not accompanied the police, the child, too, would have died. As it was, the tiny girl left the scene for the hospital where she remained for five days in emergency care.

Kathy Foster found the place unacceptable. It was a horrible to visit and no fit place to die. The cross, placed by someone well-intended, made it a mockery. Dieter had the decency to remain silent.

"How far to the border?" she asked.

"Five, maybe, eight kilometers."

Kathy hadn't been idle. She examined every page of Uncle Dieter's file. She knew exactly what her mother wore, what was in her pockets, her height and weight – if it could be observed, documented, or quantified, Dieter recorded it. The weather and the temperatures for January 1, 1974 was, likewise, burned into her memory.

"She walked, this far in that cold with sorry shoes and a worthless coat?"

There was nothing for Dieter to contribute.

Kathy was torn between amazement and anger. She considered it a miracle that any living being had the stamina, and angry that a person with superhuman qualities was too ignorant to match clothing to weather. Laboratory tests confirmed the dead woman was Kathy's mother. If Kathy's estimates were correct, the difference between being adopted and being raised by her mother was one pair of winter boots and a decent coat.

"Can you take me to the border?"

She asked after regaining her emotions.

"I won't drive up to it," he replied. "We must walk."

"Why?"

"I don't want pictures taken of the car," he replied.

She thought for a moment.

"You're afraid of the Stasi?"

He nodded emphatically.

"I've talked to a lot of people. Some of them live in the DDR; the Stasi knows all about me. They know about *you*. What happens if they get my plate number? Maybe, nothing. Still, I'm not risking your safety or the safety of my family on a *maybe*."

Kathy nodded.

They drove along a vehicle track, parked near a grove of trees – far healthier than those where Kathy's mother died – and walked within a hundred yards of an imposing wire fence. There was a single guard tower some distance to the south and no observable human movement on either side of the barrier.

"How could she get through that?" Kathy asked.

"She probably came on the railroad," Dieter explained, "there are barriers, of course, but nothing like this. Trains can't get through unless the Ossis allow. A person might hide on a train."

"Not likely," she mused aloud.

"No – but a possibility. Most likely, she walked through or under the barriers. A person can get through where vehicles can't, but speed would be important – you can't be weighed down."

"Ah," Kathy nodded. "That explains flimsy clothes and shoes."

Dieter remained quiet. She turned to look at him. He returned her look and shook his head.

"No, Kathy. I won't take you to the crossing. For one thing, it's a prohibited zone. For another, there's no way to drive to it."

"Daddy did," she reminded.

"In a military vehicle," he countered. "I don't have one."

She nodded and sighed. She studied the border for a minute more. "I've seen enough."

She led the way back to the car.

"I'd like to see where Mom is buried," she reminded.

"It will take a while. Care for something to eat?"

"I'm not really hungry, but I am thirsty."

There was a story behind the funeral. When the incident became public, Ute Foster began making inquiries. Simultaneously, the pastor of a small country church bid for the body. He was elderly and caught on the wrong side of the border when it went up. Most of his family remained in the DDR.

Since he had links to the East, he petitioned to have the woman buried in his church cemetery. The members of the congregation approved. The woman received a proper burial. It was a pauper's grave, of course, but the locals paid for it.

Dieter mentioned the possibility that Kathy should announce her visit. Though the pastor was long dead, there were country folk who remembered the episode and would welcome the orphan. Kathy rejected this. She had no interest in telling and retelling the story of her life since that terrible New Year's Day. Moreover, it was absurd and distasteful that neither mother nor daughter had an identity.

Kathy stood over a clearly marked but anonymous grave. As she stood above the spot where her mother lay, Kathy was disturbed; she experienced not the slight emotional tremor. It was as if she were looking at a channel buoy on the Oregon coast. Other than marking a spot on the earth's surface, there was nothing special about it. For a moment, she thought Dieter would put a comforting arm around her shoulders. It was just as well that he did not.

DDR

June 1989

When Heike entered the Freie Deutsche Jungend, she trembled. She was eager to follow in the footsteps of Jürgen and Nadine, but her fear was palpable; she expected the worst. FDJ repudiation was a public humiliation. Refusing membership constituted an unpardonable sin replete with criminal implications.

Unlike many of her classmates, Heike wanted to wear the blue shirt. The socialist ideal was not limited to May Day and Party occasions. She spent hours in the library composing an eight-page composition of allegiance. Her desire to work toward the fulfillment of a century-long struggle ran deep.

The Phoenix of the Spree treatise was her testament. After the authorities murdered Rosa Luxemburg and Karl Liebknecht, they tossed their bodies into the river with impunity. Heike's stated goal was to resurrect martyrs' ideals. Moreover, her adamant belief was that the murderers and those who issued the orders must face justice. Most, if not all, the perpetrators escaped. Few remained alive. Heike Jacobs would make certain none escaped history.

Ironically, she secretly hoped she'd be barred. It would give her the opportunity to produce the flaming rhetoric of her handwritten manifesto. Coupled with an impassioned oral defense, the document was certain to draw public attention. Perhaps, Heike might prod the FDJ cadre and local officials to reexamine those goals and policies shunted aside in favor of "progress."

Nevertheless, Heike was frightened her crusade might be drowned in Nadine's bellicosity. Where Heike praised and honored socialist ideals, Nadine leveled recriminations and denunciations. Once aroused, the elder Jacobs daughter would be silenced by imprisonment or worse. Both girls could be mired in the judicial system and incarceration centers; Jürgen would be expelled from university; Rolf would be unemployable; and – worse – the daughter of a socialist icon would be sent to a dark, dank institution.

It was with relief more than pride that Heike donned the blue shirt for the first time. With the golden rays of the rising sun on her sleeve, she was renewed. Perhaps, The *Phoenix of the Spree* might not attract the attention she hoped, but FDJ membership symbolized her good standing. With hard work and a modicum of prudence, she'd save her family from disaster.

A highlight of the summer was the retreat to an FDJ camp. There'd be hiking, swimming, boating and sport. It promised a replication of *Heiße Sommer* replete with music, dancing, and (assuredly) flirting. Regrettably, there'd be no Ostsee. Nevertheless, comradeship was sure to abound.

Once upon a time, Jürgen and Nadine went to camp, leaving Heike with six days of housework. She completed chores normally shared amongst three. For this reason, she harbored reservations about approaching Rolf. Nadine, as ever undiplomatic, forced the issue over Abendsbrot. Rolf exploded. It was a quiet explosion because Mutti was near.

"Heike can go," he grunted, "you stay and look after your mother."

Too late did Nadine realize she'd crossed a boundary. She opened her mouth to initiate amends but was cut short by Rolf's expression. Nadine might be invited for "a walk." Unable to speak abruptly in Anne's presence, Rolf "escorted" miscreants outside.

There'd be little walking. There would, however, be a great deal of shouting. Should anyone object to admonishment, the back of Rolf's hand would terminate the discussion. Jürgen, Nadine, and Heike understood this. The words "going for a walk" were sufficient. Rolf seldom had to make good his threat.

Heike saw Rolf's expression and, thankfully, watched Nadine's reserve. She breathed a sigh of relief but vowed to have a word with Pabst when tempers cooled. The problem was, in a tiny house, privacy was theoretical.

The following day, Rolf returned from work cranky. He showered, changed, and settled down with the more innocuous portions of the newspaper. There was general conversation, but no opportunity for interviews. Not until Abendsbrot would Rolf wax eloquent. He dominated the conversation; it was left to Nadine and Heike to append appropriate remarks and signs of approval. Unexpectedly, however, Rolf deviated from the traditional format.

"I had a talk with Frau Götz this afternoon," he began.

The girls waited for Rolf to wash down bread with tea.

Rolf was used to people waiting for him.

"She has a daughter who earns summer money doing odd jobs. She assures me the daughter can come afternoons and tend to chores. You may both go to camp."

Heike, cheeks bulging with dried fish, looked anxiously at Nadine. She issued a warning with an under-the-table nudge. She needn't have worried. Nadine was too intelligent to gloat, too cautious to smile.

"Danke, Pabst," Nadine said quietly.

Heike wanted to kiss her for this restraint. Instead, she delayed her praise. They would have an opportunity to speak before the evening concluded.

"I really didn't want to go alone," Heike confessed. "I can relax, now."

"You dare be seen with me?"

"Nadine, please."

"I'm disreputable, you know," Nadine insisted, "I've been writing *Eingaben*."

"It's your right," Heike assured.

Law stipulated that any business receiving a citizen petition must respond. The petitioner seldom got desired results, but they, at least, obtained the satisfaction of knowing the complaint was attended.

"Well, there's a way to do it, correct? One must be diplomatic."

The words "Nadine" and "diplomatic" were contraries.

"Tell *me*. I'll write them."

"Danke, but, maybe, too late."

Nadine sighed and sat on the edge of Heike's bed.

"I'm informed that my tone was *inappropriate* and *worthy of admonishment*."

Heike set aside her book.

"You think they reported you?"

Nadine nodded.

"My Stasi file must be bursting."

Heike placed a comforting hand on Nadine's shoulder.

"Let me do the writing from now on."

"If someone releases my Eingaben, you'll insist you wrote it. I get myself into these messes, Heike. Don't cover for me."

"You're not leaving here alone, Nadine. No matter what you've done, I'm with you."

Nadine walked around her bed to the door. When the girls wanted privacy, one or both leaned against it.

"I might join the New Forum," she announced.

"Nadine, no! You haven't, have you?"

She shook her head.

"But I've made up my mind."

Heike thought – hard!

"Will you wait until we get back? Can we, at least, have three days together?"

Nadine shrugged.

* * *

Heike was assigned to a cabin with two girls from Apolda and one each from Jena, Bad Berka, and Stadtroda. For mysterious reasons, Nadine was assigned to a cabin with five girls from Gera. Suspicion reared; the billeting arrangements were ominous. To make the issue acute, the cabins were at opposite ends of the compound. Nadine could be spirited away in the dead of night, leaving Heike clueless.

The girls held a hasty conference while pretending to gather their luggage. Burdened with a sports bag and a modest rucksack, the "struggle" was contrived. They were certain to attract suspicious eyes.

"Why not put Weimar girls together?" Heike hissed.

"They're six of us and only the five from Gera," Nadine whispered back. "Maybe, that's just the way it worked out."

"Let's talk with Genossin Whoseits and ask to change."

"Let's not be babies," Nadine insisted. "The idea is to meet new people. They might have split us up because we share a name."

"I don't like it."

"If they come for me, they won't need to kidnap me," Nadine reminded. "We're in the woods and many places to hide. Why bother when they can come to the house?"

"I still don't like it."

"I promise to stay alert. Freundschaft."

"Freundschaft."

The NDJ by-word was traditional. In this instance, however, Heike felt it down to her toes. If anything happened to Nadine…

Getting settled was easy. As the last girl in her cabin, only one bunk remained. It was furthest from the door; Heike must navigate through a maze in the dark should nature summon. There was an unattractive stain on the wall above her bed. It looked sinister, and she tried to wipe it away with a strap of her rucksack. The stain remained unchanged and left no residuals on the strap.

The girls introduced themselves while preparing bunks with issued bedclothes. Save for schoolmates from Apolda, they were strangers. No one mentioned politics. Everyone focused on having a good time. One of the girls expressed hope of making the acquaintance of a boy she spied on her bus.

Heike searched for Nadine. Her assigned cabin was empty.

Nadine was at the lake, her pants rolled up and her bare feet in the water. They exchanged first impressions. Heike was not keen on sharing a common bathroom with so many.

"Get up early. You can shower and brush your teeth without waiting in line," she advised.

"Getting up early was not a part of my plan."

"Heike, you can sleep at home. Let's not waste time."

Had Nadine gone vacant? "Sleep at home?" With Rolf bellowing like a wounded bear?

They wandered around and joined a spirited volleyball game. There were eight members of both sexes on one side and nine on the other. The fervor with which the game was played made clear a mutual disregard for the net.

"What's the score?" someone asked, using the pause as an excuse to catch his breath.

"I don't know," someone responded, "Are we keeping score?"

"Mind if we have a go?" One of a pair of boys asked, taking advantage of the lull.

"The more the merrier."

Heike looked at Nadine. Sweat rolled down her face; her breathing came in short, noisy bursts.

"Take our spot," Heike offered as she led the way to neutral ground.

Nadine thanked her sister for dragging her away.

Lunch was brötchen and cold wursts. It was enough, but young appetites aren't easily placated. The big meal of the first day would be at seven to allow the late comers time to settle in. There would, of course, be a short ceremony and words of welcome before dismissal to the community mess.

The Jacobs girls washed their hands and faces and changed into blue shirts. Nadine joined other veterans in arranging the neophytes into a proper assembly. When the two leaders appeared, the sixty-something campers formed a horseshoe around twin flag poles.

Genosse Sellmer stepped forward to introduce himself. He was a solid looking man in his thirties. It was obvious he'd been an athlete; however, eating had overtaken exercise. He introduced Genossin Engle, a tall, sleek blond who, despite thick wire-rimmed glasses, was used to exercising authority. She had a toothy smile and a perky delivery. Still, as she spoke, her tone suggested she'd not tolerate transgressions.

"Remember who you are, what you are, and where you are."

She stepped aside and allowed two of the senior members to raise the NDJ flag alongside that of the DDR. They sang an anthem, prior to Genossin Engle dismissing the formation.

Each cabin was assigned a table, crudely hewn out of timber, and joined with great iron pins. A long bench flanked each side. They, too, were made of wood but were professionally crafted. Doubtless, the furnishings were made by FDJ volunteers whose enthusiasm was white hot though their woodworking talents varied.

One member of each table was tasked with reporting to kitchen to fetch the food, another fetched the wooden bowls and eating utensils, and a third brought a pitcher of tea and a pitcher of imitation fruit drink. The plastic beakers for drinking were clustered in the center of each table. After the meal, it was the job of the remaining three mess mates to clear the dishes, help with washing up and wiping down the table, and seeing the clean beakers returned to the table and all other items stowed for the night.

These chores were assigned on a rotating basis.

The residents got a ladle of thick soup with potatoes and chunks of meat and bits of mushroom. This was served with a large loaf of dark bread that the mess mates carved up individually. The remaining soup was divided amongst the tables in ancient tureens. Heike found a single bowl enough. The boys at the next table, however, were polite in relieving the clean-up girl the need to dispose of the surplus.

"We don't want to waste food, do we?" the smiling delegate from the next table remarked, escorting the tureen to his brethren.

Heike wasn't certain how to respond. Two of her cabin mates did.

"Freundschaft," they said in unison.

For afters, they had a small serving of rice pudding. After the pudding and before the tidying up, there was a rousing sing-along. The newer people relied on mimeographed sheets with the lyrics printed, almost, legibly. For Heike, however, the songs were familiar. She didn't need to squint at hieroglyphs.

After singing, Genossin Engle made announcements. Genosse Sellmer was content to nod his head in approval at her every comment while taking long drags on a cigarette. Sellmer, Heike learned later, was an auto mechanic from Erfurt. Genossin Engle was a teacher at a Berlin trade school. She so enjoyed her time in the FDJ that she joined the cadre as an avocation.

As a supervisor, she continued to wear the blue shirt she loved.

"Finally, Genossinn," Frau Engle said with her glittering smile, "we need volunteers to remove the tables and make space. Tonight, we dance. We have Herr Feder, a D.J. from Eisenach arriving soon."

"Is he the one who plays Wessi music?" one Apolda girl asked of the other.

"I think so."

This reply caused the questioner to pump her fist in delight.

"We hope to see you all here at eight o'clock. Those not tidying up are dismissed. Freundschaft."

"Freundschaft," sixty voices echoed.

* * *

Nadine remained stoic as young man after young man danced with Heike. She remained glued a bench shunted against the wall to make space. Whenever Heike returned to her, she got an apology.

"A thought occurs," Nadine advanced, "if you sit somewhere else, I might be asked."

"Nadine, please. Let's not fight."

Nadine shrugged.

"I'm not fighting, Heike. I see a mirror every day."

It was always there. Normally, Nadine was confident. There were, however, times when she wallowed in the realization that she was not the pretty one. Heike didn't consider her homely. Still, after Heike's third dance invitation, Nadine turned sauer. Even beautiful women looked horrid when sauer.

There was no placating Nadine, so Heike sat silently by and waited. A boy came across the floor, intending to ask for a second dance. Heike shook her head and aimed a furtive finger at Nadine. Perhaps, the boy interpreted this as a plea to ask Nadine, perhaps, not. He sought someone else.

Heike wouldn't abandon a distraught Genossin.

"Frau Engle is having a great time," Nadine muttered.

Indeed, she was. She and the ubiquitous Herr Sellmer were the only ones wearing blue shirts. Perhaps, this was intended as a display of authority. Standing behind the refreshment counter and catering to the thirsty, Sellmer's warning scowls validated his authority sufficiently, but Engle danced with abandon. She started out with one of the older boys and, from there, grabbed the first person nearest whenever the music started. She was laughing and bouncing and having a great time.

"Let's get out of here," Heike suggested.

"No. Enjoy yourself," Nadine insisted.

Heike could not. Her brooding sister stole any enjoyment. Just as important, however, she was cool towards Wessi music. It was too abstract and too discordant for her taste. Heike considered herself "Old Fashioned."

She'd dance to Frank Schöbel or Chris Doerk, but their music was considered passé. The DJ opened the evening with the Ossie group Bell, Book and Candle. This gave Heike a glimmer of hope. Since then, however, it was all Wessi.

Frau Engle grabbed a girl whose dancing was similarly animated. Together, they began a circuit of the room as if imitating an Indian rain dance gone terribly wrong. This performance was applauded and encouraged. Several people joined in.

"I'm Ossi," Heike announced, "I don't like this music. Let's walk."

This brought Nadine to her feet. They ambled toward the lake. It was twilight and the lake nearly deserted. A couple paddled slowly around in a canoe. The girls opted to try their luck.

It took mere minutes to make two laps around the tiny pool. Obviously, it was constructed with swimming in mind, but someone placed four canoes around the circumference. It would be comical to fit all the boats into the lake at once, but two boats making leisurely circles were beyond hazard.

As ennui set in, the girls decided to give the dance another go. From a distance, the music selection hadn't improved, but in front of the common dining hall tables were occupied by people enjoying a group chat. The sisters discovered people sitting Indian style on the top of two joined tables. They were convivial and related tales from their respective cities and towns. Heike and Nadine stood quietly on the periphery before attracting notice.

"Hey, you!" the dominant male hailed. "Pull up a table and sit down."

Appreciative that Nadine was not regarded as too repulsive to join, the duo half carried, and half worried, a third table against the others. As they mounted, adjustments were made to widen the circle. There, the two Weimarians spent the balance of the evening enjoying conversation and camaraderie.

The participants drifted in and out, save for the Jacobs sisters. As one or two ambled away in search of a soft drink or a spin around the dance floor, others filled the void. They exchanged jokes, sang songs to rival the DJ, and exchanged news of their varied lives. Politics, except for historical references, was eschewed.

As darkness descended, people melted away and returned to their cabins. Heike and Nadine exchanged farewells with mutual nervousness.

"I'll be okay," Nadine assured upon parting. This was one of her few English phrases.

Heike nodded, more in the hope than as a sign of reassurance. Back in her cabin, even after lights out, there was a lively exchange lasting an hour or more. Gradually, the conversation became more and more subdued as girls drifted off.

In the morning, there were no blue shirts save for the supervisors. They were called to formation at the appointed time in observance of the flag raising. Then, the youths filed into the resurrected dining hall and enjoyed a breakfast of brötchen, boiled eggs, and cheese. There was hot tea and mock coffee followed by three songs to open the eyes.

Before dismissal, Genossin Engle gave the morning announcements. There would be organized games and activities at specified times. Events were posted on the bulletin boards. She announced the time of *Mittagessen*, the major meal of the day, and cautioned everyone to leave time enough to clean up and, if appropriate, change before assembling. Punctuality, she reminded, is an important quality.

"Genossinnen Jacobs. Would you be so kind as to come to my cabin after dismissal?"

Heike was in shock. Was this it? Had the Stasi arrived?

Everyone exited the building after clean-up. Heike couldn't find her legs.

Eventually, Nadine came.

"No use putting it off," she whispered, "maybe, it's nothing."

"Being summoned?" Heike returned. "Nothing?"

"Well," Nadine mused, "it's worse if we delay. Punctuality is important."

This was the moment for which Heike steeled herself. She knew exactly what to do. She walked with Nadine to the door.

"Don't look like a whipped puppy," Heike said. "Keep your head up. We're Genossinnen."

They locked arms. They took deep breaths and experienced the courage of solidarity. They marched, in perfect step, as proudly as if they were on their way to accept the Order of Lenin. Nadine's right arm remained free, ergo, she'd pound Genossin Engle's door.

"Be bold," Heike muttered.

Nadine said nothing, but the pressure on Heike's arm was reassuring. They marched past the twin flag poles and hurried to that place which was both the camp's headquarters and Frau Engle's cottage.

"No autos," Nadine noted.

Only the supervisors battered relics were parked beside the cabin. The Stasi would hardly come afoot. Moreover, the door was wide open; knocking was unnecessary. They marched right through the door, with Nadine leading the way, and stood at the "commandant's" desk.

Frau Engle's back was turned; she was alone. There was no sign of Genosse Sellmer or Stasi. They watched Frau Engle tidying a small bookshelf behind her desk. To the left, just under a window, was her bed made up with military exactness. A guitar hung by a strap from the far wall on a stout wooden peg. Save for the desk and three wooden chairs, there were no additional adornments.

The girls examined the Spartan quarters before riveting their attention to the back of Engle's blue shirt. When the woman turned, she was momentarily surprised to see the girls standing so stiff, erect and with arms linked. She smiled broadly as if expecting them to break into a burlesque.

"Good morning," she greeted, apparently willing to ignore eccentricity.

"Nadine, you've been here before, correct?"

"This is my third time."

Thankfully, Nadine didn't bark as if addressing a drill sergeant. She had the presence of mind to realize the tactical situation had altered.

"You have an older brother, correct? I do well enough with names, but I'm not good at details. Jürgen, true?"

"Ja; he's at university."

The girls stood stiff and formal. Frau Engle's expression altered.

"Genossinnen, I didn't call you in for disciplinary action, but your deportment suggests you have something to confess."

"Nein," Heike replied. "we assumed there's a proper way to report."

A placated smile returned.

"Relax. A youth officer approached me this morning. He was with you last night and learned you're related to Werner Ecke. Is that correct?"

"That is correct."

Heike let Nadine respond.

"Granddaughters?"

Nadine assured her such was the case. Heike appreciated the plural. She was thankful Frau Engle made no remarks about the girls' obvious dissimilarities. Instead, the woman opened a desk drawer and produced a ragged pamphlet. It had no measurable thickness but was well-traveled. The cover, originally bright red with bold black lettering in the old script, was now a dull, unattractive pink.

"I was presented this years ago," Frau Engle explained. "I think it's the only pamphlet your grandfather published, but it's a masterpiece. This prompted me to dedicate my life to the socialist cause. I'll never part with it, but I no longer read it. I memorized it years ago."

The girls exchanged a curious look. In their lives, they never learned of Werner Ecke's printed works. They knew of his courage and greatness, but neither Anne nor any of the late leader's admirers ever mentioned a pamphlet.

"I wasn't interested in politics before reading this. Everyone goes on about duty and sacrifice, quoting Marx or Lenin. Very uninspiring. You, probably, noticed I love dancing – despite my lack of grace. Your grandfather explained socialism is not words and marches and flags and rallies. He taught me that socialism is spiritual. It's camaraderie, a part of your personality. I don't explain well. Your grandfather gave me freedom. I dance, have fun and still contribute as well as any frowning autocrat."

She gave up with an exasperated facial gesture and a toss of the head. Rather than blather on, she came from behind her desk and offered her hand to Nadine who accepted without hesitation.

"It is an honor to shake hands with links to a truly great man."

After she enthusiastically pumped Nadine's hand, she repeated the ritual with Heike. More words were exchanged. Frau Engle intended to announce the presence of the camp celebrities, but the girls declined.

"We prefer to be recognized for our accomplishments," Nadine explained. "We are proud of Opa, but his work was his own."

"Well, said," the woman beamed reassuringly. "Very well said!"

They exited in a different posture. They were relieved, of course, but strangely deflated. Nadine wandered pointlessly; Heike followed at a discrete distance. Eventually, she leaned up against a young tree. As Heike approached, she discovered tears on her sister's cheeks.

"I'm already in prison," she said softly. "I'm so terrified, I can't live my life. Last night, I jumped at every noise. I don't know where to get strength, Heike. I know what I must do, but I am so frightened that – that, sometimes, I wish they'd kill me."

Heike could have – probably, should have – put a reassuring hand Nadine's shoulder. It took restraint to keep it at her side. She refused to be shallow and offer empty reassurances.

"We must get a copy of that pamphlet," Heike muttered.

Nadine did not hear. She was consumed with fear.

"I don't want to go to prison," she moaned. "I'm not strong enough. I hope they kill me."

* * *

True to her word, Frau Engle declined to announce the celebrity status of the Weimarians. However, Nadine had identified herself or, more correctly, the identity of her grandfather before witnesses; word spread. As morning lapsed into afternoon, all tablemates and cohabitants were privy to the "secret."

Soon, Nadine was being escorted by a pair of young men. In the DDR, elite status depended upon party membership. Above this, however, was ancestry. Anyone with a resistance leader or a martyred socialist in the family got special attention. Heike was the object much male attention, but, only as the "pretty one". Nadine, however, was guaranteed an escort of loyal subjects.

The moment Kathy Foster viewed the East German border, Heike was barely forty miles to the north. A trepidatious girl and her uncle approached a guarded barrier. Concurrently, Heike and Nadine, in the company of others, relaxed in the shade of two small trees near the lake.

The assembly chatted briefly about *Heiße Sommer*. Since Heike was likely to see no one other than her sister ever again, she defended the film against those who found it trite. Nadine followed the discussion in silence. Suddenly, the discussion turned serious.

"I joined the New Forum," one boy announced.

"How can you wear a blue shirt?" another challenged.

The first boy took no umbrage; he explained he found no shame in belonging to both the FDJ and the New Forum. The Soviet tanks and divisions of 1953 brought the government of the DDR under the direct control of Moscow. After Stalin's death, the DDR remained under the Soviet thumb. They maintained brutal Stalinist notions of who did what, who traveled where and when, but – most objectionable – was a total lack of concern for productivity.

"We live in a police state," he announced carelessly. "We can't talk without fear; we can't write without fear; we can't be seen together without fear; we can't report crimes without fear. Because everyone is afraid, everyone is passive and slothful. What does it matter if one makes one nail an hour or a hundred? You get the same reward.

"Productivity doesn't get you a better apartment or a promotion. There's no reason to produce. That's why we see empty shelves in the shops, and we wait years for a car or an apartment. Nobody likes it, but everybody keeps quiet. The New Forum wants discussion. When people talk, ideas are exchanged. If enough people rally behind the good ideas and the government responds, productivity increases. People are happier."

Heike eyed Nadine, expecting her to jump in. She did not. Once the boy concluded his prepared speech, three others refuted it. Each time, the perpetrator offered counter-refutations laced with anecdotal evidence. Still, Nadine reserved comment. From the expression on her face, she was bored.

Not until they were on the bus home did Heike dare make mention. First, she confirmed the seats behind them were vacant. She leaned closer to Nadine's ear and spoke in a whisper.

"I expected you to say something to the New Forum boy."

She couched her question in the form of a statement. If Nadine chose not to respond, Heike wouldn't press. Both girls prepared for eventual interrogation. If they lied, they'd be tricked into exposing themselves. If they clung to the truth, they'd be less vulnerable. The fewer secrets they had, the better for everyone.

"Stasi trick," Nadine whispered back. "They draw you out, then, denounce you."

Heike shuddered. She'd no idea how Nadine learned Stasi techniques; she was too shrewd to inquire.

"You think he was Stasi?"

"No matter," Nadine replied. "I'm a prisoner of cowardice. I don't know any of those people, but they all know me."

Three days later, as was her wont, Heike spent the free part of her day in the city library. She didn't know Nadine was engaged in research there. As Heike made notes from Marx and Adam Smith on the relationship between labor and the value of goods, Nadine approached. She said not a word, but quietly left two books at Heike's right elbow and disappeared.

Heike examined the books and found pages marked with scraps of paper. She turned to the designated page in the first volume and a portion of the United States Constitution. It was heavily annotated and footnoted with gross historical violations of the document's provisions. Realizing Nadine's recent interests, she ignored the notes and examined the text. It taxed her English, but she waded patently through ten amendments. She didn't understand much, but she understood some things.

Next, she opened the second volume to find an excerpt from an article edited by Werner Ecke. She took her time reading. It was in the crabbed, old-style German which was a chore to read.

The article relates,

"On this subject, one hears the echo of Rosa Luxemburg. The future of socialism must be built on freedom. Without freedom, the workers become ignorant slaves to anyone exercising power, be it the factory manager, a local ministry, or the government itself. The surest way to achieve socialist success is, also, the most difficult and time-consuming. It must work both with and through the democratic principles of freedom, i.e.: the freedom to speak without fear of retribution; the freedom to print the facts however unpleasant they are; the freedom to assemble and discuss without fear of reprisal. If the worker is not free to find socialism for himself and in his own way, he lacks investment. Without personal investment, socialism is valueless. If socialism is forced upon him, a man must either rebel or submit. If he rebels, he harms himself and those around him, all the while diverting valuable resources and time away from those compelled to deal with his misconduct. If he submits, he becomes a slave and resentment festers until he attempts, perhaps in league with others equally distraught, to gain freedom."

Was Nadine attempting to convert her to the New Forum? Was she merely showing her that either Rosa or Werner (perhaps, both) was aware of an eighteenth-century American document?

Perhaps, Nadine intended Heike to reach her own conclusion.

Fürth

June 1989

Kathy's vacation slid into a comfortable routine. In the mornings, Oma tutored her in preparing Swabish delights. By the end of the first week, she prepared Mittagessen under Frau Kaufmann's careful supervision. She browned meat, sliced vegetables, and created the trademark thick, creamy gravies with unexpected skill.

She made tasty bread. She loved kneading and beating the dough, and feeling flour on her fingertips and the addictive scent of the loaf as it swelled in a bowl under a damp cloth and, better still, the aroma as it matured in the oven. Opa was the supreme culinary arbiter, blunt and honest. She approached the table with apprehension, delivering her first meal.

Opa smacked his lips and tucked a white linen napkin under his chin. He took up the serving platters and bowls in turn and took generous portions. Next, he cut a slice of bread, and swathed it with a layer of (unfortunately) store-bought butter. Finally, he reached for the gravy dish and drown much of his food with the textured sauce. Kathy feared a plague of lumps and held her breath.

Oma and Kathy, nervously, filled their plates. Finally, Opa took up knife and fork. Kathy sat with hands in her lap, too nervous to eat, too flustered to remember how impolite it is to hide one's hands during meals.

She waited until she feared for her sanity. Even Oma ate but dared not speak until the patriarch's verdict was announced. Both women hoped for charity. Neither expected anything superlative. His every vocal edict was Old Testament thunder. Kathy knew his ways and thought herself prepared, but Opa's voice created havoc with her spine.

"This is good!" he roared. "You're a good Swabish cook."

Kathy nearly burst into tears. She chalked it up to beginner's luck. Still, her heart swelled. It took time to collect herself.

"Am I Swabish now?"

She regretted it instantly, but her stupid question lay on the table like a hideous stain.

"*Absolute!*" Opa roared.

Though she enjoyed her morning lessons in Swabish cookery, her nervousness about Opa's approval stressed her. If the mornings were bitter-sweet, her afternoons were blissful. Everyone, save Kathy, was so correct. Once she got to know the Bavarian side of her family, she found it irresistible.

The boys, so easily excited, were a joy. Kathy was American and, in their eyes, could do no wrong. She lived in a place they knew only through television and books. She'd sailed on the Pacific and talked with real Indians. They couldn't get enough of her adventures.

Mischa asked a simple question about breakfast and was amazed that the Ami considered the topic so pedestrian. Kathy was bold enough to sing a jingle. The boys stared at her with wide-eyed adoration. They spent several minutes gushing over her voice, how she must make records and become famous and buy a huge house with swimming pool in Beverly Hills and invite her German cousins to come spend summers with her.

Kathy dismissed this as youthful exuberance. Nevertheless, the boys pestered her into singing for Tante Marion. Kathy was flustered and inhibited; she wanted to escape. Unfortunately, the more she resisted, the greater the issue became. She relented and sang a verse of a Swabish folk song.

At the conclusion, Marion joined in praising her talent. Kathy considered it patronizing. Once she knew the family better, she understood that Dieter's family did not engage in false praise.

The trio passed a soccer ball about in the park, they biked about the city and explored the zoo together. Always, however, the boys pestered her to sing. Kathy did her best to please but lacked enthusiasm. One afternoon, however, giddy from a *spaghetti-eis* sugar rush, she launched into a Swabish folk song. Her version, however, was amended.

It was Opa's version, bellowed years before after consuming copious alcohol. The lyrics, not exactly, lewd, were suggestive. It was great fun when they reprised it as a trio.

Oma answered the phone. She hung up and entered the kitchen where Kathy leisurely nursed a cup of coffee.

"Your uncle's coming this evening," she said portentously. "He sounds *sauer.*"

Kathy realized instantly. The boys shared the song with Marion who sentenced them to isolation and called Dieter at work. Kathy pushed the porcelain cup, its contents, and its matching saucer away from her. Felicity gave way to dread. After a tenuous start, she'd created a bridge between herself and her pretend cousins.

Now, she faced the austerity of her pretend uncle. She mourned. At the least, she expected banishment from the boys' company. This prospect was insufferable. She didn't sob or blubber, but the tears came.

Oma called for reinforcements. Opa was outside wrestling with the shutters. None were, technically, broken, but he performed periodic maintenance to keep occupied. He sacrificed his habit of haunting his former business, chumming around with former employees, and looking over Dieter's shoulder. He'd became a disruption; his son was forced to order him off the premises. Opa was forced to invent household chores to keep himself occupied.

In her self-effacing style, Oma provided a brief narrative of events and showed her husband the result. Opa took in the scene and roared.

"No sulking, Schatz!"

She wiped her eyes with the back of her hand and sat up. She could not, however, look at him. Opa sat at table across from her. Though his voice was never tender, he radiated support.

"So, why should a phone create a scene?" he demanded.

She kept her eyes averted and told her side of the story. Opa demanded to know what they sang. She relied on historical references rather than actual lyrics. Opa understood. He exploded in laughter and pounded the table in his mirth.

"Classic! I can imagine Marion's eyes. I bet they popped!"

With that, he collapsed in a fit of laughter. Even Oma couldn't resist joining in.

"That's terrible!" Oma said, but her laughter belied her words.

"I feel such an idiot!" Kathy confessed, thrusting her chin into her waiting hands.

"Schatz, this is not important," Oma soothed.

"Of course not!" Opa added, choking with laughter.

"I got Bernd and Mischa in trouble," she protested.

"Egg jelly!" he growled. "They got themselves in trouble. I bet those little devils conspired to show some backbone – and enjoying every delicious second. They've been sheltered too long. They need some naughtiness."

"Now, now," Oma cautioned.

"Oh, piffle!" he snorted. "I don't want them slashing tires or robbing banks but singing Swabish porn doesn't rate."

Kathy heard but didn't listen.

"Uncle Dieter is sauer."

"You sound like a baby," Oma warned.

"Dieter will swear at you. Everyone will feel better, and it is forgotten."

"Dieter will not swear at her," Oma protested.

"Well, he should," Opa suggested. "He must stand up for his family. If he goes too far, I'll throw him out. Ha! That will flavor his sauce!"

"Nobody's going to throw anybody out," Oma announced forcefully. "We're family."

Opa let his exuberance get the better of him. He couldn't relent, but it was clear his threat would never be carried out.

"Kathy," he promised, "by tomorrow, this will be forgotten."

She took comfort in this but couldn't shed her guilt.

* * *

Kathy spent much of the afternoon in the shrine. She examined the remnants of Ute's childhood. Her radio, the books, which ranged from juvenile to young-adult fiction, two dolls propped up on either side of the radio and a few decorative figures, a small plastic puppy, Asterex, and other fictional figures Kathy didn't recognize – things that were part of the life of the girl who lived here.

The book collection heavily favored Enid Blyton and Erich Kästner. As Kathy reclined on the bed, she reached out and grabbed a title she recognized, *Das Doppelte Lottchen*. She paged through, examining the illustrations. Over the course of several nights, Kathy sat beside Ute on the same bed while the woman read it aloud.

Years later, Kathy saw the Disney version. Later still, she watched the German film narrated by Kästner himself. Instead of the vast expanse of America separating twins, it was the mountains twixt Munich and Vienna. Kathy nearly dozed during the German film. It pre-dated the Disney version and was black and white. It was more serious than funny. It was, however, set in familiar landscapes. Additionally, instead of one girl playing both parts, the Germans found twins to play the leads.

Kathy preferred the German version.

She particularly enjoyed the imbiss behind a farmhouse where the girls plotted. She thrilled at delightful scenery as mother and daughter hiked through the Bavarian Alps. She slammed the book shut and returned it. She didn't want to think of siblings split apart. Moreover, the Kästner book had a happy ending. Kathy doubted her life would prove so serendipitous.

During Abendsbrot, she tried to appear appreciative of Opa's banter while dreading the forthcoming visit. Despite the knot in her stomach, she packed away two tomato slices and a thick slice of camembert. Rather than bother Oma with starting a fresh pot, she eschewed coffee and joined them in hot tea. After, Opa went to his evening paper, Kathy joined Oma in cleaning up. It didn't take long, and she padded upstairs to think.

That huge wire obstruction, the jagged knife-wound that people on both sides refused to treat, created a "zero at the bone." She experienced seizing neck muscles. As she examined the border barrier, she imagined herself crossing over. The temperature over there dropped twenty degrees;

she couldn't breathe. There was no air, only that huge, country-splitting gash.

Out of that wound seeped the life's blood of a country. Bit by bit, the blood flowed for want of treatment – but the wound never healed, and the bleeding never ceased. On a blustery New Year's Eve, a desperate mother and her tiny baby gurgled up out of the wound. A slight prick few noticed.

Kathy Foster knew from Dieter's meticulous research how old the mother was. They knew, through careful calculation, the baby's birth date to a narrower range – November 22, give or take a few days. November 17 to December 27. Forty-five days, by her calculation, was Kathy's age when her mother carried her into a copse and died.

There were few things in Kathy's life which spanned forty-five pathetic days. Her stint as a freshman cheerleader dragged on and on and on and on across a bleak, wind-blown, dry, forbidding expanse of desert taking her through basketball season. Chronologically, it was hardly more than a hundred days, but it left her emotionally and physically drained. Gary's sojourn with the football team was less than half her sentence, and he didn't recover elasticity until Christmas break.

Kathy had yet to give birth, but it must be a draining experience. Yet, within a month and a half, a desperate mother made an impossible trek through a frozen waste in inadequate clothing across a closely guarded border. After seeing the ground, Kathy doubted her ability to walk the same distance in the summer air – never mind dodging mines, evading dogs, and sneaking past armed soldiers. Yet, her mother did exactly that. Even more remarkable, she managed it while carrying a baby!

If Kathy lived in the DDR, how long would it take her to become that desperate?

Dieter didn't ring the bell. Opa greeted him with a booming voice and bid him sit. Somewhere, Kathy heard Oma's far more melodious voice, but the words were too soft to understand. Opa asked about the business while Kathy wondered how long it would be before the inquisition.

Apparently, an employee was getting married. Oma spoke unintelligibly, but she'd insist on giving a gift. Dieter's narration of the romance rambled on. Occasionally, Opa exploded with a question, comment, or a roar of laughter. When all life was squeezed from the wedding story, Opa began a methodical examination. He inquired after other employees by name.

It was too much!

Something about Kathy's footfalls stopped the conversation. Everyone knew Dieter was there to have sharp words with his "niece." However, even a miscreant knew Kaufmann protocol: business concerns before personal matters. For Kathy to make a premature entrance was a major faux pas. No one knew how to react.

Oma looked up from her perch on the couch with a worried expression. Dieter, who faced the stairs, frowned. He tacitly reminded her that it wasn't her turn. Even Opa, who seldom reflected surprise, shifted in his chair to see if Kathy was ill.

Halfway down the stairs, she stopped. She was stunned by the silence and intimidated by the undivided attention. The boiling caldron within steamed.

"There was no identification on the body," she announced.

Dieter caught the thread. He noticed she was *not* asking.

"You know that."

She'd read the file.

"If an Ossi sets foot in the *Bundesrepublik*, he's a citizen, right?"

"Automatically."

"So, Ossis crossing the border would need official papers, right?"

Dieter replaced severity with brow-knitting concern.

"Ja."

It was a single syllable, but Dieter dragged it out.

"So, my mother and me – we weren't alone."

Oma and Opa exchanged concerned glances. Dieter remained unflappable.

"I was wondering when you'd figure that out," he sighed.

She held his stare. After several seconds, with perfect calm, she turned and walked back up the stairs. The Kaufmann family exchanged concerned looks. They hadn't expected a lack of emotion. They were concerned enough that Oma moved to check on the girl.

Even Dieter moved to accompany her. This, they mutually agreed, was not the time to leave Kathy Foster alone. Just as they reached the base of the stairs, a single word tumbled down. It was filled with anger, regret, and frustration.

"*Scheiße!*"

Even Opa, the reigning master of Swabish boisterousness, sat up upon receipt of Kathy's public announcement. The trio remained fixed where they were. They were shocked, but hardly surprised. Nevertheless, they heaved a collective sigh.

"She'll be all right, now," Oma murmured.

Dieter nodded.

"This isn't the time," he concluded, patting his mother affectionately on the shoulder. "I'll speak with her later."

Weimar

June 1989

The girls were giddy and radiated an energy that made Anne restless. There was, however, a certain felicity in her expression. Rolf Jacobs felt it as well. Did it come through his wife or daughters who, uncharacteristically, were sweetness and light? Had Heike paused to examine the cause of familial felicity, she may have deduced Rolf's mellow demeanor sprang from a secret reservoir.

The Jacobs Family had no telephone. The message arrived via relay. It arrived that morning through a friend of Nadine. Both friend and the message were entrusted to a greengrocer who, in turn, scribbled a note for his daughter, another of Nadine's friends. Upon receipt, the daughter raced to the Jacobs home.

"Jürgen arrives tomorrow afternoon."

This initiated a flurry of activity. Though the house was dusted, swept, scrubbed, and cleaned daily, the girls became especially meticulous. Heike cleaned the stairs earlier but dropped to her knees and swabbed them anew. The stairs would get an additional scrub, maybe two, the following day – as a part of the celebration. Duty assigned afternoon and evening chores to Nadine. Heike, loathing idleness, worked alongside her.

When Rolf arrived, he was informed before entering. His expression didn't change. He did, however, climb the freshly rewashed stairs and pulled himself into the stifling heat of the attic. Minutes later, Heike's pallet lay under the window as in days of old.

Abendsbrot was lively. Normally, save for Rolf's terse orders, there were few exchanges. That evening, ceaseless babble abounded.

"I'll wait at the Bahnhof," Nadine announced.

Heike made a face. It was her turn for afternoon chores, and she resented being left behind.

"Your brother might not take the train," Rolf cautioned, "he might hitch a ride with a friend or smuggle himself in with a convoy of reservists."

Nadine nodded knowingly. Jürgen was unpredictable. She'd not risk being stranded in the Bahnhof should Jürgen slip by.

The morning began earlier than normal. Heike stripped the bed, put on clean sheets and a fresh cover for the down comforter. She made up her pallet and fetched a blanket should evening temperatures drop. She hurried downstairs, drew water for the large pots on the hotplate and fetched the wash tub from its place in the shelter behind the house. Nadine readied soapy water for the stairs, she'd employ Heike's scrub-brush rather than her preferred washcloth.

Rolf and Anne came down together. Normally, he'd scold the girls for not having breakfast ready. On this day, he made no mention. Heike sliced bread and piled it in a basket. Rolf took a bit of wurst, some cheese, and a sampling of honey. Moments later, Heike arrived with cups and saucers, knives, spoons on a tray and a pot of tea.

Anne smiled approvingly.

"The water might be a moment, Pabst," she informed.

Normally, he shaved before Frühstück. That morning, he could wait. Heike hadn't thought things through. She should have put shaving water on first. Rolf, however, was understanding.

Upon Rolf's departure, Heike worked on laundry; Nadine took care of sweeping, dusting, and floor scouring. After Heike got the bedclothes on the line, she helped Anne to some bread and tea. Then, she waited with mounting nervousness for Anne to finish so she could clean both the dishes and the kitchen. Nadine was struggling in the bathroom. Heike wanted to lend a hand, but the space was too confined.

Heike waited for the shops to open whereupon she fidgeted while standing in line. She started lintel soup earlier than normal should Jürgen arrive early. Extra vegetables and wurst were diced and chopped.

Restless, Heike patrolled the streets. Upon returning, Nadine took over sentry duty.

Time lumbered past.

Few words passed during Mittagessen. Rolf pronounced the soup good, but Heike paid no heed. Under the circumstances, Rolf could consume wash-water and praise it no less.

There was tea, but Heike made mock coffee to cover for the sins of the morning.

Nadine took in and folded the wash while Heike patrolled. She charged upstairs and made certain Jürgen's bed was made to perfection. Her fussing and smoothing took only seconds. Heike took a break from sentry duty to get a head start on Abendsbrot.

Some distance from the house, Heike caught sight of Jürgen. Instantly, every sinew was stretched to the limit. Even the rapid strides of Lilo Kruger would be hard pressed to keep pace. Her feet scarcely touched the cobbles. Jürgen's broad grin turned to alarm at the approaching bullet.

The last portion of Heike's journey was completed in the air. She crashed into her brother. He staggered backward. He avoided tumbling onto the stones, but Heike's arms around his neck, impeded breathing.

Heike savored the sensation of the moment – Jürgen's reassuring, protective arms were comforting. Her serendipity was on par with Anna Ecke Jacobs's sheltering embrace of the long ago. Heike Jacobs felt no threat, worry or misfortune could find her.

This delicious feeling evaporated too soon, but Heike treasured this magic memory. Jürgen was home!

Mysteriously alerted, Anne stole away to the kitchen. Moments after his arrival, Jürgen smelled the unmistakable aroma of hot cocoa.

Fürth and Nürnberg

July 1989

If Kathy suffered from melancholia during Uncle Dieter's tour, she rebounded graciously with the help of her quasi-cousins. No American fact was too trivial; they demanded Kathy tell them everything about everything. Recognizing how disappointed their shinning faces became when pleading ignorance, Kathy created stories.

These inventions were welcome intervals between cascades of questions. Some stories were so strained that even young Mischa's gullibility wouldn't stretch. However, the brothers enjoyed the Ami's fictions more than her admitting to not knowing.

Aunt Marion, formerly despised as a Bavarian sphinx, was more animated than a Swabian dared expect. She procured three tickets to a summer staging of *Hansel und Gretel*. She intended to take her children. They, however, insisted on escorting their American cousin.

Marion Kaufmann was disappointed. Opera was her passion, and she had few opportunities to attend. Still, she willingly made the sacrifice.

Kathy had no formal attire. Opera, even when performed for largely juvenile audiences, was formal. Bernard and Michael had dark suits and bow ties. Kathy had jeans and t-shirts. Tante Marion, however, had a closet.

Kathy opposed the opera. Further, she abhorred the fashion tour. The boys, however, made it priceless. They sat on a stool while Marion fetched gowns. Adroit and critical comments accompanied each article. Their pride in Kathy demanded her making a favorable public impression. Ergo, they were brutally honest.

Tante Marion ground her teeth but did not admonish her sons for their diplomatic lapses. So long as opinions were heartfelt, Kathy's cousins were safe.

"That's my favorite dress, Mutti," the normally dour Bernard admitted. "For you!"

Marion stepped back and considered. True, the lines looked a bit off, but Kathy wore jeans underneath. Moreover, Marion was taller that Kathy.

"It might do," Marion insisted.

Michael waved his hand.

"She looks like a *Kluße!*"

Tante was injured, but it gave her pause.

"Take it off," she ordered.

When, at last, Kathy appeared in a scooped neck, sleeveless mauve dress with a high waist, the boys applauded. Kathy scowled at the mirror. True, she wore t-shirt and jeans, but the color was wrong. Girlie garb was for Molly – formal wear more so. Kathy felt like a scarecrow.

"I have pearls that go well with that," Tante announced.

Kathy cringed. Could she return the garment undamaged? The realization she might lose a string of pearls mortified her. Marion, unexpectedly, burst into laughter.

"Come the day Dieter Kaufmann buys real pearls is the day of the great skating party."

At that moment Kathy Foster truly appreciated Marion Kaufmann. Kathy recognized a woman not unlike herself. She didn't need expensive jewels to promote self-esteem. She was, Kathy concluded, more Swabish than Bavarian.

It was a chore to wear stockings, heels and carry a bag. The appalling gown – purple, sleeveless and so very formal – made her feel freakish. It was more abysmal to travel by bus accompanied by two handsome boys in dark suits and bow ties. Fortunately, her fellow travelers didn't gawk.

Kathy hesitated to sit lest she wrinkle Marion's gown but standing made her appear narcissistic. With exaggerated care for her costume, she lowered herself into the nearest vacancy. She kept the contact of gown and seat to a minimum. Her hand clutched the grip of the seat in front.

Kathy didn't notice the glow in Michael's visage when she perched beside him. Bernard, seated opposite, remained demure, but he displayed traces of petulance. At the second stop, a slender, elderly man in a charcoal suit struggled to board. There were a few seats behind Kathy and none forward of the mid-mounted double doors. Judging by the effort it cost him to mount the two steps from the street, he faced an additional struggle to reach a seat.

Kathy stood to allow him place. It was no matter that Bernd guarded an open spot. The panting man examined Kathy. The gown was a departure from city-bus norms. The high waist and scoop were designed to flatter, but Kathy had so little to flatter.

The old man shook his head and latched onto the nearest pole for support.

"I don't need to sit, thank you," he rasped. "I'm not on a world tour."

Kathy was embarrassed. She'd offered her seat to an elderly man, in accordance with accepted etiquette. Once on her feet, she refused to sit. If the man didn't need a seat, neither did a young girl.

She grabbed a strap above Bernard's head fearing the final humiliation of a sudden lurch or brake that would send her sprawling. The novelty of teetering in heels increased the likelihood of humiliation. Her grip on the strap and the back of Bernd's seat drained color from her fingers.

At the next stop, the old man turned to determine if anyone behind him wished to exit. He noticed Kathy. He leaned toward her to get his mouth close to her ear.

"When I was young," he announced, "I walked to Russia."

Though the voice was weak, his pride was unmistakable. He wasn't always stiff and weak kneed.

A moment later, he shifted to gain her ear once more.

"*And* I walked *back*!"

It was an effort to resist the motion of the carriage as it pulled away; he nearly toppled into her. Involuntarily, Kathy let go of Bernard's seat and made ready to catch him. If he went down, there was nothing she could do other than cushion his fall. At the critical instant, he caught himself, Kathy breathed again. To avoid further mishap, she leaned forward so he could speak without turning.

"I'm *very* lucky!"

Kathy Foster flooded with wonder. Few men who went into Russia returned under their own power. Her fellow passenger enjoyed a surplus of luck. Was it possible that a fraction of that luck might favor her? True, she was lucky in not damaging her dignity and Tante Marion's gown. Kathy's greed upset her.

Momentarily, she covered his hand with her own – just on the chance…

Entering the opera house, Kathy felt less freakish. Compared to the adult patrons, she was underdressed, but, thankfully, not enough to arouse attention. She followed the example of other women in clutching her dainty handbag fashionably. It contained nothing. She was too afraid of losing it. Bernd oversaw both tickets and money, but Kathy had an emergency ten-mark note stuffed in a place where she'd not lose it.

Bernard played his role to the hilt. He presented tickets at the door; it was he who led his retinue through the correct door, and it was he who found their assigned seats. Kathy thought it proper to sit next to the man in charge, but Michael launched an unseemly, if judiciously quiet, protest. Kathy redressed grievances by sitting between her escorts.

The audience sat expectantly as the orchestra ceased exercising and fell silent. Kathy expected a man in a tuxedo, like the handsome maestro in *Das Doppelte Lottchen*. Coincidently, the movie featured the same opera. *Hansel und Gretel* is, traditionally, performed around Christmas and New Year. The summer presentation, presumably, was aimed at vacationers.

A burly woman mounted the podium in a white blouse and a long, black skirt. Kathy was nonplused, but her cousins leaned forward expectantly. The overture flooded the auditorium with a richness Kathy hadn't expected. Despite her reticence, she uncrossed her legs and joined her bookends in leaning forward. After the overture, there was a burst of prolonged applause.

Once the hall quieted, there was another pause and last-moment coughing. The conductress raised her baton; the orchestra snapped to attention. The curtain flew open, and the audience was treated to an intricate set – far nicer than a genuine peasant cottage. Two girls sat on wooden chairs, pretending not to look for their cue. The downbeat came, the music played, and, with the nod of the conductor's head, the singing began.

Hundreds of children filled the audience. If any were bored or the restless, they escaped detection. Everyone was mesmerized by the unfolding pageant. Not once did the Kaufmann trio settle back in their seats. They remained poised just above the shoulders of those seated ahead.

As the final scene of the first act approached, Kathy's stomach tightened. The children were hopelessly lost; a witch lurked; the darkness was ominous. After a brief lament, the siblings fell to their knees and sang an evening prayer.

After the Sandman sang and sprinkled the lost children with magic powder, she exited stage right. The music flooded the hall. Angels entered, simultaneously, from both wings and the loft. Gradually, they formed a protective ring around the sleeping children.

The back of Kathy's neck tingled. She thought of the former infantryman on the bus. She thought of that horrible copse of trees where her mother died. She imagined herself moments from death. What, she wondered, determined who lived and who died?

Reverend Rademacher had no doubt. Kathy, however, was no theologian, nor was her religious faith strong. Kathy was a thief; she created heartbreak for her parents during the Pig War; she assumed vile things about Molly and Dieter and Marion without knowing them well enough to pass judgment; she stood over her mother's grave and felt nothing. Why was she alive?

Mischa noticed; something wasn't right. Kathy made no sound, nor did she move. He, however, sensed her pain. As he joined in the applause, he watched his stoic cousin. When the lights came up, he couldn't suppress the shock of finding her in tears.

"What's wrong?"

Kathy bit her lip and kneaded the handbag in her lap. Nothing, save her palms and the back of her hand, could tend the mess on her visage. Had she put on a face, as Marion suggested, it would be a shambles. She assuaged her aunt by applying a thin coat of gloss to her lips rather than initiate mutiny.

"Why don't you two buy an Eis?"

Neither moved. They refused to leave their Ami cousin blubbering in her seat while they went larking about. Uncertain of proper etiquette, they remained solemn and silent bookends.

"I'm sorry," she said, regaining control, "I was thinking of – things. It isn't good to think about things, I guess."

"What were you thinking?

"My real family – must be – somewhere."

* * *

The summer of 1989 was not atypical. Adolescent girls found it bitter-sweet as with previous summers. The hopes and heartbreaks were different, but the general summer motif remained as ever. There were rumblings, of course. There were always rumblings. However, vague disquiet remained a minor feature of summer's tableaux.

As Jürgen departed, chasing a few days of summer adventure with comrades, Kathy Foster boarded a plane for the long flight home. Few realized the summer of '89 marked the end of the familiar. The European fabric was unraveling. Fraying for decades, the tapestry fragmented.

Weimar

August 1989

Frau Willing rode a bus to work, drove one at work, and rode another home. A few off-duty hours were spent in the maintenance shop; she enjoyed tinkering. The boisterous Rolf Jacobs had no use for interlopers, but he always mellowed when Frau Willing pitched in.

Normally, Rolf had no use for drivers, but Frau Willing was the exception. She knew every mechanical centimeter of her vehicle. Over the years, she proved as good a mechanic as Herr Jacobs. Early one afternoon Frau Willing sought her mentor. They exchanged few words, and she departed with a key.

Minutes later, Nadine responded to knocking.

It was years since the woman's previous visit. She liked and respected Anne Ecke Jacobs, but when the woman's mind fogged, she couldn't bear witnessing the disintegration. The family never mistook it for snobbishness.

"Your father said Heike be to home."

"She is," Nadine assured. "Won't you come in?"

"Bitte, nein."

Frau Willing horded a plethora of treasured memories. She did not dare risk smothering them. Nadine understood and left the driver in the street.

"I've job," Willing explained, "Your father said you can help."

"What kind of a job?"

"Farmer near Possendorf has truck he want for the fix. I have parts we can use. I need someone with the help."

"Yes, I can help."

The woman pressed the keys into Heike's hand.

"You make the drive."

"To Possendorf?"

"Good practice? Twenty minutes, maybe, we arriving."

"What if the Polizei stop us? I have no papers."

"Not worry much. I say you steal Herr Jacobs's car and force me with to ride. Your papa get you out of jail – someday."

Willing's deadpan made Heike quake. Even with father's permission; it was risky to drive in traffic. Frau Willing tutelage was thorough, but Heike found comfort only on semi-deserted streets. Still, she trusted Willing's judgment. Her fears were buried in the promise of adventure.

Frau Willing didn't bother watching the road. She trusted Heike to drive as taught. She rested her head against the passenger window and observed the road peripherally. As navigator, she used hand gestures. She enjoyed talking and wouldn't interrupt her conversational flow.

"Is Soviet truck," the woman informed, using her thumb to indicate a right turn.

"Soviets make junk! Anything who need precision, Soviets no good. German truck much better. German truck simple and easy to make fix. Soviet truck have pickle parts and not work good. My friend have nice farm, nice family, do good work, but have crap truck. I try to tell, but, 'no;' he say, he need big truck to make one trip to market instead of three with German truck. Is crazy. One load, yes, but what good when you must pull truck instead of to drive?"

Heike half listened. She concentrated on speed, traffic, and the road. Her nerves were worn to a slender thread, and she feared her eyes or judgment might fail. It was a relief when Frau Willing signaled her to turn onto a dirt track. Twice they came to an intersection, twice the navigator gestured directions. Cresting a small mound, the truck loomed large. Heike slowed and stopped meters from a huge steel grill.

"Great Soviet dung hill," Willing announced.

Heike surveyed the huge vehicle as Willing extracted tools from the Trabi.

Never had Heike seen such a monster so close. The driver's seat was nearly two meters above the road.

"So," Frau Willing announced. "We work."

The plural pronoun proved a fraud. Willing didn't lift a finger. She directed Heike onto the solid bumper and explained how to open the cowling. Unfastening the object was easy. Lifting the great engine cover, however, initiated a struggle.

Had Willing lent a hand, the task could be quickly dispatched, but she declined to mount the bumper until Heike completed the job. After hoisting herself, Willing rested her arms on the radiator and peered at the engine. She refused to point. Instead, she directed Heike's eyes to key locations by describing the surroundings.

"You must take that off," she directed. "You need tool. Go to get."

It was clear what was afoot. Using the same techniques employed as driving instructor, Frau Willing taught through the student's doing. The work could have progressed much faster if the teacher specified a tool or, better yet, fetched it. Instead, Heike repeatedly leapt to the ground, rummaged in the heavy box, and hefted the instrument to the engine. When she erred, her mentor remained silent and allowed her to correct her mistakes.

Repeatedly pulling herself up onto the bumper left Heike sore for days.

By the time she removed the wires, hoses, and yanked useless parts, her legs ached, her knuckles oozed red, and her assessment of the Soviet vehicle was less charitable than Frau Willing's. Thrice, she crawled under the engine to fetch a dropped tool.

She was covered in sweat, dirt and smudges of oil and grease when the parts were finally replaced. At this point, she climbed into the cab and attempted an engine start. Failing, she climbed back for further adjustments. At last, Frau Willing offered advice. Since she could see the engine while Heike turned the starter, she deduced a remedy.

On the third try, the motor roared to life, Heike was jubilant. Frau Willing, however, was not satisfied. More climbing and more adjustments followed before the taskmaster was placated.

"It not good, but this will do must," Frau Willing announced. "Tomorrow, transmission fail, radiator explode, parts will burn. If farmer is lucky, truck will last a week, maybe two, if it not move. Better him drive Soviet junk to edge of cliff and push over."

Heike, wiping the worst of the blood and grime from her hands, wished the truck had gone over a cliff before her nightmarish odyssey. She used a sleeve to wipe the sweat from her upper lip. She hadn't realized she dripped until she tasted salt on her tongue.

"Can we leave now?"

"Not before you close motor."

Heike looked up at the raised engine cowling. She launched an unkind word and called upon aching legs one last time.

"Rain come and get on Soviet motor and it get soft," Frau Willing predicted. "When motor flushed down toilet is, Soviet junk become orange heap. People come long way to take photo of Rust Mountain and show friends."

Heike wasn't gentle. She hoped she broke the beast. Once the monster was made whole, Heike pivoted on the bumper and looked upon the figure putting the tools away.

"Are we finished?"

Frau Willing grunted. Heike jumped. Her teeth rattled one last time. She helped in returning the heavy box to the trunk and threw the filthy rag in after it.

"You want me to drive?"

Frau Willing shook her head.

"First, you calm down. Angry driver, tired driver not safe. You, maybe, tell me story of Comedy Mistake."

"Of what?"

"You know. Shakespeare and his Comedy Mistake."

Comedy of Errors.

For two hours, Frau Willing gave oral instructions without getting her hands dirty.

"Read it yourself." Heike responded, sparks flying from her tongue.

Frau Willing refused to take offense.

"I do read," she shrugged, "but I just spoon carver. Many words, they mean what I know not. They just words. When you tell story, I hear your voice and understand even if I not know all words. You tell stories good."

Heike's temper lurched free. Never would she expect Frau Willing to sit down with a Shakespearian play. The woman was barely literate. Attempting a slog through Shakespearian text deserved commendation.

"Maybe," Heike proposed, "we can read a play together. I will sit with arms folded and tell you how to take it apart and make it work."

The woman burst into laughter. There was no rancor, no bitterness, no resentment. She was, in her own words, a peasant girl, but she wasn't stupid.

"Good idea," she beamed. "When do we this?"

Heike relented with good grace and narrated the tale of *A Comedy of Errors*. The sun was near the horizon, and Rolf would be anxious about his auto. Nadine might be resentful about assuming Heike's chores. Nevertheless, Freundschaft is no platitude.

Frau Willing enjoyed Heike's plot summary. It was childishly simple. Recounting who was mistaking who for whom, however, was tricky. Frau Willing nodded frequently. Several times she made a sound indicating understanding.

"You did read it, didn't you?"

"Oh, yes," she nodded, "but I not understand so much. You make clear."

The tale told; they mounted the Trabi. Despite preoccupation, Heike answered several perceptive, questions.

"You'd make a good scholar," Heike advanced.

She aimed for another merry laugh but missed. Frau Willing remained stoic.

"Maybe so," she replied. "I have good teacher."

Heike glowed. Never had anyone made her feel better about herself than the praise of a peasant woman.

* * *

Three days later, Heike and Nadine "discussed" Polish elections. Official news was sketchy and terse. Rumor, however, abounded. Without Party sanction, Poles elected a prime minister. Nadine felt it a harbinger of for-real democratic socialism that Walter Ecke advocated. Heike was less enthusiastic; reform from outside the Party was a threat.

"This could be disastrous," she warned.

"Now, people have a voice," Nadine countered.

"That doesn't mean they're right," Heike countered. "People thought Hitler was a good idea."

Nadine couldn't deny that. She'd keep erudition to herself. If Heike insisted upon being a misery guts, there was nothing to say or do.

"Maus!" Rolf roared.

Heike sprang from the bed and hurried down the stairs. She felt no fear. Despite Rolf's deep, commanding voice, he never called her Maus when displeased.

"Here, Pabst."

He led her outside to the Trabi. In the trunk were six burlap sacks and more in the back seat.

"Potatoes," he announced, "and four cartons of cigarettes, payment for fixing the truck. Frau Willing says for you to divide it."

Heike was stunned. The payment was a treasure in the DDR's underground economy. In terms of barter, the Jacobs family was wealthy. The cigarettes, alone, could fetch Nadine liters of paint.

"Me?"

"Frau Willing said you did the work; you decide."

"What value is labor? Without her direction, I was useless."

"Decide," he repeated.

Heike calculated.

"We each get half," she announced.

Rolf laughed. It was not his trademark belly-laugh, but it was welcome.

"I knew you'd do the right thing," he nodded.

They carried Heike's share into the house. In the morning, Rolf would deliver Willing's share.

"Anne, look," Rolf said, setting the booty near the door. "Maus is bringing bread in house."

"Why, Papa," Nadine cooed, descending the stairs. "You're a poet!"

This laugh was more pronounced. The patriarch felt even better when Anne smiled broadly.

Oregon Coast

September 1989

Kathy Foster's music teacher viewed her as a special challenge. Kathy refused to believe in her talent. In a previous year, Mr. Davidson fumbled a similar gem by pushing too hard. The net result was a student who hated both music and teacher. He learned the value of patience; he stroked Kathy and babied her.

Kathy wanted to learn to read music. Beyond the rudiments, class time was too sparse. She volunteered to stay after school three days a week and ride the activity bus home. Kathy learned the code. More importantly, she began respecting her voice. Though untrained, she shed timidity. Her meticulous enunciation and confident voice were qualities around which the chorus rallied.

Over summer break, Mr. Davidson put Kathy from his mind. Reporting in, he fought anxiety. Through two days of faculty meetings and room preparation, he suffered. The final class lists were distributed on the final prep day. He skimmed through intermediate choir roster.

FOSTER, Kathy

She'd committed to another year. He couldn't gloat. The "final" class list is a euphemism for "subject-to-change." Still, there was a chance. He vowed not to push, but – damn – a voice like hers must be showcased! Where did nurturing become oppression?

Sunday, after church, the phone interrupted his quandary.

* * *

It was the fourth day of school. Molly, Kathy, and Jayme were as thick as ever. Where Kathy went, Gary went. Jayme was exceptionally attractive in her, unique, Tom-boy togs, while Molly, as ever, was a *Vogue* cover-girl-in-waiting. A recipe for jealousy confronted Kathy every day.

It was unreasonable of her to expect Gary to avoid feasting eyes on the Waldrons, but it pained her. Next to Jayme and Molly, Kathy was invisible – so she thought. Molly's infatuation ebbed when her boyfriend ensconced shortly after graduation. She realized that "the love of her life" was little more than a learning experience. She was sadder, but wiser, according to platitudinous piffle.

She realized her rock-solid friendship was Kathy Foster; she was her constant. Never again, she vowed, would she shunt people aside for transient emotional highs. In the little community by the bay, Kathy and Gary became "kissing friends." They'd deny it until death, of course.

Gary carried the burden of a father he never knew while Kathy's origins remained vague. She'd learned that, in Germany, people must prove they're *not* related before they can marry. Kathy, in the bureaucratic sense, could prove nothing.

After school, the girls adjourned to the tennis courts, and stubborn Gary to the practice field. He'd get bashed about, but he was accepted as a teammate. He was better conditioned and, occasionally, got in a lick. Blinded by giddy romance, Kathy missed the subtle signals of her choral teacher. His kid-gloves approach was too artful.

Mr. Davidson got another call.

He wasn't alone at the classroom door when Kathy worked her way through a crowded hall. The stocky, balding man beside him was introduced as Ed Geist. Kathy assumed he was German.

"*Freut mich sehr,*" she offered with a deferential, old-world bob curtsey.

The man hadn't had a clue. The red-faced girl apologized for her faux pas. Mr. Davidson handed Kathy a pass and instructed her to escort the visitor to the library for a conference. Flustered, Kathy obeyed – and quietly, lest she stumble anew.

She selected a table as far away from other ears as possible. Once seated, Ed Geist introduced himself as the artistic director of the amateur theatrical group. He was directing a musical revival. The actors and singers were cast – all save one. He needed a soprano to fill a subplot.

If Kathy signed on, she'd feature in one, twenty-second solo and participate in two production numbers. He produced sheet music for a duet and solo. Could she do it? She could read enough music to evaluate.

"Not here," she stammered, under the eye of the frowning librarian.

The ghost smiled. He handed her a copy of the script with her lines highlighted and his phone number on the cover. He begged Kathy to study the materials, decide and call him soon.

"I must do serious re-writes if I can't cast this part," he said, mournfully. "It would be a shame."

Kathy promised to study and call.

Mr. Davidson recommended her. That was a vote of confidence. Though she doubted her abilities, she realized her choral teacher would not vouch for her if he entertained doubts. The ghost was employed by a consortium of local businesses. All others were volunteers. To Kathy, that meant "no obligation."

Yeah, well…

* * *

While Kathy was entertaining her cousins, Molly secured a driver's license. She, eagerly, volunteered to drive Kathy to rehearsals and, hopefully, home after. Molly batted her lashes; pleaded with buttered words and syrupy voice. Jayme made gagging noises over the performance, but Kathy's resistance crumbled. When Molly left the basement rec room, Jayme made a less histrionic pitch.

"If you can help these people, you should."

"I don't want to be out until all hours every night."

"Not everyone gets an opportunity like this."

"Et tu, Jayme?"

No obligation – ha!

Kathy shared her concern with Gary. Jayme had lobbied him. Bussing to school the following morning, Gary's excited verbal arm twisting grated.

"Let Jayme do it," Kathy suggested.

Jayme can't sing.

"Let Molly."

Molly, at least, thought she could act; her basement performance vouched for that. Alas, Molly, as a singer, was worse than Jayme.

Ute and Aaron were excited and encouraged her.

"Imagine how proud Bernd and Mischa will be," Ute proposed.

No obligation – ha!

With the resumption of school, Dieter's folder faded in importance. School work, tennis and, unexpectedly, Thespianism moved to the fore. She'd digested Dieter's research and, save for formulating additional questions, it was a source of frustration and best ignored. She had "Foster parents" and Swabish-American culture. For the present, that was enough.

Kathy's fictional character was a woman in her mid-twenties. She was engaged to one man and in love with another. She's required Ed Geist's directional expertise to guide her through the maze of experiences she never had. There was, however, one major obstacle haunting her. On stage, in front of friends, family and complete strangers, Kathy Foster must kiss the baritone.

Weimar

Günther came home on leave at least twice. This news circulated and crushed Heike. The heartache of no cards or letters was compounded by his avoiding her. Doubtless, Günther was communicating with Lilo, wherever she was.

Heike was a fool to think Günther was serious about her. She had only herself to blame. She was a young, punk kid; Günther was a man in national service. She harbored dreams she had no right to. Two years on, Heike was less vulnerable and naïve, but the pain was real.

Heike vowed to march through life as her own agent. Unfortunately, she needed people. More importantly, she needed someone who needed her. If she committed to a celibate life, she had a wider range of possibilities. In a perverse way, this appealed to her.

Heike had Nadine and Jürgen. One was out of reach and the other flirted with treason. Who could predict what chaos her blood relations might visit upon her? Suffering rage and confusion, Heike did not dare ponder politics.

When Nadine learned Slovenia was serious about seceding from Yugoslavia, she insisted the New Forum was the only path. Poland was not an isolated event. To the south, the cauldron bubbled. Without serious reform, the world might explode. Heike, however, realized she must obtain Party membership. As an "insider," she'd initiate a redress of grievances. Alas, Party membership remained years away.

Heike fled to the park to consult Shakespeare.

Oregon Coast

Kathy's circle of friends increased with her foray into amateur dramatics. She was the only rookie. The cast doted on her like mother hens. Dee (Debbie), the pianist, was youngish and attractive with a quiet voice and a passion for music. Her husband, Steve, was a baritone – *the* baritone.

The couple had participated in every musical production for six years. Steve, also, played the lead in several dramas and comedies. According to Dee, he was nervous about this show; Kathy was underage. Dee thought it amusing how her husband kept his distance from the neophyte.

"I can tease him about this for months," Dee giggled.

Despite their penchant for teasing one another, Steve and Dee were a devoted couple; a quality Kathy admired.

"It's called *acting*," Athena reminded her during a Saturday café break.

"It's called kissing. I must do it in front of God and everybody."

"You kissed Gary in front of one and all," the waitress reminded.

"He kissed me. If I'd known, I'd have punched his snoot."

"Fat lot of good that did ya the first time. And don't be tellin' me you ain't been kissin'. Just cause I'm older don't mean I'm stupid. I know you two ain't hunting agates."

Weimar

School started, and Heike found herself assigned to a third floor, corner room. It was her first time to experience two banks of windows. It was eerie.

She checked the bulletin board and examined the seat assignments as determined by Herr Direktor or one of his aids. Sure enough, Heike and Heiko were paired. There were three rows of desks, and Heike was assigned to the third desk of the middle row.

"Some things never change," Heiko grinned.

Heike pulled out her chair and kicked her backpack under the desk.

In her school – she assumed, in every school – the students remained in assigned seats while teachers went from class to class. The same first-day pep talk was filled with patriotic phrases and quotations. The economics teacher, however, elaborated on his favorite topics in Marxist economic theory. He urged everyone to read *Das Kapital*; students must know the enemy to triumph.

She noticed Heiko about to drop off; she kicked his ankle. He refocused. Her thanks would come when he returned the favor.

A traffic triangle with the aging trees growing upward from each apex fronted the school. It was Heike's habit to cut across it when heading home. The first of several short cuts.

She spied a figure in a sleeveless pullover packing a pale-yellow pack. She hadn't cut across the triangle but went around to the sidewalk opposite. The girl's chest identified her.

"Hanna!"

The figure stopped and turned. She didn't smile. Hanna squinted into an afternoon sun, waiting for Heike to explain herself. Calling a person's name for all and sundry to hear was a major trespass.

"I'm surprised to see you," she stammered, "I forgot you were schooling here this year."

"Oh?"

The subtext of this monosyllabic response inferred that Heike was a) daft and b) inane. Feeling a fool magnified Heike's misery. Jürgen was at uni in Halle. Nadine remained distant for fear of interrogation. Heike needed to "bark." Hanna Müller filled a need.

"A burdened heart is the death of a healthy mind," Heike confessed.

"Shakespeare?" Hanna asked.

"Heike Jacobs."

"Oh?"

Hanna's tone communicated concern.

"May I walk with you?" She asked nervously, afraid of prying.

"I was off to the park," Hanna volunteered.

"That's on my way."

They walked in silence before Heike checked to ensure they were beyond earshot.

"What do you think of the New Forum?" Heike asked.

"Not much," Hanna replied diplomatically. "I hear it mentioned."

"Since Poland?"

"Longer ago than that. I didn't pay attention."

Hanna was cautious; everyone was. No one knew what to expect. The rules, both written and unwritten, were clear. Since the Polish elections, however, rules became blurred and ambiguous. A person was a fool to speak without a clear point of reference; Hanna was no fool.

There was no understanding between Heike and Hanna as existed among the barkers. There was no oath nor bond of blood. Regardless, Heike must speak.

"I believe – there's another."

Hanna turned to read Heike's face. The words were devoid of meaning. Heike saw the perplexity in the girl's round, babyish face.

"*Ich bin Geschwistert.*"

"Oh?"

For the third time, Hanna remained non-committal. There was, however, the hint of sympathy. Heike assumed Hanna knew of the adoption.

"I've no sympathy for my parents. Eight years in prison is too lenient. My brothers and sisters didn't conspire with them, *oder*?"

"I can't say," Hanna responded carefully. "A classmate is the baby of her family; her nearest sibling is thirty-four."

"Gott! She was a surprise!"

"Her case is unique."

"I'd be the baby of the family," Heike reasoned. "What of the others? Were they placed; did I get special treatment? Why won't the authorities allow contact?"

Hanna made certain there were no idle ears.

"Perhaps, you're the only one left?"

Heike hadn't thought of that.

"I mean…" Hanna added, "Suppose the others –?"

Heike pondered.

"That's hardly likely."

"But possible."

It would explain much.

"The problem is," Heike thought aloud, "I've developed a bond with my family. I put them first – before country, before Party…"

Heike placed her fate in Hanna's delicate hands. It was a stupid mistake. Hanna, as always, displayed maturity beyond her years. She locked arms with her. The gesture communicated an assurance that Hanna wouldn't betray a confidence.

"Jürgen, once, reminded me I have two families. How can I be faithful? What if my brothers and sisters are in the West? They cannot be held responsible. They'll be well indoctrinated. They must hate me and everything I stand for, but – they are family."

"You'd treat them as you would Nadine and Jürgen."

It sounded glib, but Heike doubted Hanna was so shallow.

"And if they hate me?"

"Heike, you can't be anything but what you are. You and Nadine are like cat and dog, but you remain loyal to family, *nicht war*? You can't deny their attitude toward you, but you cannot hate them out of revenge or spite. Or can you? Is that the kind of person you are?"

Heike pondered the times she wanted to hurt Nadine. Regardless, she was willing to stand with her against the authorities.

"I'm not sure I can answer your question."

Hanna gave her arm a reassuring squeeze.

"I have confidence in you, even if you don't."

Heike wanted to cry. *Where do these people come from? The Jürgens and Nadines, the Frau Willings and the Frau Engles, the Heikos and the Hannas – priceless!*

"Thanks, Mutti," she responded, attempting flippancy but failing. "I turn off here."

Hanna released her arm, and Heike veered toward a street emptying on the busy Friedenstrasse. She was meters distant when Hanna, imprudently, called her name. She turned to find the girl standing at the corner. Her visage was serious – almost sad. Heike retraced her steps.

"I saw him some weeks ago," Hanna reported.

My brother? Jürgen – or a brother I know not of?

The girl with a child's face and a woman's body showed her perception once again.

"Günther," she announced quietly.

Heike came nearer, slowly, cautiously, full of suspicion. *People didn't volunteer information. They, particularly, didn't volunteer information about third parties.*

"How do you know Günther?"

"I watched Heiko play with his band in the *Kasseturm*. Jürgen and Günther were there."

Plausible, Heike reflected. Jürgen liked to spend time at the tower, a place where students socialized and shared a drink or two. There were live music evenings. Heike had never been inside. Anyone noticing Hanna filling out a blouse or a pullover was likely to hanker for an introduction.

"Where did you see Günther?"

Hanna's composure slipped. She was nervous.

"Returning from Apolda. It was at the Bahnhof. Günther was waiting for a train. He's going back to the Army."

"Did you speak?"

Hanna nodded.

Did he try to kiss you? Heike stifled the question, but –

"What did you talk about?"

This question was out of bounds.

Hanna turned reticent. She'd broken a rule.

"You."

"Wie, bitte?"

Hanna licked her lips and wiped her sweaty palms on her khaki pants. She looked again for bystanders. Standing on a street corner was a sure means of attracting attention. Hanna took Heike by the elbow and led her down the street. Once in the shadow of the building opposite, they stopped.

"He talked about you," she repeated, emphatically.

Hanna didn't look at Heike. She looked at the sidewalk.

"He asked if you were healthy; if you had a boyfriend. I told him – things I – shouldn't have. I'm sorry. I've said too much and – I'm leaving."

She turned on her heel and rounded the corner. Heike didn't follow.

Was Günther a member of the New Forum? Was he involved in subversive activity? Was that why he never wrote? The Stasi read suspicious mail. If Günther was being watched, direct communication would place Heike under surveillance. Similarly, if he attempted to see her –

Oregon Coast

Homecoming came unusually early in 1989. A quirk in scheduling deposited all activities athletic at home on the same weekend. Gary, in a rare display of bravado, asked Kathy to the dance. She balked; she'd be tied up in rehearsal until late. Gary could wait.

Molly, ever faithful, promised to drive Kathy from the theatre to the dance even though she had her own date. Homecoming weather was cooperative. The wind gusts were fewer and less pronounced than the norm; the sun splashed across the coastal plain as if inviting impressionists. The gulls took turns circling overhead and stabbing the afternoon calm with their staccato cries.

Henry, a Japanese-American transfer, Shelly, his impish sister, Kathy and Molly lounged in the bleachers watching the JV football game. Kathy's attention was divided between Gary's participation and Shelly's delightful, if incessant, yammering. She envied the young sophomore because she was more American than Kathy, particularly in gestures and slang. Further, Shelly matched Molly's ubiquitous smile. Despite like-poles repelling, Molly and Shelly bonded. Together they were a diabetic's nightmare.

Kathy was on "automatic pilot." Molly realized her best friend was under a cloud and kept close. Shelly's audible antics amused no few. Gary caught a touchdown pass for the only score in the JV game.

Molly crushed her opponent in a varsity match. Kathy's match was in the offing, yet she remained taciturn and emotionally aloof. Molly and

Jayme escorted Kathy to the courts while Henry and Shelly remained to show support for the football squad.

Kathy's opponent wore a neat, white tennis outfit with an imitation pearl suspended around her neck. Her pierced ears were, similarly, adorned with fake pearls. Her strawberry-blond hair was drawn neatly back. White combs above her temples and a clasp behind her neck confined the bulk of her tresses between her shoulder blades. She sported a new racket and the handle of another protruded from her bag.

"Janet Birdham," the girl introduced, extending her hand.

"Kathy Foster. It's my first varsity match."

"Congrats! Good luck."

Luck! Yeah, right.

"Remember your service," Jayme advised.

Varsity players were forbidden to use underhand serves. Kathy, habitually, lobbed her second service, but this was the big time.

"You're Molly Waldron, right?" Janet asked.

"Yes."

"We played at district last year."

"I remember."

"I want another crack at you."

Molly turned to Jayme.

"I'll have to beat my sister first," Molly confessed with a blush.

Janet shook hands with the sisters and exchanged a few words. Then, she and Kathy warmed up. Kathy, with first serve, double faulted to love-fifteen. Jayme urged Kathy to settle down.

Janet's service was a yellow blur. After a humiliating start, Kathy began returning serves. She wasn't skilled enough to make it a contest. She was two games down when she, again, double faulted into love-fifteen. Meanwhile, the football game broke for half time with the score six to nothing, thanks to Gary.

JV players didn't trek to locker rooms; they adjourned to patches of grass. The home team congregated near the tennis courts. Gary stood with arms crossed. Kathy shriveled, realizing her retinue had grown.

She tossed up the service ball and brought her racket up to meet it.

It was perfection!

In mental freeze-frame, she enjoyed every detail – where ball and strings met, the direction of flight, and the exact spot where the ball would kiss earth. It happened, exactly as predicted. Joy surged with the vibration transferring from the shaft into her arm. Her chest exploded in euphoric celebration!

Janet hardly bothered to lean left.

"Was it in?" Kathy gulped.

"Oh, yeah!" Janet confirmed. "Great serve."

"*Ganz Genau!*" Molly cheered.

Kathy saw Gary's huge grin. He'd beheld her triumph. She should have been euphoric over her first ace – doubly so since Gary witnessed it. Inexplicably, she felt empty.

Kathy won two games in her first ever varsity match. An auspicious and respectable start, Molly decided, and a complement to her sister's off-court coaching. Once Janet got a sample of Kathy's backhand, she exploited it and cruised to victory. She joined Kathy and Molly to watch Jayme pummel a creditable opponent.

"Has she killed anybody with that serve?" Janet asked, nudging Molly.

"Not yet. She practices with me. It's scary."

Janet whistled.

"I don't envy you looking down the barrel of that gun."

Kathy remained morose. Aside from Gary's winning touchdown and her memory-making ace, she faced a dreaded rehearsal. Ed Geist was soft spoken, but he was an utter tyrant about that stupid kiss. Kathy was inhibited, and his coaching, with people standing around, was mortifying. She was holding up rehearsal while the amused cast and crew chuckled and exchanged comments. Kathy wanted to quit. However, family and friends kept hurling her back into the caldron.

Weimar

October 1989

Official news reports were cryptic, but rumors spread. Only deaf people escaped the unofficial but more accurate news. In August, hundreds of DDR vacationers scurried across the Hungarian border into Austria, under the noses of Hungarian soldiers. Soon, hundreds of citizens camped in the West German Embassy compound in Prague.

The West German Foreign Minister, a former citizen of the DDR, went to Prague and announced a negotiated agreement. He informed the huddled masses that transportation to the Bundesrepublik was in the offing. Unfounded rumors abounded. The veracity of the latest whispers, however, was gauged by Heike Jacobs's own eyes. The nearer the DDR approached its fortieth anniversary, the fewer students appeared in school.

Five empty seats haunted the corner classroom. People Heike knew from kindergarten had vanished. The time for caution was past. Heike's bizarre conversation with Hanna was a tangible sign.

Heike sat on the floor, braced against the wall below her window, an open notebook in her lap. Three weeks previously, she'd never commit thoughts to paper; they could be used against her. Suddenly, she didn't care if authorities brought her to trial. Her fear transformed into a fireball.

Rosa's Children

A Statement of Values and Beliefs

1. The basic socialist unit is the family. However, the family must enjoy democratic ideals. This is not to imply that the patriarch (or matriarch) is supplanted. The elders have wisdom and experience. They have earned the final say. However, family members must have voice in matters impacting the family unit.

2. The basic socialist tool is discussion. Just as family members help shape decisions, people must have a voice in working conditions, production, and State policies. The leaders, through wisdom and experience, are not obliged to obey *vox popoli*, but a vital part of leadership is explaining, in language the proletariat understands, exactly how and why the will of the people is overruled. To this end, State secrets are forbidden. A policy too dangerous for the people to know is too dangerous for the government to implement.

Hearing approaching footfalls, Heike closed the notebook. When Nadine opened the door, she found Heike cowering on the floor looking guilty. Nadine hoisted herself onto the bed with two notebooks and her math text. She sat Indian style and spread her work in front of her. With a fountain pen in hand, she tapped her teeth and looked over the assignment.

"Do you know someone leaving?"

Nadine looked sternly at the simpleton. Some questions *are not* asked.

"What?"

Heike made a dismissive gesture. She'd neither the will nor the patience to play the game of mutual protection.

"You'd tell me if you were leaving, wouldn't you?"

"And you'd come with?"

Heike gulped. She hadn't expected that. Still, she'd made a vow.

"I'd try to talk you out of it."

"And if you couldn't?"

Nadine forced the issue.

"I'd go."

Nadine was incredulous.

"I promised, Nadine," Heike reminded, "and I promise again: I'll share your danger."

"Even if they shoot us?"

For one horrible moment, Heike imagined Jürgen being ordered to pull the trigger.

"Especially if they shoot."

Nadine glared. Heike never averted her eyes.

"Rest easy," Nadine assured, "I'm not leaving."

Heike let out her breath.

"Do you know of someone?"

"I won't say."

Heike interpreted the answer as an affirmative. She tore a bit of paper out of her notebook and scrawled a message. She placed the paper on the open page of Nadine's math notebook.

New Year's Day 1974: Your sister, Heike.

"Are you insane?"

Nadine snatched the paper, tore it to shreds, rolled the pieces into a ball, stuck it in her mouth and chewed.

"I want it to go out."

"To whom? Why?"

Despite herself, Heike was on the verge of tears.

"I want them – I'm – alive."

"What good?" Nadine asked, chewing furiously. "You won't hear back."

Heike fell back on the issue foremost in her mind.

"They're family."

Nadine ceased chewing.

"Deliver it in person," she suggested.

Heike pounded her fists on the bed with such violence that Nadine shifted away.

"My home! I won't leave! Nein, nein, nein!"

"Enough!"

Heike grasped Nadine's hand in hers and held tightly.

The chewing of cud continued until Nadine was satisfied the ink on the tattered message was sufficiently smeared. With her free hand, she removed it from her mouth.

"Get rid of it," she commanded.

"Promise me."

Nadine nodded. It was barely perceptible, but there was an unmistakable solemnity. Heike took the wet pellet from Nadine's fingers and scurried away.

Oregon Coast

Before washing and putting away the dinner dishes, Ute and Kathy warmed up the ancient tube radio to troll shortwave frequencies. Ute would fiddle until they found Deutsche Welle. If the English language broadcast was smothered by squeals and pops, they'd wait for the German program.

They heard about mass migration.

Kathy rehearsed on school evenings; she sat by the radio only on Saturday and Sunday. However, whenever Molly and an adult delivered Kathy home; she demanded a report. She demanded they call Dieter. Ute insisted he'd call if he had anything to report.

The life's blood of East Germany gushed out. Spurt by relentless spurt, it spilled onto West German soil and was absorbed. Every minute of every day, Kathy Foster imagined her father, brothers, and sisters begging authorities to make the family whole.

Had there been no school, no tennis, no theatre, Kathy would be uncontrollable. Luckily, she had friends. Molly and Jayme, Henry and Shelly, Gary and Athena – one of them was ever near. At home, Ute and Aaron exercised boundless understanding. When Kathy was sharp of tongue, nobody took offense. When she slacked on her homework, gentle nudges rather than fiery ultimatums were administered.

Kissing Steve Davis no longer terrified or humiliated her. Other things were more important. She and Steve must waltz. Ed Geist showed her the steps; Dee practiced with her. At home, Ute or Aaron partnered her. Kathy mastered the waltz as she had her overhand service.

Singing was her delight. She wallowed in the mingling of choral voices and the blending of duets. She focused on her voice and was amazed. Alas, world events pounded her stomach and crawled up her throat. She turned despondent and, periodically, cried until her emotions were washed clean.

Staring at the TV, Kathy's brain registered neither images nor sounds. Program and commercials were merely an inane background to her cares, marching in formation like a lumbering herd of circus beasts.

"What is it!" Aaron demanded.

Ute sat stock still. Kathy was flummoxed.

"That's it, then!" Aaron announced. "I've asked you three times; now I'm telling you. You're seeing Doc Reynolds tomorrow!"

"But —"

Ute didn't finish.

Embroiled in her cares, Kathy failed to notice the unfolding drama. Aaron's ultimatum required investigation.

Ute had developed *tummy* problems. Imprudently, she complained about a "flapping butterfly." When sparrow wings "flapped," Ute sat up straight and sucked in a surprised breath. Aaron noticed and focused Kathy's attention.

Kathy hardly slept. Ute was her (known) mother. She departed for school only to return. Ute was cross, but Kathy was impervious.

Ute was ready for work. She'd have all day to think up excuses. Unexpectedly, Kathy hounded her every step. It was easier to relent than fight.

* * *

Kathy flipped through a magazine – again. She read nothing, saw nothing. She was unaware of the noise she made. Others waiting to see the local G.P. were aware – and annoyed.

After an eternity, the door opened; Ute marched out – her jaw set; her face ashen. She looked neither right nor left but hurried to the exit. Kathy followed.

"What is it?"

"Nothing."

Kathy discovered the magazine clutched in one hand and cared not. She pestered Ute without reward.

"Get in the car."

This was beyond endurance.

"Tell me, or I'll take my clothes off!"

It was a stupid threat, magnified by panicked words. Ute's eyes pleaded until Kathy heart hurt.

"Please, get in the car. I must get to work."

Looking like the wreck of the *Hesperus*? The girl expected Ute to drop dead momentarily. Angry and frightened, Kathy threw off her jacket and lifted her sweater.

It was cold and windy. The orphan cursed her inability to conjure an alternate threat. She, however, was frightened enough to make good. Ute screeched and relented – thankfully. They made a deal: first, they'd get in the car.

Further persuasion was superfluous. Angry though she was, it was cold. Kathy sat with her jacket on her lap, ready to leave the vehicle and continue stripping.

"Don't make me do this," she growled.

Ute fastened herself in. She put the key into the ignition but didn't engage. Instead, she gripped the wheel and leaned her head against it.

"I should talk to Aaron first," she moaned.

There was a long, eerie silence. The ocean gusts whistling through the car's frame were the only sounds. Kathy stopped breathing.

"Now!" Kathy warned.

"It's not butterflies or birds. It's a baby."

Ute was nearly five months along. Incredulous, Kathy exploded.

"How could you not know? No blood for five months! That wasn't a clue?"

Part of Ute's "condition" was a capricious and infrequent cycle.

"At my age – a first child. This might not end well."

"No…"

Kathy's plaintive summation no longer carried disbelief. Rather, she recognized that this "miracle" changed – well – everything!

Weimar

There was a pall over the city. People vanished. Businesses shuttered; people with aching teeth, injuries and ailments discovered medical and dental offices vacant. Traffic thinned; available workers declined; busses ran infrequently and in fewer numbers.

At school, in normal times, there were gatherings outside the massive building. Friends conversed, joked, and smoked between classes. The atmosphere, normally, was convivial and noisy. As September closed, the crowds shrank, and chatter became subdued and sullen. Blank stares and nervous ticks replaced conviviality.

Heike trudged as in a funeral procession. The streets were eerily empty. Students trekked silently in pairs or small groups. She discovered a morose, silent gathering near the school's huge, solid wooden double doors.

She weaved through silent mannequins and proceeded to her corner room. It was several minutes before class, but the room was half full. Some students sat at their desks; some looked out the windows at nothing; a few leaned against the wall as if preparing to flee.

No one spoke.

Heiko sat with arms crossed, leaning back on two chair legs. He looked squarely into Heike's eyes. She padded softly across the room, placed her materials next to Heiko's, and pulled out her chair. She turned it around, planted herself on the desk behind and utilized her chair as a footrest.

Silence.

Three students arrived singly at the appointed time. They observed the absence of an instructor. In eerie silence they took their places. Everyone studied the large clock mounted on the front wall.

Five minutes passed. Ten additional minutes passed. Heike's butt turned to stone. She wanted to move, to change her posture, but no one else moved. She kept still.

Silence.

Motionlessness.

They heard someone on the steps. The tread was slow, sad, and heavy. In unison and silently, the assembly counted the steps until, finally, the footfalls came from the landing down the hall. Finally, Herr Direktor, a stout man with close-cropped hair and grayish temples, come through the door. Established protocol insisted that students stand whenever Herr Direktor entered a room. Students and teachers were to remain standing until instructed to do otherwise.

No one moved.

If this flagrant breach disturbed Herr Direktor, he kept it submerged. He faced the silent, immobile audience.

"Frau Schulz is indisposed this morning. No English today. Herr Ganz has transferred. There will be no math class until a suitable replacement is dispatched. Announcements will be posted in the main hall."

He took a breath. He wanted to say more, but words evaded him. After an uncomfortable moment, he exited slowly. Footsteps echoed down the hall, inching towards another classroom.

"What happened?" Heike whispered to Heiko.

Her whisper cut through the silence like a thunderclap.

The boy at the desk nearest the door spun around and looked at Heike with loathing.

"Figure it out, *Frau Marx!*" he snarled.

He snatched his books and stormed out.

The spell was broken, students shuffled out the door. Eventually, Heiko stood and faced Heike, but no words came. At last, he, too, gathered his books, inched past her chair, and left.

Heike was alone. Dazed, she stood up until feeling returned to her bottom. She righted her chair, sat down, and drew up to the desk. With no need to hurry, she tore a sheet of blank paper from a notebook. She fumbled until she found her fountain pen.

She removed the cap and set it carefully aside. When her hand ceased trembling, she wrote in large, neat script.

Ich Bleibe Hier!

She slid the paper to the upper left corner and made sure the sides matched the right angle of the desk. She recapped her pen and put it away. She gathered her things and walked on legs of rubber to the stairs. She used the handrail in case her knees failed. As miserable as she was, she didn't want her life to end in a crumpled heap at the bottom of the stairs.

She passed through the entrance and squinted against the sunlight. She blinked several times before the blur in the traffic triangle came into focus. It was Nadine, wearing her blue FDJ shirt and leaning against the tree nearest the school. Heike stumbled toward her.

"Why are you wearing that?" she asked.

"In case I never get another chance," Nadine replied, unexpectedly calm.

Heike should have castigated Nadine unmercifully for the catastrophe wrought by the New Forum and the thousands of traitors deserting the country. Suddenly, however, she saw no profit in castigation. The girls trod slowly toward home. There was no reason to go there. There was no reason to go anywhere.

"Are you okay?" Nadine asked.

Heike shrugged. She was unsure.

"I've never seen a country die before."

"I'm going to Halle on Monday," Nadine announced, "I must talk with Jürgen."

Heike nodded. If anyone retained reason for hope, it was Jürgen.

"I'll do all the chores," Heike promised.

"You'll look after Mutti?"

An alarm sounded! The question was stupid and unnecessary. Not to look after Mutti would constitute neglect worthy of a public flogging. Any answer would prove as vapid as the question itself.

* * *

Doubt gathered around Heike like cigarette smoke in a crowded room. Sunday would be the best day to visit Jürgen. Why wait until Monday?

Monday.

Monday?

It gnawed at her. That day of the week had meaning, but it eluded her.

Politics and Monday.

Religion and Monday?

Heike wasn't religious, but she recognized Sunday's significance. Friday afternoons and Sundays were the religious days. Why, then, did Monday conjure religious associations?

Celebrations were in the offing. October 7 marked the fortieth anniversary of the nation's socialist birth. Monday was a poor day to seek Jürgen. He and his university chums would, likely, attend some commemoration lasting far into the night.

Heike lay in bed, listening to Nadine's deep breathing. Occasionally, the older girl thrashed and turned restlessly. Why was Nadine so restless? Certainly, the events of the past several days and the bombshell of canceled classes would account for it. By that time, however, the mystery of Monday so dominated Heike's thoughts that she ceased considering rational explanations.

Early Saturday morning, the puzzle pieces fit snuggly. Just as Heike once entered Lilo's brain, so she spied upon Nadine's thoughts. Heike knew exactly.

Fear seized her throat; she struggled with a new terror.

Heike threw off her down blanket and padded softly across the floor. Slowly and quietly, she opened the door. She felt her way through darkness to the stairs. She counted every step to avoid missteps.

Feeling her way, she groped for the bathroom door and opened it quietly. She ducked her head, closed the door, and latched it. The light switch made noise, so she knelt in the darkness. She raised the lid of the toilet and the retching commenced.

After the first horrible storm, she waited. She panted for breath and, gradually, felt better. She waited. Sure enough, the nausea returned. Nothing remained in her stomach; she gagged and choked on bitter bile until the revolution ceased.

Her ribs hurt and her body trembled, but Heike's fear had run its course. She lowered the seat and lay with her head on crossed arms to catch her breath. When she felt safe, she pulled the chain. The tank refilled and silence reigned once more. Quiet as her namesake, Maus let herself out.

A form punctuated the darkness. One of Anne's children was distressed, and maternal instincts guided Anne through the darkness. Heike found her way around the table to the couch. She settled onto it and leaned up the silent figure. Arms caressed her.

As Anne's hands stroked Heike's hair and shoulders. Fear receded. Anne's loving embrace, the warmth of her body, the magic of her soothing hands was a balm to the troubled teen.

Nicolaikirche is the oldest church in Leipzig. It became infamous via its clientele. Initially, people gathered on Monday evenings to pray for peace. Though the government rejected religion, it exploited certain public gatherings. The DDR embraced peace for propaganda purposes. While superstitious people offered peace prayers, the government harvested publicity points.

Ultimately, Monday prayers adopted an anti-Party sentiment. Nicolaikirche became a meeting place for the Stasi. They identified, monitored, and spied upon participants. Monday prayers morphed into reform rallies.

The clamor for reform spread throughout the DDR. Its beating heart was the Nicolaikirche. To visit Jürgen in Halle, Nadine must change in Leipzig. Nadine, however, wouldn't change. She was headed for Nicolaikirche – even as the government openly discussed using "the Chinese Solution" to deal with protests.

Heike shivered. The DDR, alone of the world's nations, sent congratulatory messages to the People's Republic of China for quelling protests with tanks and troops. Nadine knew the risk.

Look after Mutti.

* * *

Nadine was up and at her tasks as if it were one more Saturday morning in the Jacobs home. Rolf left for work. They heard the putter of the auto until it blended with the distant rumble of city noises. Heike took a last sip of tea and grabbed her book bag.

"No classes," Nadine reminded.

"You don't *know* that," Heike replied.

"*Doch.*"

Nadine spoke thus because Rolf was gone. Heike declined debate. She had things to do. There was a school crowd. Few bothered with books or materials.

It was a good place to discuss political issues. Likely, students had nowhere else to assemble. Heike entered without speaking. She consulted the posted bulletins only momentarily. She marched down the hall and exited through the back.

Twenty minutes later, her finger was on an apartment buzzer.

"Ja, bitte?" the speaker crackled.

"Heike Jacobs."

A buzzer sounded. She pushed her way through the door and climbed the steps to face a bespectacled woman wearing a kittle, a dish in one hand and a towel in the other. Heike knew her despite their having never met.

"Heiko isn't here," the woman announced.

Her voice was flat, a sign of abandoned hope.

"Hanna?"

The woman nodded.

"*Moment mal.*"

She left Heike on the landing. Seconds later Hanna appeared. There was color in her cheeks; she flashed a winning smile. Heike envied her. With the nation crumbling, Hanna didn't see a future filled with dread. Instead, she faced uncertainty by believing things would come to right; her confidence and self-assurance oozed.

"May I buy you a coffee?"

Hanna was younger but highly perceptive. She realized Heike had no interest in coffee.

"Mutti," she called, plucking her coat from a wall peg. "I'll be back in a few minutes."

They headed in the general direction of town.

"I need a big favor."

Hanna didn't flinch.

"If I can."

"Nadine and I are going to Halle on Monday, to talk with Jürgen."

"There is much to talk about."

"Would you look in on Mutti while we're gone?"

"Anne Ecke? I consider it a privilege."

Heike could think of nothing more. She wanted to mention the possibility that they might not return. If they were lucky, they'd be jailed. If not…

They walked without speaking. Hanna realized there was more to the story.

"Anything else?"

"No."

"Good journey."

"Danke."

Hanna turned and headed back. Heike was convinced that the girl deduced the truth quicker than Heike had. She marched to the Bahnhof, waited in line some minutes, and bought a Monday ticket. It cost more, but she only needed one-way fare.

Oregon Coast

Kathy was impatient and taut. She'd yet to win a varsity tennis match but held her serve with increasing frequency. At the theatre, she knew her lines; she knew the lyrics; she knew how to kiss; she knew how to waltz. Both as an athlete and actress, she needed polish. Similarly, her scholastic work was consistently high; she impressed teachers with her acute insight that compensated for her crude writing skills.

Aaron, Ute and even Athena expected an explosion. Kathy developed nervous and annoying mannerisms. She turned "snippy" over any task beyond immediate dispatch. She adopted self-deprecation.

Aaron and Ute were a good fit from the first. They argued infrequently and forgave instantly. They were safe. They chuckled over Athena's *faux* flirting with Aaron. Early on, the newly wed groom threatened to leave Ute for a cute, German pop singer. He reminded Ute of this whenever she became "difficult." Ute always offered to pack his bags.

Kathy learned that she was a major reason her parent's sparring seldom got very serious.

Then, baby manifested itself. Kathy was superfluous. She was an interloper. There was no room for baby in the tiny gingerbread house. There was no room for a crib, changing table or numerous other accoutrements.

Moreover, Ute's fears of age and first baby weighed heavily. If, Kathy figured, she'd get out of the way, Ute would be more relaxed, confident, and apt to deliver a healthy child. Ute nixed a baby shower. Likewise, she forbade baby items in the house. They would, she argued, only tempt fate.

She confessed, within Kathy's earshot, that they hadn't room. Therefore, Athena secreted items at her place – only things mother and child would require immediately. Kathy offered to surrender her room. She'd sleep on the couch or, even, the garage rafters. These suggestions were rejected as impractical.

She'd move in with Grandma and Grandpa Foster in Milton-Freewater, or Oma and Opa in Germany. Maybe, she could sleep downstairs with the Waldrons, or in the front room on the floor at Athena's. The Foster clan, she knew, were setting aside money for her college. It would never approach the amount required; it was, therefore, useless. With no sacrifice on her part, Kathy offered the baby her trust money. This, also, was summarily dismissed.

Meanwhile, Aaron treated Ute like fine Meißen porcelain. He sat close to her in the house, often with an arm around her. Kathy came home from rehearsal one evening to find Ute sitting in Aaron's lap. He, instantly, signaled quiet; Ute was asleep. Touching as this was, the scene further convinced Kathy she was excess.

Eventually, in a fit of pique, she expressed her opinion that, if anything happened to the baby, the fault was hers. Aaron didn't argue. His experience taught him never to reason with a female on high-octane emotion. He related Kathy's outburst to Ute, and they agreed to face her jointly.

Kathy's exhausting schedule allowed few opportunities. It was, therefore, a shock to find Ute at the family breakfast table rather than tending the breakfast rush at the Fisherman's Inn. Aaron was sipping an inviting cup of coffee while Ute nursed orange juice.

Kathy wished them good morning and settled into her chair. Ute fetched something from the kitchen counter. Kathy's back was to her. The steaming mug of coffee arrived without warning. This break with household discipline sounded the alarm.

"The doctor says I'm very healthy," Ute announced. "I get a lot of exercise at the café, and he wants me to keep working."

Kathy filled a bowl with cereal.

"Only Barker's slave will bring bread in the house," Kathy responded.

"Stop being reasonable for a minute," Aaron growled.

She grabbed for the milk carton and studied his scowl.

"Listen to your mother," he commanded.

She doused her cereal.

"Kathy, this isn't without risk, but the doctor says we're doing well."

She looked at Ute. Without make up, she looked so old. She was on the wrong side of forty and very pale.

"You must understand Aaron and I didn't bring in some stray cat. We're family. You act as if you want to leave."

"I'm not a Foster," Kathy protested. "I'm a nobody."

Aaron slapped her hand sharply. She dropped her spoon, it clattered on the table amid milk and cereal.

"Never say that again!" he warned.

Kathy was ashamed, but too proud to apologize. She recovered her spoon and forced herself to eat.

"Okay," Ute conceded, "there's no Foster blood in you – no Kaufmann blood either, but we're family. Soon, the family will get bigger. You are as much family as the baby. When it comes, I'll need all the help I can get."

Kathy hadn't thought of that. For the first time in many days, her pulse quickened.

"Any minute now," Aaron injected, "we might get word of your – people. You decide. You can leave, if that's what you want, but you'll not be forced. You have a door key. You come and go as you please."

"One more thing" Ute appended. "Aaron and I have discussed this: We want to take this chance. If something bad happens, it was our decision."

Kathy heard more than was spoken. She thought about graduation, so far away yet so near. Unless she got an athletic scholarship, which was highly unlikely, or an academic scholarship, just as unlikely, an American university education was not in her future. However, as a German citizen, she'd pay no tuition if accepted. With a baby coming, a second family would prove advantageous.

DDR

Heike left the house to check the school announcements and report back. This lie guaranteed she'd be first at the Bahnhof. When Nadine appeared thirty minutes later, she didn't go to the ticket counter, nor did she consult timetables, a clear indication of planning. From a spot near the Mitropa Café, Heike monitored Nadine as she mounted the stairs leading to platforms four and five. Heike tensed and waited.

The Leipzig train approached a mere forty minutes late. Heike walked to the base of the platform stairs and inched upward. She searched the crowd, discovering Nadine several meters away, screened by other passengers.

The train squealed to a halt. Nadine waited for those exiting before joining others in scrambling aboard. Heike forced her way to the nearest entry and pressed against the far side of the vestibule. After the door slammed shut and the train lurched forward, she scanned the platform. She failed to spot Nadine.

Proceeding according to plan, she slithered through the swinging door and worked forward past the compartments. She examined passengers without appearing to spy. The third wagon forward was a coach, open seating with an aisle running through the middle. She must find Nadine and convince her to continue to Halle.

There she was, arms folded, a scowl on her face. Of course, she faced the rear of the train. Though Nadine's eyes burned a hole through the seats opposite, she was sure to look up at any approach. It was, however, Heike who was surprised.

"You didn't fetch it, did you?" Nadine scolded.

Baffled, Heike remained mute. Nadine stood and grabbed her.

"The one thing Jürgen asked us to bring," she hissed, pressing Heike into the window seat beside her.

"You couldn't wait for the next train, could you? Oh, no!"

Nadine turned to mask her face from couple seated opposite. She motioned toward the front of the wagon and mouthed one word.

Stasi.

Heike was petrified; she couldn't make a sound. Heike's eyes popped. Message received.

"You explain to your brother about his winter coat," Nadine concluded. "You were reminded twice. I'll make no excuses for you."

Nadine sat back, crossed her arms anew and scowled at the man seated across from them. After her tirade, the aging passenger refused to look at her. Heike, however, felt obliged to say something. With the Stasi near, meekness or surrender wouldn't appear natural.

"But I felt that…"

"Shut up!" Nadine snapped, "I don't want to hear a word out of you until we get to Halle."

Heike obeyed. She leaned against the window and watched the scenery crawl past. Her stomach tightened. The icy silence continued to Weißenfels. Passengers were discharged, new ones climbed aboard, the doors slammed, and the train lurched forward.

There was rustling at both ends of the wagon. A booming voice from behind announced himself. He demanded papers; he asked questions. His partner, working forward from the back of the wagon, did the same.

Heike was shaking when the hulking Stasi agent cast demanding eyes upon them. Nadine tore Heike's identification from her hands. She presented both sets of documents. The towering menace asked no questions. He'd heard all and knew all: the Jacobs sisters were en-route to Halle to visit their brother at university, less one winter jacket.

He could (should) have asked why they weren't in school. Nadine had prepared an answer, but it wasn't needed. The hulk returned their papers and tickets prior to examining those of the man and wife sitting across. This couple was peppered with questions. Apparently, their answers proved satisfactorily.

Not until the Stasi men left the car did Heike dare to breathe again.

"Just shut up," Nadine snapped.

Heike pondered her luck. If Nadine hadn't spotted her first, they might be under arrest.

Just outside Leipzig, the train made an unscheduled stop. There were several Vopos waiting. Nadine and Heike saw the two plain-clothes Stasi men from their wagon and four others turning over nine "suspicious passengers." The girls watched the Vopos escort the suspects away.

Thirty minutes later, Nadine and Heike stepped off the train at the main Leipzig station. They observed silence until on a busy street and away from other people.

"You're supposed to watch Mutti!" Nadine snarled.

"Fat lot you care!" Heike shot back, eager for combat. "You're crazy to come!"

"Some things must be done," Nadine retorted. "How do you expect Mutti to manage?"

"She manages when we're at school," Heike reminded. "Anyway, I made arrangements."

Nadine was furious, but she could ill afford a scene.

"How did you know there were Stasi?"

"I have friends. Travel to Leipzig is monitored on Mondays."

Heike accepted that.

"So, where's this church?"

"You're going home," Nadine announced. "*Sofort!*"

"Nadine, where's this church?"

"How am I supposed to know? Why don't we ask the Vopos?"

Gallows humor, Heike concluded.

"Let's look for a crowd," she suggested.

"It's a big city," Nadine reminded.

After several seconds, Nadine moved. She didn't check to see if Heike followed. The day was warm and clear. The girls slipped off their jackets and tied them around their waists as they entered a huge, public square.

Heike recognized the baroque architecture and the colonnade from the opening scenes of *Heiße Sommer*. Nadine recognized an excellent venue for a huge rally and suspected that Nicolaikirche must be close.

They ambled about inspecting shops and paused at outdoor confection carts without purchasing anything. All the while, Nadine looked for a kind person who might provide directions.

They stumbled across the university. They loitered. Surely, members of the New Forum must be near. If only they could be identified.

"Look, Nadine!" Heike grabbed an arm and pointed to a building across a square behind a large water basin.

"Remember that?" *Heiße Sommer*," Heike cooed. "Chris Doerk stood right – there!"

Nadine spun and slapped Heike's hand away.

"Will you stop!" she demanded. "This isn't a movie! If we're arrested, they won't lock us in a fire station with a loft window to escape through."

Though her hand stung from the slap, it wasn't her deepest pain.

An hour later, they were parched. They parted with money enough for a drink. They carried juice bottles into the shade and found a vacant bench. They sipped and rested their feet.

"I'm sorry I hit you," Nadine ventured softly. "I'm hot and I'm scared."

"Why did you come?"

"Because the Party must listen. If it doesn't reform, we lose everything. The more people calling for reform, the more likely the Party will hear."

"The Party does what it can," Heike replied.

"Feeding us bananas won't still our voices."

Heike considered the appearance of tropical fruit as a major government concession. The unexpected proliferation of bananas was a tangible sign of change.

"Notice the Vopos?" Nadine asked.

The green uniforms were difficult to ignore. Though ubiquitous, they were hardly menacing. They chatted away as they strolled lazily about, enjoying the warm, autumn air.

"Notice anything else?"

Heike sampled her drink. There were scores of students in pairs, walking with purpose. A few of the boy-girl pairs weren't eager to reach a destination; their gait was leisurely. Gradually, however, she noticed older men. They weren't students and their clothes, though casual, were too nice.

It wasn't unusual to see men, similarly dressed, standing in a line for scarce goods outside a store. These, however, were strollers. Though Heike would never notice before, Nadine had spotted them. These men should be working, not wandering around.

"Stasi?"

Nadine nodded.

"That church must be close."

If the Stasi were prowling, it was wiser to press on to Halle, but Nadine remained steadfast. Heike made a vow. It was as useless to talk Nadine out of insanity as it was for Nadine to force Heike home.

When hunger haunted, they adjourned to a bakery and bought a brötchen each and two more bottles of juice. The brötchen were slightly stale and the juice wasn't made from real fruit, but the bread fended off hunger and the liquid slacked their thirst. Returning to the Karl Marx Platz, they discovered a considerable crowd.

Nadine waded in.

"If there's trouble," she reasoned, "the safest place is with the crowd."

Heike considered this logic flawed. It might be true for a herd of zebras on the veldt, but Heike doubted it served well in the DDR. Still, she honored her promise and held onto one of Nadine's belt loops.

Despite Nadine's determination, neither of them got within sight of a church. They followed the sound of chanting, but the area around the girls – though crowded – remained peaceful. Standing its ground, ripples ran through the mass. There was a disturbance toward the front.

For Heike, it was a chore hanging onto Nadine. Her fingers grew stiff and numb. She traded hands periodically to reintroduce circulation. She grew tired of standing and did what she could to shift her weight and allow relief for her feet.

Suddenly, there was a surge. The mass contracted like a python. Someone's shoulder was thrust against Heike's face; she strained her neck muscles to press back. An elbow struck painfully into her ribs from the defenseless side. Her fingers gripped Nadine's belt loop, but her sight was blocked by those immediately surrounding.

Momentarily, there was a relaxing of tension. Heike managed to wiggle her way forward until she was with Nadine. Her finger-hold tight on the belt loop, she inched the other arm around her sister's waist and held tight. She heard a scream, then a shout and cries of panic. The crowd pressed in and jostled the girls.

Heike felt Nadine lose her footing and concentrated all her efforts on keeping upright. She let go of Nadine's waist and worked her hand around to push against someone to steady herself. The cacophony grew more urgent. Suddenly, the person bracing her vanished. Heike dropped to her knees, keeping hold of Nadine. She pulled on Nadine's pants to regain her feet, it was then she saw the policeman.

He wore a riot helmet. His raised hand wielded a night stick from behind the menacing shield battering anyone in his path. Those who could, ran. Those trapped fought for room to maneuver, but there was no room.

Heike saw another brutal, black stick. Simultaneously, she was struck by a thousand kilos of panicked humanity crushing her against another thousand kilos of people unable to move. Her fingers were tenacious, but her forearm was being crushed; she couldn't breathe.

The wall of humanity melted. She lost her balance and sucked in a lung full of welcome air. Nadine was torn away. Heike screamed and lunged for her. She was bowled over backward and thrown down against the pavement.

Her only thought was to rescue Nadine. She rolled onto her hands and knees. Someone in a dead sprint caught her in the side with a knee. The sprinter went sprawling. Heike was thrown again onto her back like a helpless turtle.

She cried out in pain, but no sound came. The blow drained her lungs. She sucked greedily for air and, ignoring excruciating pain, sought Nadine. She saw more panic-stricken elephants – or blurs representing them. She saw another blur raise a club.

She heard the crack of the wood. The blur came sprawling at her, she avoided it by throwing herself in the path of something – someone. This time, the knee caught her just above the eye and sent her onto her back, again. Her head bounced on the pavement.

Heike's body was swathed in pain. She realized the futility of finding Nadine. Her sense of direction was destroyed. Still, she refused to surrender. She rolled, again, onto hands and knees and fought to her unsteady feet.

Her legs were rubber, her side on fire; thick ooze stung the corner of her right eye. The remaining eye glimpsed Nadine. She was several meters away. One of the Vopos dragged her. The oaf caught a hand full of hair along with Nadine's shirt collar.

The head was forced back unnaturally, and her glazed eyes probed the sky. Blood flowed freely from her mouth and over her shirt and jacket. Her pants were wet and a thin line of urine marked her trail. For one terrifying moment, Heike thought Nadine dead. The next moment, she saw the vacant eyes blink.

Heike tried to call out, but her voice failed. She took a step on unsure legs. The step and her stagger avoided the worst part of the blow. Heike was blinded by a brilliant explosion of light. The sensation of pain did not come until later.

Some club-wielding Neanderthal was behind her, Heike's anger swelled. If the barbarian brute thought a whack on the head was going to keep her from getting to her sister –

She rushed towards Nadine's retreating form. Her feet, however, refused to obey. Desperately, she struggled to get a foot under her, but her body refused commands.

A fog obscured her vision. Out of the fog stepped Nadine. Her face was scrubbed, her beautiful blond hair glistened; she wore a flowing white gown. There was a garland of flowers in her hair and a broad smile spread across her face. Heike gasped at the sight; Nadine was beautiful!

Her hands reached out.

"Let's go home," she said, quietly.

Relieved and amazed, Heike reached for the proffered hands. Nadine, however, was a centimeter too distant. As Heike stretched out, the image disappeared into darkness. She felt a dull pain in her knees followed by pain on her chin. Her body was no longer part of her.

From somewhere far away, she heard voices. They were excited. They spoke German. Heike couldn't understand a word. She recognized words, but she couldn't comprehend them; she couldn't understand her own language.

Hands were on her. She groaned. She didn't want to be touched. She wanted to remain one with serene blackness. People grabbed at her. She attempted to cry out. She wanted them to leave her in peace, but the hands persisted. She hated them! She tried to fight, but she had no legs to thrash, no arms to flail, no tongue to curse.

Brutal, unwelcome hands groped her and forced her back into her body. She didn't want her body. She wanted peace. She felt pounding on her stomach. She tried to scream. She wanted the pounding to stop, but words and screams refused to come. The brötchen did. It slithered up her throat and out of her mouth. She couldn't breathe.

She was drowning.

Good!

The horror would soon end.

Oregon Coast

Reports out of the DDR were thin at the best of times. Early October was not the best of times. Ute heard of a demonstration in Leipzig. Unconfirmed reports suggested 50,000 participated. The same dubious source reported scuffles.

This arrived in Oregon via Deutsche Welle, but Ute, unilaterally, considered such news conjectural. She refused to tell Kathy who, uncharacteristically, didn't ask. Kathy's major challenge was to look ten years older. Throughout rehearsals, Ed Geist offered suggestions on deportment. Kathy practiced gestures and mannerisms of a proper lady of the1930s.

Since she'd wear heels during the play, she rehearsed in alien footwear. This amended her walk considerably. Despite practicing at home as well as on stage, Kathy still looked like a precocious teenager. Highly trained in theatre arts and makeup, Ed confessed it was easier to age Kathy fifty years rather than ten. She'd arrive early to rehearsals, so the Ghost and Debbie Davis could experiment.

After tennis, Kathy went home with either Molly or the Kuriharas. She either ate with a family, or five teens would adjourn to a popular gut-bomb palace. Molly drove Kathy to practice and picked her up after. The rehearsals ran progressively longer once Geist insisted upon rehearsing complete acts. Thus, Molly found herself sitting in the theatre watching the troupe struggle with lines and crosses.

Before the cast and crew were released, everyone gathered to hear the Ghost sharing his notes. If Kathy arrived home before eleven, she considered it a treat. Normally, she showered and went to bed. She hardly saw Aaron and Ute, save for weekends. This spawned guilt.

Molly got to bed even later. Since one of her parents insisted on supervising Molly's nocturnal drives, they, also, suffered. Moreover, Ute needed help with household chores. Kathy was tired of doing homework in varied venues and on the run. She detested causing disruption for friends and family.

She missed working on the *Mary R.* and being with Gary. Not a day went by without thoughts of giving her acting début a pass. Instantly, she'd think of those who worked so hard and long; they depended on her.

Two things kept her going: Ute was pregnant, and Kathy had a sister. The former remained a product of faith, but the latter was a certainty. Kathy had known since that eerie Thanksgiving visitation.

She spent much time in speculation. If Kathy was a baby on New Year's Day, 1974, then her sister must be a year older at least. She imagined her twenty or twenty-one. She possessed a wonderful name; Anka (her personal favorite) or Nikola. Then there was Andrea, Pamela, and Charlotte – all possessing musical resonance when pronounced the German way.

She proceeded to speculate over additional siblings. An older brother would be nice; two would be better. Before long, Kathy invented an entire family, including aunts, uncles, cousins, and an army of in-laws. These thoughts raced through her dreams.

Moreover, she knew of the upheaval in Eastern Europe and realized she might meet her real family very soon. People were stampeding out of the DDR. Was anyone left? It was a manifestation of trust when she told Gary of the ghostly, Thanksgiving figure. Gary mentioned it to Jayme who passed it on to Molly and Henry. Kathy remained blissfully unaware until…

Molly and Kathy enjoyed dinner with the Kuriharas. Kathy was at her ease. Mrs. K. was proud of her cooking and took pains to serve up tasty Japanese dishes whenever entertaining. Normally, the Kuriharas feasted on spaghetti, pot roast, or "good-old meat loaf." Whenever Molly came to dinner, it was Japanese fare right down to salted soy-beans for dessert.

Kathy enjoyed every morsel. Seldom did she know exactly what she was eating. Her policy was not to ask. With a minimum of coaching and spillage, she learned to use chop sticks. She wasn't as dexterous as the Kuriharas or, for that matter, Molly whose mastery made it appear as if she'd never eaten with anything other. Still, Kathy was proud to feed herself in so novel a way.

Eating noodle soup, Japanese style, necessitated slurping and only enough chop-sticking to guide the noodles. Shelly – as ever – was chirping about something. Her soup bowl remained on the table leaving both hands free to gesture. No matter which language she used, Shelly's facial and hand gestures screamed *American*!

Suddenly, Shelly ceased the exposition aimed at her parents and, switching languages, turned to Kathy.

"Wouldn't it be neat if your sister came to the show?"

Kathy took it well. She didn't explode, nor did she demand to know Shelly's intelligence source. Molly, however, suffered a coughing spasm.

She looked for strangers at school, during tennis practice, and at ball games and matches. Anyone entering the Fisherman's Inn was studied closely. Kathy examined every ticket holder stepping aboard the *Mary R.* Rationality told her it was senseless. There was no way her sister could find her or know where to look.

Leipzig

Heike heard a moan. Throbbing pain radiated from the back of her head. There was another moan. This one was more distinct.

Did she dare open her eyes?

No.

She wanted to lapse back into oblivion, where pain, the sticky dryness in her mouth, of her sense of loss lapsed. The image of helpless Nadine stabbed deep. A sob followed the next moan. It hurt.

She felt a disturbance. A sound alerted her, but it hurt to hear. She wasn't alone. Heike opened her eyes cautiously. It was dim. A faint light hurt her eyes; she closed them. Ages crawled before she tried again. A vaguely human blur appeared. It made a gesture – one from the movies.

She didn't move. It hurt to think. She smacked her lips, but no moisture came. Aridness overtook pain. She grunted. The blur moved quickly; this made her dizzy.

Heike closed her eyes in self-defense.

"Drink this," a voice whispered.

She felt something touch her lips. She opened her mouth slightly and felt liquid in her mouth. Some flowed over her chin and dribbled on both sides of her neck. She swallowed and greedily sought more.

It was tea.

It was room temperature and fruity. It was wet; she wanted more. Slowly, slowly, slowly, the liquid spilled down her chin onto her neck and chest. What got into her mouth was treasured. It slacked her thirst only slightly.

Suddenly, she experienced another pain – one usurping thirst. Heike tried to sit. Her body revolted. If she opened her eyes, she'd be lost.

"*Toilette*," a dry, husky voice croaked.

"This way," a male voice whispered in return.

Hands helped her to her feet. Heike realized she was naked; it didn't matter. Avoiding making a mess was her only thought.

One arm was around the neck of – someone. The helper steadied her and wrapped an arm around her. The pain brought a howl. Heike gritted her teeth, greedily sucked in air, and tried to ignore pain. Decades later, she heard a door open.

She was turned about and realized she wasn't completely naked. She heard the door close and managed, somehow, to free herself of the remaining impediment.

A torrent.

For one, blissful, moment, she was free of pain. She opened her eyes.

Thankfully, the room was dark. Then, pain returned with a vengeance. She had no strength to stand, and it hurt to sit. She squeaked for help. She reached out to steady herself. The cocoon-like walls were very near. She leaned right; her ribs exploded.

How long could she remain, consumed by pain, before she died?

Another voice, female, excited and angry – It drown a timid, male tongue.

"A pot from the kitchen, dolt! Didn't the doctor say not to let her out of bed?"

The door was flung outward. Heike caught a flash of light before sealing her eyes. Hands grabbed her. She was jerked, yanked, and pulled, nearly, to her feet. She was half dragged, half carried back to the bed where her head crashed against concrete. Another blinding light was followed by a surge of pain shooting through every nerve in her body.

Then, she experienced the welcome, back blanket of nothingness.

* * *

Her head was tender, her side throbbed. Natural light seeped into the room. After a rebellion, her eyes adjusted; she looked around. Heike did not dare to move.

She half saw, half sensed a young woman seated nearby. Her blond hair was woven tightly into twin braids. Her face was long and thin. She had a needle-like nose. Her mouth was too wide, but a cupid's bow compensated for this deficiency.

She was, by the DDR standards, attractive – slight of build with a proud, proletarian face. She'd appear at home holding a scathe among wheat stalks. This image was furthered by work pants rolled to mid-calf, a work shirt and brown work shoes.

"Good morning," the young woman greeted, softly.

"Morning?"

The woman produced an earthen mug from somewhere beyond Heike's ken. She held it towards her.

"Can you sit up, or should I help you?"

Pride dictated that Heike self-advocate. It was a struggle. Though her hands and arms responded, her ribs punished. During her struggle, the blanket collapsed in a heap in her lap. She experienced an unwelcome chill as the air caressed bare skin.

"I washed your clothes and mended them," the woman announced.

"I brought you something to wear in bed. Drink this and we'll get you dressed. Then, you must eat something."

It was purplish tea. She recognized the fruity taste. Her throat wasn't as dry as before, but wet was welcome. She drank in large swallows.

"Who are you?"

"I'm Jana," the woman replied, extracting a washcloth from a basin, and wringing it out.

No last name. That made her a reformer or, at least, a sympathizer. It explained why Heike wasn't surrounded by bars and uniforms.

She sat still and stoic while Jana dabbed a tender spot above the right eye.

"I cleaned you off as much as I could," she cooed. "You were a mess. We tried not to bother you more than we could help, so you're filthy, still. When you get some strength back, we'll see if we can shine you up."

"How did I get here?"

"That was Marco. This is his apartment. We were near the side of the street and the crowd pressed us up against a building when the Vopos marched in. They didn't stay together, you see. When the people ran, they chased. Soon they were spread out and we got away. Despite their training, they aren't used to real crowds."

"Who's Marco?" Heike asked, refocusing the conversation.

"Sorry, of course. Marco is a good Catholic boy with good Catholic values. Paul, my fiancé, thought we'd run for it before the Vopos could arrest us. Marco saw you. The Vopos, probably, thought you dead. Anyway, he insisted we get you out of there."

"Paul said he was crazy and started to run, but Marco went back and tried to pick you up. He does things without thinking, you see. I was cross with him last night when he put you in the closet alone. He's very coy."

"He carried me up here."

"Sorry, no. Marco is a wonderful person, but he is not physical. If he tried to carry you, you'd both be out there, still. It was Paul who picked you up. I stayed with him. Either we all got away, or we all got caught."

Heike finished the tea. Jana finished dabbing the wounded eye. Thankfully, Heike felt no urgent need to rush to the toilet. In fact, she'd not admit to it in any case. She wasn't using a pot from the kitchen.

"Marco's very brave," Jana concluded. "I guess it's a church thing. I don't know. I'm not religious. Are you?"

Heike shook her head carefully to avoid penalties.

"Anyway, Paul and I live in the Dragon's Tooth. You know it?"

Heike nodded. She'd never heard the nickname, but it fit only one building.

"We couldn't take you there," Jana continued. "We'd be reported. So, we brought you here. It was less risky."

Heike nodded again.

"They got my sister," she moaned. "I saw her dragged away. I came here to protect her. I don't care about reform. It wasn't my idea. Now, my sister is gone!"

To her credit, Jana did not try to lift the blame from Heike's shoulders. She didn't say anything. She allowed Heike to wallow in guilt.

"Hungry?"

"A little," Heike admitted.

"We have soup. It isn't good for you to eat anything ambitious after starving so long."

"Wh -- what do you mean?"

Jana hesitated for a moment.

"I guess you wouldn't really know. It's Wednesday afternoon."

* * *

Herr Doktor arrived in the early evening.

Heike was told he was a real *Artz*, but names weren't mentioned. Everyone was secretive. Heike was at their mercy, and she knew only first names. Her rescuers, however, had her papers. She didn't care since Nadine was injured, dead or in jail. If the students or the doctor turned Heike in, it was no less than she deserved.

The doctor had lush hair parted on the left side. His temples were sprinkled with a dignified gray; the remainder was healthy brown. He spoke reassuringly.

"It would be better to go to hospital," he said.

"You know why we didn't want that," Marco, slight of build and timorous of voice announced from behind his black-rimmed glasses.

He stood in the doorway. It was his apartment, according to Jana. Still, Marco was reluctant to enter the room when Heike was there.

"Of course, of course," the doctor nodded, never taking his eyes off his covert patient.

"You got a nasty whack to the head. I'd like to see x-rays, but I doubt there's any real damage. Had you a broken rib, I'd insist you go to hospital – risk of punctured lung."

Heike wasn't bold enough to examine her injuries, but she looked on as the doctor took inventory. Both her knees were swollen with an ugly scab forming on the right one. When he lifted the night shirt Jana lent her, Heike gasped at the soccer-ball sized bruise on her side.

It was ugly, black, and bordered with a sickening purple. She knew the doctor would prod her there and ask if it hurt. She breathed an audible sigh when he did nothing more than allow the nightshirt to resume hiding the nauseating sight. He did, however, poke the painful lump on her head. It hurt, but not much.

The doctor leaned back in the wooden chair and gave her wrist a reassuring pat.

"And this?" Heike asked, pointing to her eye.

"The swelling is way down," he assured. "It might bother you for a few days, but the cut is healing nicely. Is your vision blurred?"

She replied in the negative and earned a satisfied nod. He picked up a metal bread pan and handed it to Marco.

"You can get up and walk around in the apartment," the doctor assured. "If you feel dizzy, sit down at once."

Marco and Heike exchanged glances. By tacit agreement, they refused to inform the doctor that she'd been making her own way to the bathroom. Heike thought she'd end her life on the toilet that first, horrible, night. Since then, she suffered no problems save for the pain in her side.

"You're going to be fine," the doctor promised. "Don't lift hay bales for a couple weeks."

He intended this as a joke, but no one reacted.

"Can she eat?"

The Artz nodded to Marco.

"I dare say, she can eat anything you can fix, *but*," here he turned to Heike, "don't be a pig. Take it easy on your digestive system."

Heike would have nodded, but that would hurt. He left the room. Heike heard him say a few audible but indecipherable words to Marco. The door closed. A moment later, Marco was wreathed in the door frame.

"The doctor has tasted your cooking," she speculated.

"How did you know?"

"He doesn't think much of it."

He nodded but wasn't offended.

"Hungry?"

"Ja."

He began rattling things in the kitchen. His labor completed, he wanted to serve her in bed. Heike was tired of bed. She was unable to roll onto her stomach or either side, because of the discomfort. It hurt to stand and walk. It hurt to sit. However, she needed a change of posture.

The nightshirt didn't cover much, but Heike was beyond modesty. There was very little her bespectacled benefactor hadn't seen. To turn modest would magnify her embarrassment exponentially.

She was familiar with the steps between the bed and the toilet. That path comprised nearly a quarter of Marco's living space. The kitchen was a tiny sink and hot plate behind a tattered curtain. The living room consisted of a tiny couch, a wooden armchair, and a small coffee table.

Heike judged the furnishings predated the war. Moving anything would block the door. Books and papers were kept on high shelves. Any shelf of normal height would create a navigational hazard.

There was one small window in the sitting room, a similar one in the "kitchen," and an even smaller one in the bathroom. The light struggled through a gap between the window and an adjoining building.

It was obvious why Marco had no roommate.

She gingerly settled onto the couch. A determined person might squeeze in next to her. It would be companionable, but her tender ribs would pay the forfeit.

He brought a tray with two bowls of soup, some dark bread, a saucer with two cheese slices and a single egg in a cup. He set this largess on the coffee table and fetched silverware and two mugs of tea. Heike noticed, thankfully, that the tea was an inviting brown and not the purple variety she'd been drinking.

"I'm in your bed," she began. "Where do you sleep?"

"In the chair next to you for the first night," he replied. "When I move this table, there's room enough on the floor."

Heike couldn't visualize how it was possible. Even with Marco's diminutive stature, the challenge defied physics.

"I'll sleep on the floor," she announced. "You've done too much. I can't put you out of your bed."

"It's my apartment," he responded with unexpected authority. "I decide where to sleep. That egg, by the way, is for you."

She was too tempted to be gracious. A boiled egg was unexpectedly appealing. She reached greedily, only to be arrested by Marco's fit of gestures. He was doing his Catholic ritual. Heike decided it would be beyond rude to eat while Marco was doing – whatever he was doing.

The egg was undercooked. The yoke was gooey and some of the white was watery. After Heike's expectations, it was, almost, sickening. The soup came from a can or a mix. It was bland but, thankfully, hot. The bread was of poor quality as was the cheese.

"If you get an onion or two and a sliver of meat, I'll cook us something."

She wished she hadn't said it. She apologized at once. Marco, however, took no offense. On the contrary, he promised to get a few things in if Heike could cope unattended. He didn't want Jana scolding him again.

Her hunger satisfied, but her appetite ruined by Paul's culinary ineptitude, Heike leaned back and studied him as he finished his food. She couldn't help thinking he was demented. If he'd rushed into the street, intending to carry her to safety, Marco had no respect for reality. The longer she studied him, the more she was convinced she'd a better chance of carrying him – were she healthy.

He caught her staring but made no issue. He inquired about her thoughts. Heike didn't wish to share. However, her mind returned to a haunting theme.

"The police have my sister. She was bleeding."

She relived the horrible vision until she could stand it no further.

"I'm not a reformer. I'm not a counter revolutionary. I came to keep my sister out of harm's way. I was useless. The moment she needed me, I failed."

Marco was hardly stoic. He was moved but refused to share in her remorse.

"If you knew what would happen, you'd have stayed home?

"Nein!" she hurled with resentment.

Marco didn't shy. He gestured with an upturned palm as he swallowed some food.

"How can you feel guilty if you admit you wouldn't have behaved differently?"

"That's a fair question," she admitted. "I haven't told everything."

He was all ears. It was strange, but Heike sensed he wasn't one to repeat her narratives.

"I – I knew I was going to die. I could feel it. I was glad. Isn't that the most selfish thing? I thought only of myself. Me! No thought about my sister. I should have been thinking of her. She was a reason to live – to hang on! I've read of people who were given up for dead, but they recovered because they had something to live for. There I was, feeling happy to die. How can I ever forgive myself?"

To her astonishment, Marco's reply was instant.

"There are two answers," he began with calm authority.

"The first answer is that you're human; you're as frail as the rest of us. You admitted there was nothing you could do, so it's natural that, under stress, you'd think of yourself. You were in pain; you'd been knocked in the head; your brain scrambled. You weren't yourself."

"That's an excuse," Heike said, coolly. "That doesn't make it right."

"It isn't a question of right or wrong. It's a condition of nature."

Heike cast a curious look. He'd introduced an avenue of speculation worth attention. She didn't believe herself a vile person, but she refused to embrace the first glib philosophical argument to come her way.

"You said there were two answers."

"God's will," he replied.

Later, she prided herself on exercising restraint. She rejected superstition, the basis of all religions. However, there was no doubt that Marco believed. It was bad enough to fail her sister. She'd not compound her failure by scoffing at the beliefs of a man whose food – for want of a better word – she'd consumed.

Oregon Coast

Dressing room was the designation for a table and a collection of mirrors behind two heavy black curtains. The men's "dressing room" was a less spacious but more private; it had a functioning door. When female cast members performed quick changes, the recessed area was as private as a display window. Nobody, save Kathy, expressed qualms over the arrangement. To avoid being labeled a prude or, worse, "the kid," suppressed her inhibitions.

She took her first-scene dress from the rack, threw back the curtain and entered the refuge. Working to minimize the time disrobed, she dawned her costume. After, she folded her jeans and sweatshirt, she stowed them in a shopping bag. The bag fit under the makeup table.

When Debbie slid around the curtain, Kathy presented her back. Zipping up dresses was one of the thousand tasks Dee executed backstage. During performances, the actresses would rely on each other.

Kathy didn't like wearing stockings. No matter how careful she was, she damaged them. Ute bought replacements, but money didn't grow on sea foam, so, Kathy rehearsed without stockings.

Molly thought the issue of falsies was silly. It was part of the acting experience. Kathy remained contentious. It mattered not that Mrs. Waldron sat in the front seat next to her daughter. She'd heard Molly and Kathy exchange councils before and never betrayed confidence.

Mr. Waldron was not so reserved; he never threw the girls' conversations into the public domain, but he offered observations and advice from time to time. When this happened, Molly reverted to her expected role as the perfect, gracious daughter. These time-consuming performances inhibited the conversational flow.

"Miss America I ain't," Kathy acknowledged, "but I'm comfortable with what I am…"

"You're Popeye the Sailor."

Kathy wanted to slap her. The one-time Molly decided to crack wise, and Kathy wasn't receptive. To touch the driver, however, was sure to put an end to the taxi service.

"Sorry," Molly appended, feeling an arctic wind from the back seat. "Still, it's only a play."

"So easy for you to say, Miss Perfect Figure."

"Ah!" Molly took one hand off the wheel to hold up a warning figure, "Let's not get into Barbieland again, pal. You'll be walking home. And, I don't have a perfect figure."

"There speaks a minority of one," Kathy pouted.

"Didn't you ever put on your mom's clothes when you were little?"

"No," Kathy declared defensively. "Did you?"

Molly turned coy. She never invaded her mother's closet. In a very real sense, her mother got into Molly's.

Kathy sulked. They were five miles from her home, and she realized she was sulking like a baby. However, Kathy was looking for strokes and getting none. It was particularly galling that Molly was everything Ed Geist looked for in a supporting actress.

Then, a spark lit from within. There was one thing Kathy brought to the production which Molly lacked. Despite her charm and looks and athletic prowess, Molly couldn't sing. Well, not as well.

Kathy entertained fantasy.

She imagined her sister (Anka or Monika or whoever) arriving, exhausted and destitute, at Uncle Dieter's home. There, she'd obtain sustenance, a set of clothes and the hearts of two young boys. Where, she'd ask, was her sister? She must see her.

An older sister, an accomplished and resourceful woman, searched for her. There were many things she must learn. She would need someone on whom to rely. Kathy would be there for her and help tame the tempestuous waves of a strange, new land.

Kathy's epiphany was she didn't *need* pampering. Rather, she needed a sister who recognized Kathy was a fool. They'd shout and argue. In the end, however, sisters are sisters forever, like "perfect" Molly and "rebellious" Jayme.

"Why are you smiling?"

Molly had adjusted the rear-view mirror. In the light of a passing car, she found an incongruous expression.

"Ssshh! I'm dreaming."

Leipzig

Heike examined the neatly folded shirt Jana placed near her bed. She wore the trousers Jana had cleaned and mended but retained Jana's nightshirt; it afforded greater comfort. Nevertheless, she'd change into her shirt to seek news of Nadine. Heike was tempted to walk into a police station and ask.

Alas, she promised not to leave the apartment. She'd broken a promise to Nadine; she didn't intend to compound this by breaking more promises. Jana, Paul, and Marco risked their safety for her. She could not betray their confidence. Heike must begin keeping her word, despite the misery she courted.

She returned to the living room. Marco left strict instructions to remain in the rabbit hutch. Heike Jacobs was ready to scream or surrender her mind to the same malevolent spirit which had stolen Anne's.

Where were they? What were they doing? Did the classes at uni go on as if nothing were afoot, or were the trio of street protesters holding a plenary session amongst others of their ilk? What was the difference to a young girl craving occupation? Worrying about Nadine magnified her disquiet.

She grabbed a textbook from a shelf. Her ribs protested. She sat panting, waiting for the pain to ebb. Eventually, she opened the book and learned more about civil engineering than she wanted to know. It was dull, tedious reading, but it kept her mind out of the abyss.

There were noises in the hall. She paid little attention. There were always noises in the hall. This time, however, the footfalls paused outside the door. When someone knocked softly, her stomach knotted.

"Heike."

She didn't recognize the voice. It was a low, whispered, male voice. Marco had a key. He didn't knock.

"Heike, it's Paul. Jana's friend."

She took a chance. She padded to the door and drew back the bolt. A man entered quickly and closed the door behind him.

"Jana said you need something to read."

Heike relaxed and examined a tall, burly man. She judged he could, likely, carry Heike and Marco together. He wasn't particularly handsome, but he was certainly no ogre.

"All Marco has is engineering, math texts and the Bible," she reported.

He stuck one large hand into a pocket of his work trousers and pulled out a slender volume of Kleist. She accepted it with gratitude. It was not Shakespeare, but it was not a treatise on energy coefficients either.

"I'm glad to meet you, at last," she stated, after expressing her thanks.

"We met Monday evening," he reminded. "You threw up on me."

She averted her eyes.

"Yes, I am sorry, of course, but I didn't intend…"

He was about to say something more, but Heike blocked him.

"Any news of my sister?"

"I'm afraid not, and I really have to run. I hope to be back later."

"I look forward to it."

He nodded, slipped out the door and was gone. Heike bolted the door and waited for silence before opening the book.

She read, but she couldn't hold the thread of any story. She thought of Nadine and the chaos which must have descended upon the Jacobs home. Mutti would sense something. Rolf must be *very* angry. That was to be expected.

Though concerned about the back of his hand, she was not afraid. All her fears were reserved for Anne. Someone should be with her. The guilt gnawed, worked its way up her spine, and curled up in a painful knot at the base of her neck. It diverted her attention and energy. Try as she might, she read three of the short stories without comprehension.

Heike had failed. She failed Nadine; she failed Anne; she failed her country. She failed herself. If she were dead, who would care? Her life had directed her to one critical moment on a Leipzig Square. Nadine needed her; Heike failed.

What could she have done? Heike never addressed that. Instead, she was obsessed with the image of Nadine being dragged away. If only Heike got to her, there would have been options. Inspiration or reflex would produce action.

If nothing more, she'd be sharing in Nadine's fate, but – a promise broken. Nadine disappeared behind a black curtain leaving Heike tortured by ignorance. Had she been arrested; she'd know the extent of Nadine's injuries.

Marco returned with a backpack stuffed with notes, a calculus text, and eclectic food samples. Heike examined the items set out on the tiny counter near his hot plate and realized she could be useful.

"Any word?"

She asked for want of anything better. She sensed rather than saw Marco shaking his head. Any news would be shared without prompting.

"Jana is on her way," he mumbled.

Heike's heart jumped. The young woman tended her as Marco could not. Marco was a jailer. Jana was a Genossin. She found herself waiting anxiously for a break in her confinement.

When knuckles softly trilled on the door frame, Heike rushed carelessly. Jana, in coat, skirt, sweater and tights, slipped inside quickly. She panted for breath. Heike thought she had information. When Jana pulled the woolen hat off without speaking, Heike's heart broke – again.

"It wouldn't come amiss for you to get some air," Jana suggested.

Marco wasn't keen. It was too easy to observe Heike leaving and entering. More importantly, he wondered if the doctor would endorse Jana's proposal.

"Everyone knows you have someone in here," Jana reminded.

The diminutive student made a face. Jana unbuttoned her coat but did not remove it.

"He thinks the neighbors assume he's keeping his sweetie," Jana informed Heike. "But everyone knows he's a nice Catholic boy who isn't about to risk Hell with nights of sexual frenzy."

Heike didn't pretend to understand. Marco, however, turned bright red. Jana displayed a satisfied smile. Even in her moment of triumph, she wouldn't allow him to suffer. She gave him a friendly, reassuring pat on the shoulder.

"If anyone squeaked, the Vopos would be here," she assured.

Marco conceded the point with a nod.

"There are some people who provide a good example," Jana concluded.

"I don't know anyone who shares Marco's beliefs, but everyone respects them. When he does something, it's because he wants to; not because he gains by it. It's easy to overlook his eccentricities."

Marco blushed.

"Get dressed," Jana urged.

Heike replaced the nightshirt in an instant. Her ribs ached when she twisted, but pain no longer mattered.

"We could go by the church," Marco suggested.

Jana was willing. Heike, meanwhile, looked forward to being anywhere else.

Marco procured a cap for Heike. It was old and ratty.

"In case we go in the church," he explained. "Women are expected to wear a cover inside."

Heike couldn't know Marco referred to his brand of observance. It meant nothing to him that the Nicolaikirche was Protestant and had been since the Reformation. Heike took the cap. She tacitly agreed to carry it but wouldn't wear it unless instructed.

It was a thirty-minute march under normal conditions. Heike, however, fatigued quickly and begged to rest periodically.

"I'm sorry," she uttered, her knees quivering.

"Something to drink?" Marco asked.

Heike shook her head.

"Let me rest."

There was a quick discussion about returning to the apartment. Heike protested. It was a joy to be in the open air. Her escorts, apparently, had no pressing engagements. They urged Heike to take all the time she needed.

To excuse her loitering, Heike asked Marco to tell a little about himself. She regretted it; he seized the opportunity to go on about his religious upbringing. Between encapsulations of the history of Catholicism in the DDR, he revealed that he was a farm boy from an area just south of Leipzig. The runt of the litter, he was no match for his elder brothers and sisters in the rigors of farm life. Fortunately, from an early age, he displayed cerebral proclivity and was singled out as a scholar.

Marco and his eldest sister were the family's only university attendees. The sister married and became a village post mistress, though she still lent a hand during harvest. By the time his narrative ended, Heike was bold enough to renew their journey.

"Where do you come from?" Heike asked Jana.

"*Amerika,*" she reported offhandedly.

Heike was standing when this explosive revelation clapped. She nearly sat again but recovered in time. She turned to Jana and discovered a mischievous smile.

"She says that to everyone," Marco informed. "She likes seeing people react – like you just did."

"Amerika is a village not far from Karl-Marx-Stadt," Jana explained.

"Yes," Marco nodded. "Jana, however, does not come from either place."

"Why do you have to spoil my harmless little game?"

"Harmless? It's a lie."

"Not everyone has your unyielding rules of veracity," Jana reminded.

There was an air of tension for a moment. Jana opted to dispel it.

"No, Heike, I do not live in Amerika, but I live close enough to cycle there frequently. Amerika is on a river; Amsdorf is my village."

She took Heike's arm. The longer they walked, the more Heike leaned on her. Perhaps, they should have turned back, but the injured girl relished the open air. Heike recognized the Dragon's Tooth, a high-rise designed as a monument to the design and technical skill of the DDR. Heike thought it looked silly.

Marco and Jana pointed out the scene of the disturbance. Since she was one of thousands, and since she concentrated all her attention on

Nadine, Heike recognized nothing. They passed through the area where Paul hoisted Heike onto his shoulder. She looked around for traces of blood and urine testifying that Nadine Jacobs was there. She found only the emptiness in her heart.

Still, they walked and walked. She and Nadine got nowhere near the church. The throng must have been large, indeed, to keep the Weimarians far removed from the edifice. At last, they arrived. Heike was highly fatigued.

They decided not to attempt entry but passed on to a spacious square. There, they settled onto a bench. Heike gazed upon the imposing building, mourning for Nadine. Her sister would have liked to see the object of their quest. Heike, however, felt nothing. For her, it was just one more building.

Marco left the young women to fetch them something to drink.

"Paul carried me all the way to Marco's?" Heike asked in wonder.

"Not directly. We stopped several times to make certain you were breathing. We had a heated debate about taking you to hospital. Marco wouldn't hear of it; you'd be arrested. Paul feared you'd die, but Marco – well, how does one explain Marco?"

"His superstition?"

Jana nodded.

"At least, he believes in something," Heike sighed. "Once, I believed in my country. Now, I don't believe in anything."

"You believe in loyalty to your sister," Jana corrected.

"And the sacrifice of my family," Heike amended.

If justice existed, Heike would have been left in the street. The Vopos would have taken her. By turning her back on Rolf and Anne, Heike earned the worst fate could offer. She failed to protect Nadine; she failed her duty to the family. If she had worked harder, if she had lived the words of Werner Ecke rather than just repeating them, if the socialist ideal resonated in her soul as well as in her head – maybe, she could have kept her country alive.

Alas, she was not left to fate. A Catholic boy took up the cause of a stranger. Aided by confederates, she was spirited out of danger. They hid her, nursed her, and fed her, even after she repudiated the reformers.

How do such people exist? How can they place themselves, their future, and their lives in jeopardy for Heike, a failure?

She placed her head on Jana's shoulder. The blond didn't protest.

"I guess," Heike moaned, "there is one thing I can believe."

"What?" Jana asked, hopefully.

"Freundschaft."

The Oregon Coast

The sky was overcast; the ocean churned. The air was clear and brisk, and the wind gusted with autumn effusiveness – benign in nature, ominous to the timid. Kathy wasn't there for the Saturday, inland, tennis match. She didn't regret being left behind. The pleasing October day on the Pacific would sure to be chilly and rainy beyond the coastal range.

She should be at the theatre, helping the cast and crew put the final touches on the set. After hammering a finger and splashing paint on herself and others, Kathy realized her aptitude for set construction was counterproductive. Though an extra pair of hands was welcome, her great work-day contribution was staying out from underfoot. Moreover, the ocean was too inviting, and a wedding party had booked a cruise.

Ed Geist ended the cosmetic crisis with a gracious retreat. He'd experienced many shows flirting with utter ruin right up to the opening curtain. He wouldn't panic over the apparent disarray on the eve of opening week. Kathy's participation far outweighed the advantages of her departure. She wasn't a featured player, but her brief scenes delighted both cast and crew.

"You're a volunteer," he reminded. "If it isn't fun, step back."

Set work was not fun. Steve, Dee, Ed, and several others reveled in it. Kathy opted to enjoy herself elsewhere.

It was pleasing to reflect upon the theatrical events of the past few days as the *Mary R.* smacked against the ocean swells. The wind was inviting, the salt spray intoxicating, and the motion of the boat was soothing to body and soul. Not everyone, however, was as comfortable on the churning sea. Hardly had they gained open water when the groom leaned over the rail. Her efforts to soothe her husband of four hours were unsuccessful and the bride – perhaps out of sympathy – made it a duet.

Kathy tried to hide her mirth. She'd fallen victim to rough water often enough to know there was nothing remotely funny about it. She rinsed the sides of the *Mary R.* with salt water. Fetching it in a bucket without losing it to the sea or being yanked overboard required skill born of experience.

After a few minutes, the bride and groom sat on the covered portion of the deck, looking at nothing with pin-point pupils and ghostly complexions. Aside from the fact that they were exhausted and feeling much worse for the heaving of the ocean, they were as well as anyone in such circumstances could be. Though not at death's door, they probably wished they were.

Then, something happened. Kathy had her back turned and saw nothing, though she heard much. One of the wedding party lay on his side and struggled to get up. Seeing blood, Kathy rushed for the first-aid kit. Upon her return, the victim sat on the bench in the middle of the quarter deck. He appeared to be in good condition despite the blood swabbed up by a handkerchief.

"Kathy!"

Instinctively, she looked to the bridge. She expected another catastrophe. Instead, Aaron motioned to her. She pointed at the injured passenger. His response was to motion again, emphatically. Even on the tiny *Mary R.*, the captain was the captain; debate or hesitation constituted mutiny. She scrambled up the ladder.

"Take the helm," he instructed, grabbing the first-aid kit, "I'll do this."

She obeyed, but she was pained. She knew and practiced first aid both in the county hospital and in the Coast Guard station. She was certified. Unexpectedly, her father disqualified her. It hurt, but he was the captain. She vowed to have words with him later.

"Steer for the outer marker," he ordered. "Call out when we hit the channel."

He was gone.

Kathy stood alone on the bridge wondering why she wasn't allowed to do her job. Had Aaron panicked over fears that Barker might get slapped with a lawsuit?

She hoisted herself into the captain's chair and gripped the arm rests to prevent unexpected swells from pitching her overboard. She slipped her feet into the spokes of the helm, just as she'd seen Aaron do often enough, and brought the *Mary R.* onto her new course. She looked over her shoulder periodically to measure the response of the stern. Mostly, however, she watched Aaron at work. She'd provide a critique later.

They ventured north of the bay. Kathy spied the outer channel buoy in the distance and predicted a quarter-hour run. She knew the tide was coming in and took that, and the stiff wind, into account. She crabbed into the wind to ensure a seaward arrival.

Once she set a course, Kathy spent more time watching the scene behind and below. Aaron wasn't in any hurry. After dressing the wound, he engaged in light banter with is patient and others in the party. The wind and engine noise prevented her hearing. If Aaron Foster was concerned about the conning of the *Mary R.*, he made no show.

The buoy was only a few hundred yards ahead. Kathy grew impatient. She wasn't supposed to be at the helm. If Barker found out, the air would be blue for weeks. If the Coast Guard found out, Aaron, Barker and Kathy might find themselves sharing a cell. Still, Aaron remained unconcerned.

"Channel marker!" Kathy bellowed.

"Take us into the channel," Aaron shouted back.

"What!"

He repacked the first aid kit. He interrupted this activity long enough to shoot Kathy a cold glare. When his hand made a pushing motion, Kathy turned all her attention to piloting. Convinced that Aaron Foster had lost his mind, she found herself with plenty of sea room, exactly as she planned.

She brought the *Mary R.* gently to port and watched the buoy to better judge the speed and distance. Satisfied with a favorable position, she increased the turn. The bell affixed to the buoy clanged merrily in the choppy water. She observed the stern swing in relation to the wake. Aaron had disappeared. She assumed he went below to stow the kit.

Satisfied with *Mary's* motion, Kathy kept the helm over until the bow pointed directly at the narrow entrance of the bay. Kathy kept her eyes welded on it. She clearly saw the channel buoys on either side; she was in no danger of straying. The motion of the entrance in relation to the bow provided an accurate reading of wind and current. Detecting the drift, she crabbed, gently, to starboard.

She felt sweat trickling down her back. They were near enough to land for spectators on the bridge to be identified by gender. If the wrong person noticed Aaron Foster absence from the helm, things could get nasty. She added power and allowed the bow to steady on. The two massive rocks loomed larger and larger as did the plumes of ocean spray created by angry waves.

Where was Aaron? He couldn't expect her to attempt passage through that narrow, dangerous gap. A single misjudgment and the *Mary R.* would be smashed. The passengers, even in life vests, would be hurled against the rocks. A miracle might deliver two or three. Kathy, however, would be thrown clear on impact and crushed between the rocks and what remained of the hull.

It was dangerous to lay to. They were too near the shore; the boat might wallow onto the rocks. Even if it didn't, she might drift out of the channel and into dangerous shallows. Kathy had to bring the *Mary R.* around for the safety of deep water until Aaron Foster recovered from his coma.

Her left hand was on the throttle. She readied to "pour on the coal" when Aaron's voice arrested her.

"I'd better take," he yelled over the wind and noise.

He'd been standing behind her! He clutched the back of the chair; she hadn't noticed.

She vacated the seat as if shot from a cannon.

* * *

It was late afternoon. The *Mary R.* was secure in her berth and the mariners Foster were seated at a table in the Fisherman's Inn. Despite working the counter, Athena came by to flirt. She excused her trespass by bringing two steaming mugs of coffee.

"I don't get off for another two hours, mates," she teased.

"Maybe, we can have an early dinner here," Aaron suggested. "It would save your mother having to feed us."

"Ya jus' wanna be close to me," Athena grinned.

"Yeah," Aaron nodded "That's another reason."

Though Aaron and Ute thought Athena's flirting funny and harmless, it bothered Kathy. She toyed with her mug, momentarily. Athena tarried.

"What do we have to do to get waited on around here?"

Athena responded to the brusqueness by retreating to the counter. A moment later, Ute appeared with one menu.

"I know what you want," she told Kathy while handing the menu, including the daily specials, to her husband, the *Captain*.

"I'll fix you dinner when we get home," Kathy promised.

"Unless you want to eat here with us," Aaron suggested.

"I work here," Ute responded with a long-standing joke, "I ain't eatin' this slop."

"Tuna casserole?" Kathy asked.

"With corn and peas?"

"Sure."

"Yummm!"

Ute hurried to another table.

Aaron tossed the menu aside.

"Hot roast beef sandwich," he announced.

"Again?" Kathy asked.

"Don't start. You haven't eaten anything in here but oyster sandwiches for two years."

"My birthday dinner," she reminded.

"Other than that."

Ute was on her way to take her husband's order when she caught his pantomime. She nodded and retired to the kitchen.

"When that guy got hurt this afternoon, I got to thinking," Aaron began. "If something happens to me, you'd have to bring *Mary* in."

Kathy looked at him incredulously.

"I'd use the radio and call the Coast Guard," she assured. "It would take only a few minutes for a rescue craft to reach us."

That was the standard emergency procedure drilled into Kathy since her first day on the boat.

"In a *real* emergency," he insisted.

What, she wondered, was he trying to say? She knew he was nervous about getting Ute to hospital when the time came, but if he wasn't available, Mrs. Rademacher was a phone call away. Everyone had a part in the emergency plan. What possible circumstances would Kathy face that didn't include Coast Guard assistance?

"Tell me," he began. "Could you bring *Mary* through that entrance in a sea like today's?"

She never contemplated such an eventuality. It was dangerous, sure, but no less dangerous the hundredth time than the first. Aaron made the passage the first time. Kathy studied his handling of the boat; she often knew what Aaron would do before he did it.

"Yes," she announced boldly.

Aaron nodded and patted her shoulder. For him both the subject and his concern vanished. For Kathy, however, the worries began. What did Aaron know that she didn't? Why would she ever operate the *Mary R.* without proper papers?

As if she didn't have enough to worry about.

Leipzig

Once, and only once, Marco asked how long Heike intended to stay. It was his apartment, his bed and there was hardly room for one; it was a reasonable question. Heike was mobile. Though tiring quickly during their brief excursions, she was fit enough to travel. Her family would be concerned, and Heike must inform them –

"Let me stay until Monday."

Marco was too polite to press.

Paul and Jana were proactive. They guarded Heike's papers during her convalescence. She couldn't travel without them. Neither could she stay in Leipzig without them. Harboring an undocumented person would put Marco in jail.

At the first sign of improved health, Jana returned the documents. She and her fiancé had information enough to make guarded inquiries through surreptitious avenues. Marco and Heike lingered at a café long enough to enjoy a cup of coffee and a pastry. Heike desired to loiter; she enjoyed fresh air and the freedom. Returning to Marco's broom closet would amplify restlessness and mind-numbing boredom. Behind these tortures lurked guilt.

Back in her cell, Heike lay on Marco's bed. The more she slept, the fewer waking hours she'd agonize over Nadine.

There was a rap at the door. Heike didn't stir. If it were one of Marco's friends, they'd carry on without her. If it was the authorities, there was nowhere to hide.

She recognized Paul's voice. She listened to a hushed murmur of voices ending in silence. Heike realized something was afoot but remained still.

"Heike."

Her eyes popped open, and she saw Jürgen framed in the doorway. The image alone blurred her eyes with tears. She sat up.

"It's my fault!" she bellowed.

He took her hands and helped her to her feet. Heike wept and spewed forth hurried, blubbering apologies.

"The only reason I came was to be here for her," Heike blubbered. "I'm useless."

"Heike, please."

"It's my fault!" she insisted.

Paul was as uncomfortable as Jürgen at the shameless scene.

"Why are you here?" she asked, her voice considerably subdued.

"I came to take you home," Jürgen replied, calmly.

"I can't go home," she moaned, tears flowing.

Jürgen suspected she would adopt such an attitude. He was distraught at seeing Heike in mental and physical pain. He could not lie by saying everything would be fine. It was obvious that everything was wrong.

Paul looked upon Jürgen with an undisguised look of contempt. He and Jana went through a tedious and time-consuming process to find him. Jürgen was obliged to care for his sister. They could have saved time and trouble.

Although he was most uncomfortable with his unexpected role, Paul got his arm – very carefully – around her. He guided her through the door and onto the couch.

"Why can't you go home?" he asked, since no one else would.

Heike gained control over her gasping and blubbering, but her tears remained copious. She made no effort to wipe away a steady stream running down her face.

"How can I ever face Rolf and Anne?" she asked of Jürgen as if Paul were invisible.

"How can I return without Nadine? She's their flesh and blood; I'm just a lodger."

Paul cast a curious look at Jürgen.

"You can't hold yourself responsible for what happened."

"What good is that?" she demanded. "It should have been me! Who am I?"

Marco, propped up against the frame of the kitchen cubical, exchanged a wide-eyed expression of amazement with Paul. These four eyes then drifted onto Jürgen.

"I do not hold you responsible," he replied. "Pabst won't either."

"But I do! How can I ever look at them again?"

"Look at me, Heike," Jürgen demanded.

She shook her head. She turned away.

"What will you do?" he demanded with agitation.

"I have to go tomorrow – to the church. I have to be there because Nadine can't."

Jürgen sighed again.

"And after?"

"I don't know," she admitted, "I can't go home. I can't face them."

"Mutti and Pabst need you."

"Jürgen, please! I cannot justify myself. Nadine and I left together. It was a mistake to take me in. They cared for me all these years, so I could stand helpless while Nadine –"

She coughed and gasped.

"You can't stay here."

"I won't. After tomorrow, none of you will have to see me again."

It was too much for Paul. His anger against Jürgen had diminished while his anger at Heike was growing by leaps and bounds.

"Three people risked a lot to peel you off that street," he reminded. "Don't you dare tell us it was for nothing! You have a duty. If you don't care about yourself, respect the people who do."

Had Heike anywhere else to go, she'd leave. She must be at the protest the following evening. Beyond that, her future was void.

* * *

When Jana arrived, she found her fiancé with his arm around Heike, hiding her face in his shoulder. Across from them, sat a stranger who, she assumed, was the brother from Halle. Squatting in the space remaining was the diminutive Marco.

With nowhere to stand or sit, Jana leaned back against the open door. Whispered introductions were made and, predictably, Jana's eyes reflected awe over the presence of Werner Ecke's grandson. Jana leaned forward and shook his hand.

"I've heard of Werner Ecke all my life," she said. "I'm honored."

She then nodded toward the silent and morose figure clinging to her intended. Marco and Paul shook their heads in unison and took turns whispering Heike's history. She, additionally, learned of the hysterical scene she'd missed.

"What are you going to do?" she asked of Jürgen after sliding down the door into a squat.

"I know better than to try and make Heike do something," he replied. "She might throw herself off the train."

Jana looked over at Paul. They didn't cuddle and purr as Lilo and Günther once had, but they were much closer. They did not need to speak to communicate.

"So," she concluded, "we go to the rally."

The agreement, though tacit, was unanimous. Eventually, Paul cleared his throat. Jana pulled Heike up by the arm. She half led, half pulled the girl into the bedroom and closed the door. They sat down on the bed.

"This is serious, Heike," she warned. "Last week, Vopos busted heads. This week, they might shoot. The government's been hinting all week."

"If they shoot me, it puts an end to my shame," Heike responded. "You don't seem afraid."

"We feel we can make a difference," Jana reported. "We aren't going to get killed; we're going because it's the only voice we have. Your sister felt it was worth the risk."

"Look what it got her. She may be dead."

"If she's dead, your family would be informed. Jürgen would have heard."

"And she isn't my sister."

Jana pursed her lips for a moment.

"I don't know her, Heike," she noted. "Do you suppose Nadine would say that about you?"

Jana was a poised young woman who possessed all the qualities and confidence of a simple, if intelligent, farm girl. Yet, as she spoke with such calm, Heike recognized a devious side. Jana scolded so deeply that Heike feared to speak for fear of initiating further opportunity to scourge her lacerated spirit.

Minutes later, a bold knock announced Herr Doktor's arrival.

The females stood simultaneously. The door opened; they could greet the man who had little hope of entering. He asked Heike how she felt and what she'd been eating. She responded tersely but honestly. She sensed he desired one last look at her injuries, but that was impossible without an evacuation. No one was inclined to leave.

"I think you'll be fine," he pronounced. "Just don't exert yourself for a few more days."

That would have constituted a perfect exit line. His departure would allow the assembly room to breathe. However, he lingered until every eye searched for an explanation.

"You should know," he said, finally. "The hospitals are alerted to expect casualties."

Heike could not see Jana's face, but she could see the look Paul sent her way. They realized that their spring wedding might not come to pass. The doctor quietly closed the door. The assembly listened until his footfalls no longer echoed in the hall.

"You can spend the night in my room," Paul told Jürgen. "I have a roommate, but there's place to sleep."

Jürgen silently accepted by standing. With nothing further to discuss, they started through the door.

"Jürgen?"

He turned to find Heike. After not looking at him directly since his arrival, she focused on his eyes. She squeezed around Jana, Marco, and the furniture. She slid her arms around him. She rested her head on his chest. Taking her cue from Jana, Heike communicated, like Jana and Paul, through silence.

He hugged her back before following Paul down the hall.

Heike expected Jana to hurry after her fiancé, but she remained to give Marco words of encouragement and advice. He nodded.

They all knew a largely sleepless night lay before them.

"You'll be doing a lot of thinking tonight," Jana addressed Heike. "I hope you find the answers you're looking for."

"Maybe," Marco suggested, "we should meet up tomorrow afternoon for a meal."

"Hmmm," Jana pondered. "A last supper?"

The allusion was not lost on him.

"God's will."

Jana and Paul normally took perverse delight and scoffing at Marco's superstitions. This time, however, she wasn't in the mood.

"We shall see soon enough," she responded.

Again, the door closed quietly.

* * *

The venue was a perfect place for a pre-slaughter feast. It was cavernous, dimly lit, and the atmosphere reeked of conspiracy. Both Jürgen and Heike knew it as the setting for a scene in Goethe's *Faust*. For that reason alone, it was eerie. For Marco, Paul, and Jana, it was a preferred haunt.

Many times, they, and several comrades plotted with impunity. Even with Stasi surrounding their table, the acoustical qualities made it nearly impossible to catch guarded words sliding across polished wooden surfaces. As an historical landmark, it attracted many foreign visitors. The government took pains to ensure that the food was high-quality while the prices reflected DDR levels.

The management, however, recognized students and eagerly unloaded food of questionable quality or – in some cases – items that had lingered too long. Jana and Paul habitually discouraged normal student fare by entering the cellar speaking French or English. Once, they risked Russian and were served a particularly inedible meal.

That Monday afternoon, they dispensed with pretense. The group had very little appetite. They each ordered a light meal and beer. They ate slowly and without enthusiasm; there was no conversation. From time to time, one offered up a thought or observation, but there was no discussion.

After lingering an hour over beer, a waiter cleared the table. Heike came to life and ordered a coffee. As if roused from a deep slumber, the rest of the party followed suit.

"You know," Marco began over coffee, "we could go home and wait."

Everyone nodded agreement.

The coffee finished and the bill settled, they sat in silence. One by one, over the course of several minutes, they visited the toilet. Heike made two trips. They might be standing for hours. She couldn't repress the image of Nadine's bladder failure; Heike hoped to avoid a similar humiliation.

Eventually, the matter could be postponed no longer, and five comrades climbed the stairs to street level. Unexpectedly, Heike found herself in the lead. She walked through the dark passage toward the street and waited for the others. Together, they set off with purpose towards Karl Marx Platz. Heike foolishly hoped she'd find Nadine waiting for her.

Soon enough, Heike's legs wobbled, and her strength ebbed. Jana took her left arm and Jürgen her right. Heike descended into a fog of fatigue. She heard the crowd chant, "*Wir sind Das Volk!*" several times, and she felt the crowd surge from time to time, but she was past caring.

Jana remained a buttress on her left and Jürgen a bulwark on her right. She waited for the shooting. She wished for it! If shots were fired and people fled, she'd sink onto the stones and lie quietly.

It must be horrible to be trampled to death, but it required no energy. If a bullet ripped her open, it should be quick. Whatever fate awaited, she hoped it came instantly. It hurt to stand; it hurt to breathe; it hurt to lean; it hurt to listen. She dozed several times only to wake whenever her head fell forward. Jana and her brother struggled to keep her vertical.

She didn't realize they were moving. She was awake, yet she dreamed. She noticed people around her, smelled their woolen coats and recognized the color of individual fibers. She heard people speaking, arguing, and shouting. Then, suddenly, she was lowered to a sitting position. Ethereal people vanished. There were several knots of citizens moving away, but the mass of humanity had dissolved.

"It's over," Jana announced in a whisper.

"I didn't hear shooting," Heike protested.

"There wasn't any," Jürgen assured. "I think we may have won."

"Won?" Heike protested. "Where's Nadine?"

The resulting silence stabbed her.

Weimar

It was late afternoon. The train squealed to a halt. Heike thought of remaining aboard and losing herself in Erfurt. A sense of duty forced her to step onto the familiar platform. Her ribs throbbed momentarily from the jolt.

She waited for the platform to empty, then descended the steps into the tunnel and headed for the exit. When she neared the Mitropa Café, she stepped inside. She hoped to find Nicole. Perhaps, over a cup of coffee, she might gain insight into local events.

Alas, there was a surly man and an unhealthily thin woman tending customers. Perhaps, Nicole had the day off. Perhaps…

She quickly exited and made her way onto the street. The sun danced across the cobblestones accompanied by the autumn chill. Heike stepped into the zebra crossing. She hoped a taxi or a speeding Trabi would save her the walk. Escaping unhurt, she plotted the longest course to the Jacobs's abode.

She paused frequently to regain a portion of her flagging energy. Heike should have known. Now that she depended on rubbery legs and burdensome fatigue, her body refused to surrender. Her ribs ached, but this minor annoyance could not excuse additional wayside rests.

Amazed by sudden stamina, Heike altered course and quickened her step. Fearing the sight of a familiar face, she must get home quickly. The sooner she arrived, the sooner her aching would subside. Thoughts of Nadine blurred her vision.

Her steps took her out of the way until near the *Schloß*. A tributary street emptied onto her familiar lane. She squinted into the descending sun. The familiar house quietly awaited her.

With a display of courage, she stepped to the door and inserted her key. It opened effortlessly; Heike felt the eyes of Anne Jacobs upon her. A smile spread across the face of the woman. Simultaneously, the bathroom door swung open. Heike was amazed to find Hanna, cleaning cloth in hand, peering at her.

Of course, when the Jacobs daughters vanished, Hanna took it upon herself to care for the house and its mistress. Anne got to her feet and moved sedately toward the kitchen. Heike was glad. Maybe, Anne's addled brain could not properly register narrated events, but it was better for the nerves that her adoptive mother removed herself.

"I lost her," Heike croaked.

Hanna blinked. She ducked back into the bathroom for a moment and reappeared without the scrub cloth.

"You look a fright," she replied. "Sit down."

Heike closed the door solemnly and took tentative steps into the room. She'd no right to be there. Hanna, ever perceptive, extended a welcoming hand and helped the guilty party to the sofa. Heike, knowing what was in the offing, shook her head and sat at table. Hanna pulled out the chair opposite and settled in.

"You were in Leipzig?"

Heike nodded.

"We heard there were more than a hundred thousand. Not official news, of course."

"I don't know. I don't remember much."

"Are you hurt?"

Heike nodded.

"Last week. They took Nadine. We got hurt, and the Vopos took her."

Hanna didn't press for details.

"We've heard nothing," she informed.

If Jana was right, no news was the best news.

"Pabst must be roaring."

"He's been very quiet," Hanna corrected.

Rolf would do nothing to cause Anne alarm or discomfort. Still, he'd be boiling. It would prove ill had the errant daughters returned together. It would be a million times worse for Heike only.

"I had no intention you should take over –"

The girl shook her head and rapped knuckles on the table.

"I'm proud to help." she interrupted. "I'm proud of you. Nadine, too."

Heike fought for control. She felt bad about Nadine being held incommunicado while she, the self-appointed guardian, returned – the only survivor of a shipwreck. No one would question her courage and second guess her actions more than Heike herself.

She was to blame for Nadine's beating and arrest. She knew how the girl dreaded captivity, humiliation and, perhaps, torture. If residual actions resulted from Nadine's detention, Heike would bear the burden. If only she'd been quicker, stronger, more vigilant –

If only –

She planted her elbows on the table, wove her fingers, and rested her head upon them. Tears threatened renewal, but she fought against them. Anne must not see her in distress when she brought the hot cocoa.

Oregon Coast

As Molly and Henry grew more serious about one another, Kathy found
the time she shared with her closest friend decreasing. She didn't object,
of course, but she did miss Molly's company. Kathy would devote more
time to Gary, but theatre rehearsals interfered. With Molly and Henry
off on their own, Kathy orbited around Shelly and Jayme. It was obvious
that the trio would be short lived, as Shelly expressed interest in a boy
who lived close by.

Jayme spent her time plopped – in impossible postures – before the
TV. She claimed to miss the levity and silliness she and Shelly shared.
Kathy wasn't obtuse. Jayme was interested in a classmate who, until she
turned sixteen, was strictly off limits.

Leaving Rapunzel, *nee* Jayme, staring at an electronic screen with
thoughts centered on forbidden fruit, Kathy wandered upstairs to assist
Mrs. Waldron. Raised on a farm, Mrs. Waldron was well-organized and
efficient. With Kathy's aid, they had time to spare. They dallied over a
leisurely cup of coffee before firing up the stove and oven.

"You know Honecker's been sacked?"

Coming from the north of Germany, her English acquired British
influence.

Kathy nodded. It was clear that the DDR was, quite literally, falling
apart. Her focus, however, wasn't trauma in the ruling party, but the
flood of refugees. Uncle Dieter couldn't keep atop the influx. If Kathy's
sister managed to escape, it could be months, or years, before her identity
and whereabouts were known.

Her hostess fathomed the reason for Kathy's silence. She'd not force her into conversation. Nor would she prod her into eating. She objected, however, when Kathy played with her food.

Henry was at the table also, so Molly's dinner conversation was top form. Even the morose Jayme lit up over the clever repartee. Kathy, however, possessed a heavy, iron tongue.

"Kathy," Molly prompted, "you don't mind our missing dress rehearsal?"

It was too much effort to formulate a sentence; she shook her head. Molly and Henry opted for a movie.

"I'll go," Jayme announced.

The elders balked. Molly would go solo for the first time. Risking both offspring was tempting fate. The tomboy, without becoming abrasive, pleaded her case successfully. Molly got out of the car and gave Kathy a reassuring hug.

"Break a leg," she bade.

Somber Kathy thanked her. She and Jayme watched Molly and Henry drive, carefully, away.

Kathy sighed.

"Here goes nothing."

"Nervous?" Jayme asked.

"Yeah."

She lied. Kathy was anxious about events half a world away. She'd rather be parked in front of a television, Jayme style, waiting for news. To express herself truthfully, that she was not the least nervous, would be interpreted as a show of bravado. Susceptible to pre-match nerves, Jayme could believe her, so Kathy took the path of least resistance.

It was too crowded in the dressing room for Jayme to watch the transformation from flat-chested teen to social sophisticate. Instead, the girl wandered about the house and watched people dress the stage. Ed Geist flitted here and there making terse comments and dispatching orders. No one thought to close the curtain; it was, after all, only a rehearsal.

Friends and family began arriving. They constituted audience enough. Jayme had little interest in monitoring strangers. She didn't notice Gary until he sat next to her.

"How'd you get here?"

He gestured to the aisle; Jayme discovered Athena and the Fosters taking seats in the next row. Athena and Ute shared a carefree banter which, soon, grated Jayme's nerves.

At last, ten minutes after the announced start, the curtain closed. A team of elephants stampeded prior to Geist's appearance. He and his clipboard parked in the center of the sparse assembly. In due course, Debbie and other musicians took their places in front and to the left of the stage.

Fifteen minutes late, the overture began, the curtain opened, and the audience was drawn into a domino effect of minor mishaps. Within ten minutes, Jayme was squirming. By the time Kathy, literally, waltzed onto stage, it was all the tennis phenom could do to keep burying her head in her hands.

Somehow, the cast stumbled into the intermission without stopping, though they had opportunities enough. As the curtain closed, Geist left his clipboard and headed backstage. Three of the musicians melted away leaving Debbie seated at the piano as if afraid to venture behind the curtain. There was noise as scenery was shunted about.

"I don't think this is exactly what they intended," Jayme announced for want of something better.

"Kathy's doing okay," Gary offered, defensively.

"If you say so," Jayme *almost* said.

Gary was more biased than she, but – aside from her singing – Kathy was devoid of life. Why Steve Davis, Gary or any boy would be attracted to her stage persona was a mystery. She made a mental note to come down with a serious malady Saturday night. That would free her from this torture. She was embarrassed for the cast – especially Kathy – for being trapped on the *Titanic*.

When the play resumed, the bumbling resumed. After a few minutes, Jayme examined the toes of her shoes. She longed for a bucket of balls to practice her power serve. Algebra homework would be more entertaining.

Finally, the sacrilege in the temple of Thespis was complete. Jayme breathed a grateful sigh of relief. Even Gary slid down in his seat and relaxed after the strain of a death-grip on the arms of his seat. Athena and Ute, so cheerily effervescent before, were ominously silent. No one bothered to close the curtain. Debbie ended the finale with a ramble down the keys which, even to the ears of a novice, had no place in the score.

Silently, the cast came out of their hiding places to stand uncomfortably under the stage lights or sit on the apron to hear the sentence of the presiding judge. Geist turned and looked up at the control booth, a glassed-in promontory just above the last row.

"Bring up the house lights," he yelled.

"Do you want us to bring down the final bank?" a muffled voice asked.

"Do it!"

In a moment, the lights above the audience's head came on and the stage lights dimmed. The sudden reduction in illumination caused Jayme to squint. She saw Henry and Molly sitting in the last row. At least, she had a ride home.

The cast, solemn and contrite, awaited its fate. Geist studied their faces for several moments before studying his clipboard. There were four pages of hastily scribbled notes.

"Why go over notes?" he asked in a voice which had no right to be calm.

"There's no point in telling you what you know."

Debbie, the silent Buddha at the keyboard, rubbed her nose. Her hands returned to her lap, and she looked at something miles away.

"A bad dress rehearsal means a great opening night. Get a good night's rest; look over your lines; be here at six o'clock."

No one moved. It is likely nobody would ever move. When Ed marched up into the control booth, however, the spell was broken; the cast began to melt away.

"We'll take Kathy home," Aaron announced quietly to Molly.

Jayme's sister nodded. As always, there was a smile on her face. Jayme, however, knew every shade of that smile and recognized the pain behind it. If the cheery, optimistic Molly found no refuge in hope, the rehearsal must be worse than Jayme imagined.

Kathy was as lethargic when she appeared in girlish form once more.

"I'm tired," she confessed.

"You can nap in the car," Ute suggested.

As they departed, Ed was coming down the aisle on some final, futile mission. The Fosters and the Swoffords were the only congestion in his path, and he didn't wish to seem brusque; he paused to exchange greetings. Inevitably, his eye fell upon Kathy.

"Don't hurry that kiss," he reminded. "Remember, you're in love. You look at Steve as if he had rabies."

Kathy nodded but remained mute until the party of five crossed a nearly deserted parking lot.

"The only damned note he gives all night, and I get it!" she blurted.

"Kathy!" Ute and Aaron responded in unison.

Suddenly, devoid of all feeling, Kathy retreated once more into silence.

* * *

Molly dropped Kathy at the theatre. Her intention was to wish her luck and exercise her newfound liberty by dropping in on Henry. Later, she'd return and drive Kathy home.

Once at the theatre, however, Kathy didn't get out. She didn't refuse, but she didn't move. Molly sensed her friend's increasingly morose behavior. Her buoyant personality failed.

"The play won't perform itself," she said, for this once, without a smile.

Kathy memorized spots on the windshield. Finally, she reached for Molly's wrist.

"I can't go in there alone."

"Geist will throw me out," Molly responded.

"He wouldn't dare. Crazy as it sounds, he needs me."

Molly caught the spark in Kathy's eye.

Molly opened her door. The moment the keys came out of the ignition, Kathy exited. She took one long, deep breath of the salt-laden air and satisfied herself that she could face the firing squad. No longer alone, Kathy had courage.

The moment she opened the stage door, she felt a surge of electricity. She expected to find panicked people snapping at each other and moaning over the previous night's disaster. Instead, she found Debbie seated on a worn couch chatting merrily with the leading lady. Both women greeted Kathy with toothy smiles; neither objected to, or questioned, Molly's presence.

Suddenly reassured, Kathy led Molly to the stage. They passed the men's dressing room. The door was open; neither could resist a peek. Stretched out on the floor, was Steve Davis humming softly and leafing through a worn copy of his script. Nearby, another cast member calmly ironed a shirt.

Kathy and Molly exchanged smiles.

In the wing, they discovered the stage manager with a property list. She smiled and nodded at Kathy while continuing her placement of items on the prop table. The girls crossed backstage by a narrow, carpeted causeway built to facilitate rapid movement with a minimum of noise.

In the wing, stage left, they found a smaller prop table with the items neatly arranged from left to right in the order they'd be taken on stage. The stage floor had been repainted, the scuff marks and scratches of the night before were buried. Moreover, the stage was immaculately dressed and ready for the first act.

Another exchange of smiles

Kathy led the way into the house and up the aisle. In the lobby, she found Ed Geist in a tailored white suit, red tie, and black, highly polished shoes. He spoke quietly with the light engineer about scene changes. Both smiled and exchanged witty remarks.

"There she is!" Geist smiled at Kathy's approach.

"Ah, Mr. Geist –"

"Please," he interrupted, "I think you can call me Ed."

No, she couldn't, but she appreciated the gesture. She motioned to Molly whose smile matched his.

"My friend has tickets for tomorrow," Kathy began, "but, maybe, she can stay for the show."

Molly was no stranger. He'd seen her often at rehearsals. However, he hadn't seen Molly up close. She was as attractive at arm's length as she was in the shadowed recesses of the rehearsal hall.

"Ed Geist," he said, extending his hand.

Poised as ever, Molly offered her own.

"Molly Waldron."

"Nice to meet you at last," he nodded. "You drive Kathy home."

"Yes, sir."

"Come with me."

Kathy and Molly followed in his wake across the lobby. He stopped at the public entrance and rapped at the glass of the ticket booth.

"Where's Jeff?" he asked of the empty lobby.

"On my way!" An echoing voice responded.

"Must be in the light booth," Ed shrugged.

A moment later, a younger man in a sport jacket and striped tie appeared.

"Jeff," Ed took Molly's hand and drew her forward. "This is Molly Waldron, a theatre supporter. Give her the best unreserved seat in the house."

"With pleasure," Jeff replied.

"This young lady doesn't pay for the duration of the run."

"Understood."

Ed turned back to Molly.

"Enjoy the show."

"Thank you, ah – Ed. I shall."

I shall? What was Molly reading? In the end, it mattered not. She'd made a favorable first impression on Kathy's boss; he, in turn, made clear his appreciation. Kathy's request properly attended; Geist drifted away to examine the programs arriving with another volunteer.

Jeff, the ticket manager, slid into his cell to check available seating. Unable to put off her gargantuan costuming any longer, Kathy bid her friend adieu with a warm smile. Everyone was so relaxed and unconcerned; it was a pleasure to be a member of the group. If the cast sensed disaster, they disguised well.

Kathy Foster arrived with jumbled nerves; the casualness of their pre-show routine banished her morbidity. The dancing pair who, the night before, made a mess of their featured solo, chatted about mundane matters while stretching. It was as if this was just another rehearsal.

The leading lady, who missed two cues the previous evening, chirped with Debbie about her two-year-old's mischief. Kathy wanted to review a page of dialogue with Steve, but he was engrossed in talking about sport fishing with two of the crew. She abandoned her quest.

Slipping on pantyhose and stepping into high heels, Kathy, too, transformed. There was unmistakable energy backstage, but it was controlled by a cheerful, devil-may-care attitude. Twice, Geist came around to remind them to quiet down; people were in the house.

Eventually, the ghost called the cast and crew together. He had everyone circle and join hands. He squeezed the hand of the person to his left who transferred it to the next, *und zu weiter*. As this energy circulated through every person, Geist quietly and calmly, provided last moment encouragement.

"You know the show," he reminded. "You've rehearsed it; you've sung the lyrics. It's all there. Now, you're going to share your hard work with the people. Remember, the audience is on your side."

The hand squeezing continued around.

"The papers are here tonight," he warned. "If they take a flash picture or two, don't get flustered. Keep your concentration and keep the show moving. Kathy is the rookie, so we leave the energy with her. Kathy, when the squeeze comes around, keep it."

When the person next to her squeezed her hand, she stood mute and still.

"Got it?" the theatre director asked.

"Yes."

He lifted the hands of those on either side of him and, instantly, everyone else followed suit.

"Break a leg!" Geist encouraged.

Everyone echoed the words in a group whisper.

When the circle dissolved, Kathy went to the couch. She carefully smoothed out her dress and settled down. Taking advantage of the time remaining, she slipped off her shoes and let her body go limp.

"Places!" the stage manager hissed.

"Places!" three cast repeated.

Debbie and Steve embraced and kissed. She smiled and said something. He nodded and said something in reply, and Dee made her way out front. The overhead lights went out. Save for a light in the men's dressing room and another behind the curtain of the women's, the wings and backstage areas were illuminated with small blue lights strategically placed. Save for the need to see where one's feet landed, there was no longer a need of light.

Ed Geist went before the curtain and made a short welcome speech. After cautioning the patrons to smoke, drink or eat only in the lobby, he invited them to enjoy the show. This earned an ovation. When the applause died down, Debbie banged out the introductory chords of the play's first number.

Steve came over in his suit and bow tie. His highly polished shoes glistened even in the dull blue light. He sat next to Kathy.

"Ready?"

For the first time in over a week, the smile she awarded was genuine.

"Yes."

"Nervous?"

"A bit," she admitted. "Excited, too."

He returned her smile.

"I've been doing this for years," he confessed, "This is the time I enjoy most. I have all this energy and excitement waiting to get out."

"I feel it, too," she admitted.

"The trick is, don't finish the night with leftovers. Leave it all on stage. If you're not dead tired at the end, you haven't given enough."

She shrugged.

"I'll try and remember that."

They sat quietly and enjoyed the music and the singing. There followed bits of dialogue, eliciting appreciative laughter from the audience. The second scene began. Steve and Kathy listened to the familiar lines. They looked at each other over a tangled line, but someone jumped in and covered. The audience, likely, remained unaware, but the cumulative heart rate backstage spiked momentarily.

The play advanced without any additional, audible gaffs until Steve roused himself.

"Better get to work," he whispered.

"Break a leg," Kathy responded automatically.

"See you in a few minutes," he reminded, setting off for his first entrance.

Most of the cast that were not on stage remained crammed in the wings for several minutes. Satisfied the play was not unraveling, they filtered backstage.

"It's a good audience!" the leading lady whispered to Kathy on her way to change.

Kathy, suddenly cautious, put on her shoes and started stage right. She was early. She did not dare go into the tiny, high-trafficked space. She found herself pacing in small circles.

When her time came, Kathy took three deep breaths and let them out. Assured of the right-of-way by her entry cue, she boldly mounted the steps and moved to the prop table. The tiny handbag was exactly where it always was. She knew the lipstick was in the bag – she'd checked, but she checked again. This task completed, she stepped back to await Steve's arrival.

He ignored her and headed for a towel. It dangled from a peg on the wall and Kathy never noticed it before he snapped it up. Sweating profusely, he dabbed his face cautiously to minimize damage to his makeup. He fanned himself for a few seconds before replacing the towel. Finally, he found Kathy waiting patiently as she always had during rehearsals.

There was a strict prohibition against speaking in the wings, even in whispers. Neither Steve nor Kathy would dare risk the ghost's ire; all communications were non-verbal. Steve looked questioningly at her. She nodded and, amazingly, smiled. He invited her to dance.

She slipped into his embrace clutching her bag on his shoulder exactly as rehearsed. The heat from his body radiated through her. It made her uncomfortably warm. Everything was pre-arranged. He'd count three with a subtle movement of his left leg; on four, they'd dance.

When they got on stage, they'd initiate a turn; he'd navigate for her as she backed. If performed correctly, they'd miss the two couples dancing in the opposite direction. When they swept onto the stage, Kathy closed her eyes and allowed him to steer. She was hardly aware of the audience. There was Steve and four other people on stage; that was her universe.

Kathy spoke immediately on cue as trained. She enunciated carefully and made herself speak at her normal rate. She projected her voice. There followed uncomfortable moments when the audience exploded in laughter. Steve didn't say his next line immediately; she quaked, fearing he'd forgotten it. Instead, he waited for the laughter to peak and proceeded. Kathy's line was funny, but after rehearsing it countless times, the humor evaporated. The performance went swimmingly. Twenty-four hours before, no one did anything right. Suddenly, they could do no wrong. It was impossible for Kathy to escape the spirit setting everyone aglow.

Steve serenaded her; she turned to spurn him. All the while, she must show the audience her love for him. When left alone, the music continued and out came the dancers. Kathy stood in place and shared amazement with the audience as the limber team danced and contorted impossibly. Upon completion, the audience exploded with enthusiastic applause forcing Debbie to improvise on the piano.

Steve returned to finish his serenade. Kathy cut him off in mid-sentence and made a sharp speech. Steve's response was to take her in his arms. That was the point at which Kathy's character succumbs to her own desires and kisses him. On this night, a sudden anger burned within. Kathy pressed her lips against his and maintained the pose through piano chords trilled on.

"Is this long enough, Ghost?" she thought.

Steve broke the trance. He paused, dramatically, spoke his last line and left Kathy alone with three hundred people.

For reasons unfathomable, Kathy stretched forth an arm, begging his return. She held the pose as she sang her one sentence solo then, again, without understanding, she brought her empty arm slowly back.

Fade to black. Curtain. Applause.

Geist and the light technician conspired to bring up a tentative change light when the curtain closed. After several minutes under the blaze and tropical heat of the light banks, Kathy had no chance to adjust to near dark. She inched her way off the platform. Save for the show, she never wore heels; for her own safety and self-assurance, she descended on her toes. Once on the level surface, she found the exit from memory.

Thankfully, the lights backstage came up for the intermission. She removed her shoes before confronting the steps to the dressing-room level. She needn't have bothered. The meaty hand of a scene changer was offered; she accepted it.

"Very nice," he congratulated.

She thanked him and hurried to change. Intermission was fifteen minutes. That was more than enough to change, but she would not push her luck. She ducked behind the curtain and peeled off her dress to wiggle into another. Four other women, similarly engaged, jostled for room while exchanging comments about the audience.

From a distance, Ed Geist's subdued voice was heard.

"What's he doing here?" A dress-changer asked.

"It's his theatre," Kathy reminded.

"He never comes in until after intermission," another actress informed. "He likes to schmooze the newspapers and eavesdrop on audience comments."

Kathy dressed. The evening was, so far, a delight. If the Ghost wanted to climb up on the roof and bark at the moon, it was nothing to her.

The women helped each other with zippers and minor adjustments. As Kathy caught a glance in a mirror, she saw someone's hands untangle the collar of her dress and make it right. She thanked her helper though she never knew who it was. She stashed her first act shoes in a safe, out of the way place and fetched her second pair. These would go on only when places were announced.

The couch was full, but Kathy was too hyped to care. She plopped down on the nearest arm. Almost immediately, the Ghost materialized.

"Where did this come from?" he asked, mimicking her hand gesture.

"I'm sorry. I won't do it again."

"Please do. It worked," he assured.

"Really?" she asked, sensing sarcasm.

"We tell a story, right? We don't just sing and talk; we communicate with actions. You told a story with that gesture. It nearly knocked me over."

"Really!"

He reached out and patted the incredulous girl on both arms and moved on.

* * *

After the curtain call, Kathy rushed to change. Most of the cast cooed and congratulated each other on a great show. Some made plans to retire to a quiet venue to enjoy a late dinner and spirits. Kathy wasn't hungry and unlikely to be admitted to a bar. Her place was at home, the longer she tarried, the later Molly would get home.

She bid hasty good-byes to the cast and crew she encountered on her bolt for the exit. She returned every congratulatory wish sent her way. The bracing autumn breeze greeted her. It was a balm after the roasting stage lights. She filled her lungs.

Molly was nearly bowled over. Kathy didn't see her standing near the exit. They avoided tumbling onto the asphalt by clinging to each other. Once equilibrium was recovered, they hugged.

"That was super!" Molly congratulated.

"It was fun!"

The morose, taciturn schoolgirl of the previous several days was suddenly a gurgling fountain of joy. She related anecdotes, observations and waxed lyrical about her emotional metamorphosis that evening. By the time they were halfway home, she realized her throat was parched and her lids were heavy; the adrenaline rush ebbed. Kathy Foster recalled what Steve Davis said to her as they waited to go on. Only then did she realize how much energy she'd expended.

Molly took advantage of the sudden lull.

"At the end of the first act. What you did with your arms. I heard a woman sitting in front of me sob."

"Really?"

"You didn't do that last night."

"I just – It just happened. I felt – weird and – it just happened."

Molly let it sit for a few moments.

"Steve didn't make you feel that way."

"No."

The answer was both immediate and emphatic.

"That was for your sister, wasn't it?"

For nearly three hours Kathy's emotions roared in high gear. What she felt at any given moment registered in her face, her voice, and her body. It was artificial, yet natural. The audience responded, Steve and the other people on stage responded, just as she responded to them. During her very brief solo, Kathy was awed by the voice she heard.

Her emotions created a gesture she never knew existed. It was eerie, but it came as naturally as the thrill of salt spray. Molly's words, so calmly registered, crawled into her ears and exploded amid her residual emotions. Her fatigue was great; she was defenseless.

It was her turn to sob.

Weimar

Despite Hanna's protests, Heike resumed the daily chores. Anne sat serenely by watching as if nothing had happened. However, Heike was alone in a house not rightfully hers. With Nadine missing, there was no excuse to be in the childhood home of Anne Ecke.

How would Rolf react when he discovered his flesh and blood was needlessly sacrificed at the altar of brutality while an interloper returned? When Herr Jacobs entered late that afternoon, he discovered his wife seated next to Heike, gripping her hand. The blood in Heike's veins ceased flowing; she looked into the wrathful eyes of the patriarch. Seated with Anne, Heike feared neither Rolf's words nor his touch.

The expression on his face, however, made her shrink. If she were very lucky, she'd roam the streets seeking sustenance and somewhere to sleep. If she got what she deserved, Heike would never see the dawn. Rolf glared at Heike until his breathing normalized. He mounted the stairs and moved heavy tread above them. He knew he'd not find Nadine in her room, but...

His malevolent eyes burned Heike's retinas upon his return. He didn't speak; there was no need. Rolf's only daughter was ripped from the family and the wretched excuse for a human being, responsible for Nadine's abduction, clung to his wife's protective side.

The silence continued through Abendsbrot. Heike knew, eventually, she'd must surrender Frau Jacobs. The moment that happened, she and Rolf would go for a "walk." Heike preferred to go sooner rather than later.

There was nothing Rolf Jacobs could do to her that she didn't deserve. It was much better if the matter was dispatched quickly.

Heike kissed Anne good night and negotiated the stairs slowly, on unsteady legs. She opened the door to Nadine's room and flipped on the light. She closed it. This would stoke Rolf's temper when he came for her. However, if Anne came to bed and found the door open, she'd sense something amiss.

Heike leaned against Jürgen's bed. It was exactly as Nadine made it on the morning of their departure. She imagined she smelled Nadine. Finally, she looked at Nadine's former bed – just as Heike made it up on that fateful morning.

Heike, the *Nameless*, stood alone.

She waited; Rolf did not come. She heard husband and wife come up the stairs together. She heard the door across the landing close. She listened to every movement, every squeaking floorboard, and every muted sound. The noises stopped.

Only when she heard Rolf's snoring did she move.

Heike sank to her knees at the foot of Jürgen's bed. This was not in thankful relief at her temporary reprieve. Rather, it was born of bitter helplessness. There was no justice in being alone in that room. There was no reason for her to remain in the house.

It was not her idea to return; Jürgen demanded it. She kept her promise to him; it was her duty to submit to Rolf's revenge. For several minutes, Heike considered returning to the Bahnhof. Then what? She had hardly enough money to get to Apolda.

Even that pitiful amount of money was not rightfully hers. She could, of course, sleep at the station until the Vopos objected. She'd shiver in jail – as did Nadine. She was too tired and too cowardly to think. She'd allow Rolf to force her hand. In the meanwhile, she'd sleep.

Heike had her first opportunity to sleep in Jürgen's bed. That wouldn't do. How could she betray Nadine and collect a reward? Similarly, she couldn't sleep in Nadine's former bed.

Heike switched off the light and sobbed. She fumbled to the far end of the room. She settled onto the cold floor and diagnosed, yet again, her inexcusable failure.

* * *

Rolf found her the following morning shivering on the floor under her coat. He did not speak; he closed the door and went downstairs. Heike awaited his return. Not until she heard the putter of the auto did she investigate.

Anne sat at the table with a steaming mug of tea. She smiled at Heike who forced herself to return it. There was hot water in the kettle, so Heike made herself a mug of tea and grabbed a slice of stale bread. When she sat down in her place, she discovered a twenty-mark bill under the sugar bowl. Anne paid no heed when Heike took it.

What terrible fate did Rolf have in store? Clearly, he expected her to handle the household chores and the daily shopping. There would be little time for herself, but that was only fair. After all, had she taken care of Nadine, they'd be sharing the work. Her negligence dictated her own punishment.

After sweeping the floor and scrubbing the stairs, she washed the dishes, cleaned the kitchen, and started on the bathroom. She left when the shops opened. Promising Anne, who could not understand, that she'd finish the bathroom later. She left during the morning chill to bring bread in house.

Momentarily, she thought of school. It would take but a few minutes to check in, but she dismissed the idea as a needless waste of time. Heike Neman was adrift on a lonely sea. There was no Jürgen or Günther to guide her, no Nadine to watch over, no Heiko to tease her with his broad grin, no Hanna in whom to confide, no Frau Willing to mentor. She thought again of Nicole and recalled her absence from the Bahnhof Café.

Had she, too, fled to the glitz and glam of the West?

Heike never thought to ask Jürgen about – things. Nicole recommended Heike question him, but Heike's mind was consumed with Nadine. Suddenly, the matter became imperative. When Rolf arranged circumstances to his liking, Heike would be homeless. If she starved or froze to death, she'd earn just deserts.

There was, however, a faint glimmer of hope that Heike had a family. She'd never forgive her parents for trying to steal her from the country she loved, but that country was falling to pieces, and Heike must belong.

What if her brothers and sisters were in the West? If the DDR ceased to exist, Heike could swallow her hatred for the West if – and only if – she found a sibling. In return for a blood relation, Heike Neman would endure even the depravity of the West.

Heike could not renounce her socialist ideals. They were the nutrients of her spirit. Even emersion in the capitalist exploitation could not destroy her socialist roots. So long as the memory of Rosa Luxemburg and Werner Ecke remained alive, Heike Neman would advocate to her last breath.

Her roots and her being might turn to dust. To exist, Heike required someone bound by blood. She could, and did, dream of living out her days as Frau Neubert, but that, too, was gone. When (if) she bore children, Heike's blood relations remained her only anchorage. Despite feuds and petty differences, family ties cannot be severed.

To exist outside the Jacobs family, Heike must find her siblings. Above all, Heike needed to be needed. She marched through her marketing with determination. She survived the drudgery of her chores, ignoring her physical pain. She could never repay her debt, to complain or entertain thoughts of self was unforgivable.

Abendsbrot was silent. Anne, though, showed signs of disquiet. By tacit agreement, Rolf and Heike feigned a placid atmosphere. Should Heike speak, it might prompt a discharge of hate and recrimination.

As she cleaned the dishes, she heard Rolf's heavy tread on the stairs and wondered if he was removing her clothes from the family shrunk. Would he throw them onto the street, or would he stuff them in a sack for her to take? Such a dramatic scene would be spoiled by Heike's meager belongings. Many of the clothes she wore were Nadine's. Further, she realized her paltry belongings represented Rolf's labor; therefore, she had nothing of her own.

The kitchen was cleaned, Heike discovered Rolf next to Anne on the couch. He didn't look up from his paper as she crept, cat like, around the table and into the bathroom. She made a hasty evening toilet and had a quick wipe around before slinking up the stairs. She was exhausted and in pain. All she wanted was sleep, despite the dreaded dreams awaiting her.

She paused before the shrunk and gathered courage to open it. There, hanging where she had left it, was her heavy coat. She took it into the room with her. The previous night, she shivered for hours and snatched only infrequent naps.

Heike felt her way to the far side of the room without the light. When she knelt, she was amazed to discover something. Panicked, she quickly felt to make known the unknown. Tears streamed down her face.

Rolf had every reason to hate her. Regardless, he'd crawled into the attic and brought down her sleeping pallet and a heavy woolen blanket. Additionally, he left her a pillow and a down comforter.

Weimar

October 19, 1989

From the couch, her refuge of tranquility, Anne Jacobs studied the lower end of the staircase. She heard Heike's scrub brush, saw movement though most of the girl remained beyond her view. There was a timid knock at the door.

The scrubbing ceased; nothing moved and no further sound was heard. Wearily, Heike came slowly, cautiously, down the steps. She wiped her hands on her kittle, leaned forward, and listened. She looked questioningly at Anne to discover expectant eyes urging her on.

Seconds ticked away. Had there been a knock? Heike thought she heard one. Anne's expression implied she'd heard it. A bolder, more impatient knock was expected, but nothing came. To put Anne at ease, Heike opened the door, expecting emptiness. She was startled by a frightening specter.

A person in tattered clothes, tangled hair and a disfigured face glared at her through red-rimmed, bloodshot eyes. The thin, fragile shape stood on the cobbled street, an emaciated shell. The creature's skin was jaundiced and bruised. A single tear raced down a sunken cheek.

"Forgive me, Heike," the figure croaked. "I was wrong."

Heike, unable to move or think, stood dumb. Asking this sickly person to identify itself never crossed her mind.

It approached. Sinking to its knees, the "creature" embraced Heike's legs. Panic surged. Disquiet was compounded by Anne's approach. Unable to escape the leech, Heike feared some loathsome contagion.

Anne leaned over and pried the gorgon's arms from around Heike.

"Come. Sit," Anne said quietly.

The wretched being seized the hands of the deranged woman.

"I'm sorry, Heike," the creature moaned, struggling to rise. "I'm so sorry."

Tears indicated life, but the voice was hollow and motor skills were lacking. Anne's arms supported the "thing" and drew it into the house. Heike wanted to protest the intrusion but could muster no voice. She watched, dumbfounded, as Anne helped the form to the table.

The poor woman's fogged brain mistook a street urchin for an acquaintance. How did this tattered creature know Heike's name? Against her instinct, Heike went to her seat at the table and curiously eyed the vaguely sentient being.

Anne doted on it and stroked the filthy hair of straw. The brute responded by taking Anne's hand, kissing it with deformed lips and pressing it to her hollow cheek. After several, silent moments, Anne shuffled off to the tiny kitchen.

The being, whatever it was, kept its face turned aside. When Heike strained for a better look, the thing lifted a battered hand to shield her visage.

"I didn't want it to be like this!" a throaty voice growled.

"In the streets – I went – back. As soon as they let us go – I had to. '*Wir sind das Volk*' we chanted. You heard?"

Heike gulped.

"*Ja. Ich gehört.*"

Slang. Heike was too stunned to speak properly. However, conversing might placate this ominous presence.

"We were – out there – chanting – we, when – I heard, them, Heike. Scheiße! They – they were shouting *Wir sind ein Volk*! That was – I – walked away. I want no part of it."

The dry voice struggled through the confused narrative. Aside from its grating voice, the person experienced breathing problems. All the while, the hand not hiding the face, waved pointlessly in the air.

"I am so sorry," the voice muttered once more.

The figure folded its arms on the table and buried its head upon them.

Berlin, DDR

November 9, 1989

Günter Schabowski entered the International Press Center exhausted. There was precious little time to rest. The DDR was in turmoil. With each passing day, more and more people joined street demonstrations. Days before, Berlin was the location of the largest rally in the history of the nation.

Nearly a million people chanted, marched, and carried banners without the sanction of the SED. Indeed, the swelling crowds gathered in open defiance of authorities. Honecker's resignation placated no one. On the contrary, the people's list of grievances and demands increased. The reformers insisted on real elections featuring candidates opposed to the SED.

If the party didn't reform drastically, and instantly, the people – by sheer weight of numbers – would destroy it. The entire Politburo resigned. Willi Stroph, the Prime Minister, and Erich Meilke, the despised Stasi chief, were gone. Both men sought foreign residences.

The "new" Politburo was smaller. Günter Schabowski was one of its members.

He was a large man with a high forehead, protuberant eyes, and thick hair which he kept swept back. Along with the other members of the party elites, he was working thirty-eight-hour days to return the SED to a solid foundation. There was much shouting but little time to argue.

Schabowski acquired, among a myriad of other duties, the job of party spokesman. He faced the cameras of his nation and the world. There was a meeting of the Central Committee that day, but Schabowski was busy elsewhere. Regardless, it was his job to brief reporters on the stormy committee meeting. He hadn't time to read through the sheaf of papers pressed into his hand; he didn't like that.

In former times, no SED member met with the press before every syllable was analyzed and discussed in detail. Egon Krenz, Honecker's successor, the "crown prince" and prior leader of the FDJ, was a man the burgers loved to hate. They criticized him openly for falsifying election results. He was known as a friend of the *Chinese terror* and was not averse to ordering troops to replicate a Tiananmen Massacre.

While Schabowski joined the struggle to save the Party and the nation, Krenz fought for his life. Should he be ousted, as Stroph and Mielke were, his chances of assassination were excellent. Perhaps, this figured into his decision when he added one more document to Schabowski's papers as the spokesman entered the center. There was a special reason why it was thrust upon Schabowski; he and the mayor of East Berlin had debated reformers the month previous. One of the government concessions was a promised review of travel laws.

The press conference was like many others. Schabowski was short on detail and long on ambiguity, evasiveness, and Party platitudes. He loathed to admit he had little personal knowledge of the items addressed. Instead, he reverted to tried-and-true, SED techniques. The East German press did not dare criticize the party openly. The world press could go to hell – they had no voice in matters of State. He attempted to be honest and forthright, but he was ignorant about the party stance on critical issues. Schabowski wasn't at that damned meeting of the Central Committee; no one gave him a proper briefing. Better, he thought, for reporters and editors to remain dissatisfied than to outrage the Politburo.

For all practical purposes, the press conference was over. A few reporters drifted away; more prepared to leave. The exhausted Schabowski shuffled through his papers and lit upon the one Krenz pressed upon him at the last moment. He couldn't omit that. Because of its source, the spokesman assumed it was properly screened and approved.

He began reading aloud.

Reporters settled back into their seats. Those at the exits paused, and movements ceased. Every eye and ear attended the fatigued speaker. Schabowski was arrested by what he heard himself say. He quickly reviewed the words on the page.

They were incredible, but there was no mistaking them for anything other than what they were. He hadn't misread them. He cleared his throat and resumed reading,

"Private journeys abroad can be applied for without presenting conditions…"

Pause.

He read and reread silently to make double, double certain his tired brain hadn't betrayed him. He flipped to a previous page. He returned to Krenz's paper. The words remained unchanged.

"Permission will be granted at short notice --"

"… the Volkspolitzei…are instructed to distribute visas for permanent exit at once…"

What the hell? This can't be right! Something this drastic must clear the Politburo. When and where was this discussed? Did anyone tell the Soviets? How was it possible that he, a member of the Politburo, was not informed?

He looked up to find his audience as stunned as he. After a moment, with mouths agape, reporters reopened notebooks and reached for pencils. Film cameras and audio recorders, previously stowed, were retrieved and pressed into service. They waited as Schabowski silently reread the paper. He tripled check it, then checked again. It was the paper Krenz gave him. There was no mistake.

Someone snapped out of his coma and asked, in a voice timid and unsure, a question. Soon, the other reporters came to their senses and launched a flurry of questions. What did he mean by *private journeys*? Would he explain the concept of permission *at short notice*? Had he, indeed, used the word *permanent*? Did Schabowski mean that exit visas would be issued *at the border*?

Before responding, the harried man reread the paper. He must get this right. There was no room for error. Soon, he'd face other members of the Politburo; his only defense would be the paper he held in his sweaty, trembling hand.

"Does this apply to West Berlin?" a voice demanded.

Compared with this, facing down a million angry demonstrators was easy.

He looked at the document again. It didn't mention West Berlin. The omission was significant. The Western Sector was considered an entity all its own; it was not recognized as part of the Federal Republic. If Krenz intended to exclude the city's check points, the paper would so specify.

"Well – yes," he said. "Yes."

An uncharacteristic and undisciplined buzz filled the room making Schabowski more uncomfortable. He wanted to say something to quiet the press, but nothing came. Once more, he silently read the text.

"When will the new travel policy begin?"

Yet again, Schabowski examined the paper. This time, however, he paged through the stack in search of related documents to clarify the situation. To his dismay, there was only one reference: Krenz's memo.

"Well – as far as I can see –" he paused to shuffle parchments yet again. "Straightaway. Immediately."

There was no room for maneuver. The proverbial Rubicon was crossed. The Soviets would have no warning. Well, they'd have to live with it. Concerns about Soviet displeasure were, suddenly, moot.

Oregon Coast

November 9, 1989

Molly opened the front door leading into the Waldron home. Three girls were mildly concerned over Mrs. Waldron's absence. Her car was in the driveway.

"Mutti?" Jayme called.

"Is Kathy with you?"

The reply came from downstairs.

"I'm here, Mrs. Waldron," Kathy called out.

"Come down here – all of you!"

Kathy gasped.

"Oh, God!"

She'd caught Ute's jitters and was ready to believe the baby was lost. Mrs. Waldron should drive her to the hospital. Why would she be in the basement?

Molly, sensing panic, patted Kathy on the shoulder.

"Mom wouldn't make you come for bad news," she assured. "She'd come to you."

Kathy's eyes glowed at the reassurance. Still, Mrs. Waldron was never downstairs in the afternoon. Something was very not right.

The curious trio made its way down the steps to the game room. There, in the chair so often abused by Jayme, sat the Waldron matriarch in dress slacks and a seasonal tunic. Her head was turned to spy Kathy. An inane game show was on, but the sound was off.

"They've opened the border," she reported.

Kathy understood at once. Still, she dared not hope. She had to be sure.

"The East German border?"

"*Genau*! They showed film just a few minutes ago. People are partying on the *Ku-Damm*; people are standing on the wall; cars are driving through check points like crazy."

"When?"

"A couple of hours, at least. I was listening to the radio and rushed down here to see if something was on TV."

"So, people are coming across in Berlin?"

"Not just Berlin, Kathy. People are crossing everywhere!"

Kathy Foster stood dumb. She couldn't believe the unbelievable. The TV continued with the normal vapid fare. Jayme looked at the TV with disapproval. She wanted the sports channel.

After moments of silent awe by three females and an impatient glower from the fourth, the screen suddenly transformed into a brilliant poster. *Special Report* spewed in large red letters. Mrs. Waldron fired the remote control at the set and the sound burst forth at a volume never permitted the Waldron girls.

Soon enough, Kathy saw what no living person ever expected.

* * *

Kathy lashed herself to the television without understanding why. She experienced split-second visuals sandwiched between decades of commercials and eons of insipid programming. Perhaps, her family would march up to a camera crew and introduce themselves. Perhaps, the East German Army would march into West Berlin and massacre thousands of inebriated celebrants.

She refused to come to dinner. Jayme brought her a plate. She nibbled at the food without being aware. Her only hunger was for information, and the television showed only pictures. The news, such as it was, remained confined to what media figures, politicians, and celebrities said.

Infrequently, cameras captured Ossis near the Brandenburg Gate. She listened to their delighted voices and heard them babbling in rapid German. A network translator told the English-speaking audience things the German-speakers weren't saying. This made Kathy angry.

"If they'd shut up, I could hear what they are really saying," she groused.

"We'd better get going," Henry announced when the time came.

She was oblivious to his arrival but was not surprised.

Kathy forced herself out of the chair and stared blankly at the plate in her hand. There were edible items remaining, yet she'd no idea how the food arrived or what she'd consumed. She closed her eyes and sighed. She couldn't perform that evening. Perhaps, Ed would cancel.

Kathy, the silent passenger, was delivered to the stage door and left alone. She stiffened as if caught in a horrible dream. She didn't remember a single line or a single note of the music. She must secure a script and sheet music to relearn everything in ninety minutes.

In full panic mode, she rushed to the stage entrance and threw open the door. The welcome placidness inside refreshed and calmed her once more. Everything returned. The words, music, and order of costume changes. Aided by an adrenaline overdose, Kathy changed in record time.

Once dressed, she sat down with Debbie's make-up stash. Routine guided her. Though her hands trembled initially, she was phlegmatic by the time Debbie arrived.

"I guess you've heard the news," she said, relieving Kathy's fingers of the eyeliner.

Kathy grunted. She wasn't Kathy, however. The metamorphosis into a twenty-something, depression-socialite was nearing completion. Whoever said "the show must go on" was not an actor. Regardless, once ensconced in the trappings of her alter ego, Kathy's concerns were worth scant attention.

What remained of the brooding sophomore was lost in the giddy excitement of an impending performance. Ed Geist reminded the cast that the local newspaper was also a community sponsor of the theatre. Even if opening night proved a "train wreck," the reporters would print a complementary review. Still, everyone took the keenest interest in the first edition of the *Herald-News* following the first performance.

The production marks the stage début of Kathy Foster who sparkled with all the élan and savvy of a veteran. Her vivacity, aided by a smooth-as-silk voice, so charmed us that we were amazed at how completely she stole our hearts.

Steve and Debbie were used to such hyperbole; they shrugged off the review as an interesting curiosity. The leading lady, who insisted that acting and singing were her hobbies, didn't even bother to read the report; she enjoyed her opening performance; the opinions of outsiders were superfluous. For Kathy, however, two glowing sentences constituted a tremendous morale boost.

This was icing on a cake consisting of the praises and congratulatory sentiments of her parents, friends, teachers *et al.* The greatest plaudit, however, was the expressed desire of friends and family to watch her performance again. The difficulty in reserving tickets magnified this praise. The musical was sold out; Geist added two Wednesday performances to accommodate the unprecedented demand. The Davidsons, unable to secure tickets for Saturday, paid full price so they could stand under the lighting booth.

High praise, indeed.

Further, Mrs. Rademacher approached her after church. Kathy thought it furtive if not bizarre. She took Kathy's arm and led her away as if they were fast friends and Reverend Rademacher was a KGB spy. With her husband seeing his congregation out, his wife half led, half pulled Kathy into the vestry.

"We only have a few moments, dear," the suddenly somber woman announced.

Kathy was suspicious of anyone calling her "dear". She stood silent and expectant.

"My husband's favorite song is *Stille Nacht.*"

Kathy made no sign. Mrs. R. started this; let her finish.

"Do you know it?"

"Of course," Kathy replied guardedly.

"*Auf Deutsch?*"

"*Genau.*"

"The Women of the Church are organizing the Christmas pageant," the woman said, casting conspiratorial looks out the vestry door.

"We'd like, very much, if you sang. This is a special Christmas gift for my husband."

Suspicion wafted away. Once she recognized her talent, Kathy was flattered and moved. She'd never been a Christmas gift before and imagined, in a girlish flight of fancy, that her sister would be proud.

"I'd love to," she replied.

"Here's the tricky part," the woman continued. "It was originally written in German when the church organ –"

"I know the story," Kathy nodded.

"Can you do it acapella?"

There was a moment of hesitation – the flitting shadow of doubt. Just a few weeks prior, the girl was convinced that her singing ability existed only in the mistaken good wishes of others. Now, seemingly everyone, from her choir teacher to the local newspaper, had endorsed her prowess. To sing such a revered song in public might be mistaken as an act of pride, and pride, as she knew, was one of the Seven Deadlies.

Nevertheless, she was excited at the prospect to honor Rev. Rademacher and all the support he lent her. If others interpreted her gesture as a product of pride or ego, she refused to be responsible for such conceits.

"I think I can do it," she assured.

At last, Mrs. Rademacher smiled. She patted the girl on the shoulder. "So do I."

November proceeded towards Kathy's "birthday." Her emotions were in high gear. It was as if she were piloting the *Mary R.* into the teeth of a Pacific storm. The bow would rise and crawl up to the crest of a mighty wave and drop into a trough. Thus, as her singing and acting carried her to majestic peaks and made her head swim; the events half a world away drove her into the darkness.

There was a sister, she was certain. Possibly, there were others. After their nation crumbled, would they be safe? Where were they? How could she find them? What would they think of her?

Yes, she'd sing *Silent Night* in the original tongue and as written. She'd kiss Steve Davis in front of his wife and audiences of a three hundred or more. She'd waltz before strangers and tolerate being bathed in blistering light. If any mishap manifested itself, what was lost? Kathy was too preoccupied for embarrassment.

The more Ute's stomach protruded; the more Kathy felt squeezed out of the tiny Foster abode. There was nothing in either Aaron or Ute's behavior making her feel unwelcome, but the child growing inside its mother did not share Kathy's genes. The Fosters accepted her under fallacious circumstances; they assumed they'd have no children of their own. With a child on the way, Kathy became an intruder.

Her proper place was with her proper family; the baby's proper place was with Aaron and Ute. The Fosters, together, asked Kathy if they could put the crib in Kathy's room. Small it was, there was more room for a crib than in one dominated by a double bed. Kathy eagerly assented. She thrilled at the prospect, though the room would no longer be hers; she'd become a live-in nanny. When the baby grew out of the crib, Kathy would become an impediment.

Molly was a great friend, but Kathy was no longer her best friend. That honor was passed on to Henry. Unable to feel resentment, Kathy's heart ached whenever Molly spoke in hesitant Japanese phrases. Jayme was a treasure, but she and Shelly were joined at the hip. When the Tomboy found a boyfriend, Kathy would be marooned.

During light-headed moments, Kathy imagined herself as Mrs. Gary Swofford. She conjured a small home and two (or three) little Garys. However, her imagined home was nondescript and isolated from the world. There was no context or texture to her futuristic vision. Gary would never make millions in the NFL. Similarly, Kathy was unlikely to become a pop diva or a star in the opera firmament. Even if chance provided the opportunity, Kathy's temperament would reject it.

For the final performance, each person in the cast and crew brought a covered dish. When the diminishing applause terminated curtain calls, the cast sprinted for the changing rooms and the crew began striking the set. The stagehands managed the serious labor.

Back in street clothes, the cast returned the costumes to the wardrobe matron before sweeping, mopping, and trash collecting. Once the stage was clear, tables and folding chairs, table clothes, dishes, glasses, and silverware were brandished about. Placemats, napkins, salt and pepper shakers, centerpieces, candles, and bottles of wine appeared on the tables with a rapidity to flummox a conjurer.

Slightly more than an hour after the final curtain, the buffet opened. Kathy sat next to the veteran light designer/operator and the Davis duo. Kathy, Debbie, and Steve were the only revelers not imbibing alcohol; they'd promised to see Kathy home. Molly, of course, was willing enough to respond to a phone call, but the party could go on until the wee-small.

Kathy was uncomfortable among the theatre clique, people who had worked together for years. She was further concerned when the wine bottles emptied, and a fresh legion brought out. Debbie's elbow was in constant action, but her drink came from a pitcher of ice water. Steve fancied a cola, but caffeine robbed him of sleep, so he followed his wife's lead.

He spent much of the evening casting envious glances in Kathy's direction each time she warmed her coffee. The banter was boisterous and light. Everyone laughed heartily over theatrical mishaps. When that conversational well ran dry, anecdotes were dredged up from previous shows. Kathy listened with a twinkling eye and joined in the laughter.

While Debbie blushed, one of the set-changers related how that woman sang as Eliza Doolittle when a falsie flew right out of her dress and onto the apron. Those who witnessed the catastrophe guffawed at the mastery of this latest retelling.

"She never missed a note," Steve shouted in his wife's defense.

"She kept singing," someone confirmed from the far end of the table.

"She just walked over – still singing – picked it up and tucked it back in!"

Debbie glowed red but laughed along with the crowd.

"I couldn't pretend it never happened," she concluded.

"And she couldn't have finished up the scene lopsided," someone cried from among the multitude.

"She'd have had the audience rolling on the floor."

"It wasn't funny when it happened," Debbie assured Kathy.

Kathy wondered if she'd appear in a future, cast-party anecdote.

Later, she wished she made notes of these playhouse bloopers while still fresh in her mind. Each was a gem: King Arthur sweeping on stage with a wire hanger dangling from his robe; Ed Geist caught on stage with a blank memory, calmly excusing himself from a card game to consult a script in the wings and returning with an adlibbed announcement about the maid going on strike. The woman hanging up the phone instead of giving it to her stage husband as the script called for, and, realizing her error, announced the caller's identity and suggesting her stage husband call him back. These were among the tamest stories of the evening.

When everyone was satiated with good food, Ed Geist stood and called for quiet. He made his way around the two tables and authored maudlin speeches about each person. He massaged each person's shoulders and neck while expressing his appreciation for their contributions, past and current. An approving round of applause followed each tribute. Kathy attended these snippets of fascinating biographies until realizing her turn approached, suddenly, the ghost's hands were on her.

"I guess you all knew how desperate I was to find a soprano," he began.

"I've been in theatre long enough to know that a show always comes together if we work hard enough, but I admit, now that it's over, I wasn't sleeping well. A teacher friend suggested I come by the school and speak with this young lady. I nearly didn't go. After the Christmas Carol last year, you heard me say I'd never work with kids again. Well, Kathy is no kid. She's a trooper. You notice she never missed a line."

At this point, there were mummers of agreement; three people pounded approval lightly on the tabletop.

"She saved my butt," Steve interrupted.

"Yes," Ed nodded amid subdued chuckles.

"You're lucky Kathy was on stage. She made up that great line and brought Steve back. You got a nice little laugh with that speech, Kathy. Well done."

Kathy relived the petrifying moment with a quiver and wetness in her palms. She realized something was very wrong. She assumed she'd skipped a line, and everyone waited on her. It was gone! However, she knew where the scene was headed; she said the first thing that came into her head.

It was a horrible, childish line. It fetched a laugh, however, and jolted Steve's memory enough to get him back into the scene. After the show, she and Steve consulted the script to determine with whom the fault lay. Steve was ashamed and apologized to Kathy for his mistake. Even with Ed's magic hands gently relaxing her taut shoulder muscles, the adlib sounded no better in retelling than it had before.

"Kathy," Ed continued, "You did a super, super job."

There was scattered applause.

"I thank you for all you did for this show. I wish Molly was here; I should thank her as well. These doors will always be open to you, and I really, really hope you will try out for another show very soon."

Kathy smiled appreciatively and watched the ghost passed on to Debbie. She hoped to hear another great anecdote. Perhaps, she did. Despite the coffee, her eyes were heavy and her memory impaired by fatigue.

The remainder of the evening – more accurately, early morning – evaded her. She may have nodded off. When Debbie gently prodded her, Kathy noticed, via blurred vision, that several seats were empty. Ed Geist and a select few were clearing the tables.

"We'd better get you home," Steve said, gently taking her arm.

Debbie sat in the back seat and snoozed while Kathy forced herself to navigate. Steve kept her senses alert with conversation. Days later, the girl's memory of that warm, midnight discourse delighted her.

A brisk, autumn wind drove inland from the foam-laden crests of Pacific waves. Kathy woke when her mother scolded her for sleeping in her clothes. Though the brusque tone pierced her, it was a struggle to open her eyes. For several seconds, Ute and the immediate surroundings were distorted.

"It would be best if you stayed home this morning," Ute sighed.

"I want to see Gary," Kathy croaked.

Ute pouted. Kathy looked like the Wreck of the Hesperus, and her voice resembled that of a cartoon villain. Time was short. Kathy shed her clothes and managed to climb into presentable slacks and a sweater. There was no time for a shower. Because she'd spent the evening under hot lights, she really needed a shower.

"Sit downwind of me," Ute commanded.

Similarly, Gary made signs that Kathy's aroma was unwelcome. Hyperbolically, Kathy Foster turned a church pew into a P. U. Gary gave her space but refused to shun her.

Kathy realized she needed to be with people. The theatre crowd, which proved a burden during rehearsals, became a family. Now, it was over. Her "evening family" vanished like the misty, ocean spray. Save for few exceptions, she'd never see the theatre people again.

Being alone was her greatest fear. Having Aaron and Ute – and Gary – near was more important than any other possibility. Subconsciously, she feared all the important people in her life might disappear if not continuously monitored.

Being alone equals non-existence.

Weimar

December 1989

Nadine's homecoming was difficult. In addition to her beaten and deformed face, she lived on little or no food. She was too weak to perform all but the simplest chores. Heike did not begrudge her a pass on housework. Indeed, she considered the extra work partial payment for failing Nadine.

It was tiring and hard, but Heike refused to shirk; her debt was too great. There were tears in her eyes as she helped Nadine onto her bed that first night. The girl was too weak to climb. She grunted and moaned under the pain induced by Heike's aid. Heike's sorrow mounted.

"Let me sleep in my old bed," Nadine panted.

Alarmed that Nadine could fall and hurt herself, Heike kept an arm around her waist as tight as she dared. Slowly, they shuffled to the bed. Nadine half leaned and half sat on the edge. Heike gingerly urged Nadine's bottom up and helped lift her legs. Once aboard, Nadine turned onto her side and crabbed onto the mattress.

The effort left her so exhausted, so she lay motionless long enough to make her sister anxious.

"What's that?" she asked, a feeble finger pointing towards the pallet.

"I couldn't sleep in your bed, Nadine," Heike answered mournfully.

"*Mist*!" came a weak reply. "Sleep in Jürgen's bed."

"I can't."

"You can."

Heike let the matter drop. She scurried downstairs to finish her chores. When she returned, Nadine would be asleep. Quietly, she crept up the stairs and switched off the light before feeling her way to the opposite wall.

"Sleep in the bed." Nadine snarled.

It was a pitiful example of a snarl. Nadine couldn't muster the requisite energy. Heike ignored the order and resumed her act of penance.

In the morning, she helped Nadine dress before helping her downstairs.

"When I get better, I'm going to kick you in the arse," Nadine promised, struggling with the steps.

Heike assumed this referenced was due to negligence in Leipzig. It wasn't until days later she realized that Nadine was highly upset about the sleeping arrangements.

They trekked to the dentist only to learn he'd fled West. Nadine was too tired to migrate elsewhere, so they returned home. There Nadine could eat, rest, and build up her strength.

That evening, Heike made further reconnaissance. She returned home to report other reputable dentists had, likewise, decamped.

"You'll be very lucky to find a good one," Rolf growled.

On the fourth day of December, a crowd of demonstrators stormed the Leipzig Stasi headquarters. News of the event spread throughout the country in a matter of hours. As Family Jacobs had no television and the radio remained mute most days, neither Heike nor Nadine knew what, if anything, the state-controlled media reported of the event. Everything that reached their ears came from friends, neighbors and, on one occasion, strangers who congregated near the greengrocers.

Stasi administrators were led out of the building and taken away. Records and files were examined with horror at the pervasiveness of Stasi spying. People discovered transcripts of their conversations. People learned family members reported on them.

With each revelation, the Jacobs siblings shuddered. How far could unofficial reports be trusted? All the Volk knew for certain was that "official" reports were based on lies; this had been common knowledge for decades.

Little by little, as she regained her strength, Nadine spoke of her captivity. These revelations came in single sentences injected into thoughtful silences. Each announcement was followed by the expectancy of elaboration. Nadine, however, never expanded upon her pithy recollections. Indeed, she was unaware she spoke. It was all Heike could do to keep from hugging her and begging forgiveness yet again.

Nadine was in jail for only a few hours. She was forced to stand in an unheated area until she collapsed due, perhaps, to loss of blood. She was left untended. Someone attempted to aid her only to be physically retrained, struck, and loudly berated by the Vopos.

When herded out onto the street, Nadine found herself in the company of a half-dozen locals who accepted her as a comrade. The eldest was a pensioner who offered to feed the entire crew at his apartment. When they arrived, however, they found the apartment was sealed and entry forbidden. It fell to the younger people to care for the suddenly homeless old man.

They managed as best as they could through the week and returned to the area near the university for the Monday demonstrations. Just as with Heike, Nadine's friends, physically, held her up. When subsequent crowds began chanting for a reunited Germany, Nadine, tired, half starved, broken in body and in spirit, lost all hope. She begged for rail fare and she stole several more marks to have enough.

"I've betrayed everything," she remarked. "I turned my back on my country, and I gave up on its people."

Had she railed or scorched the air with sarcasm, it would leave Heike troubled. The terse report, calmly dispatched, hurt Heike deeply. Feeling faint, Heike wondered how Nadine could be utterly devoid of emotion? How could she witness the demise of her country with such detachment? When Nadine's silence turned ominous, Heike paused in her chores to cast an investigatory glance.

"Heike, I'm the reason you sleep on the floor. You have some crazy notion you're doing me homage. You're a fool. I'm not the person you thought."

Heike averted her eyes. She thought deeply and carefully.

That evening, Nadine, after days of proper nourishment and limited housework, pulled herself up onto the big bed. Once perched on high, she looked directly at Heike as if daring her. Heike took one deep breath through her nostrils, turned out the light and padded her way to the window and her orphan's bed.

"Heike, I'm not worth sacrifice," the elder girl said angrily.

"I had a sister once who loved her country so much, she nearly got killed," Heike responded with a calm she did not feel.

Nadine offered no response.

"I owe her reverence. In any case, Nadine, it's my business and none of yours."

* * *

Another reshuffle came in December. Egon Krenz was thrown out with the trash. In his place was Gregor Gysi, a lawyer previously unknown to all but a few citizens of the DDR. What remained of the official media introduced Gysi as a defense lawyer for dissidents. To further distance the fledgling and fumbling government, the SED recreated itself.

The new party was the PDS, democratic socialists. The democratic portion of the moniker caught Heike's attention immediately; she prayed that the word would be applied as she envisioned it in her personal manifesto. She looked for reaction from Nadine, but the deformed visage of the older girl remained frozen.

Nadine had abandoned hope. Heike fruitlessly looked for something more than apathy. She and Nadine had once fought fiercely over political matters. It should please her that the fighting had ceased, but she was in despair. At least when she faced off with Nadine, she had a foe who cared. Heike preferred fighting to fatalism.

Nadine sighed, *"Alles vorbei."*

The girls walked through the town square. A light dusting of snow coated the cobblestones though pedestrians and temperature would soon clear it away. Above, the clouds boiled ominously and threatened a freezing rain. Without protection, they were near enough to scamper home should the need arise.

They'd been to school. It was an infrequent activity they shared by turns. With little instruction, there was hardly an excuse to attend. After checking updates, there was little excuse to linger. Heike crept into her nearly vacant economics class for a few minutes and walked out without hindrance.

The school was run by the state, and the state was dissolving. It was the first time the girls traveled together since boarding the Leipzig train. Once the balance of the chores were completed, they then intended to fetch daily bread. The cold weather created a natural refrigerator behind the kitchen door. Milk – if they found any – would keep for days.

Heike convinced Nadine to exercise. She managed some through daily chores. What Nadine really needed was additional days of a healthy diet. It was difficult to chew with missing and injured teeth, but the pitiful, emasculated creature who limped home from oblivion was, thankfully, gone.

The West German Chancellor visited Dresden and made a speech not many days before. Obviously, he expected reunification – under the Wessi government. Heike knew better than to mention it, though not – as in days of old – for fear Nadine would go crazy. On the contrary, Nadine, probably, didn't care.

"Hallo!"

Heike and Nadine turned to discover Frau Willing carrying a basket of purchases. No one smiled. Few citizens smiled anymore.

"I have not to ask what bus run into you," the driver commented to Nadine.

Heike and Nadine nodded a greeting. The trio's breaths came in small puffs.

"Bad joke. Sorry," Frau Willing admitted. "I'm happy to see you. Both of you. I think not I see you again. Rolf, I know, think so, too."

Rolf spoke sparingly at home. He'd bark orders when orders were called for, but he never talked; he never scolded. If he wished to admonish, he'd glare at the object of his displeasure until she wilted. Once, he made a reference to his "convict daughters," but that remark was not directed at them.

"He was worried," Nadine said.

She didn't mean it. The comment was born of sarcasm, but it came out drenched in bitterness. Frau Willing, Heike knew, was not a country dolt; however, she pretended not to understand.

"In shop, he was like tiny dog pooping cocoanuts."

Formerly, Frau Willing's remark would generate a laugh from Heike. This, however, was not formerly; it was a time of fear, anger, and regret.

"You hear about Stasi come?" Frau Willing asked.

Heike and Nadine exchanged looks of surprise and anxiety.

"No!" Frau Willing exploded. "How you not hear? I was in office, you know. I have to turn-in money and sign papers when I leave the work. I hear roar of lion. Well, I know no lion. Is your father. When he roar, all city hear. I first think to me, 'Get out! Someone to be killed. You not want here to be!'"

"But you didn't leave."

Heike knew this woman. She delivered a baby on a bus; with Rolf's blessing, she gave Heike driving lessons that could have cost her both her job and her freedom. Frau Willing was hardly one to turn her back on a crisis.

"No. No, I leave not," she said slapping her forehead. "I think to me, 'Maybe, I can stop murder.' Maybe! If Rolf, he going to kill, very much I can do, right? So, stupid me, I rush to door. There is Rolf. Two men there and everybody others standing around watching. One man, he is sitting on floor and not looking so good. The other man, Rolf have him lifted and is shaking him like toy. But he not toy; he grown man and his eyes; they are like headlights on bus.

"I think to me, 'Stasi!' I never see Stasi man before, but I know I see now. I see two! Rolf not to care. He so angry. They come, I think, to ask for you," she looked at Heike.

"I think, Fraulein Jacobs," she said turning to Nadine, "you in trouble in Leipzig. Stasi know where you are, but not other Fraulein Jacobs. They come to bus office to – fish the exposition – however, you say. Rolf, say, you sick – this I hear later. That is why you not to school. One Stasi man say is not true, and Rolf, he get very, very angry."

"He knock one man down and grab other Stasi man by coat and lift him into air. He tell him nobody call Rolf Jacobs liar – not Stasi, not nobody! Then he throw man to floor and grab the other. Soon, he have them by collars and rushing with them to open shop door. He say to them when Nazis take away Herr Ecke, they have two Gestapo men and two soldiers with rifles. He yell that if weasels want Herr Ecke's granddaughter, they need two Gestapo men and two armed soldiers when they arrest her. He say them, too, if they come to house without Gestapo and soldiers, he kill them. Then he throw out into yard. Two men vanish very fast."

Heike and Nadine exchanged incredulous looks. Heike tacitly assured Nadine that Frau Willing didn't spin stories. If she reported what she saw and heard, it was without exaggeration. If anything, Rolf's dialogue was drastically edited to fit the tongue of a spoon-carver and the ears of two young ladies.

The girls returned home on wobbly legs. It was a near thing. Rolf's temper could cost them all their lives. Had the reign of Stasi terror not ended when it did, the little house of Werner Ecke might be vacant with the doors sealed.

"I'm not Werner Ecke's granddaughter," Heike mumbled.

"Are you calling Pabst a liar?"

Heike was jolted by this unexpected remark. She examined Nadine and found the same apathetic expression she'd observed every hour since her return. However, the eyes were no longer glazed over; deep within shone a flicker of life.

Oregon Coast

December - January, 1989-1990

Reverend Rademacher was, indeed, surprised. Though each Christmas Eve service was special, they'd ossified over the years. The Sunday evening service was better attended than normal; everyone appeared in their best togs. Kathy Foster wore a red skirt and a white knit sweater with a string of fake pearls around her neck.

Her feet were adorned with a pair of red pumps. The whole ensemble came via various benefactors for the occasion. It made her uncomfortable. She learned to walk in heels at the theatre, but the horror of sprawling headfirst down the aisle was manifest.

Ute, clutching her unborn baby with one hand, applied a coat of gloss. She assured Kathy it rounded out her outfit. The moment Ute's back was turned, Kathy caught a look at herself in the bathroom mirror and cringed.

Red lips made her look like Mrs. Dracula. She grabbed for the tissues and nervously wiped most of it away. Ute was disappointed, but Kathy was adamant. Getting the recalcitrant girl to wear a skirt was a major victory. Luck stretched only so far.

Molly drove up for the event. Blustery winter winds and intermittent rain were a further test. The roads remained clear, and the Waldrons trusted her. Where there was Molly, there was Henry. It was more surprising to find Jayme and Shelly sitting together in a pew.

Were Henry and Shelly Christians? The matter never came up. Not that it mattered – certainly not to the cosmopolitan Rev. Rademacher. The church, he insisted, is not members-only.

Mrs. R. assembled the Sunday schoolers for the presentation of the Christmas story. By her own admission, the reverend's wife was not particularly creative; thus, the children's program was blessed by brevity and simplicity. There were choral interludes by the cherubs, far more well-intended than audible, and the audience was appreciative. Unless Henry and Shelly were unversed in the origins of Christmas, the performance was hardly didactic.

As the leader of his flock, Rev. Rademacher was obliged to read and expand upon certain seasonal Bible verses. The children performers became restless. Two shepherds discovered their crooks resembled cartoon-like creatures. Soon, they were acting out their own little pastiche. Kathy caught on to the game. As the armless characters performed for each other, Kathy joined the shepherds in tittering.

Ute, not privy to the amateur theatricals, kept her hand on her stomach attending to the movements of the baby. She repeatedly shushed Kathy's muffled mirth. Finally, the foundling opened a hymn book and forced herself to read silently through responsive passages. Should she look up, the boys might have her laughing aloud.

Gary was aware of her every action since the moment Kathy sat beside him. He monitored every breath she drew, every movement, every fidget. He caught her giggles though ignorant of their source. He, too, studied the hymn book thoughtfully. He burned to ask what had set her off, but his mother cast disapproving looks.

If Gary made any sound, he'd invite an elbow to the side. The choir sang a verse of "O, Holy Night" which sounded professional when compared to the cherubs. Finally, the choir closed their music folders and sat. Reverend Rademacher rose to resume the pulpit for a closing prayer, but his wife headed him off. The man suspected something, but his trust in her was absolute. He nodded and returned to his seat.

Mrs. R.'s speech was short, crisp and complete. She explained the circumstances under which "Silent Night" was composed – making no mention that the myth had been largely debunked. Kathy was invited to the platform to sing the traditional carol.

Kathy cleared her throat and got on her unsteady feet. She slithered past Ute without losing her balance or crushing the baby. She slid past Aaron without falling onto his lap. She faced the challenge of moving quickly up the aisle in heels and negotiating three steps without mishap.

She nodded to Rev. Rademacher. She couldn't resist looking to her left at the two playful shepherds who sat attentively as if expecting something profound. Unable to resist, Kathy winked at them and, perhaps, condemned them to a future of prolonged therapy.

Ute looked proud and confident. Aaron was visibly nervous. Molly and Jayme, inexplicably *not* sitting together, leaned forward in anticipation.

She "warmed up" at home, but that was long before. Thus, she began with a cautious ease. Soon, however, she hit each note as practiced. Beginning the second verse, she projected boldly, unafraid she'd forget the German text.

People don't applaud in church; Kathy didn't expect any. Once finished, she paused as she was coached in the theatre. There'd be no blackout, of course. She returned cautiously to her pew. She noticed Molly dabbing her eyes with a Kleenex. This struck her as bizarre.

It took her no little while to plop down next to Gary without smashing into feet, landing in laps, or crashing into babies. Facing forward, she realized why the service ground to a halt. Rev. Rademacher, sitting where he'd been for much of the evening, had his glasses in one hand and wiped his eyes with a handkerchief in the other.

Only Kathy appeared impatient over the time it took the good reverend to compose himself. She imagined she'd done something wrong. Finally, the man put away his handkerchief and moved to the pulpit, his glasses still in his left hand.

"Thank you, Kathy," he said. "For a few moments, I was a child again in a faraway land."

After the service, people who knew Kathy only by sight lined up to offer congratulations and complements. All the while, Gary stood proudly beside her as if to remind people that he'd known Kathy before she became a "star." Molly and her entourage joined the recessional.

"*Sehr gut*," Molly said, shaking Kathy's hand.

How Kathy loved her! There was no hyperbole or false sentiment. Barbie presented heartfelt feelings with a smile and a firm handshake.

"*Sehr, sehr gut*," Henry Kurihara said, bowing.

That, Kathy concluded, was Molly's influence. He'd added a second adjective to avoid parroting, but there was no gushing, no fawning, no hint of insincerity. Simple and dignified – a perfect blend of three cultures.

"That was sooo good!"

Shelly smiled broadly, her peach lip gloss shimmering in the artificial light. She didn't bow being – as Kathy often noted – too American to mix bow and handshake. Again, the complement was genuine. Shelly gave a typically American teenager salutation and made no attempt to spoil it by drowning it with goop.

Jayme, however, outdid them all.

She didn't shake hands. Instead, she punched Kathy on the upper arm.

"Set and match, babe," she congratulated.

Coming from a tennis prodigy with a killer instinct, this constituted the evening's highlight.

When Rev. Rademacher saw nearly everyone out the door, he made his way to Kathy. He took her hand in both of his and made clear his appreciation for the song and her singing. Though pleased, Kathy was annoyed by his implication that her performance constituted a sacrifice. Were it a chore, she'd have declined. It wasn't until Ute folded her arms around her and she felt the presence of the child inside that Kathy was moved.

"I'm so proud of you," Ute announced, maintaining the evening's theme of simplicity.

Simple though it was, the meaning went far beyond semantics. For weeks, the growing bulge in Ute's stomach underscored Kathy's status. Ute selected Kathy as her daughter, but blood is thicker. The love she felt for her own manifested itself in a myriad of ways. Not once, however, did Ute begrudge Kathy attention.

Instead of dividing a finite quantity of love, Ute produced more – and more and more. Ultimately, Ute bestowed the greatest gift; she expressed motherly pride in a foundling. Kathy returned Ute's glowing expression with a twisted smile – twisted by the struggle to keep her tears at bay.

* * *

Christmas was quiet but memorable. Ute served a special meal despite the tightening family budget. Though fit for kitchen duty, Ute relented when Aaron and Kathy agreed the mother-to-be should not exert herself over much.

Though she knew her way around the kitchen, Kathy's skill was confined to work-a-day creations. Ute's turkey a la Swabia was too ambitious for Kathy to master at one go. Therefore, Ute assisted from time to time; Kathy listened and learned.

After a delicious meal, Kathy salvaged the leftovers and stored them. Aaron dried the dishes while Kathy washed and rinsed. Later, they joined Ute in the living room. Her feet propped on the coffee table; Ute's hand messaged the baby as she hummed a Swabish folk song.

There was an exchange of modest gifts after church; no one minded. Kathy didn't feel shortchanged by family frugality. On the contrary, she suggested the money that Aaron and Ute set aside for her college be diverted to baby.

"It won't be enough to pay for college anyway," she reasoned. "I'll try for uni in Germany where it doesn't cost anything."

"Except for travel," Aaron reminded. "If you go to school there, we might not see you for years."

Kathy, employing Molly's stratagem, smiled, and kept things light. "Would that be a bad thing?"

"Yes, it would," Ute replied instantly.

Aaron's expression mirrored his wife's so exactly that Kathy's smile vanished.

The Fosters weren't ready to part with Kathy regardless of a shrinking house. This warmed her. Old enough to be the baby's mother, Kathy intended to be as much a mother as Ute allowed. The hug in the church communicated so much. Not until days later, did she realize she'd been a victim of seduction.

She and Gary sat together in the school cafeteria. They were pressed up against each other even though there was ample room. Shelly and Jayme sat across and slightly farther down. They giggled and snorted privately. Molly and Henry, who recently occupied the spot directly opposite, were bussing their trays. From there, they'd slink up onto the stage and disappear behind the curtain. Ostensibly, Molly was learning Japanese, but Kathy knew smooching was going on back there. Someday, a teacher would peek behind that curtain and a scandal would erupt, keeping the faculty lounge in stitches for days. Kathy, however, harbored no resentment despite Henry's stealing her best-ever friend.

"I'm going to be a sister," she mused.

Gary nodded.

"I'm going to be someone's sister," she repeated. "I want that baby to understand, that it will have a sister forever – no matter what."

Gary nodded again. He allowed Kathy to swathe herself in emotional garments. Kathy should have realized Gary's silence was a portent. When she planted her elbow on the table and braced her face against her palm, her eyes were fixed on something only she could see.

"You're, probably, someone's sister already," Gary said.

At that moment Kathy realized she'd been seduced. There may not be a drop of malice or premeditation, but she'd been lured into the embrace of a family which wasn't hers. Though she'd never repudiate the Fosters, her place was elsewhere. How could she allow herself to become complacent when, half a world away, there was turmoil?

What if her family needed her?

* * *

Ute heard the phone summons. Aaron stirred; the baby made a torpid movement against the side of its shelter. A shadow raced silently past the open bedroom door.

The woman woke several times on a normal night. Each time, she must satisfy herself that her child was safe. As time progressed, she feared it would be stillborn. No matter how determined she was, these thoughts were banished only after battling anxiety.

The ringing alerted Aaron. Ute wasn't certain she could manage a midnight conversation. The phone rang again. Aaron was awake; and she must get up. It would, at least, postpone a verbal exchange. Kathy and the midnight caller demanded attention.

She swung her swollen feet out of bed but made no attempt to stuff them into her slippers.

"Onkel Dieter?" Kathy's voice reverberated.

There was no certainty, save that local calls did not invade at insane hours. Aaron rolled onto his side and immediately renewed his deep breathing. Ute was tempted to lay back and wrestle with her emotions in peace.

"Cut the schmooze!" Kathy hissed.

No, Ute must get up. Kathy made no effort to keep her voice at a respectable volume. If she tarried, Ute would confront a wide awake and angry Aaron.

"Less than a month to go," she muttered to the being inside her.

She refused to hurry. A fall now could be deadly. She felt her way along the closet to the hallway. Kathy hadn't bothered with lights. Ute followed suit.

She planted her shoulder against the partition separating the living room from the dinning nook. Kathy's copious tears shimmered in the indirect light while she clutched the phone. The front of her pajamas heaved noticeably and irregularly as she listened.

"Ja," she said with effort. "I'm still here. Anything else?"

She listened for a moment before noticing Ute's huge belly pointing at her. Kathy thrust the receiver toward her. Ute half walked, and half waddled to accept it. Before speaking, she watched Kathy pull out a chair and settle onto it. She stared, momentarily, into infinity before burying her head on crossed arms.

"Dieter?"

"Ute? Where's Kathy?"

"She's here. What did you tell her?"

Ute's anxiety, for once, didn't center on the baby. Kathy didn't get overtly emotional.

"I got a message."

"What?"

"I tried to tell Kathy it might be nothing," Dieter explained. "I wanted to wait and talk with the person myself, but things are so confusing. We don't know where she is or how to contact her. It could take months to track her down."

"What is it?"

"It might be something," he repeated adamantly.

"Understood."

"Before the wall opened, floods of Ossis escaped through Hungary and Czechoslovakia. They're in resettlement centers –"

"Oh, God!"

Ute couldn't contain herself. She learned about D.P. camps after the war through her parents. She had a too-vivid picture of what the Ossis must experience.

"They interview them," Dieter charged on.

"Interrogate," Ute corrected.

Politics is politics.

"Do you want to hear or what?" Dieter snapped. "I've a business to run."

"Sorry," she said, and meant it.

"I know someone in Bonn who knows about Kathy. He helped with the adoption. He accessed something from a center and forwarded it – a message. Somebody brought a message across. It might be for Kathy."

"Oh, God!"

"It says, 'New Year's Day 1974. Greetings from sister Heike.'"

"Yes?"

"That's it."

"Oh, God!"

"We can't know, Ute."

She checked herself before repeating herself again.

"What are the chances?" she asked.

"Good, but no more than that. Still, if it's Kathy's sister, she, apparently, hasn't crossed."

"But the wall is down."

"Doesn't mean a thing," Dieter replied. "There are lots of people who won't even come across to have a look. Until I find this messenger, we know nothing. How is Kathy?"

"In shock."

"I was afraid of that. I could have written, but she'd never forgive me."

"You did the right thing, Dieter."

She hung up. It was Ute's turn to cry. Despite the uncertain nature of a cryptic message, Ute confronted something she'd dreaded for sixteen years. Ute Foster might lose a child.

DDR

Winter 1989

When the chores were finished, and the evening shadows drew in, the uncertainty of existence was held at bay by the door of the little house. The growls of the patriarch were blunted by the domestic confines. Nadine and Heike adjourned to their room. The overhead light burned bright.

A brilliant light was the only luxury in a family that repudiated luxury. Should some supercilious government official confront Herr Jacobs on the waste of one high-watt bulb, he'd reply with a snarl. The children's room was where they did homework – and so they had when homework mattered. They bent into impossible positions working math problems or reading texts. With the decline of learning and the crumbling of the nation, the girls made recreational use of the opulent device.

A sleeping-arrangement truce existed. Heike would sleep on the floor, and Nadine allowed it. Rather than continuously snarling, bickering, or resorting to fisticuffs, they settled down with Shakespeare. Heike read short scenes aloud to the malnourished creature who required assistance to mount her bed.

In the early days, it was therapeutic. Heike needed a buffer against terrifying thoughts; Nadine needed diversion. Gradually, however, they lapsed into mirth. They were so delighted with Touchstone and Falstaff that they muffled their giggles lest Rolf scold them. Frivolous behavior during critical times wasn't allowed.

Bad news and disappointments aside, their spirits soared above woe. The Bard was on hand to ensure a peaceful slumber. Indeed, the master's doggerel and the resultant pleasant dreams were the only enjoyments left.

When the Wessis began peeling off hundred-mark bills to citizens of the DDR who came West to collect, the economies of both nations swelled. Rolf called it bribery and resisted temptation – for a time. The stories circulating through the maintenance shop were too tantalizing. Finally, he ordered Nadine into the Trabi, and they set off, ostensibly, in search of a dentist.

They did, in fact, find a dentist. He was not, however, one of the many who fled to the West in search of proper monetary compensation for skills. It would be months before any Ossi could meet Wessi standards and requirements.

The dentist they consulted was Wessi born and schooled. He examined Nadine's mouth *pro bono*. His estimate brought father and daughter the realization that immediate action was beyond reach.

Upon their return, the Trabi was stuffed with two hundred Wessi-Marks worth of food. Everything Heike longed for came into the house in abundance. They feasted on fresh tomatoes, cheeses, and a myriad of fruit. There were large loaves of bread and packages of butter, jams, spices, and packaged food. Most exciting of all were three large packages of real coffee.

As they gorged themselves on unfamiliar delights, Nadine and Rolf swore every purchase came from a single store. Heike couldn't credit that, nor did she believe Nadine's claim that she'd seen no empty shelves. If an economy specifically designed to keep DDR families well fed couldn't match daily demands, there was no way greed-driven markets could manage.

There was no Shakespeare that evening. Instead, Heike listened to Nadine's account on what she experienced. Heike couldn't call her sister a liar, but her exposition was too fantastic. She attempted to end the farrago, but Nadine chuntered on – and on and on.

Had Nadine fallen under an evil spell? Heike remained steadfast. Her real parents failed to smuggle her into the Wessi mire. She'd not fall for capitalist tricks and swindles.

Three days later, His Royal Majesty, King Rolf Hardhand, ruled that Heike collect her hundred marks before the Wessis withdrew the offer. She objected, insofar as she dared. Though unwilling to "go for a walk," she protested up to a point.

She sat resentfully during Abendsbrot, making her displeasure dangerously obvious. She expected Rolf to call her out. There was little use in feigning obedience. Eventually, they'd be taking a walk.

"Take Nadine with you," Rolf suggested nonchalantly, enjoying Wessi bread-and-cheese cud.

Amazement overpowered umbrage and forced Heike to attention. He displayed no anger. On the contrary, he appeared placid.

"Pabst, I collected my hundred," Nadine reminded. "If I go, the chores won't get done."

Rolf took another bite of his open-faced sandwich and, spying a remaining slice of tomato on the serving platter, popped it in his mouth to join the other delightful flavors.

"We can manage for a day or so," he announced.

Heike and Nadine shared incredulous expressions. To see the nation's border dissolve, and to witness Rolf Jacobs dismiss daily chores was too much to expect in a single lifetime. For one moment of stark terror, both girls feared Rolf's mind might soon join Anne's in oblivion.

"Enough!" he growled.

This word made them sit straight. This was the Rolf they knew and feared.

"You run off to join a gang of counter-revolutionaries without a word. I and your mother are frantic that we might never see you again. Now, I ask you to do something legal, and you act as if I ordered you to assassinate our neighbors. Do you think I can't hold this house together?"

The girls dared not answer.

"We can slip across the border at Bebra," Heike suggested in a near whisper.

No one spoke for a time.

"Fulda?" Nadine suggested.

It was, at least, an historical location. They might find a museum.

"Go to Frankfurt," Rolf suggested.

"Aber, Pabst —"

Nadine arrested herself in time. Heike shivered.

Frankfurt was the heart of the capitalist world. The banks headquartered there. The place was infested with exploiting vermin. In truth, Heike would rather face the guns in Leipzig's Karl Marx Square than risk Frankfurt. She and Nadine might be snatched up and taken as slaves or cast into a bordello.

If going to the West was hateful, going to Frankfurt was tantamount to a death sentence. Did Rolf contemplate ridding himself of them to keep the home economy safe? Not without guilt did they board the train early Friday morning. Not without fear did they creep along the tracks into the unknown. They watched the vacant border tower slide by their window.

Heike shuddered.

It was akin to entering a dark cavern where the temperature – already bracing by German standards – dipped several degrees. They watched the DR locomotive pass them on a parallel set of tracks. A Wessi locomotive replaced it.

When the Wessi conductor came to inspect tickets, the girls were petrified. The tall, burly man's blue uniform was as menacing as those of the old SS. Moreover, the train raced away with speed unknown in the East.

The machine squealed to a halt in Fulda. Heike, petrified, had to get off. Nadine didn't argue. She was as breathless as her sister. They watched the train slowly move out of the station and proceed on its way.

"There's a slow train leaving in forty minutes," Nadine reported, consulting a schedule.

She reasoned any train making numerous stops would travel at a more moderate rate.

Signs directed Heike to her hundred-mark bribe. The sisters entered the lobby of a government structure within sight of the station. She presented her papers and was handed her money in crisp, new twenty-mark bills. The official showed no enthusiasm for her presence. She withdrew without speaking.

On their return to the station, Nadine spied a greengrocer. Heike refused to go inside, but Nadine didn't hesitate. Seconds ticked by, and Heike spent them in abject fear. In Ossi clothes, Nadine would be immediately identified. They'd throw her out – if she were lucky; if not, Heike would throw herself at the police.

She vowed not to see Nadine dragged away again.

To her surprised relief, Nadine stepped briskly onto the street with a paper bag. Inside were two pears. Heike recognized them from pictures. There were pear trees in the East, of course, but one seldom found the fruit in shops.

With pear juice dotting their coats and a sticky residual clinging to the corners of their mouths, the visitors discovered that Wessi trains ran on time. The slow train they expected to catch was long gone. They remained on the platform until the next train squealed to a noisy stop.

It was an express.

They held onto each other with one hand and wadded their coats with the other as the train flew down the tracks. They expected every moment to be their last. The supports for the electric wire suppling power to the engine were formless blurs against the widow. The other passengers displayed no concern.

Were they on a ghost train?

They arrived unsettled. The huge throng of transients boarding, and detraining intimidated them. Unlike anything they experienced, businesses abounded inside the huge arched ceilings of the station. Tired, frightened, and famished, they bought two bratwurst and two bottles of juice. They were forced to pay more than they should, but the wurst was exceptionally filling and the juice was real and unlike anything they'd experienced.

Heike fortified herself inside Jürgen's frayed winter coat. It was too large. Rolf offered to buy her a coat, but Heike refused. In the DDR people made do with what was available.

It was best to maintain a financial reserve for a rainy, blustery day. Nadine, for example, wore the same patched coat she'd worn for five winters. It was too small, but, after Leipzig, it was roomy enough. Heike hoped it would grow small again soon.

It was disquieting to notice coats of those whizzing purposefully to and from platforms. The only clothes the girls found commensurate with theirs were those of slaves to drugs, alcohol, or both. They walked through the squalor of Kaisarstrasse, the smut capital of Germany and, therefore,

Europe. On the Anlage, they witnessed addicts rinsing off needles with snow or water in puddles. They ducked into a huge department store for the warmth and found themselves confronted with the shiny glitter of abject waste.

"Who needs any of this stuff?" Nadine asked.

"Not the Turks," Heike replied.

In less than an hour, the younger girl's keen eyes noticed who performed physical labor.

"The Turks might have to go back home."

Heike examined her sister critically. She'd never heard Nadine express ethnic sentiments.

"Now, they have the Ossis to do their work."

Heike nodded knowingly.

After ridding escalators to the top floor, they rode them back to street level. Dressed as they were, the girls collected curious, unsettling glances. The Ossis were out of place amid the opulent displays.

"Heike, what if you have to buy something to get out?"

It was frightening. A moment before, the thought hadn't existed; a moment later, it couldn't be shaken off. To have unlimited amounts of glittering junk cluttering the store must cost a fortune. Though the throngs made purchases at dozens of counters, they were not making a dent in the stock. It would be in keeping with the Wessi character to charge people something to look. If one didn't buy something, one must contribute to the cost of a myriad of lights and the heating required by such a gargantuan interior.

They reversed course to seek work clothes. What they found was too attractive for serious labor and exceedingly overpriced. Similarly, kitchen towels were too attractive and expensive for practicality.

"The Wessis must need this stuff to polish gold and silver," Nadine deduced.

Judging by the kitchenware on display, Heike was inclined to believe it.

Then they headed for an exit.

"What if we have to pay?" Heike whispered frantically.

"Say something rude in English," Nadine suggested, "Amis get away with everything."

Heike inventoried her brain. She could assemble something abrupt, but would it sound American? She'd never heard American speech, save for an occasional snippet played in class. Most of the English they heard was from the forbidden BBC. Once, an American writer was interviewed; the differences in pronunciation were obvious and, often, unintelligible.

Fortunately, they burst through the huge glass doors without being accosted. They breathed a huge sigh of relief before putting distance between themselves and the Wessi horror. They found a buffet and ordered coffee. It came in paper cups. Heike felt Nadine's indignation and quickly put a soothing hand on her arm.

Whatever comment Nadine invented was stored for future use.

The coffee was rich. Heike, the family's coffee connoisseur, audibly praised it. True, exchanging valuable money for paper cups was an afront, but neither objected to the contents.

They searched for a hotel. Even the cheapest would create a gash in Heike's hundred marks. That money – real money that could buy a mountain of Ossi marks – was too valuable an asset. Squandering it on intangibles was unthinkable. Ultimately, they huddled in the bowels of the Bahnhof, sitting on a cold floor, trying to draw heat from each other.

The noises of bottles scudding on the floor and heated, alcoholic-induced exchanges from just beyond sight did not bother Nadine in the least. She was soon asleep, her head on Heike's shoulder and drooling on Jürgen's former coat. Heike did not begrudge Nadine either the shoulder or the coat. Rather, she remained alert. She had failed Nadine in Leipzig. This time, she'd not allow Nadine to be torn from her.

Suddenly, the noises died away; the yelling ceased. A few moments later, Heike saw why. Approaching them were two visions bundled in green. *Polizei*! In a typical DDR reaction, Heike's blood froze. However, she refused to show fear. If the need arose, she'd defend herself and Nadine furiously. This would not, she vowed, end as it had in Leipzig.

The policemen stood far enough apart to cut off any escape route. They surveyed the girls closely, saying nothing. Heike glared with all the malevolence she could muster.

"Is she alright?" the taller officer asked.

Involuntarily, Heike redirected her attention. With Nadine's deformed face and saliva accumulating on the sleeve of Jürgen's jacket, she could be mistaken for a drug victim.

"Except for being very tired, she's quite well."

She kept her words respectful, but her no-nonsense tone was intended as a deterrent.

"What are you doing here?" the other officer asked.

His face and voice were respectful but authoritative.

"We're waiting for our train home."

"Where's home?" he asked.

"The DDR," Heike stated defiantly.

She'd not be submissive. She was proud of her heritage. If her attitude provoked violence, so be it. Her muscles tensed in anticipation of a hostile response. To her amazement, the green-uniformed men displayed neither resentment nor condescension. They remained perfectly relaxed.

"Do you have a ticket?"

"Ja."

She'd no intention of showing it to them. To her amazement, neither issued a demand.

"It's not safe for you to stay here all night. Why don't you go into the station? There is an all-night buffet. It's heated."

So unexpected was this suggestion that Heike was speechless. The second officer elaborated.

"So long as you have a long-range ticket, you're allowed to wait there."

She blinked.

These were Wessi police. They knew she was Ossi. Was it a trick? To what end? They could beat them to death and claim innocence. With their DDR documents, they'd be labeled spies, thieves, smugglers or worse. Wessi authorities would ignore a double murder on the word of the perpetrators alone. Heike and Nadine were enemy aliens. Murdered under the Frankfurt Bahnhof amid drunks, wine, and beer residue – who'd bother asking questions?

She nudged the slumbering baggage.

"Nadine. Nadine, wake up!"

The nudges became more insistent. Nadine moaned in protest. She clung to sleep with determination. She growled and pushed at Heike's leg.

"Nadine, please!"

"*Lass mich alein!*"

"Nadine, wake up."

Her eyes opened. Upon seeing two green blurs, she sensed danger.

"Ach, Scheiße!"

Heike faced a delicate situation. Should Nadine exercise bellicosity, the girls would be trapped!

"It's fine, Nadine. It's not trouble. We can go upstairs and stay in a warm place."

Nadine moaned again.

"Don't play tricks. I'm exhausted."

"Come."

Heike called upon limbs both stiff and sore. She struggled to her feet and coaxed her sister to do likewise. Before she could protest, Heike watched a green-sleeved hand grip Nadine's other arm firmly. Soon enough, the woozy girl was on her feet.

"Where do we go?"

"Up the escalator and turn left," the assisting policeman motioned.

"Are you sure you don't need help?"

"We're fine," Heike replied. "Danke."

The uniforms stood and watched until satisfied Nadine was under her own power. The pair passed through the underground passageway without hindrance. The drunken congress had been dispersed minutes before, but empty bottles and cigarette butts littered the scene.

"Did you say *danke*?" Nadine croaked.

"Ja."

"To Wessi Bulle?"

"Ja."

"I never expected to see the day."

Nadine did not joke.

"Neither did I," Heike replied.

The Oregon Coast

February-March 1990

Kathy Foster convinced herself Uncle Dieter was right; the more hope she heaped on a spurious message, the greater the disappointment. Despite her efforts, however, she knew Heike was family. How much older was she? What memories had she of mother? Perhaps she could provide a lucid recollection of the New Year's night when tragedy divided them.

Whatever is good, let your thoughts be on these things. Kathy recalled Paul's message related by Reverend Rademacher. He looked directly at her through much of his sermon on Philippians.

Thoughts of one's own sister were, indeed, good.

Ute's child neared arrival. Despite all Ute's positive thinking, she grew nervous and reticent. She exercised cautiously, fearing the slightest miscalculation might snuff a life. Kathy tended to her adoptive mother's every need. Additionally, she was constantly supportive, but Ute's trepidation was contagious. Both Foster females turned skittish.

"If it is premature now, it should make it," Ute stated absent-mindedly over dinner one evening.

Kathy and Aaron exchanged startled looks. Ute's daze ceased once she noticed the staring. She smiled self-consciously and resumed mastication. She wasn't aware she'd spoken.

Four nights later, Kathy sat on the floor with her geometry homework spread out on the coffee table. Aaron was finishing the dishes. Ute lay in the bedroom relaxing. Since beginning her sabbatical a month before, the woman found food irresistible.

Aaron and Kathy formed a food-police detachment, but they were gone most of the day and unable to monitor Ute's "grazing." The doctor cautioned her emphatically about the dangers of gluttony. His admonition that excess might not be good for the baby put a damper on most of Ute's urges, and Mrs. Rademacher looked in twice or thrice a day. When a fatigued Ute excused herself from dinner, announcing overindulgence, her family grew concerned.

Kathy fiddled with compass and protractor, more attuned to sounds from her parent's room than the problem at hand. Similarly, Aaron was extra quiet rinsing, drying, and putting dishes away. Nothing anomalous disturbed them. Soon, Kathy's mind turned to Heike. She imagined her sister struggling with university studies.

That's why she refused to flee when opportunity presented! Heike, so Kathy imagined, was taller and hardened by the border trauma. Though not overtly cynical, she'd be wary and judicious. Bold, but never foolish, Heike was a person to mentor and guide a younger sister – not only in matters of erudition, but, also, in the practicality of daily living. The lack-luster geometrician speculated Heike could help her obtain a university billet and, perhaps, find a small apartment near campus.

"Aaron."

Ute's voice was calm. Though employing her normal voice, her husband heard her half a house away. He abandoned the dishes instantly. Kathy feigned nonchalance and as he walked by.

"You called?" he asked, disappearing into the bedroom.

"I want you to promise me something."

Kathy's ears pricked up. She lay her math toys aside and crept stealthily around the coffee table to get nearer the bedroom door.

"Ute, don't get worked up. It doesn't help."

"It's helping," Ute insisted, keeping her voice low.

She knew Kathy was spying. "When the time comes, I must not worry about anything except the delivery."

Aaron sighed.

"Okay, honey. What is it?"

"If the doctor says he can only save one of us –"

"Oh, God!" Aaron protested.

Ute shushed him. She waited, listening for movement in the living room.

"You've got to promise! I mean it, Aaron. I've thought it through. You must promise to save the baby."

"You can't make me promise that!"

Kathy's stomach knotted tightly; her breathing became labored.

"I've written it in German for Mutti and Pappi, and I'm leaving it here. It's what I want, Aaron. I honestly don't want to live if…Give the child a chance. It's one thing to lose it, but I can't live realizing there was a choice. I told Doc Reynolds and I'm telling you: that's what I want. You must promise to respect my wishes."

There was a long, long – very long – pause.

"The situation will never come up," Aaron moaned.

"That should make it easy."

There was another long pause.

"We need to talk about this further."

He was gone before Ute issued an ultimatum. He discovered Kathy on her knees nearby and knew she'd heard. Their sad eyes met, but they didn't speak.

Several minutes later, Kathy went into the bathroom and pretended to use it. On her way back, she hoped to find Ute asleep. Instead, she found her propped against the headboard, reading the Bible.

"Come watch TV with us," Kathy invited.

"No, thanks, dear. I just got comfortable."

"Can I bring you something?"

"Not at the moment."

Aaron turned on the set but wasn't watching. Kathy changed to a show she preferred. It was a smoke screen; she wanted nothing to do with it. She knelt on the sofa next to Aaron.

"I'll get Gary to take me for pizza or something tomorrow night," she whispered.

He examined her with sad eyes.

"Kathy, I can't do it. I can't let her die."

"It isn't your choice."

He knew that, of course but wasn't comforted. He wrung his hands.

"If you save her, and the baby dies, Ute will resent you, forever."

"You know everything, don't you?" he challenged softly.

"I don't have to know anything. She wrote Oma and Opa! She wants this baby even if she dies for it."

"You're going back to your family," he spat. "How will I care for a baby and make a living?"

"I promise this," Kathy whispered. "If Ute – doesn't make it, I'll stay right here and take care of it."

He snorted.

"That's very glib," he noted. "How can you promise that?"

Kathy shrugged.

"You said yourself the situation won't come up. It's easy. Try it."

"What if the situation does come up?"

She didn't dare hesitate.

"I'll do exactly what I said."

He put his arm around her and held her close.

"That Swabish sense of honor, huh? We both know you aren't really Swabish."

"That's how I was raised."

She saw it. True, it was only a shadow and was gone in an instant, but, for the first time all evening, Kathy saw Aaron smile. He kissed her forehead. She felt pleased with herself for making him feel better, but she shuddered at the potential cost.

* * *

Characteristically, Kathy kept the storm of her swirling emotions locked up. She longed to unburden herself, but it was too great an imposition on Molly. Gary, meanwhile, might interpret her concerns as a ploy to gain attention or sympathy. She heard vague reports about students who accused Kathy of limelight lust, and her tales of Eastern intrigue were a means of obtaining it.

She was confident Gary wouldn't be so judgmental, but she lacked a similar confidence in herself. Perhaps, as she tossed in bed at night, her critics were right. She enjoyed the accolades directed her way through the theatre and the use of her voice. Was she an addict?

After disturbing dreams and fitful sleep, she decided she must confide or explode. Alas, Gary didn't board the bus that morning. Kathy knew he'd contracted a cold. Had he the means to crawl to the kitchen, Athena would chase him off to school.

Kathy's spirits sank deeper. Her sudden appetite for osculation was thwarted, temporarily. This prospect paled with the certainty she was condemned to drag a dead elephant through another restless night littered with disturbing visions.

Jayme was smitten. The Tomboy was possessed by a classmate. Despite red hearts and visions of fairy-dust floating about her as she wandered, dazed, about campus, Jayme was, alas, Jayme. It proved impossible to share her feelings with the object of her adoration. Molly sympathized but enjoyed the entertaining farce. Even Shelly, never timid around boys, enjoyed discovering this Achilles heel of her, previously, fearless friend.

So, "it came to pass" that the entire entourage abandoned its lunch corner for a table in the cafeteria. There they watched Jayme sit silently while casting wistful glances in the direction of the boy who stole her appetite. Molly was there for the amusement, but she was ready with verbal salve should her sister require it. Where Molly went, her loyal subjects followed.

Kathy didn't look forward to lunch. Ute, exceedingly lethargic in the mornings, forced her to prepare her own. Further, Gary wasn't there for her, and she got no amusement from Jayme's sighs and envied Shelly who flitted about school, introducing herself to all and sundry as Kuri O'Hara of the County Cork O'Haras. It was the latest in the extrovert's lunch-time adventures aimed at amusing herself and many others. Her reputation as the school clown was tempered by her no-nonsense approach to academics.

Molly and Henry tarried while Kathy fetched lunch from her locker. They formed the van, merrily marching ahead through the halls. As Kathy passed the choir room, she heard soothing music wafting about her. She slowed her pace, then, stopped at the open door.

"Be right with you," she assured the retreating figures.

If either Molly or Henry heard, they trusted her promise. Kathy, however, didn't keep it. She was seduced by string instruments and must investigate.

She entered the room quietly, not certain if she violated school rules, but aware Mr. Davidson's lunch period was not open to students. She found him seated at his desk behind a plate with a thick slice of homemade bread, two slabs of ham and a sliced tomato. If he had a bottle of beer at his elbow, Kathy would have anointed him a German.

He looked at her and surmised what lured her in. He popped a tomato slice into his mouth and gestured her to take a seat. She went to the first level of risers and sat.

"What's that?" she asked in a whisper.

"Bach." Mr. Davidson informed. "Air on a G string."

There was humble silence.

"Could you play it again?"

He hit the rewind button and started anew. Kathy placed her lunch bag on the chair next, folded her hands in her lap, put her feet on the floor and closed her eyes. The music wrapped around her. It exorcised every doubt and fear. It vanquished the rash promise she made Aaron, and the terror that she might live life as a drudge, raising a child not her own. Concerns over Heike and the remainder of her family eased. From somewhere came the words of Reverend Rademacher, soft and melodious.

"Whatever is good…Think upon these things."

A comforting certitude washed over her. She accepted the possibility Ute might die, that Kathy would be bound to an unrelated child for years; that she might never know her real family. These troubles were shunted aside. No matter what happened, there were reasons.

When she opened her eyes, Molly and Henry sat on folding chairs opposite and several feet away. She hadn't heard them enter. Had she dozed? Molly and Henry alternated preparing and bringing lunch. It was Henry's turn, so the couple used chopsticks and shared a common bowl. They had returned to find their missing friend and perched nearby without disturbing her reverie.

They asked no questions. They required no explanations.

"Once more?" Mr. Davidson asked.

"If it isn't a bother."

Henry and Molly maintained silence. It was enough to tend a flock of one and forego the merriment of Jayme melting in sighs. Kathy didn't need their company, but she treasured it.

Kathy Foster had been moved by music before. Certainly, the opera *Hansel and Gretel* garnered a profound effect. So, also, was the intoxication of the Brenda Lee songbook she and Athena bellowed one evening under a spell that could not be broken. Their cacophony drove poor Gary home alone. The Bach melody, however, transcended anything she'd yet experienced.

It didn't tap a reverberate chord; instead, it reached into every corner of her being and engendered emotional tranquility. A small string orchestra produced an ethereal melody. It was a balm to her soul. It was as if Bach composed this therapeutic interlude as a message in a bottle. It drifted along for two hundred and fifty years to provide succor for young nobody.

Bach, Kathy concluded, set the notes to paper, but no human composed it. Humans drew lines on maps and imprisoned or killed those attempting to cross. Humans manufactured misery over the powerless until the misery became so ponderous it consumed those who created it.

Humans, unable to manage their lives, strove to gain control over the lives of others. From ignorance and vanity, a simple parchment that, somehow, escaped use as wrapping paper in a Leipzig butcher shop, survived. Eventually, it found Kathy. She was convinced that these coincidences were smudged with divine fingerprints.

* * *

The first spasms came in the early hours.

It was Saturday; Aaron took off work a week prior to be near as the critical time neared. Athena came by before and after work, daily. She claimed her purpose was to flirt with Aaron. She urged Ute to resume work as soon as possible,

"'Cuz that new girl ain't cuttin' it."

Similarly, Mrs. Rademacher frequently dropped by. However, as Ute predicted, the "performance" began in private. They called the doctor, then mounted the car and issued Kathy's instructions.

The girl, Bach playing in her head, remained unruffled. She dressed, made breakfast; strangely, she eschewed coffee. It was part of their prepared procedure: no appliance use, ensuring that none was left on. Ute slowly paced the living room floor, devoid of appetite and thirst. Periodically, she'd lean on Aaron or a wall until the pain subsided. Aaron monitored his watch.

Kathy hugged Ute goodbye and wished her luck. She dashed down the hill to buy a cup of coffee before reporting to the *Mary R.* She was disappointed, but not surprised, to find Barker piloting the craft. Aaron gave the sea mammals room, but Barker crowded them. Alas, with Aaron shore bound, Barker's most cost-effective replacement was Barker.

It was a cool, blustery day. The ocean was turgid, but not enough to dissuade customers. As expected, there was screaming at the water, but Kathy went about her duties with patience and fortitude.

She didn't yell at or threaten the "skipper" when he steered right up to a whale. Instead, she tended greener passengers with the benevolence of Florence Nightingale. It was useless, of course, but it distracted her from Barker's carelessness around her marine friends.

Her chest puffed up when a couple recognized her from the theatre. They were amazed to learn that she was merely sixteen. After a few moments of adulation, she excused herself and continued her duties. She kept a hot cup in the captain's hand. Aaron never tended the helm one-handed, but Barker assumed his seamanship was predicated on sipping coffee garnished with sea spray.

Kathy refrained; coffee required frequent visits to the head, but Barker had a bladder of steel. He hated Kathy's being below while dockside, so Kathy made three pots of coffee on a pitching craft. It was messy and wasteful, and she resented it, but Barker was the skipper; she was merely a slave.

Aaron cleaned *Mary* after each day's cruising. Barker left this to Kathy who, unfamiliar with Aaron's practice, made repeated inspections of her work. If Barker discovered something improperly stowed, or an item unpolished, he'd not spare vocabulary.

Molly waited at the end of the dock. Kathy was amazed that Henry was nowhere in sight.

"Has it come yet?"

"Don't know."

They didn't speak in the car. Once at the hospital, Molly waited in the lobby while Kathy was escorted to Aaron. The nurse on duty had problems with Ute. She'd never heard the name.

"There's a Mrs. Foster in room 208," she reported as if scolding. "And you are?"

"Kathy Foster," she lied. "My dad's probably with her."

The nurse nodded.

"Go in, but no high-fives."

Kathy wondered about recent nursing-school graduates but reserved a comment. She followed the numbers and arrows to find room 208. She pushed gently on the wide wooden door and found herself looking at a pale and subdued Aaron. When she looked onto the bed, she shivered.

Ute lay with her head arched back and her mouth wide open. The woman looked as white as the pillow upon which she rested. One white-porcelain arm lay stretched at her side with a bottle of fluid plugged into it.

"It was pretty rough," he whispered.

"The baby tried to come out feet first. They had to turn it. She's lost a lot of blood – was too weak to push – had to pull it out."

"How long?"

"About an hour ago."

"Is he okay?"

Strange, she thought, how she accepted the pronoun without qualification.

"Fine, considering the beating he took."

Aaron quivered noticeably. He'd experienced a very bad time. Judging from the motionless form on the bed, Ute fared worse.

"How is she?"

"She?"

The voice was quiet and crackled with dryness. It was a voice Kathy never heard before.

"I'm not dead yet," Ute continued.

She didn't open her eyes.

"You're supposed to rest," Aaron reminded.

"Am I running laps here? Give me your hand."

Aaron took her free hand. Ute gripped it weakly.

"Remind me not to do this again."

Kathy smiled. If Ute made cracks, her spirit remained unscathed. Aaron, however, was very quiet.

"Take Kathy to see her brother."

Aaron didn't want to leave, but Ute insisted.

"Kathy?"

"Yes?"

The woman couldn't open her eyes.

"He's your brother. Don't forget that."

Kathy locked onto Aaron's arm. He was shaken and might fall if unassisted. Together, they shuffled to a glassed-in room containing several tiny baskets. Only three were occupied; all were tucked in with heads down and tiny feet up.

"There he is," Aaron nodded at the baby nearest.

He was very pink. His eyes were tightly shut. There were tiny pimples on either side of his tiny nose. As they watched, his tiny right arm quickly moved, and the blanket undulated over his tiny feet.

"What's his name?" she asked.

There was an amazed silence.

"I – don't – know."

Weimar

March-April 1990

It began on their train return to the DDR.

"You abandoned the New Forum when the crowd chanted for unity," Heike submitted.

"The New Forum – great mistake," Nadine conceded. "I thought reform would –."

She couldn't continue.

"The system was flawed, Nadine. Reform couldn't eliminate flaws. We required revolution. Leipzig could have brought it about. No one knew the Vopos would disobey orders. No one knew how fragile the government was. If there was ever a moment for revolution, there it was. What was missing?"

Nadine lost the thread of the discussion. She saw the future in Frankfurt – open drug use, prostitution, exploited foreign workers, an industry dedicated to waste and frivolousness, a society based on stealing from mindless consumers and creating victims – money for trinkets.

"What was missing, Nadine?" Heike insisted.

"*Ich weis nicht.*"

"Leadership! The thing preventing revolution was lack of leaders. People could have seized the moment and brought about a socialist nation. The potential leaders were exiled, in prison, or under the Stasi thumb. That day when the police refused to fire – We could have won."

Nadine kept her gaze out the window. She half expected the train to lift from its tracks and take to the air.

"Too late," she groaned.

Heike physically shook Nadine until she turned to face her.

"How long do you think the Wessis can keep ahead of the revolution? Sooner or later, the workers must realize they're being exploited more than ever. They'll get fed up with drugs and whores and slavery and dependence. They'll take to the streets again. They need leaders, Nadine, people who can direct energy where it's needed the most. We have to keep the ideals alive."

"What ideals?"

Nadine had every right to by cynical – they all did. The SED required citizens to sacrifice for Party aggrandizement. She, Heike, Jürgen, and Rolf made sacrifices every day and did so willingly; they believed in the betterment of the world. They had since learned SED administrators shopped in stores crammed with goods the people could only dream about; the highest leaders lived in a resort city where they never interacted with the people.

A rumor circulated that the wife of the party leader flew to Paris twice a month to have her hair done. Instantly, people believed this without any evidence. When the rumor spread, people were aware of ruling-class depravity. No outrageous story was rejected.

"Our ideals, Nadine. The people's ideals!"

Nadine studied the blurred countryside. Her thoughts returned to Frankfurt. She shrugged. What good were ideals now?

"Rosa was right," Heike concluded. "Lenin and the rest were wrong. Democratic socialism is the only way. We must keep her spirit alive. We don't know when the next opportunity will come. We must be ready."

Nadine turned and glared. She was hostile.

"Who do you think you are?" she asked sharply. "What makes you think you can lead a revolution?"

"Stop, Nadine. I'm no fool. I know I can't lead, but I can keep Rosa's ideas alive in those who do lead. When people believe, they will follow! We require something to work for. If not, we have nothing."

Nadine examined Heike's fatigued eyes.

"*Wir sind das Volk.*" Heike whispered.

That struck Nadine with the force of a nightstick to the face.

Over the next several days, Heike fed Nadine just enough to stir the mind. Many times, Nadine pretended not hear. Heike didn't give up. She dropped crumbs – one here, a couple there.

One evening, Nadine sat propped against the headboard with her knees drawn under her chin. At the foot of the bed sat Heike, feet dangling in space and body twisted to read the words of the Bard from a thick book which lay near Nadine's naked toes.

"*Do you not know that I am a woman?*" the honeyed voice of Heike Nemo rang clear.

"*When I think, I must speak...*"

"Can you say that in English?" Nadine blurted, unexpectedly.

Heike assumed she was being mocked.

"Um, I can – try."

Moments later, she advanced her best English summation. It wasn't a difficult concept; it required neither tricky verb tenses nor advanced vocabulary. Nevertheless, Heike knew Shakespeare's knack for making profound the, seemingly, mundane. Though satisfied with the accuracy of her translation, the author's style evaded her.

Heike looked vacantly at Nadine. She sought approval, but what credentials had she? The blond with the misshapen face knew only enough English to author sentences of two or three words. Gleaned from snippets of student exchanges, these were mangled and, often, vulgar.

"So," Nadine advanced, "how do we preach revolution without ending up in a Wessi dungeon?"

Heike devoted much thought to the subject. She, cautiously, explained the concept of Rosa's Children to her suddenly receptive sister.

As the days trudged by, Heike showed her pages from her notebook. There were expositions on Luxemburg themes; others were single sentence axioms which struck Heike with increasing frequency.

"You don't give up, do you?"

"Good ideas don't deserve to die," she replied instantly.

Nadine wondered if that was Shakespeare speaking.

"What can we do?"

"I want a public gathering."

Nadine bulked. She'd had her fill of those.

"A protest?"

Heike shook her head.

"A rally, more like. I want people to have information. I want to remind them what we're working for…"

"And how the SED ruined everything," Nadine snarled.

Heike shook her head emphatically.

"No name-calling or finger-pointing. I want to remind people of something to believe in. The people are angry. They know they were lied to and exploited. I want them to realize socialism isn't dead. A good idea remains a good idea. I want names and addresses so we can send informational letters and messages of inspiration."

"Heike! It will take years to build a base."

"And?" Heike retorted. "You know how to do it quicker?'

Heike wasn't known for patience. To start modestly confirmed the depth of her commitment. And Nadine was impressed.

"When do you want to do this?"

"When the weather is good. May. June is probably better. Maybe, July?"

"And where?"

"The *Frauenplan*."

Nadine started.

"Are you crazy? You'll be arrested."

Heike shook her head.

"We don't violate law. We get permission."

"Angry people might try to stab you."

"I believe in standing for my beliefs," she asserted. "You did!"

"It got me a new face and fewer teeth," Nadine reminded. "You're willing to risk that?"

Heike didn't speak. She didn't have to. Though Nadine's expression remained lifeless since Leipzig, for the first time in ages, Heike saw in Nadine's eyes a flicker of life.

* * *

It was Nadine's turn to venture into the city and collect items for the evening table. A small residual of their Wessi stash remained, but the household economy was back in Ossiland. Taking her heavy coat from the door-side peg, Nadine noticed two pieces of outgoing mail. The letter, addressed in Rolf's scrawl, was for Jürgen. The other was a postcard; she turned it over to ensure it was stamped, it was for Günther but *not* his military address.

Something was going on. Heike had been brooding for two days. This wasn't out of character. However, a card for Günther smacked of conspiracy. Nadine was suddenly aware that Heike never mentioned his name.

She thrust the mail into her coat pocket. As per normal duties, the mail would find the first available receptacle. Nadine, however, was suspicious. A letter to Jürgen was dispatched within minutes, but she kept the postcard until her basket was as full as it was likely to get. Then, Nadine did something out of character: she entered a corner café for tea.

She shed her coat and scarf and placed them on a heavy-laden rack. She withdrew the postcard from the pocket and furtively transported it to the nearest vacant table. The front featured Shakespeare's statue. She kept it face up until her tea arrived. Satisfied she wasn't likely to be disturbed, Nadine turned the card over and was confronted by a confusion of letters.

Some were Cyrillic. Others were arranged in English. The German portion was in old-style lettering. Heike attempted a poem. The meter and rhyme worked out, but only by switching languages to make the syllables and rhyme fit.

Heike was nothing if not resourceful. Nevertheless, it took time for Nadine to make sense of the bizarre prosody. She guessed the meaning of an English verb and noun.

> *In dappled sunlight, in a park*
> > *You and I; remember?*
> *You gave me a kiss there*
> > *My first; remember?*
> *Allow me, please, to return it.*
> > *At least that to remember;*
> *Leave me free to water, with my tears,*
> > *the ashes of a country*
> *I remember.*

It was signed H. J.

Heike and Günther? Nadine knew flirting went on, at least, from Heike's side, but kisses in the park? When? It wasn't since Lilo left. Günther's supposedly secret visits to the city, weren't very secret. Had it occurred during courtship with Lilo, the Amazon would have killed her rival.

She reread the twisted and confused letters. Whatever its merit as a work of poetry, it oozed pathos. Heike's one overriding fault was feeling things too deeply, and she carried wounds forever. The postcard was no sham. It constituted a conduit into Heike's soul.

Had Heike intended her art to remain secret, she'd have posted it herself. She knew Nadine would read it! Why?

"Bitte!"

The waitress heard something in Nadine's voice that prohibited her from exercising the innate DDR quality of polite rudeness. Despite her need to record the order of a new customer, she stopped for Nadine's summons.

"May I use your pen?"

Upside down, the poem appeared a jumbled mess. Nevertheless, the waitress pulled the pen from her apron. She fully expected to see a hasty correction. Instead, she witnessed an addition.

Nadine left payment in coins beside the cup and saucer. She placed the postcard in her basket with the evening victuals. Scarf about her neck and coat buttoned to the top, Nadine boldly confronted the brusque winter weather so typical of a German spring. Moments later, she stepped up to a postbox.

"Bastard!" she spat, sending the poem on its way.

She wondered if Heike would ever learn of her addendum. If ever she did, fury would visit. Well, it was worth it, but only if Günther understood the allusion. She hoped he would understand; she hoped it would send a dagger through his blackened heart.

Nadine had scribbled *Helena* after Heike's initials.

* * *

That evening, Nadine joined Rosa's Children. There was no paper to sign, no oath to swear, and no badge to wear. Nadine's induction into Germany's newest political movement was a nod of Heike's head.

It was cold, and the ancient heating system was taxed beyond capacity. Despite the early hour, the girls enjoyed getting into warm night clothes and snuggling under the covers. If Nadine were in a receptive mood, they'd recline together on the high bed and take turns reading from the volume of Shakespeare propped up against their knees. They would alternate in turning the pages so their hands would be exposed to the chill less frequently.

There came a loud knock at the front door, they exchanged anxious looks. It was not late, but callers seldom came after working hours. Everyone insisted the Stasi would never bother Rolf. The dreaded institution was defunct; its records destroyed or seized by outraged citizens. Former agents hid under assumed names. Still –

They listened quietly. They'd closed the room's door to give the radiator a fighting chance, but they heard voices. After a few seconds, they resumed reading. By the end of the first act of *Cymbeline*, they forgot there was a guest in the house. Agreeing the story was grim, they paged back to Sir John and Mistress Ford for a few laughs.

Rolf called for Maus.

"What have I done?" she sighed.

"He isn't angry," Nadine reminded.

Despite Rolf's placid tone, Heike begged Nadine to come down with her.

"I'm not brave," Nadine responded. "If he wanted us both, he'd have called us."

Heike threw back the covers and slid off the bed until her woolen socks hit the floor. Bundled up for the night, she wrapped herself in the remnants of an old robe. It was a needless show of modesty, but one could not know who was below.

Nadine attempted to read on; it was futile. There were no raised voices and no audible evidence of furniture being smashed. Several minutes passed. No one opened and closed the front door. She closed the volume and laid it on Heike's place.

Voices filtered through the door. They were low and slow with great, troubling gaps between. Nadine's anxiety turned to alarm. She was on the verge of eavesdropping. She'd be detected if she cracked the bedroom door; Rolf wouldn't tolerate it. Yet, she could not remain cloistered with her fears.

Finally, there was movement below. She heard the front door open. The voices continued for several seconds, and the door closed. Voices began anew, Rolf's and Heike's. Then, she heard her mother say something. Nadine felt cheated.

Anne spoke so infrequently that Nadine pined to know the words and, just as much, what had prompted their articulation. More talking. Then – silence. Finally, she heard the creak of the stairs.

Slowly, a figure made its way to the landing. The door opened and Heike, face drained, entered. She looked into Nadine's eyes with an expression so catastrophic that Nadine was unable to speak.

Had something happened to Jürgen? Why call only Heike? Whatever the news, it left Heike weak enough that she must cling to the edge of the bed. Nadine, unable to think clearly, gripped Heike's arm and attempted to reel her in.

As the struggle continued, Nadine expended a strength she'd not felt since Leipzig. The renewed strength was doubled with the realization that Heike wasn't helping much. Once she gained the summit, Heike threw her arms around Nadine's neck and held close.

"What?"

Heike groaned.

"Who was it?"

"I'm scared," Heike uttered.

Nadine let go. She couldn't force Heike to speak, and she couldn't push her away. She waited with her blood bulging her veins. Finally, Heike released her grip and fell back into the space previously vacated. If the Shakespeare volume created discomfort, she ignored it. Heike leaned against the headboard and covered her face with her hands.

"Oh," she groaned, "I'm getting a baby."

That lead-hearted bastard! It will be a race with Lilo for his wretched throat!

Not until that moment did Nadine think of killing somebody. The desire was palpable. With the postcard, she intended to injure Günther emotionally. That was no longer enough. Nothing short of his lifeless, bleeding body at her feet would satisfy her.

Heike was too upset and frightened to realize what she said.

"It was Frau Willing," she moaned.

Nadine's murder plot was momentarily interrupted. She could do nothing but stare, open mouthed. Heike pressed up against her. In bits and starts, Heike narrated Willing's story as she recalled it. Heike's mind produced a perfectly clear picture of the sequence of events.

Frau Willing was preparing to pull into the designated bus stop at Goethe Platz. A baby carriage ambled across the street directly in front of her. She slammed on the breaks. A man and woman, prematurely leaving their seats, went sprawling.

Enraged, Frau Willing opened the door, jumped out of the bus, grabbed the carriage, and pulled it onto the sidewalk. The whole while she shouted her most disgusting peasant epithets at the blocks of stone standing immobile as an untended baby rolled out into a busy street.

"Whose baby is this? Where is the drunken slut of a pig's bitch who let this happen?"

Only when her insane screaming met with absolute and amazed silence did she realize the baby's plight was not due to ineptitude. Regaining her faculties, she saw. The tragedy was nauseatingly clear: A woman pushed her carriage off the walk, behind a parked bus, to negotiate a crossing. The bus unexpectedly backed up.

Why? What insane thought crossed the driver's mind?

"He can't tell us," Frau Willing reported. "He's in hospital. In shock. Can't speak. Sits and looks to nothing. Good man. Good driver. Now, his family sit with him and wonder if he ever to come back."

The tiny mother was dead – crushed like an egg. Her last living act was to push the baby into the street, trusting, blindly, that traffic would avoid it.

Frau Willing left the bus where she braked it. The infant slept through the entire drama. She stood guard while the police interviewed witnesses.

Their attempts to interrogate the driver were fruitless. No one knew what to do with the baby, so the peasant woman stayed. When the baby woke up, Willing plucked it out of the carriage and held it close. When it fussed, she bounced it and soothed it as best she could. No one would take charge of the child.

She lingered, comforting the child while alternate drivers were dispatched. Eventually, the busses rolled again. Frau Willing remained with a baby in her arms.

Eventually, the police brought the father. Eyes red, face puffy, hands trembling, he was mute and in shock. Frau Willing refused to surrender the baby for fear he'd drop it and the tragedy would compound. She returned it to the carriage, leaving the widower disoriented. One policeman steered the baby tram while another led the father away.

Frau Willing trailed behind, curious to know what would happen.

"Public nurseries closing," she reminded Heike. "No money. The one's still here close soon. Cannot care for baby. Father, he is no good. Can't even keep baby's *po* dry – never mind feed. I go to hims house, do what I can to do, but now which? Papa's family dead. Mama's family goes West last year. Disappear. Nobody know. Man work in wood factory, still have job, maybe – for now, but maybe not so long. Need money to baby. He want me to help, but I to work too."

Heike cried in the retelling. She was sad, but the tears sprang from fear as much as from horror.

"I don't know how to look after a baby," she croaked.

Nadine understood why Frau Willing thought of Heike. However, there were limits.

"Why didn't you tell her you can't help?"

"Because," Heike blubbered. "I can't!"

In the futility of it all, Heike threw her arms around Nadine again and wept openly on her shoulder.

"*Typisch Heike*," Nadine thought, holding her sister close. She won't ever cry for herself, but her pathos for others ran very deep.

Die Wende

April 1990

"It's a boy," Kathy announced, meeting Molly in the lobby.

"Congratulations," Molly beamed. "What's his name?"

Kathy gave a disappointed shrug.

"They must have discussed names before," Molly insisted.

"Only a million times."

Molly guessed the truth. Her face, for one of the few times ever, reflected sobriety.

"How's your mom?"

"Resting."

Molly didn't move.

"They think she'll be fine."

Molly accepted that, though her concerned visage remained. She was concerned about Ute because she was concerned about Kathy; the condition of the one was wedded to the other.

"Let me take you out and treat you to a gut bomb," she ventured at last.

"That's tempting, Mol, but get me home. Mom left a letter to her folks in case – well, in case. Until I burn it, I can't know peace."

Molly watched Kathy's eccentric ceremony of burning Ute's missive. The deed was done in a jungle of hearty, winter-drenched vegetation.

Kathy made a thorough inspection of the ashes to make certain only ashes remained. She then offered Molly an impromptu dinner.

"Henry won't be upset?"

"Henry and I have no plans for this evening," Molly announced.

That callous declaration startled Kathy.

"That doesn't sound good."

Molly's thoughts wandered. Perhaps, that allowed her terse comment to slip out.

"I didn't mean it the way it sounded." Molly assured. "Henry copes without me disgustingly well. The same cannot be said for me. Sorry, I'm deep into Jane Austin. Forgive my coarse mode of address, but the style is addictive. I imagine Jane and I could have a nice conversation."

Kathy assured her friend that she had no objection to eighteenth century syntax. Anyone else would sound both pompous and silly. Molly, however, did not. As with her clothes, Molly's conversational style suited her.

"You started to say something," Kathy prompted.

"The Kuriharas have family night once a week. There's nothing sinister. Still, I get restless. I daren't phone – tonight."

"So," Kathy concluded. "Tonight, is family night."

"It is not," Molly announced bravely. "It's girls' night."

Kathy would have laughed had she dared.

"You cannot expect me to believe you're punishing Henry. You aren't petty."

"Oh, I hope not! If anyone is being punished, it is I. Please, do not think I don't want to be here. On the contrary, it would be a crime to leave you alone. Still, I was sorely tempted to invite Henry along."

"He'd be welcome," Kathy assured.

"I know," Molly nodded. "Nevertheless, my attentions would be divided, and I don't think it's right. So, here I am talking about him instead of being here for you. That can't be right either."

"*Typisch Molly*," Kathy thought.

"You think I'm offended because we're having a talk?"

"Well, the topic is rather inappropriate. Of course, Gary might walk through that door at any moment. I'm content to be invisible."

"I'd like to see you try," Kathy dared.

"You, Kathy Foster, have a baby brother. Tell me."

"He's wrinkled and ugly," Kathy replied instantly, thankful to address a different topic.

"He's got zits on his face."

"And you're head over heels in love with him," Molly concluded.

Kathy sighed and surrendered a coy smile.

"Of course, I am. But there's more. It won't mean so much to you because you have Jayme, but I am so happy to be someone's sister. I can't tell you how wonderful I feel."

Molly didn't have to speculate. Kathy's visage and tone of voice communicated the depth of her emotion. After a lingering, felicitous moment, the face clouded.

"I already knew I was somebody's sister," she said. "The difference is I met this one, even if I don't know his name. My real sister's name I know, but I've never seen her."

Molly pulled up one of the kitchen chairs and sat down as a pointed reminder that Kathy invited her to dinner. Kathy caught the tacit message and opened the fridge to survey the possibilities. After a quick rummage, she brought forth the remains of a head of lettuce, two baked potatoes in aluminum jackets, and the scant remains of a roast.

"Hash," the hostess announced sadly. "I can mix up a salad to go with, but I see a burger in your future. Sorry, I didn't accept your offer."

"We won't starve," Molly promised.

She came forward to lend a hand. Without exchanging a word, Molly took charge of the salad and left Kathy to create beggar's hash. Suddenly inspired, she cracked eggs, shredded cheese, and reached for frozen vegetables. There emerged the possibility of a modest casserole.

"Anything other than lettuce? Carrots, maybe?"

Molly was given liberty to check the hydrator. Before the refrigerator door opened, Kathy launched, unexpectedly into a frustrated invective.

"My sister knows about me!" She reminded after exhausting the more emphatic portion of the Barker lexicon. "But I know nothing of her. What if she finds me, or I find her? What do I have to do to fit into my own family? I think you and I are passing each other, going in opposite directions. Do I have to start slopping hogs at three in the morning, or do I have to learn about finger bowls?"

Molly tittered as only Molly can titter.

"Finger bowls in the DDR? I don't think so."

"Who explains the rules, Mol? My sister is a stranger. I guess my one advantage is that she's older. She can explain how things work."

"You've made your mind about going back?"

"If I want to go to college, I'll have to. What kind of person would I be if I lived in a country about the size of this state and I didn't visit my family?"

The princess observed silence.

"And thank you, Mol, for not giving me this clap-trap about getting a scholarship."

Molly's smile lit the kitchen. She considered saying exactly that, but judiciousness won out. Kathy's smile matched Molly's. They laughed.

They were sitting over coffee like two middle-aged spinsters waiting for the oven to complete its work when the phone rang. Thinking it was Aaron with news of some new terror, Kathy jumped like a cat. Relief positively gathered in a puddle at her feet when she realized it was her grandmother in Milton-Freewater. The conversation became animated, and Molly amazed herself by succumbing to Kathy's lively banter.

"Grandma and Grandpa will drive over in a few days to help out," Kathy reported as she hung up.

"God! Where will they stay?"

An interesting question. There was a nice motel in town, but the prices were, also, nice. Though hardly paupers, the family Foster was comprised of pensioners save, of course, Ute and Aaron who were both, temporarily, unemployed.

"I just wonder."

Molly examined Kathy's inscrutability for only the length of her patience.

"No!" she concluded. "Aaron would kill you. When your mother gets home, she'll kill you again!"

"Don't be a prude," Kathy scolded. "We'd be chaperoned."

"By whom? Miss Oregon Territory?"

"Don't you have any faith in me?" Kathy demanded. "Or Gary either?"

Molly was in a spot there.

"Well – that's not the point."

"Did you say *whom*?"

"Where would you sleep?"

Ah, there was a question! On the floor under the kitchen table? Any other option was, pretty much, impossible.

"What is the point, by the way?"

"The point is – The point is – " Molly shrugged. "I don't know what the point is."

"Did you say *whom*?"

"Stop!"

Kathy's smile was all the warmth a shared friendship required. Molly's umbrage could not resist. In the next moment, her habitual smile returned.

"There's hope for you yet, Molly Waldron," Kathy said, waving a spatula at her friend. "I detected some temper there. Give it a few weeks and you'll be swearing like Ed Barker."

* * *

Desperation and despair were the forces lifting Heike off the floor and into the high bed. She required the comfort and reassurance of Nadine. As with every undertaking, Heike believed any issue worth consideration was worth knowing inside and out. To be left in charge of a child on, essentially, a moment's notice created near panic. She knew nothing of childcare, and, worse, there was no time to learn.

"How can I do this?" she asked.

Nadine was tempted to kick her out of the bed but feared a long journey to the floor would compound an already tenuous situation. Still, the single bed was decidedly crowded. Nadine wanted the light out and proper space.

Heike shivered from fright, but Nadine offered no succor. Heike Jacobs would never be comforted by caresses save for those of her beloved mother. Anne was a tower of strength and a treasure trove of maternal experience, but, alas, she existed in an inaccessible dimension.

It was futile for any other to extend an understanding hand. Yet, Heike simply could not recess to her crude bed. She needed to feel the warmth and the touch of another human lest she suffocate in the claustrophobia of inadequacy.

When the girl's lids grew heavy, she began nodding. Nadine entertained a plan to slide out of the bed and flee to a familiar venue. The clutches of Morpheus, however, were unable to gain sufficient purchase. Just when Nadine thought it was safe to move, Heike would wake with a start and repeat, with ever increasing bathos: "How can I do this?"

After three aborted attempts to steal out of bed, Nadine dismounted to kill the light. The moment she left, Heike sat up and watched in wide eyed terror. Her panic subsided when she realized Nadine's mission. She groped wildly for Nadine to haul her back. Testily, Nadine slapped Heike's hand aside.

Her resentment over trespass increased by the moment. In the end, she relented. They made themselves as comfortable as possible in the overloaded vessel. Nadine, finally, managed to fade into slumber. Heike, however, made no attempt until satisfied she would not be abandoned.

Neither person reaped the benefit of rest that night. One was restless by haunting fears; the other was constantly frustrated by a knee in the thigh or an elbow in the ribs. The chill, dreary, damp morning would never come, but, in perfect contradiction, it came too quickly.

"How can I do this?"

Thus, the morning began as the evening ended.

The girls, wearing winter coats in the kitchen, got coffee brewing and water boiling. By the time Rolf stirred, sliced bread, slices of cheese, and a saucer of jam were arrayed on the table. Nadine prepared three boiled eggs and, thankfully, brought them to resolve just as Rolf emerged from his morning toilet.

As always, the girls kept silent and moved with quiet deliberation. They dared not sit until Rolf took his place. When he took up a slice of bread, the serving maids placed an egg in the egg cup and poured steaming coffee into the earthenware mug which must endure the demands of Rolf's sausage-like fingers. Only then did the attendants take their places.

Nadine plucked out an egg without hesitation knowing full well Heike would refuse. Politeness demanded that she make the offer, but she had no patience with charades after their miserable night. That would leave one egg for Anne, making it sacred.

Car keys clattered atop the battered table. The girls looked in amazement at the anomaly. Then they examined the countenance of the person who had thrown them down.

"I can bus to work," he announced in a tone much softer than normal.

The girls exchanged looks but dared not speak, let alone question, the tempestuous patriarch.

"Nadine," he continued after a gulp of coffee which would have scalded a mere mortal, "you better go along."

When Heike realized her sister would not issue a word of protest, a palpable relief descended. The blurriness in her eyes vanished and her back straightened. It was troubling to leave both Anne and the morning chores untended, but Heike was developing confidence.

She was not afraid to go to battle; she was afraid of being found wanting. With Nadine at her side, Heike would wage war against a platoon of tanks – or a far more formidable and daunting task: tending an infant. Little could she know that Nadine had already decided to assist the Samaritan, with or without Rolf's blessing. It was better that Heike never know. So long as she thought her sister was under the dictatorial fist of Rolf Jacobs, the greater latitude Nadine had in exercise authority if the need arose.

Rolf departed a few minutes early to catch a bus. The girls quickly cleared the kitchen. They left Anne's breakfast out and the pot under the family tea cozy. It was a favorite of Anne's mother and, as the only surviving child, it was cherished. After the curtain descended, one found evidence that Anne still appreciated the heirloom though it was worn.

Frau Willing rapped gently at the door and was admitted at once. Heike attempted to relinquish the car into the driver's care but was refused. She designated herself the navigator. The professional driver took no pleasure in operating a vehicle except at work.

The distance was not great, but the route was convoluted. Frau Willing, unable to part with the child she adopted in the moment of rescue, knew the way only because of the ride the Polizei extended to what remained of a very small family. Even the bereaved father, still in shock, had problems finding the way home.

"Herr Zimmermann," Frau Willing announced at the door, "here are the Fräulein Jacobs."

Obviously, she promised the girls' assistance before seeking it. Herr Zimmermann, however, was too distraught to respond. Had the Bolshoi Ballet pirouetted into the tiny apartment, he wouldn't have noticed. His eyes were red and sunken; he looked as if he were drunk, as indeed he was, but from a binge of grief.

He invited them in and mumbled a few things that made no sense. Nadine did not pause to listen. She sought the baby and found her asleep in what was, apparently, the child's crib, the same stroller she had slept in during Frau Willing's rescue.

"Herr Zimmermann," Heike asked, "have you had breakfast?"

He shook his head.

"Not hungry," he croaked.

That didn't matter. Nadine was watching the child leaving Heike superfluous. Putting together a breakfast gave her a purpose. He was too tired to protest and too grieved to take umbrage. He sat at a tiny table which, for lack of any other candidate, was where he and his wife shared meals.

Heike inspected the cupboards and discovered enough to qualify as a morning snack. As she made the offering presentable, she put the water on. Soon enough, she had a plate of nourishment and a cup of steaming tea on the table in front of him.

"Eat," she ordered.

She pulled up the chair across from him and glared threateningly. She was too angry to consider trespassing in his wife's place. His incredulous expression never registered. She was determined to watch him eat his breakfast.

What kind of country was it where a grieving widower had to report to work or risk losing his job and, with it, the baby's only source of sustenance? With the economy in transition, hundreds of people lost jobs every day. It was too easy to discard employees who did not report for work. Further, there was no guarantee the government, the ultimate employer, wouldn't terminate workers in a fit of belated austerity. Herr Zimmermann was in no state to work. Any human agent would have excused him, with pay, for at least long enough to get his wife in the ground. But these were the days when malevolence had the nation by the throat.

"You need some food in the house," Heike reminded.

"And milk for the baby," Herr Zimmermann added without enthusiasm.

Yes, Heike told herself, her stomach contracting.

"There's house money in the kitchen," he stated listlessly. "Look in the tea tin. There's probably money in Blossom's bag; I haven't looked."

He wanted to be off, but Heike ordered him to sit until every crumb was gone. He was not so much mired in fatigue and grief to be unable to recognize blackmail. He gagged on the last mouthful. He snatched up the tea and took a gulp, but that made him gag as well.

Heike remained at her post without flinching. If, she decided, he throws it all up, he will simply have to remain while she prepared him something else. He would leave with food in his stomach if she had to use a funnel. A few moments later, the danger passed. Heike remained seated but swiveled in her chair to watch him approach the door and open it.

"Auf Wiedersehen," she called out.

He paused for a moment. He looked at Willing and the other women – virtual strangers. His tiny daughter was in the possession of strangers!

"*T'ja,*" he muttered. "'Wiedersehen."

The word announced expectation, but his tone and demeanor suggested that he neither knew, nor cared, if he ever saw them again.

"Blossom?" Frau Willing uttered incredulously.

She was one of the last people to see the woman before she was packaged. The pet name, as an endearment, was sickening sweet. Had Frau Zimmermann been less delicate, she might not have died. Unfortunately, Blossom was pathetically accurate.

"There is not a speck of dirt or dust in this place," Nadine observed after a tour.

Both Heike and Nadine were experts at finding clever hiding places. For either of them to make such a pronouncement left no doubt: Blossom was a hard-working mite. True, she had little space to keep clean. Still, it would require daily effort to keep the place ready for an inspection by the Jacobs sisters.

Heike was not in an inspection mood. She took the dishes into the kitchen and set them in the sink. As she let the water run, she spied a silver decorative canister on a shelf above the electric water kettle. In it, she found just over forty Reich marks and nearly as many Wessi marks. The Zimmermanns, obviously, had made their pilgrimage.

Next, she approached the sleeping child. Carefully, she reached for the decorative bag and gripped the wooden straps. After lifting it from the frame under the baby's bed, she stepped away and examined the items within. There was a plastic rain hat, a small package of tissues and a wallet.

Heike opened the wallet to discover an identification card. The woman smiling up at her from the tiny photo was identified as Monika Zimmermann geb. Dunnwald. Against her baser instincts, Heike couldn't help associating the maiden name with spoon-carvers to the south. Still, she resisted raising the possibility with Frau Willing present.

Inside the wallet were twenty-five Reich marks. Judging it was enough for a start, Heike pocketed the money and returned the wallet, and the bag from whence they came.

"Look at this," Nadine called.

Frau Willing and Heike left the dining/living room and entered the tiny bedroom, carefully dodging the baby carriage. They found themselves in a tiny space which accommodated a double bed (not slept in) built very low to the floor with a small nightstand on either side. The rest of the room was reserved for a medium sized shrunk of cheap though well-constructed wood.

On the side of the shrunk nearest the door was a built-in display case. It may have been designed as a glass enclosure, but Herr Zimmermann was a wood worker, not a glazier. The shelves contained small mementos. One of these was a wedding picture.

The shrunk was highly polished. The nightstands had only a light coat of varnish. The floor shone as if to excuse the absence of a throw rug, a welcome item on chilly, winter mornings. All of this, and more, Heike's practiced eye drank in immediately before turning her attention to the wooden-framed wedding photo Nadine held in her hands.

Heike's open-mouthed expression of amazement mirrored Nadine's. Frau Willing, who glimpsed Monika's remains, looked on with a scowl. There stood Herr Zimmerman in a pressed blue suit next to his wife in a white vest over a matching dress. The hem of the dress fell well below the knee but not so far as to spoil the effect produced by her fashionable white shoes.

"She was tiny, wasn't she?" Heike concluded.

Even in high heels, Monika's barely reached her husband's shoulder.

"Blossom," Nadine reminded.

"Blossom? She's hardly a petal."

Heike did not intend to be funny. Her companions did not find it so. However, they tacitly endorsed her sentiment. Nadine could not resist temptation and drew open the doors of the shrunk. Six eyes examined a modest collection of miniature skirts, dresses, pants, and tops.

"Doll clothes," Heike concluded.

They heard a cat mew and thought little of it until the noise became insistent.

"Scheiße!" Nadine hissed. "It's the baby."

Frau Willing, who had heard the baby's cries the previous day, simply closed the shrunk and removed the picture from Nadine's hands to set it in its proper place as the trio withdrew. If Frau Zimmermann had been tiny, Inka Zimmermann was more so.

"I can drive Frau Willing to work and pick up some milk and food," Heike announced. "Do you mind being alone for an hour or so?"

Nadine and Frau Willing exchanged a knowing look.

"I think I can manage," Nadine responded, reaching down to collect the tiny, feather-light, red-faced infant whose squalling was scarcely a purr.

Heike was out of the door before second thoughts had a chance.

* * *

It was Kathy who held the child as they left the hospital. Ute insisted that she was not as weak as the doctor claimed, but his orders carried the weight of law with Aaron and Kathy. The mother refused to be denied the presence of her son and insisted on riding in the back seat. It was a struggle for her to contort enough to gain access in the family's two-door clunker. Ute nearly lost her balance, but the attentive Aaron was there with gentle hands.

Ute panted for breath when she flopped back next to Kathy. She had to be supervised into fastening her seat belt; she complied with very bad grace. Only when she drew back the blanket and gazed upon her wide-eyed and curious son was her emotional norm restored.

Aaron Isaac Foster was named over his father's objections. It was Ute who instructed the nurse while Aaron was in the men's room. As Kathy well knew, names were discussed at length. Aaron felt naming their son after himself was vanity. The child would have his family name; that was enough.

When Ute introduced Aaron Isaac, her husband resisted because it was antique and too Biblical. Ute could not dismiss the Old Testament, however. Sarah was, supposedly, barren when she birthed a son; why shouldn't miracle sons share a name? If Aaron Foster considered himself tricked or betrayed, he offered feeble objections. He loved the new arrival as much as Ute.

A rose, by any other name, etc.

Kathy, however, was stung by the realization that Aaron lovingly held the child before Ute could touch it. That seemed very wrong. Ute, however, could care less. From the moment she knew of her pregnancy, she put the baby first; she sacrificed for it before he was born and was determined to sacrifice her life if the situation demanded.

Once home, Ute was confined to bed. Kathy, without instructions, placed little Aaron next to his mother. Because the aged mama couldn't produce enough milk, formula and bottles were marshaled. Every morning, Kathy woke early to her brother's disquiet. She'd change him, put him into something warm and dry, and deliver him to his mother.

Aaron would heat breakfast milk. Once he vacated the kitchen, Kathy prepared something for the adults. When they left for work and school, Ute and little Aaron would be together in a warm, comfortable bed. She was, in defiance of doctor's orders, never in bed when Kathy returned from school.

Kathy always found Ute visibly fatigued. She'd welcome her brother into her arms, but the sadness in Ute's eyes stung her. Regardless, Kathy couldn't keep her hands off the little guy. Any remorse over stealing him from his mother's arms was short lived.

Ute looked for the letter she'd set aside for her parents. She never asked after it. When she settled into bed that first day home, she looked towards the nightstand. Finding nothing, she looked at Kathy. The girl's visage told her everything. None of them ever made mention of it.

Athena organized a baby shower. Ute insisted they observe German tradition of a post-birth celebration. This, apparently, sprang from a time when the infant mortality was high. Athena concluded the custom wasn't a bad idea. In Ute's case, too many things could have gone wrong.

Ute wore her best robe, pajamas and slippers and sat on the couch like a queen upon a throne. Beside her was Prince Aaron escorted, as always, by Kathy, the royal governess. It was a festive ninety minutes. Little Aaron garnered some very nice clothes and playthings. He expressed his profound thanks by behaving himself and treating everyone to his sparkling, inquisitive eyes.

Dr. Reynolds's insisted the afternoon frivolities be carefully limited, but it was Kathy who made bold the strict observation of the clock. Athena, the formidable sergeant-at-arms, ushered the gathering out the door. Ten minutes later, Ute was asleep in her bed with her son who was also exhausted by the experience.

The following afternoon, Grandma and Grandpa Foster arrived. They checked into a local auto-court. Papa Foster would leave for home Monday morning, leaving Mama to assist her daughter-in-law for however long she was needed. Thus, Kathy's plans to establish camp with the Swoffords came to naught. It required only to give up her bed to Grandma and use the couch.

It was an arrangement so sensible that no one, least of all Kathy, objected. With Mother Foster and Little Aaron in the same room, neither Ute nor Kathy would sacrifice any sleep during midnight performances. Mother Foster was the gray-haired lady everyone expects in a grandmother, save that her eyes had never required glasses. Despite her matronly clothes, her quaint homespun, country manner of speaking and her firm Christian ethics, she was a young girl trapped in an elderly woman's body. She never hesitated to try new things (notably, Kathy).

Grandma Foster accepted Kathy the moment she laid eyes on her. Grumpy Grandpa remained dubious for the better part of a year, but he, too, treated Kathy as grandparents are duty-bound to – spoiling her rotten. Ute frequently lamented that whenever Kathy spent a weekend in Milton-Freewater, it took the joint efforts of both parents the better part of two weeks to get their daughter "back into harness."

Grandma Foster fell in love with Little Aaron. However, she never took Kathy for granted. They talked and laughed and played games just as they always had. If there was any friction, it was because Ute had to compete for time with her son.

"Mama," Ute complained, "you made Kathy a juvenile delinquent. I will not allow you to put Aaron on the road to reform school!"

Everyone got a chuckle over the absurd accusations, but Mother Foster could take a hint. As Kathy thought the matter through, she could recall many times when Mrs. Foster and her son exchanged heated words, but she never heard a single cross word directed at Ute.

The Spring Concert that year was late because of calendar conflicts. The choir rehearsed, of course, during class. However, Kathy stayed after school twice a week to rehearse with the jazz band. Each year, Mr. Davidson selected a talented vocalist to showcase along with hand-picked musicians. His tendency was toward seniors who possessed talent and a healthy work ethic.

Kathy realized what a great honor it was to be featured with the jazz band as a sophomore. When she discovered Air on a G String had an arrangement for acapella voices, she lobbied for it.

"We don't have enough horses to pull that wagon," Mr. Davidson admonished.

Thus, Kathy found herself singing an up-tempo song from the Big Band days of the thirties and forties. Big Aaron considered the lyrics a little "off color" for a sixteen-year-old, but he refused to make a formal complaint. Grama Foster once had danced to the tune frequently in her younger days and knew the lyrics by heart. She and Kathy could, and did, burst into a duet at the drop of a hat. Little Aaron didn't mind, in fact, he paid close attention to the pleasant harmony.

Mr. and Mrs. Foster were not as enthused.

"If Athena drops in here now," Aaron sighed, "we're doomed."

Athena did not, but Gary did. He haunted the Foster home because he couldn't lure Kathy away from either her brother or grandmother. He cultivated a habit of walking her home from the bus stop on those days when they shared the same bus. He'd tarry while Kathy commandeered her brother and devoted full attention to him until commanded to cease. At the conclusion of these saccharin performances, Gary would, politely, make his presence known.

As if to make amends for her neglect, Kathy devoted special attention to him. There were, additionally, rare occasions when Gary was invited to stay for dinner. It was decidedly overcrowded, and the portions were meager, but no one complained. In the greatest gesture of all, Kathy accompanied Gary home where she lingered until Athena ordered her out.

These domestic rituals were positively Dickensian. It was as if Little Aaron was the climax of a lengthy novel in search of a serendipitous ending. Grandma Foster got to see Kathy perform at the Spring Concert, as did Ute and her son. This event might well have served as a satisfactory ending; all the major players were present and enjoying a "happily-ever-after." It wanted only a Tiny Tim to supply the tag line.

Alas, the days dragged by with quiet tribulations that Dickens would never allow. Kathy, for example, felt a surge of panic whenever she found Ute napping. She'd never seen the woman sleeping during the day, but Ute nodded off in the most unlikely moments. Then there was personal disappointment that morphed into resentment. For ages, Kathy waited impatiently for her figure to show signs of maturity.

She frequently whispered laments in Ute's ear, and, always, she was left unsatisfied.

"Nature won't forget you," Ute assured.

Nearing her sixteenth birthday, Kathy hoped for an eruption. When that milepost receded without appreciable change, the girl concluded that nature had either forgotten or abandoned her.

Molly Waldron had a beautiful, blue-print dress Kathy admired whenever her friend wore it to school. When Kathy announced she had nothing worthy to wear for her *gig* with the jazz band, Molly, characteristically, offered a free browse in her closet. Kathy panted. She knew, exactly, what she wanted. Molly was instantly amenable. Unfortunately, Kathy had to confront the mirror in Molly's room.

"Gary would look better in this than I do," she moaned.

For once, Molly's smile wavered. Kathy looked great in the dress. However, the design left some room where no room was required. She knew better than to suggest Kathy borrow a pair of theatrical props. Moreover, she knew there was no profit in offering platitudes.

Though Kathy Foster was disappointed in her appearance, Michael Kaufmann never expressed dissatisfaction. Thrice since his cousin departed Fürth, he'd written page-long masterpieces of penmanship on unlined paper. His prose was as simple but intricate. He never let slip Bavarian or Swabish slang but maintained a caliber of German style and usage that could please Goethe.

In the end, however, the text was clearly from a young boy who suffered from an acute crush. Ute was amused by the romance. Though the letters were innocuous enough, Ute was certain neither her brother nor her sister-in-law knew of the trans-Atlantic correspondence. She couldn't resist telling Gary he had a rival.

Gary displayed jealousy. Both Kathy and Ute were amazed that he took umbrage over a child's infatuation. Care was taken to keep Mischa out of the conversation whenever Gary was present.

"Mischa is a sweetheart," she announced boldly when accompanying him home. "He's not my type, though."

"What is your type?" Gary asked, brusquely.

"Bull-headed football players who get jealous over nothing."

He didn't accept that with grace, but he didn't resist when she took his arm.

"Someday, Michael will meet a nice, quiet, blond, Bavarian girl with long lashes," Kathy predicted. "She'll flutter those lashes, and he'll become her slave forever. I'm a little jealous myself, I suppose. If she hurts my cousin, I'll wring her neck!"

Gary was pacified by her speech. He'd not show it, of course, but Kathy sensed that all was well. The very next evening, after Kathy returned from "delivering" Gary, Ute showed her an envelope with a large German stamp. Kathy thanked Ute for not mentioning it earlier.

She opened the missive, fearing it contained a proposal that would turn Ute's "little romance" into an issue.

It was as neatly penned as those that preceded, but it was much shorter.

"What is it?" Ute asked.

Ute had Little Aaron on her shoulder after feeding, but most of her attention seemed focused upon Kathy's expression.

"Uncle Dieter is driving to Hessen to talk with someone who might know my sister."

"Oh."

Kathy was amazed how voluminous that single syllable could be. She knew because, even as Ute gave it voice, Kathy's emotions were racing anew.

* * *

Rosa's Children remained confined to Heike's notebook. Inka proved a tiny tyrant. She was dependent upon others for everything in her demanding little life, and Heike discovered that a supervisory role was even more draining than the manual labor that was her lot since she became old enough to hold a scrub brush.

Regrettably, she discovered she couldn't touch the baby. Her body quaked at the mere thought. She didn't trust herself. Heike might thoughtlessly crush the child without effort. Certain was she that ineptitude and thoughtlessness would kill the innocent, and the tragedy would be compounded.

Encke!

Doubtless, her *pretend* brother made Heike cognizant of the tiny comet that raced about the sun in a tiny orbit. The name sprang to mind when Heike observed Nadine and Frau Willing racing around tiny "Inka." Without conscious thought, she adopted the celestial moniker.

Frau Willing, the spoon carver, lacked knowledge of astronomy; the allusion was lost on her. The bus driver was conversant in both applied physics and aesthetics. However, Nadine understood instantly. She marveled over Heike's talent for recalling information few people retained.

Driving illegally into the city in search of food and baby supplies, Heike fretted. Frau Willing had a full-time job; Nadine would be forced into double duty at home. Meanwhile, Heike couldn't care for a child she wasn't brave enough to touch. She sought someone to comfort the infant while Heike managed logistics.

The second day, the girls brought Encke home. Anne's maternal instincts instantly revived. She took Inka into her arms and, as with Heike years before, swathed it in love. She cooed over it and kept the comet entertained.

So long as the implements were left neatly arrayed and in plain view, she changed the baby without assistance. Someone else had to deal with the soiled diaper and heat formula when needed. Still, Anne's assistance was priceless. The auto, however, was intended for everyday use. Heike was not allowed unlimited access.

A single person could bus to the suburb, feed Herr Zimmerman, see him off to work, and deliver the baby to Anne's love. The afternoon ritual would be no less complicated. Rolf, however, was adamant. If an emergency arose, Heike would get the comet to hospital days ahead of an ambulance. Heike understood the auto was for emergency use only.

She walked into the city for supplies one afternoon and spied a blond cloud drifting above the heads of other waiting bus commuters. She gulped, reversed course, and vacated the square. Only Lilo could stand above the local burgers.

It was a question of time before Günther made an appearance. Doubtless, Heike would remain ignorant about his whereabouts, but she knew he and Lilo would resume their courtship. Finding a bench, she sat to catch her breath. There was, however, no time to linger over morbid thoughts. Nevertheless, she was shaken. Should her quaking limbs fail her, and the cobblestones precipitated a spill, Heike Jacobs would become a disastrous liability.

After a few moments, she proceeded to fill her basket, but Heike kept an eye peeled for Lilo. There must be no *chance* meeting. It was, however, by absolute chance that Heike met Hanna during a foraging mission. The brilliant Müller smile flashed the moment Heike was recognized.

"You still here?" Heike asked, forcing a smile.

This question was used with increasing frequency among locals. People assumed those who could, went West.

"Papa was asked to go over and run the World Bank, but he turned it down."

Heike couldn't help herself. She enjoyed a smile.

"Still going to school?"

Hanna shrugged.

"I need to keep busy."

How Heike burned to say that.

Hanna pointed at Heike's basket. There was no effort made to cover the contents. Baby items were in clear view.

"This is sudden," Hanna announced.

"It isn't mine."

Hanna's smile was reinforced by several thousand watts.

"It can't be Nadine's. It hasn't been that long."

Much to her surprise, Heike didn't mind narrating the events of the preceding days. When informed of the mother's demise, Hanna's smile vanished. They exchanged a few more words and parted. Early the following afternoon, there was a knock at the door. Nadine was nearest, and it was she who greeted Hanna.

"What can I do?" the buxom, baby-faced teen asked.

The daily pace intensified. Heike dodged about the city by foot or, rarely, by car. She not only kept the comet stuffed with food, she secured clothing. The seasons were changing, and the child grew at an alarming rate. The winter things she'd outgrown were taken to Goethe Platz where bold entrepreneurs sold Wessi goods from car boots.

She traded for larger items or obtained reduced prices on others, always keeping a sharp eye on Herr Zimmermann's budget. This acquainted her with the new Ossi business community. People drove West to haunt second-hand shops. They bought Wessi clothing of bright color, no matter how gaudy or ridiculous. Such items sold faster and for higher prices with a clientele whose eyes wearied of the monochromatic, drab, Ossi hues.

It took a day to drive and shop; thus, many of the "businesses" sold on alternate days. Heike found several vendors offered more items in a third of the time it took to snoop around in the declining government-run shops. Despite the pain it caused Heike, second-hand Wessi discards were often better quality than new Ossi clothes.

However, Heike was not limited to exchanging information with the first Ossi capitalists. The market was a magnet for people who wanted quantity in exchange for the shrinking Reich Mark. Prices soared, and people who previously lived comfortably, discovered a hand-to-mouth existence a challenge. People with Wessi Marks got preferred goods since Western money was stable.

By discussing current events with the burgers, Heike obtained valuable lessons in the new economy. Just as Karl Marx studied capitalism, so Heike Jacobs was greedy for knowledge of *the enemy*. Understanding evil is the key to defeating it. However, it hurt to make purchases on what was, essentially, the black market. Still, if Rolf lost his job, the grey Trabi of the Jacobs family might be required to dispense Wessi goods from the trunk in order to bring bread in house.

There was another benefit of trading at the Goethe Platz emporium: many of her former classmates flitted in and out on similar missions. Similarly, she recognized people from the FDJ passing through the gaudy displays. Frequently, friends of Nadine would stop Heike to ask about her "sister." There were exchanges of woe and expressed longing for former times. After a chat, Heike and her friends scrounged through Wessi garbage to meet basic needs.

Thus, word of Rosa's Children circulated. It began in the market, but soon filtered into the residential sections of town. In a matter of days, people from as far away as Apolda were aware of the fledgling organization. Some thought of it as a new political party and wondered when it would supplant the defunct SED.

Heike was amazed at the number of people who asked about Rosa's Children. When convinced she had a dozen like-minded people upon whom she could rely, Heike lobbied for a summer rally. She discussed the issue with Nadine who introduced several practical concerns. Heike was appreciative. It was fine to be motivated by grandiose schemes, but Nadine saw the hurdles Heike's idealism overlooked. Between them, they could chart a manageable course.

She saw Lilo from behind the Trabi's steering wheel one afternoon. This time, she didn't see the top of her head; she saw Lilo's face clearly. The Amazon didn't notice Heike. Even if she searched for a Jacobs, Lilo would hardly expect to find one driving an auto. That made it easier for Heike to avoid detection, but she did slow down enough to discover Lilo was alone.

Heike pondered a question: If she'd seen Günther with Lilo, which should she run over? Should she try for both? It was deliciously tempting, but Heike was plagued by scruples. Her greatest delight remained confined to the darkest corner of her imagination.

Heike marshaled materials that would aid the comet. She earned nothing as Herr Zimmermann's housekeeper. He was remarkably tidy. It was a minor chore to clean the tiny apartment, but tiny Frau Zimmermann left behind a high standard.

Herr Zimmermann was not eating as he should. Discovering this, Heike began preparing an after-work meal for him. She'd be assured he would have one good meal a day. This was a chore. For the first several days of their relationship, Herr Zimmermann seldom spoke and never smiled. His one thought was for his departed wife. Heike remained calm and sympathetic. Petrified over physically tending a baby, she was grateful when Herr Zimmermann changed and fed his daughter. Heike, however, was the comet's vigilant sentry; she never hesitated to dispatch terse orders if she thought Herr Zimmermann was slacking.

Eventually, the man of the house began engaging Heike in snippets of conversation. Initially, he inquired about household expenses. He suggested that Heike and her confederates be paid for their services, a proposal Heike flatly rejected. He next complemented her on the fine, thick *soljanka* she made.

Heike glowed.

She was proud of it herself, having made as large a portion as storage space allowed. It would be used as the basis for an entire week of evening meals; she need only freshen it daily with fresh vegetables and bits of meat. Eventually, Herr Zimmermann and Heike were exchanging entire sentences.

One evening, he smiled over Inka's contortions in her baby-buggy bed. From there, Heike's sarcastic remarks began eliciting tentative laughter. Conversation eased tensions. She began sitting across from him as he ate.

"You should eat something," he remarked.

"I'll eat when I get home. It's your food."

"Is it not still my food if I wish to share it?"

"Is it still your food if I refuse to eat it?"

"Are you always so cold?"

"Cold?" Heike asked indignantly.

"I cook, wash, clean, and mend for you because you bring bread in house. Do you think I'm cold because I refuse to take food off this pathetic excuse for a table?"

"It served us well enough."

"I'm certain it did, but your daughter will be crawling soon. You must get her a proper bed. No one can watch her properly once she starts to crawl. You're a woodworker; why not make her a proper bed?"

"Where would I put it?"

Heike was about to say that the large double bed was a luxury, but she caught herself. That observation, despite practicality, would prove brutal. Herr Zimmermann loved his wife very much; he missed her to distraction. The woman left behind few clues of her existence. To suggest removing furniture they once shared was a step too far and too soon.

Heike leaned forward, put her elbows on the edge of the table, and crossed her ankles under her chair.

"We had this conversation, Monika and I," he informed. "We thought of solutions. Some were utterly fantastic. The best solution is to get a larger apartment."

Heike nodded, keeping her eyes on her wrists. The apartments of the DDR were becoming fewer and fewer. Rents soared to near Wessi levels and, thus, beyond reach of most workers. Herr Zimmermann was lucky beyond reason to pay the same rent he and his bride paid three years before when they moved in.

"If only I was there for Monika —"

"It was a stupid, stupid accident," Heike concluded. "It was not your fault."

"And it isn't your fault your sister has a new face," he replied, equally emphatically.

Heike straightened. She dropped her hands into her lap and glared at her antagonist. She and her loose-tongued sister would have a serious talk, *soon*! Until then, Herr Zimmermann was a few short words from an ugly scene. Heike waited patiently for him to utter them.

He examined her countenance for only a moment before averting his eyes. He felt heat radiating from her body. He realized, too late, that Heike Jacobs would not entertain emotional argument. She demanded facts seasoned with reason. He concentrated on bringing a spoon full of soljanka to his mouth, but he sensed her eyes boring into his skull.

"I'm sorry," he muttered, no longer able to endure silent pain.

Heike's anger faded. He gave her a few seconds to accept contrition. The soljanka bathed his tongue in delight. As he swallowed, his gratitude for Heike mingled with longing for his wife.

"Monika was the best thing to come into my life," he moaned. "How will I find another Monika?"

"Don't you dare!"

He found the girl infuriated anew.

"Why?" he demanded.

He was daring her. He might not strike her, but he was ready to throw her out of the apartment. Herr Zimmermann never studied the Bard, but Heike had. She'd learned much without being aware; the widower's question awoke dormant knowledge.

"Frau Zimmerman is gone!" she hissed slowly. "No one can take her place. Find someone different. If you are very, very lucky, you will find a different brand of happiness. If you try to recreate your Monika, two people will be miserable – three, counting your daughter."

The girl's eyes flashed, but her voice was laced with sympathy. His spoon dropped with a clatter into the remnants of the soup. She sensed it; self-pity welled inside him. In a few more moments, he'd be blubbering. Enough was enough. She stood, reached across the table, and grabbed his hand.

"Bitte," she whispered.

Her hand was gentle, not insistent. Coupled with her plea, he opted to comply. She led him to Inka's rolling bed. The child kicked and flailed; one hand attempted to swat a rattle dangling over her head on an elastic cord. She attempted to swallow three fingers of the other hand; confronted by two large faces, she ceased thrashing and studied her observers with wide eyed awe.

"Here is your family," Heike reminded. "This is your purpose in life. Inka comes before everything. I've learned one thing this year: Family first. Don't forget that – I nearly did."

She released his hand. She gathered her jacket, her ubiquitous shopping bag, and reached for the door.

"Leave the dishes in the sink," she ordered, "I'll wash them first thing in the morning."

She left him alone with his thoughts and threw herself into the Trabi while wrestling with her demons. Moments before, she wanted to lecture Nadine about her annoying inability to keep her mouth shut. As she navigated the evening, she realized her own just punishment.

Heike failed Nadine. Her sister *earned* the right to tell the world. Heike told Herr Zimmerman there mightn't be a second chance. Heike hoped she'd get another!

Over Abendsbrot, Herr Jacobs hinted that Heike might be training for a servant's position in a wealthy Wessi home.

"Or auditioning for the next Frau Zimmermann," Nadine added, cruelly.

Heike refused the bait. Nadine's derision was fair recompense for the abject failure in Leipzig. If she could not vent at Nadine, she opted to attack someone not present.

"If he calls me Blossom, I'll slap his face."

No one laughed.

Later, Heike recalled Herr Zimmermann saying he and *Blossom* agreed never to go to bed with dishes in the sink. She fretted over it enough to dream of unwashed dishes. The following morning, as Nadine raced to get Inka's breakfast, Heike found the dishes clean and in their proper places.

"Scheiße!"

"What's your problem?" Nadine demanded.

"No second chance."

* * *

When Kathy opened the refrigerator upon returning from school, she found bay leaves floating in a generous marinate.

"Learning to make Sauerbraten, Grandma?"

"Lord, no. Your mother started that."

Kathy sighed.

"You're leaving Thursday."

The Foster matriarch looked up from her crossword.

"You're quite the detective."

Kathy closed the refrigerator door. The appetite for a pre-meal snack abandoned her. She sat at the end of the table to look directly at her grandmother on the living room couch.

"It takes three days to make, and it's Mom's special occasion dinner," Kathy summarized. "It's not calculus."

Mrs. Foster nodded and returned to her pursuit of a five-letter word for *large post*.

"She's feeling much stronger," Gran mused. "Grandpa's driving over Thursday morning to take me home."

Kathy realized Ute was stronger, but she still tired quickly. More disturbing, there was no talk of Ute's returning to work. It wasn't that Kathy wanted her to, but the baby was a huge drag on the family economy. It was time for Kathy to pitch-in. She could work at the café in the afternoons and weekends. She'd bring in more bread than shipping out weekends on the *Mary R*. Unfortunately, Aaron and Ute would resist the proposal. Kathy wasn't up for a confrontation.

"You'll get your room back," reminded Mrs. Foster, misinterpreting the motive behind Kathy's sudden display of sobriety.

"Isaac's room," she corrected. "He let me use it for a while."

"Oh, darling, don't talk like that. And what's with Isaac?"

"I can't call him Aaron; it's confusing. 'Little Aaron' is worse."

Granny Foster waited patiently before returning to her puzzle. She knew better than prod her granddaughter. If Kathy wanted to discuss, she'd begin in her own good time. If she did not wish to discuss, nothing could induce her.

There'd been a row. Gran Foster remained neutral, though she attempted to pour oil on the water to keep tempers in check. Ute refused to speak German to her son; Kathy refused to speak anything but. Neither Aaron nor Ute predicted any good would come from this bilingual environment, but the girl was adamant.

Isaac, she insisted, was half German and was entitled to learn his own language. The point which grated most was that Isaac was Swabish; Kathy, almost certainly, was not. No matter how much others attempted to convince her that Swabish ethics and values were not genetic, and that Kathy was as Swabish as Oma and Opa, the girl resented not possessing Swabish blood.

Kathy's problems were not limited to matters of ethnicity. Her patience with Uncle Dieter was exhausted. True, she wasn't supposed to know of the visit to a refugee center, but she did. Having no word about it irked her.

Beyond this, however, was another matter.

"I haven't seen my son-in-law around here for a while," Ute announced one morning, bouncing her son on her knee.

Kathy Foster was visited by great eddies of ambiguity since her parents made a shambles of her, previously, solid and secure existence. The raging storm within had taken her to the brink of insanity. On occasion, she may have slipped beyond. When the gossamer strands of existence wove themselves into something remotely tangible, patience ended.

Kathy knew some momentous *thing* was about to be thrust into her life and, in a very real sense, determine her future. It was as if she was large with a child; only this child refused to be born. The pressure mounted until she thought she'd explode.

How many times, she mused, within the past month, had she stood on the abyss of despair? Once, she was poised to let lose a scream so terrible it would have startled anyone within earshot. As that scream clawed up her throat, it evaporated., but it left her exhausted.

Somewhere, in a warm and comfortable compartment of her brain, there resided a string ensemble. It was a curious collection of harmless, unobtrusive, and intangible beings who kept their warm and comfortable existence aloof from the horrid, obscene, and disgusting thoughts racing through the atom-smashing shafts of her mind. When the chaos threatened to lapse into something worse, the ensemble recreated the soft, soothing chords of Bach. Within seconds, the impossible, the imponderable, and the incomprehensible dissolved into peace.

When Mr. Davidson lent her his tape, Kathy's gratitude was tainted with bitterness until, unbidden and unrepentantly, Shelly – the All-American girl – lent her tape player for as long as Kathy needed it. Always, always, Kathy thought, she collected good will and objects from those around her. The more undeserving she felt, the more largess was heaped upon her.

There were never any questions; never any conditions; never any expressed reservations. Kathy needed a dress for the spring concert, and the admired, delicate light-blue dress comes out of Molly's closet on cue. Kathy needs a tape player, and Shelly provides one. Kathy needs something for shattered nerves, and Bach reaches across the centuries to provide her with the perfect tonic.

So, Kathy played Bach's Air on a G string at night as she lay on the couch. She played it before reporting for duty on the *Mary R.* She played it while doing homework, she played it for the wide-eyed Isaac who was old enough to comprehend something not of this world. Even when Shelly's machine was beyond her reach, the notes of perfection pounced upon her torment and quelled her fears, restored her faith, and arrested her tears.

* * *

It was strangely quiet when Kathy entered the house one afternoon. The television was silent and so, too, was the radio. For a moment, Kathy imagined herself alone. Then, she saw Ute bouncing a subdued son on her hip. The expression on her face was not reassuring and, in the absence of electronic noises, disturbingly eerie. Kathy closed the door behind her and dropped her book bag on the floor.

Ute's eyes directed Kathy's attention to the coffee table. There, she found a very official-looking envelope adorned with a generous monetary amount of postage. German postage stamps boldly announced DDR.

Kathy quaked under the disquieting blandness of Ute's expression before she seized the envelope. Her hand shook. She fumbled for several seconds at the seal. Inside she found a neatly typed letter.

"From a Herr Beckmann," she announced in a quivering voice. "My father wants to meet with me."

Ute nodded stoically and walked slowly down the hall and out of sight. Kathy reread the letter with deliberate slowness as Bach's music wafted through her mind. Herr Beckmann stated that there could be no meeting until Kathy's identity was definitively established. He urged her to come to Berlin as soon as possible so that the matter could be resolved.

Calmly and rationally, Kathy Foster realized that it was impossible to make the journey. Her visit of the previous summer was an unaffordable extravagance. There remained no money in the till. Some alternate arrangement must be made. In addition, there was no way of knowing that the man seeking his daughter was her real father.

However, any official of the *Dinksboomstaamt* or whatever (it hurt her eyes just to see so many letters jammed together) wasn't likely to write her about a mere possibility. German bureaucrats are very careful to keep their posteriors protected.

There was no feeling of panic or hysteria. There was no need to propose a plan of action. They could discuss this matter in any number of ways with any number of people. Kathy wasn't anxious to be among them.

Intoxicated by Bach, Kathy set the letter on the coffee table before quelling the rumblings in her stomach. She could not negotiate the distance to the refrigerator without gaining a view of the hallway. She expected it to be empty. Instead, she found Ute leaning against the door frame of her bedroom and desperately clutching her son. Her head thrown back, her eyes shut, she allowed tears to stream down her face.

Did Ute think that she'd lost the daughter she fought so hard to get? How could she become so completely unsettled? Kathy approached stealthily. There were numerous reassurances racing through her brain, but none found utterance. Ute placed Isaac in Kathy's arms and retired to her room to be alone with her grief.

"It's going to be okay, Mom."

Kathy placed extra emphasis on the last word. She had no tangible evidence to support her prediction, but the music in her head convinced her it was so.

* * *

It was Molly's turn to bring lunch, so she and Henry were sharing PB&J sandwiches and apples. Beside them, vivacious to the brink of annoyance, but not beyond, was Shelly, her large loop earrings bobbing with her movements from the lobes of her too large ears. Eyes sparkling, teeth flashing brilliantly in limited, artificial light, the Japanese American presided over a *veggie burger* she'd prepared earlier.

Her food remained untouched. Together with Henry and Molly, she watched the scene unfolding several feet away. Kathy and Gary sat with their backs to the proceedings, not wishing to appear curious, they gauged the progression of events by the facial expressions of the trio seated across the lunchroom table.

Try as they might, Kathy and her *beau* were unable shake their somber mood. When Kathy sighed, unaware but audibly, Gary's arm snaked around her waist. She would lean into him, momentarily, grateful for his gesture of reassurance. Together, they picked over the remnants of the thick soup Ute dispatched in a thermos.

As one, Henry, Molly and Shelly expressed disappointment underscored with pathos. No one spoke, but even the effervescent Shelly's energy ebbed. Her smile faded; she forced her tightly pressed lips to curl upward, but all the gayety fled.

"That bad?" Kathy asked.

"Painful," Molly murmured.

"I think I'll be a nun," Shelly announced.

Even Henry, who knew his sister better than the others, was shocked by this uncharacteristic display of disparagement. Shelly, aware of her gaff, flashed an embarrassed and unconvincing smile.

"Who broke your heart?" Kathy asked, devoid of genuine curiosity.

"No one, yet," Shelly, who had yet to *discover* boys, responded. "Well, maybe, Jayme."

Kathy was alarmed. Two minutes prior, Jayme was sitting beside her, brooding as was her lunch-time routine of late. Unexpectedly, she banged her fist on the table.

"I'm going to speak to him," she vowed.

She took one deep breath, stood, disengaged from the bench upon which she sat and marched off. There was scarce time to offer best wishes.

The stunned expressions turned into hopeful anticipation. Kathy fought hard to refrain from turning to watch the drama.

Jayme returned as deflated as a stale party balloon. She threw one leg over the bench and crashed down to face Kathy sideways. She propped her dejected head on a fist and offered a mournful sigh.

No one spoke.

"I opened my mouth, but nothing came out," Jayme confessed.

Molly had watched Jayme extend her hand from a cocked elbow; she'd seen the object of her sister's adoration complete the handshake with an expression of amused perplexity. Next, came Jayme's idiot smile and quick retreat.

"All I could say was *hi*."

Someone groaned. It could have been Molly, but Kathy suspected it was herself. With nothing to say, tongues remained guarded. Would Jayme break into tears and magnify her mortifying humiliation further?

No one breathed.

"Kat, how'd you get Gary's attention?" she asked at, long overdue, last.

"She punched me in the mouth."

"Gary!"

"You did," he boldly affirmed.

"Stop!" Kathy pleaded, "don't make me feel worse than I already do."

She felt his reassuring squeeze and offered silent thanks that he'd said his piece. Nevertheless, guilt gnawed at her. She'd done something that could neither be forgotten nor excused.

"I don't want to punch anybody," Jayme confessed.

"Gary," Molly whispered just prior to crunching into her apple.

Kathy felt Gary's comforting arm instantly retract. Neither turned about, but they knew the *monk* was close aboard. An aging teacher trapped in Victorian hypocrisy spent the bulk of his life teaching geography. Whatever his pedagogical qualities, his chief occupation was to lace into students who seemed *too familiar*.

If it were it up to the monk, coeducational institutions would be abolished. Molly and those in her orbit had developed a simple verbal shorthand to warn the others of the monk's approach. It saved them a lengthy recitation of an admonishment speech they'd memorized over time.

Resentment surged within Kathy. She needed physical reassurance that Gary could forgive, if not forget, her thoughtlessness. As obtuse as she was, Kathy realized she would commit mindless sins in the future. Without constant reassurance, her Swabish code of honor would require her to renounce their relationship.

When danger passed, Molly gave Kathy a nudge with her foot.

"What's wrong, Kathy?" she asked, perceptively. "You've been acting like a mortician all morning."

Gary was immediately attentive. Had he noticed as well, but was too reticent to call attention? Perhaps, without Molly's comment, he'd remain unaware. It was Kathy's intention to speak with him later when they were alone. Suddenly, there was little choice but to respond.

"I got a letter," she reported, making every attempt to remain calm. "They think they found my father. They want me in Berlin."

"*Schwein gehabt!*"

Shelly's unexpected comment trumped Kathy's announcement. Everyone glared at the uncharacteristically self-conscious girl. She forced an embarrassed smile and shrugged.

Kathy was instantly inoculated. Henceforth, she'd remain immune to Shelly Kurihara forever. If she discovered Shelly in lederhosen, dancing a Bavarian jig and reciting Goethe in the original, Kathy would remain impassive.

"I don't know how lucky it is," Kathy reported. "I just got back from Germany. It will be years before we can afford it again."

"Years?" Molly asked, her eyebrows narrowed suspiciously.

"Who knows when Mom can go back to work? Then, there's Isaac. He doesn't eat much, but he's a vacuum. He sucks up money. There's no way I can go."

"Now, you're going to hate your brother," Jayme, in her black, irreconcilable mood advanced.

"No," Kathy responded emphatically. "But I would hate myself if I went to Germany and he had to go without something."

"*Typisch* Kati," Molly muttered.

Kathy ignored both the comment and the hated pronunciation of her name.

"Your father might have some money," Henry speculated.

"In the DDR?" Molly asked, saving Kathy the trouble. "The whole idea of socialism is to make sure that people don't have money."

Born of fact or simply an innate resentment of the "the other Germany," Molly's economic hypothesis went unchallenged. Suddenly ashamed of her problem and her recent public humiliation, Jayme stroked Kathy's back with the flat of her hand.

"There must be something we can do," she advanced. "I bet Mom and Dad can loan your folks some money."

Grateful for the notion, Kathy waved it away.

"Loans need to be paid off," she reminded. "We have a hard time with the debts we have. Guys, I didn't ask you to ask me. We're fresh out of ideas, but we'll think of something."

"*Schwein gehabt*," Shelly repeated.

No one was amazed. This time, the eyes turning toward Shelly were decidedly hostile. The girl didn't shrivel. She resumed her self-confident, vivacious self.

"Who ever heard of half luck?" she asked. "If you have luck, you have it. This will happen, Kathy. I don't know how, but it will happen. Keep faith."

Kathy realized Shelly was correct. With Bach's Air and Paul's advice to the Corinthians, she was prepared to battle the obstacles arrayed against her.

As with everyone, including Henry, Kathy thought of Shelly as an American in the guise of a Japanese pixie. Gradually, she warmed to her as a person who used her mischievous antics to mask a sincere and substantive nature.

Weimar

May 1990

Hanna judiciously reported once a week. Hers was a task requiring detective work. She was one of the few students who braved the chaos of an educational system in transition. Heike appreciated her terse reports. Despite her involvement in an unprecedented odyssey, Hanna's expositions were confined to the fruits of research. She omitted the epic drama in which she was a participant.

Heike, however, was not as respectful; she expounded upon her vision of Rosa's Children. Hanna listened politely and nodded when appropriate, but her attentiveness was problematic. Since Heike insisted on expanding upon tangential matters, Hanna attempted to lure her Genossin back to school.

Despite mutual disinterests, certain crumbs were eagerly snatched up. One such aside was Hanna's poignant narration concerning a young economics teacher. He'd been an ardent leader in the FDJ and an award-winning student at university. Everyone knew he was assured admission to the SED and, with it, a choice spot in local government. Of course, the demise of the DDR destroyed his career.

Hanna emotionally related how he continued to teach, but he spoke only in a monotone. Often, his voice was so weak, the students couldn't hear. One day he stopped talking and stared out the window for several uncomfortable moments.

"I didn't mean to lie to you," he announced. "I didn't know! I never meant to lie. I didn't know. I'm sorry."

With this, he marched out of class. He went missing for two days. Heike was moved enough that she came by the school to talk with the shaken teacher. They made a coffee date for a Saturday afternoon.

During their seventy-minute meeting, the broken man related how he discovered mountains of information the party kept from das Volk. When he compared this with Wessi information, he saw exactly how the disaster came upon them. It had been predictable and, thus, avoidable.

"I'm sure few at the highest levels saw it coming," he concluded with an attitude of defeat.

"The people in power knew the kind of economics I was teaching. It was ideological tripe. That, only, was allowed. Reality chugged along for decades, quite openly, but everyone was too ideological to recognize it. We were destroyed by our own ignorance."

When Heike introduced the fundamentals of Rosa's Children, she noticed a change in his expression. He remained committed to his political ideals and was enthused by the ardor and idealism of Rosa's Children. He expressed interest. If the Children became a force, he'd support it, however, he was reticent to commit.

"I was betrayed once," he reminded. "I became an instrument of betrayal. I should have seen the lies, but even had I, what could I do? I wouldn't dare tell anyone."

"We adhere to Rosa's concept of democratic socialism," Heike promised. "Discussion must be allowed and encouraged."

"And when discussion is not permitted?"

"We can't accept that. Intelligent people must always be allowed to say what they believe. If an idea is stupid or harmful, public discussion exposes it."

He nodded but with little enthusiasm.

"There were rules – very ridged rules. Certain things were never discussed."

Heike recalled Nadine's rant about lead rationing. She, together with the other "barkers," thought only of shutting her up. No one dared to view the suggestion on its own merits.

"We must not allow that ever again."

Heike's determination didn't move him.

"How?" he asked, quietly.

From that moment on, that unanswered question was draped over Heike's shoulders like a dead albatross. It began to torment her as much as it tormented the teacher and former standard-bearer of the SED. Fortunately, political philosophy is tempered by practicality. Heike found unexpected rewards in her role as Inka's guardian.

She'd taken over Frau Zimmermann's control of the family purse. Herr Zimmermann brought bread in the house and Heike directed its employment and distribution. In this role, she was frugal to a fault. Seizure of the economy by Wessi capitalists created chaos and monetary "readjustments." Above all, however, she realized the Zimmermann money was not hers to disperse recklessly.

Beyond this, she prepared the bread-winner's breakfast the afternoon prior and cooked one hot meal a day for him. It was she who kept the house clean and orderly. It was she who washed and scrubbed his and the baby's clothes. These were physical tasks she took on willingly in return for not having to fuss with the comet.

Ultimately, Hanna arrived with a written parchment. Heike studied it carefully. In the slice of time allowed for them in the afternoons, they interviewed candidates. It was a short list, but time constraints resulted in a prolonged adventure. The auto proved invaluable; they covered in minutes what public transport and foot made untenable. Even so, it was days before they conferenced with Herr Zimmermann to reach a decision.

The economy had collapsed. Most child-care facilities were closed. Boldly, a few struggled on. Lacking state support, many became unsafe. Few people could make a living on the capitalist model; if the state no longer funded business, patrons must.

Heike and Hanna matched the facilities against Herr Zimmermann's income. Two places were eliminated instantly as unclean and unsafe. The remainder were judged on quality of employees and quantity of supplies. Heike and Hanna made their recommendation; Herr Zimmermann accepted it, and Heike took the requisite amount of money from the kitchen tin.

"It is best to pay by the week," she advised.

Herr Zimmermann nodded.

He didn't bother to check Heike's expenditures and resisted sitting down with Heike once a week to review accounts. This irked her beyond endurance. She'd not steal on principle, though Frau Zimmermann's picture helped reinforce her probity.

The Wessis, however, suffered no restraints. When opportunity presented itself, the government would steal every pfennig of Zimmermann's reserve simply because it could. If he didn't, quickly, resume management of the domestic economy, Inka could starve.

Clutching bills in her hand, she closed the cash drawer.

"We will discuss this later," Heike promised.

Herr Zimmermann shuddered. Heike's concept of a discussion was a monologue berating him for slovenly habits and a careless nature. He didn't look forward to her return. The girl's lectures were made unbearable because she was, annoyingly, correct on every point.

He longed for his wife. When they engaged in similar discussions, Herr Zimmermann lost most of them. With Frau Zimmermann, however, the loss was acceptable because he loved his opponent. Heike, though a staunch ally, was an insufferable pest.

Once outside the Zimmermann "closet," Heike thanked Hanna profusely for finding Inka a suitable billet. Typically, Hanna shrugged off plaudits. Being of service was her reward.

"I catch the bus out in the morning and take Inka into town," she assured.

"You'll be late for school," Heike warned.

"*Na, und?*"

"Deliver the money as well," Heike concluded, thrusting Reich Marks into her hand.

"You trust me?"

Heike scoffed.

"We've been capitalist only a few weeks and I'm sick of it. In the old days, like about three months ago, we had several ways to pay debts. Today, it's money exchange only."

"It's pretty mercenary," Hanna agreed.

She didn't mention that Heiko and two other like-minded musicians made a small fortune playing in impromptu clubs sprouting up about town.

* * *

Government bureaucracy is a cumbersome, mammoth, and metaphysical riddle at the best of times. When a nation fails, the rules, once so ridged and weighty, burrow deep. No government employee accepts responsibility for anything. The bureaucratic waltz becomes mysterious and frustrating. Nobody knew the rules.

Heike Jacobs wasted an hour at the *Rathaus* attempting to secure official blessing for the June assembly of Rosa's Children. The low-level flunkies who deal with the unwashed masses were anxious to have Heike chase her own tail. Previously, of course, it was easy to shunt a person off to another office, the one least likely to provide succor. With so much uncertainty, government monkeys were forced into shoulder shrugs and primitive grunts. It became annoyingly difficult to misdirect people.

Heike performed her part in the proceedings with superhuman restraint. When her hour of grace was exhausted, however, her tone became crisp and petulant. She didn't care how, who or upon what subject, she was determined to get a definitive answer from someone, or some random object would be ejected through a window.

She knocked sharply on another door in the bureaucratic labyrinth but refused to hesitate respectfully before barging in. She confronted a long, chest-high counter. Behind the obstruction were hundreds of files stacked in precarious towers. Heike guessed these were divided into "destroy" and "keep" piles. A single person sat behind a too-large wooden desk. His grizzled profile leaned over the desk peering at the inner pages of a newspaper laying flat. He pretended to be unaware of her presence.

Heike leaned on the counter and waited for the man to come out of his stupor. She noticed the newspaper was a Wessi tabloid. Jürgen, always full of unauthorized information, warned his sisters about such offal.

"You have to lay it flat," he admonished. "Otherwise, the sperm and blood spills out."

Despite the effusive puffs of smoke from a cigarette planted firmly between the bureaucrat's thick lips, Heike had no problems seeing what engaged the man's attention. There was a large photo of a naked woman. The man was, apparently, committing it to memory.

"How do I address you?" she asked abrasively.

She got a bureaucratic grunt for her pains.

"Many people in Weimar have names," she announced. "Are you among them?"

"Metzger," he wheezed gruffly.

A butcher! It figures!

"Herr Metzger, I represent an organization wishing to hold a day-long exhibit on the last week in June. We seek official sanction."

She hoped the flunky language might penetrate the Neanderthal cranium. The term *exhibit* was her own invention. There was no reason, she figured, to provide details until necessary. The man didn't divert attention from photographic art. It would take him time to invent her next dead-end office; she took advantage of his delay.

"Herr Metzger, I have nowhere to be until tomorrow noon. I'm willing to spend every moment of that time in your charming company."

It was a lie, but how would he know?

He grunted.

Heike hoisted herself onto the counter and lay on her back.

"Here, now! What are you doing?"

"Getting comfortable," she chirped. "It looks like I'll be here a while. If I need to relieve myself, I can use the trash can there, right?"

"I'll have you thrown out!" he barked, but his heart, clearly, wasn't in it.

"You'll can try," she noted. "You'll not be able to do it yourself. Why not tell me where I can get permission? The sooner you do, the sooner you can get back to your — um – 'reading'."

He weighed his options for some moments. He decided she might be difficult to shove off the counter and out the door if she didn't wish to go. Then, there was always the possibility that one of the *real* officials, one who despised the "unwashed masses," might select this moment to burst into his office. That would not generate conviviality.

"Talk to the Vopos," he grunted.

Of course! Fool!

Heike should have thought of that.

She blushed. There was no one to blame for wasting her time in the city hall. Still, she wouldn't let Herr Metzger down lightly. She slid off the counter and made a show of recording the time and the office number. She hoped he'd think she recorded his name as well.

"Thank you, Herr Metzger," she flashed a phony smile. "I hope you and the young lady will be very happy."

* * *

Shakespeare sat with a foot dangling and one arm akimbo as he surveyed the disordered spring that was brought to the riverside meadow. The grass hadn't been tended since the economic collapse; it ran riot. The formerly well-manicured carpet leading up to Goethe's-garden house resembled a jungle daunting enough to give Dr. Livingston pause.

Beneath the marble sentry stood the same orphan whose pilgrimages hither were frequently rewarded with solace and epiphanies. Suddenly, advice was denied. Eyes stinging with tears and nerves frayed, Heike Jacobs brought terror with her. This unwelcome companion was not swayed by the bard. Indeed, the malevolent specter perched upon the same globe Heike once considered her throne.

The blazing eyes, all six of them, haunted her memory. She'd entered the police building with the same officious bravado she wielded against Herr Metzger. Soon, she realized the gravity of her error. The desk-bound Vopos were paralyzed with the fear and uncertainty. Already, Wessi officials gathered like vultures.

Who might the new government punish and imprison?

Into this charged atmosphere came Heike with all the haughtiness of a reigning monarch. She made demands that might lead to disorder or, worse, revolt. Wessi masters might object. Someone would be blamed; heads would roll. Who better to incarcerate than those charged with maintaining public order?

Heike read their thoughts. It would be possible to murder this troublesome girl and dump her body in the river. It might be days or even weeks before the crime was discovered. As much as Heike worshipped Rosa Luxemburg, she had no desire to meet the same end.

She left the men with a last, defiant quote and vacated the office quickly. Once the door latched behind her, she hurried to the nearest exit expecting trumpeting voices to order her seizure. Thankfully, she escaped unmolested. Reason told her that the terror was magnified by imagination. Reason, however, couldn't stop the trembling.

"I can't do this," she whispered to the master.

Rosa's Children. Such mockery. The organization should be rechristened Heike's Cowards! She fancied she could gladly give her life for the cause; then, when her hyperbolic imagination conjured a threat, she ran like the frightened child she was. Beyond her veil of shame, Heike saw Nadine, bloodied and deformed, being dragged away by a monster.

A letter arrived. Her father sought her. Angered, she ripped it to shreds. She had nothing to say to a traitor, a person who attempted to tear her from the bosom of her country. She refused to meet him; he was a Wessi. He hated the DDR; he hated Ossis.

Heike was an Ossi, a very proud Ossi. A treasonous father had no place in her life. So, that was it? Rosa's Children would languish through a summer without purpose. The child Heike hoped to bring into the world died stillborn.

Heike Jacobs would be tossed aside by history. The ideals she considered worthy of sacrifice were abandoned the moment she sensed danger. She'd proven herself a traitor on par with her unknown and detested father.

How could she face anyone? How could she admit that the summer plans she proposed and boasted about must be aborted because she was a coward? She didn't deserve the shelter of Walter Ecke's house. Would it not be better to slink away some dark night and disappear into sylvian shadows and die alone in nature's lap?

She walked. She tried to think. All her thoughts were black and self-derisive. The honorable thing would be to throw herself off a bridge and purchase a watery end. She hadn't the courage. If she couldn't defy a policeman's pistol and die instantly when his missile shred her heart, there was no way she could subject herself to the horrible seconds drowning demanded.

Until something revealed itself, Heike would trudge aimlessly about a city that no longer delighted her. Once, Goethe and Schiller, Liszt, Wagner, Bach, Herder, and countless other august personages strolled about the same paths. Heike was disgraced by her unjustified existence.

In another part of the city but under much the same motivation, Liselotte Kruger strode with a stormy brow above downcast eyes. The sport camps were closing and Lilo's dream of an Olympic medal closed with them. She must compete under the Wessi flag. Atop that disgrace, she'd be forced to sell herself to a capitalist exploiter to raise money to train and travel. Lilo would proudly run for the honor of her country, but she refused to be a pimp for the unscrupulous. She exchanged possible Olympic glory for an anonymous and pointless existence as the slave and prisoner of a hostile government.

Lured by the opportunities of the wealthy West, Lilo's parents migrated to the clutter of a refugee camp in Hessen. There were promises of better days if the Krugers submitted to "retraining." Once properly indoctrinated, they'd qualify for a *meaningful* employment – maybe.

Lilo returned to an empty apartment. It was the only home she'd ever known; she would not leave it save under duress. She meandered about the city seeking employment to meet her rent obligations. There were no jobs. She hired out as an errand runner.

She accepted any menial task. This income provided money enough for a beggar's diet and a few marks toward partial rent payments. She sold certain furnishings. Unfortunately, money owed ran far ahead of money obtained.

Lilo qualified for university, but an education would cost the home she was anxious to save. Moreover, she'd require money to pay her share with three or more other students in a university city. Until she had her home secure, education must wait.

Once, she dreamed of sharing her life with Günther. He, however, slipped into the clutches of that conniving, obnoxious ideologue who posed as Jürgen's sister. Further, it was rumored Günther was reneging on his army enlistment on the grounds that he never agreed to serve under NATO command. If the Wessis swallowed up the DDR, he'd be forced. Günther, soon enough, would compete with Lilo for food scraps.

I won't give up my home.

That was Lilo's credo and her goal. The one remaining speck of the DDR existed in her parent's third floor apartment, and she'd resort to extremes to keep it. Was she the only person left on the planet who believed in the values with which she was brought up? She heard Heike Jacobs was forming some socialist organization.

Leave it to that damned Frau Marx to whip a dead horse. Still, if there were believers enough something – however little – might be salvaged. It was worth investigating. However, to ask anything of that pompous little orphan would gall her.

Suddenly, there sat Heike Jacobs on a park bench looking blankly out across a sea of uncut grass. If Lilo turned and sped away, she'd draw attention to herself. The vision of Heike calling her out like some Prussian count summoning a groom would be too humiliating.

There was nothing for it but to keep moving. Perhaps, when she got near enough, she could kick Heike hard on the shin. It would satisfy Lilo to hear the crack of a bone. Thinking of Günther, she might murder the miserable cow.

Lilo's mouth watered as she neared her target. All her frustrations of the past months were about to be unleashed. Just short of the critical moment, Lilo saw light reflect off the tiny pool in the corner of Heike's eye.

"Hallo, Heike."

Heike's head snapped around. She discovered Lilo tickling the low-hanging clouds with her blond plumage.

"'Tag, Lilo."

She dabbed her eyes on a sleeve, hoping the Amazon wouldn't notice her tears. An embarrassing silence followed. There remained enough malevolence in Lilo to avoid breaking it. Heike must suffer.

"I watched you run at Bucharest."

Lilo nodded appreciatively. The consolation of finishing a distant second was knowing the victor was the European record holder. It was Lilo's first, and, perhaps, only televised appearance. She knew there was no television in Heike's home.

"They closed the camps," Lilo reported.

She sat next to Heike on the bench to avoid having to look directly at her.

"I heard."

Silence.

"I hear you're forming a cell."

"Not, exactly. More of a – I don't know."

"A cell."

"Okay, a *cell.*"

Silence.

"I'm looking for work, Heike. Is there anything I can do?"

"We haven't a pfennig, Lilo."

"I didn't ask you if you could pay. I asked if there's anything I can do."

"I don't know. I – we wanted to have a rally, but –"

"Go on."

"We need an okay from the Vopos."

"Get it."

"I don't know, Lilo."

Silence.

"Where do you want this rally?"

"The Frauenplan."

"You don't want much, do you?"

"It may not happen."

"Because of the Vopos? They're history. Just tell them."

Silence.

"I don't know, Lilo –"

"Scheiße! I'll do it."

"No, Lilo!"

It was and urgent, hysterical reply.

Lilo would not take orders from an impish little brat. The evil of breaking Heike's leg seized her anew.

"You make me sick!" Lilo announced, instead. "You'll break your back to help someone else, but you won't let anyone to lift a finger for you! When is the rally?'

"Lilo, please!"

The athlete grabbed the wrist nearest her and applied a vice-like force. Heike squirmed and attempted to free herself, but Lilo's strength was superior.

"When?"

"*Owa! Owa!*"

"When, *verdamnt nach mal!*"

"Saturday, the thirtieth! June!"

Lilo released the wrist which immediately sheltered between Heike's stomach and her other arm. For one brief instant, Lilo was ashamed.

"Maybe, I get too emotional sometimes," she announced calmly. "I'll help however I can, Heike, but if you take that insufferable tone with me again, I'll strangle you."

Heike thought it was an excellent time to keep quiet.

"Have you seen Günther?"

Heike shook her head.

Lilo bit her lip. She didn't know if she was angry with Heike or with Günther, but hers was a mighty rage. The desire to break bones suddenly lost appeal, but somewhere in Weimar there was some inanimate object which was going to absorb the furious energy of Lilo Kruger.

She went in search of it.

Oregon Coast

May 1990

Ute Foster sighed with relief when Kathy returned Shelly's tape player. Raised with Wagner and Beethoven, Ute never responded to Bach – he was too mellow and rococo for her romantic preference. Aaron, however, couldn't abide classical music, strings particularly. With Bach absent, Ute's husband was more amenable.

There was one advantage to Bach's sojourn in the Foster cottage; Kathy, whose patience and poise frequently lapsed, became pleasant and calm. Ute noticed the correlation and shared it with Aaron. He remained skeptical but awarded his wife the benefit of doubt.

For her birthday, Ute got a precious gift from her adopted daughter. Rather than spend her meager *Mary R.* earnings on something of tertiary importance, the girl delivered onto Ute a simple parchment rolled into a semblance of a scroll and bound with a ribbon. The old-German lettering was done in masterful calligraphy by Shelly's delicate hand.

As a schoolgirl, Ute never learned the old-style lettering and seldom read it. Kathy aided her in deciphering the text. It promised Ute one uninterrupted hour a day from Isaac's insatiable demands.

"Lovely," the appreciative mother beamed, "but how long will this last?"

"We can discuss that on your next birthday," Kathy promised.

Ute accepted this oral announcement as a sign Kathy intended to remain another year. She did not, however, press. If it were anyone but Kathy, Ute would doubt actions would match words. Kathy Foster, however, was Swabish, if only by choice. Just as Ute's father never promised lightly, Kathy's word was good.

It was delightful to have an entire hour in the evenings, but her patience was tested. Kathy's concept of an hour was ill-defined. After seventy minutes, Ute became anxious. After ninety minutes she'd meekly beg for the return of her son.

Unexpectedly, the Foster home became the focus of attention. Kathy's story circulated. A local reporter sniffed it out. She interviewed Kathy after school. The questions were innocuous enough. So was the resulting article.

First to respond was Kathy's theatre family. Ed Geist invited her to the dress rehearsal of *Blithe Spirit* whereupon she was presented with four free tickets to any of twelve scheduled performances. The gesture was appreciated. After rehearsal, however, Kathy's egress was barred. Debbie Davis, a performing member, and Steve, who was not, led a delegation of cast and crew in presenting Kathy a gift certificate from a local clothing outlet.

It was substantial.

"You'll want nice things to wear when you meet your father," Debbie advised.

Kathy was appreciative, but she accepted with guilt.

With her was Kathy's ever faithful chauffeur. With headlights piercing the darkness, Molly gushed with wardrobe suggestions. A nice dress would be in order. Molly volunteered, to assist in finding the right one.

"I know the right dress," Kathy announced.

The next day at school, Molly brought a garment bag. Kathy knew what it contained and unzipped to confirm her suspicions.

"It's yours," Molly announced.

"No, Molly. I can't accept this."

"I hardly wear it; Jayme won't be caught dead in it."

Kathy's resistance toppled. She considered the pale blue dress perfect for any occasion. She'd worn it for her jazz début. She stared at herself in a mirror for long stretches before and after that event, memorizing every detail. Athena and Ute snapped a picture of her wearing it.

Kathy made certain copies were secure in the family's fire-proof valuables box. Those photos together with her passport and "birth documents" were worthy of saving from catastrophe.

"I'll bring it back," she promised.

Molly smiled. They both realized the offer was a face-saving device.

"You should buy a nice pair of pumps to wear with that," Ute suggested.

"Flats," Kathy responded. "I want a nice pair of flats."

"Honey, they'll make you look like a child."

"I waddle in heels."

She'd managed to navigate acceptably on stage in heels, but Kathy was never comfortable. She imagined herself a breath away from disaster.

One afternoon, Kathy was called to the office. Fearing Ute or Isaac or both had met with an accident, she rushed through the hall with panic in her throat. Instead of disaster, she was confronted with a photographer and a reporter from one of the Salem papers. The Foster's didn't get a Salem paper. Kathy's relief was enough to erase the twenty-minute interview from her memory.

How would Kathy Foster get to Berlin?

No one knew, but the Fosters spoke as if it were a certainty. Kathy never gave a thought to getting on a plane for Germany. That episode banished from her dreams. If Molly could drive to Germany some drizzly afternoon…

Molly's dress was assigned a place of honor in Kathy's closet. Nightly, she collected her brother for however long Ute could suffer withdrawal. She routinely carried the child into their shared room so Ute could have the run of the house.

Ute was exhausted afternoons. Disposable diapers were a great invention, but they did not make for alluring ambiance. Therefore, she took them to the outside trash bin as required. One day, Little Aaron attempted a new world record; Ute was caught short.

She protected her son against the brisk ocean breeze and pushed his carriage to the nearest "aid station." Following this adventure, the aging mother required horizontal relaxation.

She longed for the comfort of her bed but settled for the couch. She let out a sigh and placed the back of one hand across her eyes when she heard a single, unwavering note coming from the back room.

Kathy, obviously, had arrived during Ute's trek.

How long could she hold that note?

Ute suspected something was wrong. However, the note changed beautifully before changing again. Could Kathy manage that in one breath? She recognized Bach's Air. Though the music grated, she realized Kathy's voice was amazing.

* * *

It was Shelly Big-Mouth.

From Shelly to Gary to Jayme's heartthrob. A double play!

Jayme gained a boyfriend. Though he'd never admit it, Gary took a hand. The object of Jayme's adoration was an athlete, though not a footballer. Gary, nevertheless, had influence among the *jocks*. After Jayme's lunchroom fiasco, Shelly prodded Gary who initiated a short conversation in the hall. Convinced Jayme hadn't intended to mock him, the young man found the tennis star "interesting." If things went sour, Kathy would be cross with Gary. Until then, she'd keep still; Jayme was happy. Unfortunately, Jayme didn't bring her beau into the group. She lunched with him on the steps of the stage.

"She doesn't want him to sit here and stare at Molly," Shelly deduced.

As with many of her comments, it was intended to be witty, but this one failed. Shelly and Jayme were fast friends from their first meeting. It would be in keeping with the vivacious and gregarious Shelly to amble up to the stage steps and make herself at home.

Kathy saw beyond the persona of the American with almond eyes and oversized ears. Shelly Kurihara refused to use her friendship in order to trespass on Jayme's newest pleasure.

That was so Swabish.

Kathy glanced at Molly. As ever, she looked as poised and attractive as a cover girl. Gary, often, cast envious eyes in her direction while sitting next to Kathy. Shelly's supposition about having a pig had merit.

"*Hai!*"

Shelly sent an appreciative smile across the table in a salute to Kathy's fluent Japanese.

* * *

That afternoon the post brought another communication from the old world. When Kathy entered, she discovered Ute holding a bottle to Isaac's mouth. The towel casually tossed over her left shoulder bore a spotted testament to her son's greed.

Ute met Kathy's eyes and directed them to the coffee table. The girl reopened the thick envelope and discovered airline tickets in the names of Ute and Kathy Foster. There was also a notice that an infant would round out the party.

Kathy sank to her knees and let her book bag slide off her shoulder and onto the floor. The steadiness of her fingers in returning the documents to the envelope was not lost on the adoptive mother. Though his position as the co-owner and managing head of a large wholesale business was lucrative enough, Dieter's generous act was unprecedented.

"He checked this out very carefully," Kathy surmised.

"Yep. Looks like he's found your dad," Ute confirmed. "He knew better than to ask if I wanted to come."

"He wants to see his sister," Kathy responded.

"He wants to see his nephew," Ute corrected. "Cheeky bastard!"

Kathy started and looked at the woman she thought she knew so well. Ute averted her eyes, ashamed of her words if not the sentiment.

"You don't have to go. Send your ticket back."

Ute pretended to pay undivided attention to her son's gulping. She would withdraw the bottle periodically to monitor the rate of consumption. Each time, Isaac smacked his lips, threw his arms about, and looked at his mother with an expression equally divided between puzzlement and sorrow.

"I want to see my parents," she admitted.

They had two grandsons already. Kathy thought any baby was not much different from any other at such a young age. Once Isaac formed a personality, he'd be worth showing off.

It was Dieter's generosity that grated. There was no way the Fosters could repay him properly, if at all. Swabish, Ute Foster nee Kaufmann was not comfortable as a debtor.

"You hate my dad, don't you?"

"Kathy! I've never met him."

"You think he wants me back."

Ute took the bottle from Isaac and shook it at Kathy who, subsequently, wiped stray milk drops off her face.

"Did you hear yourself? What father doesn't want his child? Do you think I'd hate a man because he wants his own daughter?"

Kathy refused to give ground, but she'd no intention of being confrontational.

"You're going as my chaperone, aren't you? Last summer, I could travel alone, but this year –."

"Sometimes –" Ute gulped.

She nearly addressed the girl by her full name. She didn't know her full name – neither of them did.

"Sometimes," she repeated in a more measured tone. "You make me so mad!"

"I'm glad you will be there."

Ute's expression was "clouded by amazement," as Ed Geist might say. Satisfied Mrs. Foster fathomed her meaning, Kathy retrieved her pack and sauntered into Isaac's room to change.

Michael Kaufmann, Kathy thought to herself, why do you not write back?

She had a spy inside her uncle's house; Mischa was the perfect insurgent. Perhaps, he was cured of his puppy love? A fine time for that to happen! It was her only hold on him, though exploiting it shamed her. Perhaps, Aunt Marion intercepted her note. Perhaps, Mischa carelessly allowed it to fall into the wrong hands.

* * *

The following day at school brought increased activity. Hardly had Kathy announced the arrival of the tickets when the "gang" mobilized. Molly insisted she be appointed hairdresser, cosmetologist, and wardrobe consultant. Jayme, struck senseless by Cupid's arrow, revived enough to agree to be Molly's leg man. Henry and Gary exercised sagacity by keeping out of the way. Shelly, as ever, flitted about on the periphery and, at exactly the most opportune moment, swooped in with profound advice.

In Molly's company, Kathy's gift certificate vanished in one voracious splurge. This daunting task was magnified by the presence of Kathy's "brother." Even under extenuating circumstances, Kathy refused to deprive Ute of her "hour of peace."

Jayme proved an adroit nanny. Despite her amateur standing, nothing in the "Isaac bag" was a mystery. Shelly, however, was alarmed by every movement Isaac made. This ceased instantly when Jayme charged her with a diaper change. Shelly, instantly, renounced "backseat babysitting."

Three hours into Ute's "sixty-minutes of freedom" was balanced by an hour of three uninvited guests stampeding through the little house on the little bay. They excused their trespass by rejecting the offer of a meal, insisting they had no appetite. Kathy, however, made a delayed forage to satisfy her guests with sandwiches and packaged cookies.

Finally, the metamorphosis was complete. Molly herded her minions out to the car. Jayme paused to thank Ute and Aaron for their hospitality. Shelly dropped her American habits long enough to fold her hands and bow to her gracious (involuntary) hosts.

The car backed into the street; an eerie hush descended. Mr. and Mrs. Foster bathed themselves in refreshing silence. They recognized such moments were as widely separated as desert oases. If either desired to summon Kathy from her hiding place, they repressed it.

Eventually, Kathy, ambivalent about her appearance, stood inspection. Her mauve slacks featured sharp creases. She had a simple but eye-catching pink top, purchased over Kathy's adamant objections. The elders' pupils dilated – not from Kathy's clothes, strange though they were. Rather, their amazement was based upon the sight of Kathy in makeup with painted nails and an alien hair style.

Kathy waited in an awkward silence. Her mirror introduced her to a stranger who, though attractive enough, was decidedly sinister. How, she wondered, could she present herself to her father in the guise of a person who didn't exist? She sensed Ute and Aaron's thoughts ran along similar lines.

"Molly wants to do my hair in the morning," she announced, as if pleading in court.

"What more is there to do?" Ute demanded.

Kathy shrugged and retreated toward the bathroom.

"Kathy!" Aaron called out.

She turned, expecting the worst.

"You look great!"

She smiled appreciatively.

In the bathroom, she reached for the cold cream and began the purge.

"*Mist!*" she challenged the image in the mirror. "Do I have to put on this crap every day?"

The answer came the moment she stepped off the school bus. Gary was shunted aside by Molly who took her in tow. As promised, she launched into Kathy's hair, but knew her client well enough to know she'd not submit to any makeup regimen.

"Are you running my life now?" Kathy demanded.

"No," Molly replied, during emergency hair care. "My mother is."

* * *

On campus, Kathy Foster was best known by her cheerleading days, an appearance with the jazz band, and as one of Molly Waldron's satellites. After Molly's make-over, Kathy became the phenomenon in her own right. Her clothes were as attractive as the person filling them. Students, who previously paid her scant attention, were saying hello and excusing themselves when wandering into her path. A few threw themselves into her path as an excuse for excusing themselves.

Teachers, who never had her in class, bid hello and called her by name. Gary Swofford was beside her. His feelings were not altered by Kathy's transformation, but he found himself seduced by the attention he enjoyed from being, figuratively, the one on Kathy's arm. Gary was in the habit of seeing Kathy to her first class; it was only a minor diversion for him. On this day, however, Gary realized he was part of a parade.

"Hey, Kathy!"

"Good morning, Kathy."

"Yo, Kat!"

Unexpectedly, Kathy spun around.

"What's wrong?" Gary asked.

"I thought someone was going to step on my heel."

"Don't be a schmuck!"

Kathy appreciated what Molly experienced for much of her life. It wasn't circumstance or obligation; it was a curse. Suddenly thrust into red-carpet treatment, Kathy longed to break free. Some girls were made for attention; some reveled in it, but not Molly Waldron and decidedly not her protégé.

It was a relief to get off the bus that afternoon and into her mousey home. Yes, *mousey*! For the first time that day, Kathy wasn't being deferred to or fawned over. She was comfortable as the slovenly first mate of the *Mary R.* – a face-in-the-crowd. There's much to be said for life on the edge of obscurity.

Molly Waldron played the regal role with dignity and class, but it was too late for Kathy to learn proper etiquette – even if she wanted to.

"Letter for you," Ute announced with a queer expression.

It was from Mischa!

"Does Gary know he has a rival?"

"Ah, Mom!"

"Don't *ah, Mom* me. Marion says he looked goof eyes at you all summer."

"Well," Kathy sighed, "I'd better see what the little twerp wants."

"Just don't break his heart, Kathy," Ute pleaded. "He'll get over it soon enough."

Kathy collected Isaac and carried him back to her lair. She sat on the bed and placed Isaac, gingerly, next to her. She tore open the envelope and scanned her false-cousin's writing.

Uncle Dieter accumulated considerable information. He suspected he'd located Kathy's sister. However, suspicion wasn't good enough for the meticulous Dieter Kaufmann. He required proof.

For Michael Kaufmann, whose feelings for Kathy ran deep, supposition was more than enough. If Kathy wanted information, he'd provide. He knew it would please her; he hoped, in his childish imagination, she'd be obligated.

Heike!

That was the name forwarded by Dieter in his cryptic New Year's message. It was Kathy's emotional overload which caused Dieter to cease regular progress reports; he refused to risk crushing disappointment. It was the object of her search which consumed more and more of her thoughts. It was a person, a living being who shared the same blood. Their mother was dead, Kathy and Heike were the closest relations on the planet.

Heike Jacobs. Weimar. There was even a street address.

Did she remember Papa?

Weimar. Kathy had heard the name but little else.

Her first reaction was to search for the German atlas. The pages were yellowed and torn; it was useless as a travel aid. Many of the highways were altered, eliminated, or replaced by autobahns. However, geographical features and towns don't change. If she searched for the book or asked for its location, suspicions would aroused and questions would be asked. Mischa might get in trouble for being Kathy's spy.

She shut her eyes, clinched her fist, and contracted every muscle in her body until her frustration ebbed. She'd force herself to wait.

"I promised Mischa a big kiss if he sent me this," she confessed to Isaac.

The baby appeared shocked by her revelation.

"That must be a sin," she concluded. "I can't believe I'm so ruthless. Still, a promise is a promise. If I find out I'm not Swabish, I'll let it slide."

She examined the child's reaction. She offered her little finger and he clutched it.

"That would exchange one sin for another, wouldn't it?"

Isaac's curiosity was aroused, but he remained mute.

"You're not the only person in this room who has a sister," she reminded.

Before class, Kathy hurried to the library and located Weimar.

Kathy was summoned to the office during second period. This time, it was a film crew from Portland, being treated by the principal and office staff as visiting royalty. The tribe was escorted in a room occupied by a teacher attempting to grade a stack of quizzes.

The principal explained the situation and asked that the room be used to provide the *atmo* the TV minions desired for their interview. It was clear the teacher's "permission" was not his to give. His relenting to circumstances was not the act of a free man.

After complementing Kathy on her appearance, the reporter perched herself on the top of a student desk. Kathy stood in front of a green chalk board presenting, in yellow chalk, a quadratic equation in search of a solution. When the camera rolled, Kathy was advised not to look at the camera and converse "naturally" with the woman holding the microphone. The "interview" took less than twenty minutes.

Kathy returned to class with relief.

That evening, Kathy saw a strangely familiar face on the TV. When a dimple winked, she left the room, crawled under her bed, and covered her ears. Aaron and Ute stared in stunned disbelief at the screen. Obviously, Kathy was unaware the news show would feature her, or she'd have alerted them.

"You must be anxious to meet your father after so long?"

"Yes, ma'am. Of course, I'm really looking forward to meeting my sister. I mean, I have a father here, but I don't have a sister – here. I'm really excited about her."

When the dinner was placed on the table, it was Aaron's job to coax a recalcitrant daughter from under the bed.

Weimar

June 1990

Lilo's note was terse. Not only did Rosa's Children have a green light for the Frauenplan the last Saturday in June, they were promised a pair of Vopos to patrol the venue. Heike was grateful, but humiliated and ashamed. She should have returned with Lilo to the office, but cowardice intervened.

Had Lilo been sweet and syrupy? Had she been as rough as with Heike's wrist? Had she introduced herself as the distance runner from Romania? Unless Lilo volunteered the information, Heike would never know.

"Hallo, Heike!"

It was the voice she least wanted to hear, but it was the voice she could ill afford to ignore. Goetheplatz was as crowded as ever. That hindered the search. Had Lilo not stood up, she might not have spotted her. Lilo was tucked away amid makeshift stalls in the unlicensed but officially tolerated market.

Unlike the competitors surrounding her, Lilo was not selling goods from a van or a trailer. She'd run a rope between two trees – only Lilo could reach so high – and draped discarded Wessi clothes from it. She, also, tended a rickety wooden table for folded items.

"Working?" Heike asked, stupidly.

"Yes and no." Lilo replied, reached into a cardboard box at her feet. She pulled out a pair of jeans, shook them and began to fold.

"I met a guy who knows my father," she explained, reaching for another item. "He started by selling out of his Trabi, but he makes runs West to keep supplied. He can't sell when he's on the road. I suggested he could double his profits if someone tended the business on his off days."

"*Profit*, Lilo?"

All her life, Heike hated and despised the word. She was awestruck when Lilo used it so casually.

"*T'cha*," Lilo replied, continuing her unpacking, and folding.

"I went to the library and studied a book. I proposed a partnership with Herr Meißner. I'd tend the stock while he's off buying and if, at the end of two weeks, he gets a satisfactory return, he'll make me a partner. Not a full partner, mind you, but I'll get a percentage of the gross."

Heike swallowed hard.

"That must have been some book," she muttered.

"Don't look hurt," Lilo warned, her eyebrows narrowing. "I haven't given up on my beliefs, but I have to survive. I'm not letting that apartment go. I promise not to hire any wage slaves. In fact, unless I can show a profit here, I'm the only slave in this scenario. Currently, I'm an unemployed socialist cast-off waiting for the sun to break through."

Heike had no response. She watched Lilo as she put her wares on display.

"I won't ask you to buy anything," Lilo said, crossing her arms. "If you put on Wessi clothing, you'd melt like Media's revenge."

The allusion went over Heike's head.

"So," Lilo continued. "What's this Frauenplan business in aid of?"

Thankful to have an opportunity to speak, Heike explained. Lilo remained attentive even as she tended to buyers. Heike could have been put off by such cavalier behavior, but each time she lost her enthusiasm, Lilo brought her back with an unexpectedly adroit comment or question.

"I don't want the people to lose sight of what we've been working for," she concluded.

"So, you need names and addresses to keep people informed of progress amid the capitalist conquistadors?"

"Well, yes."

"You're talking newsletters, petitions, manifestos, political commentary. That's going to run into money, Heike. And, in a capitalist world, the costs are higher than we're used to."

Heike blushed.

"I think you need to read that book, Heike."

Heike shrugged and turned to leave.

"Don't give me attitude!" Lilo barked. "I'm on your side, no matter how much we dislike each other. I'll help, but it will be a long, hard slog. Speak truth, you haven't looked a day beyond the Frauenplan, have you?"

"Not really," she admitted. "I thought, first we must have enough names to create an organization."

"There won't be an organization no matter how many names you get. You have to spell it all out, or you'll turn around and find no one is following."

"What do we do?

"We? I like the sound of that, Heike," Lilo nodded. "The first thing *we* need is a declaration of principles or beliefs. What do we stand for?"

"You don't know?" Heike asked, incredulously.

"What we know counts nothing. The people must understand – exactly."

There was no arguing that.

"Let me jot down some things tonight. We can sit down and plan a flyer."

"Fliers? Lilo, we have no money."

"The longest journey begins with the first step," Lilo stated patiently. "First, we decide upon a document, then we worry about publishing it."

Heike wavered. The more she remained inert, the edgier Lilo became. Finally, the distance runner realized the source of the problem. She reached out. Heike stepped back warily. Gently, Lilo put her hand on Heike's shoulders.

"Heike, I want to do this. I'll help any way I can, but I have no desire to take Rosa's Children away from you. I'm not Ernst Thälmann. I don't want to be out front leading the way. I'm a follower, not a leader. That much I've learned about myself."

"I don't know if I'm a leader either," Heike confessed.

"If you aren't, we'll find someone who is. Right now, we give this thing all we've got; if we don't attract followers, leadership won't matter. Come to my place on Thursday, and we'll talk about it."

"Okay, Lilo," Heike agreed.

"Good. Now, let me get on with my decadent, capitalist exploitation."

* * *

Lilo Kruger knew so many people in the FDJ, and not just locals. She knew Genossen from across the country. Her stint as a national athlete earned many additional acquaintances. As a lieutenant in Rosa's Children, Lilo could move a lot of horses. However, once she realized what a coward Heike was, Lilo could, deservedly, run the upstart off the planet.

Things never hold a course for long – not for Heike. She expected the other shoe to drop. When everything was placed in balance, Liselotte Kruger carried the most weight. If Rosa's Children became anything more than an amusing farce, it required critical mass. Lilo could supply it. The price was an evening in her company. Though Heike preferred being trapped on a desert isle with a hundred drunken, sex-starved Ami soldiers, she'd be brave – just this once.

Thursday evening loomed as a palpable evil.

Just off Schiller Strasse, a large tent served as Weimar's newest market. It was not so large as a circus tent, perhaps, but it enclosed voluminous space. As with Lilo's partner-to-be, a group of investors seized the opportunity and brought in goods without state-sponsored transportation links.

Inside the tent were quality goods, many from the West. The prices were, often, reflective of the frugal climate. Until the entrepreneurs negotiated their way into a proper venue, the tent trimmed overhead costs, reducing prices and, thus, luring people from the rural surroundings.

Heike hated shopping there, but Lilo was correct; Ossis must adjust to the new world. The impromptu market dealt in a wide variety of goods; Heike could purchase, in a few minutes, what once took most of a morning, flitting from laden to laden. She preferred bread and rolls from a proper baker and meat from a Metzgerei. Most everything else, from diapers to coffee; peas to cheese, lay just beyond a canvass flap.

She filled her shopping basket and two bags and met the immediate needs of both the Jacobs and the Zimmermann households. She found it difficult to manage the load but was amazed of the quantity obtained for a modest expenditure. In "the old days," i.e.: three weeks before, she'd be lucky to secure half the items in her tucker at any price.

She retired to the shelter of a nearby building to avoid a rush of pedestrians. There, within sight of the Schiller House, she redistributed her load. The eggs, for example, had to go into the basket while the less fragile items were stuffed into the bags. The bulky bags would be a challenge.

"May I help?"

A sudden frost enveloped her. She recognized the voice. She took a deep breath and allowed her eyes to travel up a pair of light brown Ossi work pants, over a blue work shirt with sleeves rolled up to the elbows. Despite knowing the face crowning this obsolete attire, Heike gasped when seeing it again.

There were a thousand things flashing through her mind. She was tempted to refuse any help. Failing this, she conjured a legion of sardonic epithets. Ultimately, she stared as if in shock, which, to say truth, was an apt appraisal of her condition.

If Heike's expression reflected ambivalence or outright perplexity, the inquisitor looked tense and frightened. They might have stood mute and immovable for hours had not Heike's fingers lost hold of the handle of a canvass bag. When it thudded to the pavement, she looked at it dumbly. There was nothing delicate within, but her expression reflected perplexity: how did it get there?

A man's callused hand took up the bag; Heike's eyes followed it as if witnessing levitation. She swallowed hard and looked, again, at the face that unnerved her.

"I've been following you, for a couple of days," he informed.

She blinked and swallowed again.

"I wanted to speak with you, but I imagined you'd be surrounded by a fleet of Knaben," he reported, feigning glibness.

Heike blinked again. He grew uncomfortable and shuffled his feet to drain off energy.

"I didn't want to – be in the way."

Had there been an observer to chronicle this bizarre exchange, Heike's nervously twitching eyelids would indicate an optical deficiency. Similarly, her powers of speech would be called into question. One might well conclude she resided in some institution for the marginally intelligent.

Little more could be said of the man who, for want of a partner, was reduced to a fatuous monologue. Perhaps, a bystander might conclude he was a trustee from the same mental institution as the disoriented young woman.

"Please, let me help you with your things. You are going home, correct?"

Again, the speaker endured a period of suspended animation before the girl nodded her head feebly, almost undetectably. He took the "lost" bag into his brawny fist. He gestured with his head and one arm to remind the retarded girl the way home.

They walked in silence because she remained stunned. Her deer-in-headlight eyes fixed ahead, oblivious to pedestrian traffic surrounding her. Nearing the Theaterplatz, she, instinctively, turned down an alley towards Werner Ecke's home. There was another way, but it included Goetheplatz – and Lilo.

"You have enough for an army," the man observed. "Giving a party?"

Heike cleared her throat.

"Ah, no – we, I, um, have to make dinner for Herr Zimmermann."

It didn't occur to Heike that her announcement would compound the confusion.

"Interesting. How long has this been going on?"

"How long? Um – Well, um, it's something I'm doing because – it's complicated."

"Indeed," he sighed.

He didn't know any Herr Zimmerman. The matter was hopelessly muddled; he surrendered hope of immediate resolution. Heike was not herself. Since discretion is the better part, he opted to postpone the discussion until Heike and lucidity were reconciled.

"Um –" never had Heike stuttered so, "What are you doing – here?"

"I came to see you."

"Me? Um – you came – um –?"

"Why wouldn't I want to see you?"

Proof positive, Heike Jacobs was under sedation. In her normal state, such a question would invite an answer of some length, high volume, and a weave of diction and syntax that would stun fastidious standers by. Heike, however, lost her bellicosity in the trauma of Leipzig.

The pair traversed a long, curving street before turning down a cobbled lane. There was no sidewalk. Heike's escort shifted his load and took her arm in case, in her dazed state, she walked into the path of a careless driver. She paused and looked at him, self-consciously, he released her arm, but she continued gazing into his eyes. It was not, from his perspective, the least disturbing.

"Um –" she began, blinking her way back to some sense of purpose, "we better – um – be going. I must catch a bus."

"That must be some dinner if you have to start this early."

"Well, I have to clean up first. I have to – do – things."

The man's patience knew no end. He burned with curiosity but felt responsible for the befuddled girl.

"*Tousend Dank*," she said at the door of the Jacobs's abode.

"A pleasure," he assured, transferring custody of his burden.

There was one last moment of extreme discomfort as each expected the other to offer a parting word.

"When will you be home?"

She shrugged.

"*Halb sieben, oder sieben oder so. Warum?*"

He was pleased she asked. It made things easier.

"I'd like to take you to dinner. It will give me a chance to tell you things and," he added with trepidation, "to explain."

"Oh?"

The staring contest was renewed.

"So?" he asked.

"So?" she repeated.

"May I take you to dinner tonight?"

She shrugged and made a face.

"*Ja. Warum nicht?*"

"Good. Seven o'clock?"

"*Es gut so.*"

"*Bis Sieben.*"

"*Tchu*."

Heike, in a haze, transferred all her purchases to their proper places as Nadine washed the stairs. Once stowage was complete, Heike transferred the Zimmermann items to the shopping basket and parked it by the door. Only then did she regain her faculties.

"Scheiße!"

Nadine hardly blinked. In a home where trauma reigned, pithy declarations were hardly worthy of note. She transferred her bucket of soapy water to the bathroom where she'd pour it in the toilet and give it a good wipe-round before flushing it away. Heike's eyes, which she could hardly avoid, arrested her.

"What?"

"Günther asked me to dinner!"

If Heike's temper was temporarily disabled, there was nothing wrong with Nadine's.

"You said yes? Heike, get rid of him! He's no good. Tell him to crap in a snake pit!"

A fraction of Heike shared her sister's sentiment. However, a second fraction wanted to keep her date. A third fraction wished her many kilometers away.

Had her "daughters" examined Anne sitting quietly on the couch, they'd have noticed her placid expression break into radiant smile. It mattered not; they'd never suspect rational thought lay behind it.

"Pabst will 'take you for a walk,'" Nadine cautioned.

"I've never been invited to dinner before," Heike mused.

"At camp," Nadine responded automatically.

Heike waved her hand. FDJ activities don't count.

"Heike, he's using you. He intends to make Lilo jealous – or some other girl. He might be married."

Heike was torn between the lure of flattery and the excesses of rage. Nadine was attempting to drench flames with gasoline.

"He never wrote! He never saw you when he was home! Slap his face and send him away."

Unexpectedly, Heike remained uncharacteristically calm. Her jaw was set, and her eyes flashed; of outrage, however, there was no sign.

"Pabst won't allow it."

Nadine knew that this remark tipped the balance. Further, discussion was fruitless. However, once Heike Jacobs decided upon a course of action, objections were dismissed.

"He'll humiliate you," Nadine predicted.

Heike took her dinner basket and left.

Nadine's pouting expression told her Rolf remained uninformed. After sober reflection, Heike realized she faced humiliation. Regardless, she itched to give Günther a substantial share of her mind and, perhaps, a portion of Nadine's as well.

"Pabst, I've been asked out to dinner – tonight."

Herr Jacobs sat next to his wife digesting the least objectionable portions of the paper; Nadine retreated to the kitchen. Rolf lowered the paper.

"Humph!" he coughed. "Who did the asking?"

"Günther Neubert," she announced with feigned courage.

"Jürgen's friend?"

"The same."

"*Viel Spaß.*"

He resumed reading.

Nadine's distorted face gasped in amazement from the kitchen portal. Her wide-eyed amazement reflected Heike's.

* * *

Once upon a time, when justice was settled with swords, the city fathers commissioned an impressive edifice for the purpose of keeping pelf secured. Through taxing the peasantry and other low citizens into a state of perpetual poverty and "inspecting" all the goods entering, leaving or in transient, these early capitalists amassed tremendous wealth. Much of what they stole were delivered in kind and distributed according to the dictates of pirate's law. However, they accumulated substantial sums of coins and precious metals. It was these valuable deposits that were stored in a guarded tower.

Of that earlier period, two highly disgraces remain: a large, round tower that once bulged with the wealth produced by those who were denied any share, and the structure's name, *Kasseturm*. In the DDR, the tower no longer served as a repository for stolen money and goods; it became a student-operated club. Jürgen and Nadine visited the Kasseturm with friends when the DDR was a sovereign state.

Heike never entered the Kasseturm. She assumed that was where Günther would take her. Once inside, they'd have a beer or lemonade and munch on bar snacks while he shared whatever he intended to share. That was her concept of *dinner*. She feared Lilo and her impromptu laden might still be in place. If so, entering the Kasseturm without being observed was problematical.

To Heike's relief, the few *merchants* still hawking wares were terminating their trading day. That space, formerly, occupied by Lilo and her gaudy wares stood vacant. Heike's consternation, however, mounted as Günther led her past the Kasseturm and across Goetheplatz. They paused at the street, where Blossom died, waiting for a chance to cross. When they stepped off the curb, Heike made certain the bus to her right remained motionless.

A grand hotel dominates the Western boundary of Goetheplatz. It was built to accommodate Russian dignitaries and merchants flocking into the city after a czar's daughter married into the local gentry. Because members of the royal family visited frequently, the hotel was palatial.

The DDR, of course, had no use for decedent lodgings and converted it into an inn better suited to proletarian tastes. Regardless, it maintained a reputation worthy of the *up-scale* proletariat. Wedding receptions and anniversary celebrations were frequently booked. It was in the capacious ballroom that an inebriated party official made a pledge to Werner Ecke's daughter.

It is customary for the man, the sword bearer, to enter public places before a lady. When Günther turned into the hotel, he had neither a sword nor regard for bygone customs. He held the door for Heike. She thought it a jest and remained rooted.

There followed an awkward silence. With a movement of his head and an imploring expression, Günther urged Heike through the door.

She remained reticent, however. If this was a joke, she had verbal reserves at the ready.

Save for the "Last Meal" in Leipzig, she'd never entered a restaurant. Her knowledge of such establishments was gleaned from literature and film. Belatedly, she realized her attire, while suitable for the Kasseturm, was hardly appropriate for a place where employees wore uniforms.

"Look how I'm dressed," she hissed urgently.

She hadn't bothered to change since returning from the Zimmermann kitchen. First, there was (she supposed) no need. Second, there was but a single dress in the house, once worn by Anne Ecke, a student. Though modified since and shared by Heike and Nadine for highly infrequent occasions, the garment would resemble a flour sack in posh surroundings.

"You look as respectable as a young proletarian should look."

Heike detected no trace of mockery. On the contrary, his comment made her proud. No matter the fate of the DDR, Heike was an Ossi; people don't "put on airs." She took a deep breath, stood erect, and passed through the door as if she were the late Czarina.

Her first sensation was the music. It was Vivaldi's seasons, and the pair arrived midway through spring. The volume was tastefully low, allowing for amiable conversation. It was as soft and comforting as a shawl over one's shoulders.

The place reeked of Wessis. Heike identified them by their posh clothes. They wore well-tailored suits and dresses. One woman filled an elaborate gown; she and her well-togged companion, apparently, had theatre tickets.

The waiter greeted the newly arrived. He was not bothered by their pauper's appearance, but every Wessi sent haughty looks their way. Heike, however, was no longer self-conscious. She was a proud Ossi and not swept up in the emptiness of superficiality. She loved her country, respected its people, remained loyal to her Genossin, and would not allow anyone to make her feel inferior.

They gawkers watched the young man pull back a chair for his disheveled companion. They watched as she accepted his gesture with an expression of gratitude. They noted how she sat ramrod straight, ignoring the multitude as her escort took his place across from her. They observed the waiter presenting the couple with menus. The tacit consensus of the

Wessie patrons was that the unsightly interlopers should be ingloriously hurried out through a rear exit.

Heike Jacobs had never studied a menu before; she examined the document with unabashed awe. The price list was above DDR norms, but not excessive. She mentally took inventory of the cash in her pocket. As Günther invited her, she expected him to pay, but she was concerned about his resources.

They enjoyed a lively conversation over their options. Heike first experience with *Vorspeise* required Günther to explain. She concluded that appetizers, and the prices accompanying them, justified a light meal.

When a dark-uniformed waiter returned, Heike opted for a house-specialty, stroganoff. Günther, apparently taken aback by Heike's Spartan taste, ordered the same but ordered a cabbage salad as well.

"And to drink?"

"Two white wines to begin," Günther announced.

"We have a nice Mosel Riesling," the balding burger suggested.

"Perfect."

"I don't usually drink wine," Heike informed with a voice not intended to travel beyond their table.

"Live a little," he replied, equally reserved.

The tartness of the grape melded with the music of Vivaldi's summer. Heike set her glass down and enjoyed the outrage on her tongue.

"Good?" he asked.

"*Sehr*," she nodded.

"What have you been doing?"

Heike began with the dark days of the Hungarian "vacations" and narrated her experiences through Leipzig and beyond. She introduced Rosa's Children. She narrated the adventures of the comet, and the trials of life in a changing world. She carefully avoided heartbreak, but Günther's attentive expression told her she didn't often succeed.

Her stomach was filled with only half her meal consumed. Heike leaned back and tried to keep her history concise and objective. Günther proved a good listener. He ate leisurely and tacitly assured Heike that his attention was hers.

"More wine?" he asked upon the waiter return.

"*Gern*," she replied.

Günther dispatched the request, keeping the interruption brief. Heike took up the thread of her narrative and continued. She was thankful Günther didn't pepper her with questions. He, apparently, decided to listen to the entire tale before speaking. This made Heike comfortable, and her saga easier to relate.

Vivaldi retired in favor of another. Heike wasn't well versed in music and failed to identify more than a half dozen works, but she was certain Schubert and Brahms contributed. Heike's odyssey concluded with the morning trip to the market. The remains of the meal were cleared away. They sat sipping their second glass of wine.

"Coffee?"

"*Gern.*"

Günther called the waiter. There followed several uncomfortable moments as he finished the last of his wine. He set down his glass with an air of grim resolution.

"Who is Helena?" he asked.

She was amazed and speechless. Unable to reply immediately, inquisitive eyes studied her.

"A literary allusion, perhaps?" he prompted.

Still baffled, Heike had some context.

"Um – the only Helena I know is an Athenian lady in love with a man who does not return it. Despite all obstacles, her love does not fade."

There was a detectable twinkle in his eye.

"Ah! Shakespeare, perhaps?"

"Ja. *Midsummer Night.*"

He nodded.

"I'm not familiar with it. The only Helena I know is from *All's Well.*"

"I'm not familiar with it," she made a mental note to study it. "Why ask?"

His visual response was curious indeed. He was anxious to leave the subject.

"I remember the first time I ever saw you," he diverted, innocuously. "Jürgen and I were playing Fußball in the street; you and Nadine came bouncing out of the house to join in. You had the biggest smile I ever saw. You don't smile much, I notice."

"There's not much to smile about," she reminded.

"Perhaps not."

They remained silent until the coffee came. Günther thanked the waiter and reached for the creamer while Heike took her first grateful sip of the undiluted brew. Günther stirred his coffee pensively. He ceased stirring and tapped the spoon against the lip of his cup. He gingerly placed the spoon in the saucer but made no move to drink. Instead, he rubbed his hands nervously and made a steeple.

"I want to explain a few things. Things I've wanted to say for months. I've rehearsed a little speech. I'm nervous, so I'd appreciate if you don't interrupt. Can you do that?"

She took a swallow and placed the cup back on its saucer. No sound escaped their table that could be heard over the music and the chatter of the thinning crowd.

"I will try."

He rubbed his hands before removing them from the table. He rubbed them on his thighs and attempted to rest them flat on the table. They weren't comfortable there. Eventually, he pushed his cup and saucer aside and folded his arms on white linen.

"There hasn't been a day I haven't thought of you," he began softly. "You were so young. I was old enough to know better. I thought I'd get over it. This will pass. It didn't. You wrote cards and that nice letter. I didn't answer because – it's selfish to interfere in your life.

"This town is full of Knaben. I knew they'd be swarming around, and your fancy might fall on one of them – someone right here, able to help you through hard times. I didn't write. *Feigling*! I'm a Feigling! If I wrote and told you what I felt – well, someday, someone would win you over and – I thought, if I kept out of the way, things would work out, and one of us could be happy.

"When I left the army, I wanted to go and beat on your door, but I was afraid that – you found – someone. So, I followed you around. If you had a friend, I would see you together, and I'd clear out."

During his monologue, he lifted his arms and wove his fingers nervously before folding them in his lap. He looked helpless. Heike was stunned. *She* was the coward. She studied the steam curling out of her cup and tapped the saucer with her forefinger.

"Günther, please – please don't tell me you left Liselotte for me."

His expression confirmed he'd predicted the accusation. It multiplied his nervousness.

"Lilo's attractive and very strong, but only physically. She's a clinger, Heike. When we were together, she had my hand or my arm or was leaning up against me like a puppy. It was pleasant, don't mistake me, but – she always deferred to me.

"It was too much. We did only what I wanted and went where I wanted and listened to the music I wanted. I realized I was her protector. She didn't trust herself to decide things for us. Well, I don't have answers, and I don't know what is right – particularly now. My judgment was certain to fail at the worst possible moment; Lilo would realize I wasn't what she thought. Worse, she'd think I betrayed her. That's a huge responsibility for a coward. When, not if, I failed her, she'd either resent me forever or grow to hate me. I didn't want –"

He ceased. His thoughts were painful.

"She might have grown out of that at sport camp," Heike suggested when the silence became uncomfortable.

"I hope she has. As much as I admire her, I don't want to live with her."

He held out his hands, palms up, then, he folded them back on top of the table. She sat still and watched her coffee cool. She committed to memory the centerpiece and the design of the cup and saucer. She cleared her throat and opened her mouth to speak but hung fire. After a bout of self-derision, she cleared her throat again.

"Am I an utter fool? Are you telling me that you love me?"

He drew in a deep breath and let it out as if greatly relieved.

"I think I could be in love with you," he admitted. "I don't know you well enough to say."

Feigling! She had deep feelings for Günther. It was difficult to handle at times. To learn, however, that his feelings mirrored her own – that was a great weight to carry. She wasn't mature enough or responsible enough.

"So, you don't consider me a clinger," she challenged, meeting his eyes.

"You have values and principles, Heike. You stand up for them and yourself. You're a fighter. I admire that. More important, you have concern for others. I see it in your eyes right now."

"Günther – I'm afraid I'm not the person you think."

"Perhaps, you aren't," he said quickly. "I can handle disappointment. You can too. The fact is – I need you, Heike. If you need me, we can rely on each other. Together, we can make up for each other's failings."

"We two against the world, huh?" she snorted.

"Please don't be trite, Heike. You lack a sense of humor."

Her eyes flashed. He showed his palms.

"I won't lie, Heike. I'm not going to try and win you over by making you think you're a wit when you aren't. In return, I know you won't lie to me about my faults. Many people can't deal with honesty; I think we can."

"Then, I shall be honest, now." she announced, leaning across the table. "Lilo is twice the woman I am, and she's seen more of life than I have."

Günther inched forward.

"But Lilo doesn't *need* me," he explained. "She doesn't need anyone for precisely the reasons you've stated. Lilo wants someone to lean on. She can stand on her own against anything, but she'd rather depend on someone else. I don't want to be leaned on. Two mutually supportive people is my ideal."

"What makes you think I'm a person who needs someone?"

They maintained their pose until people began casting curious glances. Günther, satisfied that her question required no answer, sat back. For the first time since the dinner dishes were cleared, he looked comfortable. Heike followed his example.

"You frighten me," she said. "You know things about me I'd never admit."

He had his say and didn't feel obliged to stoop to platitudes.

Sitting on Nadine's bed in a huge sweatshirt Jürgen abandoned, Heike narrated the night's events. Nadine, in a flannel shirt and sports shorts, sat Indian style atop her pillow. They spoke in hushed spurts. Nadine was uncertain if Heike shivered from emotional overload or the room's evening chill.

She dug at her blanket until there was enough to cover Heike's bare legs. The black picture of Günther Nadine kept locked in her heart began to mutate. Though he was not yet fully rehabilitated, Günther was allowed to shed the black SS uniform her imagination assigned him.

"Did he kiss you?" she asked.

"I wanted him to," Heike confessed, "but I sent a postcard, *Verdammt noch Mal!* I wrote a poem on it and –"

Nadine blushed. She well remembered the words. Heike wished to return Günther's kiss. Günther hadn't risked being dismissed upon receipt – or so Nadine believed.

"Will you see him?"

Heike shrugged.

"He's living at home. His parents still have jobs, but it isn't proper for me to go round."

"You're having doubts," Nadine concluded.

Heike nodded.

"I've been in love with Günther for years. I thought I was. Maybe, like Romeo, I was in love with the idea of being in love. After tonight – I'm scared."

"Günther tells you that he loves you, and you're scared?"

"I don't deserve to be happy."

Nadine flared.

"Get off my bed! Go! Go!"

Nadine kicked at her. Heike obeyed with alacrity though she was unaware of why.

"Scheiße! That's Scheiße! Scheiße, Scheiße, Scheiße! Get away! I thought you were the brains of this family. You're a silly fool and you make me sick. Get away!"

Heike switched off the light and retreated to her refuge on the floor. Her heart was heavy over Nadine's outburst, but she could not deny the pattern of her life: brief moments of pride and elation followed by profound disappointment and sorrow.

As for Nadine, she was bitter to the core. Heike had brains and pleasing looks. It was difficult to remain in Heike's shadow. That very morning, studying her deformed face in the mirror, she realized if her beloved mother were awarded a grandchild, it would be Jürgen's.

Nadine was deformed before Leipzig – deficient in attractiveness and devoid of personality. After Leipzig, no man attended her, even briefly. There sat Heike, her marginal beauty magnified a hundred times by her honesty, compassion, and loyalty. A handsome, worthy man of potential confesses his love, and Heike cannot accept it; she thinks she must earn happiness.

Nadine's considerable anger was directed at Heike's, but the tears she shed were for herself.

* * *

The black, dismal cloud over Heike's head gathered at the thought of attending to Lilo. It was made blacker and more ominous by the reappearance of Günther. She dared not omit mentioning him. Lilo, eventually, would find out and kill her.

Alternatively, relating the dinner conversation, would be, for Lilo, as traumatic as having the teeth ripped out of her head. The ultimate choice, however, was childishly simple; Lilo and Rosa's Children or stay clear and the Children die.

Heike had an excellent window of opportunity to succumb to doubts. She was one person who had, virtually, no chance of succeeding. Rosa Luxemburg, Ernst Thälmann and Werner Ecke forged the path and were murdered. Heike Jacobs might be following a course towards the same end. She discovered that she was not a person of courage, perhaps, she should hide and forsake an impossible dream. There were reasons why she could not surrender. If she shriveled up, she could never look upon Günther or Jürgen or Nadine ever again.

She left Herr Zimmermann fortified with his daily hot meal, potato pancakes and boiled vegetables, before catching the first bus back into town. The hike to Lilo's apartment building was lengthy, but she conquered the doubts gnawing at her resolve.

The apartment building was near the school Heike once attended – when her country existed. By DDR standards, the apartment building was a triumph of technical and aesthetic skill. Thirty years on, however, it acquired a drab and shabby appearance of most other residential buildings. It suffered greatly from want of paint. The balconies facing the street served as storage areas; they made the structure resemble a rummage sale.

The one notable exception was a third-floor balcony; it was immaculate. Of the items her parents kept there, Lilo sold what she could and tossed the remainder. In place of junk, Lilo displayed hand-made window boxes firmly fixed to the railing. The foliage taking root created a riot of color to capture the eye of the most jaded passerby.

Heike found a hand-printed KRUGER behind a yellowed plastic protector. She pressed the adjacent button and, immediately, the latch buzzed. She trudged up polished slate steps. There was no hurry, one should never be anxious to face unpleasantness. All too soon, she found an Amazon framed in a doorway. Lilo's blond hair spilled over her shoulders and her eyes burned Heike's skin; her jaw and tight-lipped expression made clear that Lilo's attitude toward her invited guest had not altered.

She wore a sleeveless white top, slightly too small. Her long legs wore Wessi cast-off jeans too large for her waist. A gaudy length of chord threading the belt loops was knotted on the right and the excess dangled like a sash. Her feet were bare.

Instinctively, Heike slipped off her shoes and left them on the landing. She entered the apartment in her socks and hoped they'd not stink as they sometimes did after a long day. She was ushered into a spacious living area, sparsely furnished. There was a small television in a corner nearest the frosted-glass door opening onto the balcony. Heike noticed the plug lay on the spotless wooden floor.

A sofa abutted an interior wall behind a small, round coffee table resting on a colorful throw rug. There was a small wooden chair near the door next to the telephone stand. Hanging from the center of the ceiling, dangled a light surrounded by a huge paper balloon so popular in the DDR.

That was all.

Lilo gestured to the sofa and Heike sat.

"I don't have coffee," Lilo announced. "I can make some tea."

"I'm fine, Lilo. I don't need anything."

Lilo picked up the wooden chair and placed it across from the coffee table to provide a buffer between them.

"I was re-reading something last night," she reported as she fished through the school bag, unused for months.

Lilo stood next to the chair.

Heike found her recently acquired copy of Werner Ecke's tract and set it on the table for inspection. It was only eighteen pages, but the bold red lettering on the cover reflected its contents. She turned it around so Lilo could read from altitude without cocking her head.

"You know it?"

Lilo nodded.

"I read it the first time when I was twelve or thirteen," she replied. "It's magnificent."

Heike averted her eyes.

"Are Nadine and I the last two people on earth to read this?"

"I think there's a young girl in Australia who hasn't read it."

The words were humorous. When Heike looked up, however, hostile eyes bored down.

"What I want to say is here," Heike gestured toward the pamphlet.

"Herr Ecke was a great writer," Lilo declared. "It will be difficult to condense him to one page."

Heike nodded. She refused to look into those eyes again. She stared at the yellowed document.

"I was reading last night as well," Lilo continued, sitting on the edge of the chair.

"*These are the times that try men's souls. The summer soldier and the sunshine patriot will, in this crisis, shrink from the service of his country; but he who stands now, deserves the love and thanks of all.*"

A chill raced up Heike's spine; her flesh turned prickly.

"Brilliant! Who is it?"

"Thomas Paine."

Heike shook her head.

"British," Lilo reported. "He helped stir up the French Revolution. I'd like to play around with the quote."

"It will get people's attention," Heike agreed.

During an awkward pause that followed, she reflected upon it some more.

"Mist! That won't get people's attention," she announced, "It will grab them by the throat!"

"Well, I can't use someone else's words. That's not fair, but I can copy the sentiment."

"Do it, Lilo."

"So, we begin with a Paine-like hook and turn to Ecke. Anything in particular?"

"There's so much. Use your judgment."

Lilo's eyes narrowed.

"You trust me that far?"

Heike met her antagonist's probing eyes.

"Yes, Lilo, I do."

The flashing eyes mellowed.

"Give me a couple days. You'd be surprised how much thinking and composing a person does while selling junk to the ignorant and the gullible. I'll type something out and bring it to you for review."

"Two days, then?"

Lilo nodded. She slapped her hands on her thighs and stood up, obviously anxious to be rid of her not-so-welcome guest. Heike wanted to leap to her feet and run for the door, but she cleared her throat and polished a small portion of the floor with a foot.

"I saw Günther."

She couldn't look at her hostess, but she sensed Lilo's momentary trembling.

"When?"

"Yesterday. He took me to Russischer Hof."

"Did he?"

Heike didn't like the tone of that rhetorical question. It flowed very mellow and very slowly. Behind it was malevolence. She tensed, expecting Lilo to assault her.

"For dinner!" Heike added quickly.

Would Lilo assume they went upstairs and spent the night?

Unexpectedly, Heike found herself looking at Lilo's naked heels. She lifted her head quickly to view of a back shrouded in white. It was a large back with broad shoulders. Cascading hair prevented a view of Lilo's face.

"How did that – come about?" Lilo asked in a low, calm voice.

"He saw me shopping. He – he wanted to talk, and – last night he – we went into town – and – we – ate."

Any moment, Heike thought, she'll pounce like a tiger. Her stuttering and stammering and amateurish syntax would not mollify Liselotte one iota.

"*We just ate!*"

A block of stone wouldn't believe that.

The oversized statue remained motionless. Heike toyed with the notion of sneaking past before Lilo came out of her trance, but she was too frightened. Finally, Lilo moved. One hand went to her face, and, despite the masking hair, Heike realized she was wiping her eyes. Any movement on the visitor's part would be an inexcusable invasion of privacy.

Heike lowered her eyes and waited. Lilo cleared her throat.

"Two days," Lilo announced. "I'll come by your house after closing up."

Heike rose tentatively. Lilo tuned about but did not look directly at her. She gestured toward the door, and Heike did not hesitate. The Amazon opened the portal; Heike squeezed quickly past.

"Danke, Lilo," she whispered.

"*Bis spater.*"

Heike picked up her shoes and hurried down the steps before putting them on. She expected the door to slam. It did not. Heike heard the thud of Lilo's back bracing against the closed door. The girl cleared the landing and froze.

She looked up toward the apartment door. Her vision obstructed by wood and plaster, she saw – as clearly as she'd ever seen anything – a blond, bare-footed Amazon. She heard as the woman slid slowly down to a sitting position. Moments before, Heike expected to hear her bones cracking. Unexpectedly, and against her will, she felt her heart breaking.

* * *

Oregon Coast

June 1990

There was a talk that Kathy would be the featured singer at graduation that year. As rehearsal time grew short and Mr. Davidson hadn't approached her, she breathed a sigh of relief. She didn't want to stay after school; she wanted to spend every minute possible with Gary.

Together, the young couple haunted the water-front establishments, snacked on unhealthy food, drank coffee, and sharpened skills with arcade games. When they reached the limits of the tourist part of town, they crossed the highway to walk along the sea wall. They talked of many things, both serious and inane and exchanged reassuring kisses along the way.

They treasured their time together. Gary feared Kathy would not return; Kathy refused to promise she would. In Germany, anything might happen. She wanted to finish school with Gary, but there was no way to predict the future.

After lengthy outings in fair evening weather and foul, the couple gravitated to the tiny cottage Athena and Gary called home. Once inside, they'd sit at the table and work a puzzle, play monopoly, or concoct food and drink experiments for evaluation by the hapless Athena. Ultimately, Kathy was obligated to retreat and provide Ute with her promised hour of peace.

Whenever Athena and Kathy bellowed through the Brenda Lee song book, Gary endured. Being with Kathy trumped the hideous cacophony. Kathy could carry a tune and had a beautiful voice. Athena, at her best, could hit one note in a dozen and her voice had all the qualities of a cow in a slaughterhouse.

It wasn't a pleasing blend, but Gary recognized his mother's bellowing was a smoke screen. Athena Swofford would miss Kathy as much as he. Anything which diverted her concern over the upcoming separation was welcome.

As May waned, Mr. Kurihara invited Kathy to sing at a business party he arranged. If she could ready three numbers that "old fogies" might enjoy, she'd earn fifty dollars. The Fosters needed the money. Though Dieter supplied the tickets and paid for three nights in a Berlin hotel, Ute, Kathy, and Isaac required money for food and incidentals. Kathy agreed to perform and adjourned to the Kurihara home where Shelly accompanied her on piano.

Kathy accepted the fact that Shelly could do anything. Piano was one of Shelly's many talents. Alas, the girl was limited in her prowess; so, too, were Kathy's selections.

Kathy applied a bear hug.

"What was that for?" Shelly demanded.

"I'm happy to learn you're human!"

Shelly was gracious, but later complained to her brother.

"What the hell was she talking about?"

Shelly's words went from Henry's mouth to Molly's ears.

The pedestrian program went ahead. There was a notable addendum which made it an adventure. Shelly and Henry secretly coached Kathy in singing the Japanese national anthem, acapella. Kathy had serious reservations.

The Japanese words were easy to replicate once Henry wrote them phonetically. Still, Kathy was ignorant of the language and feared Shelly, the practical-jokester and mischief-maker, might be setting her up.

"I'm a lumber jack, and I'm okay. That's what I'm singing, right?"

Shelly and Henry denied this stringently. When Molly provided her assurance the text was genuine, Kathy's fears receded. True, Molly's knowledge of Japanese was rudimentary, but Henry would never lie to her.

Double play: Kurihara to Fleming to Foster.

Kathy concluded her program with the Japanese anthem and drew raves from the small audience. Furthermore, there was in attendance a prominent local businessman. After the adulation died down, he hired Kathy on the spot for a local market promotion. There were two local groups paid to perform on a Saturday afternoon.

"You sing three or four numbers," he explained. "Ninety minutes later, you sing them again."

Kathy didn't like the short notice.

"It pays two hundred and fifty dollars."

"I'll do it!"

The money-grubbing teen found herself in the company of a husband-and-wife duo and a bevy of professional equipment. They were one of the featured acts; he on electric guitar while she sang and pounded a keyboard or plucked a bass guitar. The woman plied the musical stage in college. She helped Kathy with her musical selection and singing style.

For three hours over three consecutive nights, Kathy learned not only the music and songs, but how to add a visual aspect to her talent. On the final night of practice, the trio sang for a half-dozen *investors*. An audience of seven people didn't count as a performance. Devoid of nervousness or inhibitions, Kathy clutched the microphone and sang as she'd been coached.

"Man! She can belt out a tune, can't she?"

No one argued with the enthusiastic auditor.

"I want to work with you again," Kathy's coach insisted.

Her guitar-playing husband agreed.

It was a brisk, Saturday afternoon. By the time Kathy arrived at the shopping complex, the stage was set up and amplifiers strategically placed. There was an audio board and a local technician to operate it; he wanted sound checks. The performers obliged by playing their amplified instruments and singing into the microphones for a few seconds.

"Okay, deary," the sound man motioned to Kathy. "Your turn."

She'd never done a sound check. Her mentor called her to the stage and handed her the microphone.

"What'll I do?"

"Sing a few bars."

"Which song?"

The guitar player strummed familiar chords, and, without further thought, Kathy sang. It didn't take long.

"Save it for the show!" the sound man shouted.

The waiting began. She wore clothes obtained by "ill-gotten" means, the generosity of her theatre friends. She, fanatically, avoided food, drink, or dirt in any form. As others caroused and enjoyed cheerful intercourse, she remained aloof and motionless.

She was tempted to sit on one of several benches only to imagine herself stepping onto the stage with a huge smudge on her butt. Her special clothes were for her father and sister in Germany, not for a shopping mall audience. As always, Molly was her driver. Without her, the twelve-mile drive was as impossible as a trip to the moon. Molly, however, mysteriously disappeared during sound checks, leaving Kathy to suffer alone.

Ed Barker proved a pain. It was bad enough to pay someone to crew the *Mary R.* "for the whole damn summer," now, he must reach into his pocket and hire someone to first mate the *Mary R.* on Kathy's last Stateside weekend! Kathy felt not a drop of sympathy. She was presented a check in exchange for her voice, and the check represented folding money. She longed for a face full of sea spray, but she'd need more money in Germany than the coins Scrooge McBarker allowed her.

Kathy, hired as an afterthought, warmed up the stage for the *professional* entertainers. The husband-and-wife team of Sam an' Ella provided accompaniment for Kathy's *set,* after which they'd do their program, followed by a popular band from Eugene. Though Kathy wondered how any band based in Eugene could qualify as *popular,* she had the highest regard for Sam an' Ella, whose real names were Dennis and Claire.

They were eight years in the business and good enough to quit their previous jobs and earn a living playing up and down the coast. Since their needs were simple, they made a fair living. Moreover, they mentored Kathy as if working for her rather than merely lending a hand.

Kathy was only slightly nervous. The crowd was transient. People can listen while tending their shopping; no one came to hear Kathy or any of the others. Perhaps, the "popular" Eugene band might feel slighted if people didn't stand at attention during their performance, but the whole project was designed to encourage people to spend money, not feed egos.

As show time approached, however, Kathy needed to clear her bladder. This proved a career onto itself. She became more nervous when she took extreme measures to ensure her clothes wouldn't suffer from any of a dozen possible mishaps. She wished she'd worn jeans and a sweatshirt.

She debated about another last-minute trip to the powder room when Molly hove into view. She wasn't alone. The entire crew – Gary, Henry, Jayme, Shelly, Isaac, and Ute. Even Athena, jogging to catch up, was there. How did they manage to get off work? She regretted Aaron's absence mightily.

"You aren't working?" Kathy asked Athena.

"I'm very sick. Honey, I can't be passin' germs."

Kathy realized the significance of Athena's sacrifice. Either Athena or Gary must do without something to make up for a missing day of pay and tips. There was little time for reflection and no time for words.

Kathy didn't stand a chance. Molly must brush her hair; Shelly must apply Kathy's gloss before saying hello. Athena and Ute were amused. Kathy, however, became mortified upon noticing a gaggle of classmates. Someone spread the word about her performance.

Mr. Davidson and his wife, Ed Geist and, presumably, his wife or girlfriend were there. Steve and Debbie loitered nearby. None were detected by the young singer until Molly and Shelly embarrassed her by tending her like a helpless child. Suddenly, Kathy longed for seclusion.

Claire was on stage powering up her keyboard when she caught Kathy's pleading eyes and smiled. Then, she saw Dennis looping the guitar strap around his neck.

"I gotta go," Kathy protested.

"Shush! I'm almost done," Shelly retorted.

Molly said nothing, but a hairbrush worked furiously to yank every hair out of Kathy's scalp. It was beyond humiliation. Kathy Foster was prepared to exchange every penny of her two hundred and fifty dollars if she could get Molly and Shelly on the *Mary R.* and push them into the foamy water.

She was supposed to be on stage; Sam an' Ella stalled for longer than could be excused. Dennis began picking out an impromptu tune on the electric guitar while Shelly and Molly continued to fuss.

"Ladies and gentlemen," Claire said into her microphone, "we are proud to share the stage with a young lady who leaves next week for Germany. She will appear in Berlin, but she's with us now, and we're lucky to have her. Please, put 'em together for Miss Brenda Lela."

There were enough curiosity gawkers caught up in the moment to applaud, even though they had no idea for whom.

"I gotta go!"

Shelly held up a tissue.

"Dab, dab, dab," she said.

Finally, Kathy was free. She rushed to the stage but took the steps very carefully. Sam an' Ella finished playing the introduction. When Kathy didn't begin on cue, they rolled it over and started again as if it was a part of the show. Kathy took the microphone from the stand. She took a moment and turned to Claire at the keyboard.

"Brenda Lela?"

Claire's mic was open, so she didn't reply audibly. She made a facial gesture and then smiled. Kathy wanted to explain that she wouldn't be performing in Berlin, but it was too late. Fortunately, she realized nobody gave a rat's butt.

The first act over, Kathy descended to an unexpected legion of congratulations and complements. The Rademachers made their presence known as a part of the celebratory conga line. Students Kathy knew only by sight voiced their approval and offered best wishes. It was a giddy experience tempered by Kathy's comical actions to keep her "costume" away from dirt and sweat. She longed to take Isaac into her loving arms but dared not.

Eventually, Kathy had room to breathe. Out of courtesy, she attended her newest friends, filling the air with music for which Kathy was not enthusiastic. It was a relief when Sam an' Ella began their final number, the only one Kathy enjoyed. Dennis, however, launched into an impromptu guitar solo.

Judging by Claire's demeanor, it, likely, was not impromptu.

"We're closing our portion of the show with an old standard," Claire announced.

"It's a great Cole Porter song, and we know we need help to do it justice. If Brenda, would you help us? Brenda, please!"

"Damn!" Kathy let slip, next to Mrs. Rademacher.

To foil an escape attempt, Molly and Jayme pushed her gently forward. Now, she was very scared! It was one thing to sing something she'd rehearsed, but...

"I can't do this," she hissed at Claire.

"Yes, you can," she replied, microphone behind her back.

"You know the words, just come in when I tell you."

Kathy was too scared to agree. She stood like a simpleton and faced Claire.

"This is a head arrangement, right Sam?"

Dennis continued to play his vamp, but his head bobbed enthusiastically.

"We only kinda know what we're doing here," Claire continued, "I've wanted to sing with Brenda since I first heard her, so, here goes."

So, the guitar came around again.

"Pick up the mic," Clair instructed, lowering her own. "Just do what I tell ya."

Kathy's trembling fingers fumbled to coax the microphone from its cradle. Claire was nearly through the first verse before she succeeded.

"You!" Claire squeaked.

Kathy sang the second verse, tentatively at first, but she quickly gained confidence. Her eyes were riveted on Claire who uttered encouragement and smiled as her head kept time with the music. When Claire raised the microphone, Kathy relaxed and let her take over.

Claire was singing the first verse once more. Kathy panicked. However, she kept up with the lyrics until Claire nodded for her to take over and allowed Kathy to finish. Then, Claire started the second verse and let Kathy finish that. When they got to the chorus, Claire invited her to join in and they blasted out a nice little duet for the finale.

The organizers may not have been pleased when shoppers slowed their milling about and gathered in the proximity of the stage. There was a thunderous applause when Sam an' Ella Plus One finished. Claire beamed and hugged Kathy. Forgetting her concerns for her clothes, Kathy returned that hug with warmth and relief.

"That was fun," Kathy decided.

"It was great!" responded a giddy Claire.

Between sets, and while the popular band from Eugene played on, Rev. Rademacher was busy with his camera. He wanted a record of Kathy. He had her pose with Ute and Isaac, with Athena and Gary and, finally, with those she would forever call her friends. There was a nice, posed shot of Kathy and the "girls", Molly, Jayme and Shelly.

Then each couple: Kathy and Gary, Molly and Henry and, for the first time outside of school, Jayme and Cody, the "tall, dark, dream" who'd driven young Jayme to the brink of insensibility.

"I thought your folks wouldn't let you date until you're sixteen," Kathy whispered when she had any chance.

"This isn't a date," Jayme whispered back. "I'm with sis. My folks – ah, chaperones – are prowling around here somewhere."

When Kathy remounted the stage, her *groupies* made up the bulk of the audience. People, attracted by her singing, stopped to watch as well as listen. Kathy, unexpectedly, found herself the object of considerable (male) attention. Reticent to concede her talent, she considered the attention was due to the crew who selected her clothes, makeup, and hair style. Nevertheless, she was flattered by the adulation, though she considered it unwarranted.

She offered to help Claire and Dennis strike their set, but the duo made setting up and retreating an art. Kathy bowed, Kurihara style, and made the short journey from "star" to "audience." She hardly reached the steps when she felt a pull in the crook of her elbow.

It was Claire.

"Who is your voice coach?"

"Mr. Davidson. He teaches choir at my school."

"Well, ask him if he knows of anyone who can coach you," she advised, "You have a scholarship voice if you get proper training."

Kathy was too dumbfounded to respond. She focused her attention on getting down the steps without mishap. She was greeted by confusion, praise, and congratulations. There were three younger people, middle school, perhaps, who asked for her autograph.

"I'm nobody," she reminded the enthusiastic trio.

"Not for long," one of them insisted.

She signed the scraps of paper they provided with a pen they insisted she keep. Not until several hours later did she realize she'd signed the name Ute gave her despite being twice introduced as Brenda Lela. The children didn't protest. Upon reflection, Kathy realized her birth name was waiting in Berlin.

What made event notable, however, wasn't the money she earned, substantial though it was. Rather, it was Rev. Rademacher's presentation of the photos he took, thanks to a nearby one-hour film developer.

It was an appreciated gift. In addition to a series of photographs of the people she held most dear, there were several snaps of her performing. Though she knew not who she'd encounter in Germany, she'd have visual evidence of those she left behind.

All save one.

Ute Foster could read Kathy's expressions as clearly as a sleuth reads footprints. In the back seat with Isaac and Kathy, Ute studied the girl's face while flipping through the photographs for the fourth or fifth time.

"We'll get a picture of Aaron before we leave," she promised.

Kathy was taken by surprise. This was but one example of Ute's clairvoyance.

"Sometimes," she announced, "you scare me."

Weimar

"Can I cook for Herr Zimmermann this afternoon?"

Heike studied her sister as she took the basket containing the Zimmermann purchases. She'd been nervous the previous evening and was visibly nervous still.

"If you want," she replied. placidly.

Nadine didn't *want*. She did, however, realize that Heike and Lilo would prefer being alone. If Nadine tended to Herr Zimmermann and tarried on her way home, Heike and Lilo could retire upstairs for privacy. Moreover, if they were only a spark shy of an explosion, Nadine preferred being absent.

"I've made the beds and cleared upstairs," she announced. "The wash water is heating."

"Okay," Heike replied with uncharacteristic stoicism. "I'll manage. Treat yourself to a little time off."

"I can do the stairs and the bathroom," Nadine volunteered.

"I can manage, Nadine. Can you build a meal with that?"

Nadine need only to see potatoes and an onion. No matter what else Heike bought, Nadine could produce a banquet with potatoes and an onion. She smiled and a nodded.

"Off you go."

"Are you sure?"

"You've been working like a slave over the comet. Take the rest of the day off."

Nadine debated no further.

When Lilo knocked, Rolf was seated by Anne on the couch. He pretended to read the paper. He announced they would delay Abendsbrot until Nadine returned, but he was impatient. Heike quieted him with a cup of tea and some bread with cucumber slices, but he'd soon want wurst and cheese.

"Herr Jacobs," Lilo nodded.

"Lilo," he replied.

"Frau Jacobs, very nice to see you again."

Anne smiled and nodded almost imperceptivity. Heike led Lilo up the stairs and the bright light of the bedroom. Lilo had never entered the inner sanctum and marveled at the huge bed.

"This is what I have so far," Lilo announced, pulling a wadded parchment from her trouser pocket. "I penciled in corrections and improvements today when I wasn't busy."

Heike reached, but Lilo pulled it away.

"I put Rosa's Children at the bottom," she warned. "I want to lead people into the concept before making noises about the organization."

"Probably, a good idea," Heike conceded.

"Also, I thought we need an emblem or symbol. Not the flag or the FDJ sun. They might turn people off. Something, new or, something not associated with the SED. I have a friend in Apolda who does pencil sketches. He promised samples by tomorrow, so we can look at those."

"Good idea," Heike nodded.

Only then did Lilo part with her labor. Heike unfolded the manuscript. It came in three sheets. Most of the typed material was lined through. What remained was heavily edited in dark pencil.

Heike sat Indian style on the floor. Lilo, for lack of anything better, leaned on Nadine's bed with her elbow and crossed one foot over the other while watching Heike's struggle through her editing marks. Heike read each page carefully.

She compared the typing with the edits in case something was salvageable. She stacked the papers in order and read through again. Lilo's fidgeting went unnoticed.

"So?"

Heike motioned for quiet and continued shuffling through the pages. Finally, she looked up with a baffled expression.

"Und?"

"This is perfect."

The Amazon snatched the pages.

"Scheiße!" she barked. "This is serious, Heike. If you can't contribute, piss off!"

Heike got to her feet and Lilo braced. If the little pest dared to lay a finger on her, she'd find herself on the floor again – quickly!

"Lilo, I mean it. That is exactly what I want. The Thomas Paine thing, which you expressed in a modern, exact context, then Werner Ecke's spiritual socialism and Rosa's democratic ideals and back to Ecke's vision and – and your conclusion leading into Rosa's Children. I got a lump in my throat. Why do you want me to tell you it's shit?"

Lilo didn't want to believe her. She welcomed any excuse to throw Heike against the wall. In deference to Anne Ecke, she opted for control. Examining Heike's expression, however, she detected neither fear nor resentment.

"More quotations? Rosa's speech in Berlin…"

"No quotations, Lilo. If Rosa were here to deliver a speech, she wouldn't need us. Your words carry emotions. Rosa and Werner's thoughts are in your words. They're good words, Lilo."

Lilo relaxed. She'd sweated bullets getting the proper thoughts on paper. Then, she sweated more to pare it down to a manageable length. Finally, she revised and revised before revising the revisions.

"It's perfect," Heike repeated.

Set pride aside, Lilo thought. There was other business to discuss.

"I know a man in a Jena print shop. He'll run off a thousand copies for two hundred marks."

"Wessi marks?"

"Reich Marks. It's a good price, Heike."

"We don't have two pfennig to rub together, Lilo."

"Start making the rounds. There must be people with a few marks to spare. Maybe, we can talk the printer into doing the work for so much down, and we pay the balance later."

"A thousand copies?"

"Minimum. He won't run a single-page flyer for less than a thousand."

Heike whistled. Lilo retreated. She'd never heard Heike whistle; it wasn't pleasant.

"These are tough times. With so many people out of work, even if everyone chipped in two marks, we couldn't get it."

"I know some people," Lilo reported. "I'll see a few on my way home."

"I can't get out until morning," Heike moaned.

"Meet me on the Platz tomorrow."

Heike nodded and swallowed hard.

* * *

Nadine's contribution to Rosa's Children was to keep her nose to the grindstone so her sister could run the extra errands the organization required. In return, she expected to be fully appraised of Heike's progress. A chill remained between them because Heike's believed she was unworthy of happiness.

Heike's announcement of a meeting the following day left Nadine with shopping duties. It meant leaving Anne alone, but they'd done that often enough; neither harm nor discomfort visited the woman who sat on the couch and stared quietly and placidly at memories. Frau Jacobs was able enough to assuage hunger and thirst when alone.

Heike set out early. She knew where the Neuberts lived within a hundred meters. Jürgen spent enough time there in former years, but female company was seldom tolerated; neither Heike nor Nadine ever visited. Nadine, however, knew the house number.

The journey took twenty minutes. Heike looked for the number. The building was a two-story, four-apartment complex. Heike had expected a single-family dwelling. Günther appeared from behind the building.

He wore work clothes and gloves and pushed a wheelbarrow heaped with grass and dead tree limbs. He caught sight of Heike and opted to pause in his work. He peeled off his gloves.

"I'm very happy to see you," he hailed cheerfully.

Heike Jacobs kept her smile submerged.

"I need you, Günther."

"As I said," he nodded.

He gestured toward one of the two front doors with one hand while wiping sweat from his brow with the other.

"Come inside?"

She shook her head, feeling guilty.

"What's the difference between needing someone and using someone?"

Günther's expression instantly turned solemn.

"Explain it. I'll judge."

Germany

June 1990

Rev. Rademacher appointed himself as the official driver. Aaron wanted to drive, but the family agreed the bread winner should not be so cavalier. There was a proper send off. The entire Waldron and Kurihara clans were on hand. They made certain neither Ute nor Kathy bothered with baggage; they efficiently and quickly stowed in the Rademacher trunk.

They were willing to save Ute the burden of carrying her son to the car, but Ute declined this honor. Athena, as mission control, ticked off all the essential items: passports, tickets, formula, diapers, and certain "female items." Kathy feared the plane would arrive in Frankfurt before the hugging and kissing ended. Ute and Aaron enjoyed a record-setting good-bye. He wished his family best of luck and good journey. This performance made it painfully obvious how he detested the thought of an empty house.

Gary and Kathy made their good-bye pledges the previous afternoon, but they shared one final, lingering kiss at the car door. Both the elder and younger Fosters shed copious tears as the car headed down the hill and for the highway. Molly and Athena did their best to appear cheerful.

They failed.

Isaac fussed on the plane to Chicago. He objected to the change in pressure and continued his performance for most of the flight. Kathy didn't mind her brother's constant fussing, but she felt sorry for those seated nearby. When Kathy and Ute's patience neared exhaustion, a stewardess took *babers* for a stroll around the cabin.

He responded to a gentle voice and gentle bouncing. He returned to his harried mother and remained sedate – for three minutes.

"This is criminal," Ute said. "I'll strangle Dieter."

Kathy said nothing. It was cruel to submit an infant to the torture of transcontinental travel. Her heart bled for Isaac, but she'd never manage the trip alone. In Chicago, they had to rush to catch their connection. They hurried to get from the domestic gates to the international gates and, despite modern technology, the journey was endless.

"I thought the airport was in Chicago," Ute panted.

Kathy, who'd made the journey the summer prior, didn't discourage Ute by disclosing the remaining distance. They made it, just as boarding began. Ute was exhausted; Kathy was alarmed. She thought her mother had recovered from Isaac's birth, but Ute was alarmingly sluggish. She nearly asked a flight attendant to let them off the plane.

"You should see a doctor," Kathy whispered.

"I'm off my feet now. I'll be okay."

Kathy fretted. Ute, blessedly fell asleep and remained so through take off. Isaac fussed in Kathy's arms, but his malevolent energy was spent. He announced his opinion of travel, and Kathy was forced to smell it until the fasten-seatbelt sign went out. She fumbled with the diaper bag and made it to the "phone booth" where, miraculously, she got him cleaned and changed. He had the audacity to giggle.

Kathy cursed the travel gods.

Ute remained asleep when they returned. Kathy shook her awake for the meal. Ute took a few bites and went back to sleep. Eating a meal with Isaac in her arms was Kathy's special adventure. She did, however, wrap Ute's dinner roll in a napkin. When she woke, she'd be famished.

"Here!"

Kathy felt Isaac being lifted from her arms and realized she'd dozed off. Ute cradled the lethargic child and gently kissed his forehead.

"How long did I sleep?"

It was dark. Kathy was in no mood to look at Ute's watch for her. She stretched her legs, as far as she was able, and informed her mother about the dinner roll. For much of the rest of her waking hours, Kathy either thought of the friends she left behind or pondered her future. She didn't dare think what awaited them upon landing.

Bach's Air resounded inside her head and reassured her that all would be well; one step at a time. If she returned to finish high school, she might qualify for a place in a German university, saving Ute and Aaron tons of money. However, Kathy realized other options.

Claire was a very nice, musically literate person. She knew more than the jazz and rock classics she and her husband played; she knew Bach's Air on a G string. She recommended additional baroque works, a Beethoven violin concerto, and another by Mozart. It was she who used the term "scholarship voice," giving Kathy hope that an American college or university was not, automatically, beyond reach.

There was the military. Kathy could join the Army. Unlike Aaron, however, she'd not sign up for the cavalry. She'd train with computers, radio, or clerical skills. She could be a cook. The Army, also, had musical units. Might they need a singer? Could she qualify?

She'd watched a young woman interviewed on German television. She sang with the touring U.S. Army band and had a German name. Since she spoke no German, the interview portion was in English. Yes, her great grandparents came from Germany, and she was proud of her heritage. She enjoyed touring and doing what she liked best which was *singing*.

She was grateful to the Army for making it all possible. Furthermore, her dress uniform was impressive. Could Kathy follow this example? Further, if she wasn't good enough to solo, she might get into a choir. Once her enlistment ended, she could attend college at Uncle Sugar's expense.

Previously, Kathy accepted the fact that college was not part of her future. Suddenly, she discovered several options. When she returned to Oregon, she'd be a junior. It was time to get serious about plotting a course to college. German university was hardly ruled out, but there were excellent opportunities in America.

It was not a difficult walk for a young, healthy girl, but Kathy was worried about the miles they must traverse to get through passport control and baggage claim. She carried Isaac. In truth, she insisted upon it. She kept close watch on Ute as they walked and walked and walked.

"It is good to be free of the sardine can," Ute announced.

Despite these words, Kathy noticed the drawn look and how her strides grew shorter and slower. Waiting at the baggage carousel, Ute propped herself up by keeping a firm grip on the handle of the pushcart they'd muscled out of a stack. Isaac fit nicely in the portion reserved for hand baggage. He alternated between huge yawns and curious examinations of his surroundings.

With luggage collected, Kathy pushed towards the customs islands and the exit. Instinctively, Ute reached for her son. Just as instinctively, Kathy slapped her hand.

"I'm sorry," she announced. "I think he's safer where he is."

Ute didn't argue.

Once the automatic doors opened, Ute and Kathy had no problems finding Dieter and Marion. There was nothing Bavarian about the way they waved and yelled for attention. Marion snatched up Isaac and cooed at him between repeated announcements that he was "beautiful." Dieter held Ute for a long, long time – very un-Bavarian. Releasing his sister, Dieter took Kathy into his arms and held her tightly. This was a greater surprise.

The Kaufmanns bought half a loaf of dark German bread and real German butter. They had the baker slice the bread. Kathy and Ute wasted no time making pigs of themselves. After a few minutes of excited conversation, they took the S-Bahn into the city and the main station. The Kaufmanns were training back home, but the Fosters were headed to Berlin by the most expeditious route.

"I booked you three nights in East Berlin because the rates are much lower."

"I don't know how to get around East Berlin," Ute stated.

"The train will take you to the Zoo station. S-Bahn to Alexanderplatz. The TV tower is on one side and the hotel is the highest building on the other. I called Herr Beckmann. He expects you tomorrow morning."

"How do we get to his office?"

"I've marked it on the map. It's a short walk from the S-Bahn."

There was very little time to speak further. The Berlin train was pulling into the station. Kathy and Uncle Dieter quickly got the luggage onto the train. Kathy had to pry Ute away from Isaac. She kissed Aunt Marion on the cheek – very un-Swabish.

"Give Bernd and Mischa a big, big hug from me."

"I promise."

"Take good care of Little Brother."

"I promise."

The conductor blew his whistle. Kathy grabbed Ute's arm and dragged her onto the train. The tears flowed down Ute's cheeks as the wagon moved with a jerk. She kept Isaac in sight until her view was blocked. She bawled like a baby while Kathy guided her to her seat.

It wasn't only Ute who misted.

Isaac was no longer a member of their party. Soon enough, they finished the bread and most of the butter. Thankfully, Ute went to sleep. Not long after, Kathy drifted off only to be awakened by the sudden commotion in the seat next to her.

"What's wrong?" she asked, her heart in her throat.

Ute's frightened expression eased, and she swallowed hard.

"I – I woke up and couldn't find Aaron. I panicked."

"We'll call when we get to the hotel," Kathy promised, though she had no way of knowing if it was possible.

"I hope he's okay."

"Dieter and Marion have two sons who survived," Kathy reminded. "I think Isaac's chances are pretty good."

Ute nodded, but a mother has worries words cannot squelch. She took Kathy's arm and rested her head on her shoulder. When the tears stopped flowing, Kathy knew she was asleep.

* * *

It was exhausting work lugging the baggage off the train, down the stairs, over to the S-Bahn tracks and up another set of stairs to the platform. Ute and Kathy had ruminated, argued, and fussed over the things they needed and, so they thought, reduced everything to the bare minimum.

"Lewis and Clark crossed half a continent with less crap!" Kathy exploded once they gained the platform.

Ute said nothing, but she shared Kathy's urge to push a suitcase in front of the first moving vehicle. They sat on their luggage and waited for the next eastbound Bahn. It was a short wait; seemingly all trains went through Alexanderplatz.

The gaudy wagons of burnt-yellow with maroon trim rattled and whirred into the Berlin Zoo station. When the doors opened and a mob disgorged, two weary travelers half dragged, half cursed their accoutrements aboard. Due to the volume of passengers, there wasn't much place for the newcomers. Kathy spied a single seat well forward and motioned to Ute and tacitly announced her intention to remain with the "anvils." Ute shook her head and gripped a strap in one hand and a silver pole in the other.

The S-Bahn was in no hurry. The visitors viewed part of the zoo before crossing a canal and providing a clear view of 17 Juni Strasse and the Victory monument several hundred meters away. The sun glistened off the French cannon from which it was made; it hurt Kathy's eyes. The Bahn snaked into the Tiergarten where their view existed of the blur of the people waiting to board.

They viewed a small slice of the Tiergarten and the victory column from another angle before crossing the lazy River Spree into Bellevue, and a grand view it would be were the station not enclosed. As they crawled for too long, they gawked at the Pregnant Oyster, a concert venue, across the Spree. They crossed another canal, or so Kathy thought. Though the wall came down months before, any dolt could recognize where it once snaked through the city. Kathy's only previous view of the boarder was with Uncle Dieter. She gripped at her strap until her knuckles turned white.

"We're in the DDR," she whispered.

For Kathy Foster, it was a frightening ride from one country to another. For Ute, however, it was a journey she never expected to make. They caught a glimpse of the Brandenburg Gate and Ute breathed again, witnessing traffic flowing to and from without hindrance. It was a comfort to know she could return to the West again without having to be smuggled out.

Friedrichstrasse Station.

The people looked no different than the ones they'd seen at the Zoo Station. Though she'd visited Berlin several times as a girl and as a teen, Ute never saw this part of the city. Her eyes bulged and her heart raced as she viewed things once forbidden.

Crossing through the capital of the DDR without documents or confronting a mountain of hostile questions was a miracle. Noting the dilapidated condition of the area, however, brought profound pathos. It was like stepping into a palatial abode only to discover the interior was dark, dank, moldy, and crumbling.

Once again, they crossed the Spree. Their wagon was nearly rubbing up against a huge building. It was possible to peek through the windows. Kathy noted many scars and pock marks she recognized as war damage. She'd seen it before, most notably in Köln at the Cathedral, but those blemishes paled in comparison to what confronted her in Berlin.

"I want to go there," Ute whispered.

"What is it?" Kathy asked, fearing eavesdroppers.

"Museum Island," Ute replied softly.

Finally, they saw it – the Pope's Revenge!

Jutting a thousand feet into the summer sky, the East German TV Tower was a triumph of "superior socialist technology." It was visible from practically every place in the city, both East and West. The story was that the Comrades tore down a church to make way for their scientific and technological marvel.

Kathy noticed at once how the tower got its nickname. The sun's reflection on the bulbous rotating restaurant near the top of the edifice formed a cross. Heads, according to local lore, literally rolled in the East's technical world when numerous attempts failed to rid the tower of the sunlight-created image.

Kathy's knees quivered. She hoped no one, least of all Ute, would notice. In truth, Ute wouldn't have noticed Kathy vomiting. If Kathy was nervous, Ute was terrified. She wasn't ready for the DDR.

The borders may be open; the Vopos might lack authority to harass tourists; the Stasi's license to kill may have been revoked, but this was the DDR! Ute Foster found it ominous and threatening. Kathy muscled the luggage onto the platform, but Ute remained attached to the train.

"Come on!"

Ute's eyes flashed. She saw Kathy and those *damned bags.* Gingerly, she took timid steps onto the platform.

"There's the tower," Kathy motioned with her finger at the monstrous gray stem that dominated the glassed-in station. "So, the hotel is on the other side."

Just as Uncle Dieter reported.

It remained a matter of getting six tons of supplies down another series of steps and across the huge expanse named for a Russian Czar. It was warm. The subjects of this narrative were physically drained from being imprisoned in the close quarters of an aircraft and the rocking and clicking of a train which, for the last leg of their trip, was passed by cyclists. When they arrived at the registration desk, their faces were beaded with sweat, and their blouses were clinging to their arms and shoulders.

Their patience with luggage was at an absolute end! The man at the registration desk was too cheery by half and the alacrity with which he checked their prepaid reservations and brought them room keys was unbearable. Were Kathy alone, she'd have sworn at the grinning fool in Swabish, but Ute, who could summon appropriate emotions, thanked the man warmly before moving to the elevators.

"When we get to the room, don't say anything you don't want someone else to hear," Ute warned.

"Why?"

"The Stasi bugged every hotel room in this country."

"But they are gone, aren't they?"

"So, they say," Ute replied, skeptically.

There were more elevators available than the Fosters could use. With a room on the twenty-eighth floor, the fatigued pair was resigned to spend most of what remained of the afternoon in the tiny cubical.

"Let's try this one," Kathy suggested pointing to an express sign.

She pushed the call button without waiting for a vote. Soon enough, the lavish box was open for their employment. Again, they muscled their baggage. Kathy pressed the number 28.

A moment later, Kathy Foster let out a squeak. Ute gasped and moaned. The final breath they took as the door closed carried them to the tenth floor, but their stomachs lagged six floors behind.

"I hope this thing can stop, "Ute whined on the edge of hysteria.

Kathy's hopes were similar. They'd entered an express elevator and found themselves in a space capsule. The doors slid open. Ute jumped out onto the landing and dragged out what she could. If the doors closed suddenly, the rocket sled might launch again.

Ute had no wish to be trapped. Kathy would have followed suit, but she was dizzy, and her sinuses threatened to drain out her nose. It took several seconds to worry her share of the cargo out of the nightmare.

"Dear God!" Ute sighed as the doors closed.

Kathy's head was still swimming when Ute began searching for their room. By the time the card key slid into the lock, Ute's only goal was to get the "crap" far enough inside to close the door. This accomplished, she threw herself face down on the nearest of the double beds. Kathy was ready to make use of the second bed, but she must tend to Molly's dress.

Sure enough, and despite the meticulous care with which it was packed, the pale blue garment was a collection of wrinkles. She fussed for several minutes before futility asserted itself. Sighing, the girl hung it on a wall light fixture, a perfect place, she thought, for a microphone. She hoped gravity, if it functioned at such an altitude, would help the wrinkles vanish.

She walked to a huge window and looked first at the television phallus before studying the ants scurrying about Alexanderplatz. She made certain the bathroom was ready for use before shuffling to the remaining bed. She dropped onto it with her hands in her lap and her eyes on her fellow traveler.

"Mutti, this is so stupid," she blurted, finding Ute's face wet with tears. "There must be a night train. Go to Isaac!"

Ute forced herself into a semblance of composure. She wiped her face with the back of her hand, sniffed and sat up against the headboard.

"It's no good," she responded. "The moment I get to Fürth, I'll cry over you. I know where Aaron is. If I go home, I'll have no idea where you are. It will be worse."

"There's something wrong here."

Ute shook her head and sniffed.

"Honey, it was like this the first time I left you with your Oma. Aaron and I wanted to go out and have a nice dinner. I cried the whole time. He was angry with me."

It was Kathy's turn.

"Dear God!"

"I know it's stupid, but I can't control how I feel. Tomorrow, I'll be fine."

Kathy hoped so. She didn't need a misery guts with her in the morning. She'd need all her wits when she met Herr Beckmann. She didn't have enough strength to baby-sit her mother.

"Do you suppose we could get a cheap meal later?" she asked. "I need something other than airline food."

"I can't get in that elevator again tonight, Kathy. I'd die before we got halfway down."

"They're selling bratwurst in the Platz," Kathy reported.

"I'd be perfectly happy with some bread or a *brötchen* or two. Get a coffee for me, too."

"You don't like my drinking coffee," Kathy reminded.

Ute rolled her eyes. Was the girl badgering her?

"If you bring me coffee, I promise not to spank you."

* * *

The city illumination was just enough to cast eerie shadows in a hotel room hundreds of feet above Alexanderplatz. The luminous hands of the bedside clock were crawling past three forty-five. Ute Foster could make out the empty bed across from her. She lay still expecting to hear noise from the bathroom. When nothing auditory satiated her, she sat up and looked about in the dimness.

Kathy stood with her arms crossed, looking out on the lights of the city. The view to the west offered an illuminated bubble over that portion of the metropolis. The eastern view offered far less evidence of human activity.

Below, the plaza was bare, save for the leisurely gait of a policeman or the staggering of a few deep in their cups. Across the way, a man emerged from the S-Bahn station to sit, motionless near a pool of light. He placed his hat beside him on the chance some wonderer would happen by and make an offering. Kathy assumed he'd fallen asleep. She hoped so.

"A penny for –"

Kathy hadn't heard Ute stirring, but she remained calm when the quiet voice came from just behind her. She didn't turn around.

"I couldn't sleep any longer."

"Is it jet lag? Or are you getting anxious?"

Kathy shrugged.

"We must wait forever."

A prolonged silence followed. Kathy's eyes never strayed from the placid scene below. Bach's Air issued, internally, forth, and she remained motionless. She was amazed at her remarkable calm. When Ute's arms folded around her waist, it satisfied a longing. She leaned back and offered a shoulder upon which Ute propped her chin.

"I have dreaded this day," Ute whispered. "I'm losing my daughter."

"You can't get rid of me so easy," Kathy replied.

"When I was your age, I never could have done – this."

Kathy snorted. It was not, however, contemptuous. It was, instead, that peculiar variety of controlled explosion that thrived on irony.

"All you ever did was defy your family and friends to marry a GI and go off to a country that didn't exist when they laid out this square."

Ute took no offense. She warmed both to the subject and the girl who introduced it.

"That's different. I was so much in love; I wasn't aware what I was doing. I didn't care, then."

"Back home, the man you love is being chased by Athena."

It was Ute's turn to express audible mirth.

"Good luck to her."

Kathy held Ute's hands in place as if afraid her mother would let go.

"What's the difference between you and Athena? She wants a kid. Her husband walks out. You want a kid and –"

She didn't finish.

"I was very, very lucky. I wasn't certain Aaron would make a good father. He kept telling Dieter and me that we were fools. He didn't want my hopes growing large. I thought he didn't want you."

Kathy wallowed in gloom.

"What if he told you to stop?"

"That would be tough. I – I don't think I could stop loving Aaron."

"That's not very encouraging," Kathy sighed, thankful the situation never arose.

"I couldn't stop loving you either. That made it difficult."

"You didn't even know me."

This time, Kathy's sarcasm was unmistakable.

"Oh, yes I did! I loved you as I loved Little Aaron before he arrived."

That caused Kathy to think very hard. Her fingers grew tighter over Ute's hands.

"Well, you won't lose me," Kathy promised. "If I go to college or get married, you'll not lose me. This – thing won't make a difference."

"No," Ute reflected, "I suppose not. Thanks for saying that. Now, let's see to that dress."

"It's hopeless. It must be pressed. Do they have a service in this hotel?"

Ute extracted her hands and navigated through the darkness. She took the dress from the light fixture and marched it to the bathroom. In a moment, the shower gushed. Ute reappeared, closing the door behind her.

Ten minutes later, when Kathy opened the door, steam poured out and the room's air conditioning moaned. After turning off the water, she examined the damp dress. Even with the cloud diffusing the overhead light, it looked markedly better. She re-closed the door and let the garment stew.

"When do they serve breakfast?"

They never bothered to turn on the room lights, but the darkness wasn't enough to cloak Ute's visage.

"I don't want to get back in the elevator."

"Why don't we stay here and order in?"

"Well, I must see Herr Beckmann," Kathy continued. "If we start now, we can get down the steps by then."

Much later, they each showered in tepid water, got dressed, and braved the elevator. Ute covered her face with her hands; Kathy pushed the button. They experienced near weightlessness which made the deceleration of their landing sufficiently traumatic. Kathy helped Ute stagger out of the machine.

"Will we ever get used to that thing?" Kathy asked, gulping for breath.

Ute's expression announced *mal de mere*. Foreseeing the possibility that breakfast might not survive ascension, they brought down items they required. A husband and wife were seated near the door picking at their food as if waiting for the arrival of others.

Ute presented their room number to the menacing matron. When she had duly expunged the number from her roster, the dazed travelers adjourned to an area as far removed from human habitation as possible. Ute remained at the table while her unsteady legs regained consciousness.

Kathy, however, set out for the buffet. She returned with an orange juice and coffee; Ute perked up. After a second foray, she returned with a plate crowded with bread, cheese, jam, some fish and a hard-boiled egg, Ute's stomach nearly revolted.

"You'll die from all that," she predicted.

"The last meal."

Ute digested that sardonic remark. Eventually, she made her way to the buffet and selected more sensible items. She passed Kathy returning for seconds. After her juice, Ute sipped some coffee and picked at a minute portion of fruit.

Mostly, however, she watched Kathy shovel food into her maw. How curious, she pondered, that Kathy, on the brink of a life-changing experience, was so cavalier.

"When I grow up, I hope I'm as brave as you," Ute said.

Kathy looked at the speaker curiously. Had the free-fall of twenty-six floors lobotomized her escort?

* * *

It was the only building for blocks visited by the war. It was a squat, three-story, pathetic office building. The damage had been hastily patched over, but forty years of neglect had brought general degradation. Amazingly, it appeared in better condition than the post-war eyesores surrounding it.

The pockmarks made by small caliber munitions dotted the areas nearest the windows; large caliber damage was more evenly applied. In the DDR, however, if a building stood, it was used.

Kathy and Ute examined the exterior for several minutes. They frequently consulted both the map and the address to ensure they were, indeed, at their appointed location. Kathy crossed the infrequently utilized street to examine the metal plaque near the entrance. She signaled Ute to join her.

It was slightly past ten o'clock, but the visitors stood immobile as if on a stakeout. Was this, they reflected, the office they'd traversed half the globe to find? Couldn't Dieter locate an office better suited to the dignity of its function?

"The Russians really worked this place over," Ute concluded.

The comment roused Kathy from her trance. Bach provided placidness as Heike opened the door.

"Use the handrail, Kathy."

The warning was superfluous. Ute's motive was to speak the name aloud. She feared she might not get another chance.

The stairs were modern. To the left of the staircase was a narrow hallway protected by a flimsy gate. The accompanying sign announced, in four languages, that the area was for staff use only.

"No elevator," Ute noted with relief.

In America, it would be the second floor. In Germany, it was the first. Only two doors confronted them. One was unmarked with a hasp and a large lock to deter entry. The second door presented a number professionally painted in large, black characters.

To the right, at shoulder height, was a metal plaque with embossed letters announcing the existence of *PETER BECKMANN*. Ute Foster was amazed when Kathy, without further hesitation, rapped firmly on the door and reached for the handle.

The door swung open onto a scene no different than thousands of bureaucratic offices. The furnishings were bureaucratic gray, the walls were bureaucratic white, the floor was bureaucratic hardwood, and the air was bureaucratic stale. Behind the paper riot on the desk opposite to the door sat a white-haired lady wearing an unbureaucratic purple blouse.

She brandished a bureaucratic ballpoint with her right hand; the left reached for a large binder in the upper portion of her desk. The knock and subsequent entry arrested her in mid-task. Her attentive eyes, neither inquisitive nor hostile, examined the interlopers.

"Bitte?"

Ute opened her mouth, but Kathy's voice came out.

"Kathy Foster to see Herr Beckmann."

The woman lost interest in the binder.

"Herr Beckmann is on the phone," she announced. "Please, have a seat."

There were three chairs, cheap plastic ice-scoops of orange on flimsy metal legs. Ute suspected they'd been hustled up the stairs by an eager bureaucrat before some fast-food establishment detected the theft. Typically, however, they were uncomfortable to discourage loitering. The dearth of chairs announced this office was strictly "appointment only."

They sat.

Kathy looked pleasant in her yellow top, navy calf-length trousers and white canvass shoes. Ute wore a skirt, blouse, and sandals. She'd been tempted to wear Bermudas because of the heat but decided too much informality might not do.

Ute didn't realize she nervously bounced her legs. Kathy gently put her hand on a knee to call attention and encourage cessation. Ute stopped and Kathy returned the hand to her lap. She sat, calm and motionless.

The girl crossed her right leg over her left and examined the wall calendar to the side of the woman's desk. It featured a huge color picture of the Dresden Opera house. Kathy, apparently, was committing it to memory. How she could look so calm and relaxed while Ute boiled inside was as mysterious as it was annoying.

"Kathy?" she whispered.

The girl responded by a quiet noise from her throat. It was neither the time nor the place to discuss, but Ute required occupation.

"When Aaron went off to Vietnam, I moved in with your grandparents," she reported.

Kathy nodded. This was old news. Aaron and Ute seldom spoke of those dark days.

"It was great to work on the farm and tend sheep and cook and wash. Maybe, I should have got a job, but – I didn't want to be away from the house. If officers came –"

Moments later, Kathy bid her to continue. She wasn't interested, but Ute needed to speak.

"I should have come home. I could live with my parents and got a job, but I was afraid. You see, with Aaron's parents, if he was – if anything happened, we three – the people who loved him most…If news reached me in Fürth – More than anything else in the world, I was afraid Mutti or Pappy or Dieter would – sooner or later – say, '*I told you so.*' Does it make me a bad person to not trust my own family?"

Kathy held her tongue. What could she say that wouldn't sound trite? Together, they examined the woman sorting papers on her desk and placing them in varied file folders. She must know the visitors were talking. Could she hear? Ute spoke in English, but that was hardly a guarantee of privacy.

"I'm not complaining, understand. Aaron – lost friends; he still frets about that – nights. He promised, when he rotated out, he'd ask for a German posting. He said he wanted to take me home. That's why he was on the border that day. How could something so evil turn out so right?"

"Stop it!" Kathy hissed. "That was years ago. You wouldn't have felt any better if you came home. Be grateful he's alive."

"But –"

Kathy sliced the air with her hand. The conversation was over. A moment later, Ute considered charging ahead despite the warning. Deciding it wasn't worth the risk, she folded her hands over her knee. Ute wanted to cry over what she gained – and what she was about to lose. She tried to steel herself. If Kathy could remain calm, she owed it to her to retain some poise.

The whole of this scene was performed to the shuffling of paper and the resonate mumbling behind an adjoining door. Herr Beckmann, if that were the identity of the man behind the bureaucratic door with a proper ration of bureaucratic emulsion, was doing more listening than speaking. Based upon the tone of his muffled voice, there was no timidity of purpose. The longer Kathy and Ute sat uncomfortably in the office, the more assured they became that Herr Beckmann was a person used to stating facts and giving directions if not orders.

Finally, there was a brief mumble and an unmistakable clicking of a phone being returned to its cradle. The secretary, literally, abandoned her filing to cross the room with dexterity of purpose. She knocked with one hand and twisted the door handle with the other.

"Fraulein Foster is here," she announced.

"Wie, bitte?"

Kathy's heart sank. They had an appointment, and they were alone in the office. After traveling so hard and long, after such a restless night, it was too much! The man they came to see, apparently, had, no inkling of her existence. The secretary stepped into the office and closed the door, but not far enough.

"*Zwilling*," she muttered but not softly enough.

The fashion accessory Mrs. Waldron sent off with Kathy, the one she lifted over her head and rested in her lap, fell to the floor. Ute, too stunned to speak, watched as the girl uncrossed her legs and leaned forward to retrieve it. With the item clutched in her hands, she returned it to her lap. It was a great performance. It might have fooled Ute completely save for Kathy's eyes. They were directed at Ute. They were dilated and frightened.

"Did she say…?" Ute whispered stupidly.

There was no opportunity to reply. Herr Beckmann, burly and overweight, rushed out the door toward them. Instinctively, but devoid of confidence, the women stood. The large man wore a bureaucratic gray suit. His face was russet and meaty; the knot in his black tie was loosed and his top shirt button open.

His mouth was wide, his nose prominent and his ears were so flat against his head they appeared pasted on rather than attached.

"Fraulein Foster," he greeted with a bold but not overpowering voice. "Pleased to meet you."

"*Freut mich sehr*," Kathy replied, a tremble in her voice.

When Herr Beckmann cast a quick glance at Ute, Kathy woke from her daze.

"This is Mrs. Foster."

Herr Beckmann offered a bow. Shaken and flustered, Ute offered her hand. Herr Beckmann accepted it graciously. Kathy, fearing herself on the verge of a disastrous faux pas, extended her hand as well. For the briefest moment Herr Beckmann was bewildered. He saw to Ute first before taking Kathy's hand.

"Please, come inside."

Everyone was flustered. They piled into the office as if auditioning for a stint with the Three Stooges. Once inside the tiny room, it took logistical skill to move a second chair beside its mate across from Herr Beckmann's desk. He attempted to keep the conversational flow by reciting memorized apologies for the limited space. Additionally, he included a few socially approved platitudes. Finally, he bid the ladies sit. They were reluctant so long as their host remained standing, but adamancy wore them into submission.

He opened the second drawer of a filing cabinet and extracted a thick green file that he plopped on his desk. He snapped up a leather briefcase and pulled out a thinner folder. He set it beside the first. Only then did he sit down.

"Dieter Kaufmann is your brother?" Herr Beckmann asked of Ute.

Her voice caught in her throat; she was reduced to nodding.

"Thanks to him, this was child's play. He supplied me with documents and memos. This is the easiest case I've handled to date."

He patted the folder he'd extracted from his briefcase. He opened it and flipped pages. He settled on one that Kathy recognized. She had a copy among the collection Uncle Dieter ceded her. It was foot and handprints of a rescued child. A second document was segregated; it was an official paper issued from Bonn, signed stamped and sealed.

"You are Fraulein Foster, correct?" He asked of her. "I'm not being stupid, young lady; I'm simply playing by the rules."

Kathy nodded.

She opened Mrs. Waldron's gift and produced both her passports. Herr Beckmann snatched the green booklet and examined the German letters and symbols. He glanced at it the way airport customs officials do. Closing it, he paired it with its American cousin and returned them.

"Here's where we are," he began. "We know, thanks to Herr Kaufmann, that the child to whom these prints belong, was born in the DDR on November 12, 1973. There is no room for doubt. We require a set of your fingerprints, Fraulein, to verify that you are the same person whose prints are here," he held up Dieter's contribution.

"And here," he patted the cover of the green folder, "Once that is established, I'll arrange a meeting with your father."

This time, Kathy's voice failed.

"Can you take prints here?" Ute asked.

"Alas, no. My secretary will give you a card with a map to a police station three blocks away. Show your passport and the card. They do this for us frequently. It takes only a few minutes. They'll dispatch the prints and a cover letter by currier. Unfortunately, the letter takes time. I can't guarantee action today, but I'm confident we'll have an official identification by noon tomorrow."

That was disappointing. Herr Beckmann, who made this speech many times, was used to seeing deflated expressions. He'd not succeeded, however, in developing a bureaucratic heart; human feelings still touched him. He couldn't send the women away without some trinket. As an official, he'd done his duty by implying the young girl was, likely, a fraud. As a person, he wanted her to know he trusted her.

"I have here," he said, patting the green file, "something we fished out of Lichtenberg. We were lucky. The Stasi destroyed many documents when the people stormed the place. The rioters destroyed some of what remained. The Stasi wore out a fleet of shredders, getting rid of the evidence. It was like trying to erode Mt. Everest with a garden hose. Ten thousand shredders couldn't handle the material – and the DDR never had more than a few hundred."

Four eyes gazed upon that malicious green folder, filled with foreboding. That expression, also, was too familiar to Herr Beckmann. He was not allowed to let people examine still-classified, material. However, he wasn't prohibited from sharing select details.

"Fraulein," he began as he paged through, "you were born in Riesa and – how did they do it?"

"What?" Ute, in possession of the only functioning set of vocal cords, spoke for the child.

"They attempted an escape from Thüringen, but – how could they travel so far without papers? The car was found abandoned eight kilometers from the border, but – unbelievable!"

He'd done a quick page through days before, but, apparently, he hadn't been scrupulous. He flipped page after page looking for something that he didn't need to suppress or censor. He stopped after pages of interrogation transcriptions. He looked hard at the page. Then, he looked hard at Kathy.

"I wish we could forego the fingerprints, young lady, but it's the law. My doubts, however, are satisfied."

He pulled out a letter opener and fussed with a small photograph. Once freed, he passed it to Kathy. She was too stunned to take it. Ute was not. She merely glanced at the wallet-sized snapshot.

"*Gott im Himmel!*"

For Ute Foster, the exclamation was emphatic. Kathy, jolted out of her stupor and with curiosity in full bloom, reached gingerly for the photo. Kathy studied a photograph of herself. Two or three years younger, she looked impishly into the camera with her head tilted slightly forward. Her eyes were merry, and her smile was mischievous. The top button of her blouse was undone.

There were, however, two flaws: the photo was black and white, and her hair was done up in twin braids lapping over her shoulders. All known photos of Kathy were in color. Kathy's hair had never been braided. The warmth of the inner office failed to keep her blood freezing and her skin breaking out in gooseflesh.

Her head reeled. Had the Stasi snapped and doctored her picture? Gradually, she realized the nose and the dimples were hers, but the mouth and smile weren't. She looked up to Herr Beckmann for some explanation.

"Your mother," he announced.

Kathy gulped.

"How – what –?"

Herr Beckmann referred to the file.

"October of 1962. A school photo, she was – ah – thirteen."

Kathy stared in wonder. Ute stared at Kathy's staring. Beckmann's eyes flickered from one to the other. Most of his cases involved people who knew and remembered each other. Here, a young girl was introduced to a stranger. He wasn't used to seeing people in a stupor.

Timidly, Kathy tried to return the picture. She was reluctant; her fingers quivered. Beckmann waved his hand dismissively.

"Keep it," he said. "The Stasi is gone."

Kathy opened her German passport and secured her mother's picture inside. She gingerly returned both passports to her fashionable bag.

"Can you tell us more?" Ute asked.

"Not until the fingerprints are verified," he replied.

Two women deflated.

"*Unter vier augen?*" he whispered.

"I'll leave," Ute announced, getting up.

"Under six eyes, then," he amended, motioning her to resume her seat.

"I promise," Kathy said, her voice quivering and guttural.

"*Ich auch,*" Ute nodded.

Herr Beckmann felt for a paperclip he used to mark a page in the thick file. He bypassed several pages to reach it.

"You mother, Fraulein, was born Constanze Posen. The family's name was von Posen, but the 'von' because – well, the DDR."

Kathy nodded. She recalled a grave in Bavaria.

"You father is Ernst Bauer, arrested in 1974, tried and convicted of attempting to flee the country, found guilty and sentenced to eight years in prison. He was released in 1977 and sent to Eisenhuttenstadt. In 1980, he was sent to Frankfurt. Fraulein, we shall meet him there."

"We just came here from Frankfurt," Ute croaked.

"Sorry," he said with one of few English words he knew. "I'm an Ossi and I forget. Frankfurt an der Oder."

"I know of it," Ute nodded. "It's on the Polish border."

"Correct."

"What about my sister?" Kathy croaked.

Herr Beckmann's eyes locked onto her demanding eyes. He glanced at the closed door. He and his secretary would have words. Obviously, the Zwilling comment was overheard. No bureaucratic rhetoric could erase it, so he was forced to address a topic he wished to avoid.

"Your sister informs me she has no interest in seeing your father."

Herr Beckmann thought that would put a damper on the conversation. He had, however, violated common sense, administrative rules, bureaucratic regulations and, possibly, a couple of laws. In for a penny, he paged through the file to recover an item he intended to mark, but, apparently, hadn't. He tugged at a document until he freed it.

"*Unter vier Augen?*" he asked.

"*Sechs,*" Ute reminded.

"Ahm – '*sechs*,' of course," he said, clearing his throat. "You must not speak of this before tomorrow. There could be serious trouble."

"We only know two people in this city," Ute announced. "Both are in this building."

"Nevertheless, one talks on the S-Bahn and in cafés."

Ute sat back in the first semblance of composure she'd shown since entering.

"You spent time in an Ossi jail, didn't you?"

He didn't bat an eye.

"Three months," he admitted. "That was enough. I was at university. Someone asked a question – indelicately subjective, perhaps, but I was, once, an honest person. I answered the question."

"The answer was, also, subjective?"

"Indeed. Either someone reported me, or a Stasi stooge was present. Since then, I've learned to lie – even to my family. Now we're free to speak truth, I find it often causes more damage than lies."

Ute's eyes were sober and locked onto Herr Beckmann's. He stared back for several seconds before sliding the document across the desk towards Kathy. He broke the spell by leaving his chair and pretending to seek something in the filing cabinet.

Ute's eyes drifted onto the Photostat of an official document.

Heike Franziska Bauer
Sabine Aleksandra Bauer

The women studied the birth certificate. They noted location of the "multiple birth" in a Peoples' Hospital. They noted, also, the names of the parents, Ernst Albert Bauer and Constanze Marie Bauer, geb. Posen.

The room was quiet enough for Beckmann to hear breathing. Rather than interrupt the ladies' rumination, he leaned gently on the file drawer with a second green folder in his hand.

"Well," Ute said, finally, "you were hoping for an older sister, and you have one."

"By eleven minutes," Kathy whispered.

"This has gone far enough!" Beckmann stated, slamming the filing drawer shut.

He resumed his seat with the newest folder clinched tightly in his fists.

"I referenced no names. Why come here for information you have?"

Kathy and Ute exchanged glances. The young girl explained the cryptic message from across the border. Herr Beckmann wondered if Herr Kaufmann's file was incomplete. Nevertheless, he accepted Sabine's explanation.

"Notice, fraternal twins," he reminded, stabbing the document neither visitor attempted to touch.

"What's that?" Kathy asked in a whisper.

"Not identical," Herr Beckmann informed.

Sabine looked at him and tried to swallow. The distress on her face indicated she failed. Her mouth opened, but nothing came. She sat straight, took a deep breath, and tried again.

"Why doesn't Heike want to see Papa?" she croaked.

"They placed her in a proper, socialist home. In sixteen years, people can learn a lot of hate."

Kathy attempted to speak again, but she brought forth little more than a timid cough. Her throat was parched; her voice was little more than gagging.

"Frau Tiede! Have we water?"

The secretary, apparently, had strict orders not to enter the inner sanctum when Beckmann was in conference. With an official document in full view, it was just as well. They heard the woman clomp on the floor and her voice through the closed door.

"I must go downstairs."

"Bitte!"

The clomping renewed, followed by the sound of a door opening and closing. Ute got up to put her arms around her girl. How she could soothe a raw, arid throat is something only a mother can fathom. The teen patted Ute's hands appreciatively before groping for one of Beckmann's pencils. He understood and quickly tore a sheet off the notepad by his phone, placing it beside the birth certificate.

The girl breathed in dry, desperate puffs, but would not be deterred. She pressed hard and, despite her hurry, completed her message with an exaggerated punctuation mark.

I want to see my sister!

Herr Beckmann snatched up the paper and the certificate. He stuffed them into to the file. He was thinking. It was understandable Heike wished no contact with her father. Would she agree to meet her sister? He'd never arranged such a meeting. When a family was discovered, it reunited. Before reuniting siblings, he checked with higher authority.

"I'll see what I can do," he promised.

The girl leaned back. Her mouth was clamped shut. She breathed voraciously through her nose, making her chest swell, but the operation was no longer alarming.

"I will investigate," Beckmann repeated. "I promise."

She blinked and nodded.

Frau Tiede rushed back with the water. She knocked and was admitted. She brought a liter bottle and a disposable tumbler. She immediately got the water from one into the other. The young girl drank slowly until the vessel was drained.

"Danke," she said, barely audible.

Ute reached for the bottle and poured more.

"Thank you, Frau Tiede," Herr Beckmann dismissed. "We won't be much longer."

The secretary nodded, took her leave, and closed the door firmly behind her.

"My apologies," he said. "We should keep liquids up here. If we had a descent office, we would, but – well, hopefully, we won't be needed much longer. Returning to this… *problem*, the government collected children like stamps and distributed them around the country, leaving them with the *right kind* of parents."

"I want to see my sister," Sabine restated before draining the tumbler a second time.

"I understand," Herr Beckmann nodded, continuing page flipping.

"I will speak with my superiors."

He found something in the file which arrested him. He studied the paper further and he began to snarl.

"Would you care to know how your sister folds her underwear?" he growled.

Without waiting, he threw the file to the floor and stomped on it as if it were a snake. Startled, Frau Tiede let out a whoop from the next room, but knew better than to investigate.

"I'm sorry," he puffed and settled down considerably. "Sometimes, I want to bash someone."

"Why would they want to know that?" Ute asked timidly, fearing she might set him off anew.

"Because the Stasi *knows* everything. Because it's exactly the sort of thing a desk-bound Stasi slug would consider a sign of efficiency. The worm probably got a medal. I… I'm sorry, but… that's going too far! Just when I think I've seen it all, I come across… this."

Ute took the plastic cup from Sabine, poured some water, and gulped it down.

"Fraulein,"

Herr Beckmann began, as calmly as his blood pressure allowed.

"The sooner your prints are taken, the sooner we can move. Leave a phone number with Frau Tiede. I'll call the moment word comes. She'll provide our number as well."

"When?" Ute asked.

"We return from *Mittagspause* at one thirty. We should have word by then."

He stood to terminate the interview. Ute followed suit.

"Come, Sabine," she said.

Sabine rose slowly. She'd absorbed so much in a very few minutes.

"Thank you, Herr Beckmann," she said, extending her hand.

He shook it gently but warmly as Ute exited.

"I want to meet my sister," she reminded.

Weimar

Matters moved so quickly, Heike nearly lost control. Within hours of confiding in Günther, she was awash in Reich Marks. Günther contributed money from his army savings. Then Heiko, a person Heike hadn't seen in weeks, came by to press twenty marks into her hands, complements of his music earnings. Before the sun set, Heike inherited even more.

When Heike left Herr Zimmermann with his evening nourishment, she didn't notice Günther lurking. Once she boarded her bus, he knocked firmly on Zimmermann's door. He convinced him that he owed emoluments for services rendered.

The headstrong girl refused to accept payments. Regardless, she had unquestioned access to his cashbox. Heike irritated Zimmermann with her persnickety accounting of expenditures. Diplomatically, Günther shared a plan of payment. It was masterly made since Heike need never know; thus, she'd no mean to refuse.

"Shall we call it a monthly *stipend* of twenty marks?"

Herr Zimmermann sat at the mini table enjoying Heike's lintel soup and the fresh bread she'd brought. He looked over his shoulder at Inka laying in her pre-slumber torpor.

"That hardly seems enough," he concluded.

"Herr Zimmermann, if we pay Heike what she's worth, we'd have no money for ourselves."

The woodworker declined debate. In his cavalier stance towards personal finances, he directed Günther to the cash box and trusted him to help himself.

"She will scold me when she notices," he predicted.

"Tell her you made a wager at work and lost," Gunther suggested.

"I'm not brave enough!"

The two men shook hands and parted as friends.

Ossi economics, in an amended form, existed still.

Unable to supervise everything, Heike learned to delegate authority. Nadine, willingly, carried some of the burden, aided by Genossin from the nearly defunct FDJ. The trio reported to her twice a week. Heike discovered that the skills and resources of her lieutenants exceeded all expectations.

"Here's two hundred eighty marks," Heike announced less than forty-eight hours after appealing to Günther.

"That's leaves you with some money to negotiate extras if you can."

Lilo took the envelope only to return it.

"The printer keeps the same business hours I do," she reminded. "I can give you a street address, but I can't go to Jena. I have one more week before I can buy my partnership; I won't be running errands."

"I'll cover for you."

"Mist! If Herr Meißner drives up to find someone in my place, he can cancel the agreement. Take the Trabi and go."

"I don't have a license," Heike reminded.

"You never did, Frau Marx! Take the train."

"I can't spend other people's money!"

Lilo's jaw set, and her eyes flashed.

"I'll wring your neck if you don't leave me alone!"

Lilo could make good her threat. Heike secured the address and hurried away.

"I've no license," Günther confided.

"How'd you manage in the army?" she demanded.

"I rode in trucks, or I walked – a lot."

An epiphany:

"Günther, I need a job. Know any?"

"Are you insane? Nearly everyone worked for the government. The government is gone."

"Rosa's Children needs money. I can turn over all earnings since I have no needs."

Typisch Heike.

"Even Rosa Luxemburg needed something for herself. What about school? You're a year behind. You can't get into university until you finish."

Heike remained undaunted. It was so simple. Why did Günther muddy the water? She was a proud member of the proletariat; where did university enter in? Her father was a worker, why should she lust after better? If her sweat produced enough money to keep the Children afloat, she'd sweat. The days of barter and trade were confined to historical footnotes. In the *new* world, the only negotiable currency was money. Heike was prepared to exchange her labor to keep Rosa's Children alive.

"Right now, I must get to Jena," she reported. "One step at a time."

Günther turned and sniffed the air and looked at the sky.

"Sell something for train fare," he suggested. "If I can find enough for myself, I'll go with you."

Heike stepped to Günther but resisted taking his arm. She hardly considered herself a clinger, but she could have hugged him.

"What if we hiked to Jena and bussed back?" she asked.

Günther nodded. Heike wanted to make a sacrifice. Rosa made many. It's only fitting she follows the example of a hero.

"I'll bring beer and water," he suggested.

"I'll bring sandwiches and apples."

She must arrange with Nadine and Hanna, but she was confident.

"How long would it take?"

He shrugged.

"If we keep a good, steady pace, four hours?"

She thought. For Günther it was one more march. For Heike, it was *Abenteuer*!

"I'll meet you at the Sternbrücke at half six," he announced.

* * *

Günther Neubert was invigorated by his rapid march through empty streets. His backpack was secured and lighter than the "old days." It felt good to be on the move again. Once, he thought army life was all he'd wanted – plenty of time outdoors and contributing to the protection of loved ones. He knew Heike wouldn't meet him. If she did arrive, she'd present excuses.

He wouldn't wait; he'd hike to the Belvedere Palace. He'd enjoy a grand view for an hour or so before returning for lunch. On the way home, he would stop at the Jacobs' home and rattle Heike's cage. As he approached the bridge, he slipped an arm out of its strap and let the backpack dangle from the one shoulder.

"About time!" a voice hailed from across the river.

He got his free arm back through the strap and shrugged the pack back into place.

"How long have you been waiting?" he asked cheerily.

"Long enough to be halfway to Jena."

He smiled, realizing how he'd fooled himself.

* * *

The weather was warm for several days but, in honor of their hike, the sun crept over the hills with a vengeance. It was pleasing enough for a bit. They walked under the swaying green of road-side trees. Birds flitted for safety and sang merrily as they passed. The pair followed farm tracks when they paralleled the road.

Inevitably, however, they were forced to blaze a trail through tall grasses and ripening crops. They forced a fox to abandon its lair. They saw only the billowing red tail as it passed into a nearby thicket. Heike turned to catch Günther's expression. It was clear he'd witnessed the sight.

A few minutes later, they watched a snake slither ahead for a few feet before finding refuge to the side of their path. Again, no words passed between them; none were needed. They maintained a steady pace while scanning ahead, hoping for additional wildlife encounters.

Heike's thoughts turned to Jana and Paul. They had, in Heike's presence, communicated volumes merely by exchanging glances. Heike came to understand how words are, sometimes, superfluous. Her heart raced whenever she and Günther communicated tacitly.

By nine o'clock, they began taking in sail. Günther rolled up his trousers and unbuttoned his shirt. Heike removed her trousers. She wore Nadine's dark blue NDJ shorts underneath. Eventually, she unbuttoned her shirt. She wasn't modest with Gunter and oncoming traffic was of no consequence.

They agreed not to rest. Instead, they slowed their pace for a few minutes. Heike demanded they keep moving.

Her stamina awed Günther. What kept her going? Werner Ecke made great personal sacrifices. Was Heike Jacobs trying to be worthy of him? She looked comical with her bra peeking out of her sweat-stained shirt. However, no one could accuse her of slacking.

She marched on with grit and determination. *"Sunshine patriot"* sprang into his head. Where had he heard it? Lilo spoke of it years before. Well, Heike was no "sunshine patriot."

It was Heike's first time in Jena. The optic works, the university tower, and Napoleon, (against whom university students joined the Prussians in opposing) constituted the sum of her knowledge. Navigation, however, was simple. They asked the way to the market square. From there, a Vopo directed them.

The man with whom they spoke was, decidedly, *not* Lilo's friend. He was a sardonic poltroon concerned only with making an advantageous deal. Did he ever support the SED? If so, he'd converted to Mammon. The layout Heike envisioned impressed him not; Lilo's stirring text was nothing more than a word count.

If Adolf Hitler stormed in to demand a print job, the stiff-necked boob would swap morals for gold without qualms. Günther admired how Heike *reasoned* with the Chef. He admired her self-control and how she rationed her bursts of anger. She, instinctively, knew when fury was an asset.

Similarly, she knew when calm, friendly, banter and a pinch of charm could advance her cause. Ultimately, she demanded two design flourishes her adversary insisted would cost an additional hundred. Heike took a deep breath and explained the printing business to him.

Several times the harried man glanced at Günther as if seeking aid. Each time, Günther responded with an expression signaling he wasn't eager to risk his life. Twice, the besieged printer announced the deal was off; he'd not print at any price. Both times Heike pointed out the folly of his financial deleteriousness.

Damn, Günther thought. *Heike isn't above arguing like a capitalist!"*

Heike presented her foe with exactly half the agreed amount. She demanded a quality product on time, or the printer could whistle for the remainder. They retired to the market square where the Jena Tower cast a welcome shadow across a car park near a quiet copse. They settled down for lunch.

Günther felt solicitous towards Heike. She'd hiked a considerable way and cultivated a burn on her arms and chest. He wasn't certain she had reserves enough to finish her normal day.

They caught the bus and returned to Weimar in a fraction of the time it took to walk there. Heike sulked. She wanted to walk back. Brushing aside the certainty that she would never have made it, Heike felt she hadn't "sacrificed" sufficiently. She should be stronger. She should have more endurance. Somehow, she resented Günther for her own weakness. She pouted and shunned him during their return journey.

After a shower, Günther bussed to the Zimmermann's abode. He didn't enter; should Heike suspect he was "spying," he'd earn an aria.

When Hanna emerged, Günther whistled and waved. She hurried to the tree where he sat, recovering from his morning excursion.

"Forgive my not getting up. I'm sore."

Hanna didn't object to this lack of social protocol. Instead, she sat expectantly next to him.

"How is she?" he asked.

"Sleepwalking," the busty brunette replied.

He nodded.

"Did she tell you about it?"

"Only the highlights."

He nodded.

"I wanted to help," Hanna added.

"She threw you out," he concluded.

Hanna hesitated a moment.

"I wouldn't say that, exactly," she replied.

They paused to enjoy a late afternoon breeze.

"They don't call her Frau Marx for nothing," Hanna continued. "If she sees a chance for martyrdom, she jumps."

"Admirable, but martyrs have such a bad habit of dying."

Hanna smiled for her own amusement. She hoped Günther didn't notice.

"I must catch a bus."

Her announcement pierced a thoughtful pause. She stood and dusted herself off. Just as she turned to leave, he called her back for a moment.

"Am I chasing something that doesn't exist?" he asked bluntly. "Is Heike a shining example or a *Klugscheißer?*"

Hanna was astounded.

"You're asking me?"

"I'm asking you."

Hanna's chest swelled – more than normal. Günther Neubert asked a serious question. It was flattering to be considered an equal, but her best judgment was at stake. The matter demanded deliberation. Heike was a pain, but –

"She's no Klugscheißer," she decided.

"No?"

She shook her head.

"I can't admire a Klugscheißer. I admire Heike, so – there it is."

He nodded approvingly and Hanna took her leave.

Too sore to move and too concerned to want to, Günther retained his post. More than just his muscles ached. His quandary over his true feelings for Heike haunted him.

An hour passed. Had she seen him lurking in the evening shadows? Of course, she'd resent being spied upon. The Heike he knew, or thought he knew, wouldn't hide; she'd storm out of the hovel and tear him off a strip.

Something was not right.

He allowed her five more minutes. After waiting twelve minutes, he struggled to his feet and reacquainted himself with protesting muscles. He crunched across a gravel path and shuffled along the flagstones leading to Herr Zimmermann's door.

He knocked on the sturdy frame and waited. After several anxious moments, the door opened. He was confronted by the disturbed visage of a man holding a baby and a half-consumed bottle of milk. Recognizing Günther, he opened the door wide and allowed him to enter.

Günther waited between the door and the tiny kitchen while Zimmermann closed the door. He looked for Heike. Not finding her, he entertained fantastic notions; she'd escaped through a window.

"I'm glad you've come," the harried father whispered.

Had Heike's temper turned on an innocent man? That was unacceptable!

"She was waiting to clean the dishes," Herr Zimmermann began.

Günther noticed a pot, frying pan, plate, glass, knife and fork ready for Heike's attention. Zimmermann looked like a puppy expecting a beating.

"She sat down while I ate and she – she –"

Günther feared the worst.

"She went to sleep. I couldn't wake her. I was afraid she'd fall and hurt herself."

"Where –?"

Zimmermann nodded his head and Günther followed the gesture until he peered into the tiny chamber serving as the bedroom. Heike lay on the far side of the bed breathing deeply.

"Why did you put her way over there?" Günther asked crossly.

It would be a challenge to carry an inert figure sideways past the end of the bed. It would be equally difficult to extract her. Günther wasn't certain his aching body was up to it.

"This was Monika's side," Zimmermann notified softly.

Of course! Heike couldn't pass out on a shrine.

"What do I do?" the young father asked.

Günther slithered to the far side without crashing into the clothes shrunk or kicking the bed. Gingerly, he sat down on the edge and examined the body. Heike's forehead, cheeks and nose were ruddy but not badly burnt. Her mouth was wide; volumes of air and carbon dioxide exchanged places.

He shook her gently, adding force as he progressed. His efforts were rewarded with minimal stirring. Next, he started patting the sides of her face. Eventually, Heike smacked her lips, opened her eyes but saw nothing.

Günther hoped it was exhaustion. He feared an undiagnosed Leipzig injury was the problem.

"I can catch the bus into town and fetch her father," Günther volunteered. "He can drive out and take her home, but it will be an hour or two."

"I doubt she'll care," Zimmermann said.

Günther undid the buttons of her shirt.

"What are you doing?"

"Trying to make her comfortable," Günther snapped. "Do you have something she can wear?"

Had he noticed the nearby photograph, Günther would realize Heike couldn't squeeze into anything of the late Frau Zimmermann. The possibility of a half-naked girl in his bed spurred the man to quick action. He lay his daughter where his wife should be and sorted through the shrunk to bring out a thin pajama top. Where Monika's things were too small, Herr Zimmermann's pajamas were huge, but they'd serve.

Sure enough, Heike was burned below the neck. He cursed himself for being part of a hair-brained trek. He removed the filthy shirt without appreciably disturbing her. When he unfastened her trousers, Herr Zimmermann retired with his daughter to a neutral corner.

"She is wearing shorts," Gunter announced. "Help me get her arms in this thing."

Not until the pajama top was buttoned and modesty was served did Zimmermann begin feeling comfortable.

"Couldn't she just stay here the night if she had to?"

The man's eyes grew huge, and he looked at Inka as if expecting reproach.

"Well, I – it not – I mean –"

"She'd be safe enough, wouldn't she?" His tone was demanding.

Herr Zimmermann's embarrassment over a breach in propriety instantly turned into indignation.

"How could you even suggest –?"

"I'm not suggesting anything, Herr Zimmermann. I want assurance that she will be safe."

"You think her father –?"

"He's a hard man and as pigheaded as she. When I tell him what we did, he'll be very angry with me, her, you, and the world. His idea of *teaching her a lesson* might include locking her out."

Herr Zimmermann backed away and shook his head.

"No! Impossible!"

"She wouldn't stay here," Günther's frustration showed itself. "Heike has many friends."

One, in particular.

The moment Nadine learned of the predicament, she acted. Heike risked her life for her in Leipzig; she'd not allow her to be marooned in Weimar.

Berlin

Ute was stunned, unsettled, frightened, and dispirited. She'd heard more than she wanted to know. She realized she was only hours away from losing the child she loved more than herself.

Her mind slipped a cog. She wanted to go to Museum Island and see the Pergamon alter. She'd seen pictures and learned so much as a schoolgirl, but the monument was on the wrong side of a line. Now, she'd crossed that line. She insisted that Sabine come with her.

Sabine was embarrassed and ashamed. Ute refused to speak German. She acted like an obnoxious American tourist. She cooed over the alter; she examined every inch of it up close. Sabine, mortified by her guardian's behavior and language, fled to an adjoining exhibit.

The market gate of Roman Miletus was more to her liking. She was one among a hushed crowd that admired the ancient structure. She found a place to sit and studied the monument carefully.

Several minutes later, Ute arrived. She also studied the stone edifice respectfully. She turned to examine the rest of the room and her eyes fell on Sabine. This time, she did not shame the girl. Instead, she smiled and gave a finger wave before passing through the portal to examine Babylon.

Ute was a novice tourist. She opted to make the most of her visit to ancient Babylon. Sabine let her go.

"*Donkey churn,*" she grumbled softly.

That was what Ute said to the policeman who pointed the way to the museum complex. Sabine was never more ashamed of the woman. She'd come near slapping her for being loud and boorish.

Ute dallied for two hours. Sabine hadn't come to Berlin to explore museums, but Ute found it exciting and fascinating. Hopefully, the exhibits and the passage of time would allow a return to sanity or, at least, a sense of decorum.

As she waited, she imagined the men and women, the wagons, and carts that had passed through this monumental gate to the commercial center of an important city. Bach's Air wafted through her head and calmed her.

Finally, Ute reappeared. Sabine made her come to her.

"I'm sorry," she said softly. "I've settled down. Still, it will be a long time before I get used to – well, I still have Little Aaron to look after."

"No more *donkey churns*?"

Ute blushed.

"I promise," she replied.

It was Ute's idea to phone Beckmann from a pay phone in the lobby.

"Are you on the Alex?"

"No," Sabine replied, "we're in Pergamum."

"We're in business," he continued. "The prints are verified. Everything is above the table now. Your father has no phone. I'll leave in two hours to speak with him. Can you catch a train for Frankfurt in the morning?"

"Which station?" Sabine asked, translating Ute's question.

"They leave twice an hour from the Hauptbahnhof."

Ute nodded.

"I'll meet you at the Frankfurt station and take you to your father."

"What time?" Ute asked through Sabine.

"I'll meet the Berlin trains starting at ten-thirty. I'll stay until you arrive."

Before returning to the hotel, Ute insisted on a detour to the department store. Once, it was the busiest and most well-stocked of the Ossi retail outlets. There was hardly a trace of its former incarnation.

Nearly every vestige of a socialist past had been swept aside and Wessi goods assaulted consumers from every display and every shelf.

Sabine wondered what Ute sought. Their budget didn't allow for souvenirs. Rather than risk interrupting Bach's Air, the girl dutifully followed her taciturn companion.

Ute consulted the information board by an escalator and initiated a search. Moments later, they found the books – almost all Wessi and greedily examined by burgers suffering from forty years of forced literary hibernation. It was the most crowded area on the entry floor.

Ute located several atlases. She took up a paperbound road map compilation. She consulted the index, found Riesa, and paged through to a map number. Suddenly aware of the mission, curious Sabine looked over Ute's shoulder.

"Oh, no!" Ute whispered.

"What?"

Sabine scanned a portion of Germany previously unknown to her. Ute's hands trembled while searching for a letter coordinate. Next, her finger slid down the page to a number coordinate. They spied it simultaneously.

Riesa.

"Sabine," Ute announced. "You're Saxon."

"So? Do I have to invade England?"

Ute closed the book and replaced it.

"There are so many dialects in this country," Ute reminded. "I can manage most of them, but when someone speaks Sachsish, I can't understand a word. Not a word! Not *Ja* or *Nein* or *Ute*."

"So?" Sabine demanded.

"Among other things, I want to know what you're talking about."

"What makes you think I'll learn Sachsish?"

"Who made you learn Swabish?"

They burst through the swinging doors and back into the bake oven of The Alex.

"Sabine, you're Saxon. That's part of who you are. You'll learn your language. Silesian is next, I suppose."

"Silesia is Slavic," Sabine recalled from some stray information she obtained in a previous life.

"Your mother's name was von Posen, remember. Posen is in Silesia."

Ute set off. Sabine followed.

"Where are you going?"

"The hotel!"

"You plan on eating there?"

That arrested the march. Ute considered the rocket elevator and how it kills appetite. The foundling hadn't eaten since stuffing herself that morning. Ute threw up her arms betraying lost composure. She eyed a bratwurst stand suspiciously.

"Last night? Did you?"

Sabine followed her glance.

"I've got scruples, remember?"

She didn't intend to sound sarcastic, but that's how harried Ute interpreted it. She looked up into the azure sky, sucked in the burning air, and turned around. She sighed.

"Let's *bahn* West and get real food."

"It will be dear," Sabine cautioned. "How about the cafeteria."

"*Wohin?*"

"Careful, you're German is showing."

Ute made a face. Sabine motioned to the department store. The top floor featured a café. Sabine could read a store directory too.

It made perfect sense. They could wait on themselves; it would be cheap; they needn't leave a tip.

* * *

The moment they entered their room, Sabine stormed into the bathroom and turned on the hot water. She marched to her suitcase and gathered her under things. Ute watched quietly while Sabine dumped them into the steaming water.

"Those won't dry before morning," Ute warned.

Sabine shrugged.

"You're paranoid?"

"If those slugs are still around, there's no telling where their filthy hands have been."

"You intend to put your undies in the hotel safe?"

"I carry them with me."

"Sabine, really?"

"Where I go, they go."

That pronouncement was the terminus of the conversation. Sabine was no longer her little girl; she was a fanatic.

"I want to call baby," Ute moaned.

"It will cost thousands of dollars," Sabine reminded.

"If they've laid a line to West Berlin, I've got a chance," Ute speculated, picking up the phone.

Surprisingly, she got a crisp connection to Fürth. She kept the conversation as abbreviated as possible. Once Sabine's things were sufficiently scalded, she wrung them out and draped them over towel racks and the shower-curtain rod.

Sabine stood with her arms crossed at the window with Bach resonating placidly in her head. Ute sat for a moment, reflecting on the news that Aaron was fine, was in the company of Marion and the boys, and spent the entire afternoon at the house. He provided all the entertainment his Oma and Opa could wish for. That's the good news. The bad news was being stuck in East Berlin with someone else's daughter.

Across from Sabine's bed was Molly's dress, looking formidable, but somehow not quite right. Sabine brought it expressly for the purpose of meeting her father, but Ute suspected the garment had an additional story.

"Someday, I'll buy you a really nice dirndl," she promised.

"You need boobs to wear a dirndl," Sabine shot back.

Silence.

Another conversation DOA.

Ute was disappointed. Once, she'd great plans for mother-daughter matching dirndls. That ship had sailed. Sighing, Ute went to the window, hoping for companionship.

"What are you looking at?"

"Just watching the people on the Alex. Half the people down there are women. Half of them are named Sabine."

"Please."

"Half the rest are Heike."

"Don't fall into that trap like I did," Ute pleaded. "I thought a name was so important, but it's the least important thing. If it's such a bother, go by Aleksandra. Such a unique spelling."

"True," Sabine seconded.

Weimar

Her eyes fluttered open. She knew exactly where she lay. She recognized Frau Zimmermann's functional if dainty curtains. No shop in the DDR sold such attractive wares. They must be homemade.

She was uncomfortable on her back. She attempted to turn onto her side. Heike's body, from her neck to her toes, screamed in protest, so she aborted the attempt.

It was Leipzig all over.

Heike Jacobs hated her frailty. She hated her inability to absorb a nightstick blow; she hated being too weak to tangle with Lilo or defend herself should the Amazon wrap her hands around her throat. She hated being a coward with the Vopos. She hated not fending off sunstroke with impunity. Most of all, however, she hated herself because she couldn't win back her stolen country.

Death, a nemesis posing as a Genossin, urged her on, promising they'd be alone together. If only she'd died in Leipzig, the world would be the better for it. Monika Zimmermann hadn't been afraid. She thought only to save Inka. Fear did not prohibit her a last, heroic act.

There was a sharp knock at the door before it flew open.

"Guten Morgen, Herr Zimmermann."

Damn anyone so cheery!

"Hanna!"

It hurt to call out. Her voice was unrecognizable. Hanna peered into the bedroom nook. She couldn't immediately identify the person she discovered. She looked at Herr Zimmermann who sat at the table, studying Inka's crib.

"Hanna!"

The buxom girl recognized Heike.

"Bring me something to drink. Anything."

The grating voice communicated urgency. Hanna hurried to the tiny refrigerator where she found a liter bottle of orange juice and another of mineral water. She grabbed the water and fetched a mug from the cupboard. Quickly, the water was delivered to the supplicant.

Meanwhile, Herr Zimmermann waited for the commotion to rouse his daughter. Heike moved slowly. She grimaced and made sickening noises. Instinctively, Hanna used her free hand to urge the sufferer into a sitting position. Heike reached for the mug, but Hanna kept a sure grip should things go awry.

"What is it?" she asked of Herr Zimmermann.

"She fell asleep," he shrugged.

"I figured that much," she assured, fetching a refill.

"She was – sick, or something. Günther undressed her."

It was important Hanna know that.

"What's wrong?" Hanna asked, trusting Heike this time.

"Günther undressed me?" she demanded of him. "What was he doing here?"

"I think, he was checking on you."

"What happened?" Hanna demanded anew.

Heike started. Water came out her nose and splashed on the pajama top. She howled.

"Sorry!" she gasped, employing the English word sweeping the country.

Heike was in her element, suffering and derisive. Hanna was mollified. She'd been confronted with an impossible scene. She knew, instantly, that the most obvious conclusion was the one furthest from truth.

"Ah, *Liebling*," Zimmermann cooed into the stroller, "You need a change before Frühstück?"

"When did Lilo threaten you?" Hanna asked, ignoring the nearby drama.

"Tuesday."

Hanna nodded.

"On Monday, two Wessi businessmen spoke with her. They offered her money to go to Köln for training. They think she could make the Olympic team."

"They came here?"

Hanna nodded again.

"They wanted her badly enough to speak in person."

"And?"

"She threw them out."

Heike groaned. At least she wasn't the only fool. Selling junk for a beggar's income when her housing and meals could be paid for while she pursued something she loved – no wonder Lilo had been angry!

* * *

Rolf arrived in the Trabi just as Hanna carried Inka to the bus stop. Herr Zimmermann had left for work; Heike hated the house being unlocked all day. Though every movement caused her pain, she sat in the chair and left a note on the table. Then, she insisted Rolf bring the cash tin with him, hoping Herr Zimmermann wouldn't need money before her return.

She insisted on walking unassisted, but her steps were small and painful. It took three tries to fold into the passenger seat. After Rolf closed the door behind her, she put her feet on the floorboard and pushed, relieving pain in her hips and back.

He didn't growl or tell her she was stupid. Amazing! He tended to his stupid daughter and would be late for work. Assisting her was foolish and unexpected; to do so without comment was unprecedented.

Once home, he helped her out of the car rather than bully her. She watched him drive away and wondered what had happened to the universe during the night. He'd spoken only a dozen or two words during the entire episode. Not one of them was dedicated to her worthlessness.

It took all her effort to pick up her pack. She shuffled to the steps and confronted her greatest challenge. She could not lift her foot high enough to mount the first step, let alone the next. She tried several times, determined to ignore the pain. Each failed attempt, literally, sucked the air out of her body.

She began crying. Tears ran down her face and dripped off her chin; her ribs exploded each time her diaphragm contracted. Stupid, bloody, worthless fool! Her brain wouldn't fill a gnat's navel.

She was a stupid oaf, physically incapable of entering a house. The steps she mastered as a two-year-old were, now, as formidable as the Alps. She wanted to shout for help, but her pride wouldn't allow.

Ultimately, she dropped the pack and leaned forward to brace herself against the door. She sank to her knees onto the red sandstone of the first step. Her shoulders burned, her breath came in bursts. Sweat poured off her forehead, down her neck and back.

With a burst of her remaining strength and mobility, she pulled at the handle. The door was propelled open by her body weight. Her hands slapped against the wooden floor, breaking her fall. She whimpered from the pain.

Anne was instantly aroused, and immediately on her feet.

"What is it?" Nadine called from above.

Slowly, arduously, and painfully, Heike crawled into the house. Anne attempted to pick her up, but Heike waved her away. Heike feared a miscalculation on either side could send Werner Ecke's daughter spilling out into the street.

"What is it?" Nadine repeated.

A centimeter at a time, Heike crawled into the house. Each of those centimeters was punctuated with pain, remorse, humiliation, and self-immolation. She used her feet to shut the door. Heike waited for Nadine to get down the stairs and find an unworthy sister in the attitude best suited to her desserts.

Anne watched the pathetic scene and shuffled off to the kitchen. Nadine was at a loss. Heike refused Nadine's help. She crawled to the stairs, grasped the railing, and lifted herself up. Once, on her feet, Heike let her sister help her to the couch.

Nadine heard Günther's report of the previous evening. She wasn't sufficiently appreciative of the reason for an overnight in the Zimmermann Hotel until she saw the pain etched on Heike's face. Anne appeared, predictably, with a mug of steaming cocoa. Nadine abandoned the couch and knelt on the floor before the prodigal. Unable to manage the cup, Heike allowed Nadine to guide the mug to her lips.

Anne sat down in that place vacated by her real daughter. She put a comforting arm around the shoulders of the pretend daughter.

"I was changing the beds," Nadine reported.

It was the wrong day to change beds, as Heike well knew.

"Jürgen will be here tonight," Nadine explained.

Great! For the second time, he could see Heike, the failure.

* * *

Nadine did Heike's work. Once again, she avoided protest. Heike shuffled slowly to the kitchen sink and cleaned the cocoa mug. As she dried it, she searched, for the thousandth time, for the secret cocoa stash.

The bitter-sweet drink made her feel better. She added sugar to the shopping list which, of course, Nadine must fill. Heike's job was to convalesce enough to tend Herr Zimmermann later. Most of the morning, Heike and Frau Jacobs sat quietly on the couch while Nadine flew about cleaning, washing, and scrubbing. The dearth of complaints added much to Heike's guilt.

It was Nadine who produced a nice Mittagsessen. She brought to the table three bubbling and aromatic servings of toast Hawaii. Only Nadine had mastered Anne's secret of baking atop the hotplate; Heike's attempts never approached Nadine's quality.

They expected Rolf who never arrived. Maybe he confronted an emergency. Likely, he simmered over Heike's misconduct. Regardless, everyone was expected for the major meal of the day. By Rolf's own edict, anyone absent must go without; he was not above his own laws.

The open border made available items seldom seen in the DDR. Thanks to Heike's foraging, Nadine secured the right bread, sliced ham, cheese, and pineapple slices to make a delightful lunch. Further, she topped each serving with a bright red cherry. In addition, she produced a sliced-carrot salad and a banana for afters. To round out the feast was a fresh pot of tea.

Heike was starved, which all considered a good sign. Hungry as she was, she avoided gulping her food. She learned from Nadine who dealt with her missing teeth by altering and slowing her chewing.

"How did Pabst react to Günther last night?"

"He didn't shout, and he didn't make speeches," Nadine reported.

"He didn't scold this morning," Heike nodded.

Something was afoot. When Rolf failed to act like Rolf, something was wrong.

"Maybe he knows your father is looking for you."

Heike ignored her aching ribs and sat straight.

"Did you tell him?"

Nadine did not reply. She didn't have to.

"He shouldn't waste time thinking about me," Heike announced.

"You are part of this family," Nadine reminded calmly.

Frau Jacobs made a noise. It was enough to signal both her understanding and approval.

"Günther and Pabst had a long talk," Nadine reported.

"Surprise!" Heike sighed.

"I didn't hear. Papa gave me one of those looks –"

Heike knew the "look." Going to their room and shutting the door was the expected response.

"I think –" Nadine began.

She sipped at her tea.

"I'm only guessing," she tried again.

"I understand, Nadine. What's do you guess?"

Nadine stalled a moment more before taking a breath.

"I think Günther asked for your hand," she whispered.

If Heike could produce a sardonic laugh, she'd have brought one forth. Nadine, as a rule, didn't venture into speculation; when she did, there were no half measures.

"Civilized people don't ask for '*hands*' anymore," Heike pouted. "Besides, I'm not old enough. Beside the besides, Günther isn't daft."

Nadine remained placid.

"You've sworn at and fought with everybody. You've kicked or hit everybody. Somehow, you've no known enemies. Before I was banished, Günther told us how proud of you he was. He said how you haggled with that printer after hiking all that way. If the election were today, I know who'd get his vote for Chancellor."

Fearing Frau Jacobs might, somehow, be disquieted, the girls confined their conversation to whispered exchanges. Muddled though she was, Anne Jacobs was not deaf. Any morose tones might produce anxiety.

"Günther didn't ask for anybody's 'hand.' Certainly not mine!"

"Think this through," Nadine encouraged. "When you didn't come home last night, you know Pabst's mood. Suppose he found out, from someone else, that you and Günther were together. Pabst would rip his arms off if he suspected Günther and you –.

"Instead, here comes Günther, the Weiße Ritter, to explain. You were exhausted but, otherwise, okay. Most of all, he wanted us to know you were safe. After I'm sent away, Günther talked to Pabst for a while. What would they discuss? Solar wind?"

Heike remained incredulous.

"Yes, I'm guessing," Nadine admitted, "but if Günther wants to keep Pabst from treating him like those Stasi goons, he better deliver something substantial. He can't be seeing you behind his back; Pabst would smack you both. This way if you say you're off to meet Günther – well –"

"You'd better get the shopping done," Heike urged.

"Fine," Nadine said with heat. "But I'll bet you six washings that Günther and Pabst reached an agreement."

"I'll ask them both," Heike promised.

Nadine, in reply, staked her claim to the accuracy of her hypothesis. A response which, in fact, startled Heike.

"Make sure you do."

* * *

Günther waited outside. He'd imposed upon Zimmermann enough. Bound as the man was to his daughter and the memory of his late wife, the widower was easily embarrassed. Most of what he knew was surmised from limited contact and information obtained through Heike and Hanna's anecdotes. He realized Zimmermann was a slave to routine, and if Heike were part of that routine, Günther constituted a disruption.

It's best to wait.

Eventually, Heike hobbled out. She remained stiff and sore, but she picked up her feet rather than shuffled. Günther was also stiff and sore but not to the point of impairment. He abandoned his observation post. Heike's eyes remained fixed on the ground.

The smallest protuberance might create pain. Nevertheless, her peripheral vision was not impaired. She expected a reprimand for her shameless behavior of the previous afternoon. Instead, she was supplied with a helping hand.

"Danke."

He was prepared to lift her onto the bus but was wise enough to let her struggle unassisted. She made it. They sat in silence. At Goetheplatz, Heike searched for Lilo. Crossing the street, they detected no sign. In her place, seated between the open double doors of a gray van, was an unkempt, sunburned man; Heike assumed it was Herr Meißner.

"Jürgen comes tonight. He'll want to see you."

Günther was delighted. He was anxious to see his old friend. The quarter-hour journey from Goetheplatz to the Jacobs home stretched beyond the norm. Günther held Heike's arm the whole way, and she was grateful. It was a tangible reassurance that her behavior and physical collapse of the previous day hadn't severed their bond.

Jürgen's arrival was certain. In addition to Rolf's bull-elk voice, there was another voice, nearly as loud. Heike invited Günther inside and waxed emphatic in overruling his objections. At this juncture, Heike held tightly to his arm. She opened the door with one hand and strained to push Günther through with the other.

Poor Jürgen faced an untenable situation. He was forced to greet one of them first. Ultimately, he threw his arms around Günther and slapped his back. This produced obvious discomfort. Heike didn't begrudge her brother's decision nor did she mind waiting her turn.

Jürgen bent slightly to take her in his arms. She stood on her toes and threw her own arms around his neck. She paid no heed to her protesting calves nor was she deterred from lifting her arms over her head. Jürgen squeezed hard with joy. Heike was so delighted that her pain drowned in rapture.

"How was the cocoa?" she asked.

"Sweet!" he replied.

He kissed her on both cheeks and let her down. She was instantly relieved and bereaved. She could have wallowed in his loving arms for hours.

The table was set for Abendsbrot and Günther's presence made things awkward. Heike apologized profusely, first to Nadine who prepared the victuals, and to Rolf for bringing an unannounced guest.

Her motives and intentions did not meet objections. Heike, suddenly adroit in social protocol, suggested she and Günther share a plate on the couch. As provisions were plentiful, an unexpected mouth was not a disaster. Günther and Heike took bread and cheese, a slice of meat and a slice of butter and placed them on a single plate, leaving Heike's usual place at the table undisturbed. She and Günther retired to the couch.

"Ah! Is something going on here?" Jürgen teased.

No one replied. That was answer enough.

After eating, Heike took the plate into the kitchen where wash water heated. Nadine brought in the residuals and stored them with practiced efficiency. Her attempt to help in washing, drying, and putting away, was waved off.

"Stay with your brother," she whispered.

"You can't leave Günther alone."

"He's with his best friend," Heike reminded.

Gently, she nudged Nadine away.

Heike was content to hear the conversation from her workstation. It was the usual banal banter. Friends were happy to exchange news. Günther supplied army anecdotes in return for Jürgen's university experiences. Unexpectedly, however, Günther asked about the curious arrangement with Herr Zimmermann.

This was out of bounds. The visit was supposed to be light. If Günther wanted to know about the Zimmermann matter, he'd ample opportunity previously. Nadine recognized the gaff. Before Rolf could make caustic remarks, she interrupted. Her narrative was terse until Heike became a feature.

Quickly, the conversation returned to family – where it belonged. Nadine began an amazing tale, *grossly* exaggerated. Heike boiled. If anyone had a right to relate events, it was she.

Furiously, Heike wiped her hands with a vengeance and draped the towel over the rack none too gently. It was one long step to the entry way. That proved fortuitous. During that extra half-step, she heard something she'd not heard in years.

Rolf was laughing!

This was not the laugh of a man bellowing scathing maledictions. It was not a sarcastic burst nor a short, dismissive guffaw. The laugh reaching Heike's ears was the quaking, rolling roar of a person unable to harness emotion.

Bursting through the narrow opening, Heike's anger evaporated.

Anne sat on the couch, a bright smile on her face. Rolf's laughter was her tonic. The rearranged chairs faced the couch as Günther sat beside the matriarch. Nadine sat Indian style on the floor nearest Günther with Jürgen in the chair to her right. Next to Jürgen, slapping his thigh, doubled up and helpless with laughter, was Rolf Jacobs.

Nadine fed upon this unexpected bonanza. She animated her story with comical hand gestures. Drama and terror were completely expurgated by her raucous comedy. Günther's visage of mirth and Jürgen's quiet quaking kept Heike's objections squelched. Rolf's unbounded display discouraged any reasonable attempt to insert accuracy.

"Heike was terrified of the baby," Nadine continued. "She won't touch it. She won't talk to it! Even Zimmzy notices. And when it's poo time, Heike suddenly remembers she must be someplace else! And Hanna – sweet, petite, cute-cute Hanna – calls Heike *The Princess of Prude*! Can you believe it? Hanna!"

Günther was joining in, but his delight was the result of Rolf's out-of-control antics. He never once looked at Heike.

"Upstairs, Heike is moaning and carrying on," Nadine continued. "That's it, she says, I'll never have a baby! Never! Tie my legs together. No baby! Nein, nein, nein, nein!"

For one confused moment, Heike thought Rolf might fall off his chair. He did not, but he was helpless as Nadine well knew.

"And then, after a while, she says –" Rolf roared so loud, she had to pause.

"And then, she says to me, 'Maybe, after I'm married for twenty years, we'll adopt some nice, sweet nineteen-year-old boy and send him off to university, but that's it!' Then, she starts the Nein-nein thing again."

"Send him off to university?" Rolf repeated between bursts of merriment.

Nadine's recitation was pure fiction. Well, not entirely. Heike not touching the tiny comet was mostly true. Hanna and Nadine had the "delicate touch," and Heike didn't trust herself. Heike turned queasy at the sight of soiled nappies. It was all she could do to wash them after soaking.

Her anger vanished.

If Rolf enjoyment was the result, lie away! Heike was thrilled to see Rolf and Anne enjoying themselves.

It took time for Rolf to regain composure. Only after the comedy highlights ended did Heike join the assembly.

Günther stood and offered his place on the couch. He, further, offered his hand when she sat. Heike assumed he was being excessively gallant. Not until she lowered herself and experienced her screaming muscles did she understand.

After a respectful lapse, Heike asked the question everyone harbored.

"Are you off to the Ostsee?"

Jürgen swayed back as if struck. He covered his reaction, but it was wasted among those who knew him. He glanced at Heike. He was nervous.

"It may not happen this year," he announced.

Rolf was instantly suspicious. Jürgen remained furtive. He averted his eyes and cleared his throat.

"Maybe, I should start at the beginning," he said.

"Reasonable," Nadine concluded, sarcastically.

Her comment earned a nudge from Günther.

"I – um – met a girl – up there."

"I knew from your letters," Nadine announced.

That was true. Heike had sensed it as well. Jürgen's missives were mysterious. They were the basis of lights-out discussions. Jürgen was, clearly, concealing something. A girlfriend was the most obvious candidate.

"Is this serious?" Rolf asked.

"It's serious," Jürgen nodded. "Perhaps, too serious."

This confession weighed heavy. Even Rolf remained silent.

"She's Russian," he confessed. "She's from Leningrad. She studies chemistry. I never knew of her until she came to the coast – with other girls."

Nadine turned to Heike and mouthed the words *Heißer Sommer*.

Heike played sphinx.

"We began seeing each other. There are – problems."

Jürgen deliberately begged the question. The silence was profound, but no one fell into it. He looked around the group, bit his lip and stammered on.

"When her school chums found out she was coming to Germany, they'd turned their backs on her. Her family, both sides, have lived in Leningrad for generations. For them, the war will never be over. She's – home, now."

"You should have gone with," Heike said softly.

"We talked about – it," he responded.

"Marina thought it would be too great a shock. She came to Germany to see for herself. It took over a year, but she learned Germans aren't the pigs she was taught to hate. However, her family – they don't want her to come back to Halle."

"What does she want?" Rolf asked, his temper toward an unknown family showing through.

"She's promised to return in two weeks, no matter what."

"To study?" Nadine asked.

"That's part of it."

"Do they know about Werner Ecke?" Heike asked.

"For the Serovs, Germans are Germans."

They all contemplated the curse of a war that haunted the world still. Had the Thirty-Year War produced so much lasting hatred? It was hard to imagine how.

"Pabst," Jürgen began quietly. "I want to bring her here, to meet you – all. I want to ask her to marry me, but not until after you've met her."

All eyes turned to the volatile head of the family. Unexpectedly, he looked at Heike in a way which unsettled her. He turned his head and meet his son's eyes.

"If you love this girl, you don't need my permission," he stated simply.

"Nevertheless, I'd like to have it."

"And, if her family says no?"

Jürgen rubbed his hands nervously.

"I want to marry her."

"She will disobey her family?"

He continued to rub his hands and looked directly at Heike. Why, she wondered, was everybody looking at her, the Princess of Prude? What business was this of hers?

"I don't speak for her," Jürgen reported.

"What if I told you I forbid it?"

"Papa!" Nadine cried, gaining another Günther nudge.

The silence lingered.

Jürgen took a deep breath.

"I would still ask her to marry me."

All eyes were on Rolf. Everyone feared the worst. Rolf's expression provided no clue. When he stood, there was a collective gasp.

"You are determined, then." Rolf concluded, "I trust you to do as you think is best."

He thrust out his hand. Gratefully, Jürgen stood and accepted it.

* * *

Following the established routine, Heike was the last out of the bathroom. She navigated the stairs with difficulty, but her body was rebounding from her latest folly. As the last in the bedroom, it was her duty to close the door and switch off the lights. She leaned against the high bed.

"You left this girl, Marina, to come to me in Leipzig?" she asked.

"Yes."

She felt a warm hand stroking her hair.

"I know you enjoy guilt, Heike," he began, "but there are two things you must know before you start punishing yourself – again. First, think how I'd feel had I not gone. My sisters were in trouble."

"What about me?" Nadine asked from the neighboring bed. "If I hadn't decided to go to Leipzig, nothing would have happened."

"If I looked after you properly, he'd never have known," Heike responded with fire.

"There's nothing you could do," Nadine repeated for the hundredth time. "What happened was my fault. If anyone's guilty, it's me, and I don't feel guilty."

Ignoring that, Heike returned to Jürgen.

"You said two things."

"Marina insisted I go. She might not have spoken to me again had I not."

Heike accepted the spirit of the announcement. She lifted his hand from her hair, kissed it, and padded softly to her pallet.

Typically, Nadine couldn't let go.

"If she hadn't thrown you out, you'd have left Heike to rot."

Jürgen wasn't in no mood for stupid.

"Of course," he replied. "Why would a sane person leave scenic Halle for a dump like Leipzig?"

That response marked one of the few times Nadine realized her baiting had gone too far.

Berlin-Frankfurt/ Oder

They posted letters from the hotel – one to Gary, one to Aaron and another to Molly. They wrestled with their bags to the S-Bahn and wrestled again at the Hauptbahnhof. By ten-thirty, the train crawled out of the station.

It was a commuter train and not suited for people with more than a briefcase or a shopping bag. Even had there been an overhead rack, neither Ute nor Sabine could heft anything onto it. They did, however, secure adjoining seats. By cramming their luggage into one space, the women could sit across the aisle and keep watch.

Sabine was nervous. Three times she visited the WC. Each time she returned, she inspected her dress and shoes to ensure no damage was done. She hesitated to sit for fear that wrinkles would destroy the hotel-room steaming.

The square-faced, broad-shouldered conductress eyed the pair curiously as she stamped their tickets. The older woman wore foreign clothes; the young one wore a beautiful light blue dress. Where did she get it? Was she an actress? Regardless, there was nothing between Berlin and Frankfurt to justify eye-catching togs.

Sabine worried over her shiny, cream-colored flats. They were cheap and, probably, wouldn't last more than a week of normal use. They didn't go with Molly's dress, but they didn't clash.

"I'll put on my tennis shoes," she decided.

"They'll look ridiculous."

"You said these shoes look ridiculous."

"No," Ute corrected, "I said they looked silly."

"If there's a shoe store in Frankfurt, we might find a good pair."

"Sit down. You make me nervous!"

She did not sit. She refused, partly, because of her natural obstinacy but, primarily, because she hated wrinkles. Unable to pace, she went to the WC again. She examined her face in the mirror and tried to remember the make-up tips Molly provided.

She must brush her hair and put on her face – but not on a train that swayed and lurched. There must be a bathroom with a mirror in the Bahnhof. If not, she'd find some expedient means to make herself presentable – she hoped.

Sabine must get back into the air-conditioned portion of the train before her hair and dress wilted, but she loathed the idea of standing idle while the train crawled along antique tracks. She stared at the toilet and insisted she didn't need to go again. Resigned to a journey to the end of the world, where fox and hare say goodnight, she sighed and left one cramped refuge for another.

Each time the train broke the monotony of its elephantine lumber, it announced a complete stop with a deafening squeal. Each time, this event created a panic in two passengers who searched desperately for the station name. Twice, they found themselves at a station platform near a cow path with few, if any, habitable buildings in sight.

They stopped astride a country road and found it bordered by houses. The forest of lodgepole pine and the fields of grain betrayed its rural nature, but, at the first sign of a settlement of appreciable size, they clung to the window until they found a sign mounted between supporting poles.

"Pillgram?" Ute intoned. "I'm beginning to feel like one. I wish I bought a map."

"I never thought East Germany would be so empty," Sabine confided.

"Me neither. This is the frontier. I expect to see a raiding party of Comanche warriors ride out of those trees any minute."

"It looks a little like Oregon."

Ute didn't think so. Not, at least, any part of Oregon she'd ever seen. She kept the thought to herself.

Finally, they reached a platform of substance in the depth of a substantial cut. There were steps leading to ground level. They weren't unlike those bearing passengers to the *Mary R.*

"Frankfurt Rosengarten," Sabine spoke before Ute had a chance. "I think we're here."

They began hefting their luggage. They dragged, pushed, and lifted to the accompaniment of grunts and Swabish epithets until the "damned baggage" was crammed into the vestibule. There they waited and waited as the train crawled into Frankfurt proper.

It was not impressive. There were apartment buildings and businesses stretching away from the tracks on either side. It was the first population center they'd seen since Fürstenwalde about halfway between Berlin and Frankfurt. There was a drabness, a cold, chilly grayness about the place. Perhaps, it wasn't exactly the end of the world, but it would do.

Finally, the train moaned into a roofed station. Not since Berlin, seemingly months ago, had they had any such tangible evidence of a city.

"There's Herr Beckmann," Ute announced as they rumbled past.

Sabine caught just a glimpse and recognized him from his suit jacket, rotund form, and the way his tie was pulled loose off his neck. At the same instant, she realized something else.

"*Ach, Du Lieber Gott!* Someone's with him!"

Ute pressed her face to the glass and strained to see.

Sabine became unhinged.

"Make up! I must brush my hair and I – I can't get off this train! Not like this!"

"You look fine."

It was no use. Sabine tore through the shoulder bag, containing her makeup. She pulled out a compact and a tube of mascara which Ute yanked from her hands.

"There's no time!"

Sabine inched away from the door and quaked. A passenger opened the accordion doors and a herd filed off. Only a few cast curious glances at the well-dressed girl pressed against the opposite doors.

"I can't go out – not like this."

"Okay, find some gloss."

Frantically, Sabine scrounged through her bag.

"A mirror! I don't have a mirror!"

"Give it me! Hold still."

"I have to pee!"

"Shut up! Think of Bach, and – hold – still."

It was better than a slap in the face. Sabine looked at the ceiling and music began as Ute painted the frightened girl's lips. The shade was very tame; Sabine could have done as well without, but if it soothed an ounce of panic, Ute was willing to participate.

At last, they began hefting bags onto the platform. Herr Beckmann watched the drama unfold. He spoke to the man at his side and led him towards the new arrivals.

Sabine, suddenly, calm, made certain everything was accounted for before lifting the strap of her bag over her head. She smoothed out her dress and adjusted Mrs. Waldron's "passport case" so it rested again at her side.

What to do with the hands? Sabine wished she were holding something, but it was too late. The hands were lead weights at her side. What to do?

As Herr Beckmann drew near, Sabine wove her fingers together and let her hands rest in front of her. It was a preposterous pose, but there was nothing for it. She fidgeted like a guilty defendant before a judge.

Sabine examined the man to the left and slightly behind Beckmann. He was taller than the bureaucrat but not nearly as tall as Aaron. He was built substantially but wasn't as corpulent as Beckmann. The face was weathered and his crow's feet, even at a distance, were pronounced. His hair was light brown and plentiful, and he walked with a shocking limp.

Curiosity urged Sabine forward, but she fought it. She didn't wish to stray an inch from Ute or their "damned luggage" that, moments before, she'd have happily left on the train.

"Herr Bauer," Beckmann said simply and calmly. "This is Sabine."

The softness of Beckmann's voice might well have been a thunderclap. The principals studied each other carefully. Ernst Bauer was amazed to behold someone he never expected to see again. He blinked twice in disbelief and his elongated face radiated awe.

"You look so much like your mother," he croaked.

Sabine found no reply. Instinctively, he stepped forward and took her in his arms. She allowed him to hold her. Turning her head, Sabine heard a galloping heart. It matched the racing of her own.

Other than the terror of the moment, Sabine felt little emotion. This man was a perfect stranger; she had no feelings for him. However, she sensed his holding her was very important. She submitted without reservation. Her surrender might not conform with Saxon culture, but Sabine knew, it was the Swabish thing to do.

* * *

There was just enough baggage to prevent Herr Beckmann from making a single trip to the lodgings. He and Ute drove off to make the necessary arrangements while Ernst and Sabine ordered coffee at the Bahnhof café. They made a noble effort to fill sixteen years. At her father's insistence, Sabine was obliged to tell of her life as a Swabish-American. This she did with the pictures she brought.

Ernst Bauer learned Ute Kaufmann and her history. Aaron Foster's photo was more difficult. Sabine was forced to review how he discovered her. This proved difficult for Herr Bauer.

She fast-forwarded to a lively narrative culminating in slightly exaggerated accounts of the voyages of the *Mary R*. This took some of the edge off, but her listener was dazed by the memory of *that* night. Ultimately, the bulk of Ernst's attention remained on Sabine's face. He drank in every detail.

The resemblance between Sabine and Constanze Bauer was uncanny, yet he delighted in all the subtle differences. Had Giotto and Van Eyck shared the same model, the resulting canvasses could be distinguished easily by any casual observer. Herr Bauer was not a casual observer. There were hundreds of portraits of Constanze embossed on his brain; he'd studied each for nearly seventeen years. Now, Sabine was seated across from him; he admired the similarities and appreciated all the differences.

He noticed Constanze's dimples winking at him when Sabine smiled. Constanze's eyes sparkled, but not as often as he liked. Sabine didn't feel comfortable under his gaze and averted her eyes frequently. However, gestures, facial expressions, and her manner of speaking marked Sabine as a woman with her own personality.

He drank it all; the way she dropped her chin at the end of emphatic sentences, the way her hair danced so slightly when her head moved, and the peculiar effect of her mother's eyes when they focused on him. Then, there were the words. Not only was Sabine's story compelling and well-told, but her enunciation was a precious jewel. He detected a queer accent; the way she said *Ich* without a catch in her throat. When she said *brauche*, as she did frequently, her guttural was hypnotic.

"Sabine," he interrupted her torrent softly. "Do you sing?"

The question frightened her. She didn't want to answer, but she surrendered to his imploring expression. The doubts about her talent surfaced anew. People told her she was very good, but she doubted their sincerity. How could she say all that to the father she hardly knew?

"Ja."

It was the best she could do. Even that came forth with the cautious elongation of doubt. Herr Bauer nodded. His eyes glistened with tears. He placed on hand over hers and, with the other, covered his face to stifle his sobs.

When Ute and her chauffeur returned, Sabine's coffee remained largely untouched. Herr Bauer's handkerchief found much use that day. He alternated between joy and sorrow. Both produced tears.

"Frau Foster, Herr Beckmann," he said with a trembling voice. "I wish to take my not-so-little girl to lunch. I would be honored if you'd join us."

"I'd enjoy nothing more," Beckmann responded. "However, I have a small staff. I cannot afford to be away from the office for long. I'll buy a sandwich and eat as I drive."

Ute almost suggested he leave at once. Her party and she could walk to the hotel quite comfortably. She recalled Herr Bauer's limp and abandoned the suggestion. They boarded Beckmann's sedan and were ferried to the hotel.

They traversed a busy street and turned right toward the river. Not three minutes after leaving the Bahnhof, they parked outside the high-rise hotel. Herr Beckmann saw the trio into the lobby and bid them farewell.

Sabine excused herself under the pretext of escorting her bureaucratic benefactor to his auto.

Ute considered this extremely rude; she promised to have sharp words with the girl when next they were alone. For the moment, however, she was left alone with a man she dared not ignore but could never like. She smiled an embarrassed smile and felt her face changing color.

"She always impetuous," she offered.

"If we must wait, perhaps we should sit."

If he was offended, he masked it well. He hobbled to one of the plush sofas and invited Ute to sit first. When his turn came, his leg made the descent awkward and the landing sudden. He allowed himself a satisfied sigh.

"Frau Foster," he began, "I am the girl's father, but you and your husband are her parents. I owe you more than I can repay. Sabine, obviously, was well cared for and properly raised –"

"Until now," the embarrassed woman inserted, referencing Sabine's abrupt departure.

He waved a dismissive hand.

"She knows her own mind," he stated. "I respect that."

Outside the hotel entrance, in the blistering sun, Sabine held Herr Beckmann's arm with improper familiarity and an alarming firmness.

"I want to find my sister," she reminded.

"Fraulein Bauer, I must have the consent of both parties before I can arrange a meeting. It would mean my job."

"Heike refuses to see Papa. Ask if she'll see me."

"And Herr Bauer!"

"Nein!" she announced. "I promise not to bring Papa. *Verspreche*!"

Her eyes made him believe, but –

"You will find a way to bring them together."

"If Heike wants to see Papa, she will. I won't trick either of them."

He was weakening. She knew it.

"Ask if she'll see me. Bitte, bitte, bitte!"

"I will see."

"Are you saying that to be rid of me?"

It was Beckmann's turn to swear.

"I'll see what I can do. *Ich Verspreche.* Beyond that, no promises."
She nodded and released him.
"You have my room number? Call me Monday."
Once more, a nod.

Herr Beckmann planned to drive directly back to Berlin but decided to take a detour. His next appointment was the following afternoon, and the avalanche of paper wasn't going to disappear. He'd heard of Weimar for much of his life. Now, he had an excuse to have a look.

* * *

It was Sabine's first ride on the Frankfurt elevator. She hardly expected to be launched by rocket catapult, but she wasn't expecting the laborious groans as the tiny box shuttered and banged its way upward. Through the grimy vertical glass slits in the doors, she could make out only indistinguishable blurs. These were enough, however, to confirm the existence of something that moved even slower than the train from Berlin. Her bladder ached, and if she didn't reach the room very soon, there'd be no point.

Finally, the protesting doors creaked open. Sabine slithered through the opening the moment it was wide enough and, following Ute's oral instructions, dashed down the east hall to the last door on the right. She fumbled with the key. She closed the room door and accessed the bathroom to save mortification.

Once the danger was alleviated, she stood before the mirror and applied make-up to her face as well as she could, following Molly's rudimentary lessons. She wasn't much satisfied with the results, but she was a novice. Ute would have served her much better, but it wasn't acceptable to leave Herr Bauer cooling his heels, and it wasn't fair to invite him into the room only to shunt him aside while the women "fussed" in the bathroom. When her skills were exhausted, she brushed her hair.

Her plan was to return at once, but she was arrested by the huge windows on the east wall. The afternoon sun flooded the room despite white, lace curtains. Beyond lay a breath-taking view. She was drawn to the windows.

She pushed back the curtains to enjoy an unobstructed view of the Oder River and Poland. She noticed a lone fisherman standing on a Polish spit. Suddenly, she was tempted to dally to see if he hooked something, but *tempus* tugged.

The elevator remained as she left it. Sabine opened the emergency exit and hurried down the steps. In addition to saving time, it was safer. Ernst Bauer surely noticed Sabine's makeup, but his eyes responded as before.

Sabine caught Ute in a candid, conversational moment. Ute's smile beamed. Additionally, she recalled Molly Waldron's announcement that, with Henry, she need never pretend. Sabine calculated that pretense for her father would constitute rudeness.

The trio left the hotel slowly because of Herr Bauer's limp. They passed the Rathaus and turned onto a pedestrian street. There, shaded by the adjacent building, they found an outdoor café and decided to settle into a vacant table.

The waiter wore a white shirt, black vest, and a black bow tie. He had to be boiling in the heat, but he appeared composed and comfortable. He took their drink orders – beer and Wessi soft drinks were off – so Sabine joined the others in ordering tea.

Drinks and menus came together. Sabine needed only a glance.

"Papa, may I have a schnitzel?"

He looked at her curiously.

"Of course," he replied. "Order what you want."

Ute changed color. Sabine leaned forward and patted her knee reassuringly. The Pig War formally ended with neither bang nor whimper. It ceased with an appreciative gesture for a well-intended policy. To show there were no hard feelings, Ute ordered a schnitzel.

"This is schnitzel?" Sabine asked, disappointed.

"No," Ute replied. "It's paratrooper boot."

Ernst crunched away on a simple salad.

"With the collapse, the sources of supply dried up," he explained. "It's a wonder this place gets any meat at all."

"I don't think they did," Ute commented.

The women satisfied themselves with the potatoes and vegetable sides. These were hardly first-class, but they were far superior to *boot*.

Ute realized the conversation ceased, not due to poor food, but her presence. She felt no resentment, but she regretted accepting Herr Bauer's gracious invitation. She had no right to impose upon Bauer family business – of which there must be a great deal. She excused herself at the first opportunity.

Both father and daughter launched the requisite – perhaps obligatory – protests. Ute remained insistent. Pushing her chair back, her standing up forced gallant Herr Bauer to struggle to his feet. She extended her hand; the gentleman shook it.

Ute examined the girl curiously. It wasn't proper for her to stand, yet she did – in the pale blue dress Ute envied. Hands at her sides, Sabine's dimples appeared with her smile; the unnecessary gesture was a product of respect. Beyond her homage was gratitude and love.

Ute fought down tears as she departed. The twenty-four-story building had attracted her attention. She directed her feet thither. It was a short walk, crammed with a thousand memories. She found a shopping area at the base of the "tallest structure in Brandenburg," and strode into a market.

Bright colors and fancy Wessi packaging nearly crowded Ossi goods off the shelves. Fearing there may not be a restaurateur in the city capable of offering a decent meal, she purchased contingency items. Cursing herself for not bringing a shopping bag, she selected only what she could carry in her hands.

She started towards the hotel only to be arrested by a small news stand. There she fumbled with her grocery items to extract enough cash to claim a regional paper and a book of crossword puzzles. She took her juggling act on a five-minute tour of the capacious sidewalks leading to the hotel lobby. She lay her bounty upon the counter and produced her key card.

This was an annoyance created by the fact that the man who checked her in had taken his lunch break. His replacement checked her registration before fetching the key. She gathered her items and waddled for the elevator. Using her elbows, she summoned the machine and climbed inside. As the vehicle began its noisy climb, Ute took refuge in the knowledge that, should she be trapped inside, she'd not starve.

* * *

Television in the DDR has limited appeal. There was a Polish channel, cluttered with disinteresting items in an indecipherable language. Nevertheless, Ute kept the set at low volume to help her forget she was alone. She sat on the bed munching a cracker and working her fifth crossword. She'd completed almost all of the previous four, but this last, frustrating effort was wearing her down.

The bedside clock marched slowly past nine o'clock. It was still daylight, so she attempted to ignore time. She wanted to pace but resisted the urge. Sabine was out there, somewhere. Moreover, she was with her father. Sabine was officially no longer Ute's concern but unfortunately, her nerves refused to recognize reality.

She chewed the last cracker before exploding in frustration. Finally, Ute heard footfalls in the hallway. She held her breath. Her heart pounded. The knob rattled and Ute fought down an urge to sing.

"Hungry?" she asked with all the normalcy she could summon.

Sabine shook her head and walked to the window. She stood, arms akimbo, looking over the river at the Polish hills catching the rays of the setting sun.

"Posen is not in Silesia," she announced matter-of-factly. "It's in Prussia."

"The Poles might disagree," Ute tried to sound casual. "However, I stand corrected. Did you eat?"

"We had soljanka about an hour ago."

Ute inquired about soljanka and got a terse definition without elaboration. A moment later, Sabine stripped off the dress and hung it up. She gathered a few things and disappeared into the bathroom. Once her showering was completed, she came to her bed in a pajama top only. Without air conditioning, the room was very warm.

Ute attempted to remain calm while working a crossword. She'd given up trying to squeeze solutions out of nothing and carried the pretense by filling in the empty boxes with any word, German or English, that fit. However, when Sabine began talking, she set the puzzle book aside and attend to Sabine, lounging on her bed.

Constanze von Posen was the only child of Alexander von Posen, a decorated officer of the Wehrmacht. Having fought on the Eastern front, he found himself subjected to harassment by the Soviet occupation forces until the establishment of the DDR where he was routinely tormented by the Stasi seeking information on former comrades and known members of the Nazi Party. Unable to find work through "normal channels," he accepted a job from a former army subordinate at a steel mill in Riesa.

It was there that he met Greta Wellstein whose family was part of the local gentry. Because of the war, the Wellstein family was reduced to near peasant status. They were married in 1948, only four months before Constanze was born. It was a scandal at the time, but the young family was happy enough until Alexander died in a factory accident in 1953. Shortly after, Greta Posen went to work in a local bakery where she made and sold bread.

Ernst Bauer was a local lad often dispatched to the bakery on behalf of his family. It was his routine for months before finding Constanze loitering at her mother's side. He thought no more about it until he saw her in school. They became friends. They remained friends until they realized they were in love.

Ernst wanted to attend university but his father insisted he become a carpenter. Constanze worked at the bakery with her mother and had no university ambitions. Ernst bent to his father's wishes and became a carpenter's apprentice. He proposed to Constanza; they were wed eighteen months later. They continued working.

"She was a singer," Sabine reported. "She always sang in the bakery while working. People encouraged her to perform at local festivals."

Ernst loved his wife's singing. She never studied formally, but she could sing a multitude of folk songs. Then, she began singing along with popular music recordings until she knew many of them well. When she wasn't singing, she was humming. Perpetually happy, she was known as the songbird of the city.

Then, she got pregnant. Ernst was pleased at the news, but his delight turned to alarm when he realized Constanza no longer sang in the evenings. Concerned, he asked the reason. She confessed to being a simple girl with simple needs, she was happy with her simple life.

"But we cannot ask our children to be content with this," she told him. "What if they want more? What if they want to be free?"

This was disturbing. He, too, was satisfied with the simple life. He was content to be wherever Constanza was. Beyond that, he wanted little. However, the larger Constanza's belly grew, the more she nurtured discontent.

One day, she spoke the words that they, previously, shared tacitly.

"We cannot allow our children to live in this country."

They began planning. Not even their parents knew.

Their days were spent normally, but many evenings were devoted to plotting. Ernst knew a former soldier who related stories of drunken New Year's Eve celebrations while he and his mates were "on duty."

Inebriated soldiers became the dubious heart of a desperate scheme. They dared not be too bold in their planning. Frequently, they left the house to discuss things in whispers – far from structures and ears.

Ernst, surreptitiously, researched border barriers, but Constanza carelessly asked suspicious questions. If arrested, they'd lose their chance, and their child would become state property.

Frau Bauer suggested they cross along a railroad. The DDR had neither wall nor fence across international tracks. Railroads wouldn't be mined. For those reasons, Herr Bauer suggested all rail crossings would be closely guarded.

That brought them again to drunken soldiers.

The twins were born on November 12, and Constanze was quickly out of hospital. Short visits in health facilities were the norm in the DDR. She exercised and laid in supplies to take along. She wanted milk for the girls, but it might spoil. They'd have juice and water so she would, hopefully, produce enough for their daughters.

They parked as near the border as possible. They drove off the road and trekked through the woods. It was dangerous to keep the railroad in sight; Ernst navigated by a cheap compass. They were half frozen when they reached their objective.

It was ablaze with light, lights so bright they rivaled day. Several banks of lights shone down until only the studious could find a shadow.

Ernst suggested turning back. They needed to rethink their scheme in greater detail.

Constanze insisted it was as dangerous to turn back as to go forward. They must put all faith in drunken guards. They'd march slowly, parallel to the tracks. When they got close enough, they'd run.

"I suspect the guards spotted us right away," Herr Bauer confided in Sabine. "There were dogs and sentries. They probably took bets on how far we'd get."

They squatted two hundred meters from the gap through which they hoped to escape. Heike was throwing a fuss. They could do nothing to keep out of the light. They struggled to keep quiet and move slowly. Ernst did his best to silence Heike, but she was cold and wet, and her protests were like an air raid siren.

"Let's run!" Frau Bauer suggested.

She was off.

Ernst tried to follow only to stumble. He nearly dropped Heike. In the moment it took to regain equilibrium, Constanze was far ahead. Why the guards did not react sooner is impossible to fathom, but they saw him. There were shouts. Someone launched a flare which, owing to the blazing lights, was senseless.

Suddenly, his leg was on fire and refused to function. He fell, saving him from a hail of rifle bullets. He fell on Heike, stunning her, but she recovered instantly and howled. He crawled desperately, but a useless leg made his efforts symbolic. When the soldiers seized him, he was only three or four meters from where he was shot.

A guard turned him over by kicking him viciously in the side. Another tore Heike from his arms.

"I never saw her again," he reported, casually.

He monopolized the attention of the guards. Not until later did they realize there were additional fugitives. There followed shouting and recriminations, but it was too late.

"We agreed, no matter what, we'd not look back or stop until we were out of range."

Ernst Bauer was treated for his wound, but the doctors were careless. The bullet broke his leg near the knee. They, apparently, made certain it would not mend properly. He was tried and sentenced to eight years in prison, the standard sentence for those attempting to flee. Eventually, he was "bought out of jail" by the BRD, a standard DDR ploy used to coerce hard currency from the wealth creation of the capitalist world.

Herr Bauer was sent to Eisenhüttenstadt, formerly Stalinstadt, an industrial city the DDR carved out of the wilderness. He was given every fix-it job too dirty or thankless for loyal workers. Stripped of personal property and his rights as a citizen, the DDR sought to destroy Herr Bauer's spirit. However, they failed to take into consideration his monumental pride.

"I knew you were free," he told Sabine while they shared a bench and watched the Oder slide past. "That kept me going. I had something to live for."

"You knew about Mutti?"

He shook his head sadly.

"The Stasi tried to torture me with Heike, telling me how happy she was with her *proper, socialist* family. They let me know you were being fought over and abused by Western exploiters, but I knew better. I knew you were alive.

"They never mentioned your mother; I knew. They'd have used her to torment me, but they were careful about the lies they told. Should I find out she was dead, it would ruin their credibility. That would ruin their mental torture. They lied only about the living."

Ute attended Sabine as she, slowly and deliberately, relayed her father's story. The longer it continued, the more two hearts ached.

His working as a virtual slave in Eisenhüttenstadt was another Stasi failure. With each *shitty job*, Ernst's outstanding efforts earned plaudits. Word got around. He got fewer *shitty jobs*. He'd earned more important assignments.

He took jobs that would linger for months before the government could tend to them. Every business manager and factory foreman knew if they needed a job completed quickly and done well, they'd request Ernst Bauer. If they could supply quality materials, he'd do quality work.

Several months after his arrival, Herr Bauer was called into the homes of managers and party officials. He began doing home improvement. If provided materials, Ernst could build a garden fence, do wainscoting, repair roofs, walls, and, even, shingling. For such work, he received *unofficial* rewards.

The Stasi, however, monitored his bank account. When it swelled, they investigated. Upper-level managers were severely admonished; others were dismissed. Ernst was removed from the city and all *illegal* earnings seized. He was removed to Frankfurt where he was forced to compete for work with a corrupt government.

He did.

A citizen could hire Ernst on the QT months or years before the State could get on the job. Further, he'd do the job better than an entire team of government hires.

"I made arrangements to get you a single room in the morning," Ute announced.

Sabine's body deflated.

"You and your father have so much to catch up on. I want to be with *my* family and *my* son. I want to phone *my* husband without having to pay millions of marks."

These were good reasons, but Sabine wasn't certain she was up to the trial.

"I'll be in this country alone," she mused.

"Enjoy it."

Sabine sighed.

"If I leave early, I can be in Braunschweig by two o'clock. From there, it's only three or four hours to Fürth. I'll leave as much money as I can."

Sabrina refused to explore the ambiguity. Heike was – somewhere. Until she found her, she couldn't consider returning to America. Without Ute, however, she'd have greater freedom to explore.

Weimar

Jürgen came home to inform his family of his semi-secret romance and to gain parental approval.

Marina returned to Leningrad on a similar mission. The couple agreed to meet again in Halle and plan. Due to the nightmarish train connections and the distances involved, they allotted eight days. Jürgen, never more than a few hours from Halle, devoted the bulk of his time to family and friends.

After Rolf's announcement, the young man had only to bite his nails. Returning with Nadine from a foray into the city, the pair were confronted by an expensive Wessi auto parked near the Jacobs's residence. The sun was low in the sky and the street shaded, but the polished black vehicle shimmered. They rounded the curve leading to the house.

An overweight man in a white shirt stood at their door. Pricked by curiosity, they hurried. Near enough to notice the *B* on the Wessi plate, they noticed a card flutter onto the street. They heard a shrill, unmistakable voice. The words echoing down the street were *not* complementary. Before the visitor could respond, the door slammed.

Frau Ecke's serenity must have suffered mightily. Nadine vowed to remind Heike of family protocol concerning Anne and loud, angry words. Jürgen's intensions were similarly inclined.

They watched the berated man turn and slowly move to his car.

Nadine realized!

"Scheiße!"

Alarmed, Jürgen expected an explanation, but this was no time to tarry. Ignoring the lingering heat, Nadine broke into a run. The young man caught in Cupid's snare was not moved to boldness. He did, however, quicken his pace.

"Fräulein," the man began once Jürgen was within earshot, "my business is with Heike Jacobs only. I'm not allowed to deal with others."

"Don't let her have the last word," Nadine responded. "I live with her. She's as stubborn as a Polish mule, but she's sorry for what she said. She's scolding herself right now."

"She must communicate with me," the man stated doggedly.

"Don't you understand? She won't. Not after a temper tantrum. She is proud. Too proud. She'll never talk with you, and she'll regret it for the rest of her life."

The large man sighed.

"I'm just doing my job," he announced.

"A man 'just doing his job' gave me this face."

The official was shaken. As an Ossi, he was familiar with physical abuse. Still, he couldn't ignore established procedure.

"The law is very clear –"

"Are you Ossi or Wessi?" she interrupted.

"Pardon?"

"Ossi or Wessi? Which?"

"I've lived my life in the DDR," he announced.

"Jürgen, is that's a business card on the street? Bring it to me."

It had been a long day. The drive from Frankfurt was long and arduous. All Herr Beckmann wanted was a quiet hotel room, a hot bowl of soup, a glass of beer, a shower and a good night's sleep. He had neither time nor patience to deal with a loon.

"Young lady –"

Again, he was denied.

"Herr Neman, every Ossi knows there are only two kinds of people who are above the law. One is a high party official. The other is anyone clever enough and resourceful enough to circumvent the law. Danke, Jürgen. Unless you confess of your own accord, no one will know we've spoken."

Herr Beckmann was curious and amused. If he heeded Sabine's plea, he could afford to hear what this excited young woman had to say. He folded his arms across his chest and openly dared her to continue.

"Weimar is a famous, historical city. We get thousands of tourists every year from all over the world. Now, if Heike's father *just happened* to come here, he'd want to see the sites. Well, Herr Neman, I, Nadine Jacobs, am an authorized guide. Should Heike's father contact me, he won't – be – sorry."

"He may *just happen* to bump into Heike," Beckmann completed the thought.

"It's a small town."

"How long have you been a tour guide?" he demanded.

"What time is it?"

Herr Beckmann tried hard not to smile. He admired her brass.

"It would be just like Heike to tell her father the very things she told you. Still, they deserve to meet, don't you think? If she squawks to your superiors, there's nothing for it because we never spoke; you were never here. It's worth a chance, isn't it? There's no risk to you."

He nodded as he pondered.

"I'll think about it," he promised.

"Do."

"May I go?"

Nadine bowed graciously and stood aside. He climbed aboard, started the engine, and looked at the two pedestrians.

They returned his gaze.

He put the car in gear and eased his way toward town.

* * *

They wanted the visitor from Berlin to have cover if Heike persisted in making his life miserable, so Nadine and Jürgen conferred during a leisurely thirty-minute stroll before entering the house. They found Heike sitting on the couch next to Anne. She'd rush to comfort the poor woman after slamming the door, but it needn't take so long. Had she been chewing her thumb all that time?

"Where was Günther when I needed him?" she asked, timidly.

"What are you on about?" Jürgen asked, innocently.

"There was a man here. My sister is looking for me."

"Your sister?" both conspirators asked in unison.

"He says she's come from America. I thought he meant *Amerika* where Jana is from. When he – I lost it. I imagined some stuck-up Ami bitch waving money in my face and rubbing my nose in dirt because she has a country, and I don't. I said – bad things. I needed Günther to slap some sense into my big, fat stupid head."

As she spoke, tears came.

"I've really done it this time," she reflected.

Anne, sensing that one of her "dears" was distraught, put her arm around Heike's shoulders and held her close. Heike didn't whimper or sob, but her face remained taut; her gaze fixated on the unseen.

"He'll send a letter to make it official," Jürgen assured. "You will have another chance."

Heike may have heard, or she may not have. Her static expression betrayed nothing beyond disparagement.

* * *

He stayed in the *Russischer Hof* on Goetheplatz. The window of his room opened to the west; he need not look upon the improvised beer garden, the imbiss that forsook traditional bratwurst and beer to sell bananas only, or the gaudy flea market across the city's busiest street. The name and the location suggested Russian royalty, but the socialist décor and Spartan rooms made clear proletarian influences. Herr Beckmann cared not so long as he could get a good night's sleep. He intended to be on the road early to avoid traffic.

After a welcome shower, he called his wife to inform her of his whereabouts and apologized for his unplanned detour. He called Frau Tiede at her home. One of her sons answered. He left a message that he'd not be in until the following afternoon.

It was a bother not having a change of clothes, but living in the DDR schooled him on how to cope. In the past, he'd wear the same clothes two days before changing into his other suit for two days. Since the opening of borders and the plentiful supply of quality garments at moderate cost, he'd formed the habit of changing every day.

He ate in. The toxic lecture Heike Jacobs delivered killed the tourist within. The hotel restaurant, he reasoned, was probably as good as any in town. Moreover, this would save him exploring a strange city.

He ordered the house specialty, stroganoff, and a beer to wash it down. He was pleasingly surprised. Though he didn't enjoy eating alone, he took time to enjoy one of the few good meals he'd experienced. His wife's cooking was better, but she wasn't available.

The music, soft and classical, added to his pleasure. He recognized a Mendelssohn concerto and something by Liszt. Though diverted by the music, his thoughts raced far afield.

Nadine was right about one thing – the capricious laws of the DDR are flouted with ease; only fools got caught. Beckmann estimated a third, at least, of all financial transactions in the DDR were illegal. After his release from jail, he spent considerable time taking advantage of "underground" activities. Though the Stasi was omnipresent, it had one weakness: the Stasi prided itself on knowing *everything* about *everyone*. As a result, agents could not report anything they may have overlooked.

The case of Sabine Bauer, however, was not the Stasi. The Wessi law introduced a strict code of conduct in reuniting Ossi families. Bonn could slam a door hard on the fingers of any transgressor. However, the Wessis were sticklers for evidence.

Beckmann's creative juices were bubbling. He'd evaded the Stasi most of his life, save for one exception. He knew how to keep his head down.

Circumstantial evidence would not win a Wessi conviction. If anyone attempted to dismiss Beckmann, he had only to deny everything. Dismissal without concrete evidence would invite legal retaliation.

Nevertheless, he must exercise caution. He was up to the challenge. What could be proven? He'd been in Weimar; the hotel register would confirm that. The two co-conspirators and, perhaps, Heike, may have recorded his license number. At the least, they'd remember the black BMW with Berlin plates. Unless he was under surveillance (highly unlikely), there existed no evidence of malfeasance.

After paying his bill, Beckmann slipped out of the hotel to buy a souvenir postcard and a stamp. He preferred paper and an envelope, but most shops were closed, and hotel stationery wouldn't do. He ordered a cup of coffee and a slice of *Erdbeerkuchen* at a corner café. Once the waitress busied herself with filling his order, Beckmann painstakingly printed a message with his left hand. Unless someone demanded a writing sample from his sinister appendage, no one would match the missive with samples of his handwriting.

> *Frl. Nadine*
> *Private Tour Guide*
> *Werner Ecke Strasse 18*
> *Weimar*

He filled in the address.

> *Fr. U. Foster*
> *u. Sabine*
> *Hotel Frankfurter Hof*
> *Frankfurt/Oder*

Once every ten years or so, Herr Beckmann found his rudimentary English useful. However, he must include something to indicate his identity without being overt. Unable to employ a code worked out in advance, this was tricky. He hoped either Sabine or the Ami could figure it out. Still, even DDR newcomers quickly learned how to beat the system.

He used English script.

I   I   I   I

Frankfurt/Oder

Sabine woke the moment Ute sat up.

"You don't have to get up."

Sabine was not in a convivial mood.

"Then, it's up to me, isn't it?"

Wisely, Ute kept quiet.

The dawn stretched its rosy fingers into the sky. It was warm, very warm. Hot! The day would be another scorcher. After Sabine muscled the suitcase to the elevator, sweat burst forth on her face and torso. They shoved the bag into the contraption and clanked down to the lobby.

In addition to the identification and money slung around Sabine's neck and under her left arm, she totted a larger bag containing her undies. The night clerk was asleep on a couch near the desk. He'd cast aside a thin blanket and snored peacefully. His white shirt was marred by underarm wetness. The women crept past and into the dreariness of the parking lot.

Ute was surprised to find a cab waiting. She'd called from the room but suspected the dispatcher was hesitant to bother anyone at such an *obscene* hour. Thankfully, the driver hefted the luggage into the trunk and offered to take Sabine's things. She shook her head; he shrugged his shoulders.

They climbed into the cab. To celebrate the only vehicle in motion, the driver ignored two red lights and delivered them to the Bahnhof in record time. Ute paid and tipped the man while Sabine wrestled the suitcase into the building, through the tunnel and up to the platform. The train stood ready. Ute and Sabine lugged the suitcase into the vestibule.

"Let it stay there," Ute commanded.

"Someone might take off with it," Sabine warned.

"Good!"

They lingered momentarily.

"I'm going to try to snooze," Ute decided. "Go back to bed."

"Got your ticket?"

Ute looked through her handbag and pulled out the card she purchased the previous afternoon. Sabine nodded. Ute put it back before it had opportunity to escape.

"Give Isaac a big hug for me."

"You know I will."

"*Viele Grüße* to everyone. Don't forget Bernd and Mischa."

"I won't."

They hugged one last, long while.

"Viel Spaß, Mutti."

"Don't forget to change rooms before you go visiting. I left you money last night, right?"

Sabine nodded and patted the fashionable, Waldron bag.

"You know where I'll be."

Sabine nodded.

Ute disappeared into the wagon. Sabine hurried away before she burst into tears. She sat inside the Bahnhof. She hoped to see Ute emerge from the tunnel, lugging both her case and a change of heart. After twenty minutes of pensiveness and reflection, she gave up.

Sabine Bauer was all alone in a strange country. She conjured Bach's Air and her spirit revived slightly. She could speak the language; she was adaptable enough to deal with the eccentricities of a semi-alien culture. Further, she had an ally in Ernst Bauer.

A commuter train arrived disgorging an amazing number of workers. The somber, dank tunnel connecting the trains and the station was alive with people in every form of dress from the suits and shined shoes to overalls spattered with plaster and paint. Governments may rise and fall, but the ritual dance of the morning commuters didn't alter.

Sabine, however, reflected upon the morbid fact that these were the lucky people. They had jobs. Much employment was lost when the top-heavy government folded.

What better way to begin her morning than by joining the small army dispersing into the city? She learned the shortest way to the city center. Many people joined her in forsaking Bahnhof Strasse and veering off in the direction of what was once a hotel. Eager for an adventure, Sabine followed a blue suit swinging a briefcase past the hotel ruins.

There was a monument to the Reich Bahn reaching into the warm, morning light. The bronze rail wheel with wings looked ridiculous, but Sabine was adjusting to *Socialist Realism*; she concluded that the uglier the art object, the greater its importance – symbolically, at least.

After negotiating a few stone steps, the girl followed the brief case to the left and onto a street devoid of traffic. Just as well since the sidewalks abutted buildings both empty and crumbling. She noticed an ugly gash of rubble thrusting the street downhill. The exterior wall of the red-brick apartment building was an odd array of protruding brick and strips of wood and paper.

This exterior wall was, ages before, an interior wall. The rubble under the wall remained undisturbed after a third of the building was destroyed. Was it due to war damage? She'd seen many bombed-out structures in Berlin – well, in East Berlin. If Ernst Bauer could be trusted –and she had no evidence to indicate he couldn't – the German army held Frankfurt from sheer obstinacy rather than any military advantage.

The Red Army, equally obstinate, was determined to seize the city regardless of cost. When the dust cleared, the hammer and sickle floated over mountains of rubble.

She passed apartments shunted up against a derelict dwelling. The street terminated with a massive, stone, corner building. The old German script had faded. It was impossible to decipher either the name or the business that once existed within. The structure appeared untouched by war, but the years since were brutal.

Sabine had a chance to turn left on the adjoining street and return to familiar territory, but the briefcase trotted across the cobblestones; so, then, did she. There was a semblance of a bakery to the right and more abandoned businesses to her left as she continued down the hill on a pedestrian path. She negotiated more stone steps. At their base she found a cobblestone cross street, but this one accommodated trolley cars in addition to autos.

Lindenstrasse!

What German city lacked a Lindenstrasse?

The briefcase crossed, doggedly followed by Sabine, dodging commuter traffic.

She discovered herself in a park with long, untended grass and ancient, imposing trees. She spied several monuments but lacked interest enough to examine them. She trekked by a huge, gothic post office. From there, she waited for a light to assist in her crossing four lanes divided by two sets of tram tracks.

Finally, at the base of the twenty-four stories of the *Oderturm*, she abandoned the briefcase and aimed for the hotel. The next block was dominated by a massive building, the nucleus of the fledgling University of Viadrina. From there, it was one more broad avenue to cross, and she strode through the hotel parking lot.

She saw no signs of the night porter, either on the couch or behind the desk. She climbed the stairs to what was, once, *their* room. She stripped and showered, finishing with water as cold as she could stand. She ignored the towels. She threw open the windows and allowed warm air to dry her.

The sun burst over the hills and poured into the room with a vengeance. Sabine's skin prickled under its rays but she refused to close the curtains.

She cast a wistful glance towards Posen.

Once dry, Sabine dawned the coolest of her clean clothes. There was a sleeveless t-shirt with Fisherman's Inn in bold green letters across the front. She stepped into a short, pink, cotton skirt. She despised it and vowed to leave it behind in a German trash bin. She brought it for lounging rather than public use, but the bulk of her clothes were ill suited for the intense heat.

Stuffing her feet into canvass shoes, Sabine was ready to breakfast. The breakfast room was imposing, but Sabine was the only patron ambulatory at that early hour. A man in cook whites and two young women in black skirts and white blouses finished laying out the buffet.

One of the women had bright red hair. Sabine was curious to know if it was natural. Since arriving, she'd seen women with screaming red hair and no few with purple tresses.

She sat at a table and waited for the employees to finish their work. Somehow, she attracted the attention of the redhead.

"Kaffee, bitte."

The girl smiled, nodded, and turned to fill the order before thinking better of it. She retraced her steps. Sabine noticed freckles marching across her face.

"May I bring you a fresh egg?" she asked in slow, carefully enunciated English. "We have eggs boiled hardly."

Sabine resisted correcting the syntax. It was more logical the way Red expressed it.

"Thank you," she replied, imitating the speech of the waitress. "An egg sounds nice."

"Yes?"

"Yes."

Okay, so the girl wasn't a linguist. Still, one must have courage to exercise limited skills. Word reached the staff about an Ami in residence. One look at Sabine's t-shirt narrowed the candidates.

The coffee, in a gold-colored, plastic container arrived with a brown egg in a white egg cup atop a quaint white paper doily atop a white saucer. These items arrived along with a short, imitation silver spoon. The redhead served from Sabine's left. Sabine preferred the coffee server on her right, next to her cup, but this was too trivial to mention.

"Danke."

"You are welcome," Red replied in measured syllables.

The buffet was dressed. The white uniform and his remaining assistant disappeared through swinging double doors leaving Sabine and her personal servant alone. Red hesitated. Doubtless, her main duties were on the other side of those doors, but she remained hesitant. Sensing awkwardness, Sabine filled the silence.

"Where did you learn your English?"

The girl tried to stifle a smile. She was proud but cautious. She hid her hands behind her back and twisted from side to side nervously.

"I listen to Radio Luxemburg," she replied. "I know songs and I learn from the announcers."

Radio Lux: Ute used to speak of it. It played modern British music and had power enough to reach most of Europe. Sabine was incredulous. To learn song lyrics was one thing but learning conversational English was another matter. Sabine suspected Red might be a Stasi agent assigned to report on foreigners.

Sabine noticed the name tag pinned to Red's blouse.

"Birgit. I've always liked that name. Do people call you Biggi?"

"Yes," the girl nodded. "That's me: Biggi Schneeweiß."

Sabine was enjoying her first sip of coffee. She nearly spit it out. Was her leg being pulled? She came very near asking about the seven dwarfs. This query was parried by Biggi's expression.

"I think I should go, now."

"It was nice talking to you."

"Yes, me too."

Biggi took three steps towards the kitchen. She decided something, stopped, and returned timidly. She started to speak but lifted her eyes up and to her left. Due to the tutelage of Ed Geist, Sabine knew the meaning of the gesture.

"Please, en-joy your – um, breakfast."

"Danke."

* * *

She agreed to meet her father in the shopping area of the Oderturm. After breakfast, she informed the desk of the room change. She fully expected to bring her things to be stored until the new room was properly made up. However, the collapse of the government and the economy resulted in many vacancies. She was promptly presented a new room key.

Sabine opted to change at once. There were differences between her new room and the previous one. It faced west, promising blistering afternoon sun. There was only one double bed, but a larger, more modern bathroom. There was a delightful view of Karl Marx Strasse and the business district, the clanging street cars, the gothic façade of the post office, and a peek of the greenery marking the course of the defunct medieval moat. Immediately across the street was the Viadrina University building; a few students congregated there.

The cleaning crew, the day before, opened both windows so they leaned inward eight inches or so. By closing them, twisting the handle, and reopening them, Sabine could have them swing all the way open. She was tempted to do exactly that and allow the cooler morning air to fill the room. She discarded the idea. With her luck, the wind would gust, and the windows could swing wildly. Who could predict what damage might result? Better, she thought, to leave them as they were. The room would become stifling hot regardless.

Before taking the stairs, she returned to her previous room for a last view of the Oder. The man had returned and fished on the Polish side. She waved, but she was too tiny to see, even if he looked directly at her. Finally, she took one last look at Ute's bed.

Sabine sighed and left the room forever.

On her way out, she left both keys with the clerk. She placed her key card in Mrs. Waldron's bag and, hefting her under things on the opposite hip, she walked briskly to the Oderturm. She found a seat near the fountain and waited. She should have brought paper to write Gary and Molly during her wait. However, she'd hardly gotten comfortable before noticing a pronounced limp approaching.

She hadn't bothered with makeup. Herr Bauer didn't seem to notice. That was a relief. No matter how good Molly was at cosmetology, it was a burden to use all that "muck" when it was sure to melt and, perhaps, catch fire.

"You're as pretty today as you were yesterday," he greeted.

Sabine blushed. She intended to say something deferential and witty, but she came up empty.

"I brought my tools," he said, gesturing with his battered toolbox. "I promised some people to help them. I didn't know when you'd be here."

"That's okay. May I come along?"

"Of course! After we finish, we can have a nice lunch and, maybe, do some shopping."

For Herr Bauer it was important Sabine be close. He'd not seen her for over sixteen years. He recognized Constanze Posen in her. Yet, every time he looked upon her, there was a new discovery – a shadow across the face, a renegade strand of hair, a flash of the eyes, a twitch of the mouth, a peculiar tilt of the head. Sabine Bauer was clearly her mother's daughter, but she was different, and pleasingly unique.

Sabine loved listening to him. He was a living history book. His lessons spanned centuries. She drank in every word, every syllable. The more she heard, the more intoxicated she became.

Beyond the general survey, there were many chapters from the family history. There was one event that carried through the narratives like a malevolent plague: the war. It was the tragedy from which everything was measured. Herr Bauer dated events *before* the war and *after* the war by so many decades or years. The war itself was a calamitous event with no measure. Everything was so tightly condensed so the invasion of Poland and the fall of Berlin seemed simultaneous.

Ernst, of course, did not remember the war. Yet, he, Sabine and Heike were products of that war. There were two branches of the von Posen clan. One remained in Prussia and built considerable holdings near and along the Vistula. These were the family aristocrats who summered in Königsberg, who were chauffeured between estates by coachmen and footmen and oversaw scores of peasants who paid rent with a fixed percentage of their production.

Part of this family moved to Memel, presently in Lithuania, where they became city dwellers and, for a time, prosperous in the Baltic trade. This branch shriveled and disappeared from history in the early 1900s. A second branch migrated from Memel to Hamburg where they established a short-lived banking house. The descendants returned to Memel and, also, disappeared.

One hardy adventurer, however, moved southeast and settled in Leipzig. There he went into partnership with two other investors and founded a publishing house. Within a decade, he bought out his partners and published books and pamphlets until Hitler took more interest in burning books than printing them. The von Posen family either went bankrupt or sold the concern, there was no reliable information about this. The former printer became a coffee importer.

By the time bombs fell on Leipzig, the ragged survivors sold the coffee business for a song and fled to Dresden. In a *safe* city, the residuals of a once great fortune kept the family relatively comfortable in a metropolis flooded with refugees. After British bombers transformed the city to ashes, the von Posen family vanished.

The Vistula von Posens thrived until the *hard times* of the first war and rebounded. Under Hitler, the family supplied agricultural products until the Russian advance. The Soviet Army swept the von Posens out of their ancestral lands and laid waste to their lavish estates. The last thing anyone knew, only the remains of a few scattered sheds and abandoned barns remained.

Die Flucht scattered the family. Riding horses, pushing, and pulling carts or walking, the von Posens kept moving through snow and rain to keep one jump ahead of the Red Army. Those who could not keep up vanished. A half-dozen reached Germany.

With their fortune gone and only a fraction of the family treasures buried in locations long since forgotten, the surviving few began their post-war lives as laborers or farm hands. By the time the DDR was founded, the *von* disappeared along with all other aristocratic pretenses.

"What about the Bauers?" Sabine asked.

"There are thousands of stories about my family," Herr Bauer admitted, "but it isn't glorious. Most of us were farmers and, before that, as the name suggests, we were peasants. Since few of our family could read or write until the 1840s or so, there are few records. There must be hundreds of thousands of Bauers in Germany. I doubt I'm related to more than a dozen. My parents, uncles, and aunts are all dead. I think I have one or two cousins in Plauen, but I never met them."

"But your family is Saxon, right?"

"For three generations at least. My grandfather was a farmer who learned carpentry. My father was a carpenter who learned farming. He learned Morse code in the army. That was a useful skill, and he worked for the railroad until they didn't need telegraphers anymore.

"That's when he got a job as a farm hand, but he was more useful as a builder. Wood was scarce during the war and doubly so when the war began to turn. When it ended, there were many buildings in need of repair. My mother took in laundry during and after the war. We were never rich, but I don't recall ever going hungry."

Frankfurt abounded in apartment buildings. They looked similar because most shared a single blueprint. They were built quickly and cheaply. Anyone with dexterity in wood and plaster was in constant demand. In theory, the local government was responsible for maintenance, but government employees were unmotivated and notoriously unskilled.

Since every apartment needed repair, government repairmen mightn't show for months or years. When they did, repairs were generally slap-dash. They were paid the same amount no matter how well or poorly they did, so why work hard?

Ernst Bauer made a small fortune in a country where any fortune (no matter how small) was treason. He knew how to do quality work, and he delivered. Without advertising, save by word-of-mouth, his services were in constant demand. If a client needed repairs and promised Ernst the required materials, he'd begin work within days if not hours.

"Under the law, I was not allowed to work. One needed *papers*, and as an *enemy of the state,* I did not have papers. I was paid, even in Hütte, under the table. The Stasi got wise. They were clocking my bank account. They threatened to arrest me again. They probably would have if they hadn't gotten a better idea. The bank *lost* my accounts and records."

"The Stasi just took it?"

"I didn't care. If I couldn't spend it on you or Heike, it was little use to me."

"Oh, Papa!"

"So, they sent me up here and put me in a special building. It was a big house until after the war. They made it into apartments. Every person living there was under Stasi surveillance. We all knew one of the tenants was a Stasi informer or, maybe, an agent. We were always very, very quiet."

"I'd learned my lesson in Hütte. I opened a bank account, but I never kept more than two hundred marks in it. If I had no money, the Stasi was happy. Since I couldn't work, by law, the government had to support me. If I worked here, as I had in Hütte, they need not give me anything. So, they let me break the law. I looked poor. I lived poor. I had a tiny bank account. Everyone, including me, was happy."

Sabine saw a twinkle in his eye and a smirk on his face when he narrated his work history.

"But you made more than the Stasi knew."

He laughed. It was quiet but satisfied.

"I took what I needed for myself and hid the rest. If the Stasi were as smart as they thought, they'd find the money and take it. They never found it. Probably, they never hired a carpenter as an agent, or they'd have had a very big party with all that money. Stupid pigs!"

"So, are you going to buy a nice house and enjoy life?"

He shook his head and continued to assemble the second-hand shrunk he'd been hired to put into commission.

"I will do what I have done. I take what I need. The rest is yours."

"Mine?"

"Well, not exactly. Half is yours –"

"The other half is Heike's."

He nodded.

"Papa, I'm grateful, but I can't accept it. You made the money. You should have it."

He continued working.

"It's yours to do with as you please," he insisted. "If you don't accept, then it stays where it is. I'll put it in a bank when I think it's safe. I'll arrange for your children to have it."

She avoided an argument by keeping still. She leaned against a cast iron radiator which, ironically, was the coolest item in the apartment and watched her father work. After several minutes, he looked up and smiled.

"I used to make a game of it," he said. "If Constanze were alive and you children were with us, I figured how much money you'd need for clothes and food. I set aside some more for things little girls and young ladies might need. I counted out that amount and set it aside. You and Heike went cold one winter, metaphorically, because I couldn't afford to buy you proper coats. Perhaps, I should give the money to Frau Foster. A girl must be expensive in America."

"She left this morning," she reported with a catch in her voice.

"I'm sorry to hear that. I imagine she has beautiful stories to tell me about you."

"Stories of a spoiled brat."

He smiled a big, toothy smile.

"I can tell, you are not spoiled."

"Selfish, then."

He shrugged and made a dubious sound.

"Maybe," he pondered, "but instantly refusing a large amount of money doesn't strike me as selfish. However, we shall see."

"And if you find me selfish, you'll be disappointed."

"My child, you can do hundreds of things to disappoint me, but you can never stop me loving you."

She felt a huge lump in her throat. For a moment, she could not speak. Only when he turned to examine her reaction could she muster her voice.

"You sound pretty certain," she said, as evenly as she could.

His reply was a knowing smile.

The man who commissioned the job of assembling the shrunk was satisfied it could not be done. He attempted the job himself, but the result was so unstable he declared it trash and wanted it hauled away. His wife, however, argued they couldn't be so cavalier with their money and insisted on a professional to make it right. When Ernst promised to forego payment if he didn't succeed, the couple had nothing to lose.

Sabine and Ernst arrived as the wife was preparing to go to market. She let them in, showed them the job and hurried off. Sabine was petrified. She feared it was a "set up," and her father might be accused of burglary.

When the stout lady returned with three bags of groceries, she galloped noisily into the kitchen to lay down her burden. She hurried to the bedroom to inspect. She was panting from her stair climbing and her face was puffy and red. She eyed the shrunk suspiciously.

"Just putting on the doors," Herr Bauer informed needlessly.

The woman pressed lightly on the side of the chest. Nothing happened. She pressed a bit harder.

"I can't believe it!"

She leaned against it and grinned appreciatively. Apparently, her husband-assembled shrunk was marred by instability. Ernst's knowledge through experience brought success and left the harried wife positively giddy.

"My man will be very, very pleased!"

For her it was a miracle. For Herr Bauer it was little more than matchsticks and a screwdriver. Sabine took pride in the modest assistance she'd provided.

"Would you like a cold beer?"

"Anything cold," Ernst replied.

The woman questioned Sabine by her glance. Not once did she demand to know her function. The woman's lack of curiosity astonished her. Suddenly, without reservations, the woman's eager glance asked for her drink order.

They'd not been introduced. Sabine knew not how to address the hostess. To call her "Frau" without a last name was unconscionable; to say *Genettige frau* would make Sabine seem presumptuous. In the DDR, this might constitute an insult.

"I had too much coffee this morning," Sabine stammered. "What I need – really – is –"

She looked at her father for support.

"You need not ask, my dear," the woman said gaily. "You come right through."

Thankfully, the woman didn't escort her. She merely pointed the way and allowed Sabine to care for herself.

"Come into the kitchen!" the woman called.

Once there, the guests discovered a corner bench wrapped around two sides of a wooden table. It was a familiar arrangement in German apartments, as Sabine knew from films. She slid onto the bench while her father occupied one of the two available wooden chairs.

"You're from America!" The woman exclaimed.

Sabine's absence, apparently, obligated her father to explain the presence of his "assistant."

"Yes."

Ernst Bauer was suddenly invisible. After setting a glass of cold beer in front of each guest, the woman accompanied a glass of ice water to the bench and peppered Sabine with questions. Some were insightful, most were inane, but all were the products of forty years of unsatisfied curiosity. The girl answered politely, but it was an effort. She cast furtive glances at her father who appeared amused; he enjoyed the answers as much as the inquisitive woman.

Sabine felt guilty about leaving half her beer. In a land where sacrifices were a way of life, leaving something freely given was wasteful and insulting. The woman assured her that it was a matter of no consequence. She learned so much about America from one who lived there was ample compensation for wasted beer.

"You must find Ossi beer disappointing."

Sabine had no intention of being rude and admitting she was not a beer drinker. Ernst was awarded twenty-five Wessi marks for his labor. The woman offered more, but he insisted twenty-five marks was the price agreed upon in their verbal contract.

In the same building, but a different stairwell, he called upon two potential clients. He made notes of their projects. He estimated the requirements for the job and promised to return when his customer assembled the materials he required to execute his commission. He was proud to introduce his daughter from America. Sabine was obliged to answer another stream of questions while Ernst looked on with quiet satisfaction.

Once the inquisitions concluded, father and daughter were free to walk the paths of the park. They strolled slowly and spoke casually about the weather and the ducks frolicking in the water of the serpentine. They encountered a memorial to several luminaries of the former university. They paused to inspect each. Ernst may have passed by the commemorative walls many times, but he waited so Sabine could read the inscriptions beneath every stone-relief portrait.

"It says the university was moved by order of Napoleon in 1811," she reported superfluously. "What's that near the hotel?"

"A dream," he replied. "Now we have a free society again, there is a strong sentiment about a new university. They have classes, I believe, but it's only a start."

Sabine examined him for a moment.

"Why study if there is no guarantee it will count towards a degree?"

His ubiquitous, tight-lipped, Mona-Lisa smile never faltered.

"No one in my family ever went to university, so I cannot know," he said quietly. "After decades of censorship and laws prohibiting open discussion, people have an appetite. Maybe, people simply want to know things they were forbidden to know before. Unemployment is high around here, but I observe people who aren't working spend much time reading."

He did not intend it, but Sabine felt ashamed. All her life, she watched the TV shows she wanted, read the books she wanted, and listened to the music she wanted. She never imagined some people never shared such experiences.

"Let me carry your tools for a while," she offered.

He let her. He smiled at the surprise in her eyes and took it back.

"I'm used to it," he reminded.

Once more, she was ashamed. The tools were too heavy for her to carry. Her father must have had the strength of Hercules and the grip of Beowulf to lug such a load all over the city. How many times in the previous four days had she and Ute bemoaned their lot of herding suitcases fifty meters or more?

The park emptied out onto Karl Marx Stasse. Sabine spied one more monument and, assuming it was dedicated to the founder of the defunct university, turned to get a better look. It was a large bust of Karl Marx looking out upon the street that bore his name. A few feet off to the side, there was a sandwich board put up by the PDK, the Wessi Communist Party. There was a likeness of a grim-faced Marx with a cartoon bubble above his head.

"PEOPLE, FORGIVE ME!"

The bold, red lettering was too powerful to be hidden under a layer of black ink, but someone did their best to cover the last two words. The substitute words were imposed in huge letters. It demanded a physically impossible act.

"People are angry," Sabine mused.

"I don't think so. Everyone realizes Marx was used as a weapon against those he most wanted to help. Maybe, people will become angry – someday. Now, they're happy it's over."

She examined him for some sign of bitterness or a flash of temper. Ernst Bauer was shot by a border guard and treated by an East German doctor who didn't tend his leg properly. His child was ripped from his arms. He was sentenced to eight years in prison because he dared to dream of living somewhere else. He looked at the image of a man in whose name it was all done. Inexplicably, Ernst Bauer appeared to be at peace.

"What would you like for lunch, Liebschen?" he asked.

She was momentarily stunned.

"Soljanka is good," she mused.

"It's a bit hot, don't you think?"

"It must be hotter still to keep soljanka from tempting me."

"Just so. I happen to know where we can get the best soljanka in Brandenburg."

They hugged the buildings to keep to the shadows. They had to walk around sidewalk displays. One was set out by a bookseller; it featured a large collection of paperbacks. In Sabine's experience, such displays would encourage people to take without paying. In the DDR, of all places, people respected private property.

Sabine stepped quickly around and ducked back into the shade.

"*Moment mal*," Ernst said.

She turned to find his tool chest on the sidewalk. He examined a book, a paperback with a plain white cover that, together with the pages, were yellow around the edges. Herr Bauer ducked into the shop. Sabine was impatient and hungry. She resented this pointless pause but held her tongue; her father's comment about people's appetite for reading, demanded restraint.

It took only seconds and Herr Bauer picked up his tools. He presented her with the volume. Sabine accepted it. She noticed the title, *Silas Marner*. It was published in English! She examined it curiously and found the author's name and the copyright, 1931. She was about to ask about it when she noticed something.

LEIPZIG: HEINRICH VON POSEN

She realized the book was a tangible link to her mother. She flipped through the pages in search of notes or observations. Though penciled margin notes (in German) existed, there was no clue as to ownership.

"Danke, Papa," she said.

"Have you read it?"

She shook her head. It didn't matter. This item would be placed in some very special spot when she returned home. Perhaps, if she combed more second-hand shops, she'd find more von Posen volumes.

Along the edge of the park that was once the city moat was the *Platz der Republik*. It stretched from Karl Marx Strasse to the large shopping center at the end of a very long block. There were several streetcars and bus stops.

In the open field were impromptu eating establishments and the ubiquitous *Bier garten.* Such capitalist entrepreneurs were once discouraged. Under the interim government, enterprising people violated dozens of business and health statutes. Still, opening one's own business and supporting oneself during a time of high unemployment was seldom discouraged.

The best soljanka was served from a horse trailer. Mama cooked; Papa made change. The soljanka itself bubbled in huge kettles brought from home and kept heated on elements fed from a heavy-duty electrical cable plugged into the nearest power source twenty meters away. When the kettles were empty, the business closed. The kettles and heating elements returned home with the entrepreneurs.

For ten Ossi marks, one got a disposable bowl of soljanka and a fresh brötchen. Ernst opted for soljanka with pork while Sabine asked for mushrooms. Herr Bauer paid in Wessi marks. The money changer consulted a pocket calculator and ran the amount through the unofficial but more favorable street exchange. The change came in Ossi marks.

The numerical value Herr Bauer got in change came very near the numerical value he paid.

It was delicious, as promised. To wash it down, Ernst purchased two Wessi beer. Sabine preferred cola, but all they had were foul Ossi drinks.

"Would you like to see my apartment?"

"You know I would."

"Eat up and we will have a look."

Sächsisch

Once upon a time, before a war destroyed it and a socialist government prohibited people from advancing on merit or being rewarded for productivity, Frankfurt was an opulent city. Despite its distance from the sea, it was a member of the Hanseatic League with a showcase city hall. When the league lapsed into the pages of history, the wealthy class within maintained an impetus which carried it through to the twentieth century. One of the last residences of a wealthy family was one of the few to escape the Red Army's lust for destruction.

After the war, housing was at a premium; the home was hurriedly converted into seven apartments. In the 1980s, the place was taken over by the Stasi and was used to house the undesirables; keeping all the bad eggs in one basket simplified surveillance problems. The apartments on the three floors were connected by a wooden staircase, stripped of its former grandeur. The top floor was the former servants' quarters – two small rooms served by a common bathroom. The plumbing was added during the war with more speed than care.

Sabine was appalled. Her father's apartment consisted of a single, square room. There were two small windows on adjacent walls, no curtains, no carpets, and a single bare bulb hanging from the ceiling. His narrow bed fit against the wall just under the *front* window.

Whatever clothes he had were stored in small drawers he made and attached to the underside of the bed. There was a small table and a chair, both made by him. Next to a sink basin was a cupboard for storage of foodstuffs. There was one plate, one cup, one bowl and a bread knife, all kept on a custom-made shelf for them.

"Papa!"

The exclamation was out of her mouth before she could help herself. It was bad enough that the room was Spartan but the wallpaper, vintage 1930s, was faded and peeling. The wooden floor was scarred and uneven. The bed may have been *quaint* in the 1890s, but it looked like junk by the 1990s.

"How could you live here all these years?"

The self-contented smile remained fixed. He pulled out the chair and invited her to sit; she accepted the offer since the shock made her knees wobbly. Herr Bauer limped over to the bed, put down his tools, and sat. Both the bed and the floor beneath creaked under his weight. He placed his hands flat on either side of him, leaned back and examined his home.

"This is the home of a man with no wife, no family, no money and, until this day, no visitors,"

He sounded cheerful.

"It's an apartment to drive the Stasi mad. They love to find things they aren't meant to find, and they love to see forbidden items. Once a day, someone had to climb those steps to inspect the cabinet and look under the mattress. It wouldn't take long for the most dedicated man to become complacent. They had great hopes for me. They even removed the lock on the door when they put me in here."

Instinctively, she noticed the door, indeed, had neither lock nor bolt. There was nothing worth climbing three flights of stairs to steal. Even so –

"I made a lock out of wood," he grinned. "It was childishly simple, but the Stasi couldn't figure it out. They had to smash it off. That's when I knew I had them."

"You had them?"

He enjoyed a laugh.

"If they couldn't manage a crude wooden lock, there was no way they could find the money I stashed; the money I wasn't supposed to have."

"In here?" she asked, looking hard for a hiding place.

"In the attic, next to the bathroom. Everyone has access to it, but there is no lock on that door either. Nobody ever put anything of value in there. Well, almost nobody."

"It's still there?"

He nodded.

"When I'm certain the banks are safe, I'll open an account. Until then, it's safe where it is."

"What about Heike?" she asked abruptly. "Why don't you try to find her?"

The contentment on his face remained undisturbed.

"Herr Beckmann knows. What do you suggest? Should I hold a knife to his throat and threaten to kill him? Heike does not want to see me. I can't blame her. After being conditioned and indoctrinated for sixteen years to hate me, she isn't likely to change her mind."

"But – but, it must be torture to know she is out there somewhere."

"It would be, but I adopted a philosophy long ago. I only worry about things I can control. I accept what is and trust that, whatever happens, it is for the best."

Sabine sat speechless.

"I guess that sounds glib," he admitted. "But it has kept me alive. The woman I still love is dead, and my darling daughters vanished. That's something that can kill a person. Well, I decided I was left alive for a reason. What reason? I don't know. All I know is that a rifle gave me this limp. That was good luck, Sabine. There were machine gun emplacements. If one of those started shooting, there wouldn't have been enough of Heike and me to bury. We are both alive. There must be a reason. If I'm patient, I will learn it."

Sabine responded by sharing her mantra for holding anxiety at bay. Herr Bauer nodded approvingly and encouraged her to cling to Bach's Air on a G string. If it kept her from irrationality, it was a blessing. He went further and reminded her that one of Bach's sons studied for a time at the university in Frankfurt. There is, he reminded, a city street named for Carl Philipp Emanuel Bach.

They were sparing. Sabine realized it. She hoped that her father would take control of the conversation, but he ignored every opportunity. His abiding patience was clear.

"I got a message from Heike."

Beyond raising curious eyebrows, he exhibited no emotion. She told of the message passed on by her uncle from a DP camp.

"How did she know?" she asked.

"It will give you something to talk about when you see her."

"You're pretty confident."

He shrugged.

"You are young and strong and determined," he replied. "You don't yet realize some things are impossible. That's why people your age are capable of the most amazing things."

"You know that I knew about Heike."

He nodded.

"Frau Foster told me."

"Serves me right," she snorted.

He laughed again. It was an inconsequential matter and, therefore, perfect for his personal amusement. There were many things in his life that did not lend themselves to humor, so he treasured whatever did.

"I think I know where she is."

This he did not know. It was a matter of the utmost gravity. His smile was lost in a sober expression. He sat up straight.

"I'm going to look for her," she announced firmly.

"When?"

"Just as soon as I can."

He considered that carefully.

"Liebschen, I haven't seen you for over sixteen years. Can't you spare me one day for every one of those years?"

"Papa, I can't stay in that hotel," she protested. "I don't have the money. Now, you're going to be noble and say I can stay here while you sleep on the floor or a park bench. Well, that will require my cooperation, and I won't give it."

The smile returned.

"You've got money," he reminded. "Maybe, your hands are too delicate to touch it, but I bet the hotel isn't. I'll go with you this afternoon and pay for fifteen days. By then, you will be so much on my nerves I'll be happy to be rid of you."

Sabine studied this strange man carefully. He lived in a room just half again larger than the one she and Isaac shared in Oregon. He'd been denied his family for most of seventeen years. He had a mother-in-law who hated him for *killing* her daughter. He was spied upon, robbed, and abused by his government. He climbed three flights of stairs with a shocking limp to reach his hovel. To provide for himself, he carried a heavy tool chest wherever he went. He was begging her. A man who depended only upon himself and relied on nothing other than his skills was begged his daughter for a sliver of time.

She got up and examined the wall cabinet. She found what she hoped to find. She closed it. She faced him.

"I must write Ute and tell her," she announced. "She must change our flight."

There it was. She didn't intend to be brutal, but she could not remain in Germany with her father. The poor man hardly had room for himself. There was no way they could share this apartment, and there existed no guarantee they'd find another. Until Ernst Bauer had the prospect of a steady income, he could not support her.

She must return to America.

Perhaps, she expected him to object, but he wasn't a man who survived on wishes and dreams. He knew that his days as a freelance handyman were numbered. Just as the husband and wife with the horse trailer adjusted to the loss of government-subsidized jobs, there were many people handy with tools – most were not handicapped. Soon, competitors would open shops and stock goods. They'd buy vehicles to carry themselves and needed materials to their work. It was a matter of weeks before Ernst Bauer was no longer needed.

He loved his daughters, but it was impossible to support them. Perhaps, he might never be able to support them. The government might have gone and taken the Stasi with it, but Ernst Bauer remained a prisoner.

"Well," Sabine reflected, "she might change *my* flight."

"You would fly alone?"

"I did last year – both ways."

His eyes flashed.

"You're very strong."

Sabine ignored him.

"I saw Mutti's grave," she announced.

They reached another conversational terminus.

"If she knew you were free," he ventured.

He did not complete his thought.

"Knowing that you and Heike were, maybe, dead? I doubt it. She probably died from defeat and sorrow."

Ernst shook his head.

"She'd never give up so long as you were alive," he promised.

Sabine pondered that. She hoped it was true. She wanted it to be true.

"I'm going to find Heike," she vowed. "I won't give up."

"I'd expect nothing less. It's incredible how like your mother you are – no, I'm not saying that because you look so much alike. You have the same spirit, the same strength. She was a strong woman, your mother. She risked all our lives for an idea. I'll tell you straight, Sabine, if it weren't for her, I'd never have risked it. She had courage enough for us all."

"I wonder – I wonder if she'd have felt differently if she knew it would end in sixteen years."

"I can answer for her," he replied boldly, "She would have done as she did. As with any parent, she wanted her children to have what she lacked. She wouldn't have waited an hour."

Weimar

Jürgen came home to share the news, good or bad, from Leningrad. When he learned of Rosa's Children and the campaign slated for the Frauenplan, he adjusted his summer plans. He and Marina had intended to participate in a seminar sponsored by the Wessis, but they agreed to help Heike instead. If they were doomed to live under Wessi rule, they'd focus on themselves and their interests above alien economic theory.

There was doubt Marina would be allowed back into the DDR. Her family could hold her prisoner, or they could appeal to their xenophobic government to cancel her exit visa. Jürgen was ever resourceful. Heike and Nadine believed if Marina were made a prisoner, Jürgen would devise some scheme to get her out. His sisters vowed to aid him regardless of risk. They'd never met Marina Serov, but they loved their brother.

"I'll be here for your big day," he promised. "With luck, Marina will too."

He was a man of action; it wasn't enough to provide moral support. He'd become part of the cadre. Jürgen read Lilo's text and lauded her stirring composition. Still stiff and sore, but adjusting to life as a near invalid, Heike marched towards Goetheplatz with all the erectness her protesting body allowed.

They found Lilo, similarly, ramrod straight and defiant. She had been defeated by circumstances, but she refused to be defeated by life. Her single goal was to keep the only home she'd ever known. With that refuge, she'd endure the worst the "new order" threw at her.

Surrounded by goods she found gaudy and corrupt, she serviced customers she couldn't respect. Like a great tree, she bent with the wind. She forced herself to be courteous and helpful. Keeping her apartment might depend on repeat business.

Rather than approaching from the front, Jürgen guided Heike around the assemblage and other vendors to approach from behind. Lilo's broad shoulders were exposed by a halter top. That and her shorts were her best bet to stay cool. The nearby trees and buildings offered minimal protection. Her arms and neck were lobster red and great patches of skin were either peeling or in the process.

"'Tag, Lilo."

She turned her head, recognized him, and brought her body around to face him properly.

"'Tag, Jürgen!"

She held out her arms. Not even the proximity of Heike deterred her. She hugged Jürgen unabashedly. She announced how wonderful it was to see him. She gave him a kiss on each cheek. Jürgen responded in kind.

"I read your piece. It's great, Lilo."

"Thanks. Does the printer have it?"

"Ja, ja. Heike walked it over the other day."

Suddenly, Lilo turned to the pest. Heike regretted not having a camera to capture the surprise and awe registered on that sun-spotted face.

"You walked!"

It was not a question.

Heike averted her eyes. It was bad enough to crane her neck to look up into Lilo's face. When Lilo bent down as if addressing a tiny child, it was humiliating.

"We took the bus back," she mumbled as if ashamed.

"'We?'"

A fatal mistake! Well, there was nothing for it. She'd discover the truth sooner or later.

"Günther went with me," she murmured.

She stepped nearer Jürgen. If Lilo turned violent, she knew her brother would protect her. Several moments passed with no profanity and no fangs in her neck. Heike looked up timorously.

Lilo hadn't moved. Heike's eyes climbed until she saw Lilo's set jaw and dilated nostrils. Amazingly, however, the eyes did not scald.

"Mmmm," she mused.

There was no malice in Lilo's voice, but there was no amiability either. It was merely inserted into a lingering silence. Regardless, Heike decided it might not be healthy to meet Lilo on a deserted street.

Jürgen realized he had his head in a hornet's nest. Despite his sister's unfortunate gaff, he refused to wait for a change of season.

"Lilo, we have a problem."

"That's news," she said, her eyes riveted on Heike.

"Lilo, look at me."

She obeyed the command, but her demeanor suggested Heike's turn would come.

"This document will get blood pumping, but if we don't have a cause, it won't last."

"We think alike!" she responded.

"Unfortunately, it's the same cause we've had for four decades," he reminded. "The government failed to deliver and lied about – well, mostly everything. People are wary. We need something local and immediate. Something to build on. If we can bring change, even a modest gain, it will boost confidence and attract people."

"War on pay toilets?"

"Don't make fun, Lilo. We've all got to find something tangible to take to the people."

Lilo scratched the peeling skin on her nose.

"Maybe, we could get rid of the eye-sore in Goetheplatz."

"Think, Lilo!" Heike commanded with feeling, "People here are struggling to make a living. Other people buy from this market to survive on Ossi wages in a Wessi world. Banishing this market will hurt people, not help them."

The Amazon tried to appear contemptuous. She failed. Heike was a nuisance, but she had a brain.

"You're correct," she said to Heike though addressing Jürgen. "I'll work on it."

"Danke, Lilo," he acknowledged, taking Heike's arm, and drawing her away.

"Regards to Günther."

Jürgen acknowledged Lilo's sentiment with a gesture. Heike dared not turn her head for fear Lilo might throw something.

* * *

Nadine was unquestionably the better shopper; she always came home with most of the specific items she set out to fetch. Even in a market dominated by Wessi goods, this was time consuming, but she took pride in displaying her loot. Alternatively, Heike was an "opportunity shopper." Even in the restrictive days of the Ossi economy, she'd proved a genius at finding quality substitutes despite frequently empty shelves. Because she lacked the patience to track down specific items, she seldom bothered with lists.

Jürgen was partial to Nadine's method. Her insistence on pinpoint shopping guaranteed a meal to coddle the palate. Heike's meals tended to be "adventurous." She frequently substituted chicken for pork or squash for tomatoes. However, Jürgen wasn't an adventurous eater.

When at home, even for a visit, the university student was automatically reinserted into the daily chores. Of all these, shopping and cooking were his least favorite. He wasn't a bad cook, exactly. However, he disliked shopping and had little patience with boiling, simmering, and browning. Thus, when he offered to trade shopping and cooking for cleaning chores, his sisters readily agreed.

Unfortunately, Heike took over the shopping. He opted to handle the laundry. Heating and wrestling with tubs of water was better than making beds, scrubbing stairs which included the front steps, dusting, and battling the bathroom. Nadine was, innately, more meticulous at this sort of work, though she didn't derive any joy from it.

Once free of Lilo's icy glare, Heike limped away to gather the goods for the mid-day meal while Jürgen returned home to do laundry. He was faster than his sisters at this, but Heike loudly pointed out his deficiencies in scrubbing, folding, and correctly employing their wooden press. To promote peace, he'd make a special effort to keep Heike from finding fault that day.

Günther dropped in just as Jürgen finished dressing the clothesline. In the heat, he couldn't dally. He would need to press before certain items were completely dry.

"Heike's out," he told his friend.

Jürgen knew if Günther had a choice, he preferred Heike's company over his. Günther took the news graciously and greeted the venerable Frau Jacobs with a bow. She smiled, nodded politely, and returned into her other world.

"You wouldn't mind me as a brother-in-law, would you?" he asked without preamble.

Jürgen didn't care to be coy. Nadine informed him about Heike's date with Günther.

"Mind? I'd be proud, but Heike should have some say, don't you agree?"

"I told her I loved her – or as good as," he reported.

"And?"

Günther shrugged.

Jürgen understood. Since Frau Jacobs was unavailable, he knew Heike best,

"I spoke with your father," he continued.

This was a surprise. Jürgen wondered how Günther avoided broken limbs and bruises. Rolf Jacobs was very protective. Further, there was the issue of Heike's age.

"I can only imagine who did the talking."

Günther shook his head slowly.

"He says it isn't his place to decide."

A major surprise!

"He knows her family is looking for her," Günther continued. "Not that I'd want to marry soon. I put in my bid because, when she comes of age, someone else might beat me to it. I think I fell in love with her that day we were kicking the ball around in the street out front –"

"I remember!" Jürgen grinned. "You were pretending to be Jürgen Sparwasser."

Günther blushed. He'd forgotten that foolishness. Indeed, he'd never seen Sparwasser play. However, every Ossi knew his was the winning goal in the only contest against the Wessis; none of that mattered. Heike's young, innocent smile dominated that afternoon so completely that all else shrank into insignificance.

He didn't fall in love that day; Heike Jacobs was a mere child. The smile, however, was embossed upon his memory. Gradually, it gained dominance.

Whenever anything amused Günther Neubert enough to draw serendipity, it was Heike's smile that illuminated his thoughts. He began watching Heike, hoping that he'd witness that smile again. Over time, he became as interested in the person to whom the smile belonged.

That afternoon in the park, not long after he did his best to discourage Lilo, he shamed himself by stealing a kiss from her. It was his way of announcing her value. He considered himself a fool. When he entered the national service, he vowed to leave his foolishness behind.

He failed.

Rather than push her out of his thoughts, Heike came to the fore. He refused to write or answer her messages. She was too young. Unfortunately, he realized she was growing older with each passing day. Heike Jacobs wouldn't be a child forever. If he were very lucky, she'd still be available when he returned. However, the odds were good that she had several, acceptable candidates lined up at her door.

"You think you could put up with Heike?" Jürgen asked, jarring Günther from his reverie.

"She's impulsive. Dangerously so. She could have done herself serious harm the other day. I reigned her in. She wanted to walk back. She's bucking for martyrdom. I had to force her onto that bus. She was very brusque with me. After, she refused to speak to me."

"That's who you want to live with?"

"I'm too easy going," he confessed. "I always manage to get by. Heike wouldn't let me get away with that. She'd drive me. Well, not exactly. She'll get in front and lead. She'll shame me into following her example."

Jürgen nodded knowingly.

"Well, whoever ends up with Heike will have his hands full," he concluded.

"And why not me? She has spirit and energy –"

"And obstinacy," Jürgen reminded.

Günther smiled and nodded.

"That as well."

There followed a moment of mutual reflection.

"Do you think Rosa's Children has a chance?" Jürgen asked.

There it was. The subject that closely touched an ever-growing number of people. The one subject no one was brave enough to confront until Jürgen couched it as a direct question. Günther turned it over in his mind for the hundredth time. Frequently, he imagined himself on the brink of an epiphany, but it always evaded him.

"No chance at all," he whispered.

Three or four established parties vied to make inroads in the former DDR. Rosa's Children could never be more than a shadow of the SPD or the CDU. Furthermore, the childish name would advance no further than a punch line to a bad joke.

"Who will tell her?"

Jürgen's question lingered in the air and billowed between them like a toxic cloud. Günther hadn't nerve enough to practice betrayal. If Heike's brother hadn't sufficient courage, it would fall to him. Günther wanted none of it.

"What do we do when it blows up?"

Günther refused to let this pass unanswered. He resented his friend's audacity in asking.

"We help her confront reality," he promised. "It isn't as if we demand she give up her beliefs. She won't, in any case. It will go hard with her. She will need us."

"She might kick the 'stuffing' out of us. You, yourself, said she's insane."

Günther had to smile. He couldn't help himself.

"You don't believe that." he announced, accurately. "It's true she could hurt someone in a rage. One of us should be able to calm her down."

If it weren't for the sudden movement of Frau Jacobs on the couch, they mightn't have noticed. Foolishly, they took their colloquy into the kitchen. The sentry woman on the couch tacitly acknowledged the presence of an additional person.

Nadine, properly speaking, was not in the room. She stole into the kitchen arch. She must have followed them. She couldn't have been there long, but the expression on her twisted face made it clear she'd heard enough.

"Günther Neubert," she began petulantly and an accusatory tone. "Can you wait two years for Heike?"

It was not a question. It was a challenge.

This was not the time to be coy; nor was it the proper place to stammer some pathetic apology or excuse. Nadine's visage was threatening. It would take so little to transform Heike into a stampeding tyrant. All that was necessary was to repeat a small sampling Günther and Jürgen's exchange.

"I can wait longer than that if I must, Nadine Jacobs," he announced boldly. "She's worth it."

She held his eyes while judging his veracity.

"Alright, then," she snapped.

Nadine retired to prepare soapy water for the stairs.

Jürgen and Günther exchanged looks of relief.

* * *

The mid-day meal was finished, and Rolf returned to work. The dishes were cleaned. With the major meal of the day behind them, the family generally suspended activities for at least an hour. Unused to the exertion required to keep the family's wood surfaces properly cleaned, Jürgen opted for a brief heat-of-the-day nap. Nadine, helplessly under Heike's influence, wished to settle down beside Anne with a worn text of *A Midsummer Night's Dream* in German with facing pages in the original English.

It was suggested Heike go for a walk. She was suspicious when both Jürgen and Nadine proposed it. Her convalescing legs remained sore and, strangely, the area between her shoulder blades pained her. However, it cost no more to walk than watch Nadine read. Still, she knew some subterfuge was underway.

Heike headed for the city park. She wasn't surprised to see Günther step from the shade.

"Been waiting long?"

"Not very. I just got back."

"From —?"

He came abreast of her and gestured towards the park. Günther slowed to keep her from falling behind.

"I stopped to see Lilo."

He got no reaction, but he was schooled enough to know that, inside, Heike was bubbling.

"I couldn't avoid her forever, even if I wanted to," he appended. "I thought it best to get it over."

"I didn't ask," she reminded.

"That's why I'm explaining."

It was a cordial encounter. It was so polite and measured that both parties experienced acute agony. Günther broke off at the first properly civilized moment and saw relief in Lilo's eyes. He left the square with his hands sweating profusely.

Günther and Heike walked silently toward the music school.

"She's still smitten," Heike informed when they passed the bust of Pushkin and entered the greenery.

"*Smitten*? Well, I've no control over that. It's over, Heike. You must trust me."

"It's Lilo I don't trust."

The conversation was not progressing. Günther allowed it to lapse. They reached the water's edge. The level was much lower than normal. They turned south. In truth, Heike drew him along a different path.

"Jürgen is right, of course," she began from nowhere. "We need a local cause to fire up interest. Lilo's written out a great text – I nearly cried reading it, but words don't salt potatoes, do they? We must have some immediate issue."

Günther, with no suggestions to offer, continued to match Heike's pace with slow, lazy steps.

"I wish you were there when that man came," she spoke louder and with fire. "All I heard was my sister came from America. I couldn't handle it. Our country goes to smash and the Amis flock here to devour the body. I couldn't handle it. I needed you."

"What could I do?"

"You could have slapped some sense into me."

He let that thought travel with them for several meters.

"I might throw you down and sit on you until your brain comes back, but I draw the line there," he announced. "I've never slapped a girl."

"What can I do? I told that man – never mind."

"I can imagine."

"If he tells my sister, and she clears off…I really made a mess this time."

"If she's like you, she won't be put off by rude words."

She digested that and found some comfort.

"What if she isn't like me?"

"She's come all the way from America for what, the brats? She's on a mission, Heike!"

Heike's hands flailed at the air with meaningless gestures born or frustration and self-derision.

"I could have asked about her. Is she well? Where is she? Günther, I don't even know her name! All I could think – she's a gloating Ami, dripping with jewels and leaking dollars from every pore. It made me angry – very angry."

"If she is loaded with jewels and leaking dollars?" he asked, baiting her. "You'd be composed, I suppose."

"I don't know!" she responded instantly.

"You do, Heike. You know exactly. You'd be very angry. Somebody would get hurt. All I know is I won't get between you. Don't expect me to slap sense into you. This is your test, Heike. Nobody can help you."

Heike attempted to conjure speech. Instead, she threatened to bring tears. Yes, Heike who did not cry, but for whom it was fast becoming a habit, was struggling hard. She ran ahead to hold the waters at bay. Additionally, she must not allow Günther to see her in tears. He made no attempt to keep up. He knew where to find her.

She arrived only moments prior. Her breath did not heave from the exertion of the run, so she had time to recover. Her stiff muscles and joints rioted. She clung to the pedestal where one of Shakespeare's feet rested. She looked up, but not for inspiration from her silent mentor; it hurt too much to hang her head.

Heike heard footfalls and the crush of the gravel. She had no need to identify him.

"She must be older," she ruminated. "I wonder – Was it her idea to flee? If she takes pride in that –"

"Suppose she wants only to see her sister?"

Heike shivered. Slowly, with uncooperative muscles, she turned. She placed her feet in front of her and leaned back onto her hands pressed against the base of the statue. She looked squarely into his eyes.

"You promised you'd never slap me," she reminded. "Well, you just did."

"Sorry," he said in English.

"Don't be. Why do I imagine the worst?"

Günther halted his advance just beyond her reach. He watched Heike's eyes grew large.

"What – what if she's younger? What if she was born in America? A half-sister!"

That jolted Günther.

"What if she's been kicked out? What if she expects me to support her?"

"So much for dripping in jewels," Günther theorized.

Heike would not be distracted. Her thoughts raced.

"That's all I need! An older Inka."

This time, Günther thought to himself, the tactic of pushing the dirty work off on Hanna Müller was not an option. Heike would face her terror alone.

Perhaps, not entirely alone

Frankfurt/Oder

A smiling Biggi greeted Sabine with coffee in hand. She didn't need to ask for an egg *"boiled hardly"* because the breakfast buffet was fully laid out. There were several clues to suggest that Biggi got an early start in the kitchen.

The *chef* inspected the buffet with a considerably older assistant. He issued a couple terse commands and disappeared into his kingdom beyond the swinging doors. From this brief scene, Sabine assumed he was a grumpy, pompous boss.

Biggi appeared twice. The first time, she brought a cart of plates and saucers to set on the far end of the long serving table. Her second mission was to wheel a cart loaded with three smallish metal servers. These, she placed in specially designed hot-water receptacles. The contents, Sabine assumed were scrambled eggs, sausages and bacon strips, the traditional hotel fare. Biggie gave Sabine a quick wave as she, and her cart, hurried back into the kitchen.

"Your boss is a jerk."

The verdict was delivered when Biggi made a furtive attempt to get to Sabine's table. The redhead shrugged as if to say there was nothing to be done.

"Is there a bakery open this early? I want to get my father's breakfast."

This last sentence was added least Biggi think she wasn't appreciative of the hotel's victuals. Simultaneously, she recalled that sorry bakery she and Ute passed previously. If she were directed hither, Ernst Bauer would have to fend for himself. Biggi knew of one on Karl Marx Strasse. She provided directions. They were simple enough: turn left beyond the war-gutted cathedral, right at the first street and take the pedestrian passage.

Sabine thanked her and, after breakfast and two cups of coffee, she picked up her underwear bag and a shopping bag she'd acquired the previous evening. Suspicious of Biggi, she didn't follow her directions on the off chance that there were a couple Stasi goons posted along the route. Instead of turning right and heading for the cathedral, Sabine turned left, crossed the street, and headed for the Oderturm from that side.

Passing the looming gothic post office, she crossed Karl Marx Strasse then paused before crossing Heilbrunnerstrasse onto the Platz der Republik. Thrice she turned suddenly to catch anyone following. She was satisfied but remained suspicious.

She spotted the bakery Biggi recommended from the opposite side of the street. She continued to Rosa-Luxemburg Strasse and crossed with the light. If anyone followed her, he or she or they were very clever; her anxiety departed.

Her devious route transformed a five-minute walk into a quarter-hour hike, but she arrived unharmed and unworried. She waited her turn and purchased two brötchen and two sweet rolls. The paper bags went into her shopping bag, and she walked back toward the Oderturm.

Herr Bauer was an early riser, but he promised that he'd not leave for work without her. The Stasi didn't like locks; therefore, she walked into the building and climbed the stairs. She reached the end of the stairs. (Sabine refused to dignify the cracker-box former servants' rooms and attic with the term "top floor.")

She discovered her father's door ajar. With only a single knock on the door frame, she breezed in.

"You're earlier than I expected," Herr Bauer greeted while pulling on his shoes.

"You had a late night," she replied.

From the pocket of her jeans, she pulled the hotel receipt handed her when she left her key at the desk.

"I thought we agreed."

"We did. So, why did you sneak in and pay? You could have waited until today, or you could have walked me back to the hotel last night."

He shrugged. It was clear he had no intention of explaining himself. Sabine was happy he didn't invent some silly excuse. She hesitated to argue with a man she hardly knew.

"I brought you some breakfast," she informed seizing his plate, cup, knife, and linen napkin from the custom-made storage place.

"I told you I'd get something on the way," he reminded.

Her reply was a reproduction of the shrug he'd given her.

After placing the baked goods on his plate, she retrieved the shopping bag. She carefully cleaned and repacked the item the evening before, so it was ready for instant use. Herr Bauer watched her place the coffee maker atop his small food cabinet. He watched her plug it into the only electrical socket in the room, mysteriously situated shoulder high near the sink. He watched her fill the small, glass vessel half full, and pour the water into the machine.

There was a tin into which she poured the ground coffee she bought. From this, she spooned out the aromatic grains until satisfied.

"I know this takes longer, but it's better than instant," she smiled. "Here is your coffee. It should stay fresh if you snap the lid shut – and here are your filters. I'll put them in the cabinet, like so. All you need to do, *Meister Holzman*, is make yourself a proper shelf or stand for the coffee maker and *dort sind wir*!"

She turned to discover the man stunned. For over sixteen years, he'd tended to his own breakfast, his own dishes, and his own coffee. Suddenly, his daughter appears with food and coffee – and the means to brew it!

"Herr Bauer!"

A bold voice echoed from below. Whatever the Ernst's reverie, the woman's voice shook him out of it. He and Sabine exchanged a glance. He shuffled to the door. By that time, they heard footfalls.

"Good morning, Herr Bauer, I heard you were up – oh!"

The woman's gray hair was fixed in a tight bun high enough on the head to be seen from the front. Her face was wrinkled but kindly. Her eager eyes registered surprise to see a young girl in the room.

"Frau Kosyk," Herr Bauer introduced. "My daughter, Sabine, from America."

Whatever the woman's surprise before, it was trebled through the introduction.

"Fräulein Bauer, welcome, welcome!"

She scurried across the room on invisible feet. The hem of her skirt cleared the floor by a millimeter. Her hand stretched forth from a long white sleeve. Though the wrinkles betrayed age, the ease with which she moved, and the grip used to capture Sabine's hand were youthful. Sabine, who, moments before, leaned against the wall with no qualms over soiling the tattered wallpaper, stood straight.

The woman's bearing demand that Sabine's best manners should come out of hiding.

"A pleasure, Frau Kosyk," Sabine replied.

"From America."

"From America," Sabine confirmed.

Sabine was eager to have her hand back, but Frau Kosyk was as eager to keep hold. She placed her left hand over her right to make her grip more secure.

"I wanted to catch your father before he left," she explained with an unfamiliar accent. "I wanted to invite him to dinner this evening. If he accepts, I insist you come as well."

Sabine looked over the vivacious woman's head at the figure near the door.

"Papa?"

"We would be honored, Frau Kosyk," he said.

"Honored, indeed," Sabine seconded despite the unease over her hostage hand.

"The honor is ours; I assure you. Your father worked on our apartment, but with the Stasi prowling around, we had to be careful. We paid what we could, but it was not near enough. When we have guests, we eat late. If you come down around eight, we'll enjoy a drink or two before dinner."

Since the woman spoke exclusively to Sabine, she felt it incumbent upon her to speak on behalf of the entire family.

"Eight will be very nice."

"*Sehr gut!* Now, if there is one more to dinner, I must be off to get some more things."

"Please, Frau Kosyk, don't go to any trouble for me."

Finally, Sabine's hand was released if only so the woman could make a gesture of dismissal. She turned to Herr Bauer and glided.

"A visitor from America agrees to come into our home, and she thinks it is trouble. Herr Bauer, your daughter is very witty. We shall look forward to seeing you at eight."

Before she left, she turned to say good-bye to Sabine. In doing so, she tilted her cheery head just enough for the girl to respond in kind. From some long-forgotten example, Sabine put her right toe behind her left heel and bent her knee slightly. It was a "bob curtsey."

How she knew it by that name, she'd never know, but she realized – if properly done – it could be rendered in a skirt or a dress, but, normally, by younger girls. If any etiquette existed vis-à-vis the bob curtsey, the woman pretended ignorance. She left the room wearing a warm, satisfied smile.

"Polish?" Sabine whispered the moment she gauged the woman out of earshot.

"Sorb, I think."

* * *

Herr Bauer had agreed to travel to Seelow on short notice. The library suffered the crash of a shelf causing a second shelf to follow its example. The staff was hip deep in books and couldn't wait for the "*when-we-can-gat-around-to-its.*"

Someone knew someone who knew Ernst Bauer. He appeared in Seelow once a month and, occasionally, made enough to pay his fare up and back. Because it was an emergency, he agreed to make an emergency response before negotiating terms.

After breakfast and the wash-up, he took his tools and limped off to the Bahnhof. Sabine insisted on paying her own fare to tag along. She felt uncomfortable in her jeans, but she couldn't tramp around the DDR on a short pink skirt again. She'd collected curious, disapproving, and lecherous looks the day before.

As they waited for the train, Sabine learned about the Sorbs, Slavic people who migrated to Germany centuries before. They were mainly farmers. They clung to their culture and religion with tenacity. They were of Germany, but not German. Predictably, the Nazis marked them for extinction. They used the young men as cannon fodder in the Wehrmacht and shipped others to concentration camps on whatever invented excuses they dreamed up. When the DDR was born, it made life as miserable as possible. The Stasi created a special unit to spy on the Sorbs. The DDR removed as many as they could frame, their intricate Easter egg decorations were frowned upon by a country that denied religion. The Sorbs, who openly practiced their orthodox religion, populated "special" prisons.

Herr and Frau Kosyk were lucky; they were punished by exile. They were ripped from a Sorb village and were resettled in Frankfurt. They were near enough home to be tortured like Tantalus, and far enough away to prohibit the use of their language, customs and culture beyond the door of their Stasi apartment.

During their mutual imprisonment, the Kosyks dared not speak to Herr Bauer, save in whispers. The Stasi forbade fraternization among tenants, but the Kosyks offered Ernst the use of their bathroom so he could shower properly if infrequently. Initially, he refused. He feared they'd all be punished if the Stasi discovered the arrangement.

One *Orthodox* Easter, Frau Kosyk slipped an intricately adorned and brightly colored Easter egg, into Herr Bauer's coat pocket. He admired it for as long as he dared before leaving it in a public trash bin. It was too dangerous to keep. If he ate it, the Stasi might discover a sliver of shell and…

Everyone in the *Building of the Damned* knew the identity of the Stasi informers, a skinny little man, his mousey little wife and two wicked children. The adults were indolent. They had a free apartment and were too worthless to take their jobs seriously. Of course, they reported to their bosses periodically, but they were seldom pro-active. Their children, however, haunted the stairwell like malevolent ghosts.

If Herr Kosyk exchanged a word with his wife in their language, even behind the closed door of their apartment, the Stasi would know within the hour. If there was Easter production, a single shred of literature not properly supported by the SED, any sign of "counter-revolutionary" or "anti-social" behavior, the *spy* kids would tell their parents, who would inform the Stasi. Presumably, the informers earned rewards.

Ernst Bauer was very careful when stashing money. If one of the spies saw him, he'd be wiped out again. One afternoon, he was trapped in the attic because a spy kid was perched on the landing outside the door to his room; listening. Perhaps, he thought Herr Bauer talked to himself in an incriminating way. At last, when the little monster decided to prey on another tenant, Ernst tiptoed out of the attic and into his room.

When the government began crumbling, the kids became less active. One day, the moving truck arrived, and the informants packed up. They were still lugging their belongings out when Frau Kosyk shouted up the stairs.

"Herr Bauer! Come have lunch. We will celebrate Mass, dance traditional Sorb dances, and sing very rude songs about children who crawl on their bellies and hiss like snakes!"

Ernst wasn't there. He was working, as she well knew. Her performance was aimed at the departing stooges. She told him about this episode days later. Frau Kosyk did not boast; she was merely sharing an anecdote. She "confessed" to him as an act of repentance aimed at regaining her self-respect.

"The Kosyks are always eager to help others." Papa shared, "Of course, they were forced into being covert. Before, no one in our building dared get caught speaking to other tenants. Now, you can't get us to shut up. We missed forty years of conversation, and we're trying to catch up."

They left the train but couldn't cross the tracks immediately. They walked south for some distance before finding a pedestrian crossing. Sabine regretted her weakness. She wanted to help her father carry that heavy tool chest as he limped along, but it was futile.

"What's that?" she asked, pointing to a reddish base and statue in the distance.

"Battle memorial."

"Napoleon again?"

"Red Army."

Sabine conjured Berlin and Frankfurt-like visions of scared structures, heaps of rubble and gutted buildings. As they neared the main road through town, she was confronted by a squat ivy-covered, concrete building recessed from the road. Around it was an array of military equipment. Among the menacing display was a polished tank with the barrel of its turret pointed ominously west.

"This was the one tank road to Berlin and the Reds wanted it," Ernst explained. "The Wehrmacht fortified these heights with everything they had. It was a horrible fight, lasting for days. You might want to spend some time in the museum. This may take me a while."

She shook her head. Fighting and killing had a limited appeal for her.

"I came to be with you, Baba."

He laughed. It was modest but heartfelt.

"You speak Sächsisch?"

"I discovered lazy consonants," she replied seriously. "Beyond that, I know nothing."

"Isch och ne," he announced with a grin.

Sabine pondered these strange sounds momentarily.

"You – don't either?"

He nodded.

"Correct, Sabine. Let me caution you, anyone can speak Saxon if you pretend you're lazy and drunk and have a mouth full of cake. That's easy. The hard part is trying to understand what the other lazy, drunk, cake-chewing people are saying."

Even the timorous visitor cracked a smile over this homily.

"The Vandals and the Lombards lived on the Oder before they caused so much mischief in Europe and Africa," he stated. "It's only fitting that so much blood was shed here centuries later."

Clearly, Ernst Bauer had returned to more somber thoughts. Sabine honored his sudden mood swing by remaining silent. There were no gutted buildings or battle scars. Seelow, apparently flattened during the battle, was rebuilt from scratch; they weren't very successful. Of what Sabine had seen in the DDR, this place was the least pretentious. It was one step above a peasant village.

As they lumbered uphill on crumbling pavement, they passed a peculiar house. It was large, gray, and ugly. It was several meters off the street, and it had a low wall in front. The grass between the wall and the house had run riot for some while. Some windows were boarded up.

The library, further on, was a squat, ugly building with small windows. It may have been a school once. It might have been a stable. It, most certainly, was not built for use as the community library.

A small alcove with a cement floor greeted them. To reach the library entrance, the Bauers navigated around a stack of tires and two coiled garden hoses.

Once inside, they discovered a spacious room with slatted wooden shelves stretching around the walls with breaks to allow for the windows. There were four other free-standing shelves running through the center. Behind a counter, neatly stacked, were seven pillars of books. One was slightly taller than Sabine. There was room for a tiny desk littered with papers and three unmatched chairs.

Two women patrolled behind the counter. One was young; the other looked out from under a flurry of white hair and over a pair of cumbersome glasses perched precariously on the tip of her broad nose. She studied, with an air of disapproval, a pair of teenagers floating through the stacks. Her suspicious eyes diverted to the Bauers. Spying the tool chest, she lifted her head slightly.

"Herr Bauer?" she asked, moving toward the end of the counter.

"Frau Sturtz?"

"I'm glad you're here. Let me show you."

She lifted a hinged portion of the counter, ducked through it, and led the new arrivals to two neat stacks of polished wood. Some of the pieces were broken.

Ernst examined the lumber. One part of the frame was warped, and another was in the early stages. He examined the shelves themselves. Two were split and useless. Carefully, he inspected the dowels and flanges.

The person or persons who cleared away the mess made certain to pick up all the little *Dingsboomstas*. These were stored in clear plastic bags and affixed to the ruins with heavy-duty tape.

"I cannot repair these broken shelves," he announced. "I'll take measurements and make new ones. That will take a few days, and I can't guarantee to match them with the other shelves."

"Fix what you can," the lady implored. "We have new ones on order, but they may not arrive for months."

"These will only collapse again," he announced. "I can reinforce the corners and the warped sides. It won't look pretty."

Obviously, Sabine thought, if looks counted for anything, the entire building would have been condemned years before.

"I'll need some plywood and a few lengths of board," he mused. "Sabine, could you help me?"

"Of course, Baba."

They retraced their steps to the crumbling street. They returned to the gate of the abandoned house, found it unlocked, and walked onto the "estate." They discovered a faded police seal on the front door.

"Somebody was murdered?" Sabine asked.

"I doubt it. Somebody was arrested or fled West."

They walked to the back and found another door with another police seal. Ernst began examining the windows. One was boarded up with plywood. He removed it with ease.

"That's more than we need," he stated, turning his attention to the window.

It was broken. They peered in to find shattered glass and a large rock that told a story.

"Could you reach the handle on the inside and open the window without cutting yourself?" he asked.

"If I can get up there."

He used a hammer to break off the window glass nearest the handle.

"Reach underneath carefully," he instructed. "If you get cut, don't pull back. Instead, move your arm away from the cut. Understand?"

"Yes, Baba."

She lay down her underwear bag. He leaned against the house and spread his feet wide. He bent as far as he was able with a bad leg.

"Climb on my back and open the window. Take your time."

She didn't want to hurt him. Her canvass shoes were judged safe enough, or she'd have removed them. However, she was concerned about her weight. She vowed to avoid taking her time, but she wasn't anxious to spend the evening in a hospital with stitches and plasma.

She climbed on his back. He straightened his legs and gave her extra few inches. She reached through quickly but carefully. She had no chance of reaching in with her right hand. Very gingerly, she reached with her left, her fingers felt inside.

She felt the bottom of the plate of the handle, but jagged glass threatened. If she had something to wrap round her hand, she'd break the last bit with her fist. All she had, however, was her t-shirt. To use it, she must take it off. She rejected that idea instantly, but she couldn't stay where she was forever.

She gripped the edge of the glass with her thumb and a finger. She attempted to wiggle it loose, but it was solid.

"Give me the hammer!"

She got hold with her index and middle finger and managed, somehow, to transfer it to her left hand without dropping it on her father's head. She smashed the offending obstacle with all the force she could bring to bear. Broken glass fell on her wrist, but it fell harmlessly away into the grass.

Quickly, she reached through and grabbed the handle. She twisted it ninety degrees and pushed on the frame.

"Now what?"

"Climb in."

She got her feet on his shoulders. From there, getting into the room was simple. She climbed up and looked down.

"Are you okay?" she asked.

"You're light as a feather," he lied. "Go around and open the door."

She moved slowly. The sunlight hadn't shifted to that side of the house and there was more than glass and rocks on the floor. Looking about and judging by the bric-a-brac, Sabine concluded the room belonged to a boy not much younger than she. He liked soccer and horses. His bed remained unmade. There was a stale, unpleasant smell. The house must have remained abandoned for a very long time.

Sabine made her way into a living room where things remained neat and undisturbed. There was a noticeable collection of dust. She feared meeting rats or other unspeakable vermin, but her father was expecting her.

The kitchen was small yet functional. There were a few dishes in the sink. She reached the door, opened the deadbolt, and turned a latch below the knob. She opened it and Ernst limped in.

"They left in a very big hurry," she speculated.

Herr Bauer bothered only with what he could use.

"Aren't we breaking the law?" she asked.

"Whose law? This house and everything in it belong to *the people*. The government confiscates in the name of *Das Volk*. Now that the Stasi is gone, or has gone underground, I and the library staff are *the people*. We're making use of our own resources."

"Won't the family come back?"

"If they were in prison, they'd be released by now. My guess is, they found a way to get out. They're making a new life somewhere. Likely, they think someone's living here, or that it was destroyed."

"Or they've been killed."

"Always a possibility in the DDR," he agreed.

Sabine was not anxious to move about. She stood at the door as a lookout. She allowed her father to do the searching. He knew what he wanted; she hadn't had a clue.

"Does it make you angry?" she asked over her shoulder.

"What?"

The voice was partially muffled.

"These people may have got out. You didn't."

Her answer came amid a brief cacophony. There were thuds and banging. These were followed by the crack of hammer on wood and select Saxon oaths. Finally, she heard the less hostile and more reassuring sounds of boards being stacked. Finally, her father's uneven footfalls approached, and he appeared with two long and two short boards.

"Bed frame," he explained.

She stood aside so he could remove his treasure. Without waiting for orders, Sabine closed, locked, and bolted the door. She scurried to the window, slithered cautiously out, and dropped to the earth without wrenching an ankle or a knee.

"Your mother died free," he said off-handedly as they trundled back toward the library. "You grew up free. I'm alive to see the day when freedom came looking for me. Heike will experience the same – even if she doesn't appreciate it. I cannot say I'm angry."

"But Mutti is dead."

"True. Still, we were lucky – very lucky. Two people got out. It was a stupid plan, and a poor one. We all should have been killed or locked up. Your mother would agree, it turned out better than anyone expected."

"Sometimes," he admitted, meters later, "I wished I had died instead of your mother. Then, I think not. She would have lost one daughter, at least. I shudder to think what that would have done to her."

Herr Bauer needed to borrow a certain kind of saw to transform his *looted* lumber into useful material. Once he had the proper tool, he made a short work of restoring two bookcases. They weren't pretty, but they served well enough while the cash-strapped library waited for factory-made replacements.

* * *

That evening at the Kosyks, Sabine was the guest of honor. If she were the President of the United States, she couldn't have been treated better. She got the best chair, the first choice of every item on the table, and her every word was attended as if she had the power of holy writ.

Herr Kosyk was a balding man with gray eyebrows, a high forehead, and probing eyes. He was also quick to smile and easily satisfied by – well, everything. As with Ernst Bauer, he had worked on the sly. He assured his guests that he'd soon have a permanent position in a local business as a combination supply clerk and record keeper.

Together, Herr and Frau Kosyk lay siege to Sabine. They began by exhausting the normal questions: Did she have a swimming pool? Did she know any movie stars?

Later, they queried Sabine on substantive matters. Ernst kept silent. He soaked in her every word. Things she most wanted to relate to him about her friends, the *Mary R.*, and her life as a free citizen held everyone rapt. The Kosyks were amazed and bewildered that Herr Bauer was hearing these incredible reflections for the first time.

"Too much, too soon is bad," he smiled. "Each day, Sabine tells me something amazing. It's like getting sixteen years of Christmas gifts every day."

Sabine, however, was dissatisfied. Though she enjoyed sharing her life, she wanted to know about the Sorbs. She'd never heard of these people and was eager to correct the deficiency. Similarly, she was interested in Saxony. In both wishes, she was left wanting.

"We must have you back," Frau Kosyk promised.

"I'm afraid the Sorb culture would prove too pedestrian for an American," Herr Kosyk ventured.

Sabine looked at her father's contented face.

"I'm German," she stated confidently. "I'm part Swabish, part Saxon, and…"

She hesitated.

"…part Ossi."

The entire assembly paused for a few seconds of sober reflection. Eventually, the silence became oppressive. Ernst cleared his throat.

"Perhaps," he introduced, "we could take you to dinner some evening. It's only fair; you've gone to so much trouble."

"Trouble?" Frau Kosyk laughed. "I welcome such troubles. For years, we've eaten alone. Now, we are free to have guests. I long for trouble!"

* * *

It was after ten o'clock when she entered the hotel. She presented her card and collected her key. In her key box was a postcard. After seeing the address, she was amazed it reached her. Ute registered as Foster, but Sabine re-registered as Bauer.

Unwilling to risk the elevator, she trudged up the stairs. She had the information. It was the same address Michael Kaufmann smuggled to Oregon. Still, she'd like to know of Nadine. What did she have to do with anything? Also, why was Herr Beckmann so coy?

"You're so clever," she snorted aloud to Herr Beckmann in absentia. "Under four eyes!"

Regardless, he thought the information was sensitive. She tore the card into tiny bits. When she left the hotel in the morning, she shared the bits in several trash bins along her way.

She didn't see Biggi that morning. She ordered coffee from a woman, a stranger. It was unsettling. She fought the urge to ask if Biggi was ill.

Though he never said it, it was clear that her father didn't care for sweet rolls. At the bakery she settled on a pair of rye brötchen. Sabine arrived at her father's box with slices of cheese lifted from the breakfast buffet. She preferred purchasing the cheese, but she couldn't obtain it by the slice. What Baba didn't eat that morning would never survive in the heat.

She was pleased to discover Ernst had the coffee on when she arrived. He, in turn, was thankful for the breakfast, but insisted he could get his own. She was equally insistent that it was a daughter's right to bring breakfast to her father. He grumbled but offered no further objections.

She spent most of the day with him in a school where he installed new baseboards in three classrooms. It hurt her to stand idle and watch him crawl along the floor with his bad leg, but he never complained. They talked while he worked, and she enjoyed her first lessons in the Saxon dialect.

With Sabine willingness and her ability to clear objects from her father's path, the baseboards were installed in far less time than if left alone. With plenty of time before lunch, Ernst planed the bottom of a problem door. Sabine helped re-hang it. During this operation, the school director came by and asked if Herr Bauer could install wainscoting in the staff room and in two classrooms on the upper level.

The most difficult problem with their new commission was getting the material from where it was to where it was needed. Sabine was no small help. Having the proper material – imported from the West – and a level floor made the project easy though tedious and time-consuming. They left work shortly after one and walked through the park to the horse-trailer imbiss for a bowl of soljanka, a brötchen, and a Wessi beer.

"Have you ever heard of a Nadine?" Sabine asked without preface.

Herr Bauer gave the question respectful thought.

"I don't believe so. Is she a pop singer?"

"I don't know. That's why I asked."

He shrugged and shook his head.

They returned to the school, finished the project, and had time to watch the ducks paddling about in the pond behind the school. The director invited Herr Bauer back the next day for further renovations now that the long-awaited materials were arriving. The contract was agreed upon with the formality of a firm handshake. Negotiations were concluded after which the director counted out several Ossi bills for the fulfillment of that day's work.

"You are part of the economy of the DDR," Baba assured his daughter, thrusting an alarming share of the day's earnings into her hand.

"Baba! I did almost nothing."

"You did enough for us to have the remainder of the day to ourselves."

Sabine pocketed the wad of bills without further protest. If her father refused to spend money on needed items, she'd do so on his behalf.

That evening, they went to a *friend's* workshop. By day, it remained the property of the DDR; after hours it was available for Ernst to create things when special equipment was required. He made his table and chair there (contrary to prevailing law). Currently, the law was neither Ossi nor Wessi; the shop was at the disposal of anyone with a key.

He paid for the lumber he used. This procedure was simple and informal. Herr Bauer left a penciled note including the storage bin number and number of units removed. Estimating the cost, he'd leave the note folded around Ossie bills. If he underpaid, the shop foreman would collect later.

"They know how to get hold of me," he winked, sliding paper and money through a slot in an office door.

"And, if you overpay?" she asked.

"Then, they experience difficulty in getting hold of me."

She frowned. However, she made no attempt to fathom the DDR economy. It was impossible to comprehend.

"You need to make a shelf for your coffee maker," she reminded.

"In good time."

That evening's project was to make shelves to replace the ones rendered useless by the Seelow "misfortune." Sabine watched as he measured and cut the boards precisely with a table saw. Sabine was charged with carrying the fragments to the "bone yard," a euphemism for a scrap bin. In the DDR, nothing was wasted. Ernst's cast offs would be used for something.

Once home, Herr Bauer took the shelves into the attic where he placed them across a pair of home-made sawhorses. The lighting was poor, but he patiently and lovingly applied a finishing coat to the top and edges of the shelves.

"We'll let that dry and finish up tomorrow," he promised.

"Is this where you keep your money?" she asked.

"Feel free to look for it."

She made no move. If there were a secret door or a sliding panel somewhere, the Stasi couldn't find it. If they couldn't, Sabine concluded she had no chance. Besides, the money was her father's; she'd no business with it. She felt badly enough about him paying her hotel bill. She felt worse when she recalled Molly's words about socialism.

It was late, but he insisted on walking her back to the hotel. She made a valiant attempt to dissuade him, but he remained adamant.

"I'm not a baby, you know," she protested.

He made no reply, and she felt instant remorse.

"I'm sorry," she said.

He replied by taking her arm and leading her down the stairs.

The following morning, Biggi brought her coffee with one hand and an egg with the other. The previous day was her day off. Apparently, she spent some of her time thinking.

"Would you mind so very much if I could talk with you, after work?"

"Biggi, you're speaking German this morning."

The artificial redhead blushed.

"I can't say that in English," she admitted.

"What do you want to talk about?"

"America."

"Biggi, I'm not American. I was born in Saxony."

"Yes, but you lived in America, right?"

Sabine nodded.

She dreaded the thought of answering the inane questions which, apparently, came with celebrity status. Still, empathy squelched any plans for a flat refusal. Sabine longed to have an hour with Gary and Molly – with the whole *gang*, in fact.

Writing letters was an obligation she took seriously, but her heart ached when she realized there could be no replies. If Birgit were obsessively curious about America, maybe they could become mutually supportive. She'd be free to say things to Biggi she didn't feel comfortable sharing with her father. If, in her excitement, she let slip something too personal, she took comfort in the fact that Birgit Schneeweiß and Sabine Bauer would, likely, never cross paths again.

Suspicion remained that Biggi might be Stasi, but it was fast evaporating. Aside from everything else, it's too bizarre for a spy to advertise by dying her hair red. Moreover, the girl was as subtle as a train wreck. Though Sabine knew little about spying, she assumed a good spy preferred being inconspicuous.

"If I'm not out late tonight, we can meet at the hotel. Where do you live?"

"Not far," Birgit gestured. "Old University."

"The apartment building?"

"Ja."

"I know it. Why don't I come there?"

"The hotel's better," she said, evasively enough to renew Sabine's suspicions.

Biggi noticed Sabine's hesitation.

"I'll come to the lobby around seven. If you don't show, I'll see you in the morning."

Sabine forced a smile.

"Fair enough."

* * *

They spent the day at the school. There was much detailed work and very little Sabine could do to help. However, she was hardly bored. Her Saxon lessons continued. So did Baba's interesting narratives.

Ernst enjoyed talking of Constanze. It did Sabine no harm, and her father's eyes sparkled. He was sorry she was gone, but he retained a myriad of wonderful memories.

For lunch, they headed towards the river and found a place where they could sit and be waited on. Sabine was disappointed that all the menu items were potato dishes. Still, the hash-like creation she ordered was excellent. Further, despite a modest price, it was a heaping portion. She hoped they would enjoy a good supper that evening, but Sabine doubted her appetite would recover in time.

She told her father about meeting with Biggi at seven. He offered no objection. Indeed, he suggested it was a good idea.

"You need to be around young people," he philosophized.

Sabine agreed, though not without guilt. He was her father; their time together was precious and limited.

"The shelves will be ready tomorrow morning, but I have five apartments that I promised to do this week, so I can't, with a clear conscience, spend half a day delivering them."

"I'll take them, Papa," she said without thinking.

"They're bulky and heavy," he reminded. "I can borrow a cart. That will help, but you can't get it up the Bahnhof steps –"

"I'll figure out something," she promised.

He grinned.

"I'm proud of you!"

Sabine was overwhelmed. She nearly teared up.

"It's hardly worth a Nobel Prize," she responded incredulously.

He shook his head.

"You don't understand, Schatz," he chuckled. "Most girls, even here, wouldn't think to offer. They're too deferential. Some women, particularly young ones, assume certain things are beneath them and certain other things are indelicate. You want results. If something needs doing, you jump in."

She blinked.

"Ha!" he continued. "Ute Foster is a fine woman. I knew from the first. I know what your Ami father is like – *exact*! He doesn't cater to you, does he? If he sees you getting your hands dirty, he didn't discourage you, did he?"

"My *father*?"

Sabine had only one. She'd love Aaron forever, but he was NOT her father.

"He helped raise you. I never had a chance to raise you. That man – I am grateful to him. He and Ute did a magnificent job with you. I have a daughter, and I am very proud of her!"

She reflected. Aaron Foster seldom placed restrictions on her. Neither he nor Ute established set expectations beyond their mutual desire that she go to college. It was a stark contrast to Molly Waldron who was raised a *princess*. She recalled how Aaron stood aside and watched quietly as she piloted the *Mary R.* to within yards of a very dangerous situation.

"No," she concluded. "I guess he never did."

"That's exactly how we would have done," he told her. "We discussed it in detail. We decided you girls would not grow up spoiled and fastidious. We would establish certain boundaries and let you develop on your own. We did not want you dependent upon others. What are the chances, Sabine? What are the chances that you'd be brought up exactly as Constanze hoped? There must be some divinity behind it."

He picked up the remainder of his beer when he thought of something more important. He put the glass stein back on the polished wooden table and leaned forward.

"Don't mistake me, Sabine. We'd have loved you as much if you decided to become an actress and wouldn't be caught dead with a hammer in your hand, but we certainly have more respect if you were willing to take on responsibilities even if they aren't your own. I saw you climb through that window. You didn't debate or discuss it. You didn't bat an eye."

He saluted her with the stein and downed the remaining beer in two great gulps. Sabine had opted for an orange juice. When she emptied her glass, the meal was officially over, and the check was called for. Ernst insisted on paying but he made no protest when Sabine pressed two marks into the waitress' hand.

"The day before you got here, I was paid with two concert tickets," he reported. "I had second thoughts. I was about to cash them in. Might you be interested?"

"What concert?"

"A young Polish violinist. I can't pronounce the name. She's only twenty something, but I've heard good things about her. They made the arrangements long before the *Wende*, but, I guess, they decided to go ahead."

"Will she play Bach?" she asked, eagerly.

"One of them lived and worked here. I don't know what's on the program, but it would be rude not to play some Bach. Shall we find out?"

"When?"

"Next Friday. I think, you should wear that pretty dress from the first day. No one will notice the program. Everyone will be looking at you."

She blushed anew.

"Looking at the dress," she corrected.

He shrugged.

"It's a date, Baba."

* * *

They were buoyant when they left the school late that afternoon. Herr Direktor found Ernst just after four o'clock while he replaced a broken windowpane. He hadn't wanted to mention the matter before. However, the bureaucratic hurdles were cleared. Herr Direktor was authorized to hire Herr Bauer as the *Hausmeister* for the coming school year.

The pay was not princely, but it would constitute a steady income. It could pave the way for a better job later. Realizing that his days as a freelance repairman were numbered, Ernst accepted. Again, they sealed the contract with a handshake. Sabine wanted to celebrate, but Herr Bauer insisted she keep her date with Birgit Schneeweiß.

"We shall celebrate when I sign the contract," he promised.

"A handshake was always good before," she observed.

"For a *Schwartzarbieter*, indeed," he cautioned. "But a contract makes me legal. That's why I am careful. People dealing in the Black Market are honest – they must be. If they cheat, they're turned in. Legitimate workers are the ones likely to be dishonest."

"You don't trust that Direktor."

"Herr Direktor, yes. Like me, he did time in prison. His crime was to protest, too loudly, that the Education Ministry was a gaggle of foolish geese. Oh, I trust a man who isn't afraid to say what he knows is true. I don't know his superiors. Until I have a signed contract, I'm not in a mood to celebrate."

Sabine relented.

"If you're sure, Baba."

He gave her a big hug. She shivered in his arms. The meaning of the gesture – and the gesture itself – was powerful. She was someone's daughter.

"Have a good time. Oh, don't bring your underwear to the concert."

Sabine laughed. She was crying, but she'd never been so happy in her life.

With key in hand, Sabine ignored both the heat and the stale air. She bounded up the stairwell, two steps at a time, until the bounce left her legs and was reduced to one frustratingly small step after another. She ignored the protests of her lungs and negotiated the climb in the shortest time possible.

Dripping by the time she reached her room; Sabine didn't mind a layer of sweat. She showered at once. Moreover, she remained under the nozzle until she shivered from the cold. Her task accomplished; Sabine expected a few minutes of relief from the heat only to be greeted by a wall of fire upon opening the bathroom door.

She groaned.

Twisting the handle and drawing the window into the room, Sabine prayed for a whisper of breeze. She moved a chair to keep the window from swinging back. Alas, only hot air moved. Still, moving air was better than oven air. Well, perhaps not – she rushed to the sink, drenched a towel under the cold tap and swathed her upper body while ignoring the water dripping onto the carpet.

Five minutes later, without the aid of a towel, she was dry. She read *Silas Marner* for a few minutes until her hair was, likewise, dry. Had Ute remained her roommate, she'd be forced to wear clothes. Alone behind a locked door, Sabine enjoyed the freedom of lounging naked. Alas, the clock continued to march. She must decide what to wear.

She hated the pink skirt, but it was that or jeans. Maybe, she could use her earnings to get a pair of loose-fitting shorts or a less obnoxious skirt. Perhaps, she could get in a quick shop upon her return from Seelow.

Unfortunately, her date with Biggi was in the offing. So, the pink skirt and the Fisherman's Inn t-shirt must serve. She tucked Silas in her underwear bag in case she had to spend time in the lobby.

She did not. Biggi was sitting on a couch paging through a Wessi magazine and admiring the fashion trends of the celebrity crowd. She, herself, wore an ankle-length white skirt so thin the heat had no chance of being entrapped. She had a gold print top with, obviously, nothing beneath.

"Have you been waiting long?"

"I haven't been waiting at all," Birgit replied, her red hair spilling down onto her shoulders. "This is about the coolest place in town."

"Maybe, we should stay here."

"Nein! Let's get a cold drink! I know the place."

"Moment mal. You're not taking me somewhere to flush Knaben, are you?"

"No! I swear, but if you want –"

"I don't want. I've got a boyfriend at home. I don't think I'm ready for life in the DDR fast lane."

Birgit laughed and bounded to her feet.

"Neither am I. I have rotten luck with guys, but I'm thirsty."

With this assurance, Sabine handed her room key to the attendant and followed Birgit's long, confident strides. Soon, they were seated at one of the outdoor tables where Sabine had tasted her first, very disappointing schnitzel. Biggi ordered a Wessi beer and Sabine, wary of any DDR drinks, followed suit.

"They didn't have beer when I ate here," Sabine reported.

"You do need luck," Biggi replied. "Tell me about America."

There followed the expected questions about swimming pools and movie stars but quickly graduated to matters less frivolous. When Biggi admitted she had no idea where Oregon was, Sabine reminded her about the one of the two states every European knew.

"It's just to the north."

"Oh, yes. Apples."

"Too far. We have apples, but Washington is famous for them."

"And Oregon?"

"Beaver, supposedly. I've seen a couple. On the ocean, where I live, I see many seals, sea otters, and sea lions. And whales – many, many. My grandpa had a big sheep ranch in another part of the state. We have a lot of desert."

"Indians?"

"I've seen many, but they aren't like the ones in Karl May."

Birgit was disappointed. The East German film industry made several shoot-'em-ups about the repressed and exploited American Indians. For over an hour, Sabine narrated snap shots of the *Mary R.*, Gary, the Waldrons, and the Kuriharas. Birgit sat rapt, aside from an occasional question.

She drank it in with her eyes as well as her ears. She also drank her beer. She started on her third while Sabine was still working on the second half of her first glass.

"Tell me about life in the DDR."

Biggi made a horse's whine.

"Look around," she suggested with a decided lack of interest.

"Have you been to Poland?"

"Słubice, across the river," she responded. "That doesn't count. Until 1945, it was just the other part of Frankfurt. Most of the people still speak German."

"What's it like?"

"The people are dirt poor. I've seen kids over there in November without shoes."

"Can you speak Polish?"

"A little more than English. Not much. But my Polish helped me get my job at the hotel. They assumed I know more Polish than I do."

"That first day, when you spoke English, I thought you might be Stasi."

Feeling that confession is good for the soul, Sabine thought it best to be candid. Biggi's face turned to stone. She squeezed her glass so tightly her knuckles glowed.

"I'm sorry! I didn't mean to upset you. Honest!"

She flailed like a drowning person to banish Birgit's disturbing visage and alarming bellicose attitude. Whatever war raged within the phony red head, it began to ebb. After a few moments Birgit managed a tight-lipped and embarrassed smile. Her eyes remained averted, however.

"Okay, then," she began a confession. "My life in the DDR by Biggi Schneeweiß:

I was in a gymnasium, for reasons never quite clear. I was not a good student. That's boastful, I'm sorry; I was a rotten student. I won't tell you what I got on my *Abi*. Well, I don't have to, do I? If I'd done well, I'd be in university, wouldn't I? Well, I'm not at university – that was never a possibility. Someone, I guess, owed my family a favor and got me placed in a gymnasium instead of a trade school – do you mind?"

From the front pocket of her skirt, she brought out a pack of cigarettes. Sabine noticed them earlier through the thinness of the skirt. She smelled it on Biggi in the lobby. Up until that moment, Biggi refrained as if in deference to the visitor, but the urge to smoke could no longer be repressed.

"Please," Sabine nodded.

She was thankful Biggi did not offer her a cigarette.

Birgit seeded a stick in her mouth and tore a match out of a generic book. Her fingers trembled as she struck the match. A pool of light reflected off her grim face as she lit up. She took a drag so deep Sabine expected to see smoke rise from her shoes. When she exhaled, it was voluminous and choking. Somehow, Sabine kept from coughing up a lung.

"So," Birgit resumed after another drag, "Since I didn't do trade school, this was as good a job as I could get. Not that I'm complaining. It isn't rocket science and I don't mind. The boss is an ass hole, but the pay is okay.

"Other than my boss, I got along with everybody. Well, after I'd been here several months, these guys stopped me on my way home. You can smell Stasi! They wanted me to be an informer – easy work. All I need do is keep my ears open and report on anything interesting the guests might talk about over breakfast or afternoon coffee."

She sat back and took three puffs as she stared out at nothing.

"They didn't give a damn about the guests," she snorted at last. "They were after someone on staff. I could tell by the way they talked. Well, I didn't want to do it, but you can't tell the Stasi to piss off. I told them I'd think it over."

"Gott! My skin crawled for three days. They came back. We talked more, and I tried to put them off – I had a few friends, and I didn't want to inform on anybody. It was a nightmare. They reminded me people who do poorly on their *abider* might never get work anywhere unless she had *friends*. If I became an informer, they'd see to it that I'd get a better job."

"They wanted you as a spy?"

Birgit shook her head violently.

"They didn't want me at all. They wanted me to get dirt on somebody at the hotel – someone to send to prison, probably. They thought I was a fool and believed their shit about a better job. People who get poor marks don't get better jobs even with Stasi power. All I'd get is being an informant somewhere else. Well, I didn't want to work for them, but I couldn't refuse. Hell, they'd put me in prison for counter-revolutionary tendencies or – or for smoking in public. With the Stasi, if they want you in prison, you go to prison."

She flicked ashes onto the ground. She flicked again, absent mindedly, when there was no need.

"A few of us were sitting around during *Pause* – just drinking coffee and having a chat. I tell them that the Stasi wanted me to work for them. You know, I made it sound like a boast. I acted like I expected them to be impressed."

Sabine pondered this while Birgit wrestled with a nightmare.

"Biggi! That's brilliant," Sabine congratulated. "You'd have been useless to them!"

"Yeah, brilliant. That's what I thought. So," she took another long drag, "Not any of my friends dared speak to me, and my mother got fired."

"What? Why?"

"Because that's the Stasi. They didn't punish *me*. They didn't get *me* fired. They decided to punish me by hurting my mother. They're all scum."

She pulled another cigarette out of the pack and lit it with the nearly dead one. Biggi then took a long, deep drag from the new fag and crushed out the old one in the ashtray midway between them. She did not look at Sabine. She kept her eyes trained away.

"That's life in the DDR," she concluded. "That's why I don't want to talk about it."

Sabine wanted desperately to lift the girl's spirits, but her brain and speech failed her. Therefore, Birgit's brain remained in overdrive. She relived the nightmare repeatedly between billowing clouds of smoke. Inevitably, she reached an intersection; one that defined the old regime and the new.

"Now, Vati's lost his job."

Sabine was stunned. She reached the lowest emotional moment in her life since leaving "home" for the great unknown across the water. If Molly were at her side, she'd have fallen into her waiting arms and cried. If Shelly were on hand, she would douse Birgit's trouble in sugary nonsense – well, she'd try.

It was Sabine's fault. Of course, she'd no way of knowing she was opening a Pandora's box, but that did not make her blameless. It was fitting for Birgit to cry on Sabine's shoulder, but to search for comfort from a merciless torturer was to deny justice.

"You're left to bring bread in the house," Sabine's voice quaked.

Biggi took another puff. Mercifully, the statement diverted her thoughts.

"Not exactly," she replied from behind a billowing cloud followed by two jets from her nostrils.

"We put away some money. Vati is in Berlin. He thinks there might be jobs in the Wessi part of the city. Personally, I doubt anyone will hire Ossis unless they can't get anybody else."

"But, it's over, isn't it? Your mother can go to work, can't she?"

"With people losing jobs every day? Not likely."

Sabine gulped.

"How many are you?"

"Mutti und *misch* und *meine kleine Bruder*."

Sabine waited for inspiration.

Nothing.

"Can I buy you another beer?"

Birgit considered the offer before shaking her head. Three, she said, was her limit. After that she'd get silly or become belligerent.

"I'm sorry I asked. Biggi, would you feel any better if you did what the Stasi wanted?"

She shook her head sadly.

"Of course not. That's why the Stasi was so evil. No matter what you did, you're beaten."

Sabine's heart was breaking for a person she hardly knew.

"Biggi, I can't leave you like this. Let me help. I've got a job here."

Birgit eyed her suspiciously.

"Doing what?"

"A *Schwartzarbieter* – with my father. Let me buy a few things; I'll fix dinner for your family. It isn't much, but that, I can do."

For the first time since dredging up black memories, Birgit displayed a flicker of interest.

"Ami food?"

What, Sabine wondered, was American food? For Molly, it was fried rice and fish. For Shelly, it was Jaeger Schnitzel und Pommes. For Sabine, it was an oyster sandwich. For Gary, it was spaghetti with a thick tomato sauce. Well, she'd have to see what her earnings would fetch.

"Sure," Sabine nodded, "if you like American."

"Hamburgers?"

"Biggi, a hamburger isn't a meal —"

"Bitte! I've never had a hamburger. Bitte, bitte, bitte!"

Sabine relented. She imagined that if she resisted, Birgit would be on her knees slobbering on her despised skirt.

* * *

"Mutti is excited about it," Biggi reported at breakfast. "Tomorrow evening?"

"I must speak with Papa," she cautioned.

Birgit hid her hands behind her back, bounced on her toes, pressed her lips firmly together and curled them into a smile before returning to her duties.

The baker woman behind the counter recognized her and greeted her. While her order was being filled, Sabine looked about for hamburger bun substitute.

The *Milschbrotchen* were roughly the correct size and shape, but the crust was hard. It would take an expert to slice them in half. However, it was either that or sliced bread from the store. As Sabine well knew, packaged bread was little more than ipecac — sliced bread more so.

The coffee was on when she arrived. She wasn't quick enough or clever enough to steal cheese slices. Instead, she bought two serving-sized packages of butter and four packages of jam. These suited Herr Bauer just fine. He was in a hurry to be on his way. He quickly fetched the shelves and leaned them against the companion room door across the landing.

"What's in that room?" she asked.

"Stasi stuff, I guess. It's always locked, but we'll find out soon enough. A man was here yesterday and spoke to Frau Kosyk. This house was confiscated; the owners were thrown out. The man is from the family that owned it."

"Oh, Gott! Now, he's throwing you out."

He shook his head and prepared a brötchen.

"He says the family only wants ownership restored, but they live in Berlin now. They don't plan to move back."

"He's going to raise your rent!"

He paused for a moment to examine her.

"You're so pretty, but you're determined to be a pessimist. That's not very attractive."

"I worry about you," she replied with regret.

"The subject of a rent increase was not mentioned. Don't worry. Besides, worrying about rent is a pleasure I reserve for myself."

"If I want to live with you, I have the same right."

"If." he quoted the pithy laconic response. Sabine detected no trace of emotion. Even young Sabine was acquainted with that famous reply.

"Don't you want me here with you?"

He had mentioned previously that her standing up while he sat in the only chair was annoying. After the tartness of her question, he stood up and placed his hands on her shoulders. He pushed her back until she was at the bed and was physically persuaded to sit down. Sabine wove her fingers together and rested her hands in her lap. Her father resumed both his seat and his breakfast.

"I want you every bit as much as Mrs. Foster and her husband want you – no more and no less," he said evenly. "It's your choice. I refuse to pressure. If you stay, we must find another apartment. Therefore, my rent here is moot."

She thought for several moments and rubbed her palms on her jeans.

"There's a young woman at the hotel who had Stasi problems. She told me about it last night. I invited myself to cook for her family tomorrow evening. May I?"

He froze. It was the first time a child – his child – asked permission. He was moved.

"Of course."

"You say that Baba, but our time is limited, and I'm going to be away most of today. Are you certain you don't mind?"

He chewed his food while cogitating.

"I think it is good you make friends quickly. You should have friends. You should spend time with them. I'm your father, not your warden."

Still unconvinced she was doing the right thing, she nodded.

* * *

The shelves were not very heavy, but they were bulky and awkward to carry. Whenever she found herself flustered wrestling shelves, she thought of the hated suitcases. The shelves were not as taxing as the arm-wrenching battles she and Ute experienced with their luggage.

Once in Seelow, with the sun beating down the back of her neck, she stopped several times to rest. At each stop, she set the edge of the shelves on her feet so they'd not get damaged or dirty. Because she must climb the heights, she was short of breath. She feared her hands might cramp into a claw as she carried her load.

I've got it easy, she told herself. *I don't have a hundred thousand German soldiers determined to keep me off this road.*

This should have been a consolation, but it was not. When she got to the library, she lay the shelves down carefully and shook her hands to reintroduce blood to her fingers. Finally, she reclaimed her cargo and waddled through the door frame.

The woman flew from behind the counter to help. Together, they carried the shelves the last few meters. Together, they placed the shelves gingerly onto the flanges. Sabine had a speech prepared if the boards didn't fit snuggly, but her father had measured and cut with precision.

"At last," the woman said, "we can get these books reshelved."

Sabine smiled and attempted to get away, but she was not allowed to leave before the woman paid the balance of her bill. Because she hired black market labor, she must pay in cash. This money went into the same pocket as the bills Baba shared from the school project. When she returned to Frankfurt, she segregated the money before she went clothes shopping. She didn't want to cheat her father.

She knew she wanted something cool and cheap. In the DDR, the latter was the norm unless the store was stocked with Wessi goods. Frankfurt was a regional center, so people traveled distances to find shops the lesser burgs didn't have. By the time Sabine entered a clothing store, hundreds of transients joined with hundreds of locals and dozens of Poles in picking the racks clean. Resupply was always a problem in the DDR even before the infrastructure crashed.

She discovered a jeans skirt. The material was too heavy, the hem was way low, but it had a slit up the back. That promised circulating air. It was cheap – very! In another shop, she found a short, cotton skirt. It was a pair of shorts cleverly disguised as a skirt. She bought it for the optical allusion alone. Additionally, she bought two sleeveless tops.

Sabine Bauer reentered the hotel with mixed emotions. She was used to buying clothes, normally with other people's money. She considered her Frankfurt togs earned. Alas, she realized the money was little more than Ernst Bauer's version of the gift certificate she had obtained through the theatre group.

If she remained in the DDR, she'd need a job. They couldn't live on the black market forever. They required legitimate work in an economy where people lost thousands of jobs. Chances of finding vacancies were not good. Herr Bauer was the school Hausmeister to-be, a grand start. However, what could Sabine contribute?

Sabine Bauer was very lucky to be in the DDR during the final days. She wasn't confident she'd have survived the Vopos and the Stasi. When she found Heike, she would be interested to know how she managed.

And *who the hell was Nadine?*

Clouds were building. It looked as if there might be some weather. Sabine found herself wishing for rain. She missed the salt air and the breezes of the ocean.

She changed into the jeans skirt and the new yellow top. It was too bright, but she didn't buy for the color. She grabbed the laundry bag containing her smelly clothes and set out.

She stopped at the market under the Oderturm and bought laundry soap, a package of croissants and a carton of Wessi orange juice. From there, she returned to a coin-operated laundry she'd noticed earlier.

The machines were decrepit and required Reich marks, which were no longer in abundance. It was likely the dearth of *plastic money* (for so it seemed) allowed her the choice of several unbroken machines.

Sabine intended to sort her loads. After counting her resources, she threw everything together. She watched her clothes being massaged in soapy water while she chewed two croissants into extinction. They weren't good, but she never expected them to be. They and the orange juice filled her stomach void. Unfortunately, the combination brought audible protests. The few who ambled in and out of the establishment heard the rumblings and cries from her stomach, even over the noise of the machines.

She didn't care.

Sabine retrieved her clothes, rolled each item, and stuffed them into the laundry bag she'd, also, washed. She exited as the rain began. It was delicious after the misery of the week-long heat. By the time she reached the hotel, her hair was pasted to her head and neck. The desk clerk congratulated her on her appearance.

Everyone was sick of the heat!

By the time she reached her room, the rain stopped. Though clouds hid the sun, the streets and sidewalks were dry. Now, it was hot *and* humid. She discovered places to hang or lay out her laundry. She fought the urge to rush to the school and her father, but she wouldn't leave damp underwear unattended.

She tried to be patient while reading *Silas Marner*. When she reached the page where the mother dies in the snow and her baby crawls to Silas's fire, she closed the book and tossed it aside.

A century-old novel was mocking her.

* * *

It was late in the afternoon when she reached her father's apartment. If he were still out, she'd wait. The moment she opened the front door, she was relieved to hear her father's voice. Climbing the stairs, she heard another man's voice. It was coming from an apartment on the second landing, just across from the Sorbs.

Figuring she'd a legitimate excuse to intrude, Sabine walked through the open door and into the empty apartment. Standing on the far side of the room, next to the peeling wallpaper and amid the clutter of discarded bottles and cans, Herr Bauer conferenced with a tallish man in a brown suit, white shirt, and brown tie. The man's clothes showed signs of age and wear. Obviously, he was an Ossi.

"Ah, Sabine, come in, come in. Herr Schneider, allow me to present my daughter, Sabine from America."

The man's business-like expression changed to one of warmth and astonishment.

"From America!" he gasped, extending his hand.

Sabine ignored this breech of protocol. It was rude to shake hands with a woman before she extended hers. Sabine excused this seeming affront. She accepted his hand and simultaneously presented him a bob curtsy.

"Freut Mich sehr."

No need to be rude. Perhaps, this man was nervous or confused. She'd give him the benefit of doubt – for the moment.

"Fräulein Sabine, your father and I were discussing this building. My great-grandfather owned it and my grandfather grew up here. The house was confiscated after the war by the Soviets and passed on to the DDR. Our family never surrendered the title, and we have reason to believe it will be returned soon. A court must rule, of course, but similar rulings, thus far, are favorable."

Sabine caught her father's eye. She saw a radiance that gave her both patience and hope.

"My family lives in Berlin, so we won't use this house. We, of course, need someone to make repairs and provide maintenance. I don't know anyone in Frankfurt, but I've talked with tenants. Everyone praises Herr Baur's abilities as a craftsman.

"I've made him an offer. If he restores this apartment, at the cost of materials only, I'll allow him the use of the apartment, rent free for two years, if he renovates the remaining apartments. That will take a year, at least. I understand, your father has a good job, so he can hardly work full-time here.

"After completing renovations, he is welcome to remain. I cannot promise the rent will be as low as the – ahm, former administrators. We can't forecast economic conditions. However, I promise you, as

I've promised your father, we are far more concerned with keeping the property in the family than making unreasonable profit from it."

Sabine was satisfied with the man's sincerity. She looked at her father.

"You would be Hausmeister here," she announced. "That is a big promotion."

"I have to audition," he reminded. "We were discussing what needs doing."

Even to Sabine's unpracticed eye, there was much to be done. In addition to wallpaper, the ceiling plaster flaked and the water heater over the kitchen sink looked as if it was installed during Bismarck's time. Then, of course, there was the problem of furnishing the place. Everything her father owned would fit in one of the bedrooms.

"We may not be able to pay for everything," Herr Schneider continued. "We must secure a loan. That complicates matters. However, we can pay for the renovation of this apartment."

"What do you think, Sabine?" her father asked. "Is it worth a gamble?"

She couldn't reply at once. She inspected the bathroom and the two bedrooms.

"It will be a lot of work," she concluded.

"This, I know," her father nodded, "but I'm not afraid of work. Besides, I have motivation."

They exchanged another look.

"It could take months," Herr Bauer confided. "Herr Schneider says he won't let me begin work until he knows for certain ownership is restored."

Later, she sat in his chair. Her father sat on the edge of his bed. Sabine didn't dare hope, but she could not ward off a thrill. Herr Bauer felt it, too.

"You want me to have my own room – here?"

He needn't reply, so he kept quiet.

"Today, when the rain came, it felt so good. I realize how much I miss the ocean."

He'd not speak. His eyes remained fixed on her.

"I'm sure you would make me a beautiful room, Baba, but it is a – difficult choice."

Here he allowed himself a sardonic laugh.

"It is nice to be free," he said. "However freedom offers choices. Some choices are difficult. You know what I want, but I'm sure Ute and her man want the same. This is your choice, *Schätz*."

"I – I can't make it!" she moaned.

"It is so much easier when the Stasi says: 'You live here.' You might not like it, but it beats making decisions."

Sabine sighed and beat her knees with her fists to avoid crying.

"I'm going to find Heike, Papa. I promise. Beyond that – I – I – don't know. This is a different planet. It's like the old frontier in America. People suffer hardships to make something of nothing. I really want to be a part of it, but it is so hard to leave so much behind."

"It's your life," he reminded. "All of it."

He was too decent to say more, so Sabine finished the thought.

"I have Mutti to thank for that."

Weimar

When Jürgen departed for Halle, he left a huge hole in Heike's life. In a country devoid of color and man-made attractions, Halle must rank as one of the ugliest cities in the world. Walking out of the Bahnhof, he was greeted with a huge, semi-abstract sculpture of Karl Marx. Was it a deliberate attempt to impugn Herr Marx, or was it a deliberate attempt to defame art? The government commissioned the work; who dared ask?

What was there in Halle for Jürgen? He would have naught but to sit and brood in a place which fostered depression; but there he'd wait for Marina. With each passing hour, he'd drink from the cup of anguish and sup at the table of trepidation.

Had they agreed to meet in Weimar, he'd be surrounded by people who loved him. If Marina were allowed to return, he could celebrate with friends and family. If she remained a prisoner in a Soviet fortress, he would grieve alone.

As the Day of Rosa's Children grew nearer, the preparations took on an unexpected life. Heike was forced to admit that she'd lost control. Heiko, who was never a member and who expressed only mild interest, promised beer and juice to sell.

He'd make no profit. Instead, he'd undersell the suppliers nearest the Fraunplan to induce people to loiter and chat. The Children would, hopefully, gather names and addresses against the day when the organization could mail out materials.

Hanna, another non-member member, talked up the event at Inka's daycare; some employees promised to turn out. One of Nadine's friends, who possessed dexterity with things electronic, promised a turntable and a set of powerful speakers. Another knew the *former* manager of a bakery on the square. He was forced to close his doors, but the owner agreed to unlock the empty shop so the sound equipment would have an electrical access. When Heike asked how Rosa's Children would pay for the power they used and to whom, she was told,

"*Don't worry about it.*"

Herr Meißner promised Lilo the day off to attend. Nadine was driven to Jena by a former FDJ leader to pick up the fliers. A rumor circulated that a half-dozen FDJ members would erect a non-profit stand to sell Wursts and, perhaps, *Bratel.*

Heike spent every spare second with Günther. They talked about literature, politics, music, the future – and a sister Heike had yet to meet. One thing they did not talk about, however, was the event coming the last Saturday in June.

One afternoon, Nadine volunteered to prepare Herr Zimmermann's hot meal. This allowed Heike and Günther to pack sandwiches and juice. They crossed the Ilm and approached the Goethe Garden House. The grass, an uncut and flourishing riot of nature, was too inviting. They found a spot in the shadow of a towering tree and created a den. They ate, drank, and lay down.

They heard human noises but saw no one. Further, no one could see them unless they came very near. Heike turned on her side and lay up against Günther, her head on his chest and her hand searching along his arm until her fingers found his hand. He waited for her to speak, but she said nothing. Moments later her breathing betrayed her, he didn't move or speak, he just let her rest undisturbed.

Time passed. It was an enjoyable, lazy time. The scorching sun was blunted by the tree, and a steady breeze slithered through the grass. Heike's warmth against him was pleasant. She'd worked as a maid and cook for most of the day. Any "free time" was filled with Rosa's work. She deserved time to rest. He was honored to be her pillow.

"You know why people come out here, don't you?" she asked softly.
"Ja."

She squeezed his hand.

"I'm not ready," she announced, point blank.

He resisted a laugh. It was a struggle. Regardless, she had to hear his heart racing.

"Now, you're angry with me."

"Nein," he replied truthfully "I'm sure there will come a time. This isn't it."

She lay stroking his wrist with her thumb.

"Did you and Lilo come here?"

"I won't answer that."

She smiled.

"You were angry, Günther! You were angry when you threw me on the bus."

The word *threw* was an overstatement.

"If I were angry, I'd let you hurt yourself."

Even her wandering thumb stopped to digest that.

"But – I was so mean!"

"It was a trial, I confess. I thought some rude things about your temper and your amazing energy, but – no, Heike, I was not angry."

She sighed and thought about returning to school. When the new term began, there'd be no excuse for not attending. She would be a year behind. She owed it to the Children if not herself.

Maybe, at long last, she and Heiko would sit at separate desks. If he went to the next level, it was a sure bet. He might, however, be in a similar situation. She made a note to ask Hanna.

Suddenly, she thought of her nameless sister. Jürgen, as always, was right. A letter came. Heike had not the nerve to open it – old prejudices die hard. She wondered if they could meet on neutral ground.

If it didn't go well, Heike would slip back into the anonymity she found comforting.

"I'm afraid, I'm about to make you angry," Günther disturbed her reverie.

Heike's heart froze. She didn't dare move.

"What is it?" she asked, her breathing so feeble she hardly expected her voice to carry.

"I applied for a computer course. I've been accepted."

"Aren't you going to university?" she asked boldly.

"University is where all the lies were born and where they were taught," he reported. "That won't change. The Wessis invent and promote lies, too. I saw all the lies so clearly in the army, Heike. In school, I'd be blind."

"Computers then," she said to be supportive, despite her doubts.

"I don't want to do computers, either, but I know I'll need them – later."

"And that is?"

"I don't know, yet. Maybe, if you get it going, I'll come back and work for Rosa's Children."

She sighed again.

"That sounds so… childish. I didn't realize until you said it just now. It's an awful name."

"But apt. We are, all of us, Rosa's spiritual children. We cannot allow anyone to destroy Rosa's vision or her hopes. That would be the triumph of injustice."

Heike fed upon that sentiment. Günther the Magnificent allowed her to ruminate without interruption. Anybody else would speak, driven by the tyranny of silence. That's when she knew her love for Günther was not a child's infatuation. They could communicate without uttering a sound.

"Come back?" she heard herself say. "What do you mean come back? Where is this computer course?"

"Trier."

She suppressed a sob. She swallowed hard. Heike was thankful he couldn't see her face. Günther would realize what a weak, sniveling coward she was.

"Could you go any further away?" she asked.

"Brest, maybe, or Cardiff."

It wasn't funny.

"I know how you feel," he added. "Karl Marx was born there. If we're speaking of things spiritual, we might consider that."

"I need you so much, and you'll be so far away," she conjectured.

"Just for a few months. If you need me, I can be here in ten hours or so. Or," he added with a deliberately understated tone, "you can come to me."

When she didn't fly up like a broken mainspring, he knew she was hurting.

"I hate the West," she responded, but there was no fire in it.

"Maybe, but you must find a way to live with it."

He didn't ask. She didn't say. Heike Jacobs was thinking of her Ami sister.

* * *

The following afternoon, Heike was slicing a ripe tomato in Herr Zimmermann's tiny kitchen. Hanna knocked sharply twice and let herself in carrying the cargo that she, more and more, thought was her own.

"Where's the Chef?" she asked, lowering Inka into her mobile bed.

"He's either working late or getting drunk."

Inka began to fuss. Despite her resolve not to spoil the little tyrant, Hanna took her up again.

"Allowing for what Herr Zimmermann drinks, I'd say he is working late."

"More bread in the house," Heike commented with an uncharacteristically lilting tone.

Most people feared for their jobs, but Herr Zimmermann was fortunate enough to work with a small concern that, apparently, would survive the transition to a market economy. Rosa's Children, or, at least, the cadre, considered rallying around a jobless parent and his daughter. That hope dimmed.

Hanna offered her little finger. Inka grinned and grabbed for it. This was her favorite game. Only Hanna was allowed to play.

"I took Frau Willing's bus downtown," Hanna reported. "She's in a snit."

"What about?" Heike asked out of idle curiosity.

"There's a rumor the Wessis will take over all public transportation."

"Pabst heard that, but it's only rumors."

"Frau Willing thinks the Wessis will kick her out."

That was news! However, there was an avalanche of unconfirmed *news*. One was foolish to pay heed.

"Why would they do that?"

The term *they* came into vogue as a substitute for West German authorities. It was a pejorative in Ossi Land.

The words Heike used would earn her to the back of Rolf's hand.

"She said the Wessi busses are too complicated; repairing problems on the road will be impossible – only trained experts with special tools can fix them. They don't want women drivers."

Heike left her tomato slices in a pool of juice and stirred vegetables simmering in a pot.

"They would fire Frau Willing without testing her? Figures!"

* * *

When Herr Zimmermann returned, he greeted his favorite women cheerfully. This gushing adulation paled in comparison to the levity and love he showered upon his *favorite* daughter. Hanna left her charge safely in Herr Zimmermann's arms. He, in turn, lay her in her bed for that time it took him to wash up.

Inka didn't like being treated thus. She registered her protests accordingly. When the father returned, he secured a bottle of juice. Inka eyed him suspiciously before allowing the nipple in her mouth. The bed was moved next to the table so the comet could watch her father's every move. This kept her calm.

Boiled potatoes salted and sprinkled with parsley flakes, fresh steamed peas and broccoli and one very fresh, juicy tomato was a feast for a simple working man. Heike further presented him with two freshly sliced slices of rye bread, lightly coated with butter. Herr Zimmermann was most appreciative.

Heike washed out the pots, dried them and returned them to their proper places.

"Can you finish up?" she asked timidly.

"Ho! Are you and Günther off to a movie?"

He didn't wait for a reply. It was well because she didn't intend to offer one.

"I can manage very well, Fraulein Heike."

"You two behave yourselves," she said, taking her leave.

* * *

Half an hour later, she sat across from Herr Jacobs and helped herself to a slice of rye bread. There was no refrigerator and, thus, no chance to keep butter. Instead, she slapped a slice of cheese on her bread. It was sweating.

"Pabst, I must see Lilo this evening."

He eyed her carefully. Considering her recent activities, Rolf wondered if she needed his permission for anything.

"Could Nadine come too?"

He was disarmed. He could refuse a demand and feel justified. Once Heike requested something in Nadine's name, well…

Nadine didn't bother to ask. She'd come to the realization that Heike was the dominate sibling. She'd resented this metamorphosis, but the climax came in Leipzig; she realized Heike was correct in her evaluation of – everything.

Nadine's resentment melted the moment she recognized Heike's clear, cerebral vision. If Heike urgently need to see Lilo, Nadine knew an important purpose lay behind it. Similarly, if Heike requested her to come along, there was a good reason.

They did not bother taking the bus. Since Heike assumed the Zimmermann family, she declined spending a single pfennig so long as there were other options. Lilo pushed the buzzer allowing them entry.

The moment Lilo and Heike exchanged looks in the stairwell, Nadine realized her place. Lilo would rather push Heike down the stairs than speak with her. Nadine and her misshapen face would discourage the Amazon's baser instincts.

"We have a cause," Heike announced.

Lilo nodded and motioned them inside.

* * *

Nadine felt the resentment and animosity in the apartment. It was palpable. Lilo was deprived of Günther and Heike was the reason. Nadine admired her "sister's" dauntless attitude. However, Heike was wise to be afraid of Lilo; she was, also, wise enough to consult her.

Heike's hands trembled. If Nadine noticed, so had Lilo.

Nadine peppered Heike with questions on the way home. Why, for example, Lilo? Rosa's Children had a multitude of human resources.

"You read her flyer," Heike replied. "That may light a fuse."

Nadine, in the days that followed, agreed; Heike exercised great judgment. She had the limited aim of saving Frau Willing's job. She couldn't look beyond that immediate goal. Lilo, however, molded the objective and shaped it into a powerful cause. The people whose jobs touched the citizens needed reassurance they'd not be casually shunted aside by the new regime.

The DDR had had enough of political leaders who struck all the right chords in their public speeches only to devour the flesh and the souls of the people they pretended to support. Lilo took up the cause of the workers and made certain the political class must exist at the pleasure of the workers – not the other way around. Without calling for, or threatening violence, Lilo crafted a message even Wessis couldn't ignore. If the conquering plunderers expected to take the bread off workers' tables to satisfy the whims of the political elites, then serious unrest and disaffection would result.

As with her quasi-essay explaining Rosa's Children, Lilo couched mighty arguments in short, pithy phrases that fit on banners, posters, and business-sized cards. With Lilo leading the way and Heike rushing about in Rolf's Trabi, the Children were mobilized in a matter of hours. Materials were gathered and collated.

Thirty-six hours after Heike and Lilo's colloquy, signs appeared at bus stops and on shop doors and windows. One of the FDJ artists designed and produced a silk-screen image and slogan. She couldn't afford to buy t-shirts, but if the Children brought in their own, they could wear the message.

Heike and Lilo were justly proud of their accomplishments, but Günther was flummoxed.

"How did you do this so quickly?" he asked.

"I spoke with Lilo," she replied, handing him a t-shirt.

Further explanation was superfluous.

Heike and Nadine had planned to wear their blue FDJ shirts to the rally. Fortunately, they discussed the matter within earshot of Jürgen. He set about to discourage the idea. Too many people, he argued, were angry with the government. Blue shirts would associate Rosa's Children with corruption and deception. The girls, proud of their blue shirts and what they represented, rejected his advice.

After he was gone and their longing for him returned, the girls revisited the issue. Finally, they concluded Jürgen, as always, was right. They would keep their FDJ uniform shirts to wear with pride on other occasions. For the Children's rally, however, it would be the newly printed t-shirts.

Günther was dubious until Heike disclosed the idea was Jürgen's. Objections ceased. Later, as Heike was passing through Goetheplatz, she angled towards Lilo and made a terse, but civil, announcement about the uniform of the day for the rally. Surprisingly, Lilo, who was as proud of her FDJ uniform as any living being, did not object.

"You're the Chef," she responded.

Feeling thankful that the Amazon had not argued, Heike continued her shopping. Reflecting later, she wondered if Lilo had already reached the same conclusion as Jürgen. It would explain her sudden submission; if not – well…

Lilo being Lilo, and Heike being Heike, neither would ever discuss it.

* * *

Heike's emotions ran riot. She was alarmed and amazed by the interest in the information spread by Rosa's Children. There were many people, some of whom remained unknown to her, who were figuratively mounting the public podium to speak on behalf of the organization. From what she could learn, all messages were in accordance with her incomplete manifesto. Nevertheless, she took more control over public announcements. At the same time, she recognized hers was exactly the kind of control that resulted in the worst abuses of the SED.

Beyond Rosa's Children was the presence of Günther. There was a strong bond between them which grew stronger each day. They did, indeed, need each other. Perhaps, for that very reason, their emotional union transcended society's approval. When Heike lay in his arms in the park and confessed her intention to resist parting with her childhood, he responded with a calm and understanding that she'd no right to expect.

At that moment, her love for him became unbounded. He could look at her knowingly at precisely the moment she needed reassurance. His hand in hers made her heart threaten to burst through her chest. Similarly, Günther found contentment whenever he was near enough to see her. They might not speak, or Heike might be unaware of his presence, but knowing she was near was all the reassurance he required.

Günther's exuberance was tempered by pangs of guilt. Heike wasn't a Jacobs, but she was the most fortunate of them. True, Jürgen, the greatest man in Heike's life – greater, even, than Günther, but he was cursed with the same emotional chaos as Heike herself.

Jürgen was forced to endure agony until the moment his love returned to his side. Günther refused to speculate about Jürgen's suffering if Marina's family kept her prisoner like some vituperative reincarnation of the Capulets. Still, Jürgen and Günther each experienced the joy of Aphrodite's fruit. In that, they were brothers as well as friends.

Unfortunately, there was Nadine, defeated and stoic. She'd not been favored with Anne Eck's once enviable beauty. Yet, she looked most like the great Werner Ecke; his heroic features, visited upon a young woman, hardly constituted largess.

After resuming a nutritious diet, Nadine's blond hair was as silky and alluring as ever, but her remodeled visage would have repulsed Homer. Every moment Heike spent with Günther or lounging in the memory of Günther, she felt like she was stealing something rightfully Nadine's. What justice would allow Jürgen to experience an abundance of the very commodity Nadine was forced to live without?

Unexpectedly, this shadow began to diminish, however little.

Heike saw Hanna frequently at the Zimmermann home. They seldom visited for long, and their conversation seldom touched upon anything of consequence. Still, the girls liked each other despite, other than Heiko, sharing nothing in common. However, a curious, uneasy motion built in the pit of Heike's stomach.

"I went by the Schortmann house this morning," Hanna reported the matter, obviously, gnawing at her. "I'd swear someone was inside."

If Hanna Müller was prepared to swear, then there was someone inside! Heike dared not mention it for fear of false hope. However, two days later, as Nadine and Heike were making the rounds of non-Lilo organizers, Heike made a detour. Nadine didn't protest, though she was clearly resentful.

A short walk brought them down a dreary street fronted by gray and dreary houses, some in a state of decay. One of the least disreputable dwellings featured clean widows and lace curtains. The girls paused and examined the name under the buzzer. They exchanged a glance.

"Hanna said somebody lives here."

Nadine looked at the name before daring Heike.

"She's seeing things," Nadine deduced.

They looked at the nearest window, hoping to see the lace curtain flutter. Nothing moved. There was no sound.

"You think Hanna sees things?"

Nadine considered that carefully.

"She imagined something," she amended.

"Hanna?"

The question hung in the air for several seconds. At last, Heike moved, and Nadine stood unmoving and watched a finger press the button. There was no sound, but Heike wouldn't relent. She was prepared to press again, but they heard a noise from inside. They stepped back – just in case.

The door opened. A bespectacled man stared at them. He wore an undershirt and a pair of work pants. He held a folded local paper in one hand. He glared at them questioningly before the light of recognition glowed in his eyes.

"Heike Jacobs, and – Nadine?"

"Yes, Herr Doktor," Nadine replied meekly.

"We were told you had – left," Heike said.

"We did. We didn't stay."

"Your office is closed," Heike informed, perhaps, too emphatically.

"I'm not ready," he replied. "It needs repairs. I must see what will happen, but, Nadine, what happened to you?"

Nadine grabbed Heike's arm and squeezed. She wouldn't allow Heike's vapid narrative to find voice; she'd insist she was to blame for Nadine's face. That lie had lived long enough.

"It is a long story," Nadine reported, firing a warning glance to go with her grip.

"Can anything be done?" Heike asked without preface.

"I'm certain it can," the doctor replied. "Not by me. Nadine, you need a specialist."

"Do you know of any?"

"Several, but I'll look for myself first. I can't do it now. Let me get some things from my office. Come back tomorrow afternoon."

"Danke, Herr Doktor," Nadine bowed and stepped back.

"Danke viel mals," Heike echoed and duplicated Nadine's respectful gesture.

Moments later, after they rediscovered a spring in their step, Nadine spoke with more animation than Heike heard in months.

"Hanna saw somebody in the house!"

Frankfurt/Oder

Anton Schneeweiß was old enough to be a pest, but young enough to be disarming. His sister informed him of the visit of an American; he prepared for the event. Below his absorbent green eyes was a white shirt, dark blue tie, black slacks with a razor-sharp crease and brown shoes polished like nothing Sabine had seen in the DDR. His brown hair was neatly trimmed and parted with a meticulousness rivaling Molly's best effort. His teeth glistened.

Biggi, in contrast, wore a pair of cut-off jeans, an off-white tunic and sandals from the ancient seventies. Sabine assumed that the whole of her attire was cast-off Wessi junk. Though it looked cool enough, the tunic made Biggi appear seven months pregnant.

Frau Schneeweiß looked professional in dress slacks and a blouse. She was no longer thin, and she cultivated a double chin and crow's feet. These, however, did not negate the obvious: she had been a beauty. The gray creeping into her hair made her look both regal and sagacious. Sabine paid silent homage to her for not attempting to disguise her aging features.

The apartment smelled of smoke and there were ash trays on many level surfaces. They'd been emptied and scrubbed, however; there was no sign of a single cigarette for the entire duration of Sabine's visit. Sabine made a mental note to thank Biggi at the first opportunity.

Dangling from her arms were two shopping bags. Biggi took them and hurried them into the kitchen. After introductions and handshakes, Biggi took the underwear pack and placed it under the coat pegs near the door. Anton eyed the object curiously, but Birgit must have briefed him earlier.

"Do you have a swimming pool?" he asked, practically panting.

"The biggest in the world, Anton. We call it the Pacific Ocean."

He refused to allow her to deflate his balloon.

"Do you see any movie stars?"

"Every time I go to the movies."

"Did you buy that skirt in America?"

"No, Anton. I bought it on Karl Marx Strasse."

He wasn't put off by her answers. It was enough to realize their guest came from America. He continued his interrogation as she and Biggi worked side by side at the kitchen counter. Though her responses were often sarcastic, her tone was so pleasant that Anton was encouraged to continue.

It was an adventure to get the meat. The best offerings were swept up by eager shoppers before noon. What remained was fit only for hamburger, in Sabine's estimation. The Metzgerei was happy to grind the quantity Sabine requested.

She wasn't comfortable with European measure, so she asked for two hundred grams extra just to be safe. Of course, she found herself with more than she needed. She rushed to the hotel and explained she must protect her purchase. The clerk dispatched it to the kitchen with an expository note.

Sabine was learning. In the DDR, everybody required assistance sometime; people were seldom denied a favor. It was another form of underground currency. *I help today against a future need.* Sabine might not be around for repayment, but the burgers considered it dangerous to flaunt fate.

Responding to Anton's endless questions, Sabine realized her stature as an Ami was enough. Among the staff, she rated VIP treatment. Biggi was the most visible of those eager to serve. Though Sabine never saw her, the Zimmermädchen not only kept the room spotless, she took it upon herself to get Molly's dress properly pressed – gratis.

Hamburgers and fries were impossible. Sabine hadn't the patience to do fries; those sold commercially were horrid. Moreover, the German version of ketchup was vile – not that it mattered; most Germans preferred mayo with fries. Still, she couldn't make a proper meal of sandwiches.

She considered a salad, but she was lucky enough to find only enough good lettuce and tomato for the burgers. This left her staring at a bin of potatoes. Salzkartoffel might pass muster. After boiling, she could fry them. It was an option, so she began vetting spuds.

Later, she found Worcestershire sauce. Sabine's ticket was punched! Devoid of worry, she discovered fresh fruit. She was home free.

Biggi peeled the potatoes and put them to boil. Sabine chopped a whole onion and set the bits in a pool of Worcester sauce. Together, she and Biggi chopped apples and pears, sliced two bananas, and salvaged what they could of a pathetic-looking pineapple.

Sabine squeezed the best of three oranges and let the juice mingle with the chopped fruit. The remaining two oranges were sliced and added. Not trusting the fruit to be at its best, she added a liberal dose of sugar and tasked Biggi with mixing and tossing until the acid dissolved the sugar.

Next, she threw the ground meat into a bowl, added the onion *soup*, and began kneading the mixture.

"Are these real hamburgers?" Anton asked.

"Burgers a-la-Kathy," she responded. "We can't do real burgers because we don't have Ami buns or Ami ketchup. I'm making something we can have with German *Senf* and brötchen. Don't be disappointed, Anton. Unless you make it yourself, a real hamburger is nearly impossible to get in America – mass-produced burgers don't measure up."

If the complements of the Schneeweiß family were exaggerated, the eagerness with which they devoured Sabine's meal couldn't be feigned. Sabine was ashamed of boiled potatoes as a side dish, but she was proud of the fruit salad dessert. In a country that, previously, seldom saw fresh fruit, any such composition would initiate plaudits. Still, Sabine was proud of her creation. Her trepidation about the quality of fruit was confirmed, but the sugar worked its magic. It proved tart, but the sugar took off the edge.

The supreme compliment came, however, when Sabine surveyed the table and found not a shred of food remaining. There were smears of senf, a few tomato seeds and a stray crumb of brötchen, but there was nothing piled under the table and no family pet to destroy evidence. All edibles were devoured to the last gram.

"You should set up a stand on the Platz," Anton suggested. "You'd make a fortune!"

That was a compliment, indeed, but Sabine knew there was no future existing on the fringes of the economy. Anton's father learned as much when his government subsidized job went south. He fled to the West to ply his skills only to discover similar jobs required skills, methods, and equipment unknown in the DDR.

He was forced to take menial jobs for menial pay. The Wessis looked after their own. They pitied Ossis but refused to subsidize them. Herr Schneeweiß supported himself and had precious little surplus to send home.

Birgit and her mother cleared the table and washed the dishes. Sabine insisted she help. She had created the mess.

"You treated us to a delicious meal," Frau Schneeweiß argued. "You entertain Anton. It won't take us long."

So, Sabine and Anton remained at the table. Thankfully, they fell into a conversation rather than a continuation of the earlier interrogation. He described his school and hobbies; Sabine responded in kind by recounting hers. Her narration of her adventures on the *Mary R.* expanded when he began firing questions anew.

After the dishes were stacked, Frau Schneeweiß brought out a welcome pitcher of iced tea. An hour after the tea was gone, the party broke up. Amid the farewells were repeated invitations to drop by any time. Biggi offered to walk Sabine "home." Anton took Biggi aside momentarily.

"What was that about?" Sabine asked as they marched down the stairs.

"Anton wants me to get your address," Birgit explained. "He'd like to get information. It will make his schoolmates green."

Sabine let it pass.

"How old is Anton?"

"He'll be thirteen in October."

"Do you get along well?"

"No! We used to fight like wet cats. Then Vati left – we started to rely on each other to help Mutti."

They walked through the park to Rosa-Luxemburg Strasse where traffic dictated they walk all the way to Karl Marx Strasse to catch a light. Crossing the street, they walked up the hill to resume their stroll through the park. It was longer, but there were few people at that hour, and it was peaceful.

When Sabine retrieved her room key, she was presented with a letter from Fürth. Not wishing to appear rude, Sabine invited Biggi upstairs. The redhead wasn't eager to climb the steps, but she agreed using the elevator was unnecessarily nerve racking.

The first thing Birgit saw was Molly's dress. She admired it. Sabine took the opportunity to open her mother's letter. She laughed. She shared the reason with Birgit.

"Mom wrote to tell me she had a beer with Jesus!"

That got the expected reaction.

"Her brother reserved tickets months ago for the Passion Play in Oberammergau. After the show, she, her brother, and his wife explored the town. They ran into some guy in a silly party hat."

"He asked if we saw the show. We told him we had, and he got all excited. He played John. He was on his way to a party some of the cast were having that night and he invited us to come with. We weren't too sure this man was all there, but we decided to have a look. We ended up in a beer garden crammed with passion players. Dieter, Marion and I sat down with John, and we all ordered a beer. I was sitting across the table from Jesus! Two Roman soldiers sat on either side of us. We had a very nice chat!"

"Wow!" Birgit concluded.

Sabine struggled to translate. Why did she write in English? There was a single sentence in German. It came at the bottom like an ominous warning.

"Enclosed is a twenty-mark bill," it said, "Call Sunday night."

Sabine folded the money and stuffed it into the pocket of her skirt.

"Everybody gives me money."

"You say that as if it's a bad thing."

Sabine snapped back to life and remembered who was with her.

"I've done nothing to earn it. Well," she added after reflection. "I've helped Papa a bit, but not worth what he pays me. He gives me money because I'm his daughter, not because I've earned it. It's like the dress. That isn't mine, either."

Birgit turned to examine the item anew – and at length.

"Whose is it? Princess Di's?"

"Close," Sabine snickered. "It's Barbie's."

At last, Sabine was given the opportunity to pull out pictures and talk of her friends to an appreciative audience.

"She's gorgeous!"

Birgit exclaimed, seeing Molly for the first time, and looking more gorgeous sandwiched between Henry's inexplicably stern expression and a disheveled Jayme.

"Her mother grew up as a milkmaid here. She's groomed her daughter to look the way she always wanted to look herself."

Sabine continued her narration, allowing a few embellishments. After an hour, they went to the cafe and had a coffee. Sabine faded a bit, but Birgit's excited questions renewed her strength. They returned to the room where Sabine's saga continued. At half eleven, Biggi called her mother to let her know where she was.

By thirty after midnight, they were fatigued, but couldn't stop. Friendship was as intoxicating as drink and as addictive as tobacco. In addition, too vivid accounts of Sabine's life in America and the interesting people who made it more wondrous, Biggi laid aside her armor. She detailed how she, a dim child, was delivered to the Gymnasium through much string pulling.

She wasn't aware at the time, but she realized she didn't fit with the educational elite. Her school career was a continuous nightmare. She studied hard and long and passed most of her exams, but her overall scores did not lie.

"I could have been learning secretarial skills, dress making, baking, or brewing. That's what I want to be, a Braumeister. That or a vintner. Fermentation fascinates me, but the closest we got to it in the Gymnasium was if we ruined a science project.

"I did my best. Honest! I studied hard for my Abitur. I started a year early. Fat lot of good that did. Now, I'm a waitress in a breakfast room. The closest I'll ever come to being a Braumeister is taking cases off a delivery truck! I know my grandfather had the best of intentions when he fixed the Gymnasium, but –"

"Things are changing," Sabine reminded. "When the new economy settles, you can get an apprenticeship somewhere. There will be new breweries here – you can't go more than ten kilometers in the West without finding one. If that's what you want – ask around. In Belgium, they drink more beer than Germans. Hey, if you can get a job there and learn how they do it, you could come back and make this place the beer capital of Germany."

Birgit's eyes flamed.

"Sabine, I'd have to go to university."

"If you make a great beer, the university graduates will be begging you to give them a job. They run the business; you make beer."

That thought never entered Birgit's head. Once Sabine put it there, it could not be dislodged.

Biggi explained what went into the making of great beer. Obviously, she knew more than she'd previously acknowledged. She explained, for example, that Frankfurt/Oder could never make great beer because they didn't have access to the right water. Even after they cleaned up the river enough for people to wade in it; what was required was spring water.

Despite her fatigue and a lack of interest in brewing, Sabine listened closely. Birgit was excited and her discourse made her excitement contagious. The clock slid past two and they were so full of adrenaline they might have plowed on for days. By two forty, however, the adrenaline ebbed and, with it, strength.

"Gott! I'm too tired to even think about walking home."

"Stay here."

"Where?"

Sabine slapped the pillow on the other side of the bed.

"They'd fire me if they knew I was in here."

"Who will tell?"

"It's your bed."

"It's big enough for two. I doubt I'll have to fight you for covers in this heat."

"Well – I have to be in the kitchen at six."

"I'll leave a wake-up call for five-thirty."

Birgit hesitated. She imagined dragging herself home only to turn around to drag herself back. That was enough. She threw herself onto the bed and surrendered. Sabine rang the desk.

Not surprisingly, it took several rings before a groggy voice wheezed in her ear. She left the call. The night man repeated it to be certain he heard correctly. Likely, he assumed Sabine was drunk or insane. By the time Sabine hung up, Birgit's snoring filled the room.

She stirred when a phone rang in her dreams. She stirred, again, when the bed rocked. She woke, momentarily, to hear a woman's voice telling her mother she was at work and asking if she should bring something home from the market.

She stirred and blinked. Her blurry eyes protested at the flood of light. Slowly, her memory returned. Panicked, she looked for Birgit. The emptiness of the room testified that the ringing phone and the shaking bed hadn't been a dream.

She squinted at the digital clock at her side. Her heart stopped. She jumped out of bed and leaned out the window she'd propped open. There was traffic – a lot of traffic.

Karl Marx Strasse was virtually bumper to bumper. Papa wouldn't get his breakfast! He might be at work, and she knew not where to find him.

She stripped, showered, and scrubbed the yuck of the night from her body. With remarkable clarity, she rapidly and logically laid out an emergency plan. She'd check for messages at the desk. She'd grab some breakfast and ask Biggi if a man with a limp was asking about her.

She would rush to her father's room, knowing it would be empty. She would knock on Frau Kosyk's door to check if her father left any word. She'd return to her father's room and leave a message apologizing for her negligence. When she reached the end of her itinerary, Sabine would find a comfortable step in the stairwell, sit down, and cry.

This was unforgivable! She should have left a word with Biggi to throw her out of bed. A daughter has certain obligations; among these is being where one is expected. She would never not show up when slated for duty on the *Mary R.* She'd never skip school without telling someone where she was going.

She'd never leave Aaron and Ute in the dead of night. How then could she justify not bringing her father his breakfast? It was a task she had taken upon herself. That made her failure despicable. It was an insult to her father and shame upon herself.

She dried quickly and pulled on some clothes – her deceptive shorts and one of the new tops. She wrestled to get her feet into her canvass shoes. She paused to disguise the fact two people had shared the bed. The Zimmermädchen would suspect "hanky-panky." Would she express disapproval by wrinkling Molly's dress? Perhaps, she'd leave word at the desk and Sabine would be evicted.

She left the underwear bag. She'd give the garments a scalding the following morning. She did, however, have presence enough to take her passports.

There was no message waiting at the desk. Biggi saw no one with a limp. Sabine gulped down some coffee for an energy lift, but she'd have no appetite until she found her father. She left her chair just as a man with a limp entered.

Ignoring the crowd, she rushed to him and launched herself into his arms. She blubbered a hasty explanation and a tearful apology. Once he realized she was inconsolable, he guided her back to her chair and sat her down. If he noticed several people followed the drama, he paid no heed.

"Did you have breakfast?" she asked.

He nodded.

"Baba, I'm so very sorry –" and she started off again.

"I knew where to find you, *Schatz.* So, you're up late. Get rested. We're going to a concert tonight."

"But I want to be with you."

"You will. Shall we go out to dinner?"

"If you like."

"I like."

He smiled.

"Klar, Baba."

"I come at five o'clock."

He knelt awkwardly, gave her a hug, kissed her cheek, and limped away. Sabine began tearing up anew. She was awash in guilt. Birgit witnessed only a portion of the scene. Realizing her friend was battling tears, she grabbed an insulated vessel and hurried over while doing her best to avoid the appearance of hurrying.

"Kaffee?" she asked.

Before Sabine could react, Biggi lowered her voice to avoid the breakfast assembly overhearing.

"Your father?"

Sabine nodded.

"*Böse?*"

Sabine shook her head.

"Why the tears?"

Sabine gulped and choked. She attempted to speak but struggled to reign in her emotions.

"My – father," she squeaked, "my father – called – me – *Schatz.*"

Biggi, familiar with Sabine's situation and wallowing in memories of her own father was unable to speak. She was in danger of choking up herself. Unable to give voice to her feelings, she settled with a congratulatory pat on the shoulder before she returning to work.

* * *

They found a Greek place. The interior was a restaurant; the exterior screamed fast-food. Molly's dress attracted all the attention Herr Bauer expected it would. She certainly turned more heads than he did in his white shirt and thick blue tie. It was too hot for a blazer, but Sabine thought he should have worn one anyway.

Once seated, the dress brought a waiter and waitress to the table. It was an awkward moment. The waiter drifted away without the issue of a verbal command. The raven-haired woman suggested a drink while they examined the menu. Sabine recommended retsina; Herr Bauer deferred to her knowledge of things Greek.

"How long have you been drinking wine," he asked suspiciously but devoid of disapproval.

"I've only tried it. Opa – uhm, my other Opa – let me have a sip now and then. You may not like it at first. It's made from tree sap."

He smiled meekly.

"We can order something else," she reminded.

His smiled widened.

"If you recommend, I will drink."

She let the matter drop, uncomfortably. She didn't want to force her father to drink what he didn't like. However, he was proud to try anything his daughter suggested. She studied her menu between curious glances at a four-foot, plaster reproduction of David. She wondered how David figured into the Greek motif. Mainly, however, she studied his "instrument."

Guided by the experience of their first day and recalling tour of meat markets, she eliminated meat dishes. She ordered tzatziki and a farmer's salad. Her more adventurous father, settled on a lamb casserole. He claimed it was very good, but after years of Ossi food, his concept of quality had suffered.

Before the government of the DDR ruled religious expression inappropriate socialist behavior, the Konserthalle Carl-Philipp Emanuel Bach was a church. What better way to honor a German composer than to seize a religious house and turn it into a place for public entertainment? Likely, the Party lavished awards and praise on those who brought such a valuable cultural addition to the glory of the DDR.

Perhaps, Sabine was hardened and cynical through Birgit's experiences. Perhaps, her survey of the gutted Marienkirche initiated bitterness. She'd passed the ruins several times before pausing to examine them. The steeple rocketed into the sky. It vied with the Oderturm as the dominant feature in the city skyline. It was not nearly as huge as the cathedrals Sabine found in the West, but – for the Oder, the "Wild East" – it was monumental. It withstood the Soviet Army and suffered the indignity of looters. The DDR left it windowless and derelict. Amazingly, no one ordered it raised to make way for a market or parking area. To ignore its existence for forty years was more than folly; it was cruel. The DDR's demise gave rise to talk about refurbishing the imposing building.

Though proud to enter the concert hall with her father and flattered at the attention Molly's dress received, Sabine's elation was tempered by bitterness. The Marienkirche could accommodate a much larger audience, though its high, vaulted ceiling might prove an acoustical nightmare.

Perhaps, a socialist "visionary" feared a refurbished Marienkirche would have become Frankfurt's *Pope's Revenge*. Regardless, the church outlived the DDR, a major victory.

Herr Bauer found their places. Ever the gentleman, he stood erect until Sabine seated herself. He took his place beside her, making accommodations for his bad leg, Sabine surveyed the others nearest. She wondered if a few once worshipped in this place, and, further, what they thought of returning to attend a concert.

She examined the program.

There was a short biographical essay of the artist. Sabine never heard of her, but she didn't know the name of any violinist. She noted the woman was not yet thirty and wondered how famous she must be to attract such an audience.

Next, she examined the musical program. J.S. Bach was listed, but not Air on a G String. She recognized two other composers, Brahms, and Mendelssohn, by name only. She had no schooling in classical music and hoped that the evening would not be a bore.

Sabine Bauer suddenly recognized the *curse of Molly's dress*; had she worn normal clothes, she could yawn, scratch itchy arm pits or doze off. However, eyes were riveted on her. Eventually, a woman in a soft-yellow pant suit strutted proudly onto the stage carrying the instrument of her trade. Behind her came an older man wearing thick glasses and a tux. As the woman acknowledged applause, the man seated himself at a piano.

The woman stepped to the microphone and spoke a few sentences in halting German. She was privileged to be in Frankfurt, and she hoped the audience would enjoy the program. This was the gist of the message, though she employed many more words.

Warm applause followed. She stepped to the piano and tested her strings while facing her accompanist. When finished, she stepped center stage and made ready. She opened with a folk song from Poland and, after brief applause, began playing a Tarantelle by Wieniawski. Any thoughts Sabine had about boredom vanished.

The artist produced impossible movements. The fingers of the woman's left hand were little more than blurs. Sabine leaned forward to better enjoy the music produced by epileptic motions of bow and fingers.

"Why does she do that thing with the bow?" she whispered.

"You can only play on two strings at a time," Baba informed.

All that sound – from two strings? How? Sabine had heard violin music, but witnessing it was exciting – and *amazing*!

The audience provided thunderous applause. Sabine enthusiastically joined in. The performer smiled broadly in appreciation.

The Tarantelle was rapid and lively, but her treatment of a work by Brahms, though much more mellow, was no less exact. Moszkowski's *Guitarre*, however, didn't impress Sabine. She focused on the operations of the bow and fingers. She gawked over the performer's facial expressions. Her eyebrows lifted and narrowed, and her visage reflected a myriad of emotions.

After forty minutes of unbelievable bowing, the woman closed the first half of her program by playing "*Meditation* from *Thais*." Sabine watched the woman's expression turn to sorrow. When she spied a tear shimmering in light, Sabine shivered and shed a few of her own.

After the lady and her accompanist left for a well-deserved break, Sabine rubbed her eyes while regaining her composure. It helped greatly that her father's comforting arm slid across her shoulders.

"Does this mean that you are enjoying the show?" he asked.

"Much more than I thought," she admitted with a smile. "I've never been to a concert."

"I'm proud to escort you."

While most of the audience stretched their legs or sought a restroom, Sabine remained where she was and narrated her first experience at the opera.

"I cried then, too," she confessed.

She didn't explain why.

If Sabine was amazed by the Tarantella, she reconsidered when the woman finished her program with a caprice by Paganini. Bowing a violin and fingering out the notes from memory was nothing short of miraculous, but when the virtuoso – for, indeed, she was – plucked out a theme with the fingers of both hands as if she were born to it, Sabine couldn't comprehend.

She eagerly joined in the standing ovation and, as with most everyone else, begged for more. The woman relented and did an encore by another

Polish composer. The applause continued for nearly three minutes before a disappointed audience realized there'd be no more encores.

"I can't get over it," She told her father, later, at an outdoor café over not-so-real coffee. "She played the violin so well, but she was playing herself, too. I saw the emotion. I guess I knew, but I never realized a performer could enjoy the music as much as the audience."

"Perhaps, more so."

This was no platitude. Sabine knew her father well enough to know when he was being generous and when he was serious. Her stage experience, limited though it was, helped her enjoy a concert just as it helped her understand her father.

"Danke, Papa. Danke for a very special evening."

Sabine discovered music, not just Bach's Air, could console her. She vowed to explore classical music. She hungered for it.

Weimar

Liebe Heike,

Paul and I were married Saturday. Our timing is very bad, we know. We have no job, no apartment, no prospects. Still, we made a promise and we kept it. Whatever awaits, we shall face it together.

We wanted to ask if you are well. Please write this address and let us know.

We think of you often.

Your Genossin,
Jana

They were, Heike surmised, living with relatives, and catching the odd mark through whatever *Schwartz Arbeit* they flushed in and around Zittau. They could have gone West and started a life, but they held back.

Heike took a Children's flyer, turned it over and penned a terse reply. She said she was well, but Nadine returned broken in spirit and in body. They were both on the mend. She congratulated them on their marriage and wished them luck. In closing, she promised she and Rosa's Children were working for them, if only in spirit. She placed the missive in an envelope and marched off to the post.

Upon her return, she opened the door to discover Jürgen. She threw herself into his arms and held him very tight, pressing the side of her face against his strong, comforting chest. Neither spoke. It was a delicious moment.

She realized!

She pushed away to look into his eyes, dreading horrible news. His eyes danced, however, and his smile beamed. She noticed a figure next to Anne. It rose from the couch.

Heike made no effort to visualize her brother's intended – had, in fact, gave no thought about the abstract concept. Turning toward her sister-in-law-to-be, she was stunned. Marina's raven tresses spilled off her head in an ordered chaos to frame her face perfectly. Her skin was smooth and blemish-free. Her large, brown eyes, sheltered by thin brows, shimmered. Her mouth was small. She has a slight over-bite, and her upper lip formed a shapely and attractive contrast to her razor-thin lower lip. Her nose was small, thin, and slightly upturned.

She was *beautiful!*

Apart from the button earrings affixed to her lobes, there were no adornments – no other jewelry and no hint of make-up. She was thin, almost delicate, but possessed a healthy deportment. Her shoulders testified she'd done her share of lifting. This, coupled with the expression on her face, projected the confidence of an independent woman.

"You must be Heike."

Heike took the offered hand without hesitation. The fingers gripped firmly but not aggressively. Heike hoped that her hand made a similar impression.

"I am pleased to meet you, Marina Serov."

The woman was impressed by Heike's employing her full name. Her pleasure was radiated by a wide, disarming smile. The teeth, as Heike expected, were perfect.

Frankfurt/Oder to Weimar

Sabine's final evening in Frankfurt was spent in the Kosyk apartment. The conversation flowed in proportion to the wine consumed. Frau Kosyk's meal was prepared with an army of guests in mind. With only four attendees, the task of consuming a mountain of food was daunting.

It wasn't long before Sabine realized whenever her plate was nearly empty, Frau Kosyk filled it again. By tacit agreement, she and her father nibbled until only a thin layer of food remained. At that point, the copious refills ceased.

The girl repented for not having a thick note pad and a supply of pens. What she heard of the Sorbs and their traditions was encyclopedic; if only she had the means to record it. Awash in wine and weighed down by many delicious articles of Sorb food, her memory couldn't keep pace with the avalanche of material.

"I'll pack you something for your train journey," Frau Kosyk announced when, belatedly, she cleared the table.

Released from the tyranny of abundance, Herr Kosyk led the way into the living room that was little more than a continuation of the dining room. Sabine swayed and lurched when her shoe caught the edge of the carpet. She burst into laughter when her father's sure, strong hands caught her.

"I think you've had too much to drink," he stated.

For some inane reason, the girl found this so hilarious that her fit of laughter was renewed. She managed to sit in an ancient, upholstered chair worn and, in places, threadbare. This feat was accomplished under her own power.

"I'll put on some coffee," Frau Kosyk decided.

"Please, do," Sabine responded with a chuckle she immediately subdued by putting her hand over her mouth.

She maintained her pose as Herr Kosyk and Herr Bauer exchanged inconsequential observations. When they hit upon a topic which reverberated, Sabine jumped in with an Oregon anecdote. This, in turn, reminded her of another. Both men gave her their undivided attention and enjoyed the performance. When her narrative reached an appropriate juncture, they burst into laughter. This encouraged Sabine to continue performing.

When Frau Kosyk brought coffee, cups and saucers were arrayed precisely on a tray. Sabine was offered the first service. Instantly sober for fear she'd spill her coffee or break something, she took extreme care.

She declined sugar and milk with a shake of her head. This made her dizzy. When everyone was served and the tray safely removed, Sabine took a sip of heaven.

"This is very good coffee," she informed her hostess. "Is it a Sorb recipe?"

The woman laughed.

"It's Wessi coffee and Ossi water."

"My daughter is partial to coffee," Herr Bauer reminded.

"Bach wrote a Coffee Cantata," Herr Kosyk recalled.

"Which Bach?" Sabine asked, the spoon rattling on her saucer. "Johann?"

"Indeed."

"I look forward to hearing that."

"Is that the piece where the father hides all his daughter's clothes to discourage her from going to the café?" Herr Bauer asked.

"Take my clothes, and welcome," Sabine piped up.

She explained how she loathed suitcases and how her underwear, after repeated soakings and washing, were nearing discard status. Her delivery was flawless. She set down her cup, error free, and begged permission to use the bathroom.

"Don't worry," she said to her father's pained expression. "I'm not sick."

He smiled and nodded.

Before returning, Sabine looked carefully into the mirror for visible signs of inebriation. There was a trace of red in her eyes. She had to lean near the glass to negate blurriness.

A terse little prayer of thanksgiving escaped her lips for her father's failure to make public his displeasure. She hesitated to consider what Ute or Aaron would do or say over her current state. Instantly, her thoughts turned to Isaac.

Every morbid thought vanished with a memory picture of the cherub's face. Sabine's heart was suddenly full. She was eager to hold the child again. She switched off the light, opened the door, stepped back into the apartment – all very normal. However, felicity surged.

"Brüderchen, komm, tanz mit mir, beide Händchen reich' ich dir, einmal hin, einmal her, rund herum, es ist nicht schwer!"

Her uninhibited voice reverberated off the walls and through the apartment. Uninhibited by the wine, she gave no thought to the audience in the next room. Rounding the corner, she saw a gawking trio. Herr Bauer twisted in his chair to look over his shoulder. Sabine shut her mouth and ceased her impromptu dance.

For a moment there was a disturbing silence.

"Humperdinck," she explained as if expecting a scold. "*Hansel und Gretel.* I saw the opera last summer."

She didn't fathom the flummoxed expressions. The company was, suddenly, somber.

"You sing very well," Frau Kosyk said.

"Yes," Herr Bauer nodded, turned back around. "Her mother had a fine voice."

That was it. One drunken, thoughtless action and she'd sent her father into the memory of the final moments with his wife.

"Papa, I'm so sorry. I didn't mean –"

"Sorry? Liebchen, I'm disappointed you never told me of your singing. I feel – cheated."

"I never thought – Now, I'm really sorry."

She crept back to her chair and sat as if on eggshells.

* * *

Biggi saw her to the front desk. She presented her with an egg (boiled hardly), a bit of sausage and an apple. Already well supplied with food by Frau Kosyk, Sabine appreciated the hug much more.

"My best to Anton."

"Write me."

With that, Birgit scurried back to her work before the Chef discovered her absence. Sabine picked up the suitcase and resumed her weight training. She made it nearly across the parking lot before she saw a figure limping towards her. She set the case down and sat on it.

"I told you I was coming," she reminded.

"It's too far out of the way," her father reminded. "You can get to the Bahnhof in a third of the time if you go direct. I'll help."

With that, he gripped the suitcase and started off with it as if it were a ball of yarn. She fell into step. They crossed the street. For the first time, she walked behind the post office, through a gravel parking lot and into the park.

"I'm going to find Heike," she vowed for the hundredth time.

"I'm counting on it."

They crossed Lindenstrasse and worked up the hill. Other than his normal limp, Herr Bauer climbed effortlessly. Sabine burdened only by her underwear bag, experienced shortness of breath.

"I'm scared," she confessed.

"So am I," he replied. "I want you to promise you won't push her. I long to see her, but if you try to force her, it will make things worse. Let her know I'm here. She's welcome any time."

Sabine understood.

She was afraid. If Heike decided to be ugly, this expedition could end in a disaster. How could she cope if Heike were as bitter and hateful as suspected? How could she face her father again if Heike refused to be his daughter? How, in fact, could Sabine be Sabine if Heike rejected them both?

At the station, Ernst bought a liter bottle of water for her and paid for her ticket. When she opened her bag to stow the water, he slipped in a thick envelope.

"What is that?"

"Three thousand marks."

"Baba! I can't take your money!"

"You've no choice, Liebchen. You're on a mission to find Heike. This isn't a loan, or a part of your inheritance. It's a travel expense. If I went, I'd need this money. Well, I can't go. You can."

Sabine swallowed hard and zipped up her bag. What if this ended in failure? How would she make it up to him? Would he blame her if he never saw his daughters together? There's nothing to do other than her best.

She hated making promises that she might not be able to keep.

"I've got money," she insisted.

"Now, you have extra."

He carried her suitcase to the departure track. There was no train in sight. Familiar as they were with the Reichbahn, they knew it could be several minutes or several hours late. Regardless, Herr Bauer was content to wait. He got comfortable on a bench and propped his bad leg on her case.

"Baba, I can't stand this," she sobbed. "I'll cry if you don't leave now."

He examined her pleading eyes.

"I'm afraid I'll disappoint us both," she explained. "If I sit here and worry about it – with you beside me… I want to say good-bye, now. I promise to write the moment I have news – even if it's bad."

He didn't argue or debate. She'd demanded so little thus far. When she pleaded, his fatherly duty was to comply. He struggled to his feet and into her iron-like embrace.

"Be a good student, Sabine," he urged.

"Be a good Hausmeister, Baba."

Sabine studied the stairs down which he left. She half hoped and half dreaded his return. Once it was clear he wasn't returning she steeled herself for the task ahead. She'd find Heike if she must hire a detective.

She marched down the platform to a place overlooking the square and the Bus Bahnhof. A single bus sat quietly with passengers waiting, zombie-like, for the vehicle to move. Sabine noticed the limping figure of her father heading down Bahnhofstrasse. She wanted him to look back so she could give a final wave, but he limped on until he disappeared.

She paced. She ignored the few people on the platform and marched from one end to the other. At the conclusion of each lap, she checked the time by the clock hanging next to the information board. They both continued to march, but no announcement came.

Thirty minutes ticked by, then forty. No loudspeaker offered any information about the Berlin train's tardiness. Finally, the machine over the adjoining platform whirred through the prepared metal signs. The time sequence halted at 6:38. Seconds later, the destination locked in COTTBUS – LEIPZIG HBF.

Leipzig! She had to change in Leipzig; the ticket woman told her. The Berlin train was way late, and the train to Leipzig was hours late. What, Sabine wondered, was the difference? Being close to a bathroom, she told herself was the prime consideration! She hefted her suitcase and struggled down the steps, through the tunnel and up the next set of steps.

The train came from the north quietly. Perhaps, as trains often did, it would return from the direction it came. To make certain, Sabine examined the sign on the engine and each sign on the side of individual wagons. They were unanimous: *Leipzig*.

The train began moving south. Sabine's heart raced. Despite all precautions, did she get on the wrong train? She asked a man reading a newspaper across the aisle. He looked at her curiously and confirmed the train was headed for Leipzig.

There was no hurry. The train lumbered and swayed at slow speed. Sabine tried to sleep as a means of shortening the trip; it was useless. Her heart pounded, she was seized by guilt over leaving her father. She'd cheated him; she felt horrible about it.

She watched scrub grasses slide by. The monotony was interrupted by a few fields supporting unidentifiable crops. A cluster of houses crawled past. Most of what Sabine saw of the DDR was an untamed frontier.

Suddenly, springing out of the ground, a huge factory complex filled her window. Silver pipes and towers, stacks and buildings clawed at the open air. Sabine Bauer knew the name before the train squealed to a halt.

Eisenhüttenstadt!

There was no smoke from the mills, no people at the station, and almost no auto traffic. This was the socialist city created in 1950 by the DDR and christened Stalinstadt in honor of the man who defeated Nazism and liberated Germany. When Stalin became a dirty word, the city's name changed; Ernst Bauer was sent to slave here, exactly as skilled slaves were sent to factories by the Nazis. Refusing the honor brought death.

When the train continued onward, Sabine saw few signs of life. The model socialist city was apparently a ghost town. Sabine found Frankfurt backward but charming. Eisenhüttenstadt, however, was an ugly, dirty, foreboding, forgotten place.

After a lapse of (seemingly) several days, the train neared Cottbus. Sabine's heart quickened. Cottbus isn't a German name. Proper nouns, particularly names of places, don't begin with non-Teutonic consonants. Thanks to her association with the Kosyks, she theorized the name and letter were both Sorb in origin. Knowing something of the Sorb character, she envisioned a city full of extroverts who kept a clean, bright, and industrious city.

She might have kept that romantic conceit were it not for the public address system. Service would cease in Cottbus; all passengers were ordered off the train. Sabine half carried, half threw her case out the door and as an act of defiance aimed at the Reichbahn. She sat on her baggage with her arms folded until the train backed slowly onto a siding and trundled out of sight.

It was blistering hot despite the shade of the platform shelter. The only people visible were those sharing the platform. Traffic noise was distant. The sprawling rail yard was as dry and inhospitable as a desert. This image was further enhanced by a hot wind kicking up dust and delivering it into people's eyes and onto their clothes.

As they waited for some sign of transport in the nearly empty rail yard, a dowdy woman with graying hair shuffled towards Sabine. She had only a gym bag. She asked Sabine for a drink of her water. Sabine's plastic liter bottle was, hitherto, little used. She'd been pounding it, impatiently, against her thigh.

"I'm so sorry," the woman said, returning the nearly empty bottle.

Sabine didn't mind. She'd ripped an ornamental button off her shirt and sucked on it. This kept up spit production and staved off thirst. Aaron picked this up in the Army. He and she discovered the device worked as well on the ocean as on land.

"I'll be so glad to get out of this damned country!"

"Where are you from?" Sabine asked innocently.

"Görlitz."

Sabine looked incredulous.

"That's back there," she pointed, vaguely, east.

"I live in Hamburg now," the woman explained. "When I was eight, my mother and father took me off to Berlin in a summer nearly as hot as this one. We stayed with friends over night then my two brothers and my sister and I were dressed in three layers of clothes and our winter coats. We had our school packs on even though there was no school.

"My mother and we, the kids and the people we stayed with, marched to the S-Bahn. We stood there, stifling, in our clothes and half dead from the heat, watching the pass control people get onto the end wagon. My mother herded us onto the wagon furthest forward and we crossed the border before anyone checked our papers."

"You escaped?"

"Don't ask me how we got away with it. We weren't even told until we got to the refugee center. I bawled for hours because I missed our home and my school and all my friends. Everything and everyone I knew was in Görlitz. Mind you, all us children in winter coats and school packs on the hottest day of summer – how obvious could we be? Still, we would need our clothes and things, but you'd think someone would have noticed."

Sabine envied how lucky the family was. Prudently, she kept still.

"When I got word the border was open, I bought the biggest hammer I could find, and got on the first train to Berlin. I hammered at that damned wall until my hands were bleeding, and I couldn't lift the hammer anymore. Then, I just sat and cried.

"I was a fool to think I could take out decades of frustration on that stupid wall. I didn't feel any better. Yesterday, I saw home. Our house is falling down, I couldn't find any friends. I couldn't find anyone who knew of them. All I want, now, is to get back to Hamburg – to get out of this damned, damned country and live my life. Where are you from?"

The question was so unexpected that Sabine responded with the first thing that popped into her head.

"Riesa."

"Where's that?"

"Near Leipzig," Sabine replied, hoping the woman wouldn't press further.

"You're an Ossi, too?"

"Yes."

"Well," the woman concluded, "good luck to you. I can't stand another minute in this creepy country. Thanks for the water. I'm sorry I'm such a pig, but I thought my tongue was going to fall off."

* * *

The same train they'd been ordered off was the same train that pulled up to the Cottbus platform forty minutes later. No explanation was given. It was three hours behind schedule when it "quit" in a desert station but was only three and a half hours late pulling into Leipzig.

Sabine stepped into the huge building, the largest one she'd seen, to study the departure schedules.

Huge!

The Bahnhof was so capacious, it could have swallowed the whole of the Oregon bay and the boats moored therein. There'd remain room enough to fit both the Fisherman's Inn and the Foster house and a dozen other structures. Even her high school would look lonely if enclosed by the "city with a roof."

For one horrible moment, she feared that she'd be required to step back onto the "train from Hell". Fortunately, she spied a machine bound for Erfurt, a mere ninety minutes late. She checked her gate number, compared it with the number of the Erfurt train and deduced she'd reach the gate in three or four days with a favorable wind, if exhaustion didn't kill her.

For the first time since arriving in Berlin a lifetime ago, she hefted her suitcase and walked with soft, padded steps on the next leg of her journey. Soft and padded, perhaps, but steps both quick and long.

After a long hike, she found her gate and a waiting train. With renewed determination, she hustled onto the platform, checking the destination plaques affixed to the wagons. Finally, she worried the suitcase into the vestibule of a carriage and joined it.

For several minutes, she sat upon her burden to catch her breath and pamper her stinging hands. She remained until the wagon lurched forward and began an alarmingly violent tango as it switched from one track to another. Thrice, Sabine grabbed for support from an appendage across the door window just above the handle; with the opposite forearm, she braced against the compartment bulkhead. Not until the vehicle settled into a stable configuration did she abandon her perch and search for a seat. She left her suitcase unattended, but – save for Molly's dress – she didn't care.

Trains in the DDR don't run on time. Ute and Sabine learned that lesson quickly. Sabine, however, enjoyed what must have been a miracle of efficiency for the Reichbahn. The express had only four stops prior to Weimar. It halted at each station exactly one hundred minutes late. Someone may have goofed.

The miracle train lurched out of Weimar one hundred minutes late. Sabine Bauer remained on the platform atop her suitcase. Mrs. Waldron's bag with Sabine's passports and an address hung over her right hip; her much larger bag, with her discolored and lint-gathering "underneaths," hung over her left. What, she ruminated, was she doing? Had she lost the remnants of her mind?

At the end of the ten minutes, she'd conjured no resolution. She realized she was in Heike's city and obliged to do something – even if it was wrong. She wrestled the case off the platform and followed the tunnel towards the station exit. She, again, abandoned her case and ducked into a small shop to buy a liter bottle of water to replace the one she'd "lost" in Cottbus.

She was almost disappointed to find her tribulation exactly where she'd parked it. She wrestled it out of the station and into the bright afternoon sun to find herself confronted by August Herderplatz, a once alluring stretch of park currently overgrown with grass and weeds. Lacking ambition to cross the street and sit on a bench surrounded by the swaying stalks of brown, Sabine turned her attention elsewhere.

To her left, less than a football field distant, was a hotel in want of paint. How much, she wondered, to stay in an Ossi flop house? She had her father's money and much of the sum Ute left her. She was prepared to exchange a premium price for a place to put the suitcase.

Again, she struggled to drag, carry, shove, and curse her goods to the polished stone steps of the hotel. She saw enough through the frosted glass door to give her pause. Two men dressed like undertakers in black bow ties were examining something behind the counter. She removed the button from her mouth, dropped it in Mrs. Waldron's modest bag, swallowed hard, and got up the steps. To her amazement, the door opened automatically, denying her the opportunity to use her suitcase as a ram.

Two sets of dark, suspicious eyes surveyed her slovenly appearance.

"Do you have a single room for the night?" she asked, using her leg to shove the case across the floor.

"*Ausweis, bitte.*"

That peeved her. She was alone, frightened, and lacking in self-confidence. She'd asked a legitimate question in a place of business, and she got a snooty command in return. She wanted to author an Ed Barker aria but decided to play the game – for the moment.

Her blood boiled so intensely she didn't realize what she was doing. There were two passports in Mrs. Waldron's bag; they were together and equally available. Why, then, did she pull out the American passport?

Four eyes widened when that blue document was slapped onto the counter. After a moment, one of the men took it up and looked at the information page. Sabine could hear the machinery clatter in his brain; she knew he would, eventually, realize the answer was sixteen.

"Are you traveling alone, Miss Foster?" he asked in perfect English, making clear his distain.

She took a deep breath and counted to a hundred – by fifties. She refused to speak English to this pompous oaf. She looked at his mute partner when replying in exacting German.

"My sister is in this city. I'm here to find her. Until then, *yes*; I'm alone."

The man stiffened slightly and his expression softened. Perhaps, he understood. Perhaps, Tweedle dum deciphered her cryptogram, as well. He continued in English. Apparently, he acquired a bit of respect for the lethal edge in Sabine's voice.

"We have a smaller room available for twenty-seven marks," he informed, and not before time.

"Ossi oder Wessi?" she asked snappishly.

"Ah, Reichmarks, Miss Foster."

She wanted to slap his face, but that would require acknowledging his presence. Instead, she set her underwear bag on the suitcase, unzipped it, and counted out sixty marks for Tweedle dee.

"Two nights."

A registry card and pen were placed on the counter. She glared at Tweedle dee until he understood and delivered both paper and pen to his side of the counter. She used the name on the passport, neither knowing nor caring if she broke a law. For her address, she wrote, in bold letters, her father's address in Frankfurt/Oder – that would give them something to think about.

Tweedle dee counted out change and passed it over together with a room key. She accepted them with a frosty thank-you and began worrying the suitcase upstairs. She missed the clanking elevator of her previous hotel. Though dangerous enough for personal use, it was safe for hauling a suitcase.

Neither of the penguins offered to help her – not that she'd allow it. That denied her the pleasure of snapping "*I can do it myself!*" By the time she reached the third floor, all the fight was gone. She left the case at the stairs and searched for her room. When she found it, she inserted the key and discovered that it was, indeed, small.

The twin-sized bed was shoved against the opposite wall and the bathroom was a sink, shower and toilet that nearly overlapped. Accessing the shower, required one to duck under a cross beam; any sudden movement risked barking her shin on the toilet or knocking herself out on the beam. There was a single large window and a small shrunk behind the door. There was a waste can, a non-descript painting on the wall above the bed and an ancient radio on a corner stand between the window and the wall opposite the bed.

Sabine was beyond caring. She tossed the suitcase on the bed and opened it to retrieve Molly's dress. It survived the journey better than expected, but she smoothed it out before grabbing a hanger from the shrunk. The interior of the clothes closet smelled musty. She hung it, instead, from a hook behind the door. She need not worry about crushing the dress against the shrunk; the bed was in the way. The door could open completely only if the bed were removed or turned on its side.

After guzzling half her water, she left the bottle and the suitcase on the bed and vacated the room. She'd have asked for Werner Ecke Strasse but rejected the notion. After leaving her key at the desk, she returned to the Bahnhof to examine the large city map displayed there. She found the street, looked out the large doors several times to orient herself, and plotted a route.

She left the station and navigated the jungle park to emerge on the other side of the square. She walked through a wide street down a gentle hill and passed a large school where, unknown to her, Heike occasionally attended classes. Next, she circled a huge, empty building to discover Karl-Marx Platz; in a previous era Adolf Hitler Platz. Once, the politically-correct heart of the region beat inside those massive offices. Currently, more and more of the complex was abandoned.

Several minutes later, she waited to cross a busy street. While waiting, she watched a huge Army truck roar past with Soviet soldiers crowded into the back. She followed the sight for as long as the billowing and toxic exhaust allowed.

Was something happening? Was she in danger? Surveying the area, Sabine discovered only she felt concern over the Russian soldiers. Familiar with American military installations in Germany and America, she concluded nothing was amiss.

Sabine viewed Goethe Platz for the first time. It was a gaudy array of capitalism, Ossi style. The imbiss that, in the West, would offer wurst, pommes, beer and other fast-food delights, specialized in a single item: bananas! Judging from the crowd, it was doing a land-office business.

Past the imbiss was a *beer garden* comprised of display tables for the standing customers only who sipped their Wessi beer with the serenity that belonged only to those for whom idleness was a constant and convivial companion. Recessed further from the street was a colony of open-air shops specializing in used Wessi goods. Across this amazing stage strode a single Soviet soldier in his heavy woolen uniform. He was disheveled and in a daze. He had a sense of purpose, but he looked and acted like a bemused child.

There were plenty of people to choose from; Sabine asked for directions to Werner Ecke Strasse. After collecting peculiar expressions and evasive answers, she asked after a landmark the Bahnhof map indicated was not far from her goal.

Effusive directions were quickly obtained.

It was a leisurely, five-minute walk to the landmark, but she spent an additional twenty in a systematic search. Finally, she found the street sign. She could walk into the sun or away from it; she chose the latter and found the house numbers progressed agreeably. There was a large gap where buildings no longer existed on the right side of the street, while the row of houses on the left continued.

Finally, the dwellings on the left ceased, leaving a single house alone and forlorn on the right. As with most dwellings, it hadn't seen paint in years. It was half a football field from its nearest neighbor, and as far again to the next street corner.

She knew the house number. She kept a glimmer of hope she was wrong, but Sabine learned to accept that *hope* is a Wessi concept. Slowly, she approached. The house was ominous and sinister.

There were three metal plates visible in the bright sunlight. Shaped like grotesque flowers, they were evenly spaced across the front and on a plane marking interior levels. Sabine had seen them before; her grandfather explained their function. The metal "flowers" were attached to iron or steel rods running through the house and attached to other "flowers" in the back. These were inserted to keep the walls from falling outward.

She approached from the far side of the street on cat's feet. She was in no hurry to get near enough to see the house number because she knew what it was. While procrastinating, she noticed a woman coming toward her.

She was not old, but her gait was that of an ancient. She wore a dark housedress and carried a small canvass bag. The woman didn't come along the street but cut diagonally across vacant ground fronting a street running perpendicular to Werner Ecke Strasse. She paused and set her bag on the steps of a house since vanished.

The woman paid no heed to Sabine. It was doubtful she noticed her standing immobile yards away and on the opposite side of the street. She turned to look back in the direction from whence she had come. She turned completely around before taking up her bag and continuing her journey. The woman headed for the house with the weak walls.

Sabine quaked. She'd been prepared to stand sentry until someone, preferably her sister, forced her hand. However, when the woman pushed open the door, Sabine stepped forward.

"Excuse me! Ah – excuse me!"

The woman ignored her. She stepped into the house but didn't close the door behind her. She stood in a dimly lit room – hardly surprising. The two windows were shrouded against the summer brightness. Speak, the woman tacitly bade, I am turned to hear.

"Excuse me," Sabine repeated. "I'm seeking Heike."

Hearing that name, the woman smiled. It wasn't pronounced, but it radiated pride and, perhaps, love.

"Does Heike live here?"

The smile broadened slightly. Yet, the woman remained mute. She turned slightly and gestured with her hand. Sabine hesitated before crossing the threshold. The woman waited patiently before repeating the gesture.

Sabine stepped in further. The silent woman closed the door and took Sabine by the elbow. She led her to a table covered with a hospital-white linen cloth. She patted the back of a wooden chair. Sabine interpreted this as an invitation.

The visitor looked at the door and measured the distance. The stony silence frightened her, and she was uncomfortable about being inside a dwelling of questionable structural integrity. Still, she didn't feel threatened – yet. If the need arose, Sabine could flee without hindrance.

She sat warily.

"Heike?" she asked.

The woman nodded and motioned for her to wait.

She shuffled through a miniature arch. Sabine was certain Heike was not in that next room. Sabine realized the woman was a mute. There was nothing to do but await developments. This she did by appraising possible threats and making certain the path to the front door remained free of obstacles.

Several minutes passed, and the silence was troubling. Sabine considered tiptoeing to the door and fleeing. Each time she was tempted, she considered the penalty. If Heike did live here, Sabine must return later. Her disappearance might be interpreted as a hostile act.

Finally, the woman shuffled back with a mug of steaming liquid. She set the mug in front of Sabine and motioned for her to drink. She didn't wait for Sabine to accept. Instead, she shuffled to the couch and sat as if watching a performance.

Hot cocoa! It must be over ninety degrees outside and only slightly less inside. Praying it wasn't laced with poison, she took a tentative sip.

"Very good," Sabine lied.

The woman smiled her smile and nodded.

It was horrible. It was made of hot water. True, there was a lot of sugar, perhaps, too much. However, the woman looked on expectantly, so Sabine did her best to make it look as if she enjoyed the drink. If Heike, or any speaking person didn't appear soon, the farce would continue endlessly.

A car motor approached the house and stopped. Heike? Dare she hope? The door opened but very little light entered. There stood a huge, hulking figure not only filling the door frame but, in Sabine's estimation, overflowing it.

She stood instantly. This giant was a decided threat; her only exit was barred. Her only refuge was through the small door into the kitchen. Was there a back exit? Could she find it before Goliath grabbed her?

There was no option but to look directly at the gorgon. He eyed her with extreme suspicion garnished with dislike. He examined the placid face of the woman on the couch. That appeared to soften him slightly.

"Who are you?" he demanded.

"I'm looking for Heike," she replied, not realizing she'd avoided his question.

"Why does that not surprise me?" he scoffed. "She's on the Frauenplan. They're all on the Frauenplan – have been for hours. Fat lot of help you are!"

Sabine gulped.

"How do I get to the Frauenplan?"

The giant's eyes turned stony.

"I asked before, who are you?"

"I'm Sabine. Sabine Bauer."

That was as far as she'd go. She thought it neither wise nor healthy to claim her blood relationship until she knew how the news would be received.

"You're not from around here or you wouldn't be asking directions," the man concluded.

"I came from Berlin."

His voice remained conversational insofar as volume was concerned. His tone, however, adorned words with ice.

"Berlin? Looking for Heike? Not Nadine?"

"I've heard of Nadine," she gulped. "I'd like to see her too, but I – must see Heike."

He digested this. Sabine imagined he debated with himself how far he could throw her into the street.

"You know how to get downtown?"

"I've just come from there."

He nodded coldly.

"Well, get back. Ask someone to direct you. Don't tarry," he cautioned. "I imagine they'll shut down at six."

"Thank you," she replied with a bob curtsey.

There remained only one thing. The man divined what it was and stepped away from the door. Sabine thanked the cocoa woman, offered another curtsey, and made for the door – quickly. She was prepared to duck and run if the man made a grab.

He didn't.

The door closed quietly but firmly behind her.

* * *

Heike was fading. Since nine o'clock that morning, she'd been on her feet as an expository speaker advancing Rosa's Children and its mission to see the workers are treated fairly under the new regime. As the event organizer, she rushed about putting out brush fires that plagued the event. These minor problems mounted and made her uneasy.

The food venders upset a restaurant and nearby pizzeria. They appealed to the Vopos who warned the students grilling wurst, who complained to Heike, who appealed to Jürgen who, along with Lilo, established an uneasy truce. Two Rosa signs had been brought into the square; judged by Heike and Nadine as confrontational and counterproductive, they had to be quietly removed, and their creators placated. It was stressful duty to persuade these dedicated few to remove their works of art without destroying their fervor. She felt she succeeded. She hoped she succeeded. However, the episode taxed her emotional resources.

There was the presence of Lilo!

She was the best and most reliable of Heike's lieutenants. However, when the former Olympic hopeful found Heike and Günther together, her face became tempestuous. Thereafter, Heike steered clear of Günther who, likewise, exercised prudence.

Her greatest fear was Jürgen and Marina. The last thing she could bear was those two slobbering over each other during a serious activity. She needn't have wasted emotional energy. Jürgen was a rock. He asked Heike for instructions and followed orders with exactitude.

Marina found the event beyond her understanding, save for the obvious: it was important to Heike. She contented herself with admiring Jürgen from afar and lending a hand when she perceived a hand was required. She brought water to heat sufferers, fetched Senf when the grillers ran low, brought fresh supplies of flyers to those too engaged with the public to fetch them, and willingly performed a score of minor services for any of Rosa's Children who had only to ask.

Heike bid her to come to her aid.

"Could you please tell the Genossinn to turn that music down?" she asked. "There are many older people just now. I don't want them driven off by loud music."

"*Sofort*," Marina responded.

The Russian rushed to the vacant bakery as if delivering ammunition to desperate troops at the Battle of Borodino. There was no sign of sarcasm, no condescension, no questioning glances, and not a trace of disappointment over being charged with such a minor office. She not only carried out her instructions, but she did so with such charm and élan that the disc jockey and his "sound engineer" cheerfully complied. *Die Neue*, obviously, was far more than a pretty face.

Prior to the incident, Heike viewed Marina with skepticism. She didn't fully understand *Rosa's Children*. However, it was important to Heike who was Jürgen's "sister." That, alone, justified her full cooperation.

Heike didn't believe they changed the attitude of a city, never mind the country. Rosa's Children, however, captured peoples' attention. It was a vital first step, though light years from what the organization must become.

Shortly after five, Heike's attention was directed to a curious form approaching from the east. She wore a sleeveless shirt, a yellow miniskirt and hefted a transient's bag. From a distance, the person appeared oddly familiar. Heike presented a flyer to a middle-aged passerby and verbally stressed the need for citizens to remain in public service. Those with jobs in public works must be retained and those dismissed must be brought back. She included her rehearsed anecdote about Frau Willing and her possible dismissal despite her stellar driving record (*and* her stint as a midwife).

"The city cannot make a profit," she stated for the hundredth time, "but the people deserve the expertise and services of those who make our city function."

Twenty minutes later, she noted the yellow miniskirt on a portable bench – one of several hurried into the square at the last minute by Children who, acting independently, predicted a need. The "familiar stranger" sat isolated from three others populating the orange painted surface supported by green iron legs. She chewed like a grazing cow on a wurst. A clear plastic container of beer was clutched in her other hand. She raised to her lips and greedily drained it despite her overcrowded mouth.

Heike turned to attend anything less revolting. Spying a younger couple ambling her way from the Goethe House, she dismissed thoughts of the uncouth to attune herself to a more resonant chord. A few minutes later, the sweethearts departed with a flier and (hopefully) a favorable opinion of Rosa's Children.

Heike next discovered the miniskirt girl leaning against a water pump, a residual from a previous century. One foot was planted firmly on the street; the other rested alongside its working partner. Her arms were crossed below two miniscule bulges, but her eyes were directed at Heike.

She felt an inexplicable shiver and quickly averted her eyes. This was the third time! She knew that girl. She'd seen her before – or…? Why did the sight of her make Heike feel so queer?

The next time she saw her, the interloper was conversing with Günther.

That made it personal!

Heike moved to invite herself into the conversation. However, that damned Lilo was lurking nearby. Once again, Heike redirected her attention.

Moments later, Marina was speaking with *her*. This was not a beauty-and-the-beast confab. The beauty-and-the-cutie might, perhaps, be more apt. Regardless, the phenomenon was out of place. Heike refused to be tortured further.

There was no prohibition against associating with Marina. Lilo could get stuffed!

The distance between them was minimal. Normally, Heike could negotiate space in a time so inconsequential it wouldn't be worth recording. The speed of her fist steps, however, slacked considerably when she noted Jürgen's signal. She looked to see with whom he communicated. She discovered Nadine response.

Nadine was engaged with a small group of classmates or FDJ comrades, but she monitored her brother. She left the group, abruptly, and moved towards Marina. Heike cast a questioning glance at Jürgen and discovered him in a lazy lope toward Marina as well.

Marina and the stranger noticed Heike's advance and observed her curiously. Heike froze. The situation was surreal, and time ceased. Everyone moved as If caught in some dream-like goo.

The stranger's eyes created a queer sensation. It was not unpleasant – exactly, but it wasn't normal. Finally, Heike noticed the girl's legs. They weren't particularly attractive, but they were familiar – very, very!

Heike noticed Nadine stop when she stopped, but Jürgen ambled on with an exaggerated casualness. Was this a trick? The air of conspiracy made Heike reluctant to proceed. Why would Jürgen and Nadine conspire against her? Whatever the reason, the girl in the yellow miniskirt was the cause.

Tentatively, she crept forward on legs no longer reliable. She noticed Nadine returning to the hunt. Heike suspected; she conjured grave doubts.

A palpable suspicion gripped her.

It explained the guise of conspiracy. It explained Nadine and Jürgen's obligation to be on hand. But – it was too incredible! Heike's wariness was shunted aside by insatiable curiosity.

Marina divided her attention between two visages as if recording every nuance. With Jürgen and Nadine flanking them, Heike placed the entire matter before the stranger. She dared her to respond to her demanding gaze.

"I got you message," the familiar stranger reported, her voice quaking.

"Message?"

There was a silent pause. No one breathed. The familiar stranger swallowed. Her voice croaked.

"New Years, 1974; Greetings – from your sister – Heike.'"

The words pounded her ears. Heike's vision blurred. Then, it darkened.

"You – got – my – ? In America – you got – my – message?"

"*Stimt.*"

Heike's legs no longer supported her. She crossed her feet and sank to the cobblestones. When her amazed eyes refocused, she found the familiar stranger mirroring her Indian-style rest. It wasn't a mini skirt.

"You – knew," Heike accused her brother.

"For, maybe, twenty minutes."

Heike didn't hear. Her mind raced.

"How old are you?" she demanded.

"Eleven minutes younger than you."

Heike heard, but her brain didn't register. She was stunned. She was senseless.

Two young women sat mute and immobile surrounded by a silent scrum. Confused expectation dominated the air. No one knew what to do; no one knew what to say. Something profound had transpired, but there were no pyrotechnics.

Lilo was attracted by the unexplained huddle. She and her uncertainty drew near. Heike was obtuse. Sitting on the ground with a perfectly good bench so near was proof enough.

Who was *die Neue*? What childish game was this? Did they parody some Indian parlay? What purpose had the silent audience?

"Nobody told me about a *Pause*," Lilo scolded. "What's this?"

"Shock, I think," Marina volunteered.

Alone of the principles, the Soviet visitor was coherent. Lilo assumed it was a Jacobs family matter. Recognizing herself as the odd person, Lilo thought it best to retreat. Marina locked arms with Lilo and led her away to explain.

Lilo's voice jarred Heike out of hibernation.

"We need to start tearing down," she croaked.

Nadine shuddered. Heike's words were appropriate and rational, but her voice indicated she'd no concept of what she uttered. She shot a glance at Jürgen who caught the tacit plea. He stepped around to take Heike by the shoulders.

"Trust us, Heike," he said softly. "We can handle this. You two have much to say."

"Where?"

He gently turned her to face the new girl, standing now but uncomfortable.

"Oh," Heike said.

The sisters looked as blankly standing as they had while sitting.

"You need to talk," Jürgen prodded.

"Ahm – ja," she drawled without breaking her trance.

Once more, the two biological siblings exchanged silent messages.

"Go get an Eis or something," he suggested.

When no one moved, he gave Heike a gentle shove.

"Would you like an Eis?" Heike asked as she passed.

"Okay."

This was the American invented word used in virtually every nation on earth. Sabine used it precisely because she'd nothing to say. However, she felt obligated to make a sound. Heike walked slowly towards Schillerstrasse followed, in lockstep, by *die Neue*. After several paces, it was obvious they had no objective. Reticent to speak, Sabine forced herself.

"I didn't know – I mean – my father – uhm, my Ami father told me – well, that I – was, uhm, found in the woods. It was – well – a shock. Mutti – she died – in the woods – that – night. My Uncle Dieter worked so hard to find – I mean – well, I got your message through him."

Heike swallowed hard. Sabine was choking back emotion.

"One night – I – well, I – I – saw you!"

They stopped walking. Heike was too overwhelmed by events to comprehend much, but this announcement transformed the outlandish into the creepy. Heike didn't speak, but her penetrating glare was demanding. Sabine, wiping away copious tears, stuttered, and stammered through her recitation of an eerie birthday epiphany.

Heike's eyes grew large. She understood but could not believe the recitation. She could not believe – but she understood. Her sister had found her!

* * *

"I better keep an eye on them," Nadine pondered.

"Good idea," Jürgen seconded. "When Heike comes to, she might try to kill her."

"If she doesn't, I might."

"What are you on about?" he demanded.

"That's our sister," she reminded. "Do you want some Ami to take her away?"

"If that is *our* sister, as you say, don't you think she's the one to decide?"

Nadine left him with an ice-cold glance and launched her career as a spy.

* * *

Jürgen kissed his darling good night at the front steps and departed. Marina closed the door quietly and joined Nadine in washing dishes. Billeting became a major issue due to limited funds. Bunking in with Gunther, Jürgen willed his bed to Marina.

Heike's primitive bed pained the Soviet visitor. Nadine attempted to explain that Leipzig left Heike with masochistic tendencies.

Where was Heike? If she remained out all night, sleeping arrangements were moot.

Anne sat beside her husband on the couch. He devoured the local paper with ominous grunts and mumbling. Only splashing water and the clattering of dishes competed with him. Nadine remained dismal and mute, unaware of the discomfort this caused. Marina resisted striking up a conversation; it might violate some family custom.

Nadine, eventually, confronted the awkwardness she'd created. Marina was between her and the kitchen arch. Unless she physically shoved the guest aside, there was no way to exit.

"Sorry to be such bad company."

"I understand," Marina replied softly. "It's quite a shock."

"Do you need us for anything, Pabst?" Nadine asked, accompanying her new friend to the stairs.

He broke the back of the paper and peered at them. Normally, a dismissive grunt from behind the paper was enough. Nadine suspected he wanted to feast his eyes upon their guest.

"We're fine."

Nadine was used to his terseness. Rolf could defer a little for a future daughter-in-law. Without special dispensation, the girls weren't allowed out of the house. Marina, however, was a guest, not a prisoner. However, being the model of decorum, the Soviet girl was too polite to claim special privilege.

They discovered Heike sitting on her pallet with knees under her chin. She studied a small photo.

"We didn't hear you come in," Nadine announced. "I followed you to the park – just in case."

She expected Heike to explode.

Nothing

"You seemed to be getting along with your sister."

"*You* are my sister," Heike insisted.

Nadine looked to Marina for support. Sad eyes looked back. Yes, Heike was Nadine's sister, but Sabine was of the same blood. A prior claim existed. It was wrong for sisters to be ripped apart – particularly twins.

Nadine sat down next to her traumatized roommate. She wanted to put her arm around the person who had shared both the home and the room for most of her life.

Marina knelt quietly in front of them. There was nothing she could contribute other than tacit support. Nadine's eyes conveyed warmth and thanks.

"What's that?"

Heike replied by offering the school photo. Nadine examined it.

"Does she think braiding her hair makes her look German?" she scoffed.

"That's my mother."

Nadine gasped and reexamined the photo. Prolonged study did not help. The girl in the photo was identical to Sabine. She handed the evidence to Marina expecting vindication.

"She's planning some mischief," Marina concluded. "You can see it in her eyes."

Heike retrieved the photo. With three heads touching, Nadine and Heike searched for Marina's discovery. The seed was planted. The girl's eyes and facial expression were obvious.

"Sabine said she liked to play games," Heike sniffed. "She thinks Mutti made fun with our names. She wondered if Mutti ever intended to share it with us."

Sabine wakened from a dream one hot night in Frankfurt and carried the entire formula from dream to reality. The more she thought, the more convinced she became. Heike Franziska was born first and Sabine Aleksandra arrived soon after. Ernst confessed he had no say in the girls' names. It's bad luck to select names prior to birth. Nevertheless, Constanze either schemed before labor or was exceptionally adroit after.

Heike and Sabine were each a *peasant*, i.e.: *Bauer*. A common name, of course, and not flattering. *Franziska* and *Aleksandra*, however, were aristocratic in sound and nature – a celebration of the von Posen heritage and, therefore, discouraged by the regime. As consolation for her status as the younger child, Sabine was given the weight of an extra letter in both given names.

"Alexandra has only nine letters," Marina announced, her logical chemical-formula mind calculated with little conscious thought.

"Not with Mutti's," Heike responded with solemnity. "It's spelled A-l-e-K-S-a-n-d-r-a."

"That's Russian," Marina confided.

"It is? I'd never seen it before. Sabine thought Mutti invented it."

"Either way, Sabine got an extra letter," Marina smiled.

"There's more," Heike went on. "With that spelling, we get letters switched. S K in my name becomes K S in Aleksandra."

They grinned as if they'd broken a code. It was preposterous and silly, but it was also cunning.

"You spoke of your mother in the past tense," Nadine noted.

Marina noticed as well, but thought discretion was best. Heike's face wrinkled and clouded.

"She froze to death – that – night."

It was easy for Sabine, Heike supposed. She could speak clinically about Constanze's death as if it were fiction; for Heike, it was far different. Had Constanze lived, Heike would view her with contempt and hatred. News of her death smothered these base emotions. What remained were Heike's feelings for the only mother she knew, Anne Ecke Jacobs; the woman who had housed her, fed her, and showered her with love, and who, slowly, was stolen away.

Sabine lost a mother. Heike lost two. It was beyond her strength to fight back the tears that came unwanted and unbidden. All that remained of Constanze Bauer was a cheap, school photo. It was a pathetic remnant made poignant by Sabine's fairy-tale deductions.

Had the escape to the West been another of her mother's *games*? A game gone tragically awry. Heike's loss was shared by the doting Nadine, but Marine felt it profusely. Her delicate chin quivered.

The focus shifted. It was precisely what Marina didn't want. However, Marina's concerns could not be repressed. Heike, unintentionally, opened the cell door allowing demons to escape.

"My family has renounced me," she said in battle to maintain composure. "I'm sorry, Heike. I didn't want – this –"

"Because of Jürgen?" Nadine asked.

Marina nodded but avoided speech until she brought her tears under control. It wasn't her desire to steal the attention from Heike who deserved it. Heike and Nadine merited an explanation. Marina needed to undergo a catharsis, or she might explode at the most inopportune moment.

"It isn't Jürgen," she began.

"It's his nationality. My parents hold the Germans responsible for the deaths of much of our family and many family friends. The grandfather of a boy in my class survived the siege because he found a bucket of wallpaper paste. He hid it away for himself. His brother starved to death. You don't get over something like that. What my family went through, I'll never know. It's forbidden to speak of it, but it's our family duty to hate Germans.

"I came here because no one would speak about the war. If I must hate someone, I'll do it myself, not because I'm ordered to. So, I learned German and came to study. Mostly, I wanted to ask questions no one at home will answer. I hadn't been here long before I realized I can't hate *all* Germans. It is easy to hate some people, but I hate some Russians. I was ready to finish my studies at home. When I met Jürgen, life got complicated.

"So, I went home to explain. No one listened. I was told if I left the house, I would not be allowed to return. It's not easy to make that choice. I could be miserable if I left Jürgen and be with people who loved me, or I could be miserable amongst strangers and be with one person who loves me."

Heike sighed.

"And I thought I had problems," she said with typical self-effacement.

"I decided to make my family happy," Marina continued. "It was the hardest decision –"

Heike and Nadine exchanged an awed expression.

"What happened?"

"I'm the middle child," Marina continued calmly. "I have an older sister and brother and a younger sister and brother. Alexi, my younger brother, came to my room. He's fourteen. He never comes to my room except to tease me or make me mad by going through my things. I was sitting and staring at myself in the mirror. He walks in behind me. I thought, maybe, he wanted one of my books.

"He doesn't pay any attention to my books. He puts his hand on my shoulder and he tells me that I'm his sister no matter what. He thought the sister between us feels the same. He gave me a big hug and left. The moment the door closed, I started getting my things together. I wanted to leave before I could confuse myself more. Early the next morning, I take a taxi to the train station.

"I got very drunk on the train. It was the only to keep from bawling the whole trip. When I got to Halle, I checked into a hotel. I knew Jürgen was waiting at our apartment, but I couldn't see him before I sobered up and had a bath. He thinks I came direct from the Bahnhof and – and I didn't tell him. He'll have to know, of course. He wants to get married in the spring. Well, we might go back to Leningrad for the wedding, but he's bound to notice when none of my family shows up."

"You can get married here," Nadine suggested and was rewarded with Heike's elbow in her ribs.

Marina didn't notice. She remained focused on the floor.

"Jürgen, will have to know," she reflected. "I'm not ready. I don't know when I can gather the courage. It's my place, though. Promise to not tell."

"He's our brother," Heike reminded.

"I know, but this is my responsibility."

This was a very serious commission and neither Nadine nor Heike was eager to comply. Ultimately, the sisters decided to sleep on it.

Heike lay on her back, staring into the gloom of another stifling night. Her mind was occupied with two mothers and a sister she'd just met. She thought of Nadine and the doctor's recommendation to wait to see if the health system of the reunited country would allow the reconstruction of her face. She thought of Marina and the hardest decision she'd ever confront. In the end, she thought of Jürgen. She made a vow: if he didn't treat Marina with reverence, Heike, would never let him enjoy a moment's peace.

Behind these weighty matters, however, there was one thing bubbling to the top. It remained a persistent nuisance. Marina's slow, even breathing made clear she had succeed to in making peace with herself. The Soviet expatriate found repose in a tiny room shared by three.

Marina, with four siblings, had her *own* room!

* * *

She found Heike. That was the only satisfying part of her day. Sabine wrote a quick postcard to Baba, but the elation she feigned in the limited space didn't reflect reality. Though she and Heike talked incessantly for over two hours, there existed a huge gulf between them, a sixteen-year-wide trench.

Heike was cold, calculating, remote, and abrasive. She was Ossi from the tips of her toes to the ends of her hair. Moreover, she was crushed rather than elated by the dawn of a new era. Her resentment over her father's attempted *kidnapping* was palpable. Any attempt to bring her together with Herr Bauer would not only be time wasted, it could destroy the fragile bond between them.

Once she returned to her room, Sabine confronted the residuals of a Sorb meal and the snack Biggi prepared. She picked at these morsels absent-mindedly while reviewing the afternoon with her newest companion, despondency. For months Sabine convinced herself that finding her sister would be the happiest and most important moment of her life.

Steaming in a tiny Ossi hotel room, she regretted leaving Frankfurt. Vati was kind, loving and respectful. When she needed a confidant, Biggi proved attentive, responsive, and practical.

In Weimar, she discovered an insular sister with a hair-trigger temper waging war against reality. Sabine needed Gary, Molly, or Biggi. Were Shelly at hand…well, Sabine was alone.

For the first time in her life, Sabine confronted a disinterested and menacing world. Her only comfort was the money her father forced upon her. It was a mockery. The only comfort in money was predicated on the choices it offered. She could return to Frankfurt and face the humiliation and disappointment of a man she loved. Alternatively, she could go on to

Fürth and love Isaac until she hurt and be among the people who would accept her regardless of her many failings.

After brooding, however, Sabine remained alone and despondent. If she left, no matter in which direction she traveled, she'd be forever haunted by the realization she could have done more. What more could she do? Molly would have had a sound advice and Gary would rattle off a legion of ideas, most of them impractical and outrageous, but, in his own bumbling way, he'd exhaust himself in the mission to lift her flagging spirit.

Devoid of plans, she drew back the curtains and threw open the window, hoping for a hint of cool air. She stripped and, careful to duck her head, showered in water as cold as she could stand. She toweled herself off and threw herself onto the bed. Later, she slipped into as little clothing as her resources allowed.

Sabine lay on her back to await the passing of the night.

She slept for a few minutes at least. The room was lighter. She shifted position and attempted to doze off again. After several minutes of flailing, she gave up. Her feet struck a thin layer of carpet, and she padded over to the window to gulp outside air.

In the distance was a huge tower rising out of the wooded hills. Could there be an abbey or a large convent up there? It was improbable that something so grandiose would be nestled on those heights.

Suddenly, realized where she'd heard of Weimar!

She groaned. It wasn't enough for fate to leave her alone and disconnected. Sabine was forced to loiter in the shadow of unspeakable evil.

* * *

Heike was the first to stir. Deprived of sleep, it was a relief to pretend no further. She was in the kitchen preparing breakfast when she heard Rolf's heavy tread straining the wooden steps. He'd be in a foul mood to discover breakfast was not laid out; it mattered nothing that he'd risen earlier than usual.

Heike decided she wouldn't put up with him. Today was the day she would no longer tremble before his mighty roar. She would declare her intolerance toward unreasonable expectations; breakfast would be ready based upon her ability to prepare it rather than his capriciousness. This was the day she'd experience the back of his meaty hand and taste the blood in her mouth. Today, she'd demand a voice in this family. Today, she'd look upon Nadine's facial deformity and not feel shamed by her own lack of disfigurement.

She forced herself to work at her normal pace despite her trembling hands. She waited for the slam of a fist on the tabletop, or the growl of the bear. Nothing came. The water was nearing a boil and still no sound of impatience.

Heike could tolerate the silence no longer. She moved to the narrow door and found Rolf Jacobs sitting on the couch looking more pensive and vulnerable than she'd ever seen him without Anne sitting at his side. He turned his head towards her, but there was no fire in his eyes.

Heike's defiant speech died stillborn.

"I'll be a few more minutes," she announced meekly.

"That was your sister yesterday," his baritone voice was muted.

"She came here?"

"She was drinking cocoa when I walked in."

Heike nearly dropped the knife she was holding.

"She was here?" she repeated, stupidly.

"She didn't look too bright. I assumed she was one of your lackeys. She said she came from Berlin, but she didn't know Nadine. I knew that smelled."

"I didn't know she was here."

"She didn't know what you were doing. She didn't know how to find the Frauenplan. I thought she was daft. If I had known –"

Heike waited. She'd never seen Rolf Jacobs at a loss for words.

"You'd have thrown her out," she completed the sentence for him.

He did not speak for some moments.

"I don't know what I would have done," he confessed.

Heike was called away by the demands of the moment. It was some while before she returned to lay the table. Rolf moved to his place. He didn't speak, nor did he move as Heike brought out bread, meat, cheese, and jam in relays.

Finally, she brought the tea server in one hand and coffee server in the other. She was tempted to put her hand on his shoulder when he began helping himself. She took her chair across from him instead.

She took her first sip of coffee and was chewing a slice of bread with cheese when Rolf spoke. Instinctively, she froze. That was customary whenever Rolf Jacobs made an announcement at the table.

"When you came here, all I could see was a few extra government marks a month –"

"Oh, Gott! They've stopped payment! Pabst, I'll get a job. I'll bring bread in house."

He was shocked. No one interrupted Rolf Jacobs, but Heike composed an entire speech. Moreover, her words were muffled by the wad of food in her mouth.

Had he thought about it, he'd return her impudence with rage. He didn't, however, think about it. Her unexpected breach of protocol caught him completely off guard. He was unable to formulate a proper response.

"*Halt mal!*"

It was a limp response for a man used to launching warnings with a facial expression and a movement of his eyes. She placed her bread on the plate and folded her hands repentantly in her lap. She averted her eyes. Her jaw remained motionless; her food would remain untended until sentence was handed down.

"I don't care about the damned money," he began anew. "Not anymore. I stopped caring about that when I watched Anne coo over you like you were her own. You made her very happy. That made me happy. I'm – used to you."

She chewed surreptitiously. It was either that or choking. Rare it was to discover Rolf maudlin, it wouldn't do to spit up food.

"Heike, don't let those dimples steal you away!"

She choked on amazement. She gulped the bread before worse happened.

"Why would I go to America?"

"Everyone goes to America. I wanted to when I was your age. I pictured myself on a farm so huge, we'd seldom see our neighbors."

If eyes popped out of heads, Heike's would be rolling on the table between the tea vessel and the breadbasket.

"I'm not going to America! There's nothing for me there. This is my country. I'm not running away when it needs me."

He sighed as if not certain she could be trusted.

"What will you do?"

"What I've been doing."

"And your sister?"

How could she say? She wrestled with that on the floor all night.

"I can't speak for her," she decided.

Storm clouds formed above Rolf's head.

"She told me where she's staying. I'll go see her. She hasn't insisted I go to America. My country needs me, Pabst."

* * *

Sabine tarried over her breakfast, plotting her next move. To walk the short distance to the Bahnhof was an option. She could plant herself at a gate and allow fate to determine for her, Fürth or Frankfurt. Whichever direction the first, *late* train pointed would settle the matter. Still, aborting her mission was distasteful; there was nothing to warrant her staying beyond her room rental.

Unbidden, Bach escaped into her head. Within seconds, reality became manageable. Gone was her hysteria about formulating an instant plan of action. She had time; there was no reason to rush, literally, into the heat of the day.

While fumbling for some promising avenue leading to resolution or acceptance, Sabine depended upon some outside influence. Rev. Rademacher often included in his sermons anecdotes of fortuitous events provided by, in his view, the same source that sprinkled manna in the desert. Sabine concluded if divine forces existed, this was a good time to assert themselves.

Crossing the lobby on the way to the stairs, she saw the automatic doors sweep inward followed by Heike in jeans and a blue shirt with sleeves folded above the elbows. Nothing in her appearance hinted divine intersession. She was barely welcome.

"Morgen." Heike stated blandly.

Sabine replied with a nod. An uneasy truce existed. The slightest infringement might engage Sabine's fingers around Heike's throat. She imagined a reciprocal feeling existed.

"I wanted to return your picture."

"Keep it," Sabine responded brusquely.

"Why?" Heike dared.

The question was a challenge. Fortunately for them both, Tweedle dum sauntered up to the counter. A public brawl would not do.

"Come up while I change."

Sabine had no plans to change anything beyond her location. If Heike followed, she'd have the satisfaction of annoying Tweedle dum. If Heike refused, she knew where to find her. Perhaps, when cooler heads authored words both civil and meaningful, they'd cease sparing and settle into meaningful congress.

She didn't look back, but she heard feet on the stairs behind her. Suddenly, Sabine was nervous. Nervousness produced an annoyingly predictable symptom. When she opened the door to her room, Sabine stayed where the door met the bed. This forced Heike to move left into the room.

"Nice room," Heike commented.

Sabine didn't accept this as sincere. She'd been in rooms full of decaying fish that were roomier and nicer than the current hamster cage. She vowed, however, if an explosion was in the offing, Heike must initiate it. She shut her mouth and allowed the door perform the same function.

When Heike saw the back of the door, her eyes melded with Molly's dress. Sabine might as well be invisible. She watched Heike's eyes survey every stitch from neck to hem and then begin a return journey.

"Excuse me," Sabine said on the chance Heike would hear. "I drank four cups of coffee downstairs."

She scurried into the recess and drew the sliding door closed. It took no longer than usual, but she wished it could have taken a hundred times longer. She made meticulous work washing her hands, hoping she'd discover an empty room when she emerged.

No luck.

Heike sat on the unmade bed.

"I'm sorry I interrupted your – thing yesterday," Sabine said, for want of a better conversation. "I read the paper you were passing out."

"Are you interested in politics?" Heike asked.

"No."

Why pretend? What purpose was served by telling lies or making excuses?

"You're a fool."

That, Sabine thought, is the price of honesty. It was so tempting to serve up a knuckle hors d'oeuvre. Gary Swofford received one of those, and that turned out well enough. Dare she hope history could repeat? Still, Sabine was committed; Heike must initiate the first hostile act. However, enough was just about too much.

Sabine thundered past Heike, picking her feet way up least she be tempted to kick something – a sister, for instance. She leaned against the wall next to the window.

"Look at that," she commanded, gesturing to the monument four kilometers distant. "Politics put that there. It's politics made it necessary."

This, Sabine decided, would be exactly the wrong time to learn the stone candle was not in commemoration of a KZ. Better to make her point before Heike corrected her.

"Politics drew a line on a map. Politics drove Mutti and Vati to cross that line. It was politics that got our father shot and our mother killed. It was politics that kept us apart. If my opinion of politics is uncharitable, I have good reasons!"

She was ready to defend herself if Heike snapped at the bait. Several seconds ticked past. Sabine's hope that Heike would charge underwent a metamorphosis into a hope. She wanted the opportunity to apologize for her provocative tirade.

At least, Sabine managed to draw Heike's eyes away from Molly's dress. It was a shallow victory, however. The eyes that stared blankly out the window were Orphan Annie's. They presented no emotional clue.

"Why don't you want Mutti's picture?"

Heike's rational question and her placid tone disarmed Sabine. It wasn't a deliberate change of the subject. It was the subject that Heike brought with her. Suddenly, Sabine realized a reasonable question deserved a rational answer. Turning so both shoulders were braced against the wall, Sabine folded her arms and took a breath.

"I have no memory of Mutti," she began. "She's a concept. I've been to her grave. I felt nothing. I try to feel guilty about that, but nothing comes. Maybe, you can tell me I'm an evil person for being so cold. That might work."

Why did she end with a dare? What purpose was served? Heike opened her left hand and stared. Sabine realized their mother's photo had been there all along.

"Tell me about her."

Who, Sabine wondered, was the cold, unfeeling one? Had her initial prejudice toward Molly taught her nothing? Seated on the sweat-soaked sheets of a hotel bed was a complex young woman. Human drama touched her heart.

"I told you what I learned from Papa. He can tell you everything."

She left it there. If the hunger in her expression was any indication, the hatred of her father was being overridden.

"Strange, isn't it?" Sabine reflected. "I love Vati because he's alive and I've met him. You're in love with a person you don't remember."

If Heike heard, she made no indication. The way she drew her thumb across the ancient photo stirred Sabine's emotions enough that she could no longer stand. She stepped to the foot of the bed and sat with her back to Heike to avoid being subjected to further pathos.

"How did you get to America?"

The adventure was told in the third person with unintended pauses. Sabine realized how fantastic the tale was. Heike was either bored or simply too respectful to step on her lines. It didn't matter. It was more important for Sabine to tell the story than for Heike to hear it.

"She's nice, this Swabish woman?"

Not without tears did Sabine tell the heart-wrenching episode when she learned how Ute feared a thoughtless girl might not want her for a mother. She wiped the water away easily enough, but it was an effort to keep her voice even. It wasn't the answer Heike expected, but it was an episode that needed telling.

"The Swabish are cowards in folklore and literature," Heike stated quietly.

Sabine came so close to violence. Was Heike trying to provoke her. If so, the best response was to leave her wanting.

Rommel? A coward?

"I've never seen any evidence to confirm that," Sabine replied with a neutral tone.

If Heike was trying to start a fight, she gave up easily.

"She had her own baby in March," Sabine continued. "I'm happy for them both. He's lucky to have such a mother."

Catharsis, however necessary, is an energy pig. Sabine, suffering from sleep deprivation, was as limp and drained as a washcloth. She neither knew nor cared about how Heike received her narrative. It was one more thing over which she had no control. She guessed, however, that Heike was moved to some degree.

The bed reacted to Heike's evacuation.

"I'm meeting some people in a few minutes," Heike announced. "Would you like to come?"

No.

What Sabine needed was to lie on the bed and grab some sleep while passing through medium on the way to well-done. It took nearly all her strength to get to her feet; it took what remained to speak.

"Okay."

If she collapsed on the stairs and broke her neck, she'd die peacefully. Sabine couldn't turn down the invitation; she'd no assurance there'd be another. With reserves she never suspected, she hoisted her underwear bag onto her shoulder and held the door open for her sister.

They walked and walked and walked and walked. Sabine's legs, rubbery from the start, became more and more unreliable. It was well Heike didn't feel the urge to speak. Sabine needed to focus all her attention on putting one foot in front of the other. If it were not for the heat, the fresh air might have restorative powers. Luckily, from the hotel to town was either downhill or level.

They passed the school, Karl Marx Platz, and the National Theatre with Schiller and Goethe's bronze reproductions shaking hands in a spacious square. Only her determination to remain glued to her sister kept Sabine moving. Finally, they turned onto Schillerstrasse. At an outdoor café, she recognized Jürgen and Nadine among others surrounding two tables joined together. Everyone perked up as Heike approached.

"*Ah, Heike und Die Neue, aus Amerika.*" Jürgen greeted cheerfully.

"Where everyone owns a gun!"

Sabine didn't see who launched that bitter appendage, but it did not matter. She was too fatigued to battle or, even, take offence. A muscular blond stood up to pull out an empty chair.

Lacking the strength to look up into the stratosphere and direct her thanks, she settled down into the proffered chair. She muttered thanks, hoping the cloud-tickler would hear. She waited, however, until the woman came in for a landing before she could examine her face.

"Sorry I'm late," Heike said. "I know we all have things to do, so let's be quick. We'll decide on a place and time for a proper meeting."

"My place," the tall blond volunteered instantly. "Anytime, evenings."

"Wait a moment," Jürgen interrupted, "let's not forget our manners. Not all of us have been properly introduced."

"Sorry," Heike said in English.

There was an awkward and momentary pause. Heike expected Jürgen to put matters right He suggested it.

A woman in dark slacks, white blouse and a white apron approached the newest customers. Heike made her wait during the performance.

"Sabine, you know Jürgen and Nadine from yesterday. That's Lilo next to you. Around the table, here is Hanna and Günther. This is Bastian – right? – yes, Bastian, one of Jürgen's many friends, and next to Jürgen is Herr Gartner, who is a local FDJ leader. Everyone, this is Sabine, my sister from America."

There were nods and muttered greetings. The waitress stared at the blowsy newcomer with an entirely new attitude.

"May I bring you something?" she said in overcompensated English.

"Mineral water, bitte," Sabine replied.

Heike held up her thumb and forefinger. The waitress nodded knowingly and set off on her mission.

As the discussion began, Sabine realized Rosa's Children was not as tightly organized as she supposed the previous day. Indeed, it was markedly unorganized. Nevertheless, there was a clear purpose and a considerable following. To establish a sense of order, Lilo pulled out a notepad and took copious notes *after* asking Heike's permission.

Seated at Lilo's elbow, Sabine noticed she wrote rapidly and in detail. She'd developed a personalized shorthand. When she recorded something important or spurious, she'd place a black dot in the margin.

Sabine's presence was objected to twice. On the first occasion, Heike bid the speaker to continue. When a second objection was raised, Heike grew impatient.

"No secrets!" she proclaimed. "If we start keeping secrets, we must protect them; then, we will need a Stasi; then, the Stasi will have to know everyone's secrets and we're no better than before. No one must compare us to the SED…Ever!"

Sabine watched as Lilo's pen flew across the paper and ended with two black dots in the margin.

"Open agreements arrived at openly," Lilo muttered, hinting her reading habits were not in accord with government sanctions.

"Another quote from Chairman Mao Tse-Heike," Jürgen smirked.

Heike cast him a sharp look, but later surrendered once she realized he was making fun. Sabine found the discussion both esoteric and exceedingly dull. They could have laid out plans to invade West Germany and set up a communist dictatorship without her realizing.

The worst *faux pas* imaginable was Sabine snoozing at the table. It would bring mortification to herself and amplify Heike's truculence. The flow of words about issues she didn't understand produced a powerful anesthetic. To keep her eyes open and her mind active, she began surveying the assembly.

She started with Günther; he was the most pleasing to the eye. He was strikingly handsome with his alert eyes and angular features. If there was any conceit in his nature, he disguised it well. He attended every speaker with rapt attention and, when he spoke, his words were brief and carried a clearly defined purpose. Unlike others who attempted to gather their thoughts as they spoke, Günther refused to talk before he knew exactly what he would impart.

Jürgen wasn't quite so handsome. His features were softer and less well-defined. He had a natural reticence in his expression that matched his deferential mode of address – particularly towards Heike. His eyes wandered; Sabine caught him staring at her several times during the colloquy.

He wasn't as muscular as Günther, and he lacked the devil-may-care attitude his closest friend radiated with every gesture and expression. Jürgen was serious in a way none of the others approached, yet, as his playful aside about Heike demonstrated, there was an optimistic, even jovial, side to his nature that tempered his sobriety. In Sabine's estimation, Jürgen would be both easy and interesting to engage in conversation.

One could never ignore Lilo. Aaron Foster stood a shade over seventy-two inches, but Lilo certainly bested that. Her blond hair was not particularly well-tended, but it had an enviable sheen and texture that was sure to collect envious looks. Nadine's short, well-groomed hair had so much in common with Lilo's that Sabine speculated they shared some of the same genes.

Lilo had a trim, lanky, body but her shoulders were broad. Sabine was amazed at the way she managed to fold and twist her legs to fit into a confined space. They flew out of the chair that was designed for *normal* people. They were like a raging waterfall, spilling to the ground far beyond the brink; she wove one, vine-like appendage, around the other or wrapped her feet around the rear legs of the chair.

Aside from the dexterity of her legs and the fingers of her pen hand, Lilo had a sharp, thin, aerodynamic nose. Perhaps, the nose was compressed by her close-set eyes that glistened when she spoke. Somehow, Sabine imagined that those same eyes could look very stormy when her blood was up.

Then, there was Hanna who sat silent through the entire discussion and never took her eyes off Günther. It was an unfair conclusion since Sabine didn't watch her every second. Hanna's face was rounder than any of the others. Her red cheeks made it appear she retained some baby fat. She was the prettiest girl at the table. Her most prominent feature threatened to send two of her blouse buttons on a long journey.

Unquestionably, Hanna was a child still, but her child's clothing wasn't designed for such abuse. Perhaps, she realized as much and enjoyed keeping people, particularly men, in a state of nervous anticipation. Perhaps, she remained too innocent to realize.

Hanna was a dirndl-designer's dream. Should she show up at the Oktober Fest in München, public relations teams would abandon movie and television stars and fly to Hanna's tent. She'd be the girl in every photographers' lens.

Aware of her own deficiencies, Sabine could look at Hanna only through a green lens. Nevertheless, Hanna's movements were so innocuous that Sabine could conjure no ill-will. If her purpose was intended to capture Günther's attention with her "attributes," she was a bungler.

As the sun began intruding onto the assembly, the discussion came to a speedy close. Lilo capped her pen and Jürgen called for a round of *Korn*. Sabine knew the drink through Aaron who described the drink to Ed Barker as a rocket fuel. Moments later, small glasses of clear liquid ringed the table.

"To a good start," Jürgen proposed.

The glasses thumped on the table, held high momentarily, then, down the hatch. Sabine held her breath and got the vile liquid out of her mouth as quickly as she could. It burned all the way down and her eyes began to water.

She couldn't keep a small cough from exploding, but she willed herself to limit the damage. She noticed Hanna quietly place her glass back on the table. She sat with her arms folded as if nothing were amiss. Too late did Sabine wish she had her example to follow.

"I'll type up my notes tonight," Lilo announced. "We may want to start an archive."

It was Jürgen who paid for the drinks. He informed the waitress that he was settling for Nadine, Heike, and Sabine as well. Sabine thought that too generous and protested to no avail.

"You can pay next time, if you like," he announced.

It was unreasonable. The waitress, with an amazing display of memory and mathematical agility, announced the extent of the damages. Jürgen peeled off a single bill and received change. By Wessi standards, the cost was sinfully low, but Sabine still felt guilty; she knew from Biggi that Ossi marks are earned in tiny amounts.

Günther got up and stretched – and Hanna took it all in.

"I've got to deliver some money for my folks," he announced. "Want to come, Jürgi?"

"I'm going for Marina. I'm helping with chores."

"You better," Nadine added, resenting Heike who pretended not to hear.

Together, Jürgen and his real sister headed toward the theatre square while Günther, after bidding a farewell to all, walked in the direction towards the large, yellow Schiller House Museum. As the others melted away severally, Lilo stuck her pen and notebook into a small satchel, pushed back her chair and ambled away down Schillerstrasse.

"Sabine," Heike began. "Meet me at half five in front of the Kasseturm. I want you to meet some people."

Sabine responded with a nod, as if it made a difference. The older twin got up, thrust her hands into her pockets and sauntered casually down the street in the wake of Günther and Lilo.

"I think I've been dismissed," Sabine muttered.

Hanna hummed a response and turned in her chair to watch the comedy; Günther was followed by Lilo with Heike following her.

"You didn't say anything," Sabine noted by means of starting a conversation.

"I'm not one of Rosa's Children," she announced turning back around. "You're very pretty. You're prettier than Heike. I didn't expect that."

"And you're very pretty," Sabine responded, simply to dispense with the chit-chat. "Are you thinking about joining?"

"I'm thinking about it, but not very hard," the girl admitted. "My family made more than its fair share of sacrifices. I'll help when I can, but I don't want to be obligated. I'm not surrendering my life to politics like my parents did."

Sabine nodded. She wished Heike had heard that. It might make for an interesting discussion.

"The only reason you came was to ogle Günther?"

Sabine hardly expected to fetch a blush. When she did, she found it charming.

"It costs nothing; no one was injured," Hanna informed. "I've reached a point where Knoben aren't so annoying as before. I can dream about finding one as special as Günther."

"He is very handsome," Sabine agreed, "but that won't make a relationship."

She thought of Gary. If Günther were in the same building, Gary would be invisible to everyone but Sabine. She'd learned that character is more important than appearance. It was the same lesson she had relearned from Molly who, in truth, would make Hanna look plain.

"Günther has infinite patience," Hanna advanced.

"How do you know?"

Sabine was curious to how young Hanna could be so precocious.

"He must be patient to put up with Heike."

The Korn aided in renewing her energy, but the jolt delivered by Hanna upped the voltage even more.

"You can't be serious! Heike never mentioned it. They sat here as if they hardly knew each other."

"Well, they would with Lilo around."

Sabine realized her mouth was open. She slammed it shut, but the bafflement on her face was not so easily disguised.

"Lilo and Günther were close once," Hanna explained. "I mean, very close – make-a-baby close."

Sabine looked down the street, but the principals were beyond view.

"They didn't make-a-baby, I hope."

Hanna shook her head.

"Foolish, but not stupid. Lilo can't let go. She's still in love with him, but she knows it's over."

Sabine leaned forward in the chair.

"How old are you?" Sabine demanded.

"Fourteen, but there's nothing wrong with my sight and hearing."

She was calm and confident.

Sabine was offended because Hanna showed no signs of being offended.

"Sorry," Sabine sighed, ashamed of herself.

"We grow up fast in the DDR," Hanna explained. "Between the Pioneers and the FDJ, there aren't many social issues left untouched. Anyway, that's why Lilo and Heike are at drawn swords. It's also why Günther is on eggshells when around those two."

She continued with a sigh, "And, that's why Heike was so rude just now. She wants to make sure that Lilo isn't stalking him."

Sabine pointed to the glass of Korn.

"Are you going to drink that?"

Hanna shook her head. Sabine grabbed it and sent it after the first one. This time she made no effort to conceal her response. She shivered, blinked rapidly, and screwed her face up before letting go with an un-lady-like wheeze.

"Are you in love with Günther as well?"

Hanna considered that for a long time.

"No," she concluded. "I'm in love with the idea of being in love with someone *like* Günther. There's no way I am brave enough to take on Lilo and Heike. Besides, I prefer that a man make the first move. It isn't very nineties, I know, but it fits with my idea of romance. That might cost me, I know."

"I have a boyfriend at home. Shall I tell you how I got him to make the first move?"

Hanna leaned forward and folded her arms on the table to prepare to accept a confidence. When Sabine told her, Hanna's face exploded into silent mirth. It was a sign that something important passed between them.

It made them friends.

"When I hit him, he was the last person I intended to fall in love with."

Hanna smiled.

"I doubt I could do anything like that," she confessed.

Sabine's mood shifted.

"So, do you think – Günther and Heike? Make-a-baby –?"

Hanna leaned back and shook her head.

"I can't know, but I doubt it. That would mean they are foolish *and* stupid. Not those two – not at the same time."

That was a relief!

"Günther, I think," Hanna continued pensively, "would make a good father. I worry about Heike. Still, she adores her mother – uhm, Jürgen and Nadine's mother. That might work. Daughters tend to imitate their mothers, so I'm told. Frau Jacobs is an excellent example."

"She's the one – she isn't –"

Thankfully, Sabine didn't have to finish.

"She wasn't always that way."

Sabine waited for elaboration, but nothing came.

"I'm not feeling so well," Sabine confided. "I ate not two hours ago, but I'm suffering. Where can I get a nice bowl of Soljanka."

"Dozens of places. Take your pick."

"Show me. I'm new in town."

Hanna smiled and got to her feet.

* * *

Sharing a soljanka and a brötchen is a great way to cement a friendship. By the time they were through, Sabine leraned many details about the death of Frau Zimmermann and how Heike orchestrated the rescue of a widower and his daughter. Hanna's narrative was more complete. The details Heike omitted were those dealing with herself. They were important details, however, and Sabine remained grateful to Hanna for providing them and, thus, preventing Sabine from saying something unwise.

Herr Zimmermann wasn't dumbfounded to discover Heike had a sister from America. He was nonplussed by the entire performance. Heike cooked and served his meal, then cleaned up after. Sabine held and entertained Inka and she even changed a diaper. She noticed Heike's reluctance to come near the poor thing.

As they waited for the bus, Heike confided in her sister. Günther was pilfering money from Herr Zimmermann on her behalf for "services rendered."

"He thinks I don't know, so don't say anything."

Was Heike trying to bind Sabine to her by taking her into confidence? Was it some sly trick?

"He puts the money in the kitty for the Children, so I can't fuss," she continued. "If he shoves any of it under my nose, I'll make him eat it."

"If you are in love with Günther, you have a poor way of showing it."

That stung. Sabine intended as much. She resented being presented as a celebrity on the one hand and treated like an interloper on the other.

"Hanna! I should have known."

That ended the conversation for the remainder of the bus journey. Neither spoke again until they entered the house.

There was a complicated arrangement for Abendsbrot. With so little room at the table, Jürgen and Marina shared the couch with Frau Jacobs; the girls kept Rolf company. There was good coffee. Sabine was willing to tolerate tasteless bread and the lack of butter if the coffee was good.

"The shops will have fresh bread tomorrow," Nadine assured.

When it came time to clear away, Sabine insisted on lending a hand. This made Marina superfluous, so she and Jürgen went for a short walk before setting off for Günther's room.

"That was kind of you," Heike whispered in the kitchen. "They need to be together just now."

It was on the tip of Sabine's tongue to offer a retort, but she balked. What purpose would be served?

"You and Sabine might be able to share a room at the hotel," Nadine suggested, handing items through the narrow archway. The tiny kitchen wouldn't fit three.

"Jürgen should be here with Marina."

Heike waved one hand in front of her face – the universal sign among Germans that someone was deranged.

"What would we use for money?" Heike asked crisply.

"I have money," Sabine volunteered.

Too late did she catch Nadine's frantic signal. Heike's response, however, was relatively reserved; she drew out the silverware drawer just far enough to slam it shut.

"What's going on in there?" Rolf's voice boomed from the other room.

"Nothing," Nadine assured, returning to the table to fetch more items.

Later, Sabine saw the room where Heike spent much of her life. She saw the pallet upon which she slept. There was little wonder how she'd become so callus. Marina came into the room looking exhausted.

"I told him," she announced, ignoring the over crowdedness. "I know it wasn't a good time. When would there be a better time?"

Heike and Nadine were instantly supportive. Nadine stepped forward and gave her sister-in-law-to-be a comforting hug and kept that posture until Marina could check her tears. Heike shot a warning glance at Sabine.

"I hope Günther doesn't have anything breakable in his room," Heike mused.

"He wasn't happy, that's certain," Marina nodded.

"Would he be happier if you hadn't come back?" Heike asked bluntly.

The question was rhetorical. Even Sabine, who knew nothing of the details, realized her sister's timing was brutally off. It was best that the sisters exit shortly after this gaff. Nadine was the first to comfort the refugee; it was with her that Marina felt most comfortable.

"I'm walking Sabine back to the hotel," she announced blandly.

Despite the prohibition of children leaving the house after Abendsbrot, Heike couched her communication as a statement, not a request. When Rolf ordered her to halt, she whirled around to face him. This once, Anne's demure presence beside him would afford Heike no protection. Sabine was a part of her family too, and there were such things as extenuating circumstances. If Rolf wished to ply backhand justice, Heike was in the mood to follow Marina's example and become an exile.

Rolf was unmoved by the ferocity of her glare. He was busy leaning to his right and digging through a pocket. He extracted a brace of keys. He tossed them to Heike.

"Don't be long," he warned, "I must speak with you."

Heike's defiant anger changed to timorous curiosity. "I want to talk *to you*" was the ominous preface to a monologue. These never augured well for the listener. Never, had Heike heard the patriarch use the word "with" in such a context. It was unsettling.

Had he made a mistake or was there some design? She took refuge in Rolf's consistency. It was important that any action he took, no matter how abrupt or painful, was predictable. Lately, however, Rolf was becoming inconsistent. Even Jürgen found it disquieting.

"I won't be long," she promised.

Once on the other side of the door, Sabine pleaded to know about the scene upstairs.

"I know it is none of my business," she began but thought better of it. "Well, technically, it is my business."

"Get in," Heike motioned to the gray Trabi. "When Pabst says, 'don't be long,' he really means 'why aren't you back?'"

Sabine obeyed. She watched Heike slide behind the wheel and put the key in the ignition. In less than forty-eight hours, she'd been shaken by many surprises. Heike's command of the family car didn't qualify for a moment of wonder.

As she jammed the car into gear and checked the side mirror, Heike quickly summarized Marina's situation. It came out quickly, honestly and without a shred of emotion. It, also, made Sabine boiling mad. How could anyone be so devoid of feeling? Sabine was beginning to feel ashamed for even knowing this monster.

She knew that she was in for a long evening of composition. She must report to her father; she wouldn't bother with diplomacy. Further, she must write Gary, a task she'd not allow herself to postpone a moment longer. If she had to mail two letters, she may as well get one off to Molly and let her know how desperate she was to speak with her.

"I'll be very busy tomorrow morning," Heike began. "Could I meet you at thirteenth hour? At the Kasseturm?"

"As good a place as any."

"Fine."

She slammed the door after getting out. The Trabi lurched instantly and cat-mewed forward in a cloud of toxic smoke. Heike turned left without checking for traffic and set about to round the Bahnhof square before pointing the mound of compressed sawdust down the hill for her return journey.

Sabine didn't watch. She bounded up the steps and through the automatic door to find a matronly-looking woman behind the counter.

"Can I make a call to the BRD?"

"Ja," came a cautious reply. "Use the booth there. Dial *null eins* for the switchboard, but you must pay the tariff here, after."

Sabine threw her bag at her feet and closed the door behind her. She dialed the desk, gave the number, and waited. She was serenaded with buzzes and clicks and pops as her call went through a Leipzig exchange to another in East Berlin to another in Kaliningrad and Helsinki to – who knew? – Ulaanbaatar, Port Moresby, Mexico City, Tunis? Thirty seconds stretched into two minutes with Sabine growing more despondent and impatient with every gush of static. Finally, FINALLY! There was ringing. One, ring and –

"Kathy?"

Ute must have camped next to the phone. Likely, she'd been there all day. When the phone rang, she tore it out of the cradle.

Sabine leaned her head against the wall of the booth and sobbed.

"Kathy – Sabine, are you okay?"

"It's horrible!" she gushed. "Heike is nothing like I imagined. She's head of some commie gang and she is in love with some guy she doesn't pay attention to and she's cold and bossy and – and – and I want to hit her!"

"Kathy, stop it. Listen. Listen to me."

"What?"

"Where are you?"

"Weimar."

"Weimar? What are you doing in Weimar?"

"Heike's here. I came to see – her."

She broke down again.

"Where in Weimar? Kathy, Uncle Dieter and I can drive up there in three or four hours. Where are you?"

It was like ice water in the face. Instantly, Sabine turned brave. She stood erect and gripped the phone hard. In the background, she heard a conversation in Spanish.

"No, don't. I'm not done yet."

"Kathy, I'm not going to leave you there roaming the streets and blubbering until you walk in front of a car. We're coming to get you."

"No! I'm okay, now. I promise. I – I can't leave yet. I owe it to Vati. I'm too selfish. I wanted this for myself, and it didn't work. Now, I'm working for Vati."

There followed a long pause. The Spanish people spoke excitedly.

"Sabine – okay. Do what you have to do but call me every night."

"This will cost a lot of money –"

"You call every night!"

"But – listen, I don't see how –"

"If I don't hear by nine o'clock, I'm calling the police, the Embassy, and we're coming up there. Do you understand?"

"Yes."

"You sure you're okay now?"

"Yes. It's good to know you're only a tank of gas away. I guess, I needed to know I'm not alone."

"Not ever. It ain't gonna happen."

"Thanks – Mom."

"We love you, sweetie."

"Love you, too."

She hung up refreshed and revitalized. She needed pampering, but got a scolding instead; close enough.

She'd been selfish. This was now her father's mission, Ernst Bauer deserved her best effort; she vowed he'd get it.

After a few moments to compose herself, she was ready. She took a deep breath, opened the door, and returned to the lobby. The woman was gone. In her place was the beloved Tweedle dum. Sabine wasn't going to allow the goon any chance to jump on her one remaining nerve. She ignored the working man leaning against the counter and slapped both hands flat upon it.

"How much for the phone call?" she demanded.

It was a struggle to keep her voice civil.

"Herr Krug has paid for your call," the arrogant dunce reported, nodding toward the man next to her.

Doubtless, Tweedle dum expected to irritate her through his dismissiveness, but it was wasted effort. Sabine's attention was on the man in the paint-spattered dark blue work clothes. He was as casual as Tweedle dum was pompous.

He was thin despite the bulges around the middle which came with middle age. His skin was weather blistered and his lips were creased by burning or chapping. The hair under his dark blue, paint-spattered cap was thin and white.

"Herr Krug?"

She was polite towards generous strangers. It was part of her Swabish upbringing. The man whisked the cap off his head and wrung it between nervous hands. He projected a deferential attitude.

"Pardon, Fräulein, if I've taken a liberty, but I – I honor a mother's wish."

What were the chances, she wondered, that a derelict could walk into a Weimar hotel to accost a teen-aged girl? Sabine didn't bother to calculate the odds, but she reckoned that they were small. Her curiosity active, she didn't hesitate.

"How?"

Oh, God! She thought. Whatever the malady the eavesdropping Tweedle dum possessed, she'd caught it. She intended no offense, but her request cracked like a whip.

"Ah – well – um, this might take a moment. Could I invite you inside for a drink?"

Why not? She could hear people in the hotel café. Moreover, even the DDR, there were laws about molesting young maidens. She was perfectly safe. A drink was a modest price to pay to satiate a new acquaintance.

"Very well," she agreed before giving Tweedle dum a withering glance.

They had no problems finding a vacant if ancient wooden table hiding under a worn and frayed tablecloth. Herr Krug set his hat down as unobtrusively as possible near the edge of the table. Thankfully, he didn't embarrass Sabine by pulling a chair out for her. She set her bag under the table.

Sabine asked the waitress for an orange juice. Herr Krug wanted beer. When the waitress fled, Herr Krug leaned across the table.

He had a story.

Didn't everyone?

Why, Sabine wondered, was she subjected to an endless stream of stories? Was it her luck to be the confidant for a defunct nation, or was there something in the Ossi psyche that must be purged? After her experience with Marina's plight and her conversation earlier with Hanna, she appreciated what Ute meant when she announced there are some things she did not want to know.

The war was over, Herr Krug explained, though there was still fighting to the east. His little sister was deathly ill. His frantic mother chased him out of what remained of their house so the ailing girl could have some quiet.

He chose to play in the street with his broken toys. It was safe. There were few cars and no gas. Suddenly, a U.S. Army jeep came speeding around a curve and up the crest of the hill. It was atop the boy before he could react, the jeep swerved and braked with a defining squeal. At the wheel sat a young G.I. wearing a dented helmet and a frightened look. He appeared relieved he hadn't killed the boy.

The waitress returned with a beer for Herr Krug and an announcement that there was no orange juice.

"Chef wants to save what we have for Frühstück," she informed. "We have lots of beer."

Sabine didn't care for beer. After two shots of Korn, she'd been unsure of foot and light of head for over an hour. Figuring she'd exceeded the minimum daily requirement for alcohol, she ordered coffee.

The waitress fled and Herr Krug continued.

The GI was thrilled he hadn't killed anybody. He jumped from the jeep, hugged the boy, held him high over his head and plopped him down in the jeep. He spoke English. Young Krug had no idea what he said, but he understood when the driver took him for a nice ride through the deserted streets of the village. When they returned to the starting point, he gave the boy five packages of instant soup, two chocolate bars and an Army flashlight.

"There were strict orders about fraternization," Herr Krug reminded. "That soldier could have been punished for touching me. Giving me food was – black market. He could've gone to jail for decades."

The coffee came, thick and steaming. Sabine let it cool naturally. She feared if she stirred it down, she'd get only half the spoon back.

Herr Krug's mother was frantic. She saw a soldier drive off with her child. There were no police, only U.S. martial law. How could she hope to get her baby back? One child lay dying, and the other was spirited off by an Ami.

"She cried her eyes out when I came back unhurt," he reported.

The soup and candy bars were the bulk of the family's diet for the next eight days. Their soldier father never returned from the war; his fate remains unknown. It was very sad, but –

"What does that have to do with me, Herr Krug?"

"Most of the soup and candy went into my sister," he explained. "She got better and stronger. Mutti swore it was GI food that saved her. She wouldn't tolerate anybody speaking ill of the Amis after that. All through the DDR times, whenever the paper or the radio ranted about the Amis or some politician made a speech about the evil Amis, Mutti would swear something terrible. She'd turn to me and tell me not to believe a word. The Amis saved her little girl."

"But, Herr Krug," she insisted. "What has that to do with me?"

"When Mutti knew she was dying, she said to both of us, many times, if we ever have a chance to do an American a good turn, we must do it. She made us promise. When I found out an Ami was staying in the hotel, I came to see if there was anything I could do. You were on the phone, long-distance, and I was standing there. It was the least I could do."

She shuffled her feet under the table and kicked her bag.

"Herr Krug, I'm German. My mother carried me out of the DDR sixteen years ago."

He never batted an eye.

"You have American passport?"

"One of my passports is Ami, yes."

"Well," he stated boldly, "that's good enough for me. Mutti would agree, I'm sure."

"Still, I feel that you are helping the wrong person."

"Nonsense!"

He grabbed a beer coaster from the stack on the table, produced a pen, and wrote around the edges where no printing interfered with his own.

"This is my address and my phone number," he said, pushing it across the table.

"If you need anything – anything, let me know. I promised my mother. Now, I promise you."

"Thank you, Herr Krug. I appreciate it very much but let me pay for your beer."

"Nonsense! Enjoy your coffee, it's on me."

He signaled to the waitress.

"I have a wife and children of my own," he explained. "They must wonder what happened to me. Remember, anything I can do…"

The waitress took his money and made change. He told her to keep the change. Judging by her expression, it must have been a generous Ossi tip.

"Good night to you, Fräulein. Anything more?"

"There is just one thing," she replied, hoping it was not an imposition.

"Name it," he challenged eagerly.

"Who was Werner Ecke?"

He smiled. Most everyone in Weimar knew, but an Ami girl asked him.

He settled back into the chair.

* * *

Having no reason to get out of bed, Sabine enjoyed a few extra minutes of sleep. The brightness of the morning cut short her design. She was tempted to draw the curtains, but that would rob her of what little air there was. She pulled the pillow over her head and found it stifling. She stormed out of bed and into the shower.

Tepid water flowed over her body, and she examined the expansion of heat rash on her arms. She closed her eyes and wished for a bathtub where she could lounge for hours and perhaps steal a few more minutes of sleep. Sabine couldn't sleep standing up, but she tried.

Each time she thought she was sufficiently soaked, she persuaded herself to linger. Finally, fearing Tweedle dum would scold her for using all the water, she turned the knob as far left as it would go and remained in the freezing spray for as long as she could stand it. She ducked under the cross beam to scrub her teeth. As usual, there was no need for a towel. Medium hot air served her well. The great debate of the morning was socks or no socks. Without them, her feet would slosh in her shoes; with them, they'd perspire double. She opted for socks noting that they were her last clean pair. To these she added her jeans skirt and Fisherman's Inn t-shirt. Since it was not yet dry, her hair dampened the garment when she pulled it over her head; by the time she got downstairs, it would be dry.

There was, she remembered, that flea market near the Kasseturm. She might find light clothing there. She would have to discard; Sabine refused to add anything to her heavy suitcase. She'd begun by trashing the cheap, never-worn flats.

She avoided the window. It was enough to know the monument still stood. Breakfast was finished and her plate removed. The room was packed when she arrived. She was forced to sit near a small tinkling fountain, home to three bewildered goldfish.

It was dangerous to sit there with her hair-trigger bladder. When the crowd dwindled, she considered moving. However, the nearest bathroom was only seconds away. She waited for her coffee to cool before drinking it. This was freshly brewed and not the sludge she struggled over the previous evening.

She poured the last of the coffee from the server when she caught sight of someone in the doorway. The woman demanded attention. She was curvy in a sun suit that showcased her shapely legs. Sabine didn't want to be caught staring. She turned her attention to the rim of her cup.

She heard the woman say something to an unseen person. In profile, the stranger's ski-jump nose identified her. Sabine pushed her chair back and stood. Jürgen took Marina's arm; they advanced together.

"I tried your room," Marina informed. "I thought to check here."

Was there a point to this? Sabine stupidly reached across to pull out a chair. She couldn't manage, but Marina took advantage of the gesture and seated herself. Only after she was properly situated did Jürgen settle down in the chair directly opposite Sabine.

The waitress hurried over with a disapproving expression. Breakfast was for guests only. The café did not open to the public for another two hours. Jürgen assured her they were there to discuss, not consume. The waitress remained suspicious and disapproving, but she returned to her morning routine.

"There was a big blowup last night –"

"Heike's been joy riding! Was she hurt? Is she okay?"

Jürgen smiled grimly.

"Well, joyriding was the charge, but even Pabst knows better –"

"Even *I* knew better," Marina inserted quickly.

Sabine turned her full attention to the young run-away with the raven tresses. The unofficially engaged woman patted the back of her intended's hand with fondness.

"Jürgen told me much about his sisters; I know them intimately," Marina explained. "Heike would never be so irresponsible."

The young man cleared his throat and picked up the conversational thread.

"She gave no explanation for her being out so long. Pabst has pronounced her guilty and sentenced her to all the household chores. She's a prisoner."

Good! That meant Sabine was free. She needn't report to the Kasseturm as ordered. Maybe, she could find someplace with air conditioning. Maybe, she'd get on a train.

Marina, alas, proved too perceptive. She recognized Sabine's relief. Marina, a vision of grace worthy of fine Meißen porcelain, made haste to clarify.

"She told you about – my problem?"

Sabine's eyebrows narrowed.

"She went to see Lilo," Jürgen blurted. "They had it out. I guess it got ugly."

"That's the same as joy riding," Sabine concluded.

Jürgen quickly responded.

"That's not the reason she went."

Sabine had read and heard about pregnant pauses. Until that moment, she'd never experienced one. Her eyes widened. She turned to look at Marina who drew her lips tight and, thereby, accentuated her overbite -- damn! even that was beautiful!

"She went because of me."

Sabine turned sharply to Jürgen who didn't hesitate.

"Lilo lives alone in a two-bedroom apartment," he explained. "Heike went to see if Marina and I could stay in the other bedroom figuring that we – we shouldn't be apart when – we need to be together. Somehow, Günther was mentioned and – *zu weiter, zu weiter –*"

"UND," Marina added sharply without looking up, "*zu weiter!*"

"Why didn't Heike explain last night?"

"Because, she knew she'd done wrong. She didn't ask permission; she thought of it after you two were in the car. It need not have taken two minutes, but – the conversation got out of hand."

"Jürgi," Marina cautioned very softly.

"What?" Sabine demanded when no further explanation was forthcoming.

She stared at Marina since she'd introduced the subject. The Soviet felt Sabine's eyes upon her despite refusing to meet them.

"Heike seeks out punishment. She blames herself for Leipzig."

"Leipzig?" Sabine demanded of them. "What about Leipzig?"

"Not now," he pleaded quietly.

Marina mumbled something in Russian. Sabine thought she heard the word "God" in the midst the brief text but couldn't be sure. Marina, then, ended in German with an echo of Jürgen's previous words. Sabine clinched her fists and resisted saying what she thought. When she was as cool as the coffee, she renewed her interrogation.

"So, if Heike didn't say anything, how do you know?"

"Lilo came by on her way to work," Jürgen informed.

Sabine groaned.

"Rolf left for work," Marina said, suddenly deciding to rejoin the conversation. "Nadine left, I suppose, to give Jürgen and me a chance to talk. Heike was heating wash water. Jürgi was upstairs and there was this angry knock at the door –"

"And it started up again," Sabine concluded.

"No. She left me with a cryptic message and stormed off. Then, Jürgi and I confronted Heike. The whole story came out."

There was another pause that Sabine did not tolerate for long.

"So, Heike's off the hook, right?"

"Not by a long chalk," Jürgen replied in English with a phrase he'd picked up somewhere.

Once again, Sabine's appeal went to the woman from Leningrad.

"Lilo said, *I'll take the twins.*"

It was Sabine's turn to invoke divine intercession.

* * *

With great trepidation, Sabine checked out of the hotel but left her bags for later pick-up, except, of course, for her clean under things. She thought she'd explore the possibility of cooler clothes and, if successful, would discard equal weight by giving the Jacobs girls first chance at them.

The first thing confronting her in Goetheplatz was a micro-sized backpack. It was a gaudy, multi-colored bit of plastic, but it was decidedly more portable and more convenient than the shoulder bag, so she bought it. No matter how cheap it was, it need last only a few days.

Next, she searched for items better suited to the evil summer that descended upon the German nation. It wasn't long before she discovered Lilo hawking wares. She tried to hide under a St. Louis Cardinal cap a gray sleeveless tunic and cut-off jeans, but she couldn't disguise her long legs or her cascading hair. The tepid anxiety she harbored over confronting the woman transformed into a pain in her stomach.

Quickly, she devised a strategy. She'd not run. Instead, she'd reserve her anger until she possessed both sides of the story. She'd been down this avenue before; Sabine had learned it's a mistake for facts and emotions to stray too far apart.

Lilo was tending a customer and didn't notice Sabine approaching from behind. Slithering around behind a clothesline of displayed garments afforded no screen.

"'Tag, Sabine."

"'Tag, Lilo."

"Looking for something special?"

There was a very suspicious look in her eye, and the tone of her voice was hardly welcoming.

"Something cooler than jeans and slacks."

Lilo pointed to a table, one of three, upon which were piles of freshly folded cast offs. Sabine turned her back and examined clothes that went out of style when Ute was a baby. Perhaps, there was a touch of hyperbole in the assessment, but there were many tragic items spread out on those tables.

She found a curious sort of top with an elastic band along the bottom that would leave both her arms and her lower torso bare. That allowed more air in contact with her skin, but her natural modesty would make her uncomfortable. Additionally, there was the threat of a sunburned stomach.

A red pair of culottes, part cotton and part synthetic, whose owner must have been overjoyed to see them go; this had possibilities. They'd cling to her bottom, however. She hated that! Nevertheless, there weren't any loose-fitting wares among the cast offs.

She found a printed blouse featuring periwinkles that may have come from the closet of a heavy drug user, but it was extremely light. There was a print sundress (well, "*sunish*" dress) with an empire waist, a design feature wasted on a girl with no "empire." However, it promised comfort. Also, she discovered a surprisingly attractive yellow cotton shirt that would go well with her yellow shorts. These items, plus the culottes, she lay before Lilo.

The woman needed no calculator. She glanced at each tag and announced the sum. It was ridiculously low; Sabine suspected Lilo either erred or awarded her a discount.

"Why are you taking Heike and me in?" she asked, peeling off four bills.

"Heike sleeps on the floor, and you sleep in a shoe box," Lilo replied evenly. "Both of you can use a change?"

Sabine made a face. Lilo saw.

"You heard Heike yesterday," she reminded. "No secrets, right? If you're trying to keep your hotel room a secret, bad luck."

Sabine saw her opportunity and took it.

"No secrets, huh? What's this Leipzig – thing?"

Lilo rolled her eyes. She'd been caught in her own trap.

She swore and made a pair of comments but settled down to narrate, second-hand, the events of November. It took several minutes – not due to embellishments, but from frequent interruptions of browsers and two paying customers.

"Heike didn't believe in us, the reformers," Lilo concluded. "She went out of loyalty to her sister. For the same reason Jürgen stood out of loyalty to them both. That's the way they are – the whole gaggle of them."

Sabine, once again, was on the brink of tears. However, she refused to blubber in the city center. To avoid embarrassing herself, she reached into her arsenal of inane questions to embarrass herself with one of them instead.

"Are you still sleeping with Günther?"

Lilo leaned forward – and down – to meet her tormenter with a malevolent expression.

"How'd you like your face slapped?"

"Sorry," Sabine responded at once, partly because she'd been very rude. Mostly, however, she didn't want her face slapped.

It was a relief when, after a slight hesitation, Lilo returned to her side of the counter.

"It's because of Günther that you don't like Heike," Sabine pressed.

"Heike Jacobs is a precocious, boorish, abrupt, know-it-all prig. I'd love to wring her neck. That's how I've felt about that obnoxious Klugscheißer for years – before Günther ever looked at her. If the DDR lasted another five years, Heike would go to prison."

"On what grounds?"

"In the DDR, it's against the law to be an asshole – unless, of course, you're a party member."

"Then why do you want her in your apartment?"

"Because, Frau Ami snoop, if I'm ever in a bind, I want her on my side. She isn't afraid of anything or anybody when she knows she's right – and that annoying pest is right way too often!"

Sabine took a step back to keep out of arm's length. At precisely that moment, an old lady stepped up to buy three items of no use to an old lady. Lilo waited on her patiently. She managed a smile and a little light banter during the transaction. The moment the woman walked away, Lilo glared at Sabine.

"I don't want to fight with you," Sabine announced boldly. "Heike's my sister. I still don't understand why you want to care for her if you hate her."

"That's a fair question," Lilo agreed, her expression easing slightly. "I'm an only child, right? I never had anyone to fight with or to stand up for. I feel cheated."

"You're evading the question," Sabine challenged. "Doesn't this come under the heading of no secrets?"

Lilo's face contorted as if to say she considered Sabine as pushy as Heike. However, there was one influence she'd inherited from her "associate" for the past several weeks: at infrequent intervals, Heike Jacobs would stifle her ever-ready, invective tongue in favor of a few moments of respectful reflection. If, Lilo reasoned, Heike could manage it –

"Is it within you to understand?" she asked bluntly. "Heike and Jürgen went out into the streets when they knew the police had orders to kill. They knew that, can you understand what I'm telling you? Heike was still hurt from the first time. If something happened, she, literally, couldn't run for her life."

She continued, "Jürgen would never leave her. They'd both be killed. What was she doing there? She didn't believe in reform. She'd been opposed to it from the first. She wasn't there to strike a blow; she wasn't looking to change the world. She was there because it was the only way she could be with Nadine."

She paused and reflected.

"I couldn't do that. I must believe in a cause before I'd even consider walking out in front of loaded guns. There is no way I'd have courage enough to face death just to make a gesture. Could you?"

Sabine reflected mightily over that. How far would she go for Isaac, a person she hardly knew? Anything, she concluded. Unfortunately, she was faced with the uncomfortable fact that hers was a hypothetical case. How different the problem was for Heike – particularly when she knew Nadine was not a blood relation.

If Sabine were afforded only seconds to ponder the question, Liselotte Kruger had the luxury of several months. She had examined the situation from several angles, starting from the purely objective to the entirely emotional. It was no less a wonder for her in July as it was in December.

"I admire Heike more than any person I know."

There was nothing histrionic in this brief speech. It's a simple statement, quietly related but with an undertone of awe.

Sabine's head began to spin.

"I began with all the enthusiasm Heike has now. I lost faith years ago," Lilo confessed.

"Heike hasn't missed a step. She believes in something more important than herself. She won't go down that road alone – not as long as I'm around."

"And when she crashes?"

Lilo pursed her lips.

"Then, I'll be there with Jürgen and Nadine to help her pick up the pieces. The important thing is that she leaves nothing behind. She is *voll gas*."

Sabine pondered the matter while Lilo returned to her job. When she came back minutes later, Sabine still lingered.

"I ran a race several months ago." Lilo began. "There was a European record holder out front. I decided to match her pace. I wasn't running the race I trained for. I was running *her* race. I wasn't up to it. I lost by a greater distance than if I ran as I was trained. I might have made it a genuine race. Instead, I lost by several seconds. That was my only big race, though I didn't know it at the time.

"My trainer scolded me no end. I was so stupid. Now, I'm glad I did it. I gave it everything! It wasn't near good enough. The blessing is, when I can't sleep nights, I won't ever wonder what would have happened if *I* was voll gas. Whoever said doubt is much worse than failure knew the score."

She examined Sabine and calculated that she was getting through.

"That's where Heike is now. I don't want her to wonder what would have happened if we tried just a little harder. I'll give her the best. I hope she succeeds. Better people than Heike couldn't do it. Rosa Luxemburg, Ernst Thälmann, Werner Ecke – every one of them murdered. Fortunately, I don't think Heike will face that end. She's shown me a world where I want to live. She deserves my best effort because she earned it in Leipzig. If I can't get Heike to be on my side, I'm going to make damned sure I'm on hers."

Lilo tried to avoid emotion, but her words struck deep. Sabine was impressed.

"One more item under the heading of 'no secrets,'" Lilo appended, struggling to get her hand in her pocket.

"Günther's leaving Saturday morning to start a life in the West. Everybody knows except Heike. Tell her if you want but jump aside quickly. It's going to be very unpleasant for everyone if she finds out."

"You want her in your apartment when it hits the fan?"

"Why not? When she blows her top, she'll take it out on me. She's taken Günther away, what more can she do? I've thought of many things I didn't say last night. This will give me a second chance."

"She's my sister," Sabine reminded. "I'm with her."

"I expect no less. Here," she handed Sabine a key ring with two keys dangling from it, "get your stuff and take it to the apartment."

Sabine looked at the keys, then at Lilo.

"I don't know where your apartment is."

"When you walk out of the hotel, turn left and walk downhill almost to the end of the street. It's the only apartment building with balconies. Third floor. Left side."

"What if I get the wrong apartment?"

Lilo looked at her incredulously.

"Then, the key won't open the door."

Sabine shook her head to clear it. Her mind was crammed with so much.

* * *

The temperature in Lilo's apartment was ten degrees less than on the street. Sabine was grateful for that. She noticed the phone. In the disused bedroom, there were twin beds; Sabine ignored the irony.

There was a refrigerator, the size of a small dishwasher, but it contained a carton of whole milk and not the *H milk* to which she'd been subjected (because it needn't be refrigerated). There was a washing machine which Sabine, initially, mistook for a dishwasher. She knew it was a sin, but she couldn't resist peeking into the other bedroom.

It was neat and pleasant though the bed looked too short for Lilo's length. There were two athletic trophies perched atop a shrunk. On the wall above a bed was a photo of Lilo in a track uniform with a large DDR splayed across her chest. Obviously exhausted and near collapse, Lilo was straining to finish, her eyes wide but fixed on that white line. Was this taken during her "big race?"

There was another picture on the wall nearest the door. It was a labeled charcoal sketch of Werner Ecke. On the nightstand, under a small reading lamp, was a book, in French, about Abraham Lincoln. She was burning with curiosity but refused to touch anything or open the shrunk.

She crept out of the room and into the bathroom where she discovered the first bathtub she'd seen since leaving Oregon. She pulled off her top and had a cooling basin bath. The apartment was modest but clean. It wasn't as clean and neat as the Jacobs home, but neither were hospitals.

Not wishing to make a mess before being properly sanctioned, Sabine lay on her back on the living room area rug and snoozed. The proper thing to do was to hurry back to Goetheplatz and return Lilo's keys, but she hadn't the energy. When the phone rang with a heart-stopping clatter, the sun was decidedly lower in the sky. It flooded through the thin curtains of the glass, back balcony door of the kitchen, but the room temperature hadn't increased substantially.

She turned onto her stomach and crawled to the phone.

"I'm on my way to Herr Zimmermann's to fix his dinner," Heike explained without preface.

Sabine yawned.

"Do I have to?" she asked, sleepily.

"You can play with Inka."

Sabine's cloudy eyes cleared.

"It will take me a while to get there," she reminded.

"It's a ten-minute walk," Heike assured. "Keep to the left and stay off the main street. You'll cross in the middle of Friedenstrasse – that brings you out a block behind Goetheplatz. There's a set of keys hanging near the apartment door. Lilo says to bring her keys back and we can use that set."

"Okay."

Before Sabine had a chance to say more, the line went dead. There was no phone in the Jacobs house. Heike must have used a public phone and, she suspected, Lilo was within earshot. Herike was still alive.

That was something.

* * *

As a very young girl, Heike heard Rolf Jacobs apologize openly and genuinely to his wife on several occasions. He was a man who jealously guarded his private feelings. Despite his public displays of anger and gruffness, he always begged his wife's pardon. For her own part, Anne was patient.

It was useless to attempt to stop or even curb her husband's emotional excitement, so she never bothered. When he cooled and realized he'd been hasty or unfair, he possessed all the penitence of a medieval monk. Anne was ever gracious and willing to forgive.

When Anne's mind began to recede into a cloudy darkness, the apologies ceased. Never had Heike heard him apologize to his children. However, his sense of justice was precise. He didn't allow Heike opportunity to defend herself the previous evening. She was found guilty, sentenced and served her sentence. Jürgen and, perhaps, Marina supplied him with the facts, after the verdict was handed down. Typically, he refused to recant. Besides, Heike declined the opportunity to defend herself.

Shortly after Heike and Sabine returned from the Zimmermann home, the family gathered for Abendsbrot, following the seating arrangement previously established. Despite Nadine's insistence on setting the table and preparing the food, the sentence of the Chief Justice remained intact. Thus, everyone was obliged to wait an additional forty minutes while Heike prepared the meal.

Rolf, as was his wont, was first into the breadbasket, the first to select from the slices of meat and cheese, and first to pour a cup of coffee. Jürgen and Marina were allowed the next round so they could retire to the couch. The girls were left to satisfy themselves in a confused democracy free of a pecking order.

"Heike," Rolf began. "I think you should show your sister around the city. I think Jürgen and Nadine can share the chores."

"We'll manage," Jürgen agreed, exchanging a knowing look with Nadine.

"Me too," Marina insisted. "I'll do the shopping if you allow. Heike, is there anything you want me to fetch for Herr Zimmermann?"

"Some maize, if they have fresh," Heike replied. "Sabine tells me it's tasty with a little butter and salt."

Everyone, including *die Neue*, knew Rolf was offering a public apology; it was accepted. Heike still had to clear away and do the dishes, but Rolf broke with tradition and remained at the table. He asked Sabine several questions.

His queries were unique and born of genuine curiosity. They were absent his normal, abrasive, inquisitorial style. Sabine responded timidly at first, but she soon found the head of the family a congenial conversationalist. Heike would have loved to sit in on this unprecedented entertainment but settled for catching snippets from the kitchen.

The symposium remained in session when Heike finished. Sabine fished out photos from her gaudy, plastic backpack. Heike joined her brother and his fiancé in leaning over the table to examine each exhibit. The first photograph her eyes lit upon were the Kuriharas, Henry and Shelly. They were, so Sabine related, from Japan and were her dear friends.

"I thought Amis are racist," Heike said automatically.

"And Germans are Nazis," Sabine replied, calmly.

There was nothing irksome in her tone, but it was a slap in Heike's face. She realized she'd merely repeated one of many platitudes drummed into her head through government schools, the Pioneers and the FDJ. She, and most of her Genossinn, were learning that many dogmatic slogans had proved false. Heike was sorry to thoughtlessly echo what she should have realized was tripe.

"*Touché*," she replied.

It was more overt than Rolf's apology, but it kept with the general theme of forgiveness. Out they came – gorgeous Molly and rebellious Jayme; Aaron at the helm of the *Mary R.*, and Gary who looked scrawny and unprepossessing until Sabine identified him as her boyfriend. With that important information on the table, Gary collected universally favorable comments.

It was late when the twins set about for their new "home." As they made for the door, Rolf reminded them to return for Frühstück. It was an abuse of Lilo's hospitality to expect Lilo to feed them. Neither girl objected though it was a long way to come for so light a meal.

"I'm glad that Jürgen and Marina can be together, but I know who is sleeping on the floor, and I feel bad about that. Poor Nadine. She's trying so hard to take her turn, but it's always something."

Heike expected Sabine to ask about her statement, but nothing resounded beyond their footfalls. This pleased Heike. Once inside the apartment, they found Lilo bent over the kitchen table scribbling on a notepad. Most of her script was lined out.

She was barefoot and wore only a pair of old athletic shorts and a sleeveless pajama top she hadn't bothered buttoning. Her bra was of the same kind elderly maidens preferred, so modesty was satisfied if, indeed, there was any point.

Sabine asked permission to use the phone and explained why.

"Well, we don't want the Vopos charging up the stairs," Lilo said. "Give it a try and good luck."

"It will cost, I'm sure."

Lilo waved her off.

"We can work out payment later. Call your mum."

Sabine expressed her thanks and withdrew.

"We have to come out with a statement concerning the coming elections," Lilo explained, displaying additional pages looking much like the mess Heike suffered upon entering.

"I can't nail down a proper theme. What do you think?"

Heike came around and looked over Lilo's shoulder. She examined all four pages individually and found great Kruger prose lined through.

"That's beautiful, Lilo," she said about one discarded pearl. "Don't throw that out."

"I'll remember," Lilo assured. "We can use that, but it doesn't fit here."

Heike reconsidered as words filtered through the apartment from the phone near the front balcony. Heike reached down and pulled the notepad off to the side.

"Let me see your pen."

Lilo surrendered the instrument and watched Heike's bold lettering flow across the page, drop down and continue.

> *Without general elections, without unrestricted freedom of press and assembly, without a free diversity of opinion, life dies out of public institution and the bureaucracy remains the only active element. Public life gradually falls asleep. Such conditions must inevitably cause a brutalization of public life.*

"That's all I can remember," Heike reported, setting down the pen. "If you want to quote that, you must check to make sure it's correct."

Lilo read it over.

"Rosa?"

Heike nodded.

"Murdered in 1919, but she could have written that this morning."

"We can't let the Wessi propaganda machine dictate the terms of the new order," Heike insisted. "Ossis decide what is best for Ossis. Just because the government was corrupt doesn't mean our ideals were."

Lilo agreed.

"That ties in with the general theme we took to the Frauenplan. Look, Heike, I'm beat. Let me sleep on it and I'll mull it over at work tomorrow. I'll have something by tomorrow night."

"Thanks for taking us in," Heike said. "It was out of line to suggest it, but Marina was in tatters last night. She had me in tears."

"There's a confession I never thought I'd hear! How is she tonight?"

"She's fine. She and Jürgen, together, can cope with anything."

"If we miss each other in the morning, help yourself to whatever you find."

"We've got orders to eat at home," Heike replied. "Is there anything we can get for you?"

Lilo yawned and shrugged her shoulders.

"Use your own judgment. *Bis Morgan.*"

* * *

Sabine woke up to the sound of Lilo in the kitchen but didn't stir for fear of waking Heike. As she lay waiting to sneak out to the bathroom, she recalled Heike was an early riser. She turned onto her side in time to see Heike slip something under her pillow. Sabine knew what it was, but she refused to press.

"I was afraid to wake you," Heike said, realizing she'd been caught.

"I was thinking the same thing."

Sabine hopped out of bed and tended to her morning habits. Upon her return, both beds were neatly made; Heike sat, fully clothed, waiting her turn. While waiting, she sat at the end of her bed looking at the dress.

"Molly gave me that dress to look good when I met Papa."

"You didn't need it," Heike assured. "You're very attractive."

Why did the Ossis dwell on that? Sabine received more complements on her appearance in just a few days in the DDR than she had in all her years on the Oregon coast. Was there some psychological reason behind this? Fond of being complimented on her looks, Sabine found this unexpected frequency unsettling.

"Would you like to have it?"

Heike was nearly out the bedroom door. She stopped as if caught in a net and turned a suspicious eye.

"I thought your friend gave it to you."

"I got the use out of it for what I wanted," Sabine shrugged. "I'm so afraid it will get torn or stained. All my packing and unpacking can't be good."

Heike cast an envious eye on the garment.

"Could Nadine wear it?"

"You're asking me? For all I care, Jürgen can wear it."

Heike's eyes shone above the brightest, broadest, most disarming smile Sabine had ever seen. Before that moment, she considered Molly's smile as the warmest and most beautiful ever. Heike's smile, however, could melt iron.

"You can smile! You should smile more often."

Heike shrugged.

"The thought of Jürgen in a dress struck me as funny."

Perhaps, Frau Marx was assuming human form.

The coffee was cold, as Heike promised it would be. Still, there was plenty of brötchen and cheese, though Sabine opted for jam. Jürgen and Marina sat at the table keeping the twins company while Nadine cleared things away.

Heike requested Marina to fetch a half dozen brötchen for Lilo and passed money across the table. Clearly, it was too many for Lilo and, with no preservatives, the brötchen wouldn't keep. Wisely, everyone declined to ask what Heike was up to.

"Would you mind if we hijacked your tour for an hour?" Jürgen asked. "I'd like to show Marina something. You might find interesting."

"The *Friedhof*," Heike guessed.

Unlike Heike of the previous day, Nadine was not a captive. She and her "roommates" divvied up the daily chores. Herr Jacobs wouldn't return until the midday meal; an hours excursion to the cemetery couldn't matter.

Heike welcomed the opportunity to speak with Jürgen. Marina and Sabine were not yet *official* family. Once they started off, Heike took her brother's arm, and they walked briskly ahead to discuss family matters. The remainder of the party followed at a discrete distance.

Playfully, Marina took Sabine's arm. The girl was startled at first, but she relented with good humor. It was very German to walk arm-in-arm; Sabine was no stranger to the custom. She was, however, momentarily amazed that the Soviet citizen was culturally acclimated to German folkways.

"I'm happy to see you in high spirits," Sabine announced.

"I know things will work out," Marina bubbled. "There are no walls or guard towers around my family. Someday, when tempers cool and pride erodes, we'll discover a way to be reconciled. I have faith in Jürgen and he in me. I haven't a single doubt. Not anymore."

"Will you excuse my asking? How will you two – I mean, you can't stay in Weimar – not in that tiny house. Will you be able to keep your apartment in Halle?"

Marina laughed. It was the laugh of a buoyant woman oozing with confidence.

"We have contingency plans," she announced. "Jürgen says he can quit school and get a job, in the West if he must. That will allow me to get my degree. When I get a job, I can bring bread in house while he finishes."

"That's horrible!"

"Not at all, my young American friend. It's an adventure! I told him if we got married right now, I'd be eligible to work, but he's stubborn – like his papa. He says we promised each other a spring wedding; so, it shall be. Yes, it will be difficult, but we're hard workers. If people work hard, things happen. When Herr Jacobs married Frau Jacobs, they started with less than what we have now. They don't live in a mansion; they don't have grand vacations in Königsberg, but they have a fine family; one that works well together."

Sabine braced when the city of Königsberg was mentioned.

"You mean Kaliningrad."

Marina laughed again.

"You've done your homework. I don't imagine anyone goes to Kaliningrad looking for a grand vacation anymore."

"And Frau Jacobs? Is she happy?"

"Don't be a misery," she responded in mock anger. "With all these great changes going on, Frau Jacobs copes well. That's one of the first things Heike said to me – her mother can cope better than any of us. She responds to the warmth of the family. That is her world and she's very happy there."

It was impossible to be near such effervescence and not find it contagious.

* * *

At the cemetery, the quartet moderated their boisterousness out of respect. No one needed a guide to the major monument. In many respects, it looked like a small, stone cottage surrounded by ancient trees of impressive girth. No one spoke. Beyond the wrought-iron gate and in the heart of the cottage, lying side by side, were the two literary giants of Weimar and the German nation: Schiller and Goethe.

Dead people had no appeal for Sabine. She could be reverential with the best; after seeing the place where the great men were "planted," but Sabine was eager to see something more animated. Marina's giddiness at her side added to her impatience.

Marina saw the onion domes. She saw the crosses – Russian Orthodox crosses. She realized, directly behind the German monument, there existed consecrated Russian ground. Marina was in a trance as they rounded the crypt and studied the adjacent structure. It was, they were assured, the smallest Russian Orthodox Church in the world.

"Actually, it's the Grand Duke's burial chamber," Heike whispered to her sister.

"They put Goethe in there, but some believe the real Schiller is buried somewhere in town. Nobody knows who they put in there thinking it was Schiller. There's a tunnel leading from there to the grave under the church. You see, the Duke's wife was the daughter of the Tsar. She was buried in Russian soil. That's how they could build this church. Because of the tunnel, she's with her husband."

"How do you know this stuff?" Sabine whispered back, unable to trust the DDR version of history.

"Jürgen," Heike replied proudly.

Marina was enthralled. She recognized a substantial bit of home in the center of her soon-to-be adopted country. It was a great dome surrounded by four sentry towers all crowned with ornate onion domes, each with its own cross. There were numerous narrow windows (*slits* more like) below each dome, three larger widows above the entrance and seven more adorned the apse.

She'd brought a shawl with her. Sabine thought that eccentric on such a warm day, but someone tipped off Marina. She pulled the shawl over her head, signaled Jürgen, and tacitly bid him to join her. Together, they walked through the open doors into the church. Sabine, ever curious, started to follow.

"Sabine, stop!"

She obeyed, not knowing why.

"Women aren't allowed to go inside without covering the head."

"I'm not Catholic," Sabine reminded.

Heike gestured toward the church.

"*She* is."

Sabine understood and relented.

After several minutes, the couple returned. Marina offered Sabine her shawl. She politely deferred. It was an imposition to expect everyone to wait on her to make a secular examination. Seeing Marina's glowing face, Sabine recalled Philippians, chapter four.

Was that, perhaps, the source of Marina's certainty that life with Jürgen would be felicitous? Had she said a prayer during her visit, or was it enough to know a tangible portion of her culture was so near? The answer didn't matter.

Marina was glowing which made Jürgen equally happy. The couple left with a cheerful *Auf Wiedersehn* and returned to the secular, work-a-day world of shopping, scrubbing, mending, and washing. They possessed renewed energy and were visibly happy to be together.

"Exit the love birds," Heike murmured wistfully. "You want to take a peek now?"

Sabine was no longer in the mood. If she ever entered that church, she'd follow the customs of those who built it. Her Swabish upbringing would demand it.

Heike led her sister from the cemetery to the archive for Friedrich Nietzsche's writings. Sabine expressed no interest; she'd never heard of the man. Heike was thankful to give the building a pass. After his death, the man's sister made a career of polishing Nazi boots with the tip of her nose; thus, Heike's interest in him and his work was extremely limited.

They strolled down tree-lined residential streets and seldom had to bother with traffic as they crossed and re-crossed streets to take advantage of the shade. They followed Shakespeare Strasse to August Bebel Platz and headed to Abraham Lincoln Strasse where Heike pointed out the apartment building where Hanna lived. She volunteered the story about her fright the day Heiko played "forbidden" music.

Sabine perked up at this and asked questions about Heiko's music and their school days. Heike soon tired of it. She didn't like speaking about herself.

When they came to a church, the girls sat in the recess of the side door and listened to a riot of birds in the lush trees across the street. Sabine slipped off her shoes and socks to wiggle her toes in the gentle breeze wafting down the street. Heike couldn't resist following suit.

"You say Papa has a lot of money?" she asked abruptly.

Sabine made a noise of assent but refused to speak. Heike concluded she wasn't alone in her ambivalence of wealth.

"You've been to Mutti's grave?"

Sabine eyed her suspiciously. It was quite a leap from money to a grave. She nodded, figuring there was some purpose to the question.

"Could you take me someday?"

"You're the one with the driver's license," Sabine replied. "I can direct you – I think."

Heike let the license remark pass without comment.

"Does she have a stone?"

"Not a proper one. They didn't know her identity."

Heike rubbed her feet.

"Why don't we use the money to buy Mutti a stone?"

"I'd be willing," Sabine nodded. "Rosa's Children needs money, too."

Heike snorted.

"Papa would never allow me to use his money for that."

Sabine pursed her lips.

"You don't even know Papa!" She snapped.

Sabine's temper was influenced by the heat.

"How can you make judgments about someone you don't know? That's unfair, Heike. It's cruel and petty. He told me the money belonged to us. I take him at his word. He wants us to be happy. How can anyone be happy if someone tells you how to spend your own money?"

"I wouldn't feel right about it!"

Sabine's temper evaporated.

"Well, that's different. Do you get the concept of *freedom*, Heike? You do what you think is right, and you don't do what you think is wrong. Deciding which is which – that's the tricky part."

"I believe in my country," Heike retorted with defiance.

"Don't pick a fight with me, Heike," Sabine warned. "I've no argument with your country. Take time to believe in yourself. I'm lucky to have two countries – maybe, three, now, but I, also, have my own life."

Heike was beginning to understand how the British felt when confronted by Gandhi. How do you fight someone who refuses to fight? It's maddening! After her Vulcan experience with Lilo, Heike felt partly cleansed. Things that should have been said long ago were thrown at Lilo's feet; Heike didn't need to carry them further. With Sabine, however, there was no chance to lighten her load; her sister refused combat.

"Tell me about Leipzig."

"Nein!" Heike shot back.

Perhaps, five minutes lapsed. The birds, that were so charming before, became annoying. There were too many, and they were too loud. Heike began putting on her socks and shoes. Sabine, without any prompting, followed suit.

"I'm scared to think of it," Heike began softly. "I failed Nadine and my stubbornness might have got Jürgen killed."

"You could have been killed as well," Sabine reminded.

"If there were justice in the world, yes, I would have died. There's no justice. That much I've learned. Nadine is beaten and arrested; Jürgen is killed because of me – how could I live with myself after that? I have dreams, Sabine, my nightmares. I dream I'm the only survivor."

There was a long, disturbing pause.

"If you'd seen Nadine when she returned…Mutti recognized her. I thought she was a diseased beggar. It's a wonder I sleep at all. I caused that. It'd be different if I were arrested too, but –"

She bowed her head and fought back tears.

"I don't – want to talk about it," she announced meekly. "Don't ever ask me again."

They continued their trek back towards the city. Sabine saw, yet again, the national theatre where the short-lived Weimar Republic was created. Thankfully, Heike didn't have to introduce her sister to the statue of Goethe and Schiller. It was difficult with an annoying and boisterous crowd of Japanese tourists taking pictures of the monument and everything else, to include the twins.

They toured the Schiller House, but Sabine wasn't enthralled. She did, however, take some while looking upon the desk where the master penned *Wilhelm Tell*. What, Heike wondered, was *Wilhelm Tell* to Sabine? The way the interloper appeared to memorize the writing desk indicated it was of great significance.

They toured the Goethe House on the Frauenplan, but Sabine was bored and showed it. She wasn't alone. Early nineteenth century accommodations, even for the well-to-do, held little fascination for a pair of schoolgirls who had yet to adjust to the waning half of the twentieth. Had it been some grand palace with ornate amenities, it might be interesting. Schiller and Goethe, despite their wealth, were content with simple surroundings.

They toured the market square. Sabine's eyes lit up. It was an oasis of color amid monotonous grays. The three-tiered city hall was so heavily influenced by the Italian style that one expected to see Juliet step onto the balcony overlooking the entrance.

There was a fountain featuring Neptune brandishing a trident and behind him was a quaint building with a painted boast above the entrance proclaiming its use as an Apotheke since 1567. Directly across from the city hall was the former home of the city's wealthiest family. Of course, it had been commandeered and suffered neglect under Das Volk.

Heike intended to make a counterclockwise circuit of the ornate square and end at the city hall where she'd once battled with a lecherous clerk. They'd pass the Hotel Elephant, the haunt of visiting party officials, both SED and, before them, Nazis. It was here Sabine paused. Heike patiently waited for her sister to examine the marker commemorating the home of J. S. Bach.

"He lived here?" Sabine asked stupidly.

Heike nodded.

"Destroyed in the war, I suppose."

"In a way," Heike began. "The Nazi pooh-bahs needed more room to frolic, so they ordered the house demolished so the hotel could expand."

Sabine's eyes filled with sadness. She sighed. She reread the sign. Displaying a pathetic gesture, Sabine placed both hands and forehead against the stone.

This scene was far more melodramatic than her performance near Schiller's writing desk. Heike was as ignorant of Bach as she was with Nietzschean philosophy. She'd likely heard Bach's works, but her musical preferences were catchy tunes, like *Heißer Sommer*, FDJ sing-alongs and a select hit-parade numbers. Anything composed prior to 1950 was as alien as a didgeridoo.

"I'd love to see Bach's house," Sabine whispered. "To walk where Bach once walked –"

"You have," Heike stated impatiently.

Sabine's sad eyes turned to Heike.

"You must have done," the elder sister insisted. "He'd hardly fly across the square."

Sabine stepped away from the wall. She examined the ground near her feet.

"Come with me."

Heike didn't notice if Sabine obeyed. She marched out of the square at a brisk pace. They passed through a second square featuring an equestrian statue of Duke Carl-August riding away from the imposing building housing the music school. From there, they skirted the edge of the park until they came to a large, but ordinary "cottage."

Franz Liszt.

The name conjured vague memories for Sabine. She eagerly followed her sister into his former home. The museum, if the interior were reflective of the original furnishings, was more opulent than the Goethe and Schiller residences.

Liszt's home belayed the simple exterior. It reeked of wealth and a desire to display it. Sabine examined the musical instruments, but her attention was frequently diverted by a sparkling vase or intricate carpet.

"Do you suppose he had Bach here?" she asked, reverently.

"I – don't – think so. I don't think they lived here at the same time. Ask Jürgen."

Sabine vowed to do exactly that.

"I wouldn't mind meeting this – Liszt guy," she reported.

Heike examined her sister, noting her dimples and proud chin.

"He'd have you in that bed before you said hello," she informed. "Nine months later, yours would be one more child in his collection of miniatures."

Sabine looked straight into Heike's eyes. Heike didn't shy. Ignorance of Liszt's compositions aside, her attitude toward his personal life was not charitable.

"I'd bet twenty percent of the population of this city can be traced back to one of Liszt's bastards."

"Jürgen?"

Heike shook her head. Her refusal to identify any reference material forced Sabine to conclude someone had planted a vile seed in Heike's ear. Perhaps, this man's biography might stand a dusting off. Her interest flagged with Heike's failure to confirm Bach once trod the squeaky wooden floors, but it revived again with Heike's poisonous aspersions.

* * *

Heike's furtive examinations of mother's photo, and her agreeing to providing a proper marker encouraged Sabine. Sooner or later, Heike's adoration for a woman she never knew would propel her to Ernst Bauer's door. Sabine was confident that the properly timed nudge would topple Heike from her precarious perch atop the fast-crumbling wall of prejudice.

She was tempted to apply that nudge as they sat in the shade at Shakespeare's feet. Amazed to find a reproduction of a famous English scribbler an object of veneration in Weimar, Sabine listened as Heike related the part the man and his statue played in her maturation. Dropping her guard, Heike related two anecdotes about her "conversations" with the Bard.

"I doubt he'd understand my German," she confessed, "but a man with universal spirit understands emotions, don't you think?"

The question was, thankfully, rhetorical. Sabine heaved a sigh of relief when her twin charged on without waiting for a response.

"Later, I came here to recite my English lessons for him. Probably, he wouldn't have understood my English either. Now, Nadine asks me to read Shakespeare in English. She understands almost nothing, and claims his words are more 'musical' in German. Personally, I think it sounds silly in German. I know she laughs when my back is turned."

The sisters had developed a conversational format where one mirrored the other. Since Heike opened their shade-blessed conversation with stories, Sabine was obligated to contribute. Baba related an episode Sabine opted to repeat.

On the morning when Frau Bauer, whale-like, suffered contractions, Ernst was summoned from work. Between the car and the house, he lost his keys. Franticly he searched while Mutti called a cab. The taxi arrived before Ernst found his keys. In his excitement, he put them in his shirt pocket. Somehow, they remained hidden despite frequent bending and bobbing.

Frau Bauer won the race to the hospital by a few minutes. Indeed, Heike was well on her way by the time the doctor arrived.

At that time, there was a small brewery in Riesa and near the hospital. Constanze, ever the sprite, took the fullest advantage of circumstances and geography to concoct a myth that spread like measles through the modest steel town. Though lacking the vivacity and comic timing of her father, Sabine brought the major elements together.

The twins were born in a taxi parked in front of the brewery. They were christened in beer. Their first toy was a rattle of keys that fell out of Ernst's pocket.

It was a poor re-telling of a story related second hand sixteen years after the fact.

Heike, however, was mesmerized. Whatever image the girl had created for herself of Constanze Bauer geb. von Posen, this labored narrative fit snugly into it. Sabine noted Heike's pensive expression.

"Why would she tell such lies?" Fräulein Bauer asked, eventually.

Silence, at this juncture, was Sabine's best ally. She embraced it until Heike shot her a look of impatience.

"It cost nothing, and no one was injured," Sabine replied quietly.

She prayed Hanna hadn't used this verbal device around Heike.

Heike averted her eyes and retreated to her ruminations. Sabine wanted to steal away and let her discuss this episode with her marble mentor, but that would be rude and counterproductive. After several awkward moments, she broke the silence.

"We're going to the garden house, right? Mind if I go ahead?"

Heike looked at Sabine momentarily. She made no sign she heard. Heike dropped her eyes and contemplated her shoes.

Sabine exited the scene quietly.

* * *

The evening Lilo allowed her the phone, Sabine called Ute; it was the Fourth of July. Twenty-three years earlier, Ute Kaufmann signed papers in the Fürth Rathaus that made her Frau Foster. Herr and Frau Kaufmann were on hand with Dieter in a pressed blue suit, dark tie, and a white carnation in his lapel. Mr. and Mrs. Foster, during their only trip abroad, were also on hand. It was an event as far removed from Riesa and Saxony as circumstances allowed, but it had profound repercussions.

Aaron called earlier. He thanked her for putting up with him all those years and closed with the reassurance he still loved his wife and time passed very slowly in her absence. Hours later, with Sabine's call, her day was complete.

Sabine congratulated her "mother" on her anniversary. During their conversation, Sabine's heart broke. Great actress though she was, her voice remained chipper, and her laughter sounded genuine. Ute heard only the voice and deluded herself into thinking all was right. Had she seen the copious tears streaming from Sabine's eyes, she'd have ample reason to be alarmed.

After hanging up, Sabine leaned forward and propped her forehead on the heels of her hands. Her elbows planted on the small table, she struggled to keep her breathing normal and avoid sniffing like a wounded child. She made no effort, however, to stem her tears. At last, when she regained a modicum of composure, she wove her fingers together and propped up her chin on her thumbs.

She made her decision and suffered the pain of it. After swimming in sorrow until much of it was spent, she'd face up to the world as it was. She knew what must be done, and she knew what it would cost.

It wasn't easy, but she must be brave. Tears purged emotions temporarily, but they couldn't purchase peace. She must be strong and brave; tears were decidedly out of context.

She rubbed her face with the back of her hands, slapped her knees, and stood resolutely.

That evening, after Heike's guided tour, Sabine idled in the front room while her sister used the bath. She looked hard at the phone and was tempted to take it up anew. Instead, she reviewed her conversation of the evening before.

Had she made the right decision? It was painful. She began shedding tears anew. It took time to regain control. When she, finally managed, her first sight was one she least wished to see.

Lilo stood stock still, a mug of something in her right hand. Whatever course she'd set across the apartment, she stopped instantly and looked at the pathetic figure at the phone. How long she'd been there was Lilo's secret. She asked no questions; she offered neither comment nor succor.

"I must talk to Heike," Sabine announced.

"Make sure she isn't starting fires in there," Lilo replied.

Sabine moved toward the bedroom door. Lilo extended a restraining hand.

"Drink some of this," she commanded gently, holding forth the mug.

"What is it?"

"It's wet."

When Sabine accepted the offering, Lilo retreated to the tiny refrigerator. Sabine took a sip an unidentified juice. If it was Ossi, there was no means of detecting its source short of chemical analysis. If it was Wessi juice, it was exotic but pleasing.

Heike sat on a bed studying several pages Lilo left her. Her hair was damp. Her "night clothes" consisted of a thin, gray shirt that fell half-way to her knees. She sat so her eyes rested on the blue dress when requiring a break. She was making notes in pencil and drew circles around clumps of text. She failed to notice her sister until the door clicked shut.

Sabine's face was red and tear residuals became smears beneath her eyes and across her cheeks.

"What did she do?" she demanded, getting to her feet.

"Bitte?" Sabine asked innocently.

"Did she slap you?" Heike asked, throwing down the papers. "I'll kill her!"

Sabine leaned against the door. Amazed that her sister would be so bold, Heike hesitated.

"Lilo hasn't done anything –"

"What did she say to you?" Heike demanded.

"Sit down, please. This has nothing to do with Lilo."

Heike, suddenly contrite, worked around the bed and faced her sister. Sabine took a sip of the drink and squatted against the door.

"I'm going to Vati," she announced. "I can't – now. I'd be a mouth to feed, but he has a future, Heike. He's the Hausmeister of a local school; he'll probably be Hausmeister of his apartment building. I'll go back to Oregon and school, but, next June, I'm moving in with Baba. He invited me. I'm going to do it."

Heike was flummoxed.

"You're not happy," Heike concluded.

"I'll be leaving behind my best friends. Ute and Aaron were my parents, and I must leave my little brother. He's about Inka's age."

She stopped abruptly. She had to suppress the urge to cry again. Wisely, Heike waited.

"I'll be leaving Gary behind. He's as stubborn as you, Heike, but he's the sweetest – I had the craziest idea that we would get married someday."

"What's to stop you?"

"He lives in a different world. I can't expect him to come here."

"He'll wait," Heike suggested.

"I can't ask him to do that. Maybe, he would wait, but for what? What if I want to stay here? It doesn't matter, I must tell him when I go back."

"You could tell him later," Heike suggested.

"That's lying," Sabine snapped. "It's worse; it's the lie of a coward."

* * *

The following day, Heike was presented with another unexpected stay from chores due to Marina's insistence. Heike expressed her gratitude, but only after the Soviet refugee overruled her vociferous objections. As a result, Sabine was invited for another outing. She refused, suggesting Heike and Günther enjoy some time together. Again, Heike protested; again, she was rebuffed.

Sabine, additionally, insisted that she share household chores. Rolf wouldn't hear of it, but Sabine remained adamant. She admired Marina's example and refused to be an imposition. Rolf bellowed, of course, but the Ami refused to be bullied. Eventually, Rolf "retreated" hastily to work. He promised to resume battle later. Sabine promised to do her share in his absence. He slammed the front door and the car door. He abused the vehicle as he puttered away.

Much later, Jürgen explained that she was the first to thwart Rolf's orders without suffering memorable punishment. Sabine had no desire to initiate an international incident, but if Rolf lay a hand on her, she'd be waving her American passport at the nearest diplomatic goon. She was every bit as brash and determined as Rolf Hardhand. Sabine had not asked to take part in helping run the household, but she was accepted as a guest. That, according to Swabish custom, obligated her.

Marina opted to air the bedding, clean the bathroom and remake the beds. Jürgen would scrub the stairs, dust the downstairs, and sweep the front steps. Nadine, who was the appointed cook, was assigned the laundry and preparation of the mid-day meal.

Since Nadine's duties seemed the most daunting, Sabine offered to aid her. It wasn't, however, without ulterior motives; she couldn't bring herself to ask Lilo for the use of her washing machine. If she helped with washing, Sabine would suffer little guilt about "throwing in" a few things of her own.

She returned with her old shoulder bag stuffed with sweaty, grimy, gamy items. Nadine had the wash and rinse water heated and more heating up. Sabine never used a washboard, but she became adroit after a few minutes of coaching. It was work, but she insisted on taking on the bulk of the task so Nadine could focus on preparing the meal. Nadine was amenable, but supervised Sabine critically.

There was time to explain the choice she made the previous evening. Sabine also reviewed, largely for her own good, the sacrifices the washerwoman made due to her decision.

"My place is with my father," she decided. "He lost everything. I'm no prize, but he deserves a family – even if it is only me."

Nadine declined comment. When next she came to check on the novice, she was confronted.

"You don't like me, do you?"

Nadine was startled by this directness. Nevertheless, she knew superficiality wouldn't serve.

"You're okay," Nadine replied, wiping her hands on the towel she kept draped over one shoulder. "You're better than I expected, but I don't want you taking my sister away."

Sabine straightened, leaving a wad of wet, soapy clothing on the washboard.

"How long have you known she wasn't your sister?"

Nadine could have taken offense but didn't.

"I've never considered her anything else. Jürgen and Mutti treated us the same. Pabst was short with her for a few years, but he treats her the same as the rest of us."

"That's good," Sabine concluded. "Thank you."

"Danke? What for?"

"I was an only child until a few months ago. I don't recommend it."

The *boss* wiped her hands again and sighed.

"We fight a lot, Heike and me," Nadine revealed. "That's not fun."

"Believe me, Nadine, I'd have welcomed a good fight now and then. I'd have loved sharing, too. You've had that your whole life. Heike won't thank you; I'm doing it."

Nadine nodded.

"Günther is an only child. So is Lilo. They manage."

"I can't speak for them. I'd have loved having someone to be proud of and be proud of me when I earned it. I'm not taking Heike anywhere. If she comes, it's because she wants to. If she visits Vati, that's her choice. Would you try to force her into something?"

Nadine shook her head.

"She would redesign the other side of my face. I tricked her a few times, but that isn't the same."

"Heike is your sister," Sabine pronounced, "She's my sister too. No matter what happens, we both have a sister."

* * *

Heike returned in high spirits and ready to gather up items for Herr Zimmermann's evening meal. She discovered Anne alone on the couch, but there was an anxious debate going on upstairs. The voices were low to prevent disturbing Anne, but they were definitely agitated.

She rushed upstairs and through the door. The heat of the room struck her first. Both the door and window had been closed for some while. Sabine sat on Heike's sleeping pallet with her back to the wall, just below and to the side of the window.

Nadine sat in the corner next to her in much the same pose with a sour expression on her deformed face. Jürgen and Marina sat on the smaller bed facing the others. Everyone was beaded with sweat.

"What is it?" Heike demanded.

"Shut the door," Jürgen demanded.

Carrying out the order, Heike wished she'd avoided this viper's nest.

"What is it?" she repeated.

All eyes were directed to Sabine; she looked hurt and contrite.

"She was shoving things into her bag," Nadine began. "I scolded her for being careless. She says she doesn't fold underwear like we do."

Despite the temperature, Heike's spine shivered.

It was up to Marina, the only person not accused, to summarize. The information about folded underwear came from Heike's Stasi file. Sabine claimed she never saw the file, but the photo of Constanze and the laundry information came from Stasi documents.

Someone in the Jacobs home was an informer!

"I can't believe it!" Heike protested. "It isn't possible!"

She turned to Sabine for support. Her sister was too busy pouting to notice. Jürgen laid out the case against everyone in the house except Anne Ecke. Family members *only* had access to folding information.

Rolf might curry favor with the authorities by spying on his own family. He might get certain favors in return: extra money, access to hard-to-get goods and, maybe, several jumps ahead on the waiting list for the Trabi. Jürgen could secure a better place at the uni, and he'd gain important favors from the authorities despite courting an *Auslander*. Nasty details surrounding resident visas could be "expedited." Nadine might have spilled her guts in Leipzig while under arrest, voluntarily or under the influence of drugs. It would explain her quick release. Reportedly, nearly all those arrested were quickly freed; however, there was no documented evidence to confirm that.

Further, Heike may have been blackmailed to provide information in return for Nadine's release, or she could have squealed under threat. Moreover, the State put her in the Jacobs' home.

This was merely a portion of the items they discussed. Once the Stasi got its hooks into somebody, the wiggling could continue for decades.

"There is something more," Jürgen added. "We have no real proof Sabine is your sister. She may be Stasi. That would explain how she got information."

"I don't believe it!" Heike announced to Sabine's amazement.

"There is another possibility," Nadine advanced. "The Stasi searched the house."

"When?" Heike challenged, "Mutti's always here."

"Where does her cocoa come from?" Jürgen asked. "Maybe, they bribed her with cocoa. They'd have the run of the house."

"I can't believe that either," Heike objected. "Even in her condition, Mutti wouldn't allow strangers in here."

Jürgen eyed Heike sharply.

"Pabst says Sabine was sitting at the table drinking cocoa when he came home Saturday."

"Frau Willing can come in, day or night," Nadine added. "She's certainly no stranger."

Heike looked at them each very carefully. She couldn't accept the idea that someone she trusted would cravenly betray the family.

"I told them your mother was out of the house when I first arrived here," Sabine injected. "I watched her come down the street and unlock the door."

That was the most obvious lie. It initiated general agreement that Sabine was a Stasi agent. However, there remained one disturbing fact. If the Stasi were finished, why send Sabine?

Keeping tabs on Rosa's Children, they could infiltrate the organization easily. The Children had no secrets. The Stasi could learn everything about them merely by standing on any street corner and listening to people talk. Why put someone in the house?

"Wait," Heike said. "Nadine, you were here when Lilo came that day. She said, *'nice to see you – again.'* She said it to Mutti. What other time did Lilo see her?"

"Let's ask," Sabine suggested, clutching at straws.

"If one of us is an informer, you know what it means, don't you? It means we no longer have a family. I'd rather die."

Heike's speech was melodramatic, but inescapably true. Sabine was a virtual captive though no one said so. She knew she dared not leave the company. If Lilo got advance notice, she'd have time to prepare a story.

They left for the Zimmermann abode early. Heike was upset. Sabine went Vopo style: the one on the right watched the one on the left while the one on the left watched the one on the right. They didn't speak during their walk to Goetheplatz. They didn't speak on the bus. They didn't speak while waiting for or boarding their connecting bus. They didn't speak at their destination. Not until inside the tiny apartment and the food parcel was dumped on the kitchen floor were words exchanged.

"If any one of us is an informer, I'll never trust anyone again."

"You must know if you've informed."

Heike clinched her fists, not with rage but with frustration born of helplessness.

"I had a girl friend who moved away to Apolda several years ago. I didn't see her again until Saturday at our rally. She told me her father was arrested and sent to prison just a few weeks after he began a job here. She wonders if it was some silly, childish thing she'd said that had got him arrested. She'll carry that to the grave – unless they release the records."

"When did you ever talk about folding clothes outside the house?" Sabine demanded.

"That's why it's so despicable," Heike agreed. "It must be an informer or a spy. Frau Willing or Hanna could come in anytime, but I cannot believe they'd roam around the house without disturbing Mutti. They had to go upstairs, open the shrunk and open the drawers. I just can't imagine Mutti sitting there while that's going on. No! It must be one of us or a Stasi goon."

"I wish I'd kept my big mouth shut," Sabine muttered.

"Me, too, but there is nothing for it now. How much of that file did you see?"

"Just the cover. Herr Beckmann was careful not to let us see any of the contents."

"He gave you the picture," Heike snapped.

"It isn't quite the same as identifying the person who reported on the clothes closet, is it? He got very excited when he found it. Swabish doesn't have swear words to cover what he said."

"Do you think we could go to Berlin and ask to see it?"

"We could ask. He's afraid of two governments – *three* if the Americans get involved."

Heike nodded. She leaned on the table.

"I suspect they sealed the files because too many people were learning who informed on them. Bodies were being found. Not even Wessis can put up with that. Damn! Damn! Damn! Damn! If I could know it wasn't one of us."

"How do you think I feel? I'm accused of being a Stasi agent."

"Nobody believes that." Heike stated abruptly. "Most of them left the country. Only a fool would stay around and wait to be killed by any of the hundreds of thousands whose lives they ruined. You're not a fool, Sabine. If you're Stasi, you'd be in the Soviet Union or Chile or Cuba by now. Meanwhile, we're all suspects."

Sabine stood for several minutes and watched her sister fret. Finally, she asked if she could fix Herr Zimmermann's hot meal. Heike, whose heart was no longer in it, nodded.

Sabine took up the package of goods and found onions, carrots, beans, and a bell pepper. All were fresh from the greengrocer. There was a goodly portion of sausage and two aromatic rye brötchen. Keen enough to realize the menu Heike had planned, Sabine began searching the cupboards for those things which were lacking and, therefore, must be on site. Salt, pepper, and dry beef stock were found in moments.

"If we live through this," Sabine asked while peeling carrots, "will you teach me to make soljanka?"

For the first time in several minutes, Heike displayed signs of life.

"You like it?"

"Very much."

"The only great thing the Soviets brought here," Heike affirmed. "Will you take it to America?"

"I'd have four families addicted inside a month."

Silence descended.

Sabine checked to see if Heike was creeping toward her with a carving knife. She was not. Heike remained seated. Apparently, she was checking Sabine's work.

"Yes," she promised. "I'll show you how to make soljanka."

* * *

When Hanna and Inka arrived, Heike made no move until Sabine rushed to get the comet in her arms. Heike got up to monitor the soup. Hanna and Sabine exchanged a few short words, but the younger, remarkably perceptive girl, realized her presence was not welcome. She quickly excused herself, said good-bye, and beat a hasty retreat.

Sabine was sorry to see her go. Hanna was smart, caring and amiable. If Hanna were her sister, Sabine and she could talk freely for hours and enjoy a good laugh or two. Heike, however, was guarded and annoyingly sober. Perhaps, life had not been kind to her, but Sabine didn't understand why she rejected levity.

Jürgen and Nadine relieved Heike of Lilo's extra house key. Traveling together Vopo style – the one on the right, etc., they let themselves into the apartment and left a note Heike authored. Lilo was to come to the Jacobs home on a matter of grave urgency.

Lilo would come without any opportunity to be coached on what to say. Heike was convinced Lilo was unlikely to be pressured or swayed by anyone in the Jacobs camp. She always said what was on her mind, save for when she was Günther's dedicated parrot.

The sun was low; the shadows were long. Heike's face was partially obscured by the brightness of the sky behind her. It was difficult to read her expression, but Sabine squinted hard making the attempt.

"We might be walking into a hornet's nest," Heike said. "This might be the last time any of us will ever speak to the others. While I have the chance, I want you to know something."

Sabine braced herself, expecting some grand philosophical pronouncement. She wasn't certain she was prepared to hear her sister's "last words." Sabine swallowed hard and nodded. It was not easy to swallow with precious little moisture in her mouth. She began feeling nauseous.

"While you were making silly with Inka, Herr Zimmermann told me something important."

"What?" croaked.

"He said my soup is better than yours."

Sabine stood dumbfounded.

Against her will and with total disregard for the gravity of the moment, she laughed. It was the first real laugh since entering the DDR. It was both a relief and a sorrow.

* * *

The silence was nerve-shattering. Everyone attempted conversation to keep Anne from being alarmed. She sensed, however. The way they picked at their food put the woman on edge. She sat silent, but her expression suggested tears were in the offing. The more the girls spoke with forced cheeriness and laughed in short, timid, apologetic laughs, the more somber Anne became.

Rolf commanded the girls to shut up. Everyone, including Rolf, ached to say something – anything. Without sincerity, no words would bring Anne succor.

There was a knock on the door.

Sabine was rearranging serving plates, encouraging people to reach for something. Nadine, standing stupidly with a carafe of tepid tea, snapped to attention. She looked first at Rolf and then at Jürgen. Neither made any sign. She put down the tea and went to the door.

"'Abend, Lilo."

"'Abend."

The giant stepped into the room and joined the oppressive atmosphere. Sabine noticed the blond shuddered visibly when the door closed behind her.

"We have to ask you a few questions," Rolf said, looking across the table without looking at her.

"Of course, Herr Jacobs," Lilo replied, as if reading from a script.

Marina cleared her throat. Jürgen answered his cue and rose from the couch.

"Won't you sit down?" he asked.

Lilo stuck her hands finger deep into her jeans' pockets.

"I'm quite comfortable," she reported.

Everyone recognized the lie.

"Coffee? Tea? Something to eat?" Nadine asked.

Lilo shook her head nervously.

"Lilo," Jürgen began, "how do you know my mother?"

Lilo made a face.

"Many people know Frau Jacobs," she informed. "I've seen her picture in the paper, of course; and there is the photo of her in the museum standing with Party-Secretary Stark."

Jürgen showed no signs of impatience. If he interrupted and refined his question, she'd realize she was being interrogated over specific points. He needn't have bothered. Lilo knew she was accused of something. In true DDR fashion, she avoided seeking information and was very careful when dispensing it.

"When did you first see her in person?"

"At school," her response was instant. "I was very young. She was there to speak to the Pioneers, but my class sat in."

Heike watched her brother. Sabine noticed Heike's chin quivered.

"When did you see her again?"

This reply didn't come immediately. The nervous Amazon searched her memory.

"It was, I think, four or five years ago."

"And where?"

"In the park. Not far from the Sternbrücke."

Heike and Nadine held their breaths.

"What was she doing?"

"Walking along the river."

The girls looked at each other. As children, their mother, frequently, took them on walks through that stretch of the park.

"Did you ever see her after that?"

"A couple times," Lilo nodded. "Once, just before I left for sports camp. I spoke to her. She smiled at me."

Nadine and Heike sobbed and hugged each other. Two independent witnesses observed Frau Ecke outside the house. Even a novice Stasi agent could wait until Anne left home. Once he was inside, he could do whatever he intended. Everyone knew the Stasi had a key to every lock.

Slowly, Rolf Jacobs stood. The entire assembly waited with trepidation. He stepped to the couch.

"Anne, dear. Would you care for a walk?"

The woman looked at him and smiled. She stood and took her husband's proffered arm. Together, they walked to the door and through it.

Until the door closed with a barely audible click, there was no sound. Once Herr and Frau Jacobs were gone, there wasn't a dry eye in the room.

* * *

"I can't believe we held her prisoner all those years," Heike moaned.

The heat was ebbing slightly. As the sisters strolled toward Lilo's apartment, they remained unaware of the temperature.

"She wasn't a prisoner, obviously," Lilo responded.

She remained shaken by her part in a dark family drama.

"She had to steal out of the house like some pubescent sneak," Heike moaned, pathetically. "It never occurred to us to take her out. Before we started school, she had Nadine and I out every day, once in the morning and once in the afternoon, rain or shine."

"And the Stasi running loose in the house." Sabine concluded.

"I don't care about that!" Heike pouted. "Not even Jürgen thought of it. We all felt if she went out, she'd be taken by the authorities and put in one of those – awful places!"

They walked nearly an entire block.

"It was me," Heike reported. "The Stasi was checking up on me. Lilo, do you realize if I wrote anything stupid, we might all have gone to jail?"

"Why would they be spying on you?" Sabine demanded.

"Because," Lilo injected with a bitter tone, "in the eyes of the State, your parents were traitors. That made Heike guilty of counter-revolutionary tendencies. Heike's right, if they discovered anything, jail is the least they could expect."

"We, any of us, never had a chance of getting into the Party, did we?" Heike raged.

"Because of me, Jürgen and Nadine would be barred. I'm a curse!"

Lilo flared and went for Heike, but Sabine stepped between. The Amazon pushed the unsuspecting girl out of her path causing her to stagger. Confronted with a tumble she couldn't avoid, Sabine twisted so one arm could break her fall. Suddenly, she felt an iron grip on her other wrist. She was yanked back to her feet and found herself locked in Lilo's iron embrace.

"Hold me!" the Amazon commanded.

Her voice trembled. Her body trembled. With Lilo's strong arms making it impossible to escape, Sabine was too frightened to react.

"Hold me!" Lilo repeated.

Sabine obeyed. She'd no choice. Escape was impossible. She prayed that Heike might come to her aid, but neither sight nor sound betrayed her presence. Her arms overlapping behind Lilo's back, Sabine decided docility was her best strategy. Should Lilo explode again…

"I'm so sorry!"

Lilo said it with a voice neither Sabine nor Heike had heard before.

"Did I hurt you?"

The voice was steadier and her arms relaxed enough that Sabine could breath normally again.

"I'm very sorry," she repeated. "My fit of temper is spent."

Lilo released her prisoner. Sabine took a cautious step back and formulated an escape plan if one were required. Instantly, she realized her folly. Lilo could run faster and farther. Launching a scream on the deserted street would, likely, prod her nemesis to more violence.

"If it were only you and me, I – I might have – murdered you."

Heike stood stock still. Her eyes were huge and bulging. She was frightened into mute motionless.

"Sometimes, you make me so angry! Believe me, Heike, I'm as frightened as you are."

Heike's eyes locked onto Lilo's with fire and defiance. Amazingly, she found Lilo's eyes were languid and sad.

"You're so certain you're to blame for everything," Lilo began softly. "Heike is the cause of everything. Heike gets Nadine bashed around and beaten. Heike brings the entire Jacobs family to the brink of ruin. Anything Heike touches turns to shit. Not once, not a single moment in your entire life could you see that Jürgen and Nadine – even Rolf – would do anything for you."

She paused and continued,

"They would trade their lives – any of them – all of them – for you. They love you so much, it makes my teeth itch! But all Heike can do is whine about how everyone would be better off if Heike never existed."

She turned her head to see if Sabine remained within earshot. She wanted to be certain the Ami could hear.

"Heike is give, give, give, give, give – not out of love, but out of guilt. I know I'm not the only one to tell you this, Heike, but you're a pain in the ass!"

"I'm not giving up on Günther. You can't keep him, you know. He thinks you're so cute and so smart. When he finds out you have no respect for yourself, he won't want you. When that day comes, I'll be standing right there."

Lilo turned her attention to Sabine.

"I'm sorry I made you a part of this," she informed Sabine. "I'm glad you were here. Your holding me helped bring me to my senses. I could have – gotten arrested tonight. I could have hurt your sister – I mean, really hurt her. I was – I was insane for just long enough to – Please, I'm okay, now. No sudden moves or raised voices for a while. I include myself. Okay?"

There was but one answer to that question.

* * *

They sat on the floor between the beds, behind a closed door. Both knew if Lilo came at them in a nocturnal rage, the door was no defense. However, with nerves in taters, the psychological edge provided by a physical barrier was worth more than hiding under the beds, clutching teddy bears and sucking thumbs.

Sabine felt no further compunction to adhere to diplomacy. Her nerves were frayed. She must flee for her sanity if not her physical safety. She couldn't write Gary and she couldn't write Molly. The words wouldn't come. She was suffocating.

"I have to leave this place," she announced. "Jürgen and Marina are leaving Saturday; so, will I. You can have your room back in your own house, and we'll all sleep easier."

"I'm sorry you're disappointed," Heike replied. "It's a long way to come for – this."

"I got to meet you. That's what I set out to do."

Heike was about to say something only to think of Lilo's condemnation. How, she wondered, did one go about developing self-respect? She'd pay any price for Günther, but there was no means of figuring a rate of exchange.

"Heike," Sabine began with considerable unease, "you're my sister. Because of that, I cannot leave this place carrying a secret. Günther is leaving Saturday as well."

Heike glared hard.

"How do you know?" she demanded.

"Heike, you're the only one who doesn't know."

This exposition relieved Sabine of the icy glare, but the look Heike devoted to the floor was far from reassuring. Sabine observed her sister's body tense. A vein bulged on the side of the face. Fists clinched. Instantly, all was gone. Any sign of emotion evaporated. Heike sighed.

"I knew he was going but not so soon," she heaved. "Well, I was stupid to think we were ever a couple –"

"What makes you think you aren't?"

"Couples share," Heike spat.

Sabine took a breath and made ready for the worst.

"Not everyone is like you," she advanced. "Everyone thought it was better this way. I don't agree. I think you have a right to know."

"So, do I! Jürgen, Nadine, and I will have words. Hanna too. And Lilo. Well, she's here…"

She started to get up, but Sabine scooted to the door and braced against it. Heike got to her knees and reached to pull Sabine away from her post. It was the first time, in conscious memory, the sisters touched!

An electric tingle shot up Sabine's arm and lodged in the back of her neck. Her skin prickled. When Heike's bold action was arrested instantly, Sabine knew her sister shared the sensation.

Heike rocked back with an awed expression. She reached for Sabin's hand and held it tightly. They sat and stared. Time ceased; they existed only in a progression of emotions which swirled about in delicate, unhurried eddies.

Heike was the first to recover from the stupor. She cleared her throat and gently shook free of Sabine's hand.

"I must speak to Lilo," she said without conviction.

"Heike, please, don't do this."

Heike settled back onto her haunches.

"Why not?" Heike asked with curiosity rather than hosility.

"Because many people were trying to lessen the pain."

"By keeping secrets? I hate secrets."

"It was wrong," Sabine conceded. "That's why I told you, but I don't know you. I don't know them, either. Maybe, I'm the one who is wrong."

"It was wrong," Heike insisted with vehemence.

"Heike, please. It's called friendship. *Freundschaft*. Maybe, it's wrong and misguided, but it isn't selfish. If Lilo wanted to hurt you tonight, why didn't she throw this in your face?"

"You're on her side?" Heike accused.

Sabine smiled. She couldn't help it.

"You don't expect me to fall for that, do you?"

Heike studied her carefully. However, the hostility that existed earlier was gone.

"No," she concluded. "You're too smart. Okay, I'll play the game. But – someday Günther and I will have words."

Sabine reached out and took Heike's hand once more. Heike did not object. She relished the sensation produced by Sabine's thumb stroking the back of her appendage. It was physically soothing; it was, also, a tangible affirmation that Heike and Sabine were family.

A timid knock at the door roused them. Both girls were averse to the company of their malevolent hostess, but the pitiful noise of the timid knock communicated supplication. Regardless, they expected the door to burst open and a daughter of Wotan, in a bronze breastplate, warrior cape, her golden locks flowing in a supernatural war-wind, her mighty hand brandishing a great broadsword emitting miniature lightning bolts. Instead, there was a second knock, less insistent than the first.

Heike and Sabine looked at each other. When Sabine squeezed her sister's hand, a tacit agreement was struck.

"Bitte," they called in unison.

They scooted away from the door.

The handle moved slowly until the latch lost its hold. It swung open just enough for a blond head to peer around the edge. It was not the daughter of a Norse god, but the face of a penitent cherub. Well, a penitent cherub fresh from a mighty salute to Bacchus

Earlier, she came very near beating, if not murdering, someone. She was frightened. Lilo's eyes were dull and sorrowful. Her face was sad, yet expectant. Her hair, far from flowing in the wind of vengeance, hung limply in mourning.

"May I come in?"

Disarmed by her pleading tone and her pathetic appearance, the sisters nodded. Lilo was as wary of them as they were of her. She slithered through the door as if afraid to open it further than necessary. Once inside, she was unsure what to do.

Heike watched with amazed dread. She'd never seen Lilo deflated. She looked as timid as a child in a thunderstorm. She remained as tall as ever, but her entire demeanor was that of a field mouse.

When Lilo took the embodiment of Viking ferocity, she'd clear a room just by entering. This disturbingly morose figure, however, looked as if she intended to curl up in Heike's lap and begin sobbing uncontrollably. Faced with a choice, Heike preferred the Viking.

Lilo produced three small glasses clutched in one hand. In her other, she carried a bottle of Korn. She dropped to her knees. It was a long descent made more pronounced by the slowness with which she carried out her action.

"I'm so ashamed of myself," she began. "I know you can never forgive me, so I thought I'd forget the whole thing with my friend here. But – but – that's so selfish. I thought, maybe – well, all of us could use a jolt."

She held up two glasses which the sisters examined closely. Heike, however, looked at the pitiful creature offering them and decided the scene was too heart-rending to endure without support. She took one of the glasses and leaned against Sabine's shoulder.

"I don't want to get drunk," Sabine announced prudishly.

Lilo held up the bottle. It was three-quarters empty.

"If three of us get drunk on this little bit," she concluded. "It will constitute a scientific breakthrough."

Sabine had her doubts. Nevertheless, she didn't want to spoil Lilo's contrition. The brute was attempting to apologize. In the best interests of the moment, Sabine decided to take the risk. Lilo poured. It was a down-the-hatch moment, but the trio, without prearrangement, sipped their rocket fuel.

"I suspect you'll be glad to get out of this place," Lilo speculated.

"She's coming back," Heike informed, deadpan.

Lilo's interest was renewed. She regarded *die Neue* with renewed interest.

"Why would you do that?"

Lilo didn't live on the moon; she'd been to the West and was as mesmerized by the color and the glitter and the plenty as was everyone else. For Lilo, it was a novelty. Having grown up in, what Wessis called *the squalor of want*, she knew her life was not dependent upon material things. Sabine, however, was brought up in a world where denial of one's wants is considered a catastrophe.

"My Papa needs me."

Momentarily, Lilo cast an accusatory glance at Heike.

"Is he well off?"

"Not really. He's a school Hausmeister."

"What's wrong with that?" Lilo demanded. "We're all good proletarians here, correct? Remember, Heike, how we all used to think we'd end up at the Humboldt Uni in Berlin because they reserved so many places for children of the workers?"

Heike suspected Lilo was deep in her cups. She was recalling conversations they never had. If Lilo was miffed at Heike for failing to respond, she disguised it well.

"You must give up much," Lilo warned. "I know they plan to make us a Wessi province, but that might take time. You must learn to get along without so many things: reliable phone service or service of any kind, just for one example. If you have a special craving for certain foods, you can bet against satisfying it."

"Some sacrifices are worth making," Sabine stated simply.

Lilo rested her hand holding the glass on Sabine's shoulder.

"Congratulations," she said with conviction. "You're an Ossi!"

"Of course," Sabine replied, making certain to avoid sounding confrontational. "I was born here."

"Hundreds of thousands of Wessis were born here," Lilo insisted. "To be an Ossi, you must make sacrifices – every day."

"It's best if you think the sacrifices are in aid of something," Heike injected.

"Don't give up, Heike. We are disappointed. We were betrayed, but we believed. That's what mattered. A sacrifice is wasted if we don't believe."

"How do we know that our current sacrifices will result in anything?" Heike challenged.

Lilo didn't hesitate, nor did she become antagonistic. She nodded toward Sabine.

"You sister can answer that," she assured. "Is your father worth the sacrifice?"

Sabine looked squarely at Heike.

"Yes."

"There you are," Lilo joined Sabine in studying Heike. "Based on no tangible evidence, your sister will sacrifice on behalf of her father – your father, too. We believe. If we didn't, the country would have been deserted and empty twenty years ago."

"Sometimes, it is difficult to believe," Heike objected.

"That's when the sacrifices become more important. You believe in Rosa, don't you? That's stupid. Of course, you do, or you wouldn't be working so hard. Heike, can we forget our differences long enough to toast Sabine, the newest Ossi."

"To the Ossis," Heike saluted with her glass.

The two others gulped down the remainder of their Korn, and Sabine felt it would be rude not to follow their example.

* * *

Sleeping in was a luxury Heike rejected. Each morning in the alien apartment, she'd spring up and have her feet on the floor before realizing she wasn't home. Somehow, she felt obligated to drag the sun up over the horizon.

Korn didn't dull her internal clock. She woke up, as usual, but panic gripped her. She'd slept in a bed, not on her pallet. She heaved a sigh of relief; she hadn't overslept. Even had she, Rolf was unable to administer a penalty.

The door opened and Heike jumped to attention. If Lilo swallowed her remorse and was determined to attack her, Heike must be ready. The figure, silhouetted by the weak light slinking through the living room and bouncing off the walls of the hall, was too diminutive to be threatening.

"I'm sorry," Sabine whispered. "I didn't think anyone else was up."

Heike brought the *house rules* across town. It was carved in stone: the bathroom was used according to age, both morning and evening. As the youngest, Sabine should be last. She'd violated the rule before, but no one dared suggest a punishment. Perhaps, they chalked up Sabine's transgressions to the eccentricity of Wessi life.

"Not to worry," Heike assured. "I just woke up."

Sabine stashed her dirty things in a bag designated for soiled laundry. She sifted through fresh clothes. She decided upon the red culottes and a yellow top. It was a nightmarish combination, but, considering the younger Ossi women she'd observed, Sabine stood an excellent chance of remaining inconspicuous.

She was unaware of Heike sneaking up behind her until she felt the brush in her hair. Momentarily startled, she allowed her sister's attention. It was unexpected but appreciated.

"Do you really have to leave in the morning?"

"Not really," Sabine responded. "But with Jürgen and Marina setting off, you'll want me to stay with you, right? That means hours of debate over who sleeps on the floor. Please don't be offended, Heike, but I've had all the Jacobs family melodrama I can take."

"I couldn't allow you sleep on the floor," Heike confirmed.

"The situation won't exist," Sabine reminded. "Discussion is pointless."

Heike contemplated in silence. Suddenly, she disappeared with the promise to return. Sabine sprawled out on the bed and contemplated a few extra minutes of sleep. When she heard muffled voices down the hall, her heart raced; Lilo was up! Not hearing screams or gun fire, she relaxed.

There was activity in the bathroom. If Heike adhered to established custom, that would be Lilo.

"Sit up a minute," Heike commanded, switching on the light.

Sabine obeyed because Heike was, decidedly, less aloof. Any form of domesticity resembling that existing between Molly and Jayme was welcome. Having Heike brush her hair was an appreciated gesture.

The brushing was soothing. Sabine closed her eyes and enjoyed. She heard the brush plop softly onto the bed, but Heike produced a comb from somewhere. Sabine was only mildly curious. It was, she assumed "an Ossi thing."

"Wait a minute!" she protested. "What are you doing? Don't you dare! Stop!"

"What is wrong with you?"

"Braiding my hair won't make me look German," Sabine reminded.

"It won't kill you, either."

"I've never braided my hair. Never!"

"You're not braiding it now."

"Heike, that's enough! I'm Sabine, not Mutti."

That struck home. Heike ceased her efforts and allowed her sister to reclaim her hair. Sabine seized the brush and began smoothing out the damage.

"Bitte."

It was Sabine's turn to be shaken. That single word dripped pathos. She was defenseless. If Heike wanted to imagine her as her mother reincarnate, there was no real harm. Moreover, it might provide that final bit of play that would allow her to lodge a hook.

"This will cost you."

"Capitalist pig! It's always about money with you Yanks, isn't it?"

Sabine couldn't believe her ears. Heike's words tumbled out of her mouth with all the practiced ease of a professional satirist.

"Heike Franziska, I think you made a joke. Yes, you did! I'm proud of you."

Heike allowed herself an appreciative smile. It was beautiful and disarming. Sabine regretted not being allowed to see it more often.

"What will it cost me?"

"I want a picture of you to send to Papa."

The smile vanished and Heike was left to struggle with her bigotry. Sabine waited patiently as only a person who frequently caught her sister studying a small photo can be patient.

"Let me finish."

"Do we have a deal?"

"I don't have any photos," Heike explained. "Those kinder photos of us on the walls were taken when Mutti was well. She arranged the sittings. Pabst doesn't think of such things."

"There must be a camera in this town," Sabine insisted. "We don't need a professional."

"Maybe."

"Heike, stop. You aren't touching my hair until we have a deal."

The elder sister realized she'd no option.

How did Sabine Bauer avoid thinking of pictures earlier? In the three hurried notes to her father, it never occurred that he'd want a picture. On her first evening, she spent some while describing Heike through her amateurish composition skills. She'd exhausted all her adjectives in the first two lines and groped for phrases, she hoped, were sensory and accurate. Why hadn't she thought of a camera?

She imagined Ernst Bauer ripping open each envelope with anxious fingers and a beating heart. He'd desperately want to see his daughter. His repeated disappointments must have been devastating. Suppose he was so upset that he forgot some important matter at school and was fired – because Miss Moron couldn't think of the obvious.

She'd get a picture off at once. She'd buy a camera with her father's money if she must. She had ample stamps. She scrawled a hasty message on a post card and mailed it at the cost of a letter. It was better, and quicker, than waiting for the post office to open.

Sabine helped serve breakfast and clean up after. She charged upstairs to air bedding. She scrubbed the stairs but not, according to her critics, very well. How, she wondered, could they tell? The stairs remained sterile and pristine from the previous day's wash. However mild the rebuke, it made her more meticulous. She swept and dusted and made the beds with the greatest care, all the while convinced the chores would never be finished.

There was enough time before the midday meal to check with Lilo in the square. She'd dispatched a messenger to the day care facility to intercept Hanna and Inka. She'd yet to hear back; Sabine cursed. She cursed again when she realized she'd no time to search for a photo shop.

If she weren't home when the meal was served, Anne would get the fidgets. This, in turn, would earn a sharp scolding from Rolf and additional if more gentle rebukes of the others. She had no appetite. She forced herself to eat her soup and picked at a slice of bread leaving the boiled potatoes and steamed vegetables to the others.

Her leg bounced nervously under the table. She wanted to drag Rolf out the door, stuff him in his tiny car and hurry him back to work so she could rush into town and buy a camera and film. The others talked and joked quite casually.

Sabine Bauer went mad.

Finally!

Rolf hoisted his bulk out of his chair and started for the door. Mentally, Heike had her starting blocks out. The moment she heard the putt-putt motor engage she would disappear in a vapor trail.

As if to annoy her further, Rolf left the door open upon departing. Was he coming back? Had he transported something in the car over which he'd loiter for an additional twenty minutes before setting off? Sabine leaned forward and gently rapped on the tabletop with her forehead.

"What's she doing?"

Sabine sat up straight upon hearing a familiar voice. It was Hanna! Noting her approach, Rolf left the door open to allow the girl free access. In her hand was a camera.

In answer to the question, Jürgen, Marina, Nadine, and Heike made gestures indicating they were unsure of Sabine's sanity. Hanna assumed she was being played for a fool without knowing why. Despite their bizarre game, she had a mission to perform.

"Heiko let me borrow this," she reported, presenting the device. "It's a Wessi camera with a roll of Wessi film."

"I'll pay for the film," Sabine promised.

"No, you won't," Hanna objected. "Heiko needs the camera this evening. He and his group are playing at the *Fest*. He wants to take lots of pictures."

"Tonight?" Heike asked.

Hanna turned her attention to the sister with whom she was more familiar.

"They won't play until tomorrow night, but, of course, he's coming tonight. Are you coming?"

"Marina and I are," Jürgen assured. "I suspect we'll all be there."

Fest? It was the first Sabine heard of it. The anxiety washed away by Hanna and her presentation returned with a fury. There would be duty at Herr Zimmermann's followed by Abendsbrot and a fest after. She calculated how she could take twenty-four pictures in so little time.

"Hanna, I'd like to get a snap of you and the others right now."

The busty young brunette was convinced the family's mime accompanying her entrance was based upon truth. Why would anyone beyond her own family want Hanna's picture? It was an alien concept until she recalled the collection of Sabine's presentation over soljanka. It must be a Wessi thing. However, she wasn't certain she wanted her picture flouted before that glamorous blond who was Sabine's close friend.

Hanna's protests melted before Sabine's insistence. She had Heiko's camera, after all. It wouldn't serve to make her angry. Marina nudged her intended and whispered something in his ear. Jürgen nodded before offering an arm to his mother. Nadine and Heike blushed when they realized neither of them thought to offer.

Had the camera been a more expensive and intricate device with an adjustable lens, Sabine would be helpless. However, Sabine was frequently asked to take snaps with cameras of passengers on the *Mary R*. Forced by circumstance of limited space on board, she never included grand vistas;

she'd learned to capture clear images of faces. The thought of including the house in the photo never entered her head.

She cajoled the group to squeeze in close so she could get good resolution. Confronted with the task of making twenty-four exposures before her deadline, she snapped the shutter thrice.

Jürgen, on his own initiative, suggested he take a photo of the sisters. On his third attempt, Sabine insisted on Nadine. Heike deserved to appear with both sisters. The deformed girl was reluctant but acquiesced.

Next, Sabine ordered Heike to Lilo's apartment. She wanted to send a picture of Heike in her new dress. Heike insisted the plan, and the trip, were silly and time consuming.

"We made a deal," Sabine reminded, wagging one of her braids at her.

Heike launched a six-letter speech before surrendering. She was smart enough to realize that Sabine would insist on a pound of flesh. Transporting Zimmermann's food basket would save her the time and expense later.

Never had Heike experienced such a light, delicate fabric. Despite Sabine's assurances that the garment was durable, she handled it as if it were made of smoke. Once inside it, she felt different – very regal.

"I want a picture of you with Shakespeare," Sabine beamed.

"Are you crazy? It will take half an hour to get there."

Sabine wiggled both her braids. This overruled her sister's exaggerated objection. A circus parade marched through town. People stopped and stared at the attractive young girl in the Wessi dress. This made Heike exceptionally nervous and self-conscious; Sabine more so.

She hated her culottes because they hugged her hips. It was a fashion trend she didn't honor and habitually eschewed. In a moment of weakness, she sacrificed modesty for comfort and practicality.

True, Heike and her dress drew stares, but Sabine knew the odd by-stander would spare a moment to survey her butt. *Die Neue* told herself *everyone* is gawking at Heike; if they weren't, well, she was a stranger. The following day, she'd disappear.

In the end, the expedition came to naught. The statue was mounted too far from the ground. To capture William and Heike, Sabine must stand way back. She took two photos but realized her father would be sorely disappointed over a poor view of Heike's precious face.

She suggested they march to the Römisches Haus where Heike could pose between perfect Ionic columns. Heike put her foot down. It would take them away from busses and the Zimmermann dwelling.

They compromised. They returned by way of the Platz Die Demokratie where a score of people set up tables, benches, and a stage for the evening's fest. At the end of Puschkinstrasse, there was a bust of the great poet. Here, with the sun behind her, Sabine got two close ups. The second featured Heike with her arm around Alexander, a writer she admired.

"Now, let's get moving."

"What's the rush?" Sabine asked, quite reasonably she thought.

"I'm making Rouladen."

"What is he, royalty?"

With this pithy comment, Sabine opened the bag and took frantic inventory. There was no safe way to digest Rouladen made from meat lugged around half the day in the heat. Her nose told her there was no spoiled flesh, but her mind couldn't fathom the concept. She knew people in the DDR relied on substitutions, but Rouladen without meat –??

Heike explained she purchased pork the previous day. It waited for them in Zimmermann's refrigerator. Heike stood on the bus. As did Sabine before, she wouldn't risk wrinkles or, worse, dirt or any of a dozen renegade substances.

"Heike, you can't cook in this dress!"

"I'll take it off."

Sabine's modesty was a curse, as she knew well enough, but the image of her sister laboring over a stove in an apron and very little else was one more affront to her fastidiousness. They could, of course, swap clothes. That, however, would doom Sabine to standing about, shifting her weight from one foot to the next, for a couple of hours without Inka to relieve the tedium.

"I'll do the cooking," Sabine barked.

Heike scowled at the dictator who sat comfortably in a seat designed for two. She'd planned this meal for three days. Her sister intended to displace her because of a damned dress! It wasn't enough that photos were taken for the purpose of being ogled by perfect strangers. She remained reluctant to acknowledge the existence of a man who, in a very real sense, tried to kidnap her.

To be denied the opportunity to create something special for her satisfaction, as well as the sustenance of Herr Zimmerman, was an affront. She was tempted to lay down the law. However, every passenger was ogling her; the passengers in the forward end of the bus were craning their necks to keep her in view. If ever there was a time Heike didn't intend to create a public scene, this was it.

"Can you make Rouladen?"

"If you tell me what to do."

Here was a challenge! To cook by remote control; the idea had appeal. Moreover, Heike was beginning to trust the autocrat who burst into her life uninvited and unannounced. Sabine, as grudging as it was for her to admit, was not a bad sort. Her allegiance to her father was admirable.

"I know Herr Zimmermann doesn't think I'm the cook you are," Sabine continued, "but he ate my not-so-good soup."

Heike smiled. Sabine was instantly suspicious. However, it was a treat to look up into Heike's beaming expression.

"I'll make another deal."

It was Sabine's turn to smile. She couldn't help it; Heike's mirth was contagious.

"If you make good Rouladen, I'll take a picture of you and Inka."

That was too good to refuse.

* * *

It took longer than planned to prepare the dish for simmering. The best feature of Rouladen, however, was once on simmer, it required no further attention. The bad news was that Herr Zimmermann must wait for his dinner – a small enough inconvenience, but it pushed back washing and cleaning. Sabine and Heike would be late for Abendsbrot which, in turn, would delay their arrival at the fest.

Hanna delivered her charge and Sabine made sure to get a nice picture of her with the child in her arms. Next, Heike kept her word. Sabine wanted to hold the comet in her lap, but that was impossible in natural light. They were forced outside where Sabine stood, holding her delightful cargo.

Herr Zimmermann was not concerned over the delay of his evening meal. He appreciated what Heike did for him and would not scold her for a break in the routine. Sabine, however, suspected he wasn't keen to try her cooking again. Hanna and Heike kept Herr Zimmermann entertained with local topics of interest while Sabine kept the child's ears filled with merry nonsense. Inka's giggles were the measure of *Die Neue's* success.

"Do you think that, just maybe, when you grow up, you might marry my brother?"

It was merely more nonsense. Inka couldn't understand; all she cared about were Sabine's comic tone and exaggerated facial expressions. However, Sabine was suddenly aware of three pairs of eyes riveted upon her. For a moment, she'd no clue as to why. She, herself, paid no attention to her own baby babble.

"I'm not matchmaking," she assured, upon realizing her gaff.

No one acknowledged her statement. Sabine sighed with relief when the assembly resumed their inconsequential banter. Sabine kept her mouth shut and resorted to tickling. Isaac loved to be tickled, and Inka was similarly addicted. All the while, however, Sabine wondered what, exactly, was her faux pas? If she knew, she'd apologize.

Sabine brought out a serving platter of the Rouladen surrounded by small, whole potatoes. Herr Zimmermann started with a potato. After summoning his courage, he sliced into the Rouladen. It was exceptionally tender, Sabine observed, but it was in the man's expression that counted.

"Very good," he pronounced.

He looked at Sabine who transferred it across to Heike. She smiled her thanks for the instructions and her patience in watching her fumble through them. Heike returned the thanks with one of her rare high-voltage smiles. Sabine basked in its brilliance. She hoped that one day soon, Herr Bauer would see this heart-stopping sight.

After earning her sister's approval, Sabine could have cleaned the entire Zimmermann establishment, inside and out, to the same exacting state as Heike's own residence. She differed to Hanna, however, and allowed her to help scouring the dishes, the pot, and a saucepan. When everything was in its proper place, the trio left Herr Zimmermann to enjoy Inka's company.

On the bus to town, Sabine wanted her sin clarified. Heike and Hanna confessed of there was no overt breach of protocol. However, they were flummoxed by the notion of Inka marrying an Ami. It wasn't easy to get past their years of indoctrination.

"My brother is half-German," she announced with malice. "I can assure you he'll be brought up a proper gentleman; he will speak two languages equally well. He won't be a slave to politics – at least not when it comes to loving someone."

"We never said otherwise," Heike assured.

She was growing tired of standing.

Sabine turned to glare at Hanna seated next to her.

"Not me," the girl said.

* * *

Marina appointed herself the scullery maid for the evening. At her insistence, everyone was seated about the table, save for Jürgen. He kept his mother company on the couch. Heike could have changed into something more appropriate, but she reveled in her first formal gown.

Heike protected Molly's dress by draping the skirt over the back of her chair. It was a colorful bunting that fetched a communal laugh. It was incongruous to wear such a beautiful dress while sitting with her dreary underpants showing.

"We're all family, right?" she asked.

There was a knock. Who else could it be but Günther? Everyone stared at Heike.

"He's not family," Nadine hissed.

She *attempted* to hiss, but her mangled lip and lack of certain teeth blunted the effect. Heike turned obstinate. This remark struck her as supercilious and unfair. Jürgen admitted his friend. Günther's reaction was almost identical to Marina's. He couldn't stifle his reaction.

Heike, sullen and in a fit of pique, slid her chair back and stood up.

"That's about enough!" she said louder than was necessary.

She smoothed the dress, stormed to Günther, spun him around and hooked her arm through his.

"We're going for a walk!"

All eyes fell upon Rolf. They all knew the ominous nature of those words in former times. There was no doubt, either from Heike's tone or her attitude, that an unpleasant scene awaited Günther. Sabine reached for her camera, hoping to get a snap of Heike and her beau. Nadine placed a restraining hand on her arm and shook her head.

* * *

"We'd better find out where Heike's hiding," Jürgen suggested. "Sabine, *kommst du mit?*"

"Ja, *gern.*"

That wasn't proper procedure as the plotters well knew. No one dared look at Rolf for fear of tipping their hand. He was no fool. He knew that Jürgen was off to the fest, but he grunted, out of habit, with just enough malice to create sweat production. Nadine, gambling that her father's attention on his paper was absolute, furtively sidestepped her way towards the door and slipped out just ahead of Sabine.

Rolf chuckled. His children couldn't be certain they'd gotten away with something. They were smart enough to know they hadn't, but they'd carry doubt throughout the evening. Perhaps, when they returned, he'd bark. With proper rationing, he could use this "mass escape" as a means of keeping them in harness for months.

"Well, Frau Jacobs, now that we've gotten rid of them, shall we have a nice walk?"

He wasn't sure how much his wife understood, but she recognized his gesture readily enough. After she rose and took his arm, they moved, without hurry, to the door.

Rolf Jacobs was a happy man. When his wife began losing her faculties, he was deathly afraid he couldn't hold the family together. He became a martinet to compensate for doubts and lack of child-rearing skills. He knew he could never take the place of a loving mother, so he maintained order through force and the threat of force.

It may not have been the best strategy, but he found no fault with it. He had a son and two daughters who were brave and independent. He was proud of them. Moreover, he recognized that none of them needed him to direct their lives. They'd proven themselves in Leipzig.

* * *

Lilo established a *Stammtisch* at one of the bright orange tables. The evidence of her premeditation consisted of the bulky pants and her equally bulky shirt. Her svelte figure was adequately disguised which, when coupled with her towering stature and sour visage, encouraged others to seek more convivial atmosphere. Hanna wasn't easily frightened and helped fill the space. Frau Willing gravitated toward the pair.

There were plenty of empty places when the Jacobs entourage arrived; the evening was quite young. No one suggested it might be better to avoid Lilo. If they avoided her, she'd join them eventually. It saved energy and angst to take advantage of the space she reserved. The extra-large blond was casual and unconcerned when the new arrivals settled in, but Sabine noticed the sharp glance she sent Günther and Heike. If Heike noticed, she disguised it.

Heike introduced Frau Willing and Sabine. As a spoon-carver, the unprepossessing bus driver could hardly be expected to observe established social norms. She did, however, respect the reunification of East and West in this one very special area: she stood and offered her hand. Sabine, struck with the awkwardness of the situation, fallowed suit.

On the platform serving as a stage was a folk group consisting of a bearded guitarist and a not very attractive female tambourine player. Their place on the entertainment bill was, apparently, determined by the early hour. The organizers realized there'd be fewer revelers to frighten away. The woman stood too close to the microphone and her partner too far away. The result was an ear-splitting shriek masking her partner. The guitarist was heard only when he began singing a shade too soon – or she came in a shade too late.

"They should be finishing up soon," Lilo reported.

Welcome news, confirmed by a team of four musicians gathering nearby.

"I haven't finished the roll yet," Sabine informed Hanna. "Can you send me the prints?"

"Snap away," Hanna grinned. "Heiko may not be here for a while."

Sabine nodded.

Despite Hanna's loose-fitting, sleeveless pull-over, her healthy chest remained much in evidence. Jürgen made certain that Marina was comfortably situated and asked to fetch her a drink of her choice. She observed ritual by denying thirst. When pressed, however, she asked for red wine. He played the game cheerfully, achieving his goal: the pleasure of serving her.

Noting (even in the DDR) chivalry was not dead, Sabine turned her attention to Günther.

It was *his* turn.

He and Heike sat opposite his friend and his Soviet fiancé. He noted Heike acquired a considerable audience among the not-yet-a-crowd strolling and lounging in the square. He didn't think it amusing when she straddled the end of the orange bench so that she'd not sit on her dress. It wasn't as immodest as the display they found so funny minutes prior, but the expression on Günther's face made his feelings clear.

Günther excused himself and headed for the mobile imbiss with Jürgen. Sabine didn't approve.

"Can I get you something?" she asked from across the table.

"Günther will bring me something," Heike assured casually.

"He didn't even ask," Sabine noted.

"He's *sauer*."

Sabine nearly pressed but checked herself. Instead, she extended an offer to Hanna who, of course, insisted it wasn't necessary. Sabine was in no mood to play games. She launched herself after the guys.

She asked for Orangensaft. The young man behind the counter with disheveled hair and a day's-worth of stubble, looked as if orange juice existed through his life without his ever being aware. Giving him extreme benefit of doubt, she asked for *Apfelsinesaft*. He didn't understand that either. She pointed at a large wooden crate filled with bottles of orange juice. It took him no time to extract a bottle, open it and pour out the amount required to fill two clear plastic tumblers.

"Drei Mark, Ossi," he said, apparently perturbed over her peculiar drink order.

Sabine had a Wessi five-mark coin; she was tempted to see what he'd do if she slapped it on the counter. She fancied he'd thank her and not bother making change. It was a foolish thought. The juice was Wessi.

Selling it at a Reichmark and a half was taking a loss. She counted out three "play-money" coins.

"Does your father work at a hotel?" she asked.

"Bitte?"

"Never mind."

Lilo and Frau Willing stood near the end of the brief line chatting merrily away. Sabine silently scolded herself for not asking if she could get them something. Hanna, who asked for nothing, flashed an appreciative smile when the juice was set in front of her. Marina sipped at her wine. Jürgen guarded a beer.

Sabine was tempted to ask Günther if there was an Ossi word for orange juice. Perhaps, when ordering, one was expected to exercise sign and countersign. She didn't bother. It wasn't important.

When Frau Willing returned with a beer, she detached herself from Lilo and sat next to Sabine and directly across from Heike.

"As you from America come, I speak to you, if is not to bother."

There was a trick to understanding Frau Willing. The words were couched in a queer dialect. Understanding her grammar was a challenge, but her syntax was an even greater one. As they chatted, however, Sabine's ear and brain adjusted with ease.

Yet again, she was peppered with questions about America. These, however, were light years from the norm. Frau Willing was interested in American busses, streets, and highways. When she was informed of the *Mary R.*, Frau Willing broke out in a rash of questions about sea navigation and all things mechanical.

From across the table came plaudits for the "spoon-carver" in the form of local history. Sabine learned Frau Willing routinely pulled maintenance on the city vehicles and, several times, fixed an engine or replaced a tire while on her route. Heike explained how the bus driver taught her to drive and shared a few "professional secrets."

"When driver have license not," Frau Willing chuckled, "is best to avoid attention too much, oder?"

There was a reference to the baby she delivered followed by a lively question and answer period. Inevitably, this led to the story of Inka Zimmermann's rescue. Despite the intervening months, the narrative was as melancholy in the retelling as it was in the original. That end of the table became very quiet.

"I knew that Heike with problem was good to leave," the woman said, deflecting attention from herself.

"The city should have handled this," Heike added, unwilling to play the heroine.

Frau Willing snorted.

"Country is falling apart," Frau Willing spoke disapprovingly. "Maybe, city do what city do, but baby and baby father need care. Heike care about people. Better when people do when people care, not do because orders say."

That left an unpleasant gap in the conversation. The band, an amazing string quartet, consisted of students from the music school fronting the square. It played a varied selection and generated a good deal of applause at the conclusion of each. When they began a waltz, Jürgen and Marina joined a score of other couples while the Zimmermann Saga continued. When the morbid tale ended and everyone thirsted for levity, no one rose to the occasion.

"Fräulein Bauer," Günther jumped in at last. "Do you waltz?"

"Yes," she replied with silent thanks to the Ghost of Musicals Past.

He got up, extended his hand, and guided her around the end of the table. Once on the dance floor, that is the cobble stones, Sabine was self-conscious. Her butt was sticking out, Günther's arm around her waist and his hand pressed against her back caused her emotions to race in directions she knew were improper. Concentrating on counting her steps compounded her problem. Günther, however, was practiced; he waltzed and talked at the same time.

"She knows," he whispered in her ear.

Sabine kept counting and pretended not to hear.

"She hasn't said anything, but she knows," he insisted.

Her hand in his, his arm around her, her brain keeping her feet in step and his introduction of a sensitive topic caused her to perspire more profusely than before.

"It was you who told her, wasn't it?"

"She's my sister," she hissed rapidly.

"You ingratiate yourself by revealing confidences? Perhaps, it was bribery?"

"*Moment mal*, Pal!" she protested.

If he read Huck Finn, he'd probably know *pal*. Regardless, Sabine's emphasis made certain the word wasn't complementary.

"Go on," Günther encouraged.

"She doesn't like secrets," she reminded. "You heard that morning. I don't like keeping secrets. Oh, Scheiße!"

"I won't break," he said simply after her minor misstep. "Just relax. Let's start again."

Further flustered by stepping on his foot, Sabine was ready to abandon this distasteful inquisition. She promised herself she'd break away if he crossed the line again. Until then, she was putting the dance into her mental scrap book. She'd never been attended by someone as handsome. She wanted to pretend the dance was more than what it was.

"Let's start again," he repeated, though in a different context. "I'm in love with your sister – let me do the talking, okay? I've been in love with her for years, but she was a child and there are laws. She's grown now, but I'm walking in a mine field. One false move and this thing will go bad."

"And Lilo?"

"Is that supposed to hurt?" he responded. "You can't make me feel any worse about it. I tried to convince myself that I could love someone else – someone my age. When I was in the army, I gave Heike the opportunity to live her life. When I came back to find no boyfriend – well, I let her know how I felt. I want her to wait for me, but I don't want to chain her up."

"You should have told her," she advised.

"I was afraid we'd fall into one of those war-time good-byes. I don't have to paint a picture."

Fortunately, not.

"If I gave into that – well that might put chains on her – on us both."

"It didn't matter to you," she dared.

"But I am not Heike."

"Thankfully I am."

"Bitte?"

"Forget it. How do you get chains off Lilo?"

"I wish I knew," he sighed. "I intend no offence, but there's a reason I asked you to dance and not one of the others."

The music stopped and Sabine fell out of his hold, but not gracefully. She stood and stared at him, adding to her mental scrap book.

"Maybe, they'll play another waltz," he suggested. "Let's wait a moment."

It was a long and uncomfortable moment. The quartet began an up-tempo number. Sabine didn't realize it was Bach. She might have suspected when she took an instant liking to it. Unfortunately, it was suited more to a highland jig than a waltz, so the dance couple executed a retreat.

"You should ask Hanna to dance."

"She makes me nervous," he confessed.

"Well, she's not in love with you. She told that much, but she likes you. Ask her. It costs nothing and I doubt anyone will get hurt."

She didn't confess her thoughts. As with a certain flower vendor, Sabine could have danced all night. Heike remained much as they left her. She noticed Günther taking her sister away to speak privately. When she scanned Sabine's sheepish expression, she smiled impishly. Sabine returned it.

Jürgen and Marina did their best to dance Wessi style. They weren't very good, but they had no experience; the Ossis had rules about dancing. They knew they looked ridiculous, but they were having fun.

"You enjoy, I think," Frau Willing smiled at Sabine.

"Frau Willing, of all the people here, you're the only addressing me as *Sie*. In Swabia we have a custom –"

"We, too, in the Wald where I come."

Sabine took up her orange juice in her right hand and held it high. Frau Willing mirrored the action and they rose to their feet. The rest of the assembly looked on as they linked arms and took a healthy swallow.

"Ich heiße Sabine."

"Ich heiße Annegret."

Annegret! Heike heard her new friend's forename for the first time. This was not uncommon in a country where one's neighbors and closest associates remained Herr and Frau to each other. Indeed, since the day Frau Willing first addressed her as Fräulein, Heike became *Sie*. Until Sabine called her attention to it, Heike never gave it a thought.

There'd be whispers and smirks. Regardless, Heike Jacobs swallowed her stubborn pride. She took up her drink, swept around the end of the table, and caught Frau Willing before she had a chance to resume her seat. As if it were planned, Jürgen and Marina were returning and were sure to witness a humiliation. Well, Heike thought, it was her fault for being remiss. Annegret wasn't merely a mentor; she was a friend.

"Now," Sabine announced with satisfaction, "we're all *du*."

As one, the others stood and toasted the occasion. Günther proposed and the others echoed.

"Du!"

"One moment, please," Jürgen injected. "May I propose a toast to the only Swabish-Ami in the DDR."

Warm smiles abounding, they drank up in salute to Sabine.

"We're Saxons," Sabine whispered, not inconspicuously, to her sister.

"Don't be pedantic, *Schwesterlein*," Heike whispered back.

"What the –" Sabine almost used Ed Barker's favorite word. "What is *pedantic*?"

"Read *Taming of the Shrew*."

Sabine didn't need to read anything. Heike called her *sister – dear sister* to be more accurate. Coupled with a radioactive smile, there was only one more thing Sabine could desire.

The music slowed. The quartet didn't play a waltz, but they came close enough.

"Hanna," Günther asked, "may I have this dance?"

Hanna was amazed. She thought nothing of the fact she couldn't dance. She accepted graciously.

"That was *your* doing!" Heike accused.

"Am I in trouble?" Sabine asked rhetorically.

"I wish I'd thought of it. Maybe, it's time to press my luck. Lilo, may I have this dance?"

Lilo's laser eyes snapped. It wasn't unusual for women to dance together, particularly at informal gatherings. Normally, however, the practice was predicated on a dearth of men and a surplus of spirits.

Liselotte Kruger was not, for all her tempestuous habits, devoid of humor. It was clear Günther wouldn't dance with either of them. Two "spurned" women could aim a joke at Günther and remain within the evening's theme of merriment. Lilo extracted her long legs by snaking them between bench and table.

"Who leads?" she asked.

"As badly as I dance, it won't matter," Heike admitted.

"Freundschaft."

When in doubt, employ the FDJ-sanctioned noun.

Sabine reached for the camera to get a photo of Mutt dancing with Jeff and, for good measure, Günther with a timid, but giddy Hanna. She was suspicious. Someone else had been taking pictures. There were plenty of suspects.

She crept about stealthily and got some good candid shots. It was a contest to see which came first, finishing the exposures, or the setting sun. Twilight wouldn't come before nine o'clock and darkness an hour or so later.

Sabine witnessed Annegret and Nadine repeating the *du* ceremony.

"It awkward is, for me," Annegret mused. "I mean, to be familiar with Werner Ecke's granddaughter seems not right."

"I had nothing to do with Grandfather's work," Nadine explained. "If he shows up tonight, we shall all use *Sie*."

Annegret nodded and turned to Sabine.

"When I start work here, everyone make fun of me – stupid peasant girl who talk not so good. Herr Jacobs, teach me how fix busses. Good teacher. He not care my talk not so good. Then, he have me to house and I meet Frau Jacobs, daughter of the great Werner Ecke. Even in the Wald we know this man.

"I expect his daughter to be such a grand woman, a great daughter of a great man. What I find is great woman who not think herself special because of father. She treat me like old friend and not to be bothered by peasant girl with not so good talking. Never make fun, never make jokes about spoon-carvers, never think me anything but good friend. I cry much when she go away."

It was an autobiographical entry which Nadine knew well, but she was visibly moved in the retelling.

"We all cried much when Mutti went away," Nadine admitted.

"You were blessed," Sabine said. It sounded trite, but it was heart-felt.

"And cursed," Nadine responded. "Something like that skips generations, doesn't it? I think my face, even before the 'accident,' might make me immune. I know what Jürgen and Marina must be thinking. Heike won't have to worry."

Sabine shrugged.

"Papa never said anything."

Nadine accepted that as a good sign.

"Not to curse darkness," Annegret warned. "Enjoy what is and accept what comes, no? Live life, think me, better than stop living because afraid, *oder*? And Nadine, you (a hesitant *du*) good woman are. Some man think good woman worth more than good face, but when not, I say life alone not so very bad. Good work, good friends make for happy enough. You (a bolder, more assertive *du*) always have good friends."

"Heike tells me that they can fix the face and teeth."

Annegret held out her hands and made a "just-as-I-said" gesture. Never mind that Nadine wasn't so attractive even before Leipzig. Was she being dark in fear for her children, or had she surrendered to disparagement?

There was no time for reflection or further exploration of that conversational tributary. Lilo was back. She wasn't in a foul mood exactly, but she situated herself curtly. For a heart-stopping moment, Sabine thought Heike might be bleeding to death on the cobble stones.

"Some guy cut in," she reported, wiping her brow with the back of her hand.

Sabine caught sight of Molly's dress. There was, of course, a trace of "*why-her-and-not-me?*" in her tone. Of course, Molly's dress attracted more flies than Lilo's suit of armor. Moreover, even Lilo noticed the interloper picked someone his own size.

"Should we give it a try?" Sabine asked of Nadine.

The girl shook her head vehemently. Maybe, she was too inhibited. Likely, she preferred to wallow in her "I'm-ugly" theme.

"Lilo?"

"Nein, danke."

Sabine reminded her that she didn't have to let some Klugscheißer cut in. If that upset her, she could prevent it from happening again. Lilo refused to argue the point.

"Annegret?"

"Not until they play polka," she giggled.

"A string quartet?" Nadine challenged.

"I don't polka," Sabine admitted.

"Me too not," Annegret replied, "but how can know anyone?"

Even Lilo laughed at that; the mood lightened decidedly. Except…

"I want to dance," Sabine pouted.

* * *

The quartet concluded with an unidentified number Sabine recognized from the Frankfurt concert. The student musicians gathered up their sheet music and put their instruments away, amid prolonged applause. The venue was getting crowded and, if the applause was any indication, serious music lovers constituted a majority.

Heike returned fatigued and beaded with sweat but wearing an electric smile. She had one man after another cutting in. Flattered but not overwhelmed by the attention, Heike wanted to dance as much as Sabine. Jürgen and Marina, referred to as "*the both,*" returned in a similar state of elation.

The group surrendered to the crush of the crowd. They'd been squeezed to one third of the table. It was very cozy. Heike studied Molly's dress for signs of dirt and damage before straddling the end of the bench. One knee dug into Günther's leg; he made no indication that he minded.

Hanna, bubbly from being guided about the square in Günther's arms, squeezed up against Sabine so much she threatened to send her tumbling off the edge. No one complained about the cramped quarters, and their objections over the price of orange juice doubling were subdued. Heike slapped Günther on the back and kissed his cheek. He was flummoxed. This was a betrayal of her habitual reserve.

He didn't respond well to her tactlessness. Heike asked what troubled him. Everyone knew, of course. However, only three knew that both Günther and Heike knew.

"I'm jealous," he responded. "You've danced with every man in town."

She found the hyperbole much funnier than it was. She was giddy.

"Don't think I didn't see how you were dancing with Hanna."

To prove the degree of her disapproval, Heike wrapped her hands around Günther's throat and made growling noises. Even Lilo failed to repress a smile. Hanna beamed at the jest; her imagination working overtime.

Little persuasive effort was required on Günther's part to get the ladies together for additional pictures. Hanna, Annegret, Lilo, Marina, Nadine and Sabine – all squeezed into a huddle around Heike and her amazing dress. They enjoyed the intoxication of fun and Freundschaft.

There was a spirited debate over a series of trivial matters, fought out with great zeal through exaggerated parodies of pompous bombast. There were no rules. By tacit agreement anyone who failed to keep a straight face while advancing their argument lost their case and was forced to yield.

Conversely, anyone who couldn't resist laughing at the raucous oratory was derided by both the speaker and the remaining "delegates." Even Annegret had a go. Her peasant grammar and woodland expressions gave her a decided advantage. Abandoning her habitual reserve, Nadine shook with laughter.

During this amusing interlude, Sabine expended the last of her film. She placed it in its plastic container, snapped the lid shut and stuffed it inside her mini backpack to keep company with her passports and her last clean set of undies. Heike was not so distracted by the verbal gymnastics that she didn't notice. Spying a blue document with gold lettering, her curiosity shifted into high gear.

"May I see your passport?" she asked.

Sabine had difficulty hearing over the din. Without hesitation, she handed over both documents. Heike suspected Sabine traveled under an assumed name but never bothered to ask. When she opened the German Ausweiss, she beheld the hand-printed information in the precise bureaucratic script so familiar to the Ossis.

In the right corner was the official photo held in place with chemical cement and two, small copper-ring staples. Sabine's picture was taken four years previously and resembled the dimpled visitor very little.

"Ka-TEE Fos-TER?" she struggled.

Jürgen was orating when he sensed sudden sobriety and broke off. Curious others focused on the twins. The sight of an official document was a dose of cold water on the proceedings.

"Ka-THEE," Sabine sounded carefully.

Heike asked for a repeat. The *th* sound was rare in Weimar. Thüringen, the state, and Gotha, a neighboring city, were pronounced with a hard T. Softening the combination is difficult for German speakers. Heike persisted, however, and managed to get within range of the English pronunciation. It was important: *Kathee* was her sister's alias.

"I've seen the name," she admitted. "I've never had to say it."

Heike turned to Günther.

"I've been saying it wrong!" she whined, referring to the bothersome *th*. "Why didn't you tell me?"

Günther replied in faultless English.

"How many times have we had conversations in English?"

"Why did you never tell me your name was Ka-THEE?" Heike demanded.

"Speak German," Annegret requested. "That is enough difficult for me, but English is too much."

"My name is Sabine," she responded. "Mutti gave it to me. What I used before isn't important."

"You never knew your name?"

"Not until a few days ago."

That took a while to comprehend. Heike realized the name Bauer was, also, days old. She examined the document further.

"This picture makes you look so ugly," she noted.

"Ausweiss photos are supposed to be ugly," Sabine insisted.

The jazz band mounted the stage began to play. It was the signature tune from *The Pink Panther*, familiar enough to the Ossi crowd to generate several nostalgic comments and a small smattering of applause. Amid a sudden attack of quiet, Günther came to the rescue.

"Care to dance, *Kathee*?" he asked, extending his hand to Sabine.

She took back her documents and stowed them. She slithered into the straps. She and her backpack got up.

Heike monitored them for a moment before looking squarely at Nadine.

"Ka-THEE?" she asked.

Nadine shrugged. She refused to replicate it without a complete set of teeth. They both rose as one and headed for the square. A young man, who loitered nearby, swooped in on the abandoned girl in the attractive dress.

"Care to dance?" he asked.

His boldness was not authentic. Heike judged him harmless enough. He was her age or slightly younger. And his visage was not unpleasant.

"They're your shins," she shrugged.

They followed Günther and Sabine to the dancing area. Nadine distinctly heard Heike question her dance partner.

"Do you know anyone named Ka-THEE?"

"Come, Hanna," Lilo ordered. "I'll get you a dance partner as well. Frau Willing can watch the camera until I get back. This won't take long."

Hanna was excited by the prospect though she lacked Lilo's optimism. However, it was worth a try. In any case, the table was too sober at that moment; she welcomed a diversion.

The band didn't play a waltz tempo. Once Günther got his arm around her and her right hand in his left, he led her in steps of his own invention. After she stepped on him and stumbled twice, she took his advice and relaxed. Swaying with him and adjusting to his gentle shifts in weight and direction, she followed him with ease; her only concern was maintaining balance. Magically, her toes unerringly found stone rather than leather.

She glanced at him with a smile of accomplishment on her face. He looked directly into her eyes and held them as gently, yet as surely, as his arm held her body close to his. Her heart raced. She thought, for one heartbeat, he would kiss her.

He didn't.

Ute Foster's memory book included drinking a beer with Jesus. Sabine Bauer trumped that with a romantic turn around an East German square in the arms of a very gentle, very handsome partner. Thinking of Ute was a mistake.

Sabine strove banish thoughts of her proxy-mother, but the damage was done. From Ute, Sabine's brain jumped to Gary and his standing, arms akimbo, while she served up an ace – then to Molly and the dress

Heike wore – then the romance between Heike and Günther. The circle was complete; the house of cards cascaded to ruin.

Here she was, in the arms of her sister's boyfriend, doing her best to fall in love with him. Who could be so base? Who could be so cruel? Short hours before, she cried over sacrificing Gary to be with her father.

Günther felt the change. Sabine's body tensed, and her brows narrowed. Serendipity escaped, and she ceased moving. A moment later, she stepped away. Spooked by her strange behavior, he let her go.

"Scheiße!"

The comment was not directed at him, but the vehemence struck hard. He watched in stunned wonder as she turned and began a rapid march for the market square. There was no premeditation in her action other than the desire to get away and clear her head. Maybe, a good cry would purge her toxins. She didn't deserve her sister, she was no longer certain she deserved her father.

Solitude!

If she had a few minutes, Sabine might find some way to deal with the shame that contracted around her like a malevolent serpent. In the depths of self-derision, she discounted the most essential feature of the Ossi spirit: no Genossin is abandoned.

Marina noticed the red culottes receding and alerted Jürgen who hurried after, trusting others would follow. Lilo was, predictably, dismissed by a young man eager to take a turn with the cute, busty brunette. Satisfied that her function for the evening had been dispatched, she was puzzled when Frau Willing and Nadine stood at her approach.

The bus driver grabbed the camera and moved around the table to follow Nadine. Instantly, Lilo did an about face and set off as well. Nadine whisked by Hanna on her way through the dancers.

"*Die Neue*," she announced.

Hanna required no explanation. She stepped away from her dance partner.

"Danke viel mals, aber –"

She couldn't complete the sentence. She didn't know why, but she realized her comrades were in a hurry. Motioning with her finger after her Genossin constituted the entirety of her excuse.

Heike completed a turn and caught sight of Günther alone. She detected no sign of Sabine; she followed his eyes. Unlike Hanna, she took no time to excuse herself.

"What did you do?" she demanded of Günther. "What did you say?"

"Nothing."

"Where is she?"

He gestured; she caught a glimpse of red with a very tall blond following with long strides. Heike took Günther's hand.

"Come!"

He snapped out of his coma and matched her pace. The entire fleet was under sail. They kept the blond beacon in sight and trusted her to maintain surveillance of Sabine. Consternation erupted when Lilo broke into a run.

She was first to overtake the expat. Sabine attempted to step around her only to find Jürgen closing fast.

"I have to be alone," she said. "I'm so stupid – I – *lass mich alein!*"

Jürgen wouldn't be ignored. He asked what was wrong. Sabine repeated her desire for aloneness.

"She thinks she's Greta Garbo," he whispered to his intended.

Many times, Jürgen's encyclopedic knowledge helped smooth over rough spots and keep friends and family upbeat. The Party constantly sprinkled fairy dust on the ignorant and the gullible, but Jürgen dredged up information not officially sanctioned. Reaching into his vault to formulate a jest left Marina with no point of reference. She knew nothing of by-gone film celebrities. She reacted on instinct.

Marina gently restrained Jürgen. With unexpected adroitness, she locked her other arm through Sabine's. Tacitly, she told Jürgen to remain where he was while leading Sabine away.

"If you wish to be alone, fine." she soothed. "But – I'm not leaving until I know you're okay."

Sabine was amazed at the Russian's mastery of English. Her calm voice and placid vocabulary reminded her of Ute. They continued to drift across the market square. There were few people milling about. The businesses, both commercial and official, were shuttered.

"When will I grow up?" she asked. "I'm so – so petty and weak."

"I don't believe it," Marina responded.

They stopped after gaining several meters of separation. Marina let go Sabine's arm. They stood, motionless, with little space between them.

The others caught up with Jürgen. By tacit agreement, they allowed Marina and Sabine a private exchange. They were surrounded by buildings. To leave the square, they'd have only four possible exits; two were behind them. There was no way Sabine could get away. They tacitly agreed to keep distance.

"What the devil?" Lilo asked.

"Something upset her," Jürgen reported superfluously. "Were you searching for a code book?"

The question was directed at Günther. Everyone understood his meaning.

"You know me better!"

"Of course," his oldest friend replied, "Sorry."

"Something set her off," Heike concluded, gruffly and with an accusatory tone.

"Maybe, she's knitting a Soviet flag," Hanna suggested.

Günther, an only child, looked first at Jürgen, who lived with two sisters. He found nothing in his expression. He looked squarely at Hanna.

"Can it do that?" he asked.

Hanna crossed her arms and rubbed them as if warding off a chill.

"Don't make this personal," she warned.

"*Verdammt!*" Günther whispered not daring to look at Heike.

Marina was doing most of the talking. Twice Sabine nodded her head. After the second nod, Marina stepped away and moved slowly towards the congregation. She looked over her shoulder to assure herself Sabine wouldn't bolt. When she got to Jürgen, she offered a silent apology for her recent treatment. Next, she looked at Heike.

"She wants to talk."

Heike went solemnly forward.

"What's wrong?"

"That's all I could get," Marina replied. "She wants you."

Heike took a deep breath. She didn't feel sisterly, but she was curious. Moreover, she considered compliance an obligation.

"Sabine says she doesn't deserve to be happy," Marina whispered, once Heike was out of earshot.

The remark directed at no one, but Nadine reacted.

"Scheiße!" Nadine said, quietly. "They're sisters, sure enough!"

"One of them will clear out tomorrow," Lilo reminded.

"Mist!" Hanna spoke up. "Will anybody be left around here?"

The others turned to stare at her. Hanna stood as she before, arms crossed and hands messaging them. She cared not that everyone glared at her, nor did she repent over employing a word she'd never exercised in public. She appeared to be pouting.

Just when things were becoming interesting, the Genossinn were scattering to the four winds.

"This look like football crowd at bad match," Annegret observed gruffly.

"She's right," Günther seconded. "Let's stand off a little and not look like a mob."

He set the example by moving, however slowly, toward the music.

Sabine told Heike everything. She had two reasons. First, she'd examined herself and despised her findings. If she was evil enough to be tempted, then she was weak enough to give in. Second, she warned Heike not to trust her.

Heike listened in silence. Sabine might be speaking in Braille for no more sense than she made. She couldn't imagine Sabine Bauer successfully vamping Günther – or anyone else. Her gorgeous dimples were alluring, but Sabine's personality was too transparent. Sabine would never let herself get away with anything contrary to her staid beliefs.

"I'm no good, Heike," Sabine said. "I wouldn't blame you if you never want to see me again but go to Papa – bitte! He deserves a daughter he can be proud of."

"You're still coming back?"

Sabine nodded.

"I can't live with myself if I don't. I'll do my best not to make him ashamed."

Heike knew how it felt to meet an obligation when lacking confidence.

"I can't imagine anything that would take Günther to Frankfurt/ Oder," she concluded. "I think we'll be safe."

"Aren't you angry at me?"

"Didn't we agree that we wouldn't keep secrets?"

Sabine averted her eyes and nodded.

"Then, how can you expect me to be angry?"

"But –"

"Run off with him, and I'll strangle you," she proclaimed. "Until then, I think I can handle it."

Sabine and her party had skirted the south side of the market square, marching past the Hotel Elephant with its dining room windows open to provide guests with free musical entertainment. The hotel patrons weren't the only people interested in the musical proceedings. On the east side of the square were five Soviet soldiers seated on and around the Neptune fountain.

Forbidden by both their government and military superiors from "mixing" with the locals, they contented themselves with loitering in the nearly deserted square to talk, smoke strong Georgian cigarettes and enjoy the music.

They wore the Russian wool and the black no-lace boots. They staked their claim at the fountain. Once ensconced, their presence discouraged locals from strolling too near.

The townspeople were no more interested in approaching the soldiers than the troops were interested in having them do so. Naturally, they were on their guard the moment Sabine made her dramatic entrance, but she showed no interest in approaching. The arrival of the entourage was more unsettling, though hardly threatening.

The soldiers were content to watch the drama. They speculated as to the nature of the performance and laughed at some of their more imaginative suggestions. They watched as a woman took red pants aside; however, all eyes were riveted on the girl in the blue dress. The dress was beautiful – and evocative; it was easy to imagine the Fräulein wearing it was equally so.

It was no surprise when the comparatively plain woman came back to fetch the blue dress. The soldiers liked the way the dress moved to the girl's hesitant gait. There was moderate interest in the animated discussion between blue dress and red pants. When the eclectic retinue slowly drifted back from whence it came, the soldiers were satisfied the drama was at an end.

Suddenly, one of the figures left the rest and began walking towards them. Someone swore. Soldiers hate to surrender a prepared position, more so when attacked by a lone, unarmed woman. However, they were under strict orders. If the woman insisted on taking over the fountain, they must retreat.

The figure halted suddenly.

"Soldiers of the Rodina!" she hailed with a loud voice, using crisp, perfect Russian. "Greetings, comrades."

There was a moment of hesitation.

"It's a trick," a soldier warned. "Potato choppers learn Russian."

"That well?" another challenged.

"Who the hell are you?" the senior among them demanded.

"Marina Sergeyovna," came the immediate reply. "My grandfather won the Order of the Red Banner during the Berlin Campaign."

"Take Berlin, did he?"

They snickered at that. The soldier who captured the German capital single-handed was a standard joke of long-standing.

"Almost. He lost both his legs in battle. Angermunde. He died in hospital."

The soldiers exchanged looks.

"She's one right pot," one concluded.

"She's trouble. I still think she's a spud."

"I wanna get a look at her close up," another murmured.

"She's probably got ugly she hasn't used yet," the timid one speculated.

"Don't look like it from here."

"Where the hell is Angermunde?"

"It's a spud name! That's good. The old man died in Germany."

While the debate continued, Marina Sergeyovna advanced slowly as the others behind her watched.

"Damn! She's too good lookin' to be German!"

"I ain't hangin' around to find out," the timid one announced. "If she's German, we're for it."

"Wait for me," another followed.

"What is it?" Sabine asked innocently.

"I don't know," Heike replied. "It looks like Marina spooked the soldiers."

The sisters hadn't forgotten the substance of their discussion, but they were interrupted by unexpected developments. Heike was quick to join her formation as she'd been slow to leave it previously. Her natural inclination was to take charge when a situation was vague.

"What was it?" Günther asked Heike.

"We'll talk later," she replied.

Sabine had no notion what Heike was about to do, but there was purpose in her step. She drew Günther off. The others, who halted their migration, watched Marina. Sabine thought her Russian friend might be courting trouble; she walked towards her.

If the soldiers made any threatening moves, the adjoining square was but a short sprint away. However, Sabine wanted to be near Marina – just in case. She wouldn't allow her newest friend to be alone.

Sabine didn't know Russian, but she sensed no sign of confrontation. She softly approached from Marina's left and halted a few feet behind. If she had to, she'd rush in and, hopefully, drag Marina to safety.

"What are you doing here?" Heike demanded of Jürgen.

"If she wanted me to go with her, she'd have invited me," he responded coldly.

He was nervous. He was offended by his sister's scold. It wasn't in his nature to abandon the woman he loved, but he wouldn't impose himself uninvited. Marina was a Soviet citizen. If she wanted to exchange greetings with Soviet soldiers, it was hardly tragic. Furthermore, his presence might stampede them. Two soldiers had already fled; Jürgen took comfort in their departure. Heike viewed Sabine stationed near Marina. That, she decided, was good. If something unexpected happened, Marina would not be alone.

"Somebody find the Vopos," Nadine suggested.

"Not yet," Heike said, taking command. "We aren't at war. If something goes wrong, you run for help."

"Me?" Nadine objected.

"It's your idea," Heike reminded.

Nadine didn't respond, but she knew Heike's real reason.

"This might not end well," Lilo mused, watching Marina and the soldiers negotiating across distance.

"That's why we're not leaving her alone," Heike replied.

"Can you understand what they're saying?" Günther asked.

"Just leafing through family albums," Jürgen replied in a soft voice. He monitored as much as possible.

"That's what it sounds like," Lilo confirmed.

"Russian Fräulein is sick for home, maybe," Annegret conjectured.

"I know she is," Jürgen replied as if he were at fault.

"See if we can't work out a treaty," Heike suggested.

"My Russian is fair," Lilo volunteered.

"Unless you go over on your knees, you'll frighten them," Heike injected. "I'm dressed for it."

"What does that mean?" Günther asked with more emotion than curiosity.

"How threatening do I look?" she responded in kind.

Nadine watched Heike walk slowly and calmly toward Marina. She swallowed hard when she passed Günther.

"You be ready, Günther Neubert," Nadine whispered. "Don't you dare let anything happen to her."

Günther convinced himself that Marina and the soldiers merely wanted to share nostalgia in a familiar tongue. Nadine brought him back to the ready. In reality, no one need do more than they had thus far to get into big trouble.

"Who are they?" the nearest soldier demanded, pointing to the others.

"Friends," Marina assured. "They won't start anything."

"We can't stand out here like this," the senior in rank decided. "There will be shit for sure."

"We can't talk here," the spokesman repeated.

"Vasile?"

Everyone turned to glare at Heike who squinted through the shadows.

"Vasile, is that you?"

Two soldiers turned to look upon the third.

"You know her?"

The baby-faced, stocky soldier looked at the blue vision with mouth agape. He didn't know her, he was sure. How did she know him?

"I see someone must have cigarettes," Heike resumed.

The Russian was mangled, but recognizable. The soldier looked at his right hand and appeared surprised to find a lit cigarette.

"There's a park on the other side of the palace," the spokesman announced, making a command decision. "We can meet across the river."

Marina agreed.

"What was that about?" Sabine asked when Heike drew near.

Heike explained. After the soldiers vacated the square, Marina followed at a discrete distance until they met up in the park. With that, Sabine hurried off toward the Russian girl.

"I'm not letting her go out there alone," Sabine announced.

Heike rejoined the others. On the way, she and her brother passed in opposite directions.

"Is this wise?" she asked.

"Maybe not," he concluded, "but I'm not going to dictate to her."

Heike walked directly to Günther and put her arms around him. He held her.

"Scared?" he asked.

"Not as long as you're around."

"You won't leave me, will you?" Hanna asked.

"We could all get in big trouble," Nadine reminded.

"Then, why are you going?" the cute girl demanded.

Lilo looked at Heike secure in Günther's arms for only a second before storming off to join Marina and her escort.

"I must get the camera to Heiko," Hanna reminded. "I can't go."

"Know you trees by Kegelbrücke?" Annegret asked.

Hanna did.

"I meet you there."

Hanna set off at a trot for the festival and alive with the hope that Heiko would arrive early. The market square was deserted save for the Russian, and a few couples making their way towards the fest. The locals and the transients from the Hotel Elephant decided it was wiser and safer to be elsewhere.

Marina gave the soldiers a sufficient head start before following. Seven wary people shadowed her. They treaded carefully on the path, through the park, and across the quiet river. Marina spearheaded the advance with Sabine at her elbow.

The nervous girl turned frequently to make sure that Günther, Jürgen and the imposing Lilo were only a few meters away should they be required. Marina didn't speak, but she made no signs of resenting her escort.

The DDR was about to fall under Wessi control; that meant NATO. Soviet and Ossi authorities punished unsupervised contact between their respective populations. The Wessis might consider unsanctioned congress an act of treason. Every Ossi knows how duplicitous Wessi authority is. It was not yet dark, but the sun was sufficiently down to make figures in the distance appear as sharply defined silhouettes. Perhaps fifty meters distant was a figure with one hand in a pocket and a red glow on the other.

"Where are the others?" Sabine asked nervously, checking to make sure her posse followed.

"This one will take us to them."

They drew nearer. The lone soldier moving off the path and into the high grass.

"My father – my Ami father was a soldier," Sabine explained. "He told me enough stories about Soviet soldiers. They aren't very nice."

"These are my countrymen," Marina reminded. "They have no weapons."

Sabine kept her peace, but she gulped and checked over her shoulder. When they reached the place where the soldier crushed out his cigarette, Marina and Sabine followed him into the grass. Roughly twenty meters off the path, there was a small copse rimmed by untended bushes. They saw the glow of the cigarette as another soldier took a long drag. Within a few feet, Marina stopped, Sabine was happy to follow her example.

"So, Marina Sergeyovna, who is this?" the soldier motioned with his cigarette hand.

"A young friend. There are others, following. They are all friends."

"Germans?" he asked, suspiciously.

"Friends," she repeated. "They are afraid for me."

"The Indians and the American cavalry," a voice came from somewhere in the copse. "Maybe, we smoke peace pipe and hunt buffalo!"

This generated nervous laughter from the spokesman and his unseen person companions.

"We must be careful," the smoking spokesman cautioned.

"Understood, Comrade. My friend here comes from America."

That got their attention. The laughter ceased to be replaced by an ominous silence.

"You have strange friends, Marina Sergeyovna."

"A friend is a friend," she stated simply. "There can be nothing less strange."

"Well said," a voice from the darkness concluded.

"You want to smoke peace pipe?" the spokesman extended his cigarette.

"I don't smoke, Comrade, but I give my word we won't make trouble or bring harm."

Sabine felt her knees trembling. Thankfully, it was too dark for anyone to notice, but her fear was compounded by being talked about in a language she didn't understand.

"There's someone back there," another voice from the shadows announced.

"I have more than one friend. They're the people from the square."

"Why did they stop?" the only visible soldier demanded.

"They weren't invited. We thought it best to come ahead. I'd ask them to leave, but they won't. If you wish, I'll tell them to stay where they are."

There was a brief conference. Three soldiers weighed their options. As soldiers, they knew that an unseen enemy is much more dangerous than those under observation.

"She's okay," someone suggested. "There's plenty of room here."

That, apparently, was the deciding vote.

"Get the others?" Marina asked of Sabine.

"Just call out," Sabine replied, her quivering knees influencing her voice.

"How would they know they don't have a gun to my head?"

"Probably because they don't have any," Sabine quickly replied.

"There's a way to do these things," Marina hissed quickly, "One of us has to reassure the others that it's safe while the other stays here as a hostage. Bring them, please."

"You get them."

Marina didn't argue further. Their conversation in German renewed suspicions. Marina thought it brave for Sabine to remain alone. It was not, of course, brave. Sabine's weak and quaking legs wouldn't support her.

It was tense; the soldiers engaged in a hurried conference. One became agitated and another asked a question. Sabine assumed the question was aimed at her since the spokesman glared at her, expectantly. His attention was arrested by disturbance in the long grass. A sizable body drew near.

Marina was arm and arm with Jürgen whom she quickly introduced in Russian. Then, one at a time, the others came forward and were introduced.

"That's all," Marina assured.

Six Germans and an Ami constituted a queer definition of "that's all," but the soldiers appeared placated enough for their "leader" to escort the group a few more feet until the shapes of his two companions became clear. Heike found the one she knew even in the darkness. She knelt beside him and, in her very broken Russian, reminded him of how they met.

Günther kept close and Lilo, whose Russian was the best, settled down nearby to provide translations. Marina and the soldiers chatted merrily in rapid bursts. Jürgen remained close but had little interest in the proceedings. Annegret and Nadine were left to entertain each other; Sabine found them the most promising company.

Soon enough, Sabine was called forward by Marina. Vasile and his attendants moved in to be a part of the audience.

"They've never known anyone from America," Marina explained. "They know you don't have a swimming pool and you haven't met any movie stars."

"Thanks," the girl replied, her patience for fielding those questions was exhausted.

"Didn't you say your grandfather raises sheep? I want to get it right."

"He did. He sold out and retired."

Marina translated and fielded responses.

"They say you must be a peasant. These are all peasant sons. This one, Nicoli, is from a village two hundred kilometers from Leningrad. Andri grew up on a collective farm southeast of Moscow. Vasile, over there, is from Georgia. Believe me, when these men call you a peasant, it's a compliment."

Sabine was encouraged to speak of her life on the ocean. She prudently avoided any references to life as an army brat. Marina translated in minute-long bursts. The soldiers weren't the only interested listeners; the silent German contingent eagerly absorbed every word. They'd heard some of the narration, but the Russian questions were pin-point precise. These added considerably to their knowledge of Heike's sister.

They wanted to know every detail of the *Mary R.,* the whales, the seals, and her school. When she mentioned the community theatre, they insisted on knowing the measurements of the stage, the playhouse, and the parking lot. They thirsted to know about costumes, lights, and acting tricks.

The interrogation continued until Annegret excused herself to fetch Hanna, this renewed trepidation. It was possible the bus driver was in search of a policeman or other Germans who might not be amiable. Far worse was the fear she'd return with a Soviet officer. Marina vouched for Frau Willing. That eased much of the tension because the soldiers remained satisfied Marina was "one right pot." Nevertheless, Annegret's departure was followed by a prolonged silence.

It had to be Heike.

Unexpectedly, she boosted morale. She began softly singing *Die Internationale.* Everyone knew the melody, of course, and, save for Sabine, the lyrics. The Germans joined Heike and, soon enough, the soldiers jumped in with gusto. It mattered not that they sang in two languages, everyone's blood, including Sabine's, raced.

The moment the socialist anthem ended, one of the soldiers sang a Russian folk song in a bold baritone. The lyrics were Russian, but the Georgian joined in almost at once. Moments later, they became a trio. When they finished, Lilo started an FDJ campfire song. The other

Germans joined her. The Russians began with another folk song, followed by another FDJ selection.

"You're not singing," Nadine teased Sabine.

Die Neue didn't respond. None of the songs the Germans revived were known to her. She felt a fool to sit quietly while everyone else had a grand time. For her the sing-along stretched into eternity.

There was a momentary break when Annegret returned with Hanna. The soldiers wanted to be sure these two were the only arrivals. They listened carefully between bursts of interrogation.

Hanna was eager to expand her horizons. She was interested in anyone from the outside world. Lilo had been abroad and related "exotic" experiences; Sabine sailed on the Pacific; Marina and the soldiers were from beyond the horizon. Save for a family journey to Leipzig and Dessau, she'd never been outside Thüringen.

Hanna's Russian was indicative of her keen interest in everything foreign. She wasn't as fluent as Lilo, perhaps, but she understood most of what was said. She attempted translations and helped Lilo when Marina was occupied on the other side of the group.

She was particularly interested in Vasile, Heike's "boyfriend." He added verbal snapshots of home. The young man was so gregarious, his soldier friends frequently cautioned him about saying too much.

Vasile realized, if they get caught, there would be trouble. Any *security lapses* would be harshly met. In a country where telephone books were rare because of the "sensitive" information contained within, Vasile was not alone in his fear of paranoid Soviet State.

Annegret, the spoon-carver, had knowledge of Russian limited to whatever might appear on the Soviet equipment she saw on busses or in the shop. She was interested in listening to the soldiers. Hanna was mesmerized, and Nadine exhibited clear signs of the awakening of her long absent effervescence.

"I must to go," Annegret announced.

"Me too!" Sabine echoed. "One glass of juice was too much."

"No, Sabine. I must sleep. My work begin at ten of clock, and it not good if enough sleep haven't."

There was general laughter. Someone translated the nature of Sabine's problem.

"Just go into the bushes," Lilo suggested.

Lilo, Nadine and Günther had excused themselves during the choral interludes, but their journeys were not openly advertised. Everyone knew Sabine's problem. She was unbearably embarrassed. An announcement in Russian won the laughter of the other soldiers and the bilingual Germans.

"He says, if anyone interrupts you, they must answer to the army," Marina translated.

Sabine wasn't amused. She'd been around soldiers and knew how they should look. These pathetically blowsy Russians didn't look competent enough to dig a slit trench. Nevertheless, the longer she tarried, the more urgent her need, and the more humiliating the circumstances.

"Don't leave before I get back," she pleaded of Annegret.

She did her best to ignore the send-off she got in two languages.

Before she returned, Annegret began singing a folk song from the Wald. Sabine was unable to make out the bulk of the text. The bus driver's voice was poorly modulated, and her inability to strike a proper note made her offering painful. The dialect was so thick, the auditors were forced to guess at and translate the lyrics. Despite her handicaps, Annegret earned a rousing ovation. It was a salute to her courage.

"I used to sing this as a little girl," she explained, giving a summary of its contents.

Vasile sang next. His voice was as abrasive as the bus driver, but he managed to avoid straining the tune through barbed wire. It was moderate in length and melancholy.

"What is he singing?" Sabine asked Marina.

"I don't know," she whispered back. "It must be Georgian."

Vasile, also, garnered a nice round of applause for a song of the Black Sea. He did not elaborate.

Jürgen sang "Lili Marleen."

This song must be in the blood of every German. One of the first Nazi defeats of World War II resulted from the government's attempt to prohibit military radio stations playing that song. The troops continued to sing it and demanded a resumption of its airing. Soon, the Nazi Party countermanded its own order.

The tune crossed the lines. British and American soldiers commandeered it. There were documented cases of German and Allied troops singing together across their positions at night. Aaron Foster was first subjected to it soon after he enlisted; he sang it occasionally over the roaring of the *Mary R.*'s engines.

The Russians, apparently, escaped the virus. They listened approvingly as the Germans joined as one to render this odd, historical melody. Sabine knew only a smattering of lyrics in English and fewer in German. Nevertheless, she sang what she knew and hummed the notes of unknown text. When the group stumbled over the second verse, they followed Jürgen's lead. Finally, they repeated the first verse.

The Germans applauded themselves energetically.

The man tacitly elected the soldier's spokesman said something to Marina. Though directed at her, his voice was loud and commanding. Sabine's stomach knotted when she detected a reference to America.

"He says that we haven't heard from the Ami yet."

"I just sang," Sabine objected.

Marina passed on the information. With no need of translation, Sabine realized her excuse was rejected. She reminded them, through Marina, she wasn't an Ami. This feeble excuse was neither translated nor conveyed. The German contingent urged her to sing something.

"Sing what?" she asked, stalling for time.

They suggested the National Anthem, but Sabine knew it contained notes she couldn't reach with a ladder. The Brenda Lee songbook flashed by, but none of these selections were suited for a cappella. The more she thought, the less she retrieved. The others, however, were both persistent and incessant. Finally, to quell the commotion, she opened her mouth wide and sang a single note.

She hit it perfectly and held it.

Suddenly, everyone was still.

The note hung, unchanging, in the warm summer air. She paused for breath and started the theme. There were no words. She sang vowels, until ceasing a few seconds later.

"This is silly!" she announced.

"Go on, go on!" Jürgen encouraged.

"Bach," Nadine recognized.

"Bach?" Heike replied incredulously, recalling the scene in the market square.

"They want you to go on," Marina transferred the wishes of the suddenly boisterous soldiers.

Sabine suspected they were either humoring her or plotting something. Well, they asked for it. She cleared her throat and began anew. Every note was burned into her brain by repeated playing on Shelly's machine. It flowed effortlessly through her head, and she voiced each note from memory. She struggled to maintain the tempo. In her nervousness, she wanted to race, but she resisted the urge. It took most of five minutes to reach the final note.

Silence.

Not a person moved, not a sound was heard. Sabine was defeated, but they goaded her into it. If they didn't like it…

"I sure know how to kill a party," she whispered, leaning on Annegret's shoulder.

"It was beautiful," the peasant bus driver replied. "I'm glad I stayed to heard it, but I must, must leave or tomorrow not too good is."

Thinking she'd worn out her welcome, Sabine offered to walk with her. Before she could execute her plan, the soldiers were on their feet. Each one wanted to shake her hand and wish her well before she left. Then, by general consent, the evening's détente concluded.

* * *

As the youngest, Sabine waited for the bathroom. The great advantage was she could take her time. Because Lilo lived in an apartment building, showering was prohibited after ten o'clock. That didn't prohibit her from filling the sink and scrubbing thoroughly.

She felt relieved and refreshed when she padded barefoot back to the adjacent bedroom. The light was on. Molly's dress hung in its usual place with no visible signs of having spent the night out. Heike lay on her side with one leg atop the thin blanket. She breathed heavily.

Sabine backed out cautiously. She'd noticed a light filtering from under Lilo's door and assumed she was awake. Dropping her clothes, Sabine padded past the arch of the kitchen and knocked softly on the Amazon's door. There was an audible, if muffled, invitation to enter.

Lilo wore her blue shorts and a long white t-shirt. She sat atop her bed, her back against the headboard, her feet wide apart, but her knees drawn together. A book was held open against the incline of her legs. On her nose was a pair of small, black-rimmed glasses.

"I wanted to thank you for having me," Sabine said softly. "And – to ask a favor."

"You got bit tonight, didn't you?"

Sabine lifted the sleeve of her t-shirt to examine, for the third time, the redness on her upper arm.

"It's just heat rash," she explained. "It won't last."

"I meant Günther."

Sabine was flustered.

"He never – oh!"

"Yeah. *Oh*! That's why you ran away."

Sabine felt redness travel up her neck and across her face.

"You'll get over it," Lilo added.

Die Neue had suffered enough.

"Like you did," came a sarcastic reply.

The former distance runner never batted an eye. Perhaps, seeing Heike in Günther's arms took some of the wind from her sails. Perhaps, she'd experienced a reconciliation with her own feelings. Whatever the cause, umbrage remained dormant.

"I grew up with Günther. I know him as well as I know my own parents. You just met him. He wasn't very good tonight, was he? You took command. I was disappointed. Perhaps, I expect too much of him."

Sabine was momentarily awe struck by the calm assurance of the speaker. There was no regret in her tone. Further, there was no hint of bitterness. For a fleeting moment, Sabine reviewed what Hanna meant about being in love with someone *like* Günther.

"A favor, you said," Lilo prompted to bring her visitor back to the moment.

"It depends on you not killing my sister."

It was Lilo's turn to blush. She averted her eyes and shifted uncomfortably on her perch.

"I'm ashamed for – *that*," she repeated. "I'll be careful. I promise. Heike is too important to me."

Here, she looked through her glasses at the girl standing at the foot of her bed to see if her words sounded convincing. It was difficult to read the Ami.

"One day – soon, Heike will want to meet Papa."

"Are you sure?"

Sabine nodded emphatically.

"So, she writes to you; you tell her where to find him," Lilo concluded.

Sabine looked nervously over her shoulder. She exercised affrontery by closing the door. It was an action worthy of reprimand, but there were certain times when risks are worth the taking.

"I think I know Heike enough to know she runs hot and cold. When she gets the notion, she'll want to leave for Frankfurt that very hour. If she must wait for word, she'll talk herself out of it."

Lilo made a face. It was disturbing that this annoying visitor was so perceptive. It was possible Sabine knew Günther better than Lilo suspected. That made things more complicated.

"Leave the address with Nadine."

"She doesn't like me," Sabine informed casually. "Nor Herr Jacobs either. They think I want to steal Heike. I suppose, I'd feel the same in their place, so I can't get an attitude over it. The only one I trust is Jürgen, and he's leaving."

"I'm not leaving."

Sabine nodded.

* * *

Sabine slid into the bedroom. Heike remained in a deep sleep. She left her clothes on the floor. Better not to risk disturbing Heike than to pack her things. She switched off the light, resenting the loud click it made.

Slowly, she padded the few steps to her bed, pulled off her t-shirt and settled down onto the mattress as if it were made of glass. She felt a sense of relief after her talk with Lilo.

Everyone praised Sabine's voice and her selection which ended the "unofficial" social function. During their return Heike avoided her. The younger sibling was much concerned. Had she offended her sister?

When the couple parted at Herderplatz, Sabine watched her sister and Günther exchange a lingering kiss. There was just enough artificial light to lend a surreal dimension to the scene. Lilo saw, turned on her heel and strode away before the performance ended. Sabine drank it all in, heavily spiced with the salt of anxiety and the bitterness of envy. When the pair separated and pursued different paths, Heike saw Sabine waiting for her on the edge of the square; she hesitated for a moment before crossing to the other side.

Sabine could take a hint. She followed Lilo who had built a considerable lead. Hanna waited in the shadows unseen until *Die Neue* was within a few steps. A movement startled her.

"I thought you'd gone on ahead," Sabine growled more out of fright than resentment.

"It's my big night out," the girl confessed. "I danced with Günther. If I couldn't kiss him, I'm glad someone did."

So, she'd been spying. Sabine swept by Hanna and tried to match Lilo's pace. It was fruitless to gain ground or even hold her own against those long strides, but she did her best. Behind her, she knew, was a sister who, pointedly, loathed sharing the same street.

"Hey!"

Hanna sprinted a few steps to catch up. She grabbed Sabine's arm and jerked her back into a civilized gait.

"What is with you two?"

Sabine had a reasonable explanation, but it was the property of the Bauer sisters. If shared, it would be Heike's doing.

"An hour ago, Heike looked at you as if you were Werner Ecke himself."

"Hanna, I don't think that's even a little funny!"

"Funny? If I tried being funny, I'd be more clever than that."

That stilled the Ami for a few moments during which Hanna expected some acknowledgement of her existence. When none came, she tugged on the arm she still held captive.

"It was dark," Sabine snorted.

"Oh, you're still alive. Good. Did you notice how Lilo kept near Günther's side? There was Heike down on her knees for, practically, ever – trying to keep that precious dress from getting soiled, but I felt it.

One of those two was going to do or say something unpleasant. I worked my way between them."

"Getting closer to Günther," Sabine finished.

"I admit, my pulse went up a bit," the girl confessed. "Still, I was close enough to Heike to see her face – even in that poor light."

Sabine wanted to believe, but she continued to look at the matter through Heike's eyes. Knowing what she knew, how could she feel anything but disgust for the interloper?

"It was dark," she said doggedly. "No matter what you thought you saw, you didn't."

Hanna wouldn't be baited. She knew what she had seen and wouldn't be bullied into doubt.

"When you started singing – I got chills, Sabine. It's a beautiful piece, I know, but – well, I've never heard a voice like that. You're very good."

"Thank you, Hanna," she said, discovering her chance. "What did Heike think?"

"She was crying."

"What!"

"The whole time! There were few tears running down her face, but there was a bucket of water in her eyes. I thought she was going to fall apart, but – ha! Heike never cries! She knelt there like a statue so no one would notice."

"Günther?"

"He was a slightly behind giving the sweet-sugar back message; he couldn't see her face. It was so funny but so pathetic. She couldn't wipe away the tears without drawing attention to herself, so she let them go. You don't have to believe me, but don't tell me I didn't see."

Sabine looked over her shoulder to find a lone figure following in the darkness.

"So, why is she angry with me?"

"She's afraid."

"Hanna! You can't expect me to believe that."

"I don't care if you do or not," came a calm reply. "I've seen her act that way around Inka. It isn't you that frightens her."

Sabine checked over her shoulder again to make certain the shadowy figure remained on station. Why would Heike be unnerved? She'd had plenty of time to come unraveled since they met on the Frauenplan.

"According to Lilo, Heike isn't afraid of anything."

"Not of anything out there," she gestured with her free hand.

Sabine lay in bed listening to her sister sleep. How, she wondered to the point of distraction, could someone so angry or, if Hanna was right, so frightened, and sleep so soundly?

Not a word was exchanged between sisters upon entering the apartment. Lilo and Sabine went directly to the refrigerator and gulped down juice mixed with water to replace the pounds of liquid they'd lost during the evening. Heike made directly for the bedroom and removed her dress.

When Lilo shut herself in the bathroom, Sabine remained at the kitchen table half hoping and half fearing Heike would join her. The moment Lilo retreated into her room, Heike rushed to the bathroom. Sabine took her glass to the sink to wash and rinse it studiously and realized that was best to stay out of the bedroom.

After Heike was safely behind a closed bedroom door, Sabine hurried to the bathroom not a moment too soon. She rid herself of her shirt and the culottes she'd leave behind. A basin bath and freshly scrubbed teeth made her feel human again. Printing her father's address on a notepad by the phone made her feel even better.

Upon finding Heike slumbering peacefully, she dropped her exterior clothes and conferenced with Lilo. Fatigue quickly drew her thoughts away. Heike's breathing was reassurance enough that matters were sedate enough for the moment.

What woke her? Was it some noise Heike made, or was it an unexpected movement? It was amazing to discover herself in a sitting position and wide awake. A chill went through her body at these disturbing happenings. The last she remembered, she was on her side snuggling up to her pillow then, seemingly, an instant later, she was sitting straight-backed and staring into the darkness.

She couldn't hear breathing! Had Heike closed the door behind her on her way to some nocturnal appointment. Perhaps, that's what startled her awake. She threw her feet to the floor and made ready to pursue when she heard an unidentified but muffled noise from the other bed. It was difficult to see more than blurred shadows, but Sabine realized Heike was seated on the edge of her bed, leaning forward with her arms folded across her knees. The sound of her breathing came in short, shallow spurts.

"What is it, Heike?" Sabine asked, forgetting they weren't on speaking terms.

"What's wrong?"

"Nothing," a croaking, almost baritone voice responded.

"Nothing, my sweet Savannah!" Sabine scoffed, lifting a phrase of Athena's from some long-forgotten crevice.

She was on her feet and in the kitchen in record time. She was heedless to any possible obstacles and relied on her memory to guide her to the refrigerator. She leaned forward and found the handle.

There was no light inside, but she found the bottle of orange juice without difficulty. Similarly, she unerringly found the glass exactly where she left it. She poured it half full of juice and mixed that with water from the liter bottle Lilo kept next to the sink.

When she returned to the room, Sabine judged she'd pushed her luck far enough and switched on the light. The sight of Heike sitting on her bed, hugging her knees, and squinting vacantly startled her.

"Drink this."

Heike was surprised by Sabine's approach, but the glass was too tempting! She untied herself, slapped the floor with one foot, and accepted the mixture. It disappeared in seconds.

"More?"

Heike shook her head. Sabine resisted reaching for the glass.

"What is it?" Sabine asked again when Heike resumed staring at the wall.

"*Verdamnt noch mal!*" she replied bitterly. "I was dreaming about Leipzig – again!"

"Again?" Sabine asked, retreating to her bed. "How often does this happen?"

"Not often."

As the silence that followed, Sabine realized it is possible for a person to have nightmares while awake. It was a disservice to remain silent, but Sabine was at a loss.

"Want to talk about it?"

It was the best she could muster.

"No, I don't want to talk about it!"

The weight of the message was magnified many times by clearly enunciated English. It left Sabine with nothing. However, Heike was concentrating on something other than a dream. Heike allowed her sister to retrieve the glass, wash it and return it from whence it came.

Heike sighed with great relief. The quaking inside was fast receding, but a few chilling tremors raced about. Four times since the terror in Leipzig, Heike saw Nadine's bloody form dragged away with Heike screaming and helpless, unable to get to her. The theme remained the same, Heike lost hold of Nadine; her incompetence won Nadine a smashed face.

On this hot, July night, the dream took a more sickening turn. There was no restraint; Heike was free to move. She saw the hooded Vopo raise his stick. It was possible for Heike to rush forward and arrest that malevolent arm, but she saw another hulking Vopo raising his black bat.

At his feet knelt an amazed Sabine. Her braids were clutched in the policeman's other hand; he used them to draw her head back. He intended to crush Sabine's face! Heike was free to move; she had time to stay a single blow.

She hesitated; Heike hesitated! She was free to make a choice but froze. Whack! Whomp! The Vopos left both girls lifeless in pools of blood. Heike screamed an obscenity. The Vopos eyed her briefly before marching past her.

Heike wasn't worth notice!

This shook her from slumber. The image of two bleeding corpses was horrific. Heike's hands shook. She wondered if she could ever sleep again. It was a relief to see Sabine alive and whole.

"Fräulein Modesty isn't wearing a pajama tonight," Heike observed, grasping for reality.

"You were asleep," Sabine replied, self-consciously.

Heike watched the girl in discolored bra and panties sit down on her bed and make herself small. Despite her recent fright – perhaps, because of it – Heike laughed.

"At home, we think nothing of running around like that."

"In front of Rolf and Jürgen?" Sabine asked incredulously.

"Of all the simple pleasures, walking around in next to nothing on hot summer nights rates very high. We're family."

This had the greatest influence on Sabine. Did immodesty define the family? If so, Sabine was doomed to be forever denied. As if to underscore the theme, she went to her bed and plucked the t-shirt off the floor and pulled it on.

It was Lilo's. The shirt formed a tent which covered Sabine nearly to mid-thigh. Heike watched the entire performance with an amused expression; seeing her sister ambulatory in life was a reassurance that her terrifying dream was, alas, a dream.

"Make fun of me," Sabine dared and returned to her bed.

"Why?"

* * *

They left Lilo's apartment with sheets and pillowcases to be cleaned in the Jacob's vat. Breakfast was very much like all the others Sabine experienced since her arrival. There was, however, more banter than normal. Were it a normal day, no one would speak unless Rolf gave them leave. Amazingly, he'd become exceptionally tolerant whenever guests were present.

Marina was more beautiful than ever. Sabine considered Jürgen as special as his sisters to win the heart of such an intelligent and attractive girl. Should the Soviet stand shoulder to shoulder with Molly Waldron, it would be difficult to say which was more alluring.

Sabine recognized Molly was a creation of her mother's expectations and the daughter's effort to avoid disappointment. Marina, on the other hand, needed no prodding; she brushed her hair in the morning and, if she applied make up, it was minimal. Sabine never caught her lingering in front of a mirror.

Sabine, the intruder, was ill-clothed, unkempt, and careless of speech. If Rolf's growl was moderated, it was his enchantment with his future daughter-in-law and not because of anything Sabine brought to the table. Still, he was tolerant with her and, frequently, deferential.

Typically, Marina helped Nadine clean up. Heike arranged earlier. In return for remaining house-bound, Nadine would have the following day to herself. The Trabi was loaded with Jürgen and Marina's luggage. They hugged Frau Jacobs good-bye and Nadine as well. Rolf received a polite handshake from each.

Sabine shook Nadine's hand and then Rolf's. No one was keen, but none would spurn ritual. When turning to say good-bye to Frau Jacobs, she found herself in the woman's arms. She hugged Sabine as fervently as if she were of her own.

Marina sat in the roomy front seat – *roomy* being a relative term in a Trabi. Jürgen and Sabine contorted into the back seat. Heike drove to the station prior to hurrying to Lilo's to fetch her sister's suitcase.

Lilo arranged for the morning off. She was at the station, standing like a figure in an Icelandic saga while the principals waited in line at the ticket window. The moment Jürgen began his transaction, Lilo swooped in, gathered up the couple's luggage and hurried to the tunnel. Sabine watched her go and marveled at the ease with which she transported the stuffed cases.

It took a while for her ticket. The RB employee was not familiar with Fürth; she aided him in geography. He consulted two bound volumes before he could make out a ticket and announce the fare.

Sabine peeled off a series of Ossi bills from her impressive collection and traded them for the document. She cleared the ticket window and waited patiently at the wide double doors for Heike's return. It was cooler there. The station's tunnel facilitated a welcome draft.

The Trabi sputtered and smoked to a stop in a clearly identified no parking zone. Heike jumped out and opened the trunk. Together, they hoisted "that damned case" out of the car and onto the cobblestones.

"I'll park and return," Heike promised.

There was no time for Sabine to protest. She feared Heike might keep on driving. She decided that battling with her luggage was her most essential task. She knew where Heike lived.

"We will meet again," she muttered.

Sabine worried about her return. Where would she obtain the money? A one-way fare to Berlin and an hour train ride to Frankfurt would be cheaper than a round trip, but…

That was eleven months away. Perhaps, she could get a "real" job, one that paid "real" money and not the under-the-table trinkets Barker offered. Well…she had hours of train travel to ponder the issue, but a resolution would have to wait until she got home.

Home?

Pausing to catch her breath at the top of the stairs, she found Günther standing in a knot of familiar people on the platform. They had discussed taking the same train. Apparently, he intended to do just that. Lilo towered by his side. Heike's arrival might not prove serendipitous.

"I think we're waiting for the same train," Günther announced once Sabine drew near.

The announcement shot through Sabine like an arrow with a shaft of ice. If Heike and Lilo didn't try to kill each other, they might ally long enough to kill her.

"I've never been in the West before," he continued. "Maybe, you could help me."

"The trains run on time," she cautioned. "Why go through Fulda?"

"If I go through Berlin, I must change four times," he reported.

On the *Deutsche Reichbahn* that could take days! Changing in the West promised a far more expeditious journey. Regardless, if an ox cart were available, Sabine would consider hiring it. The journey from Weimar to the border, by train, promised a myriad of delays.

Sabine's dark thoughts were erased by a familiar voice.

"Good," Heike wheezed from the steps. "No one's left, yet."

Before Heike and Lilo could exchange daggers, Sabine reached into her mini backpack and pulled out the wad of bills she'd stashed.

"Take this," she pleaded. "It's no good where I'm going."

"I can't take your money," Heike objected.

"Put it away. We agreed to get Mutti a stone, correct?"

Heike accepted on that condition.

"What if you need something?"

"I've got a few Wessi marks. When I get home, Oma and Opa will treat me like a queen. They always do."

That, Sabine decided, was exactly the wrong thing to say to an Ossi socialist. If Lilo at Günther's side weren't enough to set Heike off, this thoughtless comment might put her over the edge.

Fortunately, Heike didn't bite.

"I'm glad," she said softly.

Sabine tried hard to find hidden sarcasm or criticism in her tone but came away empty. Even her sister's expression, for once, matched her sentiment. There was nothing to do except wait impatiently for the next late train. Everyone looked gloomy and morose. Conversations were quiet and guarded.

Jürgen and Heike took a long walk east to the end of the platform. Simultaneously, Lilo and Günther conferenced, he with his hands in his hip pockets and she with her arms crossed. Nothing in their expressions gave a clue to the topic of discussion, but neither were concerned about being observed.

Marina sauntered over to Sabine perched atop her suitcase. There was a vacant bench not three feet away, but the Leningrad quasi-orphan found a place for herself atop the luggage. Sabine slid aside as far as she dared. They leaned against each other to avoid tumbling.

"I hope I shall see you again before long," Marina said in a near whisper. "It was a pleasure to meet you. I look forward to hearing you sing again."

"Thank you," Sabine replied, not without feeling. "I'm proud to know you. I hope all will be well with you both."

The young Soviet woman smiled.

"It will be hell for the next several months; maybe, longer."

"How can you smile?"

"Because some troubles are worth it, as you know well."

Nothing in that response made any sense until Marina gave her new friend a nudge which nearly displaced her. Assuming the push was in sport, Sabine examined the Russian's smile. It radiated cheer.

"I'm so lucky to find the man I dreamed of as a child," she continued. "Unexpectedly, he turned out to be the enemy. Country or family allegiance: the one does not, automatically, overrule the other."

Sabine agreed.

"I'm coming back to live with Papa," she responded. "If he'll have me."

Sabine knew nothing of the future beyond returning to Frankfurt/ Oder. She knew naught of how or what her new school would be – or if she would be allowed in; she knew nothing of how she and her father would live together or how they'd live in a re-united Germany with a higher standard of living and inflated prices; she knew nothing of starting life anew without Molly and Jamie, Henry and Shelly, Athena and – Gary. It was as if she volunteered to walk the plank without giving a thought of what to do once she was in the water.

Marina found trouble in Sabine's eyes. She nodded in the direction of Jürgen and Heike, two quiet pedestrian images compared to the towering Amazon and the slightly uncomfortable Günther in the foreground.

"They're talking about you," Marina said.

"Did you put him up to it?" Sabine challenged.

Marina shook her head.

"I don't need to tell Jürgen what's right. He knows. That's one of the things that makes him special. He loves both his sisters, Sabine. Right now, Heike is the one in pain."

Sabine wrestled with that thought.

"Everybody thinks Heike always knows what's right," she ventured.

"Probably true," Marina acknowledged, "It takes her longer to get there. She has to convince herself."

That was no help.

"What does she do now? What do I do now?"

"I can't guess," Marina admitted. "Heike is your sister, and she knows it. Somehow, you'll get through this – eventually; just as I know I'll resolve my problems."

Jürgen took Heike's arm and began a slow walk back. They kept their eyes to the ground and conversed with their heads turned towards each other. They wore serious expressions.

"If we can get a couple bikes," Jürgen announced when they came near. "We can try for that other apartment."

"I thought we agreed things were too unsettled," Marina responded.

Jürgen cocked his head thoughtfully. This intrigued her enough to coax her off her seat. She joined him on a stroll of the down the platform.

Heike hovered uncomfortably. Sabine tried not to look at her, but it was unnerving to ignore her for long. When she relented and looked up, Heike was studying her resolutely.

"As long as you're sending pictures," Heike began timidly, "would you send me one?"

"Of you in that dress? It will be in the mail tomorrow afternoon."

Heike shook her head almost in sadness.

"I want your picture."

"Mine? In braids and those god-awful red pants? I intended to burn them!"

"Send them to me instead," she insisted.

Once armed, Heike could use those images to display her dowdy, naïve, retarded sister. It would be unnecessary to invent scathing stories; the photos would keep the locals in stitches. However, Heike's insistence provided Sabine with an unexpected lever.

"Promise to write me?"

"You know I will."

That was too easy.

"I don't want minutes from a Rosa's Children meeting or what you've been cooking for Herr Zimmermann. I want to know about you."

"You shall," she promised.

Sabine nodded.

Heike remained for several awkward moments. When neither sister thought up a conversational gambit, Heike slowly turned and waddled away to reclaim Günther.

* * *

"It looks like you're up," Lilo prompted after the train announcement.

Sabine stood to rush for the nearest second-class wagon. It was premature; the train was not yet in sight, but she was anxious to get underway. The sooner she held Isaac again, the sooner she'd feel human again. Of course, she owed Mischa a kiss – that was a chore she did not look forward to, but a deal is a deal.

Heike held Günther's arm tightly. After Jürgen's ardent handshake, Marina insisted upon a big hug. Heike was forced to surrender. The Russian hardly knew Günther; he was Jürgen's best friend, that was all

738

she needed to know. Shunted aside by Marina's action, Heike approached Sabine. She held out her hand, and Sabine took it.

"Auf Wiedersehn, Sabine Aleksandra."

"Auf Wiedersehn, Heike Franziska."

When?

Sabine barely managed to keep from crying. Auf Wiedersehen – the classic German platitude *until we see each other again*. When? Where? How?

Jürgen was there as the final representative of his family. In a clear violation of protocol, he extended his hand; Sabine accepted it without hesitation.

"I'm glad I got to meet you," he said sincerely. "If you are ever in Halle, you will have a place to stay."

Sabine was moved despite never imagining any scenario that would land her in that city. However, who knew? She might end up attending university there someday. Then, three people would curse the day Jürgen made the offer.

Marina, as ever, was more effusive. She threw her arms around the departing party and squeezed her tightly. She whispered something Slavic in her ear. Sabine didn't ask; she assumed it was an Orthodox blessing.

"Pray for us," Marina pleaded softly.

Only then did Sabine realize the young Soviet woman was the first professed Christian she'd met since arriving in the DDR.

"If Protestant prayers carry any weight," she replied.

"I'm certain they do," Marina insisted.

"Pray for us, too," Sabine appealed.

"I have, and I shall," Marina promised.

Slowly, laboriously, like a wounded elephant dragging a load of logs, the train swayed into the station. It braked with a squeal causing everyone either to cover their ears or wish they had. Sabine turned to grip her suitcase only to discover that Lilo hefted it from its place and held it, casually, in her bulging right arm.

The doors swung open and several passengers, with that expression of relief so common among *Reichbahn* travelers, realizing that, at long, long last, they'd reached their destination. Glued to the windows were hollow-eyed passengers who looked on enviously at the former passengers and longed for the day when they, too, would experience an arrival.

Lilo waited until the crowd was clear of the vestibule before heaving the suitcase up without so much as a grunt. Sabine thanked her and hurried after it. She didn't bother to look for Günther. He and Heike would be in a clutch; steam would be shooting out Lilo's ears.

To avoid an unpleasant scene, *die Neue* worried her luggage through the swinging glass door and up the passage, checking the compartments as she went. She despaired of finding one vacant; however, she discovered one containing a single traveler. She left her suitcase where it was and slid open the door.

The man sat on the far side next to the window. He was thirty-ish, slovenly, and smelled, of sausage. He eagerly stared at her breasts (was he looking *at* them or *for* them?) Sabine's heart sank. A man so desperate required vigilance. So much for shortening her journey by sleeping away the hours to the border.

She forgot about Günther.

He entered the same compartment and heaved his own bag into the luggage rack above the seat. Without any wasted movement, he reached back for Sabine's case and launched it into the rack above her head. As one, they returned to the narrow passageway and pulled down the nearest window.

A hand gripped Sabine's and squeezed hard. It belonged to Heike who suddenly acted desperate. Sabine looked down at her sister standing tip toe to increase her reach.

"Tomorrow you will send the pictures!" she reminded fervently.

"As soon as they are developed."

Heike's eyes flashed at Günther.

"Take care of her!"

It would have been comical if it weren't so heart-wrenchingly pathetic. Heike was acting like some hysterical mother sending her only child off to war. Take care of Sabine? All the way to Fulda? What was likely to happen? Once in Fulda, Günther and Sabine would go their separate ways.

"Write me, Günther!"

"Every day," he promised.

The train lurched forward, and Lilo gripped Heike by the shoulders to prevent her from leaving the station. Once detached from Sabine's hand, the girl's normal composure returned. Though Jürgen and Marina waved and Günther and Sabine returned the gesture, Heike stood with her fingers shoved in the pockets of her jeans. Lilo towered behind her.

Sabine could stomach no more. She fled to the compartment where the lecher renewed his examination of her torso. She shot him what she hoped would be a scorching glare before throwing herself into her seat. She crossed her arms to further confound Mr. Creepy. It was a relief when Günther returned; he sat across from her and slid the door closed.

"I'm pretty nervous," he confessed for no apparent reason. "Of course, for you – well, you're going home."

Home?

"What's it like?" he prompted.

She considered for a moment.

"The war is over," she reported. "You won't see bombed-out buildings and neighborhoods. There's plenty of food; the markets are full. You can buy fresh vegetables and fruit all year round. The trains run on time. Public transportation is reliable. You can go for days and never see a uniform."

He smiled to encourage her.

"I will see my baby brother," she continued wistfully. "He's probably grown a foot since I've seen him. Mutti will bend my ear about everything he's done. Oma and Opa will carry on and on about every noise and movement their grandson has made since his arrival. My cousins will be after me, night and day, to teach them lewd songs –"

Images and memories began swirling. An episode thrust itself to the fore; it was the bridge of the *Mary R.* She heard Aaron's voice telling her she was an orphan. From that moment, her own history haunted her. She plotted the course she chose to steer. Events and personalities popped up and fell in place like the tumblers of a lock.

Gary and Athena were well represented – and Molly, who was no small part of what Sabine had become. Then the other images rained down like a soft, ocean drizzle – Ernst Bauer and Biggi, Nadine and Günther, Jürgen and Marina, Lilo, Hanna, Inka, and Annegret – and

Heike. Embossed on her brain, was the Thanksgiving image of her sister looking at her as if from a reflecting pool.

Heike, ever sober of expression and serious in discourse, always just out of reach – just beyond understanding. The Heike chapter was not resolved. It mustn't end on a rail platform in the shadow of Buchenwald.

The tears filled her eyes. Günther watched timorously, not knowing what to do or say. Worse, he'd no idea why she behaved so. Sabine's dimples hid and her face contorted.

"You're that happy to get home?" he asked, finally.

Home?

Sabine shook her head and blubbered. A mighty realization gripped her stomach, and a sudden pain robbed her speech. Moments later, she regained some control.

"I'm going away," she choked. "I'm *leaving* home!"